RYANN FLETCHER

Era's End

First edition

This book was professionally typeset on Reedsy.
Find out more at reedsy.com

To everyone who's made it this far – you will go further than you ever dreamed you could.

Contents

Chapter 1

Rosie had been pacing for days. From one end of her small but comfortable room, clean to an almost sterile degree, to the other, and back. It wouldn't be long before she started to wear a hole in the grey, minimalist rug, the sight of which felt entirely suffocating.

She hadn't seen much of what she guessed was her new home, at least for long enough that she could escape. It had been nearly a week since they'd taken her, since they'd nabbed her in the alley behind the Purple Pig as she took out the morning's trash. Four of them, maybe five, she couldn't quite remember because they'd put a burlap bag over her head before anything else.

Their ships were efficient and fast, much faster than almost any ship she'd been on, except the one that belonged to Councilor Tarand. Even that felt like a lifetime ago, another existence, a chapter in a book about someone else. And yet, it was her who was nearly clawing at the stark, bleached-white walls, tugging at the ill-fitting jumpsuit they'd left her with, all grey with one embroidered patch over the left breast pocket. Obsidian Enclave was emblazoned there in black and white, a contrast to the bright pops of yellow and purple of the Coalition.

One more trip around the room, dragging her feet more this time, wondering how long it would be before she figured out something like a plan. Sure, she'd escaped Turas-Mara, but that had hardly only been *her* plan. Carmen and Delia helped, along with Officer Abara, wherever they were now, and General Fineglass, who inexplicably didn't shoot seventeen holes in her when she was trying to escape.

The vents in the room were small, too small for the slightest adult, too small for most children, even. Much too small for Rosie, and she suspected that was intentional. The door was fitted with a digital lock and a bio-scanner, neither of which she'd been able to remove, despite long hours of trying, in pure spite of the camera trained on the knob.

There would be no getting out of there, not without help. Not without assistance, and certainly not without compliance. Clearly, Gregor Zink had meant what he said when he told her that she'd stay in her room, cared for, fed fresh food from the gardens, given almost anything she could ask for, but only in her room until she agreed to cooperate.

Rosie knocked on the inside of the door, quiet at first, and then more insistent. "Hey," she said. "I'm ready."

There was no response from the other side of the door, and for a brief moment, she wondered if they'd left her unsupervised. She turned, glaring at the camera, shrugging her shoulders dramatically, an almost comedic emphasis.

She knocked again, almost pounding now. "I'll play your little game, Zink, just let me out," Rosie shouted through the door.

It swung open, throwing her off balance. She caught herself on the door frame and looked up to see the man himself, smiling down on her benevolently, as though he considered himself to be a gift from the gods, sent down to the mortals to fix their mistakes.

"Ms. Gordon," he said, beaming. "It is truly wonderful to see you here at Lucent Base."

"Oh, it's not mutual." She crossed her arms over her chest, tilting her chin up. "But I'm tired of being locked up in here."

"Are your accommodations not suitable?"

"You're keeping me prisoner."

"No, not a prisoner," Zink said with a kind smile, one that hid a sneer, or maybe that was just Rosie's imagination. "A trusted, respected, well-regarded ally to our cause."

"And what is your cause, exactly?"

"An end to the chaos, Ms. Gordon. A fresh start for everyone across the Near Systems and beyond. Let's not skirt the subject. You and I both know that the Coalition needs to be stopped. No longer content within the Near Systems, their focus on expansion beyond the Rim endangers us all."

"Endangers you all, I think you mean," Rosie shot back. "You call me an ally, yet you ignored my emphatic refusals. You kidnapped me, tossed me on a ship, and dragged me out past the Rim, and for what?"

He blinked at her. "Ms. Gordon, we're not beyond the Rim."

"You're trying to tell me that this base is within the Near Systems?" she asked, barking out a laugh. "I saw three greenhouses as they marched me from the docks. Two launch pads. Something that looked an awful lot like a science and tech building, you're telling me that you've been under the Coalition's nose all this time?" Rosie laughed again, shaking her head this time. "Impossible."

"Bradach isn't the only place that's learned how to shield itself from the Coalition's panopticon, Ms. Gordon. We've built on that technology, and we've perfected it." He moved away from the door, clearing her path. He gestured out to one of the nearby greenhouses with a calm, collected demeanor. "Come, let me show you what we have achieved here."

"I already said I'd cooperate. You don't have to sell me on it, Zink."

"Please, call me Gregor. I'd prefer that, if we are to be working together. And I'm not trying to sell you on anything—I am merely trying to show you our way of life, and why it's so important that we preserve it."

Rosie followed him, leaving her room behind for the first time in days. "I've told you time and again, I am not my grandmother's granddaughter in anything other than name, yet you insist that I am the only viable catalyst for your—"

"Respectfully, Ms. Gordon—Rosie, if I may call you that—you continue to tell me this, and yet the evidence doesn't bear out. You escaped Turas-Mara, one of the most heavily guarded stations in existence, using a High Councilor's ship. You took multiple prisoners with you, and you escaped to the relative safety of Bradach. That's something Norah Gordon would have done."

"I'm not sure I would have described what happened quite like that," she replied, tugging at the jumpsuit. "I had help."

"As do we all. Cooperation is the backbone, in fact, the very marrow of Obsidian Enclave." He scanned his chip against the lock and pushed the glass door open into the greenhouse, giving a sweeping gesture with his arm. "Welcome to paradise."

Rosie stepped over the threshold and struggled to stifle a gasp. Racks upon racks of fresh produce, grown in hydroponics, stacked at least seven feet high. Fruits and vegetables alike, with fat squashes ripe for picking, fresh herbs that drifted their aromas through the air, a deep bucket with what looked like potato leaves sprawling out over the edge. "I can't say it's not impressive," she said, swallowing back her awe. "It looks like you've managed to find peak efficiency."

"We are proud of what we've achieved here, it's true. In the early days of Lucent Base, we struggled to filter enough water for ourselves, much less a greenhouse, and even less so, three greenhouses." He plucked a raspberry from a curiously un-thorned bush and tossed it to her. "We have spliced and cross-pollinated to create the best of the best. These raspberry bushes don't have any thorns!" He examined a few leaves, frowning at a bud that had failed to produce a fruit. "They don't need thorns here. No predators to steal from us."

"Interesting," she replied, popping it into her mouth. It tasted the way summer sun felt back in Dubh Moor growing up, despite being much further from the light, cloistered and confined on a base, not growing wild in a field. "Why show me this?"

"I know that you have an affinity for cooking. I thought you might appreciate our efforts."

"I could get fresh produce just fine back in Bradach, this is nothing new."

"But other settlements? What about food production there? And, I hate to be the one to correct you, truly I am, but Bradach imports a good deal of its food, does it not? I can't imagine the community gardens there would be enough to feed everyone in the event of a blockade."

"Why, are you planning to blockade it?"

He tilted his head, considering her face for a moment before he stepped into another row of racks. "My fight is not with Bradach."

"Yet you destroyed their communications spire."

"A repair they are more than capable of carrying out, and it was only a means to an end." He ran his thumb over a pumpkin leaf, the resulting sound like quiet sandpaper. "I don't wish any harm on Bradach. It has been a useful place to stop and rest in the past, to refuel, sell goods, and buy others. It's a fool's errand to try to eradicate piracy. It is omnipresent, much like the necessity to breathe, or the inescapability of progress."

"I suppose that's what you think you're doing here, is it? Progress?"

"In a sense, but it's much more than that. The Coalition has stifled innovation for decades now, focusing all their greatest minds on weaponry instead of exploration and improvements to space travel." He shook his head. "What may have been accomplished has been lost forever, but we can still recover our humanity, our ordained legacy to the stars if we can topple the structures that fight to keep us grounded."

Rosie examined a tomato, large and ripe on the vine, the scarlet temptation of its flesh almost too much to bear. She picked it, holding it up to the light. "I'm no shill for the Coalition, Zink, but neither am I interested in more blood-soaked wars and infighting. My grandmother fell to the wrong side of things and paid the price for it. I don't want the same for me and mine."

"Yours. Delia Forrest, I presume?"

A knot formed in Rosie's stomach in an instant, pulling down on her like an anchor. She was silent for a long moment, considering her answer. "Why, are you going to kidnap her, too? If you are, I would politely request we be allowed to share a room."

"If we'd wanted to capture her, we would have," he said simply, dipping a small strip into the water and examining the color as it shifted. He frowned at it and laid the paper aside on the rack. "Slightly too alkaline," he announced. "We will have to adjust."

"If you so much as lay one hand on her—"

"Please, Ms. Gordon, be calm. Rest assured we will not harm Delia Forrest." He took the tomato from Rosie, examining it. "This one was still two days from peak ripening."

"It looks fine to me."

"You might think that, but we've spent decades perfecting the process. Surely a chef such as yourself would understand those delicate intricacies?"

"Tell me what you want with me." Rosie straightened, squaring her shoulders. "I've had enough of these games you are playing, and I want to know, without any of your flowery reasoning."

He looked at her, astonished. "Ms. Gordon, I thought I'd made myself clear even on Terringgough Gulch seven months ago. You are to be our paragon, our light in the darkness, symbol made flesh of what we are capable of."

"Because my grandmother was Norah Gordon?"

"Because she held something miraculous in her veins, and that same blood courses through you as well."

Rosie snorted. "I do not carry her metabolic immunity to poisons and truth serums. I did not inherit anything from her beyond danger. I spent a good part of my life being hunted by people like you."

"I don't wish to hunt you, Ms. Gordon, and neither is that the case for anyone else who wears the Obsidian Enclave crest. We wanted to rescue you from mundanity."

"Maybe I prefer a mundane life."

"It would be a gross miscarriage of destiny to allow that." Zink pointed up through the roof of the greenhouse, past the partially terraformed atmosphere to the stars above. "All that we are was written there, long ago. We all have a mission, a way we can improve things for others."

"Was your mission to kidnap me?"

"To help you realize your own potential."

"I would have preferred to be left alone. I was happy in Bradach, for the first time in my life, and you've taken that from me, because you want me to be your advertisement to the rest of the Near Systems." Rosie shook her head, pressing a hand to her hip and regretting the scratchy feel of the fabric against her skin. "You found the wrong woman. I never wanted any part of this."

"I believe you will change your mind," he said airily, setting the tomato on the shelf. "I believe that you will shock and surprise us in new and wonderful ways."

"My grandmother wasn't who you thought she was, either."

He frowned for a moment, busying himself with pinching leaves from stems to ensure better growth. "I think that few in history are who we thought they were. Even what is written is incomplete, only one morsel of their being."

"Did you know my grandmother?"

"Not as such. I was very young, a child at most. I saw her from afar a number of times, and I met her on a few occasions."

"She put her entire family in danger."

"To save us all from tyranny."

"To inflate her own importance, she let the rest of us drown, and in the end, it didn't matter. They caught her, they killed her nonetheless, and that isn't the ending I am searching for."

Zink considered this as he continued to prune the plants in silence, the only sound the delicate snapping of stems. "I appreciate your view on the matter, but I feel compelled to explain that it's not the full story. Yes, I'm sure your mother and grandfather felt discarded at times by her, but it was for a greater good than family harmony."

"What did she achieve, then? None of this was her doing," Rosie said, gesturing at the greenhouse. "All of this technology you boast, that wasn't her, either. She wasn't a scientist."

"No, she was a leader," he said. "She orchestrated the ability for us to do all of that. Our home beyond the Rim wouldn't exist if not for her sacrifices. Thousands live there, Ms. Gordon. Thousands that wouldn't be alive but for her sacrifice."

"They could have lived elsewhere."

"Not when they were being picked off by Coalition Intelligence agents.

One by one, we started to disappear. Mothers, fathers, corporals, generals. We were thinning out, and desperate, and she saved us all with her bravery and leadership." He looked at her now, his face poised with concern. "I believe the same innate heroism exists in you, too."

"It doesn't," Rosie said flatly. "Can I go home now?"

"You aren't a prisoner here, Ms. Gordon."

"Oh, aren't I? I've been locked in my room since we arrived."

"When have you ever seen a prisoner with such amiable surroundings? Is your bed too firm? Are you not getting enough to eat? Whatever the complaint, I'm sure we can remedy it."

Rosie rolled her eyes. "My complaint is that you brought me here against my will, and I'd rather be back home."

"Give us a week, and I'm confident you will change your mind."

"And how is that?" she asked, examining a lemon growing from a grafted branch. "Some prized produce isn't going to shift my opinion on the matter."

"One week," he reiterated. "And if, at the end of that week, you wish to return to Bradach, then we will escort you back. You will be free to leave, and you will never hear from us again. At least, not personally."

"I find that very hard to believe."

"I may be many things, Ms. Gordon, but I am also a man of my word."

"Is that how you managed to convince Barnaby Meier and William to sell you the weapon instead of Cassius Calvetti? Being a man of your word? That little incident on Terringgough Gulch set off a chain reaction, and now there are things in motion that can't be taken back."

"I never had any deal with Calvetti, not verbally or otherwise. How can I break my word to someone I never had an oath with in the first place?"

"You knew it was meant to be hers."

"And she got it, in the end." He pulled a grafting knife from his pocket, attending to more of the propagated cuttings. "Ms. Gordon, it is not my intention to lie to you, or bamboozle you. I am merely hoping that you will choose, of your own accord, to join us in our mission."

Rosie plucked a grape from a vine, popping it into her mouth. "I want to contact Bradach."

"I'm afraid that isn't possible at this juncture. We have had some dealings with those that make berth in Bradach, and it isn't unreasonable to suggest that one word from you will have them screaming across the galaxy, guns blazing, in order to retrieve you." He shook his head sadly, as though he wasn't the one calling the shots. "It is impossible, at least for now. Perhaps in a week, or perhaps if you decide to join us."

"And if I join you, what does that look like?"

"First and foremost, we would take you to Ceru."

"And where is that?" she asked, playing along.

He smiled, raising his arms above his head. "Beyond the Rim, my dear Ms. Gordon. Deep in the stars, where we are hidden and safe."

"So hidden and safe that the Coalitions station at Turas-Mara posed enough of a threat to come out of hiding?"

"Hmm," he said, lowering his arms. "It is true that our hands were forced. Given the opportunity, we would have been happy to thrive, isolated from the rest, developing the technology to find new worlds light years away." He snapped a bud from a cucumber plant and frowned, tossing it to the ground. "Unfortunately, the Coalition's never-ending quest for power and colonies wouldn't cease. We remain hidden, and will for a time, but their expeditions circle near Ceru, much to my dismay."

"What's in Ceru for me?"

"Whatever you like, once the war is done."

His final words rang like threats in Rosie's ears. "And until the war is done? What is there for me in Ceru while you still need me?"

"Ceru is like nowhere you've ever seen, Ms. Gordon. More technologically advanced than any station, any settlement. It puts the Capital to shame, to hear some talk about it, those who have seen both places."

"Have you ever seen the Capital?"

He shook his head. "I have not."

"I have." Rosie plucked the cucumber bud from the floor, the delicate petals already bruised with damage. "I don't know what to say about it, other than that it is not somewhere I wish to spend my years."

"Then perhaps Ceru is a positive move for you."

"Or a detrimental one."

"You shouldn't discount it until you've seen all it can accomplish," Zink said, returning to his pruning. "The medical advances alone are enough to amaze those who have seen them. We are growing new organs, Ms. Gordon, we are delving deep into the mysteries of human consciousness, of what we can achieve as a species. Space travel was only the catalyst for so much that is yet to come."

"Mr. Zink—"

"Gregor," he interrupted, keeping his attention on the plants in front of him. "But go on."

"I'm sure you can understand that I have some concerns."

"Of course."

"If you want me as the face of your faction, I need to know more than what you are telling me. I need information on alliances, on existing technologies and weaponry, and I'll need more access here on Lucent Base until I make my decision."

He looked up at her with a raised eyebrow. "Those are quite the demands."

"You snatched me up from my home and dragged me halfway across the galaxy. It's not even as much as I deserve to ask of you."

"My concerns are that you will take this information straight back to Bradach, to whomever is still there causing problems, now that the bans have begun, or that you will use it to sell us out to the Coalition, buying you and your friends clemency."

Rosie laid the crushed yellow blossom on the rack, turning to pluck another grape from the vine. "I hadn't even considered that as a possibility," she lied. "It seems you have quite the suspicious mind."

"Some call it suspicious or paranoid. I'd call it careful and considered." He nodded, maybe more to himself than to her. "There are some things I cannot share with you, not until you are ingratiated into Obsidian Enclave. However, there are some things I can share, and those I will."

"And access?"

"Most of Lucent Base runs on bio-scanners. It's the most transparent way to track access, and to prevent treachery. With that in mind, I can grant you access to a number of locations, provided you don't abuse the privilege. The greenhouses, to start, along with the kitchens and the east wing of the technology building."

"What about the south wing?" she asked, running a finger along the ridged grape leaves. "And the docks?"

"Those, for now, must remain restricted."

"So I'm not a prisoner, except for when I am. Is that correct?"

He sighed again, quieter this time. "It is not my intention to imprison you. I'd hoped that I'd made that clear, Ms. Gordon."

"What's in the south wing?"

"Classified medical testing." He pressed his palms together, as if in prayer. "It is classified to protect the identities of those undergoing treatments, you understand. Though we may seem odd to you, foreign, rigid in our methodology, one thing you can expect here is privacy."

Rosie's eyes followed a surveillance camera as it shifted its view from one end of the greenhouse to the other. "Privacy," she repeated.

"No one sees these feeds except security staff," he answered, glancing up to follow her stare, "and they are heavily vetted, never fear. Whatever you say here on Lucent Base stays between us. I am not in the practice of throwing my colleagues to the wolves."

"How many microphones are here?" she asked, innocent but with a tinge of judgment, just like her mother used to, and the memory of it twinged something inside her.

"Oh, here and there. I don't know the exact count. But as I said, it's only for transparency reasons. If I am physically unable to have a private discussion, unwatched, then those who count on me know that they can trust me beyond the shadow of a doubt. I cannot commit a crime if everyone is always watching."

"An interesting theory," Rosie said politely, while internally reeling at the idea of being watched every moment of every day. "It will be interesting to watch that bear out."

"So you'll stay with us, then?" he asked hopefully, inspecting a sprinkler spigot.

"I will stay for one week, and then you will take me back to Bradach."

"I hope that seven days will be enough to show you everything we have to offer you, Ms. Gordon," he said, straightening. "And that in seven days, you will see that Obsidian Enclave is the only feasible answer to ending the bloodshed that has become so commonplace across the Near Systems."

"Mr. Zink, I would be remiss if I were to suggest that I thought there was any chance in any of the multitude of hells we know of that I would agree to be the face of your faction. I expect that in one week, seven days, I will be on a transport back to Bradach, after being given wire privileges to let Delia know that I'm not rotting away in a prison somewhere."

"We would never—"

Rosie held up her hand to silence him. "Seven days, Mr. Zink."

Chapter 2

Larkin sighed as she wiped down the bar for the sixth time that night. It was nothing unusual, not for the Purple Pig, and certainly not lately, and maybe that was the problem. She scrubbed at a sticky patch, an amorphous circle left from a cocktail glass, and the slightly pink hue let her know exactly which drink it was, a blend of gin, pea flower, lemon, and raspberry. A popular choice for patrons, and a showstopper of a drink, one of her best creations.

Evie had been so proud, and Larkin had beamed under her praise, but something in the tavern was feeling strange, ever since the Cricket crew showed up with a spy, a prisoner, and stories about how Terringgough Gulch blew up. If she didn't trust them all implicitly, she would have thought they were lying.

Another rag, another wipe, another patron, another drink. Most of her motions were automatic, and it was comforting, but she couldn't shake the odd, nagging feeling that was pulling at her spine. She'd been trying to ignore it for weeks, months maybe, but every day revealed a new atrocity, every day the danger of the Coalition crept closer, and she felt more powerless than she had since she was a child.

"How come the menu is so reduced?" a woman asked, a hand on her silk-laden hip. "I thought this was supposed to be the best place in Bradach."

"Chef is out sick," Larkin lied. Some knew that Rosie had been taken, but she couldn't bring herself to explain it to a stranger. "Sorry."

"Oh. Fine, can we just get the sandwiches, then?"

"Aye," Larkin answered, offering what she hoped was a normal smile, and not the odd grimace that kept staring back at her every time she looked in a mirror. "Eves, two specials," she shouted into the kitchen.

"Be right with you!" came the reply, so bright and sunny with her newfound confidence that it made Larkin want to melt into a puddle all over again.

She'd be nothing without Evie.

Nothing but a busted-up former assassin with long-held grudges and an affinity for beautiful mixed drinks, and probably not even the latter without her. She'd shown up at exactly the right moment, heartbroken in the next cell over, and she'd turned everything upside-down, and Larkin was forever indebted to her as a result. Evie was everything, and Larkin was hiding.

Something itched, but below the skin.

A parasite of old habits, maybe, or roots that were trying to pull her back to the place she said she'd never return to. She shook her head to clear her thoughts once more, pulling an ale for the burly man at the end of the bar. He'd spent nearly every evening there for a week, never saying more than his order, never meeting with anyone, just sitting in silence, and she knew.

He was hunting someone.

She'd done it dozens of times, she'd lost count over the years. Find a tavern, lie in wait, don't be too noticeable, keep to the shadows, hit your mark and get on the first transport out of town. Walk, don't run to the docks, be polite, avoid MPOs, never risk what you're not comfortable losing, especially if it was your own skin. She watched him, waiting, wondering, but as he hunched over the glass, something twisted in her stomach like a knot, or a knife, or razor wire.

"Order up," Evie said, sliding two plates through the window.

"Thanks, Eves," Larkin said, reaching through the window to squeeze her shoulder. "I know the kitchen isn't where you'd rather be."

"Not many options until we find someone else. I have three interviews lined up for tomorrow, I feel like we should just pick one. You're run ragged."

"Me? I meant you! I'm just out here slinging drinks, you're back there cooking and plating, and that's after you were up half the night working on that code Henry left here."

Evie sucked her teeth. "I wasn't up half the night."

"Oh, no? Then why did I find three empty mugs on your side of the bed this morning, hmm? Did someone else stay on your side, drinking endless cups of coffee?"

"Excuse me, we're waiting," the woman said, tapping the toe of her boot against the ground.

Larkin rolled her eyes, making sure that Evie saw, before flashing a smile and taking the plates. "My deepest apologies, ma'am, I was merely conferring with—"

"Sure, whatever." The woman took the plates, marching off back to her table.

For a split second, Larkin hoped the woman was the mark the burly man was looking for, and then regretted having the thought. She was rude, not deserving of death.

Probably.

She jangled the rope of the bell at the edge of the bar, letting loose the rusty clang that echoed into the rafters. "Last orders in five," she announced. "Kitchen is now closed."

A few came to order final drinks, and she prepared them with the same candor and patter she always used, despite the snake of guilt and festering curled around her heart. Ale, three glasses of the house red wine, two cocktails, and five straight up shots, served as a flight to a table of scrappers who'd probably had enough already, but she was too tired to argue.

The burly man drained his glass, cast another guarded, cursory look around the tavern, and left, just behind a group of pirates who'd just landed in the docks with twenty-two refugees from Skelm. With the rotation schedule there, Emeline had been able to get some people out, the most vulnerable who wouldn't survive waiting more months or years for the settlement's liberation. More tents erected, more hands needed to help, more hungry, desperate people and what in hells was Larkin even doing, slinging booze when she could be out there making a difference?

One by one the patrons filtered out, and the group of scrappers left last, one of them falling over not one, but two chairs on her way out. She was a regular and preferred whiskey. But she tipped well, better when she was drunk, and she was always congenial, and Larkin was glad to see the back of her, nevertheless.

"Locked up," she called over the bar as she slid the padlock into place. "How's it looking in the kitchen?"

"Almost done," Evie answered over the noisy clatter of metal on metal. "Just cleaning up. You hungry?"

"Not really."

"Okay, I'll make you something."

Larkin snorted at the reply, shaking her head. No one had ever taken care of her the way Evie did, except maybe José, but that was a time in her childhood so abbreviated and fraught that she spent most of her time trying not to think about it. She wiped down the bar once more and rearranged the bottles on the lit shelf, making sure the labels were facing out, perfectly lined up and on display for everyone to see.

"Here," Evie said, sliding a plate along the bar. "I made you a sandwich."

"Oh, and toasted too," Larkin said, dragging the plate closer to her. "I'm being spoiled tonight."

"I'm sorry, it's just been chaotic all day, I've barely had time to breathe back there."

"Eves, I was being serious. Thank you."

"Oh." Evie stayed standing, hovering at the door.

Larkin lifted an eyebrow. "Aren't you eating?"

"I will, I just..." she trailed off, rubbing a hand over the merfolk scale tattoo that peeked out from beneath her sleeve. "I'll wait until you're finished."

"I'd rather you told me now."

"No, I'll wait. You should eat."

"And you should eat, too, yet you're hovering around behind the bar and you aren't making eye contact with me." Larkin took a bite, chewed, swallowed. "And you're doing that thing you do when you're nervous."

"What thing? I don't have a thing."

"Eves, you have a thing. You mess with the sleeve of your shirt, folding and unfolding the edge."

"I'm just trying to make it even with the other side."

"Oh, really? Because there are so many people here looking at you right now?"

Evie sighed. "Just eat your gods-damned sandwich, Mabel."

"Mabel," Larkin replied with a scoff. "Why did I ever choose that name?"

"Because no one named Mabel ever got into trouble with the law." Evie dropped her hands to her sides and leaned against the bar. "Not until you carried that name around, anyway." She gave Larkin a strange look, a cross between frustration and fear. "It's a good thing you won't need to use that moniker anymore, right?"

"Right."

"Larkin."

"What?"

Evie sighed, reaching into her apron pocket, and producing a cutting from a plant, the small, white flowers bunched into tight heads. "Care to explain?"

"Cow parsley? What of it?" Larkin asked easily, feeling the bile begin to rise up, burning her throat and along with it, the last vestiges of hope that Evie hadn't noticed anything was wrong.

"Don't treat me like I don't know what you're doing." Evie held the stem to the light with an accusatory glance before setting it back on the bar. "Smells strange, not like parsley, and the stems are mottled with purple, like a bruise."

"How long have you known?"

"Do you think I'm a fool, Larkin Flores? I've known from the moment these came up in the back garden. I didn't press you on it, because I know who you are, and I know your past, but this morning when I was out there collecting herbs, I noticed it's been cut." Evie set it on the bar, and even from four seats away Larkin could see the shake of her hands, and it drilled nails deep beneath her metal rib cage. Evie kept her eyes trained on the flowers, not even glancing away. "Why are you growing hemlock, Larkin?"

"Insurance."

"Against what?"

"Any of it, Eves! The Near Systems are starting to fall apart around us, and this place—we—are sitting ducks."

"We aren't sitting ducks, we are dealing with things the only way we can. The only way we *safely* can."

"I just wanted to have something ready, just in case."

"We've talked about this, Larkin. Time and time again, we have talked about this, and you promised me at least a hundred times that you were done with that—" Evie picked up the stem again and dropped it onto the bar. "With this, for good."

"Rosie was taken right out from under our noses a week ago, and you think I'm overreacting?"

"What would you have done, dosed them all with poison from ten meters away?"

"No, I have knives for that."

Evie gave her an exasperated sigh and reached for a bottle, pouring herself a hefty glass. "I know that you have knives for that."

"If you drink that on an empty stomach, you're going to feel sick."

"Don't think you can talk to me like that when I discovered you've been growing poison. I was willing to accept that you needed it to feel safe, to feel secure here, but harvesting it? This garbage has grown out there for years now, untouched, and I was fine with that, but now you're hiding things, and you promised me that you never would." Evie turned away again, and her voice shook as she spoke the next words. "Not from me."

"I'm not—hiding—Eves, I'm not hiding anything, I just have this terrible feeling that something worse is about to happen, and I can't shake it. I just thought that if I was prepared, I could protect you—us—and not be so wide open to threats."

"There's no way that you alone could have saved Rosie. Obsidian Enclave is organized, they are diligent, and they are dangerous."

"I could have saved her, but I've grown soft, Eves. I sleep in a bed every night and I eat three square meals a day and I take gods-damned bubble baths once a week and they took her, and I slept through the whole thing." Larkin pushed away the plate, her stomach sour with regret. "What good am I if I can't even use these skills to keep people safe?"

"It's not your job to keep everyone safe."

"No, my job is a barkeep."

Evie raised an eyebrow. "I thought that was enough for you."

"Under normal circumstances, sure, but not after having our chef snatched right from under our noses, carried off only the gods know where."

"And so your plan was what, to make your little vials of poison, and what? Where do you go from there?"

"Cole." One name, but the silence from the other end of the bar let Larkin know that Evie understood. "Two birds with one vial, Eves. Get him out of Bradach, find out where they've taken Rosie."

"You're going to kill him because he won't leave Bradach?"

"Because he's putting all of us at risk! Because he made a deal with Obsidian gods-damned Enclave, because he probably helped them take her, and now we haven't seen Delia in days, she's such a wreck."

"None of this is your responsibility, none of it is your job to fix. Bad things happen to good people sometimes, and you just have to weather the storm because there aren't any other options."

Larkin tensed, her shoulders seizing up against her will, and she poked at the crispy bread of the sandwich, leaving small, crunchy divots with the tip of her finger. "It's not about responsibility, it's about being able to help and not just sitting around waiting for someone else to do the dirty work."

"Haven't you done enough dirty work?" Evie asked. "Hasn't there been enough times where you nearly got caught, nearly died, nearly lost everything trying to chase after justice?" She made a quiet scoffing noise, turning her head to the side. "What does justice even mean, anymore? How do you chase after that when there's nothing but bloodshed and chaos across the entire known galaxy? And why does it have to be *you*?"

"I never said anything about how it had to be me."

"You didn't have to."

"It's not like I was making firm plans for this. I told you, it's just insurance. Truth be told, we should have been preparing like this all along," Larkin said. "We don't know how many people might be gunning for us. Hells, your ex-girlfriend might be plotting her revenge for all we know."

"Holly has been back in Bradach for months, and hasn't exacted any revenge, so I think we're safe on that front, don't you think?" Evie asked, a hint of sarcasm playing on her tongue. "Whatever goes on out there, it doesn't concern us. It doesn't concern *you*."

"What concerns me is your safety, Eves. What if they'd taken you, and not Rosie? How do you think I'd be coping then? Do you think I'd be calm and reasoned, running this place on my own, hoping you turn up? Or do you think I'd be a melted puddle of mess and disaster on the floor, unable to do anything for anyone because you were missing?"

"No one is coming for me."

"I'm sure Rosie thought that, too."

Evie inhaled a deep breath, exhaling slowly. "I thought it may come to this," she said softly. "Deep down, I knew that someday, there would be a contract you couldn't resist, a job—"

"This isn't about a contract or a job, Eves, it's—"

"Don't interrupt me, Larkin." Her tone was quiet but insistent, tired, exhausted even, but somehow still rooted in a warmth. A long moment that passed between them like a shooting star in the night— either a star to make a wish upon, or a satellite falling from orbit. "I knew someday this would happen. There's something in you that I don't understand and won't understand. You grew up alone, you fell in with a strange crowd, they trained you to be an assassin and now that's part of you, for better or for worse."

Evie pulled a box from her pocket and set it at the edge of the bar. "I had this made a while back, around the time I found this hemlock growing below the window." She nudged it towards Larkin, and it slid easily across the polished wood.

"What's this?" Larkin asked.

"Just open it."

"You're scaring me."

"The feeling is mutual. Open it."

Larkin stared at the box like it was a cobra poised to strike. Whatever it was, it couldn't be good, not after the conversation they'd just had. "I hope you're not giving your key back to this place and leaving me on my own."

"No."

"No, it's not a key? Or no, you're not leaving?"

"Do you really think I'd let you have the Purple Pig to yourself? Get real, Flores."

"Is it a key to a new apartment, because while we will remain business partners, you can't stand the sight of me anymore?"

"It's not a key!"

Larkin poked the box, expecting a rattle but hearing nothing.

"It's not going to bite you," Evie said, untying her apron and hanging it on the peg near the kitchen door. "Open it, for all the gods' sakes."

"Alright, fine." Larkin eased the hinge open, panic rising in her chest with every passing moment. Her breath caught in her throat, and suddenly the waves were crashing all around her, and she was drowning in ten thousand different emotions all at once. "It's a ring."

"There's a secret compartment if—"

"I know." Larkin took it out of the box, the silver shining in the dim light of the tavern. Intricate, filigree skulls were carved into the sides, and the segment at the top had a tiny, almost invisible access panel. "It's a poison ring."

"I thought it might help."

"I thought you didn't want rings and dresses and all that," Larkin said, trying to play it off like the joke it so obviously was, despite the quiet yearning in her heart. "Now you're giving me murder jewelry?"

"Larkin, I want to make sure you come home safe to me." The words hung in the air like molasses, sweet but thick and heavy with the weight of itself. "If I have to put up with rings and dresses to make sure you don't do anything that will get yourself killed, then so be it."

"Are you joking?" Larkin whispered. She'd asked Evie four times to marry her, and every time she'd laughed, saying she was happy to just exist together, build a life together, and that she'd never been one for big parties where she was the center of attention.

"I am not joking."

"Are you asking me to—"

"Will you be my wife?" Evie asked. It was soft but matter-of-fact, and she was just standing there, leaning casually against the bar, sipping at whiskey like she hadn't just sent Larkin's world crashing down around her.

"Are you sure?"

"Of course I'm sure. I already knew I wanted to spend my life with you the moment we signed the deeds on this place with Tansy and you immediately lost your composure planning events, looking for new artwork, reworking the menu. You threw yourself into this place, and look what we've made it, Larkin. Even Tansy can't deny that it's beautiful, and she fought you really hard on that mural."

Larkin laughed, despite herself. "But marriage, Eves?"

"Are you trying to tell me you changed your mind?"

"No, of course not, I—I want to make sure that you're not just bribing me."

"When have I ever bribed you?"

"Never." Larkin flashed her a wry smile. "You always make me work for it."

Evie stepped closer and took Larkin's hands in her own. "Larkin Flores, I love you. I am scared to death of what you're planning, of what's going to happen to us if you do it, but I'm trying to show you that I'm trying to understand this part of you."

"You don't want to understand this part of me."

"People have died at my hands, too, unless you've forgotten the little shootout we had at the Armory all that time ago."

"That's different. That's self-defense, it's automatic and compulsory. It's not... hunting."

"Maybe some people need to be hunted."

Larkin frowned. "You're not allowed to think that. I'm allowed to think that, because I'm the twisted up, mangled ex-assassin with a black heart beating in my fake rib cage. You're supposed to be the rational one who keeps me from getting into more trouble than I'm already in."

"And I know that rationality only goes so far until it's superseded by necessity." Evie shrugged half-heartedly. "Maybe necessity showed up at our door last week when Rosie was taken."

"We can't just let them have her, Eves."

"I know. But Captain Violet said they'd head straight back to Lucent Base to find her."

"And that was six days ago and we haven't heard a gods-damned thing." Larkin clenched her jaw, and then released as she ran her thumb over the ring. "No radio contact is rarely a positive thing."

"They may just be running stealth, trying to surprise Obsidian Enclave."

"Or they got tangled up in a blockade, or they ran into Josie again, or the Coalition yanked them straight out of dark space to pay for their crimes. It could be anything, and you know that as well as I do."

Evie nodded and leaned forward to plant a kiss on Larkin's cheek. "I'm not stopping you from doing whatever it is you feel you need to do."

"Cass isn't going to be happy if I kill him. It will look like assassination from The Splintered."

"Then don't kill him. Just scare him a little, enough to get some information."

"Cole is just stubborn enough that he might dig his own grave just to spite Cass," Larkin said. "He's never been the most level-headed."

"And after Cole, then what?" Evie asked. "Who will be in your crosshairs, then?"

"Eves—"

"I've always told you that I want one thing from you, and that's your honesty. But it seems like you can't give me that, because you're too busy planning murders, so fill me in, Larkin." Evie sat on the adjacent stool, swirling what was left of the whiskey in her glass.

"After Cole, I don't know." Larkin opened the ring's small compartment and closed it again. "I just want Rosie back."

"She's a better cook."

"Sure, but I prefer you at the bar with me, or upstairs working on those codes, at least getting a full night's sleep and not running on caffeine and optimism alone."

Evie laughed, draining her glass and setting it on the bar. "You want one?"

"No."

"We will get Rosie back, one way or another. We don't leave people to rot."

"Marina Sykes did," Larkin said. "Others did."

"That had nothing to do with us."

"Doesn't matter."

"Rosie Gordon is a force to be reckoned with, they'll figure that out soon enough. Anyone who can run our kitchen single-handedly can probably take on an entire army alone." Evie nodded towards the ring. "Try it on."

"I'm scared."

"Of a ring, or of marrying me?"

"Scared that you'll remember who I really am and take it back."

"I'm not taking it back." Evie shrugged. "No refunds."

Larkin slipped the ring on her finger, and it fit perfectly, snug and right as though she'd been made for it, and not the other way around. "It fits."

"I see that." Evie leaned in, snaking an arm around Larkin's waist. "So, what's your answer? Will you marry me when you're done cleansing the world of evil?"

"Evie Anderson, I'd marry you in a heartbeat." Larkin kissed her, full and soft with summery promises. "I've known that from the moment I met you in this bar." She kissed her again, feeling tears prick at her eyes but blinking them back. "I think, somehow, I've known since before I even met you."

Chapter 3

Alice tucked her large wrench into the tool belt that hung at her hips, and when she released it, the leather sagged, dragging down against her thigh, a familiar weight sitting against her that was both reassuring and indicative of what was to come.

The boilers of the ship were on their last legs, patches over patches, the metal held together by hope and prayers to long-dead gods. They wouldn't last much longer, especially not if they kept winding up in shootouts all over the Near Systems. The Cricket needed retirement as much as she did.

"Should be good," she said into the radio, examining the condensation along the safety valve with a frown. "For now, anyway."

"Great," her wife replied, her voice crackling through the speaker. Alice waited to hear more, but the boiler room fell silent except for the rumble of engines and the light crunch of flames against biofuel. Violet had been distant, not angry or upset, not sarcastic—well, no more than usual—and yet something between them felt strained, like rusted bolts trying to hold bowed steel together against the elements.

She sighed, leaning back against the workbench, wiping the sweat from her brow with the back of her hand. It came away black with grease and dirt, not unusual but always irritating. It wouldn't be long before they reached Lucent Base, and they'd scoop up Rosie and be done with Gregor Zink and all his gods-damned mind games. It was exhausting having to deal with him. He'd barely allowed her the materials to repair the ship the last time they were there almost two weeks back, and the patches were beginning to curl at the edges. She needed much longer to repair the ship to an acceptable standard, but it didn't look like she'd be getting that anytime soon.

"Hey, Al," Ned mumbled from the doorway. He leaned against the rusted metal, taking pressure off his leg.

"I told Vi already, I've got the boilers going again."

"I know, I heard from the bridge."

"So why are you down here in my boiler room?" Alice asked with a smirk. "You already know that the good whiskey is gone from the stash, we finished it last week on the way back to Bradach." She turned towards the work bench, sweeping a selection of nuts and bolts into a small wooden container. She set aside the brass cog for later, placing it carefully into the drawer.

"She wants to know if we can get any more speed off these boilers."

"Okay," Alice said. "She could have asked that over the radio."

"She said she knew that you would say no."

"I *am* saying no. We're lucky these are holding at all, one more hit to the wrong section and this whole ship could disintegrate along with us inside it."

"She's just trying to get us to Lucent Base as soon as possible. Delia hasn't stopped sending out broadcasts for days."

"I understand that, but we don't even know if Rosie is on Lucent Base. They could have her halfway carted past the Rim by now, knowing their technology and access to rhodium." Alice picked at an old burn scab on her hand, savoring the light prickles of pain that emanated from it. "I'm doing the best I can, but with Ivy out with Tansy, I'm limited in what I can accomplish. Not to mention we're woefully low on supplies, and I can't exactly disconnect a boiler while we're flying to solder it, and—"

Ned interrupted her with a sigh. "I know, Al."

"Okay."

"Is everything okay?"

"Is anything right now?"

"A fair point," he replied with a sardonic laugh. "We're all exhausted."

"That doesn't even begin to explain it." Alice glanced at him for a moment before returning her focus to the workbench, trying not to look alarmed at the state of him. "You look tired, too."

"Are you suggesting that my skin isn't glowing like a Bradach mirror on a summer's day?"

"I'm suggesting that you need a nap, Nedrick. Or a vacation. Or both."

"Don't we all?" he asked.

"Don't we all," Alice repeated. "Even if we manage to nab Rosie, what then? Spend the rest of this—war, whatever—running from Obsidian Enclave and the Coalition? From The Scattered, now that Cole Marion is shouting all kinds of lies about what happened to Jessop and Donaldson? How long before Cass turns on us, too?"

"Cass isn't turning on us. We're aligned with The Splintered, we have protection from them."

"There are about fifteen ships on that charter. We're one of them, and we know four of the others. I don't know how fifteen ships can overturn everything that's happened." Alice shook her head. "I know Vi disagrees, and so do you, but I think we should have remained neutral. We've painted a target on our backs, and it's only a matter of time before it comes to bite us all in our asses."

"It was the right thing to do."

"I'm tired, Ned."

"We're all tired. That doesn't mean we get to give up."

Alice huffed quietly, trying to ignore the shifting air of tension in the room. "I'm not suggesting we give up, but we're basically running on fumes. The biofuel reserves are almost depleted, there are no beacons around, not since Terringgough Gulch took them all out, the boilers are on their last legs, we don't have any medical staff with Hyun and Jasper back on Lucent Base, I have no mechanic assistant and haven't for months, and Vi will barely speak to me." She flushed and turned away to hide it. "Sorry. I shouldn't have said the last part."

"It's not as though it's not obvious."

"That doesn't mean I should acknowledge it by saying it out loud."

"We just need to get past this hurdle, then we can lie low for a while, give you time and resources to repair, we can refuel, pick up more supplies, we can see if Hyun and Jas can rejoin us earlier than we anticipated." Ned tried for a smile, but it looked more like a grimace. "You never know, maybe he's all fixed up. Maybe he's right as rain."

"I think Hyun would have told us by now if that was the case."

"Unless Zink isn't allowing her access to the wire station."

Alice growled under her breath, bending to organize another pile of screws, sweeping them into a crumbling tower. "It wouldn't surprise me. The man isn't two faced, it's more like five-faced. Maybe even six, depending on who his contacts in the Coalition are."

"Jhaveri?"

"I don't know, we haven't been able to contact her in a long time. She's under observation, and we don't need to turn up the heat on her or on us."

"Do we even know if she's still in her post?"

Alice tossed a hammer into a box with an angry thud. "We don't. Vi is hoping that Olivia Guisette will be able to pass us some intel, but I'm not so sure."

"You don't trust her?"

"I don't trust anyone anymore." She sighed again, wiping her hands on the thighs of her green jumpsuit. "Except you, and Vi, and the others. You know."

"I know." Ned stepped into the boiler room and began poking through a box with curiosity. "I don't suppose you've heard from Barnaby then, either."

"Ned—"

"I know," he repeated, staring down into the box. "I know, Al, but I can't help but wonder."

"He's not so special, you know. He's kind of horrible."

"You've told me that at least a hundred times."

"Yeah," she said, "and it's still true. That nonsense at Kilper Station with that gods-damned weapon was just more evidence that he hasn't changed a bit. Still grifting, still hustling, still doing his best to line his own pockets. For all we know, he's had a deal with Zink since the beginning, and that's why they dragged him off Terringgough Gulch seven months ago when Allemande showed up with her cavalry."

"Or he's sitting in an Obsidian Enclave prison."

"Or he's busy selling us all out again to the highest bidder."

Ned picked up a small droid, examining it before dropping it back into the pile with a metallic crunch. "I wish I didn't care."

"Me, too. But I do care about him, the bastard, even though he sold me out."

"You did marry her, Al. He sold you out to a pirate captain, sure, but in the end, things all worked out."

"We'll see about that."

He looked up at her, his brow furrowed. "I didn't think things were that bad."

"They're not. Maybe. I don't know." Alice turned away again, rubbing at her eyes as though she could erase the thought. "But the point is, things could have gone differently. The point is, he got caught stealing from us, and then showed up at the worst possible moment to complicate matters even further."

"Do you think he loved William?" Ned asked quietly.

"I don't know if he's ever loved anyone, at least, not more than he loves himself."

A quiet moment passed, and Alice was grateful for it. She'd done her best to keep her mouth shut about Barnaby around Ned, if only because she didn't want to cause him any more pain than Barnaby already had, the louse. She picked through a container of spare parts, hunting for a coupler she was fairly certain she'd already used weeks back. Still, it was at least something to focus her mind on that wasn't Violet, or Barnaby, or the treason they were all continuing to commit.

Ned ran a hand over the surface of the work bench, brushing dust onto the metal grate floor. "Davey Klein tried to talk to me back in Chalidon."

"And?"

"And I don't know, Al, he's so persistent."

"In a good way?"

"In a frustratingly sweet and thoughtful way." Ned tossed her a glance with the hint of a smirk playing at the corners of his lips. "He wrote me a stack of letters."

"Is that what you've been carrying around in your breast pocket?" she asked, nodding at the obvious bulge in his waistcoat, the warp of the fabric distorting the intricate brocade pattern. "You know, if Mae saw that, she'd yell at you for ruining her line work on that tailoring."

Ned snorted a laugh. "What Mae Machenet doesn't know won't hurt her." He pulled out a stack of papers, each of them folded and creased, the edges worn from their unconventional storage. "He said he's thought of me every moment since we last met."

"Wow."

"I don't know, Al, despite everything, it's kind of nice to have someone chasing me, for once."

"So have a drink with him, what harm could it do? You're both Splintered now, and as far as I know, Calvetti hasn't said anything about workplace relationships." She breathed a laugh out of her nose, nudging the box aside with the toe of her unpolished boot.

"I don't know if all of us will even make it out of this alive," Ned muttered acerbically. "Which just figures. I finally meet a nice man who writes me beautiful love letters, and not only am I hung up on Barnaby, we're also all staring down the barrel of an all-systems war."

"Don't ask me. I tossed everything aside to be with Vi."

"One of your better decisions?"

"It's made for a more exciting life, anyway. Plus, I like Ivy far more than that trainee recruit I had back on the Stronghold." Alice examined the pressure gauge with a frown, tapping at the glass covering the tiny red line that wavered back and forth. "Please tell Vi that she's going to run this ship into the fucking ground if she doesn't give me time for better repairs soon."

"I'll try, but if she's not listening to her wife, I doubt she'll listen to her navigator."

"Make Kady tell her then, she always listens to her second in command." Alice grunted, smoothing a silver hair back behind her ear. "Don't tell Kady I said that."

Ned crossed a finger in an x over his chest. "I would never."

"I can't let her know that I like and respect her now."

"I think she might know, Al."

Alice smirked. "Damn."

* * *

Alice slid beneath the sheets, grateful for the simple luxury of a hot bath. Clean and scrubbed, her hair still damp but back in their braids, she breathed out a quiet sigh, folding her hands on top of the covers. Another long day packed with repairs as she tried to stave off the inevitable.

"Hey," she said as Violet entered their room, closing the door behind her.

"Mm," Violet mumbled in response.

"Everything alright up on the bridge?"

"Handed over to Kady for the night." Violet shrugged off her waistcoat, draping it over the wardrobe door. "Should be a quiet one, not many ships around."

"That's good."

"Mhmm."

"So..." Alice trailed off, searching for the right words to say. She shifted in the bed, sitting up against the wooden headboard. "So, did Ned tell you about the boilers?"

"He did."

"And did he explain that—"

"It's nothing you haven't said before." Violet shot her a look, and Alice withered beneath the crushing weight of it.

"Vi, I can't help that the boilers need more than patching. We've been flying flat out for months, I have no help down there, and there's only so much I can do without the ship being docked. I'm not trying to be difficult."

"I know you're not trying to be difficult."

"Then why are you acting like I am?"

Violet turned away, unbuttoning her shirt. The gesture sank into Alice, and she looked away. If Vi didn't want to be seen, then she wouldn't look. "I'm not acting like you are," Violet said simply, dropping her shirt to the floor with the quiet hiss of fabric against the woven rug below that covered the cold metal grate. "I'm just trying to get through this."

"I know there's a lot of pressure on you."

"It's fine. Nothing I haven't seen before."

"Vi, come on, just talk to me," Alice pleaded, squeezing her eyes shut.

"I am talking to you."

"You know what I mean."

"If you don't know why I'm upset, then there's nothing more to discuss." Violet dumped her laundry into a basket, the soft thunk of her discarded belt buckle the only sound other than her heavy, weighted sigh.

"So this is about joining The Splintered?" Violet didn't answer, and Alice matched her sigh. "I just worry that getting all caught up in this will get us into trouble, or worse."

Violet tugged on a clean sleep shift, lilac silk that fell to her mid-thigh, and lace that draped prettily over her collarbones. "You think I don't know that?"

"Of course I know that you know that."

"I've been at this far longer than you, Alice. I saw the last rebellion, even if you didn't. You were safe with your aunt and uncle, raised within the Coalition to be a respectable member of society."

"If you'll recall, *Captain*, I left the Coalition to be with you."

"Is that the only reason?"

Alice gave her an incredulous look. "Of course not, but it was certainly a weighty factor, don't you think?"

"Then you should have known it would be like this. Isn't that why you joined this crew in the first place? To help people, to atone for your role in the Coalition, to right the wrongs? Isn't that what you said to me?"

"Yes, but—"

"Then what I can't understand for the life of me is why you're surprised I made this call."

"I'm not—hells, Vi, I'm not surprised, I'm just concerned."

"How about this? You do your job, and I'll do mine."

"That's it?" Alice huffed. "After everything we've been through?"

"What are you suggesting?"

"I'm not suggesting anything, you are!"

Violet stood at the bathroom door, arms folded across her chest. "We are quickly running out of allies. It wasn't an easy decision to make. Ned agrees with me, as does Kady." Violet tied a silk scarf around her head with a tight knot, smoothing it down and tucking in the ties. "Nevertheless, we told Delia we would check Lucent Base, and that's what we're going to do."

"And if Gregor Zink starts firing at us the moment we're in range?"

"Then you do what you always do, patch the damned boilers, and I'll fly us out of there. Alright? Is that a good enough plan for you?"

Alice bit back a grimace, trying to keep her face neutral. "We don't have our med staff, Vi."

"I am well aware of that. Did you think that I forgot?"

"No, but—"

"Hyun made the decision to stay behind with Jasper. That was her decision to make, and despite my hesitance, she chose that path. I can't say I wouldn't have done the same if it was you in their medical building instead of Jasper."

"If it was me, I'd expect you to keep everyone else safe, rather than risk everything just for me."

"I already risked everything for you. That's how we wound up in this mess in the first place."

"Me? What did I do?" Alice asked, wanting to fling the covers off her bare legs but somehow remaining beneath them. "How am I responsible for any of this?"

"I never said you were responsible for this."

"You just said—"

Violet hissed out a sigh. "Do you think you can make it five minutes without trying to undermine me?"

"I'm not trying to undermine you, I'm just trying to—"

"To question every decision I make? To whisper in corridors about how much you hate the idea of us joining with The Splintered, despite the fact that staying neutral would surely get us killed faster?"

"You don't know that."

"I do know that."

"There are plenty of neutral ships—"

"Not who have done what we have done," Violet interrupted, turning to face her. "Not with our records, not with the price that's still on all our heads, despite what Ivy did to wipe information from the server. Not who have cavorted with Cassius Calvetti, not who have infiltrated how many prisons now to break our people out. Not any of that, Alice, and you know it."

"Okay, I will admit we've had our fair share of run-ins." Alice shifted in the bed, suddenly too warm, heat crawling up her neck. "But this ship is going to disintegrate unless we schedule in time for some real repairs. I am floundering, Vi, and I don't know how long I can keep this up."

"You're not the only one struggling to keep up."

"I never said I was!"

Violet glared at first, and then blinked. "It's only another day or two to Lucent Base. It would be less if we could get more power from the boilers."

"Vi—" Alice interrupted herself with an aggrieved groan. "Vi, I already told you, there's no more power to get from them. If we keep pushing max speeds, the patches won't hold and we'll be dead in the water. Then we'll be actually dead, all of us, because the ventilation system can't run on the spirit of rebellion. We barely have any biofuel left!"

"Where do you want me to go for fuel, Alice? There are no neutral beacons, not for days. They were all taken out by that explosion, which I'm sure is just a nice added bonus for the Coalition." Violet sucked her teeth and rolled her eyes. "It doesn't help that the rest of the beacons no longer accept grey market chips. We are running out of options."

"I understand that, but the physics of flight don't change just because we can't get fuel."

"As I said when we left Delta-4, our best bet is to get to Lucent Base, sweet talk Zink into letting us barter for fuel and whatever it is you feel you need, find Rosie, and get the hell out of there."

Alice threw off the covers, relishing the brief breeze the fluttering fabric created as it skated across her skin. "He barely gave me what I needed last time, what makes you think that two weeks will make the difference?"

"Because if he does have Rosie, we can use that to our advantage."

"What, so she's leverage now?"

"Yes, Alice, she's leverage. What would you have me do, land in their docks and demand to have her? Do you really think that would work, given that man's penchant for manipulation? We already know that he lied to us, he lied to Cass, and he lied to Cole."

"I'm not debating that he's a liar, Vi."

"Then surely you should see where I'm coming from."

"I don't think he'll be quick to strike a bargain with you when you've aligned us with a competing faction!"

Violet flinched, almost invisible, but not to Alice. She sighed again. "Please don't shout, Alice."

"I'm not shouting."

"Not now, but you were a moment ago."

Alice covered her face with her hands, speaking through them so that her voice was muffled. "I wasn't yelling."

Violet waited for a beat, and then another. It was a punishment, and Alice knew it. "I am patently aware that our alignment with The Splintered is disadvantageous in dealing with Zink, which is why we aren't going to tell him. As far as he is concerned, we have remained neutral."

"Did you tell Ned that?"

"Not yet, and don't you tell him, either. I will discuss it with him tomorrow, or some time before we land. Joining up with The Splintered was the best way to keep Ned with us, and not off on some other ship with captains who are more than happy to die for the cause." Violet rubbed at the bridge of her nose. "I don't want to talk about this anymore. I'm tired."

"Alright, fine, we won't talk about it anymore," Alice said bitterly.

Violet got into bed and turned off the light, turning to face away from her. Alice waited a moment, unsure of what she should do, but couldn't resist the painful yearning to feel Violet's skin against her own. She reached out, caressing a bare shoulder, fingertips trailing across dark skin, and for a split second, it felt like everything might turn out okay.

"I said I'm tired, Alice."

"Yeah." Alice pulled away, wounded, her heart thudding painfully in her chest, and it was more specific and acute than when she'd taken shrapnel to her eye. She was losing her, one fight at a time. In a cruel twist of fate, Alice wasn't sure what would stop her heart first, the ship imploding or losing the woman she'd fought so hard to hold.

She turned over, tears pooling in the corners of her eyes, and she pressed her pillow over her face to stifle the sobs that gathered in her throat. It was perhaps an overreaction, but she was overwrought with exhaustion, wracked with worry, and not having Violet made it feel like her world was coming apart faster than poorly riveted iron girders. Her stomach clenched, and she tried to ignore it, wrapping her arms around herself for comfort.

After a time, her breathing slowed, and she vowed to make things right in the morning. There was still tomorrow, even if there wouldn't be many days after that. As she began to drift off, the ship's alarms began to sound.

Chapter 4

Chalidon was a strange city, built up with bricks and concrete, a desperate, futile attempt to recreate the Capital on Gamma-3 but without any of the pomp, circumstance, or opulence. The streets were not tree-lined, as on Gamma-3, but lined with slender towers created to send electricity, communications, and sedition off-world.

Georgie stapled the last of her flyers to one of these towers, stepping back onto the sidewalk to admire their efforts. Four hundred pages on four hundred towers, buildings, benches, and notice boards, and every single one of them read the exact same thing.

"All done?" Henry asked, snaking an arm around her waist.

"All done," Georgie agreed, planting a kiss on her forehead. "That took less time than I thought it would."

"We'd better get out of here before someone realizes that was us."

"Patrols are down lately, ever since Terringgough Gulch. I'm guessing the MPOs are too busy scraping metal out of that sector to notice what's been going on here on Delta-4."

Henry pulled her away from the street, but gently. She tucked a stray hair back into her elegant low bun and started up the back path that led to the Brushstroke Inn tavern. "Even so, we should get off this planet before things tighten up again."

"There's still plenty of work to be done. The election in Skelm is soon, and we don't know yet how that will play out."

"I need to get back home to work in the lab. Even though we don't have the weapon anymore, or know where it is, that doesn't mean I can't be doing research to plan for a defense against it. If the Coalition made one of those things, they'll definitely be building another one."

Georgie nodded, following her down an alley littered with broken iron bars, torn from old construction and abandoned when they were discovered to have rusted. "Home isn't safe anymore, either. Bans on any political or rebel groups? What happened to it being a bastion of neutrality?"

"Given what Cole has been up to, I guess they thought it was the only option."

"Cole," Georgie grumbled under her breath. "I wish I'd never laid eyes on that man."

"A lot has changed in just a few years."

"None of this would have happened if not for him." Georgie kicked a fractured brick, sending a chunk of dried clay spinning across the ground. "Maybe Emeline would have stayed on the damned ship if not for him."

"Your sister is just as stubborn as you are, so somehow, I doubt it."

"If she hadn't known she could go back to the Twisted Lantern, though? She might have stayed on the Cricket. She might never have been—kidnapped by that—"

"Georgina, we've been over this a million times. I know you're angry, but you can't change the past."

"Maybe not, but I can sure as hells make his life miserable in revenge."

"Would that really make you feel better?"

"Obviously."

Henry turned and shot her a look over one shoulder, an eyebrow arched in judgment. "I bet he won't even be there by the time we get back."

"Mm." Georgie didn't know how to tell Henry that she wanted to break one of the only promises they'd ever made to each other. "Maybe you're right."

"Of course I'm right. When am I ever not right?"

"When you're wrong."

"A rare occurrence, then."

"Rare, maybe, but certainly not unheard of."

"Have you heard from your mother?" Henry asked, stepping over an empty, cracked barrel, the metal belt around it missing, leaving a stripe around the middle pale and unsettling. That part of the wood had never been meant to see the light of day. "I know she worries when you're away."

"Can you blame her, after what happened to Em?"

"Did you send a wire or not, Georgina?"

"Of course I did, last night. I said we'd be leaving on a transport, and we'd see her and Lucy soon."

Henry hummed quietly, opening the back door to the tavern. "Ladies first," she said, holding the door open.

"Very funny," Georgie replied, taking the door from her. "I don't think anyone has had the audacity to refer to me as a lady other than you. Ruffian, rebel shit, woman with a big mouth, sure, but never *lady*."

"Are we here again tonight?" Henry asked, ignoring the comment.

"As far as I know."

"Good, I'm tired of dragging everything across town every other day."

Georgie laughed, closing the door behind them and latching it from the inside. "I did tell you to pack lighter."

"You didn't say we'd be running a marathon with it!"

"I sometimes wonder if Stockton has the same problem with Mae."

Henry tensed, glancing back at Georgie like she was anticipating something. When Georgie only shrugged, she nodded, picking at the cobwebs of the tavern's basement. "It's nice that you don't hate Bailey anymore."

"I never hated her. I just thought she shouldn't have been trying to steal you away when I was trapped in Skelm, having to dissolve bodies of The Scattered and dodging explosions left and right."

"She wasn't—"

"She was, but I don't care anymore. You left to find me. She found Mae." Georgie inhaled deeply, releasing it as a quiet hiss of mild contempt. "I am trying to learn that life isn't an easy straight line of consideration. She didn't know me then, and if I'd been in her boots, I'd have tried to steal you, too."

"Oh yeah?"

"Please, there was no stopping me."

Henry laughed, and the bright vibrancy echoed across the shelves packed with spare metallic components and tools lining the walls of the basement. "I was always going to choose you, Georgina Payne, no matter how we met."

"Any regrets?"

"Only that I moved in with a woman who always steals the blankets."

"Oh sure, says you. Every morning when I wake up, I'm half frozen, and you're wrapped up like a newborn kitten, all snug, and happy, and spoiled beyond belief."

"I'd hardly say that bunking out in a tavern basement is *spoiled.*"

"Please, you didn't see where Em and I were living for a few months back in Skelm."

"No, but I did fold myself into a crate of cleaning reagent and nearly die."

Georgie grabbed her hand and kissed it, still following behind her through the labyrinth of shelves and boxes of supplies. "And I will be forever grateful that you came back for me."

"After that first night we had together, could I really not?" Henry threw back her head with another laugh, this one rough at the edges, showing the slight rasp that had settled in her voice even despite the lung treatments she'd endured for months after that happened. "Did Marv say anything else, by the way?"

"No, not to me, anyway."

"I think he's lying."

"Why would he lie? He's letting us stay here, he's hosting an unofficial meeting space for The Splintered. Cass said she trusts him."

"He's too friendly with Josie for my liking," Henry whispered. "She's caused all of us plenty of strife over the years, and she's been too quiet for too long."

"She paid well, so can you blame him?"

"I just think we have enough to worry about without her messing everything up again."

Georgie reached out for the wall, running her hand along the cinderblock, looking for the light switch. She found it, turning the knob to pull light from the single bulb hanging from the low ceiling. "If we're lucky, she'll stay quiet. She's pissed off Captain Violet, The Scattered, The Splintered, Obsidian Enclave, and every Coalition ship in the Near Systems. There's no way she tries to rear her head again."

"I wish I had your confidence, Georgie."

"And I wish I was back home, laying next to you, digesting four plates of pancakes, but we can't all get what we want, can we?"

"Not in the middle of a war, anyway."

Georgie frowned, pushing open the door into the tavern. "Hmm," she muttered, pulling a string of cobwebs from her ponytail. "I guess this is a war now."

"No going back from Terringgough Gulch."

"No, there isn't."

Henry slid onto a tall stool at the bar, arranging her skirts around her, the dark blue fabric whispering against the unfinished wood. "The usual, Marv, I think."

The barkeep turned, glasses already in hand. "Food or drink?" he asked, shrugging his shoulders. "Both?"

"Both," Georgie answered. She turned to Henry with an apologetic look. "I'm hungry."

"You think I'm not? I had half those flyers, I'm run off my feet, thank you very much." Henry turned back to Marv, resting her forearms on the wooden bar, the varnish chipping at the edges. "No word from any of them yet?"

"Not a peep," he answered, scribbling their order on a slip of paper and shoving it through the kitchen window. It was barely a kitchen, really, hardly even fit for purpose. "But the Capital will be monitoring more and more now. You never know who might be listening."

"Nothing from Evie Anderson? Nothing coded?"

"Listen, Weaver, I told you I'll tell you when we hear something, and we haven't, alright?"

"It just seems strange that it's been almost a week with no contact." Henry smoothed her skirts angrily, rustling the fabric. She always did that when she was frustrated, a strange, archaic habit from her time at finishing school. A way to show annoyance without impropriety, even if she'd long since given up any illusions about what polite company meant. "Surely you understand our concerns?"

"I can't make the wires run any faster. We're lucky to get a channel down here at all with being underground, and we wouldn't without that antenna that Georgie strapped to the roof."

"You're sure you've not heard from Josie?"

Marv tossed the rag down on the counter, leaning forward. "If I told you once, I've told you a dozen different times—"

"We've got it, Marv, no need to take a threatening stance," Georgie interrupted, being sure to keep her tone sounding bored and neutral. "She'll be out of your hair soon enough, anyway."

He rolled his eyes, pushing through the swinging door into the kitchen with a loud, percussive huff. He was an odd man, quiet until he wasn't, guarded, collected, and easily riled. It was the combination of all of those things that put Georgie on edge whenever he was around, which was nearly always.

"What do you mean, *she?*" Henry asked?

"Hmm?"

"You said *she'll* be out of your hair, not *we.*"

Georgie grimaced. "Oh."

"Care to share whatever it is you've been planning without me, Georgina?" Henry's full lips were set into a frown, one eyebrow arched to show just how annoyed she really was. "I thought we'd agreed, no secrets."

"It's not a secret, I just haven't brought it up yet."

"The same could probably be said of most secrets. The definition of a secret is something you're keeping from someone else, and here you are, sitting on the stool next to me, keeping secrets."

"I didn't know how to tell you."

"Tell me what?"

Georgie breathed out a sigh, soft and methodical, camouflaging its existence. "I think you should go back home. They need you there, the lab needs you. Roger needs you. He can't do it without you, and he's said as such on multiple occasions."

"I am going back home for precisely all the reasons you've mentioned. What I don't understand is why I'm getting the impression that I'll be boarding one of the last safe transports off the planet alone."

"I have some concerns about the underbelly in Chalidon," Georgie explained slowly, considering every word before it passed her lips.

Henry cast her a withering glance. "*We're* the underbelly."

"You know what I mean. Talk of unions is starting to catch on here, especially with all the churn in and out of Skelm, but I have a feeling that the Coalition isn't going to take all this lying down. It's not going to be long before they send someone in to clean up the mess my sister made, and I worry they'll go after her next."

"Emeline already said she doesn't want to see you."

"And she won't. I don't have any intention of going back to Skelm." Georgie pulled at one of the snap buttons at her cuff. "I know that would be a death sentence."

"And then some."

"Yes, and then some," Georgie agreed. "I know."

"Let me get this straight." Henry folded her hands on top of the bar with that unsettling, manufactured poise that always showed through when she was angry. "You want to stay here, in Chalidon, sleeping on the floor of some speakeasy basement instead of our lovely bed at home, because you want to put up more flyers?"

"The ones we put up today will get removed sooner or later."

"Yes, and if you get caught putting up flyers encouraging people to commit treason, what do you think will happen? Do you think they'd give you a little slap on the wrist, a small fine, and that would be that?"

"No, of course not."

"*Of course not,*" Henry repeated, her eyes flashing. "Georgina, not only would you get thrown into prison, which I might add, is becoming increasingly more impossible to break our people out of, they would drag you through the streets. They'd make an example of you, a seditious janitor who tried to rise above her station in order to help The Scattered murder everyone in the city."

"But—"

Henry put up a hand to silence her. "Not only all of that, my love, but they would use you as a way to undermine and discredit your sister. Do you really think she'd get voters on her side with those kinds of connections to piracy and rebellion? Those records are sealed, at least as far as we know, but one wrong move, and Overseer Allemande will use your capture as a way to get what she wants. Again."

"I know, Henry."

"Then explain it. Tell me, for all the gods' sakes, why you'd choose that, instead of safety with me back home."

"Because—"

"And don't even get me started on how this little stunt would be undermining the promise we made to each other when I finally found you again. I do not want to be away from you." Henry reached out, cupping Georgie's face with the palm of her hand. "I don't ever want to be separated from you ever again."

"If there's a way to actually secure Chalidon for The Splintered, I think that I need to try."

"Alone?"

"There are others like us here, you know that."

Henry turned away, letting her hands fall back to her sides in defeat. "I don't know what to tell you half the time."

"What does that mean?"

"I know that losing your sister has—"

"I didn't lose her," Georgie interrupted. "She was stolen from me. I know that she's different now, she's even dangerous maybe, but that's all the more reason it should be me who tries to find out."

"And what am I supposed to tell your mother?" Henry asked. "What do I tell Lucy? She's getting older and you're gone half the time chasing after Emeline."

"Lucy is fine. She's living her dream. She's training with some of the best, you included. She's safe, she has her own bed at night and a roof over her head, and she has my mother to take care of her. Emeline is on her own and she's vulnerable."

"I don't think she's as vulnerable as you've convinced yourself she is."

"She's not even twenty years old, Henry."

"And at her age, you were already supporting all of them, Georgina. Would you say that you were weak and vulnerable then?"

Marv pushed through the kitchen door, the hinge squeaking angrily. "Food's up," he declared, sliding two steaming bowls across the bar. "Fresh, at least mostly. Made this morning."

"It's perfect, thank you," Henry said politely, pulling the bowl in front of her. "It smells scrumptious."

"Smells the same as it always does," he grumbled.

Georgie poked at the noodles, oozing with a vibrant green sauce that smelled like meadows in summer. Skelm mostly smelled of pollution, and she'd left Gamma-3 so long ago. Bradach was one thing, but meadows were another. She sighed, setting down her fork. "Maybe I wasn't weak or vulnerable, but it was too much pressure, and I nearly collapsed underneath it. I don't want that for her."

"She chose this, George."

"Maybe. She could have been forced."

"You and I both know that's not what we've heard from the reports." Henry took a delicate bite of the noodles, chewing thoughtfully, swallowing before she said anything else. "I thought you agreed to give her space?"

"I am giving her space. I'm here in Chalidon, aren't I?" Georgie looked away, fixing her stare on a bottle behind the bar. The label was new, glossy and black, embossed with gold leaf at the edges and over each of the letters, stamped from a script so florid, she could barely read it. "Hen, I just feel like I can do more to help here on Delta-4 than I can back home."

"You're needed back home, you're a valuable—"

"Stop."

"I'm not going to stop, it's true."

"I'll board the transport with you tomorrow if you want." Georgie shoved a forkful of noodles into her mouth, despite her waning hunger. She'd regret it later if she didn't, when she was lying on the floor and her stomach was rumbling, and that experience was too like Skelm to endure again. "I won't fight you."

Henry softened, letting a quiet sigh escape from her lips. "Whatever you feel you need to do, you should do it. I'm not going to stand in your way, but I'm also not going to stay here, if that's what you choose to do. I feel I have an obligation to help the others find out more about this weapon, try to find some way to overcome it, perhaps."

"I wouldn't ever ask you to abandon your own responsibilities."

"I know." Henry traced a fingertip along Georgie's jawline. "So I shouldn't do that, either. I just worry. I worry, your mother worries, Lucy worries. Everyone worries about you, except the person you worry about most."

"At least we know she doesn't want me dead."

"A small reassurance, I suppose."

Georgie swallowed another bite, feeling the knot in her stomach begin to loosen. "I wish there was a way that we could both do what we needed to do, but not be separated."

"Maybe someday, George."

"When this is all over."

Henry nodded thoughtfully, chewing her last bite of food, swallowing, balancing the fork on the empty bowl and gently nudging it towards the edge of the bar. "When this is all over," she repeated. "Whenever that might be."

"What will life look like then?"

"Hard to say. Perhaps it will look the way it does back home. Work, family, friends. For me, that's enough, so long as you're there to share it with."

"Come every hell or high water, I'll be there," Georgie reassured her. "I'm damn well going to miss that bed back home."

"Then hurry back to it." Henry rubbed her thumb over Georgie's callused knuckles. "Hurry back to me, and make sure you're in one piece."

"I'll send a wire every other day. Coded, the same way we did before. I'll have it bounced through the relays. It will look like jargon." Georgie's heart ached in her chest at the promise, knowing it meant they'd be separated again. "And I promise I won't stay here if it starts to get dangerous."

"Don't go to Skelm, Georgina."

"Why am I the only one with restrictions?"

"Because you're the only one who wants to go there."

"I could tell you not to go to Gamma-3, but I know that you're too smart to make a decision like that, so I won't."

Henry huffed quietly. "I'll go wherever I have to, in order to track this thing down."

"Why is this weapon your responsibility?" Georgie demanded. "You weren't on the team making it. It's not even your line of expertise! The last one, maybe, but you figured out the storm generators. This has nothing to do with—"

"George, do you really think that a weapon that strips atmosphere from a planet isn't within my scope?"

"A weapon that *what?*" Marv asked, standing in the kitchen doorway with two plates of salad. "It does *what?*"

Georgie shot Henry a look. "Nothing, Marv, she's just exaggerating."

"So there isn't a weapon that could do that?"

"No," Georgie lied, convincing him with a broad, friendly smile. "Nothing like that."

He stared at them both with suspicion before disappearing around the corner to the adjacent seating area to deliver the food he'd prepared.

"People will find out sooner or later," Henry protested.

"People will panic."

"They have a right to know."

"Chaos in the streets, Hen," Georgie countered. "Stampedes, fires, looting. People will die."

"They'll die regardless if that thing goes off."

"We don't even know where is safe right now, and with fuel shortages, it's not like people can just all board transports and float around in dark space, waiting for the all clear. There aren't enough damned ships for that, first of all." Georgie leaned in, resting her chin on Henry's shoulder. "So you have to figure out how to stop it. You figured out the last one, you'll figure out this one."

"No pressure."

"Still no word on Dr. Arteo?"

"Nothing. She vanished into the wind." Henry leaned her head against Georgie's, reaching up to pull her fingers through Georgie's ponytail. "So I guess we're really doing this. Separating, again."

"I guess we are."

"It had better not be as long this time around."

"It won't," Georgie promised, knowing that she had no right to make it, not when she had no idea what she was really doing in Chalidon other than trying to help her sister from afar. She leaned back onto her stool when a small, cloaked figure entered the tavern, sitting by themselves in the corner, face hidden. Something about them turned her blood to ice in her veins. There was rarely an unfriendly presence in the Brushstroke Inn, but something emanated from them that settled uneasily beneath her skin. "It won't," she repeated, offering Henry a wide smile.

"It had better not, Georgina Payne." Henry leaned in once again, whispering, "Please don't go to Skelm."

"I won't," Georgie replied, watching the stranger over Henry's shoulder. "Unless it's absolutely necessary."

Chapter 5

Mae drummed her fingers against the table, staring at the fabric in front of her. Deep viridian silk pooling in on itself, draping over the edge and hanging suspended, just a hair's breadth away from the floor.

"Are you going to draft that dress, or do I have to?" Abigail asked, standing in the doorway with two mugs. "Here, I made coffee. You look like you need it."

"Thanks."

"Didn't sleep again?"

"No." Mae took a deep sip of the coffee, wincing at the sweetness. "What did you put in this?"

"Four spoons of honey."

"Why?"

Abigail rolled her eyes, as though it was the most obvious answer in the Near Systems. "Because you look like you're half asleep, and I thought the sugar might help."

"If you want me to eat sugar, you could have just opened that fresh tin of sweets under the front desk."

"Since when is there a new pack?"

"Since I put one there yesterday. Nabbed it off the docks. They've been selling out in minutes once they hit the market." Mae set the mug down, frowning at it. Honey in coffee wasn't her favorite combination, it turned out. "And fine, I'll draft the dress. I'm just distracted."

"When are you leaving?" Abigail asked, tossing the question over her shoulder as she dug through the desk's shelves, looking for the treats.

"Leaving?"

"I don't know why you're kidding yourself, Mae, we both know you're going to go after her. You did last time."

"That was different."

"Different, different how? It looks the same to me. Your girlfriend goes off on some ill-advised mission, you bail her out."

"I didn't know she was going to be on Gamma-3 last time. That was a coincidence."

"No word yet?" Abigail asked, returning with the tin. She pried off the lid and offered it to Mae, taking several gold wrapped toffees for herself.

"Not a single one. Nothing. She disabled her tracker, not that I blame her, and no one has seen or heard from her since she told Captain Marshall that she was going to join up with the Cricket." Mae popped a sweet in her mouth, savoring the familiarity of it. It was the only thing that felt familiar, despite the muscle memory of her job. "I trust her, Abigail, but I don't trust her sister."

"No ideas where they might be?"

"None. I keep pestering Delia about reports from the Rim, but there's been nothing coming out of Turas-Mara other than more of their damned recruitment campaigns and boring, useless, redacted exploration reports."

"Would Bailey really go all the way out there?"

"I don't know. I'd say I hope not, but I don't know where I'd hope she would rather be. Nowhere is safe in the Near Systems, not anymore, not for any of us." Mae crumpled the wrapper in her hands and dropped it into the wastepaper basket at her feet. "For all we know, Olivia Guisette is a snake, and that information was poisoned, and Bailey is already sitting in a prison somewhere, awaiting sentencing." The thought dropped into her stomach like a rock, again, the same way it had with every worried thought that had crossed her mind from the second Bailey hadn't showed up with the rest of the crews.

"You aren't powerless, you know," Abigail said, nonchalant and leaning against the table. "You know people. You have connections."

"Useless out here."

"So I'll ask again, when are you leaving?"

"Where would I even start? I don't even have a single clue where she's gone, other than that it's about her damned sister. That would mean the Rim, but Bailey wouldn't be that foolish." Mae unwrapped another sweet. "At least, I hope not."

"If not the Rim, then where? Her home?"

Mae shook her head. "Hjarta was destroyed, there's nothing there now."

"She wouldn't go back to the Capital, would she?"

"Gods, I hope not." The thought had crossed her mind, but with the way they'd both crashed through the thin veil of decorum at the gala, it would be almost as risky as Turas-Mara. "Although I might be able to find out."

"How?"

"My parents." Mae grimaced at the thought of facing them again, when the last they'd seen of each other was when she'd been dragged from the front steps, drugged with truth serum, delirious, yet happy to be arrested because at least it meant getting away from them. "I don't think they'd answer a wire from me, though."

"Not from what you've told me."

"Not without blackmail."

"Extorting your own parents is certainly one hell of a line to cross," Abigail said lightly, taking another sweet from the tin. "These are always better than I remember."

"It's a line they crossed with me years ago. It's why my sister left home and never looked back, and it's why I followed suit. They treated us the same as they treated any of their contacts or clients, anything was useful. Every passing comment about a classmate had to be dissected for hints of information, every date was interrogated." Mae cringed at the memories. "I didn't really date then, that was more my sister."

"So what do you have on them that you could use?"

"It depends who I'm willing to make deals with. Unfortunately, the ones most ravenous for that sort of information are the ones who are also most likely to have me arrested." Mae glanced at her arm, at the tiny bump that indicated where her chip was buried beneath skin. "I imagine they had my arrest expunged, but if they didn't, I'll be arrested on sight."

"And if they did?"

"Then I'll have free rein over the Capital, more or less." She began to straighten the silk, preparing it for drafting, almost sad that she'd be using all of it for a customer. "This silk really is stunning."

"I told you so."

"I'm sorry I ever doubted you."

"I'm choosing the next batch, especially if you leave me on my own here again." Abigail turned, her head tilted as she took in the empty front room. "Although it's been awfully quiet lately."

"People are hurting for disposable credits now that grey market chips have been banned at all fuel beacons. It's a mess." Mae straightened, reaching for the measuring tape on the shelf above her head. "We'll be fine. We always are."

"But you are leaving, aren't you?"

"I don't know yet," Mae answered. "Yes." She brushed against the silk again, savoring it. "No."

"What happens if you don't?"

Mae measured and re-measured, forgetting the number as soon as she attained it. "That's too difficult to answer without knowing where in hells it is she went." She set the measuring tape down again and sighed. "Maybe you'd better do this. I can't stay focused, and I don't want to ruin this fabric. It's the last of it."

"Just leave it, I'll take care of it. We've got time. The initial fitting isn't for three days, and it's not like we have tons of other work lined up right now."

Mae stared out the window, blinking back the tears gathering in the corners of her eyes. "I can't believe she didn't tell me that she was going."

"Maybe she thought you wouldn't let her go."

"*Let* her? She does whatever she likes, whether I approve or not! It wasn't so long ago that she took off to that mining camp, dressed up as her sister. She was gone for *weeks*, Abigail."

"I know, I was here."

"I'm sorry that my love life is always so stressful."

"Not always. Only when she's gone." Abigail took one more sweet before returning the lid to the tin and setting it on the shelf. "If we keep these in front, I will eat every single one of them before you even notice that's what's happening." She sighed, brushing her hands against the aubergine wool of her skirts. "Thomas asked me to have dinner with him again."

"And?"

"And I said yes?"

"So you like him, then," Mae said, glad for the distraction from her own mess of a life.

"Well enough. He's sweet and kind, which is more than I can say for the last three I dated. He's been working the radio desk with Delia, now that Carmen's focus is split between that and trying to help track down that weapon."

"Makes sense," Mae said absentmindedly. "It's almost time for you to clock off, isn't it?"

"Why, are you trying to get rid of me?" Abigail asked, arms folded over her chest. "Afraid I'll stand here and hold the seam rippers hostage?" She jangled her keys in her hand, hesitating at the door. "I'm going to pick up dinner from the Pig. Do you want anything?"

"Noodles, if there are any left."

"Good." Abigail smiled. "I'll be back in a while, then. You'd better be sewing when I return." She flipped the sign to closed and locked the door behind her, leaving Mae alone with the beautiful fabric, running through her fingers and cascading to the table in a waterfall of potential.

With every passing day that Bailey was gone, and no word from her, Mae's ribs clenched a little tighter around her heart. Every moment was a cinching of the vise squeezing the air from her lungs, an opportunity for adrenaline to surge into her veins anew, despite her stasis. She could not fight, and she could not flee, because too many mysteries surrounded both.

When—if—she found Bailey, they'd have a long talk about how it wasn't appropriate to be running off without even a damned word. She could have told Marshall, or Violet, or anyone. She could have left them a note, if she was afraid they'd keep her from leaving. She could have sent Mae a cryptic wire, even just so she knew that she was alright. But she hadn't.

For some reason, she'd chosen to keep Mae in the dark, to keep her wondering and afraid, and Mae couldn't understand it. It wasn't how they lived their life together, so why all the secrecy? Why the lies? Something wasn't adding up, and with every basted stitch of the dress she worked on, what she needed to do became clearer in her mind, coming into focus like an unfamiliar room on a bright morning upon waking. She bent, stitching, lining up seams, pressing them flat, preparing the dress for the machine.

Abigail unlocked the door again, holding a stack of boxes in her arms. "I didn't know which noodles you'd want, so I got a little of everything."

"I hope you didn't put Evie out for that, they're barely scraping by without Rosie."

"Nah, she had them all ready. Said it's the same noodles, but different sauces. I got you some of that crispy fried tofu you like, too."

Mae nodded. "Thanks," she said, taking half of the boxes from Abigail. "Really, thank you."

Abigail nodded towards the stairs, still holding the boxes. "Eat in your apartment?"

"Yes, that is probably best." Mae followed her up, setting the food on her table and collecting a couple of plates and forks.

"Evie's a better cook than she thinks," Abigail said, already tucking into her dinner.

"She'd rather be working back in the code division, especially now. More coded stuff flying around than ever before, some of it so intense that it just looks like glitched jargon, not even whole characters."

Abigail chewed thoughtfully, gesturing at one of the boxes with her fork. "I think I prefer the spicy ones."

"Me, too."

"So when are you leaving?" Abigail asked, never one to leave a topic alone, always picking and pushing, and it was one thing Mae both loved and hated about her.

"I haven't decided yet," Mae answered, preparing her fork for another bite. "There's a lot to consider."

"Please, we all know you can't stay here while all this is going on. Look at you, all poised and ready like you're ready for battle."

Mae loaded up a fork, dragging the noodles through thick, viscous, spicy sauce. "I'm fresh out of armor."

"Not all armor is made of tempered steel." Abigail let the silence hang in the air, the weight of it crushing down on them both. "Some of it is silk and lace."

"Sometimes."

"Maybe even usually, but especially in the Capital."

Mae sighed, the sound of which wound up oddly strangled in her throat. "You don't have to tell me that. I'm more than intimately familiar with the social mores of that place." She huffed quietly to herself, adding, "Unfortunately."

"Then what's the plan?" Abigail asked, a notepad at the ready. "I want to know everything, in case something goes wrong."

"Why?"

"So that I know if I should book the painter to stencil my name on the door, obviously."

"Oh, right," Mae said with a snort. "Obviously." The noodles were delicious, and she savored the gentle stinging they left on her lips. "I don't have a plan."

"You'd better get one, and quick."

"Right now, my plan consists of questions rather than answers."

"Isn't that how the best plans start?" Abigail asked innocently, batting her eyelashes comically. "What good plan was ever born of months of research and dedication? No, surely the best plans are the ones we make up on a transport, once we're halfway to the destination."

Mae lifted an eyebrow. "You sound like you're speaking from experience."

"More or less. It was more about a man I thought I loved, and less about trying to topple the Coalition on the way to rescue my fair maiden beloved." Abigail smirked. "Though, for you, all of that tends to exist in the same space, doesn't it?"

"Perhaps more often than not," Mae admitted, huffing softly into her food. "But the fact remains that I don't even know where to start."

"I said it already, but I'm saying it again now—your parents would know."

"Maybe."

Abigail shook a fork at her. "Probably. Didn't you tell me that they are some of the finest political strategists in the Capital?"

"Is that what we're calling extortion now? Strategy?"

"It's a dangerous game, but a lucrative one if they have any information on where Bailey or her sister are hiding out."

"They'll want to know why."

"It's my guess that they already know why." Abigail shrugged easily at the idea of dealing with them, of asking them for help, as though it wasn't a poisoned chalice or a lifeline spun from barbed wire.

Mae's skin twinged with the inevitability. "I'll try to be back within two weeks."

"Bring back more of that candy, and we'll call it even."

Chapter 6

Olivia checked her appearance in the mirror outside Tarand's office, the same way she had for over eight and a half years. She tucked a hair back into the loose chignon at the nape of her neck, frowning at the greenish cast over her cheekbone, a souvenir from one of her fights with Cass.

Cass, who was probably ready to undermine her, to betray her, to send some anonymous tip to the High Council to say that she was a traitor, but even days after she'd reached the Capital, she was back at work, undisturbed.

"Ma'am?" she called through the door, tugging at the bodice of her dress. Gods, her heart rate had barely settled since the moment she boarded that transport back in Bradach, since she fought with Cass, since she'd gotten out of her cell in the first place. A whirlwind, and one she'd yet to recover from. "Ma'am, we have that meeting in a few minutes, to discuss the logistics of—"

"Yes, yes, Olivia, please calm down. I'm just finishing some paperwork. Open the door."

She did as she was told, turning the knob and stepping into Tarand's office, familiar like poison oak. She'd never seen it before—the scheming hidden in plain sight, camouflaged between meetings and paperwork, but now it seemed on proud display. "Good morning, Councilor."

"No coffee today?" Tarand pouted, looking up at her. "But you always bring me coffee."

"My greatest apologies, I was running late. Too much traffic in the tunnel this morning." Olivia offered her a sympathetic smile, shifting the files in her arms from one to the other. "I hear the meeting is fully catered."

"Oh, well, that's alright then, I suppose." Tarand stood, sweeping around the front of the desk, her silk robes floating behind her, whispering against the hand-woven rug. "I did miss you when you were gone, you know. Officer Abara isn't very good at making coffee."

"At least I'm back now."

Tarand cupped Olivia's chin, stepping closer to her until their lips were almost touching. "I cried for days when I thought I'd lost you. You have no idea the depths of my despair." She released Olivia, skirting around her to the door. "I wasn't sure I would survive it."

"I can only apologize for my absence." Olivia followed her out, locking the door behind them. She didn't have proof it was Tarand who ordered the missile to be fired at Terringgough Gulch, but somehow, she knew. Deep in her core was a fiery scrap of certainty, and it scorched at her bones from the inside out. She was within enemy territory, a strange feat after spending most of her life defending it. "I was so happy to be back in the Capital, doing exactly what I should be doing." Olivia smirked beneath a smile. At least that much wasn't a lie. She *was* doing exactly what she was supposed to be doing. Setting fire to the Coalition from the inside out.

"Such a terrible shame what happened out there. So many lives lost, but who could have foreseen such a malfunction? Not even you did, my dearest, and you were there!"

"I am lucky to be alive."

"Yes, very lucky that you managed to get into your shuttle and ferry yourself to safety. It's just unfortunate that the shuttle was lost in the subsequent blasts."

"Unavoidable, ma'am, given how quickly the fuel beacons went."

"Perhaps next time, we will send you with a pilot." Tarand looked over her shoulder with a bright, beaming smile. "Although with any good fortune, there won't be a next time. After all, Cassius Calvetti is dead."

"She is," Olivia lied. "I killed her myself, just before the malfunction."

It was a risky lie, but it was the only way to get her back in the building. The moment that folded, she'd better be long gone from Gamma-3. "A deserved execution."

"In any case, that little problem has been solved. Unfortunately, a new one has sprung up in her place, a Cole Marion, and he's already a thorn in our sides. Our intel, before our intel disappeared, suggested that he was forming an alliance with Obsidian Enclave."

"Try though he might, it's a worthless alliance. Obsidian Enclave has no bases within the Near Systems." Olivia glanced at her reflection as they passed another mirror. She looked almost the same as she had before, but the landscape was vastly different in her mind, a world built on lies and coercion and for the first time since she'd left the field, she felt alive again. "With fewer fuel beacons and the outlawing of grey market chips, even if they had a fleet, which I doubt, they'd be dead in dark space. Cole Marion's methodologies are no more than a puppet show for the masses."

"While I suspect you are right, Olivia, I urge you not to underestimate them. You're too young to remember, as am I, but the history books don't lie. Obsidian Enclave caused a good many problems for us, back in the day, when Norah Gordon was at the helm." Tarand fluffed the silk of her robes as she walked, pausing just before the conference room. "Her death was like cutting off the head of the snake, and we'll do the same for whatever other rebel faction leader shows up and starts to agitate things." She paused, checking her reflection in a mirror, adjusting the broad necklace at her throat, studded with gemstones and arranged into a peacock feather. "The same should be said for political candidates who threaten the status quo."

"Agreed," Olivia said, and her stomach turned again. Emeline Allemande's days were numbered, if Tarand had her way. She cleared her throat quietly, trying to urge her on, or they'd be late. "But we already have a team on that, do we not?"

"Oh, yes," Tarand said, waving her hand in the air. "Just a small reconnaissance team, gathering information from the people there on the ground. It has been a challenge, with all of the churn in Skelm, but we cannot risk a revolution building there again if we allow people to stay longer than their rotations."

"Has there been any interesting intel as of yet?"

"Not yet, but have faith, dearest. Right will triumph over wrong in the end. Reason over chaos, and innovation over regression. We will not fail, because we cannot fail." Tarand pressed a fingertip to her cheekbone, smoothing over her skin with precision. She scowled at her reflection, turning away from the truth that it told. "You're making us late, Olivia. Keep up."

"Sorry, Councilor. My apologies, once again."

"The meeting with the rest of the High Council must go ahead next week. We've already lost too much time with the initial rescheduling due to the explosion at Terringgough Gulch. Until we could confirm that it was a malfunction, it was too risky for Jacobs to travel from Delta-4, and Fredericks from The Armory."

"Understood, ma'am."

"This needs to go off without a hitch. The gala needs to be flawless and impressive, some crumbs for the press to report on. We need to get things locked down, and fast, and without most of our loyal citizens figuring out that Calvetti was loose in the first place."

"I can only continue to offer my deepest shame for allowing it in the first place."

Tarand laid a hand on Olivia's arm, dropping back to walk alongside her. "The fault lies with me. I did not adequately prepare you for the realities of your position. I did not share with you the dangers that we must keep at bay."

Dangers you created in a weapons lab, Olivia thought, but she only smiled, lowering her gaze out of mock respect. It didn't matter if it was a mockery; Tarand didn't realize it. "I will spend the rest of my life working to make up for my failures."

"I am just glad that you have a life to spend, Olivia. When I heard of the explosion, I was inconsolable. A glimmer of hope, when Officers Abara and Miller reported that their vessel had survived, but barely—but when they said you'd been on the base when it happened, all was lost."

"I'm here now, ma'am."

"Yes, you are." Tarand crossed in front of her again, entering the conference room with grandiosity, a spectacle to be admired, a force of nature clad in purple silk with yellow embroidery. Briefly, Olivia wondered if she ever tired of wearing the same two colors.

Councilor Tarand stood at the head of a long table, where others were already seated. Kimura sat, arms folded over her chest, her assistant drumming his fingers against the empty notepad in front of him. It had been months since Olivia had been in the room, but it was gorgeously, venomously familiar, all the same. Sparkling sunlight filtered down through the refracted glass above them, casting a glittering palette across the deeply varnished wood that glared up into their eyes, beautiful and sharp.

"Welcome," Tarand announced, still standing. "Thank you for joining me this morning."

"I have a lot to do, Cecelia, so how about we get to the point?" Kimura retorted. "It's not you having to organize secure transports for three of our six, it's me, and I would have thought you of all people would realize just how dangerous that is right now." She shook her head, coiled braids immovable atop her head. "The High Council meeting needs to be postponed until we can confirm that the mess made by Terringgough Gulch's detonation hasn't caused any further issues with transit or piracy," Kimura said.

Tarand tilted her head easily, staring the other councilor down. "We have things well under control."

"Do we? Because last I heard, the area was rife with unsanctioned scrapper crews."

"Who are being dealt with appropriately."

"And you want me to send three high councilors through all that?" Councilor Kimura asked, scoffing noisily. "Have you lost your senses, Cecelia?"

"Histrionics aren't going to help us. As you may well remember from your elementary school education, not all flight paths cross through that area. Thus, your security protocols should be largely unchanged."

"The damage extends far past the initial explosion, and you know it. Six fuel beacons added to the list of collateral damage, not to mention the three frigates that got caught in the fray."

Tarand smiled at her. "Only three? I would have thought that would be good news, Flora."

"Not when most of them are still tied up sending supplies out to the Rim, and the lack of raw materials makes the manufacture of replacement ships slow and arduous."

"Then mine the rhodium faster."

Councilor Kimura smiled back, and something about it made Olivia sink back in her seat. She might be the newest addition to the High Council, but she was no fool. "I propose we add a seventh councilor, one who would sit at the Rim and oversee operations there."

"Absolutely not," Tarand said, barking a laugh. "At the Rim? Flora, when I recommended you for this esteemed position—"

"You were doing so to save your own ass." Kimura raised an eyebrow, leaning forward in her chair. "You messed up, Cecelia, and everyone knows it. I was about to break the entirety of the rebellion wide open, and you panicked. You set fire to the entire mission, and for what? Because you felt threatened?"

"Because you were liaising with rebels."

"Something you have to do when you're trying to root out corruption, not that I'd expect you to understand that."

"What is that supposed to mean?" Tarand demanded.

Councilor Kimura paused for a long moment, allowing the silence to seep into each of them, a strange, hovering power granted only to those who could harness it. The former Judge had honed those skills over decades of service to the Coalition. "I would nominate Amaranth Allemande for the seat."

"You must be joking."

"I am not. She is already established at the Rim, she spends more time out there than in her own sector. We can easily fill her role, and she would step in, working with General Fineglass to increase efficiency and productivity out there, and ensuring successful exploration and construction."

"She's a nuisance, Flora."

"She's easy enough to handle."

"Why not Fineglass, if you're so desperate for another seat? Which, by the way, I am not going to be advocating for."

Councilor Kimura picked a grape from the plate in front of her, chewing slowly, methodically. "You don't have to advocate for it. I've already pitched the idea to the other four councilors, and they've all agreed that another seat is necessary as the Coalition expands." She tilted her head slowly. "And I think you would agree as well that none of us wants to be going out there on a regular basis. Not with the levels of shrapnel flying around after that explosion, and not with—how many factions have you managed to miss, now? Three? Three factions, all of whom want us dead."

"We can't provide adequate security to her out there."

"She has General Fineglass and the might of several squadrons. Taking into account the civilian contractors, she'd be as protected as we are here in the Capital."

Tarand, still standing, tapped the back of the chair, rhythmic and irritating as her nails clicked against the wood. "And so you called this meeting for what reason, then? To gloat? That's not very becoming of a high councilor, Flora."

"I am not gloating, I am informing you."

"You could have informed me earlier."

"I could have, but then you'd have run to the others the first chance you got to undermine me. You see the addition of councilors as a threat to your authority, a diminution of your stature, rather than as a sign that the Coalition is healthy and growing." Councilor Kimura tore another grape from the stem, tossing it lazily into her mouth. "You think that you have the upper hand, Cecelia, but the truth of the matter is that I am just as powerful as you are. You should have thought of that before you hauled me into your office last year, moments before I boarded my flight."

"I know you were joining the rebellion."

"That is preposterous, and as several inquiries have shown, you have no proof."

"We can't ask Allemande, it's her adopted daughter making waves in Skelm. How do you think that looks?" Tarand asked. "It makes us look weak. Inept. Prey ripe for the picking."

"It makes us look progressive, and wouldn't you rather she be far away from that girl? It will be easier to deal with Emeline Allemande if she isn't standing in the safety of her mother's shadow."

Olivia reached for a slice of melon, retracting her hand when Tarand shot her a withering glare. Her stomach growled quietly in protest, and she was regretting not stopping at the bakery despite the traffic. She cleared her throat, a polite interruption. "Councilor Kimura, have you ever met Emeline Allemande?"

"I have not."

"She's formidable. Don't underestimate her. While her star has risen thanks to her mother's meteoric rise—especially if she is to be appointed as a member of the High Council—Emeline often operates behind her mother's back. We would be smart to keep her under that surveillance."

Councilor Kimura stared at Olivia and then blinked. "She is under plenty of surveillance at present."

"I understand that, but—"

"Our Intelligence agents are working around the clock to keep tabs on that girl, and on the election, and so far, we have no need to worry. The election will proceed as planned, and the results will bear out that Governor Das remains the governor of the settlement."

"Governor Das is an insipid fool," Tarand hissed, smacking her palm against the table. "She jeopardized several missions in her desperation to be front page news."

"Would you rather have Das or Emeline Allemande?" Councilor Kimura asked. "Those are our options right now, Cecelia. We cannot rock the boat so much in Skelm, not right now. Patience is key."

"Don't talk to me about patience, you little wretch. I've been in this job far longer than you have."

"If you think I didn't have to exercise extreme levels of restraint in my role as Judge, then I beg of you to think again." The final two words were staccato, pointed in their attack. Kimura smiled, but it was wan, and she stood. "You have underestimated me for too long, Cecelia. We need a cool head at the Rim, someone who knows the station, can handle investors, and who would do best to keep away from Skelm, no matter what the election result is."

"You think you've won this morning, Flora, but mark my words, I will not stand adding a new member to the High Council, and the gods as my witnesses, it will not be Amaranth Allemande."

"It's all but done. Fight it if you wish, write letters to undermine me, but once the official votes are in, the decision is final. You know that, and I know that."

"Then I have until the full High Council meeting to be heard."

"Do as you must, but sooner or later you will realize that I was right to add another member, and right to suggest Allemande. Who do you think could handle the isolation and deprivation of the Rim? You? Me? No, we enjoy our silken sheets too much. The others aren't interested in spending their days on a cramped station, either, and a new recruit would take months to train, and they'd spend their time being undermined by Allemande."

"So you think we should reward that behavior with a promotion?"

"I think we reward her for keeping her mouth shut when prisoners escaped on *your* ship."

Tarand stilled, letting her hands drop to her sides. "I don't know what you're talking about."

"Please, it was the same day the weapon was stolen off Turas-Mara. If I didn't know any better, Cecelia, I could point the finger of treason right back at you. You're the one who allowed it to be stolen, and for prisoners to escape. We have no idea where any of them are now, least of all that damned Scattered agent, Carmen Rojas."

"The Scattered are less of a problem, now that I have personally seen to Calvetti's demise."

"True enough, maybe, but Cole Marion teaming up with Obsidian Enclave is going to keep you rather busy, I would think." Councilor Kimura turned towards the door, waving for her assistant to follow. "Trevor, please call ahead to our lunch meeting and let them know that we can push up the time. I think we're done here." She floated out the door, purple chiffon trailing behind her.

Olivia risked a glance at Tarand, and immediately regretted it, wincing from the residual hatred in the councilor's stare. "Ma'am, I—"

"You could have said something, you know."

"I did! I said that Emeline is best left to be watched by her mother, something I think is the truth. Kimura is underestimating her, and—"

"And then you rolled over like you were Kimura's lapdog." Tarand stalked to the door, slamming it, closing them in, trapping Olivia between rage and a seventh-floor window that looked out over a beautifully landscaped rock garden. "Did she pay you for you to sell me out like that?"

"What? No!"

"You're telling me that in all of your meetings, and surveillance of Kimura's office, and her irritating little assistant, you didn't hear a word about any of this?"

"No, of course not." Olivia shifted in the chair, and the arm of it began to dig into her side, a painful reminder of the predicament she was in. "I would never betray your trust like that," she lied. Lying was becoming a second nature, or rather, she was uncovering her natural predilection to it, like blowing dust off of long-buried bones in a desert. "Kimura must have known you would react this way."

"We don't need another member of the High Council, we barely need the ones we already have! In my estimation, at least half of them could be demoted. Do we really need someone whose sole purpose is determining the structural integrity of docks on settlements we barely use?"

"Dock collapses accounted for many deaths before infrastructure was prioritized—"

Tarand clenched her fists at her sides, tightening and releasing, over and over. "And that needn't have been done by a member of the High Council."

"You're right, ma'am, of course," Olivia demurred. "What do you want to do about this?"

"If Kimura is telling the truth, then it's all but a done deal. However," Tarand said, and the hope and opportunity shimmered in the air like mist, "if she is obfuscating the reality of the situation, then we have an opening to stop this charade from happening. Allemande on the High Council would be a mockery of justice. She's a frustrating little snake, slithering around, thinking she knows what's best for the Near Systems when she doesn't have the slightest clue."

"I can make contact with other assistants and get a feel for what they are moving for." Olivia averted her eyes, wanting to escape the sheer rage present on Tarand's face. Somehow, jumping out the window to painful freedom was looking more palatable by the second. There were three railings on the way down. She'd probably only break one leg, not both. "It's possible that Kimura only sold them on the idea of another councilor under duress, or the potential thought they might have to travel to Turas-Mara themselves."

"Possible, yes. Most of them don't have our fortitude, Olivia."

"Yes, ma'am."

"How did she find out about the prisoners escaping on my ship?"

"If I had to guess, ma'am, I would wager that Overseer Allemande let it slip in exchange for consideration of the position. Who else would know that, other than General Fineglass, maybe a select other few?" She glanced towards the door, knowing that Officer Remy Abara wasn't far. "Though, to my knowledge, those are all being kept under close watch as well."

"They are." Tarand sat in the chair next to Olivia, taking her hands. "I believe you're right about the overseer. We have to consider her as an enemy now, as someone who wants to undermine us, overthrow us. You know how Amaranth Allemande is. She would sell out her own daughter if it meant she got to have what she wanted."

"What if we made her?" Olivia suggested. "Put her in a position where she was forced to choose."

"Explain."

"Kimura mentioned the election, which I'm assuming will be..." Olivia trailed off, finally meeting Tarand's stare.

"Rigged."

"Well, before that happens, we make a big thing of it in the press, that Emeline is too young, that she needs guidance, the kind of guidance only a former governor could give. Make it so that we may let her win, but only if her mother comes home to roost."

"It has potential, but it needs more teeth, Olivia."

"If Emeline Allemande wins the election, and Governor Das is deposed, and Overseer Allemande is stuck ruling with her daughter over petty nonsense in Skelm, even if the others want another appointee, it would take months to find someone. Years, even, if we're lucky."

Tarand stood again, pacing, her hands clasped behind her back. "It could work, I suppose, but first, you must find out how serious all this is. For all we know, Flora Kimura is playing us for fools."

"She very well may be."

"I never should have brought her into the fold. I should have had her thrown off a balcony when I had the chance."

Olivia flinched, but said nothing. It wasn't a surprise now, hearing it. Not after what Tarand had ordered for Terringgough Gulch.

"Sort it out, Olivia. I depend on you to keep this kind of nonsense from my doorstep."

"Of course, ma'am," Olivia answered, scribbling notes in the margins of her notepad. And then, in tiny, illegible script, a tiny pair of initials in the left-hand corner. CC. A reminder of who she'd left behind, and who could still throw her to the wolves if she so wanted.

Chapter 7

Cass was so tired of late night transport hopping. Bone tired, and exhaustion settled in her like a damp cold, clammy and oppressive. With the entirety of the Near Systems after her, and even some beyond the Rim, she couldn't afford to be taking any risks. She climbed into the cargo hold of another rebel ship, one more that had cautiously aligned itself with her. Loyalty, but with a steep price. Freedom, but only if it already looked like they'd win.

She sighed, settling herself atop a stack of dilapidated wooden crates, her legs dangling off the sides. Whatever they were carrying as cargo, it smelled like rancid bog water. Cass didn't even feel tempted to look, afraid that when she pried off a lid, that the smell would only get worse. The last thing she wanted was another thirty-six hours of stench. The last transport had been bad enough, loaded full with half-rotted produce that people were more than desperate to take. The food shortages were getting worse, and with grey market chips outlawed, many weren't just hungry, they were destitute.

Most nights, she laid awake, staring at whatever identical ceiling was above her, tapping incoherent rhythms into the wood as she tried to envision what a victory would look like. She didn't want to lead, she never had. Besides, heading up a rebellion was one thing, and long meetings about infrastructure were another entirely. In one way she knew exactly what she was fighting for—the safety of every scared, displaced refugee she saw along the way—but in another way, she was lost in the ether, grasping for answers that weren't there.

Maybe she was just tired.

Or maybe, if she was lucky, she was already dead, and none of this was actually her responsibility.

She tossed a wormy apple at the wall of the bay, and it exploded into a fine mist of juice and mealy pulp.

"Throwing things around again, Calvetti?"

Cass sat up, crossing her legs beneath her. "I didn't know this was your ship, Captain Tansy." She eyed the crutch under her arm with concern. "What happened there?"

"It's not my ship, it's one in the fleet, and what happened is some Coalition bastard blew the bottom of my cybernetic leg off."

"I'm sorry to hear that."

"Better it than the other leg. Less mess." Captain Tansy cracked a smirk, leaning heavily against a nearby crate. "What brings you onto a ship in my fleet, throwing fruit at the walls?"

"Transport hopping."

"I'd heard you were somewhere with that going on. Where are you headed?"

Cass ran a hand through her short hair, ruffling it. "Originally, I was headed back to Chalidon, but I heard there have been extra checks at the docks again."

"There are," the captain replied with a nod. "Nothing we can't get past, if you're desperate."

"No, I should get back on the trail of this damned weapon. Cole sold it off to Gregor Zink and the rest of the Obsidian Enclave, and we're all scrambling. The gods only know what Zink is planning to do with that thing."

"Knowing him, and I hate to say it, but we should prepare for the worst."

"My thoughts exactly."

Captain Tansy leaned over, pressing the button to close the cargo hold. "How did you wind up on this beacon, then?"

"Hopped a frigate."

"With permission?"

"Better to ask forgiveness than permission. Isn't that what they all say?" Cass asked, raising an eyebrow, and letting it fall immediately back into place. She didn't have the energy for verbal sparring. "Beggars can't be choosers."

"I'll be swapping ships at the next beacon if you wanted to come back to Bradach."

"Can't. Splintered, Scattered, everyone has been banned."

"That hasn't stopped Cole Marion," Captain Tansy replied with a shrug. "Why should it stop you?"

"Because I don't have the weapon, I don't have my own ship, the rebels who do support me don't want to tell anyone they do, and because my integrity is the last shred of anything that I have left." Cass swallowed back another sigh, squeezing her eyes closed as though everything would be fine once she opened them. "Never thought that would be the case."

"Because you didn't foresee being ousted?"

"Because, historically, my integrity has fallen far short of anything admirable."

"Ah."

Cass played with the zipper of her jumpsuit, tugging it up and down over the jagged teeth. "I never really wanted any of this, you know?"

"Did any of us?"

"I guess not."

The ship's engines kicked into gear, emitting a constant, low hum that was a strange sort of comfort, despite her resentment of jumping from ship to ship, alone, the rest of her crew spread across the Near Systems. Lights flickered above them for a brief moment as it lifted off the ground, exiting the beacon and picking up speed as it entered dark space.

She allowed herself the briefest breath of relief before cycling right back into the doom again. Cass rubbed her palms against her knees, savoring the light roughness of the worn twill, pilled on the surface, tiny blobs of grey collecting under her fingertips as she pulled at them. "What are you doing in Bradach?"

"Need my leg repaired, don't I?" Captain Tansy said with a grimace. "I've gotten so used to relying on it that I feel too vulnerable without it. Not to mention, I need at least a few days of break. I need to sleep in a better bed than I've got on my ship. I need to soak in the mirrored sun, and I need time to harass Evie and Larkin about the accounts."

"I wish I could go with you." Cass bit her lip, trying to blink back the tears that continued to threaten to come. "I wish a lot of things."

"We all do."

"What would life have looked like for us, if we'd have lived through better times? Peaceful times?" Cass asked. "Who might we have become if this wasn't what stole so much of us away?"

"No such thing as peaceful times, Calvetti," Captain Tansy replied softly. "Just different people feeling the imbalance, the inequality. Different people, in a far-off settlement, and so we all convince ourselves that it's fine, but it's not, is it?"

"No, it's not."

"The Coalition has gone too far this time. Too many are suffering, while too few soak up the benefits of their labor. Too many have lost people." The captain adjusted the crutch, scowling at it for a moment, the padding at the top tangling in the fabric of her loose, white blouse. "Plenty are starting to question what happened at Terringgough."

"Unsurprising. Hard to hide an explosion like that. What does surprise me is that they didn't just immediately blame it on The Scattered."

"Too public, plus, why would people believe that you'd blow up your own base?"

"It wasn't the base, it was—never mind, it doesn't matter. It's gone, and The Scattered are fracturing, and I'm dragging myself across the Near Systems looking for a gods-damned weapon that Zink has probably already hidden away somewhere far away from Lucent Base." Cass buried her face in her hands and groaned. "Maybe I should just pretend I'm dead again. Let someone else deal with this."

"I don't think you have it within you to give up on this."

"Damn."

Captain Tansy snorted a quiet laugh, tossing a braid over her shoulder. "I'd be lying if I said I wasn't looking forward to at least a few days of down time. The past few months—years at this point—have been hard on all of us. My crew is suffering. The rest of the refugee relocation fleet is struggling. This time last year we were laughing and throwing a party every time we had a successful mission. Now, it's all we can do to keep hot food on the table, and keep whatever medicines we can flowing into the settlements."

"It's a shame that High Council meeting wasn't within the blast zone of Terringgough. That would have solved a lot of our problems."

"They never would have fired that missile if they were."

"No," Cass agreed. "But it would have been amazing."

"For about ten minutes, until someone worse stepped in. Power loves a vacuum."

"At least then it could be someone else's problem for ten minutes."

The airlock swished open, revealing a young woman with shoulder length green hair, wielding a frighteningly large wrench.

"You're Ivy, right?" Cass said.

"I am. What are you doing on this ship, Calvetti? We're not headed to Bradach."

"Good, neither am I."

Ivy slotted the wrench into the tool belt at her hips, pushing her hair over her shoulder. "We're aiming for one of the settlements. There was some kind of outbreak there, they are in dire need of supplies."

Captain Tansy sighed angrily. "I keep telling Zane to let me relocate his people, but he never listens. Says everywhere is just as dangerous, and maybe he's right, but damn if I don't hate having to fly out there to save his sorry ass every time something like this happens."

"We're about a day to the next fuel beacon," Ivy said, inspecting an open box of copper wiring with interest. "And from there, another two days to the settlement Tant. Are you coming with us, Calvetti?"

Cass rubbed at her temple, the delicate throb of a headache already beginning to pulse. "I'm not sure. I'm trying to track down the weapon."

"We haven't seen it, and we haven't heard anything, either."

"No, I suspected not. Cole is playing this all very close to the vest. We're lucky we found out he sold the damned thing to Zink in the first place. I'm on some wild chase across the Near Systems, basically just hoping that something jumps out at me before I get arrested or killed."

"Are you aiming for Lucent Base?" Ivy asked, bending to tie the lace of her mid-calf boots.

"I hadn't planned on it, he wouldn't be foolish enough to take it there. If he sees me, he may well shoot me on sight, now that he has what he wanted from The Scattered. His politeness and candor were only extended because he thought I'd have what he wanted." Cass smacked the wood, immediately regretting it when a tiny sliver embedded itself in her palm. "Even if I did, I wouldn't let him get his grubby little hands all over it."

Captain Tansy sat on a crate, leaning the crutch against it. The empty bottom half of her pant leg draped over the side, and she scowled at it. "I miss my leg."

"Won't be too long to get you back there," Ivy said. "The gods know we all need you back in the air as soon as possible."

"With all these blockades everywhere, I don't even know how much good I'll be. Every day, a new cordon with gunships. Every day, more unwarranted searches of transports and cargo vessels at gunpoint. There are some days I wish I'd just stayed at the Pig."

Ivy nodded, tracing a grease stain on her elbow. "I wouldn't trade anything for what I have now, but some days I wish I could fit in a nap. Maybe even two, if I was lucky."

Lucky. The word burned in Cass' ears, and she had to turn away before the sound of it slipped into her stomach with an angry roil. She'd never been lucky, until she had, and then she'd lost her immediately, proving that it hadn't been good luck at all, just another piercing cosmic joke. "Are you staying with this ship, Ivy? Or are you hopping onto another vessel at the fuel beacon?"

"I haven't decided yet," she answered sheepishly. "There are still some repairs I could do here, but I feel guilty staying, knowing that so many are in such dire need of repairs out there. It feels selfish to stay in one place too long."

"*Breathing* feels selfish, lately," Captain Tansy mused. "Using too much oxygen, when someone else might make better use of it."

"Most people aren't out there, day in and day out, ferrying refugees across the Near Systems," Cass said, her back aching from the last transport where she'd spent the entire time inside of a crate of rotten melons. "You are."

"And yet, I find myself just waiting for it all to be over. I'm tired. Someone else needs to take over for a while. I'll go pull pints of ale with Larkin and listen to her prattle on about the properties of pea flowers and violets." The captain groaned, pushing herself off the crate. "I shouldn't complain. She's done more to innovate in that place than I ever did. I lost interest after a while. Poured my heart and soul into it, and then the wanderlust set in."

Cass nodded. "I know the feeling. Like an itch under your skin that tells you everything will feel better if you can just be somewhere new."

"I'm running out of new places, Calvetti."

"You and me both."

Ivy bounced on the balls of her feet, nervous energy seeking an outlet. "I can grab some food from the galley if you're both hungry."

"I don't know, I probably still smell like rotten melon," Cass replied.

Captain Tansy snorted. "I was wondering what that was."

"There's a crew shower on the other side of the loading bay—we don't have any spare rooms, unfortunately. We're overfilled as it is, I've been sleeping on the floor in the boiler room."

"I think if I did that, I'd never make it off the floor," the captain said. "What about you, Cass?"

"I had to sleep on the floor in that cell, that was enough for me." It had only been a few weeks, and yet her time in the Coalition prison already felt like it had been years ago, a fading, distant memory that was also uncomfortably visceral when she dreamed, an inescapable curse. "I'll sleep on some crates."

"I don't know if that's any better," Captain Tansy grumbled, "but it will have to do. Ivy, some food sounds great. Whatever you have would be fine."

Ivy nodded, heading back through the airlock with a passing pneumatic hiss. The captain shifted, looking at Cass but not saying anything.

"What?" Cass asked.

"I'm waiting for the moment you ask me why I haven't directed my fleet to officially join up with The Splintered."

"You don't have to explain. I understand."

"Do you?"

Cass glanced away, focusing on a tall stack of boxes against the far wall. They were battered, beaten, and weather-worn, but the faded Coalition logo was still emblazoned onto the sides. "I am a dangerous person to be affiliated with. You have your own concerns, your own responsibilities."

"I do. But still, there must be a part of you that's frustrated."

"Even if I was, would it matter?"

"I don't want you to think I'm not on your side, Calvetti. I may be working in another arena these days, but my heart has always been with the rebellion. I just can't risk the people that travel with my fleet any more than I already have. They're vulnerable."

"You don't have to tell me that, I know."

"Off the record, I think Cole Marion is a dangerous fool who never should have been put in charge."

"There was no one else. Not really." Cass flicked a pebble from the tread of her boot, and it skittered across the metal floor of the bay. "I probably should have thought about that before I gave myself up. Not that I'm sure I would have done any better."

"You at least never used Bradach as a political outpost."

"No, I never did that."

"He's going to get people killed, Calvetti."

Cass pushed herself off the crate, pacing past the rest of the cargo. "You think I don't know that? I tried talking to him. He's as stubborn as he is dense, though that's nothing new. He was never quiet about wanting to go back to Skelm, to finish what he started, he said."

Captain Tansy nodded and pried the lid from a crate, frowning at the contents. "This shit is barely fit for consumption."

"Not much else to go around lately, unless you like the taste of protein bricks."

"I don't think anyone likes the taste of those things. They have a strange texture that I just can't handle, you know what I mean?" Captain Tansy asked, examining a head of lettuce with browning leaves. "Horrifying," she said, grimacing at it before dropping it back into the crate. "And to think, both Obsidian Enclave and the Coalition have as much as they want of whatever they want."

Cass shook her head. "I don't know about that. Not for the Coalition, anyway. When I was back on Gamma-3, they were putting up razor wire around the granaries."

"That explains the influx of relocation requests from Gamma-3."

"I thought your fleet didn't go there."

Captain Tansy gave her a guilty glance. "We don't. Too dangerous."

"Where do they go?"

"Some try to smuggle themselves off-world, although that's become increasingly more difficult. If they manage to get somewhere like Skelm, or Chalidon, or one of the fuel beacons, we can do our best to schedule a pickup. The problems arise when they aren't prepared to wait the amount of time it takes for us to plan and get there. Some leave before we arrive, they were too desperate, or maybe some ran into trouble." She shrugged. "Some nights I stand in the shower for forty-five minutes, wondering how in hells I'm going to sleep at night, knowing I let someone down."

"I wish I could say I was unfamiliar with the sensation," Cass said, pausing at a crate, "but I'm not. I spend too much time wondering which of my decisions caused pain. It wasn't my call, but thirty-eight people in Skelm died, and maybe they wouldn't have, if I hadn't convinced Lawrence Tripp to join up with The Scattered. Jessop is dead, and that's my fault. Olivia is—" Cass squeezed her eyes shut, trying to forget. "Who knows? She could be setting a trap for me, for all I know."

"Then use it," Captain Tansy replied.

"What?"

"If she's trying to trap you, trap her first."

"And you have so much experience in that?" Cass asked with a laugh.

"I have enough."

Ivy burst through the airlock, barely even waiting until the door opened. She was gasping for air, bent double, trying to catch her breath.

"Ivy, what's the matter?" Captain Tansy demanded, heading to her side, the crutch under her arm. "What happened? Are you alright?"

"I'm—fine," Ivy gasped. "We're—fine."

Cass took the burlap sack from Ivy's hands, guiding her to a crate to sit. "What's the matter?" she asked, a knot of dread kneading her stomach, squeezing at her lungs.

"Cricket—hit. We got—" Ivy took a deep breath, gulping for air. "We got a distress call. We don't know where they are, the signal has been bounced between too many relays. They're hit and dead in the water, and we don't know where they are."

"Fuck," Captain Tansy said.

Cass turned, vomiting into an empty crate. *Fuck* was right.

Chapter 8

Nox Beacon was cold, dark, and frankly, slightly disgusting. Bailey trailed a finger through the thick layer of dust atop the table she was sitting at, frowning at the residue. She'd taken the fastest transport out there, and still, it had taken over a week. The clock hanging from the peak of the beacon chimed, and she sighed angrily. Maybe her sister—if she should even be calling her that—had lied. She was probably back on Turas-Mara, making an order for her immediate capture.

"You couldn't have at least dyed your hair?"

Bailey turned, surprised to see her out of uniform, clad instead in a nondescript, matching grey training set with purple piping at the sides. Bailey flipped her braid over her shoulder. "Why would I dye my hair?" she asked.

"So that you're not running around the Near Systems looking like my twin, obviously. Yet here you are, my mirror image, apparently. Still." She sat across from Bailey, her mouth set into a frown. "Why did you bring me here?"

"I didn't bring you anywhere, Wilhemina."

"You summoned me, then."

"And you could have ignored it, but you didn't."

"So here we are."

Bailey nodded. "Here we are," she repeated. "You're not in uniform."

"What an astute observation, little sister. Did it occur to you that I may not want to look quite so obvious in this scum-infested hole?"

"I'm surprised they let you leave the station."

"When you're a general, people don't tend to question you." Wilhemina leaned against the table, her meaty forearms braced against its surface. "Not until recently, that is."

"They know you're up to something."

"I'm not up to anything, thank you very much."

"What do you call this, then?"

"A mistake." Wilhemina stood, but Bailey grabbed her by the wrist.

"Wait."

"Why should I?"

"Because you're curious, or you wouldn't have come in the first place. You'd have had me arrested the moment you got my letter."

Wilhemina searched her face, and finding nothing, sat back down. "That was a clever little trick. How did you manage that?"

"Someday, I'll tell you." Bailey was hesitant to spill her guts, knowing that this could all still be an elaborate trap, if not set by Olivia Guisette, then set by Wilhemina Fineglass, who was continuing to glare at her.

"It's not every day you get mail from the right hand to a member of the High Council."

"I'm sorry if you'd hoped that it would be something better than this."

"I don't think I was hoping for anything in particular, beyond maybe a stay of execution."

"For Marina?" Bailey asked, still bitter, still angry.

"For myself." Wilhemina sighed, leaning forward. "Tell me what you know about them watching me, and I'll tell you what I've found out about us. Who we are, why we were separated."

"Okay." Bailey cracked her knuckles, one at a time, and Wilhemina mirrored her. "We have contacts on the inside."

"Obviously."

"One of them suggested that the High Council is watching you. Your erratic behavior—"

"I think you mean, *your* erratic behavior. I was a model citizen before all of this."

"Sure. Anyway, they're not happy, and they're keeping a close eye on you."

"Can't be too close an eye, not with me all the way out here. The only one out here qualified to check me is Overseer Allemande, supreme pain in my ass."

"Welcome to the club."

Wilhemina almost cracked a smile, but stifled it. "How that woman rose through the ranks is a mystery to me. I've almost convinced myself that she's not human, once or twice."

"I wish," Bailey agreed, watching silhouetted shadows cross her peripheral vision.

"What else did they say?"

Bailey averted her eyes, staring up at the huge clock just as the minute hand dredged itself forward with an oppressive clicking noise. She was almost surprised she'd heard it over the din of ships arriving and departing every few moments, the fumes lingering potent in the air. "Have you been protecting me?"

"Of course not, don't be ridiculous. You're the reason I'm in this whole damned mess in the first place. If I'd had my way, you'd be pushing up daisies."

"You had the opportunity, and you didn't kill me. Why?"

"Dead bodies require paperwork. Paperwork requires witnesses, and your face would strip me of my military clearance in about four seconds flat. I haven't worked my entire adult life to let some pissant ruin everything for me by sticking her tongue down some débutante's throat at a gala." Wilhemina drummed her fingers against the greasy wood of the table. "I hope she was at least worth it."

Guilt burned in Bailey's chest as she nodded. "She is. Although, she might boot me out when I get back."

"Why is that? Have you been sticking your tongue down another débutante's throat?"

"No!"

"Honestly, Stockton, the state of you. Ruining my life and then ruining your own at the first opportunity." Wilhemina cocked an eyebrow. "If it was even much of a life to ruin in the first place."

"I didn't tell her I was coming here."

"A secret mission?"

"I left the ship I was on. I lied to my captain, lied to another captain, and lied to Mae, just to come here and sit across from you to be berated." Bailey dusted off her jumpsuit, wondering why in hells she'd even bothered.

Wilhemina sucked her teeth, an odd little sound, but one she made often. "Why did you really come out here? Why did you really ask to meet again?"

"I needed to know if you were protecting me."

"Why?"

"Because—because none of this makes any sense, Wilhemina. Neither of us knew who we were, the truth about us, and I can't help but be curious. Can you?"

"No." Wilhemina pulled several rumpled pages from her breast pocket, sliding them across the table. "Which is why I went looking for this."

"Birth certificates?"

"Yes. Look, here is the one I knew about." She unfolded one, facing it towards Bailey. "My adoptive parents' names are listed, as customary, as guardians. Born in the Capital, date of birth, et cetera."

"You're only eighteen months older than me?"

"Just wait. Now look here, this is one I found in the archives. It's redacted to hells and back."

Bailey examined both pages, squinting at the paper like it would help her to understand the incomprehensible. "How did you get access to the archives?"

"Allemande."

"I didn't think she'd want to help you track down your long-lost past."

"I convinced a few of your little friends to break into her office. They found a file, hidden in a false drawer. I'm sure you've heard all about that by now."

Bailey nodded. "There's no photo of me, and my name is crossed out."

"It's for the best." Wilhemina jabbed a fingertip against the wood, creating an oddly hollow sound against the din of the beacon. "But in that false drawer was something they missed, a passcode for remote access to the archives. It took some time, wire delays being what they are out here, but I finally managed to have copies sent out."

"Generals don't get archival access?"

Wilhemina scowled at her, scoffing at her ignorance. "Of course I get archival access, but it's monitored. This way, if anything gets flagged, it looks like Allemande is the one sniffing around, not me."

"Could that be why some of the higher-ups back in the Capital are watching you?"

"I don't know. Maybe." Wilhemina took the papers, stuffing them back into her pocket. "There were no records for you, obviously, with you being born off-world."

"That's to be expected, I guess."

"What are they hiding from us? Why are the names of my biological parents redacted?"

"To protect you?"

"No, you ignorant banana, it's to hide something from me. From us. It must be important, but I don't know what it is."

Bailey leaned back on the bench, the unfinished wood biting into her thighs. Across the beacon, a ship lifted off, leaving a cloud of steam in its wake. It made the air thick, heavy with humidity and something that felt like regret. "So what now?"

"Tell me what you know about your own mothers. Maybe we can piece something together."

"Belinda Stockton and her wife, Pilar Stockton. As far as I know, Belinda was my biological mother."

"How do you know for sure?" Wilhemina asked, glaring. Everything she said had a bark to it, an edge that kept Bailey off-balance.

"Well, I guess I don't know for sure, but I—we—look like her. A lot." She pulled an old, tattered photograph from her breast pocket, the only thing she'd saved from Hjarta before its destruction. Three figures against a background of black and white landscape, a small Bailey with both of her mothers. Bailey held it out with trepidation, almost afraid that Wilhemina would tear it in half, or set it on fire, or something equally destructive. Instead, she took it almost reverently, with an unfamiliar softness.

"Wow. We really do look like her."

"Strong genetics, I guess."

"What—" Wilhemina cleared her throat. "What was she like?"

"Strong. Brave. They both died when I was young, not long after this was taken. They gave their lives to protect the settlement from the Coalition."

"Rebels."

"Kind of. Mostly they were just people who wanted to be left alone, to try to build lives for themselves outside of Coalition control."

"But why would they want that? Why ignore the decades, centuries of progress? To live in some backwater?"

Bailey bit her tongue forcibly until the taste of copper filled her mouth. "It's about more than that, Wilhemina."

"Enlighten me, then. Explain why our mother—assuming we're not wrong—would lay down her life to prevent her people from accessing medicines and advanced equipment?"

"You have no idea what goes on, do you?"

"Of course I do. I'm a general in the Coalition military. I've seen more blood and firefights than you ever will." Wilhemina's jaw tensed as she looked at the photograph again, pulsing just beneath her skin. "Rebels attacking frigates and pirates looting freighters, nothing more than people who don't want to work for what they have. They'd rather steal it."

"People are starving."

"People want what they aren't entitled to."

"People are *dying,* Wilhemina, and it's because of Coalition policies. Can you seriously look at that redacted birth certificate and think that you're the only one they've lied to?"

Wilhemina set the photograph on the table, still looking at it. "I don't know what to think. A year ago, I was at the top of my field, building a research program at Turas-Mara. I didn't have any family, and then *you* showed up."

"I told you before, it wasn't my intention. I was as surprised as you were."

"It's difficult to trust you, Bailey."

"Then what are we even doing here?" Bailey asked with a scoff. "Why did you bother to show up?"

Once more, the clock ticked forward, as though it was forcibly counting down their moments together until they'd be torn apart again, just as they had been before. Wilhemina pointed at the tattooed skin peeking out from under Bailey's sleeve. "What's that?"

Bailey rolled up her sleeve, showing off the melon vines that curled around her forearm and bicep. "I may not have dyed my hair, but we're not identical. I had to do something to prove to people that I'm not you."

"Why did you have to prove that you're not me?"

"Because you're terrifying, obviously." She rolled her sleeve back down, buttoning the cuff at the edge. "You have a reputation for bloodshed."

"Hardly." Her sister tried to dismiss the comment, but when Bailey continued to stare her down, she continued. "It may be slightly overblown, and I may allow that. Keeps the troops in line." Wilhemina huffed out an angry sigh, smacking her palm against the bench with a hollow thud.

"You beat the hell out of Thomas."

"Who?"

"The prisoner on Turas-Mara. Not the pirates, the other one. The broadcaster." Bailey pulled at a piece of her braid, snapping off ends of her hair with quiet, almost inaudible pops. "You could have let him escape."

"I did!" Wilhemina protested, pushing against the table with a meaty fist before releasing, her shoulders slumped in defeat. "I don't—want you to hate me. For some reason. I don't know. It's confusing." Wilhemina flattened her palms against the table, her eyes closed against the dim, yellow lighting of the beacon. "I thought that the longer I stayed, the more I might be able to find out about me—about us, and I wanted to be there for the exploration missions." She opened her eyes, blinking. "I didn't think we'd find Obsidian Enclave out there. That... was a surprise."

"I think that's true for all of us."

"By the time I figured out what their plan was, the ones on the station, that is, I had to make a snap decision. Kill them all in the corridor, or let them go. I chose the latter." She grimaced. "You should have seen Allemande's face when she realized that they'd escaped on Tarand's ship. I thought she was going to toss all of us out an airlock. I think, given the opportunity, she still would."

Bailey put the photograph back in her pocket, suddenly overcome with an overwhelming sense of dread. She swallowed hard, fighting back the growing lump in her throat. "So what now?"

"We use your information to look through the archives. Find whatever we can on Belinda or Pilar Stockton, why they abandoned Gamma-3 for some backwater—"

"That backwater was my home. Hjarta was my home, Wilhemina."

"Regardless—"

"You're not going to find anything. I've looked. Others have looked. It's all sealed, all of it redacted, there's nothing. We'd have to go to the Capital to find the original papers, and we both know that's a death wish in the making. With the High Council watching you, you'd never even make it to the city before they dragged you back to the Rim. Or worse, threw you into a cell."

"Trust me, a cell might be preferable to dealing with Allemande. The gods help us if she ever gets promoted again. Gods willing, she won't. Hopefully, she's pissed off enough people that they leave her to rot on Turas-Mara."

"So if we can't get the files, then what?" Bailey asked, pulling at the fraying cuffs of her sleeves. The loose threads made her think of Mae, which twisted another knot into her stomach, and suddenly, bile was hovering in the back of her throat. "Where do we go from here?"

"I don't know. You're the one who called this meeting."

"I thought you'd have more than a redacted birth certificate to go on by now!"

Wilhemina huffed, a tiny growl lingering in her mouth. "Easy for you to say. You're walking around with nothing more than an old photograph!" She pressed a hand to her forehead, pushing hard against her skull until her skin flared red against the pressure. "If they know that I'm looking for information, it's not going to be long before that comes back to bite me."

"Then stop."

"And what, we never find out who we are, or why we are?"

Bailey shrugged. "Sometimes you don't find out."

"Horseshit. There's always an answer, and I'm damn well going to find it if it's the last thing I do."

"Willa, it might be the last thing you do if you're not careful. What good is an answer if it gets you killed?"

Wilhemina jerked backwards, a light but fervent gesture. "I don't think anyone has called me that since I was little."

"Your name is a mouthful."

"I—it's fine. You can call me that, if you want." Wilhemina tapped her thumb against the wood, drumming an odd, repeating rhythm. "I don't have any family, Bailey. My parents—adoptive parents, that is—died years back. My husband divorced me, though I'm sure you knew that."

"I did. He sent a letter to Mae after... well. After the papers."

"I never should have married him, the bastard. Good riddance to him. I hope he rots." Wilhemina met Bailey's eyes for just a second before looking away. "My point is, it's hard to not wonder who you are, or if there's some other reason why we exist. Maybe Belinda fooled around, maybe she left Gamma-3 to start over." She covered her face with her hands. "Gods, I'm a fool. Spending all these months wondering if she just didn't want me."

"I don't think that would have been it. She never left anyone behind, not even at the end." Bailey reached across the table, feeling like she should comfort her, but not knowing how. "I think it's normal to wonder where we came from."

"A luxury." Wilhemina looked away again, focusing her attention on an empty bay across the beacon, steam still rolling against the tiled walls in waves. "A luxury that I shouldn't be making time for in the middle of a war."

"A war." Bailey tugged at the ends of her braid, pulling at the split ends. "What happened to Terringgough Gulch, Willa?"

"Your guess is as good as mine. They said it was a malfunction."

"There was a missile. Yellow and purple, emblazoned with the Coalition crest."

Wilhemina shook her head fervently, unwilling to see the truth. "No. It can't be."

"Two witnesses."

"No one could have survived that."

"They almost didn't. They got lucky." Bailey let her braid drop with a soft thwack against her jumpsuit, the new twill fabric soft against her skin. "Who sent it?"

"I don't know. I can tell you—" Wilhemina interrupted herself with a heavy breath. "I can tell you that it may not have been the first time."

"When was the other time?"

"I always thought it was just rumors. Stories the MPOs tell, you know, they get bored. Conspiracies are fun, as long as they don't go too far. I don't know. It would have been a long time ago, years back, long before either of us were even alive, but there was an explosion during the last rebellion, the one that sent Obsidian Enclave scattering like roaches."

"I've never heard of that."

"You wouldn't, most of it is classified. Not exactly something they teach in schools."

"Mm." Bailey didn't answer, because she was wondering if Rosie knew about the explosion. Wondering if Wilhemina knew who she was, if she'd been tracking all of them the entire time. "Probably for the best," she said simply.

"In any case, I think it's best if we formulate a plan. We need to get into the archives to find the original, unredacted documents."

"I think we should take a breath first and maybe just..." Bailey trailed off. "Maybe just get out of here?"

"You want me to abandon my post?"

"They're going to catch you, Willa."

"Not if I'm careful, and we need me on the inside if we're going to find out what happened to us."

"Why can't we just leave? You can come back with me, start over, choose a new life. You don't have to join the resistance, but—"

"Have you joined the resistance?"

Bailey stared at her, unblinking. "I'm a rum-runner."

"One who knows where that secret settlement is, though."

"Yes."

"Would you tell me where it is?"

"No!" Bailey shouted, standing up from the table. "I should have known this was a fucking trap. Are they about to jump out of the shadows and arrest me, Willa?"

"Shut up and sit back down," her sister growled, yanking on her arm with an oddly tender, insistent force. "No one is going to arrest you unless you keep fucking yelling." Wilhemina waited until she was seated again before she continued. "This is going to be hard if we don't trust each other."

"You held me prisoner for a week in that office in the middle of nowhere. It's not exactly an outstanding foundation for trust, Willa."

"I didn't kill you, did I?"

"Small mercies, I guess."

Wilhemina bounced her leg beneath the table, balancing on the ball of her foot. "If you're in the rebellion, no matter which faction you've aligned yourself with, you need to know that it's going to get worse. Much worse."

"The blockades were a clue to that."

"More than blockades, Bailey. Gunships, and big ones. There has been movement across the Near Systems for weeks already. I don't know what they're planning, but it can't be good, and you can't be there, wherever *there* is."

"Are they going to attack Bradach?" Bailey asked, wincing at herself for having said the name aloud.

"There are whispers. Don't go back there. Promise me you won't go back there."

Bailey shook her head. "I can't promise that. Mae is there, and my friends, and hundreds of refugees."

"And political heads."

"Cole Marion is barely the head of anything. Cass took the rug right out from under him, and—"

"Whoa, hang on. Cassius Calvetti is alive?"

The air pulled itself out of Bailey's lungs. "What?" she asked, stalling for time, knowing it wouldn't be enough.

"She *is* alive, isn't she?"

"I... don't know."

"If Calvetti is alive, all the more reason you shouldn't go back there. They're going to rain down their might the moment they can."

"I have to go."

"Bailey, wait. Come with me."

"Go with you *where?*"

"Back to Turas-Mara, just long enough for me to gather myself. I'll hide you, and then we can go to the archives, and then I'll go wherever you want me to."

Bailey snorted. "You've got to be kidding me. That's the worst idea I've ever heard."

"It's the best one I've got."

Something about the desperation on Wilhemina's face, and knowing that having her on side could save Bradach, and Mae, and turn the tide of the war, made Bailey reconsider against all her better judgment. "Alright, fine. But if you lock me up again, I will make sure everyone knows exactly what you've been up to."

Wilhemina smiled broadly, and it was almost foreign on her face, jarring, like a crocodile or a dragon from one of the picture books Bailey had read as a child. "Deal."

Chapter 9

Violet squeezed her eyes shut for the fifth time, willing herself to wake up from the nightmare. Once more upon opening them, she was reminded that it wasn't a dream at all—it was reality. "Kady, send the SOS again," she said, and the words strangled in her throat.

"I've sent it three times already," Kady replied, more resigned than frantic. "But with the way we've been bouncing relays, they'll never figure out where we are. Not before we're taken."

"It's better than nothing."

"Boss," Ned whispered, already sitting at the navigation desk despite the ship's lack of forward motion. "They're closing in, and fast."

"Alice?" Violet called into the radio. "What's our status?"

"Whatever they just did, it fried our boilers and half the electrics. I rerouted the remaining power grid to ventilation and navigation."

"You can't fix it?"

"Maybe if we'd stopped for parts when I asked, but no, Vi, like I said three minutes ago, I can't fix it. Not unless you're hiding a few spare boilers in the cargo bay that I wasn't aware of."

Violet seethed, gripping the radio so fiercely in her hand that the aluminum strained against the screws holding it together. "Fine. Come up to the bridge if you can't fix it."

"I'm a mechanic, not a gods-damned miracle worker."

"I never asked you to perform miracles, Alice." Violet rubbed the bridge of her nose, and the knot in her stomach tightened into steel. There was no way out. Not this time. "Ned, report."

"Coalition tags, Boss. Two minutes, maybe three."

"Kady, what are the odds we can stealth?"

"Negative, Captain. We don't have enough power, and besides, they already know that we're here. Vanishing wouldn't help us."

Violet sighed. "I know." She pulled the manual override lever again, hoping against all the odds that it would magically power up the ship. It clicked into position, but the ship stayed silent, just as she knew it would. No boilers, no power. No power, no escape. They were trapped, and it was her fault, and no one was coming to save them, because no one even knew where they were. Even if they did, it would be too risky to put themselves between the Cricket and a Coalition ship. No one, not in The Scattered or The Splintered, had the kind of firepower it would take to shoot out a ship that size. "Ned, is there a signature?"

"Hold, I'm tracking it. The signal is in and out." He leaned closer to the screen, squinting at it.

"Vi." Alice was standing in the doorway to the bridge, her jumpsuit rumpled, unevenly toggled together from dressing in panic as the alarm sounded. "What's the plan?"

"There is no plan. This is it."

Alice blinked, her fingers brushing the rounded top of the large wrench hanging at her hip. "Who is it?"

"Shit," Ned uttered, leaning back in his seat. "Fucked gods."

"What is it?" Violet snapped, immediately regretting her tone. It wasn't just going to be her that went down, after all. "Who?" she asked, quieter that time.

"It's the C.S. Blackwall."

"That can't be," Alice said, now gripping the wrench, her knuckles white. "There's no way it would be out this far."

"I don't know what to tell you, Al, that's the signature on it." Ned twisted a dial on his desk, his brow furrowed. "This looks bigger than I remember."

"Is it a larger cargo vessel than before?" Violet asked, the panic rising rapidly in her chest. There was no sense in breathing exercises, not when the panic was well and truly warranted. "It is a cargo vessel, right?"

"I hate to be the bearer of bad news, Boss, but it looks more like a gunship."

"So much for being taken prisoner. I guess we just die instead."

Kady pushed off the wall she was leaning on, moving to pull at the same lever that Violet had been yanking at ever since she'd made it to the bridge after the alarm. "No," Kady said, flipping switches one after the other, despite the entire console being dark. "There has to be something. There must be a way. This can't be it, this can't be how we go down."

"We were playing a dangerous game," Violet answered. "We should have known that one day we'd overplay our hand and get caught."

"Why are you just giving up?" Kady shouted, whirling on her. "You're the captain of this gods-damned ship, do something!"

"There's nothing more to do. Alice can't fix the ship, I can't pilot with no power, and they're going to be at the bay any moment." The ship shuddered softly, and Violet closed her eyes as though that would make it all go away. "They're here."

Ned stood. "What if we hide in the compartment, and then we—"

"This is an old Coalition ship, Nedrick. You and I both know that's the first place they'd look."

"Corridors then, closets. And one by one, we sneak onto their vessel, and—"

"With the size of that ship, they'll have a crew of at least ten, probably fifteen. We're a crew of only four now. If we were still flying full, maybe, but we're not." Violet unholstered her revolver, checking the chamber before snapping it shut. "Six shots won't be enough to take them out."

"We should at least go out fighting," Ned offered, reaching for the heat gun propped against the navigation console. "Take as many out as we can. I'm not going back to a cell."

The sound of footsteps on the stairs to the bridge turned Violet's blood to ice. Even, rhythmic, the calling card of a competent captain. Alice saw her first, lunging forward before Ned held her back at the shoulders. "That won't be necessary," the captain said coolly. "We don't need to make this messy."

"Captain Josie Keller," Violet said, a simmering rage settling under her collar. She squared her shoulders, keeping the revolver in her hand. "What a surprise."

"Yes, I imagine you'd hoped you'd never lay eyes on me again, Violet Vear."

"If I'd wanted to ensure that, I'd have killed you myself the last time I had the displeasure of interacting with you. Instead, we granted you mercy."

Josie threw her head back with an irritating laugh, boisterous and noisy like the jangle of too many keys. "I would have thought you'd be thanking me, Vear, not threatening me."

"*Thank* you? You've done nothing but cause us trouble for years. Shooting at us, giving up our position to the Coalition, trying to sell us off to the highest bidder at Kilper—"

The lights flickered three times, and strange shadows danced against the wall before falling still once more. Josie flicked a long lock of hair over her shoulder with a nonchalant gesture. "And I'm the reason you're getting out of trouble. A little gratitude won't kill you." She holstered her pistol, inspecting the main console, running her fingers over it while holding Violet's stare.

"What in every known hell are you doing here?" Violet demanded.

"Saving your ass, obviously."

"Funny, it seems like you're boarding my ship, not saving my ass."

Josie snorted. "I'm not interested in your ass, Captain. I'm interested in all those fun weapons we just ripped off this Coalition ship."

"Weapons."

"Yeah, Vear, what did you think this was, a fun training exercise? I heard that Calvetti needs guns, and I need some clean credits to lay low for a while. I also heard that you're Splintered now, are you not?"

Alice shot Violet a look, but she ignored it. "Yes."

"Then you should be grateful that I commandeered this vessel an hour ago, just before it ran directly into you."

"Those bots nearly tore our ship apart, Keller. Those weapons shouldn't be in use anymore."

Josie threw out an aggrieved sigh, petulant and dramatic. "I didn't know about the bots, Violet. But you're alive, and you have me to thank for it. Once I part out your ship—"

"*Excuse* me?"

"Did you think this was charity? I just told you, I need clean credits. Whatever Calvetti gives me for the guns—and the bots—will be a good start, but it's not going to be enough."

"I swear to all the gods, whenever we're down, *you* show up to kick us," Violet spat.

Josie blinked at her with a bemused expression. "Isn't that what I promised? You murdered my captain, Vear. I told you that I would never let you rest, and I meant it." Josie smiled, a broad grin that was mocking and toothy. "You're lucky that even I'm not so heartless as to let a Coalition ship rip you apart."

"You're better off without him. He wasn't half the captain you are, and you know it. Leo never would have been able to pull off a heist at Turas-Mara, and he wouldn't have touched this job with a five thousand kilometer radius."

"You seem to be under the impression that I don't know all that," Josie said, glancing around the bridge. "Leo was cruel, and he was a fool, but he was still the father of my child, and you killed him."

"You'd have done the same in my position."

"Maybe. We'll never know, will we?" Josie strode across the bridge, looking out at the dark space outside the window. "He was charming when we first met. Enigmatic, you know the type. I didn't have anyone, and he asked me to join up with him. Things moved quickly after that, and before I knew it, I was pregnant."

"Where is your daughter these days?" Violet asked.

"None of your gods-damned business," Josie shot back. "As if I'd tell you anything, after what you've done." She unholstered her pistol again, swinging it around in circles by the trigger guard. Violet took a step backwards, and Josie laughed. "Not so tough when it's your own blood on the line, are you?"

"I'm not going to let you do this."

"You and what army? You've got this junker understaffed, there are only four of you. What happened to everyone else? Did they desert you?"

"Of course they fucking didn't," Alice sniped. "It's all well and good for you to be flying around, doing whatever you want without consequences, but we've had to make hard decisions."

"Like joining The Splintered?" Josie asked with a laugh. "The most underpowered of all the factions? You could have at least joined Obsidian Enclave. I hear they actually have ships that aren't falling apart."

"We don't all have the luxury of neutrality," Violet said. "Some of us have to lay what we have on the table and hope for the best."

"Do you even hear yourself?" Josie asked with a snorting laugh. "You think you're this moral paragon, but you aren't, Vear. You killed the father of my child. You let me and my crew get picked up by the Coalition, you—"

"If you hadn't been trying to shoot us out of the sky, that never would have happened!"

"You stole from me, Vear! Millions of credits, gone in a puff of smoke, and I don't know how you did it, but it's one more thing in a long list of horseshit from you."

Violet barked out a tired laugh. "The credits you were taking from Barnaby Meier for the *hostages* you took?"

"Please, you act like they were treated poorly. They were fed and watered, and I didn't hold them any longer than I had to. I'm only doing what I have to in order to survive. What the fuck are *you* doing?"

"Surviving! In spite of you and your spectacular levels of morality bending rationale."

"You don't even have the good graces and manners to thank me for bailing you out. They'd have found you one way or another, at least now they won't have a ship's signature to track." Josie unhooked the radio from her belt. "Dirk, take us to max speed. We need to get the hells out of here before reinforcements arrive, and we're already going to be losing speed towing this damned boat."

"I'm not letting you dismantle my ship, Josie," Violet said.

Josie spun the revolver around her finger again. "Alright, Vear, because I'm a reasonable woman, I'll give you an option. Either I tow your ship to the first scrap beacon we come across, or I let you keep your ship, but I take your mechanic."

"Don't you dare touch her," Violet hissed, her fists balled uselessly at her sides. She stepped forward, reaching for Alice even though she was on the other side of the bridge.

Josie held out the gun, pointing it first at Violet, and then at Alice. "You're in no position to be making demands. I've given you two choices. Choose."

"I'll go," Alice said, holding her hands up in surrender.

"Alice, no," Violet said firmly. "We're stuck out here without you, it won't make a difference."

"I'll go, on two conditions." Alice locked eyes with Violet, nodding gently. "Josie, tow the ship to a quiet location, and let me send encrypted coordinates to someone back in Bradach."

Josie laughed. "No."

"You need me, don't you? Something is wrong with one of your ships. Why else take me, and not Ned? We can't go anywhere without him, either, but you chose me."

"Fine. Agreed." Josie snapped a pair of iron cuffs around Alice's wrists, shoving her towards the door. "See you soon, Vear."

"Alice, wait!" Violet shouted, taking three steps to follow after them before Josie pointed her gun back at her.

"Not one more step, Captain."

"Vi, it's alright," Alice said over her shoulder as she was being nudged down the stairs. "I've done this before, remember? I'll be fine."

Violet nodded, tears gathering in her eyes, because what else could she do? Josie was right, she had no leverage. "I'll rip you to shreds for this, Keller."

Josie stepped forward and pressed the barrel of the gun to Violet's chest. "Stay the hells away from me, and we'll call this even. Test me, and I'll change my mind about what to do with her."

Chapter 10

Someone was pounding on the door, and it was the middle of the night, and Evie was so bone tired that she briefly considered letting Larkin murder whoever was on the other side. "Hang on," she called, untangling herself from the blankets on the couch. She'd fallen asleep working again, not that it was anything unusual, not lately. Larkin stirred, reaching out for her, trying to pull her back onto the couch. "Shh, it's fine," Evie whispered, kissing Larkin's hand before lowering it back down.

Flipping four deadbolts and unhooking four chains, she opened the door to find Delia, eyes puffy, and the now-familiar dark circles dragging at her face. "Sorry, I know it's late."

"Almost early, actually." Evie glanced at the clock on the wall behind her. "What does that say, three-thirty?"

"Yeah."

"What's the matter?"

"Carmen got a wire about an hour ago. It's encrypted. She's been trying to crack it herself, but she said you might be able to help. We don't know who it's from, but if it's encrypted, it could be Rosie. It could be her, right, Evie?"

"I—yeah, I guess it could be." Evie yawned, ruffling her hands through her cerulean hair. "Do you have it?"

"No, Carmen does, in the wire room."

"Alright, but I need coffee first."

"I hope you don't mind, but I already put some on in the kitchen. Carmen likes the dark roast."

"Yeah, I remember," Evie said, trying to force herself into something more like a waking state. She blinked and wiped the sleep from her eyes, stifling another yawn. Behind her, Larkin shifted, stretching her legs out to take up all the space on the couch. She could have slept in the bed, but she never wanted to be far, even when Evie was up late working on codes. Gods, how much sleep had she actually gotten? An hour? Two?

Delia started to cry, tears flowing freely down her face. "I'm sorry, I know I shouldn't be doing this, I just can't wait a single second if it could be her. What if she's in trouble? What if she's calling for help?"

"I'd do the same," Evie reassured her, closing the door and starting down the stairs. "Coffee, you say?"

"A fresh pot," Delia answered.

Evie nodded, rubbing sleep from her eyes and willing them to adjust to the light. "That's a great start. You said it was about an hour ago?"

"Yeah," Delia replied with a sniffle. "Bounced across at least a dozen relays, no way to know the place of origin."

"Standard these days, I suppose." Evie pushed into the kitchen, inhaling deep the scent of coffee, willing it to drown out the exhaustion that was pulling at the corners of consciousness. "No cipher markers?"

"None that either of us could see, but we're not the expert. You are."

"I don't know if I'd say that. Henry is probably better than me."

"Henry isn't here, she's in Chalidon."

Evie poured herself a cup, drinking it black, the way she liked it, savoring the taste of the bitter liquid as it slid down her throat. "Did you send her a wire?"

"We did, but there's no telling when she'll get it. For all we know, she and Georgie are already on a transport back this way. It could be days before we hear from them."

"Coffee?" Evie asked, holding the pot up.

"No thank you."

"You look like you haven't slept in days, Delia."

"I haven't. Not longer than twenty minutes at a time, anyway."

"Have you eaten?"

Delia shook her head. "Not much. Don't you start, I already have Carmen trying to force feed me, always showing up to the wire room with cookies and slices of cake."

"Okay, I won't." Evie rifled through a bread box, hunting for the last blueberry muffin. "I need to eat. I can't run on fumes." Locating it, she slid the lid back down, taking a bite of the pillowy sweet confection. "Damn, that's good."

"Did Rosie make that?"

"Hers never last the day. I think Sandrine made these. She's been helping out when she can, thank the gods. I'm barely keeping up."

Delia sniffled again, burying her head in her hands. "Rosie loves baking."

"And she's damned good at it," Evie replied, taking another bite. "We'll get her back, Delia, no matter what. We will."

"I don't even know where she is."

"I'm sure we'll hear from the Cricket soon. They're probably just quiet to keep any tracking attempts to a minimum."

"I was a fool, Evie. I left her once, years ago. I left her and I regretted it every single day after. I couldn't believe it when I found her again out at the Rim, after all that time, and now she's been taken from me, and I've forgotten how to function without her."

"Let's take a look at this code then," Evie said, after scraping the remaining crumbs into her mouth. "I bet we can handle it."

"I'll grab another coffee for Carmen. I don't think she's thrilled to be awake at this time, either."

"We do what we have to." Evie drained her mug and refilled it, handing the pot to Delia. "I'm sure she understands." Pushing open the basement door, she descended into the darkness, one creaky step at a time, until the soft glow of the desk lamp pooled against the floor. "Morning," Evie said, throwing a half-awake wave to Carmen.

"Oh good, you were awake."

"That might be an overstatement, but it doesn't matter. I'm here now."

Carmen's usual shiny, bouncy curls were tied back, frizzy and matted at the nape of her neck. "I'm sorry, I tried my best, but I can't get my head around this code. It doesn't look like anything else we've gotten before."

"Do you have a list of the relays it bounced across?"

"Only about half. The rest are scrambled."

"Hmm. Damn." Evie took the page from Carmen, squinting at it. "Nope, no cipher clues. Who in what hell sent this without a cipher code?"

"That was my question, too." Carmen glanced at the stairs and leaned forward in her chair, closing the gap between them. "I'm not so sure this is Rosie. She'd know to send a cipher, she's been around the wire desk enough over the past months to know that."

"Unless she didn't want to alert Zink?" Evie suggested, returning the whisper.

"Possible." Carmen leaned back with a sigh. "Yeah, that's possible."

"He's crafty, and maybe she didn't want to give him any reason to check this. I mean, without a cipher, it looks like jargon. It looks like it went through three scramblers."

"Maybe it did."

Evie nodded. "Maybe it did," she agreed. "Who else would be sending a cryptic code?" She examined the page again, frowning at the characters, all printed in Carmen's neat, legible handwriting. "Bailey?"

"We shouldn't rule that out. She could be trying to let Mae know she's okay, wherever in whichever hell she's in."

"How much does Bailey know about the cipher keys?"

Carmen shrugged. "I have no idea. She's not down here much. Almost never. So, it could fit. It could be her."

"It feels like we're fracturing," Evie said, and the future glimmered in front of them, dark and mysterious, filled with unknown dangers and more sleepless nights. "Like trying to hold on to a wine glass that's already shattering in my hands."

"Everything okay?"

Evie shook her head, forcing a smile. "Yeah, of course. I just don't like that so many of us are unaccounted for when everything is getting so dangerous. It's not just the blockades anymore, it's the grey chip ban, and fuel shortages, and what happened at Terringgough Gulch, and new factions..." she trailed off, looking back to Carmen. "Sorry. I'm just tired."

"I feel like we're all tired, where that's concerned." Carmen heaved a sigh, flapping the skirts of her butter yellow dress, sending them to brush quietly against the legs of the chair. "I was ready to die for The Scattered, and now I've renounced my alliance so that I can stay in Bradach. I don't know where to go from here."

"I don't think any of us know what in hells we're supposed to do."

Delia descended the stairs, a mug in each hand. "I brought more coffee, Carm," she said, and it was obvious that she was trying to suppress a lump in her throat, the words strangled and the tone unfamiliar. "Any ideas?" she asked.

"Not yet, there isn't a cipher key," Evie explained. "I'm not surprised, though, because if there was one, Carmen probably would have caught it. There may yet be one that I'm not seeing."

"How long do you think it will take you to figure it out?" Delia asked.

"That depends on many factors, I'm afraid." Evie placed a hand on Delia's arm. "I'll make it my top priority. Whoever it is trying to contact us, it must be important."

"Thank you, Evie. I don't know what I'd do if I didn't have you to turn to."

"You'd hunt down Henry and put her to work," Evie said with a laugh. "Hopefully she'll be back soon, so if I can't figure it out on my own, we can attack it together."

"We sent her the code, so maybe she'll get it before they both leave Delta-4." Delia checked her wrist watch and frowned at it. "They should be leaving today, so maybe she'll get it before they board the transport." She sighed, slumping back against the nicked support beam, the unfinished wood snagging on the satin of her emerald green blouse. "I just don't even know what to do anymore. I feel totally powerless."

"Just keep doing your job," Carmen offered kindly. "That's all any of us can do." She shuffled some pages, all of them neatly written, reordering them as she worked. "I think we have the morning bulletin done, though."

Delia glanced over Carmen's shoulder. "Anything interesting?"

"More blockades, as per the new usual. New polling numbers from Skelm—Emeline is still ahead, but Governor Das is pulling closer, probably due to the influx of Coalition loyalists they're pushing into the settlement."

"Bastards."

"It's to be expected. If they can't win fair and square, they'll cheat." Carmen scanned the pages, reading over them one at a time before handing them over to Delia. "And from what we can tell, the Coalition still thinks Cass is dead, although it's only a matter of time before they figure that one out. If Olivia Guisette is really on our side, having someone on the inside could really make a difference."

"Do you think she isn't?" Evie asked, sipping at her second mug of coffee.

"I think it's hard to know, given I saw her for all of five minutes before Cass let her escape off the docks." Carmen sighed. "She was nothing but business when I met her on Turas-Mara, but that's not necessarily a condemnation. Fineglass was all business, too, but Guisette said she thinks the general is covering for some of us. For Bailey, at least."

"Gods," Delia said, rubbing her eyes. "I miss when we knew exactly who was on what side. It made everything easier."

"Says the woman who was feeding rebels information for years before she got out."

"It was still better than this mess. Three factions now, assuming another one hasn't cropped up in the past five minutes. Hey, who wants to start a new faction?" Delia asked bitterly. "I hear it's all the rage these days."

"You can't blame Cass for that," Evie said. "Cole backed her into a corner."

"Cole is the biggest load of rotten produce I've ever seen. He's going to get more people killed, and he doesn't even care."

Evie nodded, thinking of Larkin asleep upstairs. "He's a liability."

"Someone should take him out," Delia said, locking eyes with her.

"Maybe someone should," Evie replied, averting her eyes, "but I wouldn't know who."

"Really? You don't know who should do that?"

"Delia—"

Carmen cleared her throat, holding her mug aloft over her head. "I need more coffee. Who wants a fresh pot?"

"Another?" Delia asked. "That will be your third since I got here."

"You keep me up late, this is what happens. I will run on caffeine and spite alone." Carmen stood, heading for the stairs. "You coming, Evie?"

It was an offering for an out, Evie knew, but she decided to stay. "I should get started on this code."

"Okay, if you're sure."

Evie sat in Carmen's seat, examining the code, scribbling notes in the margin of the page. No cipher key, but some consistencies that might point towards a conclusion, or at least another piece of the puzzle. Still, even the consistencies were running thin, and after just a few moments, she could still feel Delia's stare boring into her. "It can't be her, Delia," Evie said, without looking up. "She's retired."

"You don't think this is grounds for coming out of retirement?"

"If you're so concerned about Cole Marion, you go kill him, then."

"I'm not a trained assassin."

"She's *retired*."

Delia scoffed, pressing her loose curls against her scalp. "It could be the only way to save Rosie. To save Bradach, even, and you know she wants to do this."

"I don't think we should be making assumptions about what Larkin does or doesn't want to do."

"The only reason she hasn't done it yet is because of *you!*"

Evie bristled, suddenly regretting that she hadn't followed Carmen up to the kitchen. "You have no idea what she had to do in her old life. How she was used to do the Coalition's dirty work, chased across the Near Systems. Ralph Baker—Lionel Cabot—killed her parents in front of her. Tried to kill her, too, when she refused to keep taking contracts."

"We're not the Coalition, Anderson."

"I shot that man in the head to keep her safe. What makes you think that I'd let her put herself back in danger? She's had so many near misses it's a gods-damned miracle that she's even alive and not in a cell, and you want me to ask her to go kill Cole Marion?" Evie exhaled slowly, gripping the pen with so much force she thought she might snap it in half. "No."

"You don't have to ask her, you just have to *let* her."

"I don't tell Larkin what she can and can't do. You want her to do this, you ask her."

Delia huffed quietly. "If it was her that got taken, you'd burn down this whole settlement, including this tavern, if that's what it took to get her back. Why are you acting like me asking for help in doing the same for Rosie is an imposition?"

"An imposition? You're asking me to throw her back into a life she's now spent years getting away from. An imposition is waking me up in the middle of the night—which, for the record, I am not upset about—but what you're asking for goes so far beyond an imposition." Evie closed her eyes, breathing methodically to force her heart rate back to a normal speed. "There may yet be other ways to find her." She waved the pages above her head. "Like this code, for one thing."

"And if it's not Rosie, what then?"

"We can cross that bridge when we come to it."

Delia snorted, a derisive sound probably born of sleep deprivation and frustration, but still, it ground its way down under Evie's skin, rubbing angrily against her bones. "I should have known you'd say that," Delia said. "The two of you have barely left Bradach since you got here."

"There's plenty here to keep us busy."

"You've got her on one hell of a short leash."

For some reason, Evie was finding it harder to breathe, the fog of conflict being so dense and hard to swallow. It was manifesting itself in her lungs, wet and heavy with rot. "That's not how it is. If she wants to go, she can go."

"But you'd be angry."

"No."

Delia rolled her eyes, pushing off the beam with the toe of her polished boot. "Please, you've made it pretty gods-damned clear to all of us and everyone around that you don't want her doing that anymore."

"Because people would use her, given the opportunity."

"What exactly are you accusing me of?"

"Nothing!" Evie shot back, her hands shaking as she continued to make notes. "I don't want to argue with you, Delia."

"Who's arguing?"

"You are."

"I'm just asking why you're holding back one of our most powerful weapons," Delia said. "It's not like we have the luxury of choice.

Evie looked up at her, knowing her expression was pained. She could feel the tension settling between her brows and the wetness of her eyes. "She's not a weapon, she's a person."

"A person who can do what most of us can't. Not with the same precision, anyway."

"I already told you, if she wants to go take out Cole Marion, she's more than welcome to. I'm not stopping her. My hesitation is that he's probably got eyes all over that place. He knows that we don't want him here. He's resisting being tossed out, and the only reason no one has done it yet is because most of the people in Bradach are still sympathetic to The Scattered, with or without Cass."

Delia picked at a sliver of wood sticking out of the pillar, looking at Evie from the corner of her eye. "Then make it public Cass is still around. I wanted to put it on the airwaves the second we knew, but I was outvoted. Maybe if we had, Rosie would still be here."

"You don't know that."

"And neither do you."

"If we do that, then we put a target on Cass as well as Olivia Guisette," Evie explained. "They'd both spend all of their time being hunted, and running from that, instead of gathering intel that might turn things in our favor." She looked at Delia, meeting her eyes. "Like finding Rosie, for example."

"For all we know, Guisette is busy selling us out right now. We don't owe her allegiance or protection."

"And Cass?"

Delia huffed a sigh. "Cass can fend for herself, she's done it before. She's got the new faction to fall back on."

"We can't sacrifice everyone for this. Trying to fight against the Coalition is like trying to stop the gods-damned tide, and already we've lost so many. The price is too fucking high."

"What price have you paid?" Delia asked with a sneer. "Your love is still upstairs, sleeping soundly. Mine is probably halfway across the galaxy by now, maybe being dosed with truth serum for all we know, thanks to Kady forking over the recipe to Zink."

"You want to know what price I've paid?" Evie asked quietly. She pushed up the sleeves of her soft sleep shirt, displaying the web of tattoos that only just covered the scars. "I got sliced up by Allemande, and then she tried to kill me again when I went to Skelm for Larkin. Do you know how much iodine burns hurt, Forrest?"

Delia didn't answer. She only recoiled, looking away.

"Don't act like you're the only person who's lost something. We're all hurting, trying to do our best by the people who are still here, with whatever we have left of ourselves, despite spending years being slowly hollowed out by the Coalition." Evie pushed her sleeves back down. "Don't ask me to ask her to do this. If you want Larkin to do this, because you think that it will save Rosie, then you can damned well ask her yourself."

"I'm sorry," Delia whispered. "I know that I'm being a monster. I don't know how else to be when I'm so powerless."

"You're not a monster."

"I just can't shake the feeling that Cole knows where Rosie is. If she's not on Lucent Base, she could be anywhere. She could be on her way beyond the Rim, for all we know." Delia buried her face in her hands, stifling another sob. "With their technology, she could be out there already, outside radio contact. I just—" She sniffled, the sound strangled and painful. "I so wanted this code to be her telling me that she's alright, that she's on her way back to me, and that I don't have to worry."

"I know."

"She's the only thing that makes sense to me. I can't lose her again."

"I understand."

Delia uncovered her face, giving Evie a pathetic and guilty look. "Don't hate me, Anderson."

"I don't hate you."

Carmen's footsteps on the stairs drew their attention as she descended. "Hey, Larkin, I have that coffee," she said brightly, holding the steaming pot aloft.

"She's upstairs sleeping," Evie said, and already there was a pit in her stomach, rapidly filling with bile.

"No, she's not. I just saw her in the kitchen. She asked where you were, asked for coffee, and then I went to the bathroom. I assumed she came down here."

Evie and Delia exchanged a look, Evie's driven by panic, and Delia's by horror.

"She heard us," Evie said quietly. "She heard us, and now she's going to kill Cole Marion."

Chapter 11

Henry shifted in her seat, already uncomfortable. She never felt quite right when Georgie wasn't nearby, and the absence of her was like missing a chunk of flesh, as though it had been carved right out of her the moment she kissed Georgie goodbye on the dock and boarded the transport alone.

She understood why Georgie had to stay, and hadn't fought it much, but that didn't mean she had to like it. Despite the chaos that the destruction of Terringgough Gulch had caused, Chalidon was still a dangerous place to be, especially for someone who had been wanted by the Coalition for years. They both had, which was why most of their time was spent back in Bradach.

"Attention, passengers, boarding closes in five minutes. Please be sure to stow any luggage in the appropriate compartment and fasten your seatbelt for liftoff. We will reach the transport beacon in approximately three hours, assuming ideal conditions."

The puddle jumper transport only had hard, unforgiving seats, and the varnished wood, chipped from years of careless use, bit into the backs of her thighs. She'd been uncomfortable for weeks, nothing but a constant shifting roil in her stomach and a strange pressure beneath her navel. She'd known almost right away, of course. Henry had always had an understanding of her own body that told her when something wasn't quite right.

It was right—maybe not the ideal *time*, perhaps—but then, was there ever for something like this? Guilt prickled along her spine, heating a flush across her collarbones and neck that she hoped wasn't visible to any onlookers. The less attention she garnered, the better. Pulling her coat into her lap to hide it, she laid a hand against her stomach. She probably shouldn't have lied to Georgie, but Georgie never would have stayed if she hadn't, and that was a level of heaviness that Henry couldn't bear.

She'd told Georgie it hadn't worked.

In fairness, at the time, she thought that was the truth. Telltale signs in the following ten days after suggested the opposite, but knowing that Georgie would want to stay, she kept her mouth shut. Back to Bradach, back to the lab to figure out that damnable weapon, and she'd wait there for Georgie to return. If she could get out of Skelm when the entire settlement was on the hunt for her, she'd be able to slip off the Chalidon docks once she'd secured more support for Emeline. Henry couldn't take that from her, not when she'd spent years trying to track her sister down, to save her, to help her escape the clutches of Overseer Allemande, and to pressure her away from that now would be unfair, despite Henry's quiet desperation to have her near.

Passengers fumbled with luggage, stumbling over each other and mumbling against the quiet hum of the engines, already primed with steam and ready to carry them to the moon transport beacon. She'd catch a flight there back to Bradach, maybe with a pirate vessel or a rum-running crew, whichever left first.

Henry tore open a packet of crackers she'd stolen from behind the bar, crunching on the delicate salty flavoring, swallowing it down and willing her stomach to calm. It hadn't been easy, hiding it from Georgie, not when she had such an eagle eye for anything out of the ordinary. She'd been pouring her drinks into the plant in the Brush Stroke Inn, and to her horror, the plant had already begun to wilt. The guilt of that ate at her almost more than the nausea. She'd have to send Marv a new one as penance for what she'd done.

"Attention, passengers, boarding is now closed. Liftoff in sixty seconds."

She fastened her belt, leaning her head against the glass. The crackers were helping, but only a little. What she really wanted, inexplicably, was an enormous plate of mashed potatoes and boiled cabbage, and some of that dense bread that Rosie made.

Henry frowned, wishing there was a better way to keep contact with home, but with so many frequencies being monitored, and wires being intercepted by Intelligence agents, it was a risk that none of them felt comfortable taking, even in the instance of an emergency. Rosie had been taken, and no one knew where she was, and the last she'd heard, no one knew where Cass was, either.

Splintered, indeed.

The ship listed in the bay as the thrusters engaged, and the rocking motion threatened to bring up the crackers she'd just eaten. She covered her mouth with the back of her hand and closed her eyes, trying with all her might to suppress the almost irresistible urge to vomit. Gods below, no one had told her it would be quite like this early on. Eight weeks and counting, if her math was correct, and it was, because she'd spent hours poring over the calendar, marking off days with an almost undetectable x scrawled in the corner of each day, so that even if Georgie looked at it, she wouldn't know what it was.

Henry would tell her the second she was back in Bradach.

The transport heaved itself out of the bay, and her stomach lurched with such an intense discomfort that the only thing keeping those crackers inside was dedicated breathing and sheer force of will. Maybe she should have told Georgie already, but she didn't want to get her hopes up, in case it didn't stick. That happened, sometimes, frequently, even, especially with the procedure they'd used to create a whole from their two halves.

The others would probably wonder what in hells they were thinking, doing something like that when the entirely of the Near Systems was about to implode on itself, but if they waited until things felt stable and calm, the timing would never be right, and the both of them would miss out on something they both agreed they wanted so desperately that it ached inside them.

A family.

A small one, to be sure—Henry especially wasn't keen on repeating this process, given how she was feeling in that present moment—but a family, nonetheless, with Sandrine as a doting grandmother, and Lucy an excited aunt, and Emeline... well, she'd be more than welcome, if she ever changed her mind, not that it seemed likely that she would, despite Georgie's efforts. Sometimes, you just had to let people go, and hope that they came back to you when they were ready.

"Attention, passengers," said a different voice over the intercom. Henry's ears perked up, fearing a search by the Coalition military. "This is your captain speaking. We will be making two stops on this journey. The first, in about ninety minutes, at the Quisin Trade Beacon, and then the moon transport base will be our second and final stop for this vessel. Now that we are airborne, please feel free to move about the ship, and as a friendly reminder, there is no smoking allowed in passenger or cargo areas. Refreshments are available at the rear for a small fee. Grey market chips are not accepted."

The speaker clicked as it disconnected, and Henry sighed in relief. She had a new standard-issue chip, bought at an extremely high price with a fake name and identification, but that didn't mean she was completely safe from harm. Georgie had the same, both purchased at Kilper Station as soon as they were able to, after the grey market chips were banned in all Coalition-controlled zones. They were so high in demand that Georgie had to offer twice what they were usually worth, in rhodium, to beat out the others who were hoping to snap them up.

They were safer than most, at least for the moment, but how long would that last? How long could all of it continue before everything unraveled? Terringgough Gulch was only the beginning, a natural consequence of what had started in Skelm with the storm generators, and even earlier with the last real rebellion. Now there were three factions and counting, all hoping to overthrow the Coalition, none with anything resembling a cohesive plan for what they'd do if they managed to pull it off.

Once, she'd felt like she was at the center of it all, making the important discoveries, helping to locate and dismantle the storm generators, flying across the Near Systems to stop the Coalition in its tracks. But with the chaos of recent events, she felt small, adrift, as though things were now so much bigger than her that she didn't even know where to begin, other than to go home to Bradach, work on some research, and wait for her Georgie to return.

In some ways, maybe that was enough.

She didn't need to be the heroine that the galaxy needed. She just wanted to do her work, make some discoveries, help Roger run the lab, and, if everything went to plan, raise a little family with Georgie, and they'd all be safe, and warm, and happy.

Someday.

"Excuse me, is this seat taken?" A woman with an almost comically large hat stood next to the empty chair, eyebrows raised in question.

"Uh, no," Henry answered politely, despite being quietly irritated at no longer being alone.

"I'm so sorry, I got tied up at the docks, barely made it onto the transport before the ship left. I had to strap in back near the staff area! Can you even imagine?"

Henry glanced at her. "Mhmm," she mumbled, hoping that her lukewarm response would discourage further conversation. Given the turbulence of the ship, she wasn't sure how long she could keep the contents of her stomach contained, and preferred to focus on that, given half a chance.

The woman sat down in the adjacent seat, flapping with her things, un-buttoning her coat with a dramatic flourish, but leaving the hat obscuring her face. "Heading home?" she asked with a distinctly academic tone, condescending around the edges with a false sense of interested propriety.

"Something like that."

"Me, too. First time in a long time, in fact. It's been too long."

"I know the feeling."

"Have you ever been to Skelm?" the woman asked, adjusting her hat with the quiet crunch of felted wool resisting her manipulations.

"No," Henry lied. There was no sense in admitting to something that could potentially ensnare her into getting caught. "Never been to Skelm."

"A pity, it's such a fascinating settlement. I was only there for a short rotation, several years back."

Henry's breath caught in her throat. Rotation. The woman was either an MPO, management, or a scientist, and she didn't particularly look like the former. Silently, her heart began to race in her chest. "Oh?" she prompted innocently, wishing she'd have thought to wear an enormous hat, too.

"It was before all that business with the storms, and before it was rebuilt. I hear it's even better now that so much has been replaced."

"I wouldn't know."

The woman tilted her head, her face still obscured by the large folds of the hat, stuffed with a dizzying array of fake florals. "No, of course you wouldn't." She returned her attention to her bag, digging through it, small receipts fluttering to the floor in the almost-breeze of the air filtration system. "Damn things," she swore, picking them up and stuffing them back into her bag. "How long were you in Chalidon?"

Henry closed her eyes, trying to swallow back the bile that was creeping into her throat. "Just passing through." A lie, but only a technicality. "I don't much care for Chalidon." That much, at least, was the truth.

"Why not?"

"It's not home."

The woman faced her again, this time, her face more intent. "And where is home?"

"Oh, you know," Henry said, waving her hand vaguely. "A little town on Gamma-3."

"Ah, my favorite place to be, where the sun shines directly on your skin, not bounced off some mirrors. I do detest the mirrors, don't you?"

"Sure."

"There's nothing quite like the smell of a summer breeze on Gamma-3. Nothing really at all like it."

"I suppose not," Henry offered, wishing the woman would stop her endless prattling. She'd always hated the false interest of academic circles, and the current conversation had more than a few landmarks of the same sort of useless chatter, intended to achieve better rotations and tenure and nothing else.

"The food is always better, too, don't you think?"

Henry's stomach flipped angrily at the mention of eating, and she turned towards the window again, half expecting to revisit the crackers against the glass, splattering against the twinkling possibilities of dark space in the distance. "Transport restrictions haven't helped matters," she said after a moment. "Food arrives moldy before it's even out of port."

"It's the damn pirates," the woman said loudly.

"Uh huh," Henry mumbled, wanting to shrink back in her seat. The last thing she needed was to be sitting next to someone so mouthy and so likely to draw attention to them.

"Always stealing everything that's not nailed down, do you know what I mean?"

Henry only nodded this time, wishing the woman would stop talking.

"Thieves, that's all they are. Common ruffians, disrupting the business of everyone else who just wants to get on with it. I couldn't possibly put into words just how much disdain I hold for these pirates, these rebels, some are calling themselves, not when they're the reason that so many go hungry."

Something about it felt like a trap. Like bait, almost, but Henry hadn't spent thirteen years at private boarding schools without learning how to hold her tongue, even if the company was less than polite or respectable. "It will be good for things to return to normal," she demurred.

"Normal? What even is normal, these days? Mining camps exploding, killing hundreds. Fuel shortages as a result. Prices soaring, too, and for what?" The woman shook her head, the floppy brim of the hat undulating in a distinctly distressing way. "Things were better in my grandparents' day, you know. People actually had respect for business, then. Respect for their fellow person."

"My grandparents would probably agree," Henry replied, and that, too, wasn't a lie, because before they'd died, it was more or less all they spoke about. Derision for political upheaval, and a deep-seated obsession with tradition. Her parents were the same. They'd told everyone she was dead, and as far as she was concerned, that was for the best.

"You know," the woman said, tilting her head so that the side of her face was only just visible, olive skin glistening with a fine sheen of sweat, "some people say that there's a secret pirate settlement in the Near Systems."

Grateful for her finishing school education, Henry plastered a shocked expression across her face. "*Really?*" she asked, despite the panic that was rising steadily, one rib at a time. "I've never heard that!"

"Oh, yes," the woman whispered now, leaning closer. "I hear that some dissidents seek shelter there. Refuge, or sanctuary, if you will."

"How strange that the Coalition would allow for such a thing!"

"Some say the Coalition doesn't know where it is, that only those who have already been there know its location."

Henry offered up a light laugh, the same way she'd been trained to, so that it sounded like wind chimes on the wind, inoffensive and deferential. "Oh, I'm sorry to say, madam, but that sounds rather fanciful, don't you think?"

"Stranger things have happened in the course of our history."

"Even so, the Coalition military has power and might on its side, along with technologies we couldn't even dream of." Henry patted her arm with a smile. "I wouldn't worry about such things, dear."

"I don't know that worried is the right turn of phrase, more that I am fascinated by the idea of such a place. Ha! Can you imagine? A pirate settlement would probably look like the tenements on the outskirts of the Capital!"

"No doubt," Henry agreed, turning to the window once more. By the gods, she'd give almost anything for the woman to stop talking to her. She was exhausted, and nauseous, and the only thing she wanted was to get on a transport home, so she could get back to work, and wait for Georgie to follow her. Mercifully, the ship seemed to be moving along at a steady pace, and unless something happened en route, there wouldn't be any delays getting to the transport beacon. Her only worry was that the woman would follow her there, thinking they'd formed some annoying sort of bond on the way.

She closed her eyes, pretending to sleep, hoping that it would ward off any further conversation. The woman quieted, for which Henry was grateful, and after a few moments, she drifted off into an almost sleep, the kind where things aren't quite dreams, and aren't quite waking, wrapped in the veil that separated consciousness from whatever was on the other side.

Some amount of time passed, though she didn't know how much, and it was the telltale sound of a revolver hammer being slowly pulled back that yanked her from her rest, her eyes snapping open. In the reflection of the glass, there was the woman, that ridiculous hat pulled down over her face, and a gun pointed directly at Henry.

"I didn't really want to do things like this, you know," the woman whispered. "I tried to engage you otherwise."

"I don't want any trouble, I—"

"Nor do I, but you've made this difficult. I know who you are, Henrietta Weaver, and I've been tracking you for the better part of a week. I thought I'd lose my opportunity, but much to my surprise, you boarded alone, leaving Georgina Payne back in Chalidon."

Henry turned slowly, holding her hands with palms facing up as they lay in her lap. "I don't know who you think I am, but you've made a grave mistake. Ask a guard to check my chip if you don't believe me."

"I don't need to check any chip. I know exactly who you are, and where you're going, and you're going to take me there."

Henry's mouth dried out, leaving her parched and choking on the thickness of her own tongue. "I don't know what you're talking about."

"If you think I won't shoot you on this transport, you are sadly mistaken," the woman said, her voice barely above a whisper. "Desperate times call for desperate measures."

"Who are you?"

"It doesn't matter who I am, and you won't ask me that again. Are we understood?"

Henry nodded. "We are."

"Excellent." The woman nodded at the clock on the wall, and Henry was surprised to see that several hours had passed while she was dozing, and she had completely missed the first stop. The woman raised an eyebrow, nearly invisible beneath the drape of the hat. "You're going to take me to Bradach."

Chapter 12

Delia's stomach roiled, and she laid her head against the bar, the opulent furnishings of the Purple Pig undulating gently around her, drifting in and out of focus. She groaned, unwilling to move from her stool or even open her eyes to the harsh light of mirrored sun, already streaming through the gaps in the purple velvet curtains.

"Rise and shine, Forrest," Carmen said, throwing the drapes open. "You can't stay on that stool all day, we have work to do."

"You're not my boss."

"I might as well be."

"Leave me alone," Delia grumbled, turning her head to face the wall. Guilt and shame sat within her heavier than bricks and twice as deadly. "You can do the broadcast without me."

"Rough night?"

"You could say that."

Carmen sighed, sitting next to her and gently prying the mostly empty bottle from her hands. "First of all, you are the voice of the people, not me. I prefer being on the other side of the desk, you know that. Second, you looking like someone steamrolled you into the carpet isn't going to do anything to help Evie."

Even the mention of her name shot spikes through Delia, and she groaned audibly, dragging it out so much so that the guttural sound echoed off the chandelier hanging over them. "It's my fault, Carm."

"Yeah, it is, but feeling sorry for yourself isn't productive."

"I've just been so worried about Rosie that—"

"No one blames you for that."

Delia grimaced, her eyes still squeezed shut. "No, they just blame me for being the reason Larkin disappeared."

"It's barely been twelve hours. She'll be back."

"Unless Cole fucking Marion figured out what she was doing."

Carmen slipped behind the bar, turning towards the fancy coffee machine that had only been installed a few months prior. Installed because Rosie had requested it, and the memory pulled at Delia all over again. Yellow dress swishing as she worked, Carmen made a strong cup in silence, the only sounds that of the steamer and the gentle clink of the metal spoon against the delicate porcelain. "Please, as if that pineapple could outsmart Larkin. You forget that I knew him, Delia, better than most."

"I didn't forget."

"I told him not to stand for the leadership. If I told him once, I told him a hundred times, but he didn't listen, because he was so blinded by grief after Judy's passing that he didn't even hear me. To him, the only thing that mattered was revenge." Carmen slid the coffee across the bar, still steaming. "Now, he's completely forgotten why he started this in the first place, and it's only about hanging onto power because he thinks that's what will save him."

Delia recoiled from the mug, the familiar, bitter smell turning in her gut. "He's a fool."

"He's always been a fool, just ask Georgie. The two of them went toe-to-toe in Skelm more than once."

A long, uncomfortable silence passed. "Do you think she did it already?"

"Hard to say. I doubt his little minions will be running here to tell us, if that's the case. He's basically banned them all from coming in here."

"I wish he had just left when The Scattered were banned."

Carmen raised an eyebrow at her before turning to make her own mug of coffee. "Do you, really?" she asked, her tone light but quietly weighted. "If Larkin comes back with information, I somehow think that you won't have any regrets about what you asked for."

"I just want to get her back." Delia nudged the mug away from herself, her skull pounding with every regrettable heartbeat.

"I know. But if it's not too much to say, I don't think stealing bottles of gin from behind the bar will help."

"What else am I supposed to do? All I can do is wait, and hope, and listen, and—"

"And yell at Evie?" Carmen said, stirring frothed milk into her tall, oversized mug.

"I didn't yell at her."

"Delia, I know you're accustomed to getting your way, but if we're all going to survive this, we need to work together. I believe in the rebellion, in The Scattered—well, Splintered, now, I suppose—but I renounced it and stayed because getting accurate news out to the people is more important than my own ego, my own wants and needs."

"Easy for you to say, Roger is still here in Bradach. He wasn't snatched up by Zink and his ilk."

"Roger has struggled ever since what happened beyond the Skelm barrier. He'll carry that the rest of his life, and I'll carry what happened to my settlement when the Coalition raided it. We all have things to carry, so pick up your baggage and stop throwing it at everyone else."

Delia picked her head up off the bar, trying to ignore how the room spun around her, letting the anger cut through the fog. "You have no idea what this is like."

"My people were taken from me, too. Almost all of us have lost someone to this pointless gods-damned war, conflict, whatever they're calling it now. I know you're scared and upset, but now Larkin is missing, and we can't even go looking for her, because that could put her in even more danger."

"You think I don't know that?"

"I think you need to realize that the big picture is about more than just Rosie."

"She's *my* big picture, Carmen." Delia pushed out an aggrieved sigh, frustrated at the bile turning in her stomach. "Are you telling me that you wouldn't be like this if someone had infiltrated the city just to take Roger? To press him into service, make him their little mascot? Put him into danger with his face at the forefront? Do you really think she'll ever know peace, now that they've done this?"

Carmen sucked her teeth and sipped again at her coffee. "There haven't been any transmissions to that effect yet."

"*Yet*," Delia replied, emphasizing the word.

The silence in the tavern hung thick and discontent like a muddy fog. That was just how things had become, always tense, always mixed with the strife, and Delia was just so tired of all of it. Twenty minutes until the morning broadcast, and her head felt like it might split along the invisible seams, and there was no news of Cole Marion or from Larkin.

"Hey," Evie said from the upstairs landing, closing the door to her apartment behind her. She looked ragged, and guilt lodged itself in the crevices of Delia's ligaments, a feeling that was becoming altogether too common. Evie ran a hand through her short, unkempt hair, leaning against the banister. "I assume there's no news, or someone would have told me."

"No news," Carmen confirmed. "Coffee?"

"Might as well."

Delia couldn't face her, couldn't look her in the eyes, not when it was her fault that Larkin had gone off on the mission half-cocked. Maybe Carmen was right. Maybe she really was a spoiled, snotty little rich girl. It wasn't the first time someone had suggested that. "Morning," she mumbled, returning her attention to the mug in front of her.

"We'd have heard by now if he was dead," Evie said quietly, sitting at the other end of the bar. Obviously, she wasn't a huge fan of Delia at the moment, either. "And hopefully we'd have heard if she'd been arrested, so we can only assume that nothing has happened yet."

Carmen poured another coffee, settling a cloud of stiff milk atop it, and covering it with a fine mist of cocoa. "It could just be reconnaissance."

"I doubt that. She's never not followed through on a job."

"She's never had one in Bradach before, nor did she have you, or any of us." Carmen set the mug on the bar with a delicate thud, and patted Evie's clenched fist. "She'll come back. We just have to wait."

"I really hope you're right."

Delia kept her stare focused on her cooling coffee, annoyed at the presence of her own emotions. Her stomach growled, and she coughed to cover the sound of it. Despite the cue, the idea of eating filled her with disgust. "Maybe I should go prepare for the broadcast," she said to her mug.

"Maybe you should," Carmen replied. "Thomas is on deck today."

"Alright."

Evie said nothing, which was her right, of course, but the absence of her usual kindness slid through Delia's ribs like a curved knife, fileting her open for all to see. She couldn't blame Evie, not after what had happened, and yet something cold crept into the room, an ice cube on a winter's morning, unwelcome, a bad omen for things to come. Delia cleared her throat again, taking the mug with her as she slipped, noticed, reviled perhaps, into the kitchen.

She took a slice of stale bread from the counter and stuffed it into her mouth. If nothing else, it would quiet the angry, sharp gasps from her gut, absorbing the guilt along with the excess acid. The thought of consuming anything else was extremely unappealing. Sipping at the coffee, she grimaced at the bitterness, trying not to dwell on the fact that Carmen hadn't frothed any milk for her, but had done it for Evie.

Glancing at herself in the reflection of the window, Delia wondered what a villain looked like. Could you tell, just by looking at them? Did they see their own monstrosity, or was it just one more mirror?

"Dee, are you coming down?" Thomas asked, standing in the doorway to the basement, just a few steps down. "I thought you might want to look at revisions beforehand."

"Yeah, I'm coming." She tore her stare from the window with a belated blink, grasping the mug between her palms, grateful for the warmth. It wasn't cold as such, but the heat was a reminder of reality, and that she had a job to do, even if everyone hated her. "Are you on for the evening, too?"

"Yeah." He turned to descend the stairs, holding tight to the railing. Even months on, he was still unsteady at times, his bones weak from all the time he'd spent in that cramped cell on Turas-Mara. "I heard what happened."

A statement, and not really a request for more information, nor was it an invitation for her to defend herself. She'd worked alongside him long enough to know that. She didn't know what to say, so she followed him down the steps, silent except for the quiet, impolite slurp of coffee against her lips, resenting that it was helping to quell the painful beat in her head.

Thomas waited at the desk, leaning against it, his frame still slighter than it had been before the imprisonment. Before, he'd been lean, lithe, muscular like a swimmer would be, but he'd morphed into a shadow of his former self, willowy and fragile, by the looks of him. "Stop looking at me like that, Delia, for all the gods' sakes."

"Sorry."

"I'm fine," he said firmly. "Sandrine says I'm fine, so I'm fine."

"Alright, Thomas, I hear you."

He picked up the morning's script, straightening the pages with a soft tap against the desk. "I hung around the back entrance of the Bronze Bell this morning. I didn't hear anything."

"You shouldn't have done that. What if someone saw you and started asking questions?"

"They didn't, so relax." Thomas sat in the operator's seat, on the other side of a pane of glass. He fiddled with two of the knobs, frowning at them until the quiet fuzz dissipated. "Damn thing. I swear it hasn't been the same since Zink smashed into the tower."

"Alice said it's a patch job. We'll need more rhodium for a full fix."

"Yeah, and there's no chance of that happening any time soon, not with the shortages and restrictions. Gods below, that business at Terringgough Gulch really messed things up for all of us."

Delia nodded, sitting in her chair, perched at the edge of it like she didn't belong there. Maybe she never had in the first place. "Hopefully the beacons will get rebuilt quickly."

"I doubt it. Almost every conscious body is being pressed into the military nowadays. Conscription is a curse we never should have signed our names to." He sighed heavily, pressing a bony hand to the side of his head. "Sometimes I wonder what would have happened if we'd never gone out to the Rim."

"Hard to say."

"I'd be married by now. She wasn't my love for the ages, but it would have been a nice enough life."

"She sold you out the second she had the chance."

"She only did what most would do in that situation." He sighed again, angrier this time, tugging at the too-short cuffs of his shirt, as though pulling on the fabric would magically lengthen them. "Don't you ever wonder what in hells we're doing out here?"

"No."

"No?" he pressed.

Delia sipped her coffee. "No," she repeated. "I feel like this was always where I was meant to be. I have a freedom in broadcasting that I never did with the Coalition. I can talk about whatever I want."

"A cursed freedom, and barely even a freedom at that. There's plenty we can't talk about."

"Right, because to talk about it would be to give the Coalition the upper hand. It's no secret that they listen, they even reference our broadcast in press releases now and then." She drained the mug, setting it aside on the desk. "It's better to be safe than sorry."

"What happens if the Coalition is dissolved? What happens after that?"

"We keep reporting. That's our job."

"But to what end?" he asked.

Delia searched his face, finding nothing out of the ordinary. "Are you sure you're alright? What are these questions this morning?"

"Didn't get enough sleep, I guess."

"Maybe you should have coffee. Carmen made a fresh pot."

"Can't stand the stuff since I got out. Not sure why, but the idea of drinking it makes me queasy." He stood again, dropping the pages in front of her. "Not too many revisions from last night, just a change to the bit about the new shipping lane being infested with MPOs, and that there was something going on out at Turas-Mara."

Delia looked up at him. "What's going on at the Rim?"

"Not sure yet," he answered with a shrug. "Something about an official transport showing up, but no one knows why."

"Do you think Tarand is back on the station?"

"I don't think she would deign to get on one of those relay vessels, especially not that one. It was older, about three years."

"Fineglass?" Delia asked, tapping a pen against the edge of her chin. "It's not impossible, right?"

"Could be disciplinary." He smirked, stretching his hands up over his head. "If it's that, then I'm glad we're long gone."

"We'd be shrapnel if we hadn't."

"I would be, anyway."

Delia chewed the inside of her cheek, scanning through the script. "What's this about mandatory chip checks on transports?"

"It's been going on for a few weeks now. At first, we thought it might just be coincidental, or a general uptick in identity verification, but it's every vessel with civilians now. All of them."

"Looks like an invitation for more stowaways, if you ask me."

Thomas drummed his fingers against the desk. "With all these additional checks, it's only a matter of time before the Coalition figures out what she's been doing. Her cover operation of scrapping is thinly veiled as it is. I'd be surprised if they weren't already watching every ship in that fleet."

"Mm." Delia scanned the rest of the script, noting sections in her mind that would be trickier to read and memorizing them. She set the pages down, looking at him through the glass. "Sometimes it still feels strange to be talking to you like this. Open sedition, after years of working together with that part silent."

"It's what had to be done."

"I know. I just can't help wondering what we might have achieved if we'd known what the other was doing."

He blinked at her. "What do you mean?"

"You know, if I'd known that you were passing information to the rebellion. If you'd known that I was."

"Delia, I always knew that you were. It was a surprise, at first, but I didn't question it. I couldn't afford to, not if I wanted both of us to stay safe."

She sat back, staring. "What?"

"You're not as covert as you think you are." He laughed, flipping a few switches on the control board. "You really didn't know?"

"Of course I didn't know. If I'd have known, I would have gone looking for you sooner on Turas-Mara!" she protested. "I would have guessed earlier that they had you locked up somewhere, drilling for information."

"You got me out. It's done."

"Maybe I could have done it sooner."

Thomas glanced at her, his bright green eyes shining in the dim light of the basement. "It happened the best way it could have. If not on Tarand's ship, we'd have been rounded up and executed." He looked back at the desk, twisting a knob back and forth. "No sense dwelling on it now. I plan to spend the rest of my miserable little life making them pay for what they did, even if my best contribution is working this desk for you."

"What we do is important."

"Of course it is."

"Five minutes to broadcast," Delia said after a moment. Something felt strange, off, but she couldn't put her finger on it. "Thomas, are you sure that you're alright?"

"I told you, I'm fine."

"I know, I just meant—I meant otherwise, you know. Other than physically."

"Would you be?" he asked, fidgeting with a button on his cuffs. "Are you, with Rosie gone?"

"No," Delia admitted, dangling the headphones around her neck. "I feel like I don't even know myself, with her gone. It's like watching myself from the outside."

"Yeah," he agreed. "That's how it is." He flipped another switch, this one glowing orange. "Test the intro, let me check audio levels."

Delia nodded, clearing her throat and pulling the microphone towards herself. "Good morning, I'm Delia Forrest with the morning news."

Chapter 13

Larkin twisted the ring around her finger once more for the hundredth time in just a few hours. She'd headed straight for the Bronze Bell the night before, intending to sneak in and kill Cole, but she'd hesitated.

Hesitation was new.

She'd never hesitated before on a job, but then, things had changed since then. She'd realized she was being used by the Coalition, bought part of a tavern, moved in with Evie, built something that looked like a real life. Not a glamorous one but a real one, and knowing that one misstep would take all that away was staying her hand.

With another heavy sigh, she leaned back against the dirty brick exterior of the building, picking at a half-pulped flyer on the ground with the toe of her boot. She banged her head against the bricks softly, trying to jar the right answer to the forefront. After an entire night of doing that, though, she still didn't have the right answer.

Cole needed to be out of Bradach, and he wouldn't go. His continued presence was putting the entire city in danger, including Evie, including her friends, including her tavern. Doing nothing wasn't an option, it was stasis. It was waiting for someone else to solve the problem, and if the best solution was death, well, then, she was the best one to carry out the job.

The hesitation was new, but everything else was coldly familiar. She'd already mapped out entrance and exit, and memorized how often the guards at the back door swapped over, even when the tavern was closed.

Cole was obviously living at the Bronze Bell, not just conducting business there, which made things more difficult. If he had a room somewhere, killing him in secret would be easier. Quieter. It would give her the opportunity to move around unseen, and be back home before he even croaked.

She'd wait for someone to break the news.

She'd pretend to be surprised.

They all would.

Guilt surged through her again and Larkin swallowed back a growl. Gods-damned if she killed him, and gods-damned if she didn't. Her promise to Evie that she was done for good seemed nebulous with the introduction of the ring. Did Evie want her to kill Cole, or did she just see it as an inevitability?

Did she think that Larkin was a barely controlled killing machine that needed one for a release?

The tears cascading down her face seemed to suggest otherwise, even as she wondered it about herself. Wiping her cheeks with the back of her hand, she sniffled, tilting her head up to blink back further tears. It had only been a few years, but it had been enough to go soft.

One time, this wouldn't have fazed her. She'd already be done. She'd be back in bed with Evie, asking what she wanted for breakfast.

Maybe. Evie had changed everything the moment she'd shown up. Calm and kind and loving, depositing tiny bits of affection throughout the day, every time she walked by. "Love you, Larks," she'd say as she ran from the kitchen to a table to serve up. Or kisses on her shoulder as Larkin shook out a cocktail, or a brush of her hand as they cleaned up at night.

"Enough," Larkin hissed to herself. Cole had to go. He was putting everyone in danger, including the refugees down at the dock. Especially them. They didn't need another home going up in smoke. Larkin was the right person for the job. She could still fit through the small windows on the top level, but barely. Three square meals a day and comfort had softened her harsh edges, rounding her off into a pleasant shape. Her hands remembered how to scale the back side of a bar, reaching for uneven bricks, drain pipes, long-dead ivy showing off its crisped leaves like they were prize-winning and not an embarrassment.

Her boots easily found footholds, her eyes scanned across the alleyway every three seconds, looking for any semblance of movement, any shifting shadow. Her tavern was competition, and if anyone saw her, it would be obvious, and she'd get banned from the city, and he'd still be there, a shining beacon of bullshit for the Coalition to rain down missiles upon, vaporizing everything and everyone else in the process.

The window wasn't even latched. Cole was complacent.

She landed inside the office, boots silent against the large rug. Larkin found herself flinching from the faded blood stain in the center. She'd never been squeamish before, and despite her relative ease in climbing into the window, the turn of her stomach was odd. Foreign, like she was inhabiting a stranger's skin. The stain would have been Donaldson. Another life lost because Cole wasn't fit. His incompetence was putting people in danger.

It was early, so early that Bradach's mirrors hadn't even begun to shift inward yet, the only vague light the shifting, yellowed glow of the street lamps outside. She stayed in one spot, waiting for her eyesight to adjust. Cole wasn't in the office, he must have another room on the floor. No matter, she didn't need him present to seal his fate. She'd never been a fan of the bloodier means of murder, even before. Blood was hard to wash out, and she hated doing laundry.

Silently, she sifted through the contents of the desk, scanning files for useful information. There was nothing, only ship movements they already knew about. Nothing on Rosie. Larkin frowned, opening an unlabeled file. The only thing in it was an old, unsigned invoice from Captain Marshall for a crate of mediocre ale.

The second drawer held only a single revolver. Larkin's fingers brushed against it, considering stealing it so that he couldn't use it. But that wouldn't really solve anything, so instead, she emptied the revolver, pocketing the ammunition with a quiet series of clacks.

One more drawer down, a deeper one, and she raised an eyebrow. How in any hells did Cole Marion have a bottle of *that* whiskey? Bailey's crew had the last batch, and it went to the Capital. Given Marina's arrest, it was probable that the Coalition officers had seized whatever had been left. Something sick turned in her stomach, and enough of her hesitation fell away in that moment that she unscrewed the lid, opened the ring on her finger, and watched as the golden dust disappeared into the amber liquid.

Almost a pity she'd had to grind it from the roots. Harvesting seeds was easier, breaking down into a fine dust in moments, but the roots had more sinew. It would be more than enough. It didn't take much, and she'd tripled the usual dosage because there was no point in doing any of this if it wasn't done well. Part of her was unbalanced, the memorized movements awkward. She'd spent most of her life doing exactly what she was doing, but it had only taken a few years of her tending bar to wipe away the vast majority of her confidence.

Larkin picked up the bottle and swirled it, watching the dust dissolve in the tiny, contained whirlpool. She'd added a tiny bit of sugar, just enough to aid absorption and make sure the poison wouldn't settle to the bottom. A trick she'd learned almost fifteen years ago, and used dozens of times. Satisfied, watching the liquid calm, she set it back inside and closed the drawer almost soundlessly. All she had to do was leave. Just climb out the window, walk back home, and slide in between the sheets, and pretend like she hadn't just killed a man.

A man who, at the present, definitely deserved killing, but still.

She was a changed woman now, or something like that. Something was certainly different, whatever the hell it was. Being out of practice, maybe, or the soreness in her limbs from the climb, it being an unusual activity for her of late.

Larkin rifled through the other three desk drawers, finding nothing of use. Some old pens, an empty inkwell, papers with information thoroughly scratched out, the remains of the previous day's lunch, unfortunately enough. The smell of it roiled in her stomach, and led her to believe that either the Bronze Bell was serving up old food, which was plausible, or Cole had left it in his desk for a few days, which was, unfortunately, also plausible.

She couldn't help but remember her last contract, the security controller. A strange thread of dread sewed parts of her together that didn't fit, when she realized she couldn't remember his name. How callous, to take a life and not even remember the name. At one time, that wouldn't have bothered her. Now, it married bile to flesh in an unpleasant union at the back of her throat. "Bob?" she whispered aloud. "Was that his name?" She shook her head. "No, that wasn't it."

The last drawer closed, she turned for the window but stopped dead in her tracks at the sound of heavy footsteps in the corridor. Cole? Or one of the armed guards?

Larkin slid backwards towards the window, groping out for it with her fingers. Her palms met the rough, unfinished wood, and before she had another half of a moment to think, she was hanging from the window, reaching with her boot for a foothold in the brick. If she was going to get caught, now would be the time. It was always the escape that did assassins in, never the breaking in.

She dropped silently to the ground, pleased that she'd stuck the dismount, and not gone sprawling across the cobblestones, scraping up her hands and knees in the process. Larkin dusted herself off, squared her shoulders, and exited the alley as though she hadn't just signed a man's death warrant.

It was fine.

She didn't really need to sleep at night, after all.

* * *

She hadn't gone back to bed. By the time she made it back to the Purple Pig, for some reason, everyone was already awake. Larkin slid into the kitchen, starting morning prep the same way she always would, slicing citrus for the bar, and trying to ignore the persistent sting of the lemon juice in the tiny, nearly invisible cut on her hand, a reminder that she hadn't dreamed it.

Muffled voices from the basement told her that Delia was preparing the morning broadcast. Quiet chatter from the other side of the swinging door told her that Evie was in there with Carmen, but Larkin couldn't bring herself to face them yet. They'd know, and there was power in the knowing, and a distinct shade of weakness that Larkin hadn't managed to resist the urge. Maybe she really was a monster, underneath whatever she'd used to dress herself up as a real person. Fancy cocktails, clothes that fit, three meals a day. It was all an illusion because underneath all of it, she was still someone who had killed dozens.

She sliced up too many limes, the pile growing too tall, but she couldn't stop. Every press of the knife, the sound quiet as the blade met the soft wood of the cutting board, kept her present. It had never been like this before, but then, she'd convinced herself, too, that she wasn't a monster anymore. That she wasn't responsible, that she'd been used and manipulated, but no, it was in her, even still. Even without the pressures of the Coalition, of her handlers, of the threat of an empty credit account hanging over her head.

Too many gods-forsaken limes, and she knew it, but continued to slice through their waxy flesh anyway, piling the dismembered sections on top of each other. A mass grave of fruit.

"Larkin?" Evie whispered from the doorway, tears already filling her eyes.

Larkin couldn't say anything. She only nodded, slicing through one more lime.

Evie surged forward, wrapping her arms around Larkin's middle, burying her face in Larkin's shoulder. "I'm so glad you're alright," she said. "I missed you."

"I'm fine," Larkin replied, and heard for herself the strange, robotic tone in her voice.

"I wish you hadn't left without talking to me first."

Larkin shrugged.

"I'm glad you're back."

"Yeah."

Evie stepped back, searching her face so intently that all Larkin could do was look away. "*Are* you okay?" Evie asked.

"Sure," Larkin said, reaching for another grapefruit. Evie took it from her, placing it back in the crate.

"You don't look okay."

"I'm not bleeding, and no one saw me."

"That doesn't mean—"

"Eves, I'm fine." Larkin turned, shaking off her concern. "What's the menu today? Did we get more flour?"

"Are you going to tell me what happened?"

"I'd rather not."

"Okay."

Larkin reached for the grapefruit again, and this time, Evie let her have it. She rolled it gently against the board before sinking the knife into it, slicing it in half, and then quarters, and then eighths. "He had some of that whiskey."

"What whiskey?"

"You know, that stuff Bailey carted out to the Capital when all that happened." She waved the knife in the air, a casual gesture, as though she wasn't waiting for a man to die. "I don't know where he got it. I was under the impression that the stuff Captain Marshall had was the last of it."

"Maybe he got it before that," Evie offered.

"I doubt it. Captain Marshall was the only contact for it, so much as I'm aware. It was small batch stuff, Eves, hard to get your hands on. It's why I don't even offer it to customers anymore."

"So, you think he's working with someone?"

Larkin shrugged again, tidying the edges of each grapefruit section, pulling the rough fibers from the edges. "It would seem so."

"I guess we'll find out."

"I guess we will."

Evie reached over, taking the knife gently from her hands. "I think you have enough fruit, Larkin. It's not even a weekend, we're not going to get busy enough to use all of this."

"You never know, we might. Better to be prepared, right?" Larkin extended her arm to take the paring knife back, but Evie stepped out of her reach. Larkin frowned. "What, you don't trust me? You think I'm going to lose it and start stabbing customers?"

"No, I'm worried you're going to lose it and go through all the damned limes when we don't get another produce shipment until next week." Evie laid the knife flat on the counter and approached again, slowly this time. "I think you should tell me what happened."

"No."

"Larkin—" Evie started, but was interrupted by the basement door opening. Her mouth set into a frown at the sight of Delia, and turned towards the wall, reaching for a kitchen rag to busy herself with wiping up invisible crumbs. She did it whenever she was pissed off, a strange little pantomime of productivity that Larkin had never understood.

"Larkin," Delia breathed, pausing. "You're back."

"Yep."

"And he's...?"

"The tavern is closed until lunch," Evie said loudly. "Without Rosie here, we just don't have the capacity for anything until then." She nodded towards the swinging door. "Sorry."

Delia opened her mouth to say something, but only nodded, sidling past them with Thomas following close behind, through the swinging door.

"Don't be hostile, Eves," Larkin said quietly. "It's not her fault."

"Yes, it is."

"We'd already discussed it before that."

"It's not her place to ask that of you, Larkin."

Larkin sighed, reaching for a lemon, rolling it over in her hands, focusing on the familiar feel of the dappled skin of the fruit against her palm. "She didn't ask, I decided."

"Because of what she said."

"Maybe the call sign I found will be useful."

"Or not," Evie countered, still angrily wiping the rag across the counters. "Or you put yourself in grave danger for lateral movement at best."

"I'd have said the same in her shoes, if it had been you that was taken," Larkin said softly. "I can't blame Delia for being terrified. Eves, I'd be lost without you, and I mean that."

"Don't you think I feel the same way? Yet you make a huge decision like that without even telling me." Evie threw the rag into a laundry bag with a furious whip, rounding on her. "You didn't even *tell* me, Larkin. You left without a gods-damned word."

"I'm sorry."

"You bet your ass you're sorry," Evie said, but it was softer now. "Don't—don't fucking do that again."

"Alright, Eves."

"Let's get you some breakfast. Carmen made coffee already."

Larkin nodded, pushing through the swinging door. "Okay. Breakfast. Stop being hostile to Delia."

"I'll think about it." Evie followed her, pressing a hand against Larkin's hip. "We're not done talking about this yet."

"I figured."

"You're not getting out of this that easy, Larkin Flores."

"I'm getting the picture, yes." Larkin grabbed a large mug from the stack. It was her favorite, double-sized blue glazed ceramic, the same color as Evie's hair. She almost didn't notice the odd look on William's face. "Morning Will," she said. "You're in early."

"Someone's died at the Bell."

A knot clenched in Larkin's stomach. That had been quick, even considering the enormous pile of citrus slices in the kitchen. "Oh?" she asked.

"Cole?" Delia asked, her voice almost too hopeful to not be suspicious. William shook his head. "No. His bodyguard."

Chapter 14

Henry spent ninety minutes plotting her escape in her head. Scenarios played out against her closed eyelids as she leaned against the glass, trying to look as inoffensive and nonthreatening as possible to the woman holding the gun, still, just out of view, the rigid bulk visible beneath the loose-fitting cloak. But every option ended in death or arrest. There was no way to lose her on the transport. It was far too small for that, and nowhere to go.

She'd have to try to lose her at the beacon, but her roiling stomach and dreadful exhaustion would make that more of a challenge than she was confident she could tackle. Gods below, she shouldn't have left Georgie in Chalidon. She should have forced the subject, but she hadn't wanted Georgie to give up on her sister just yet. Yet, despite all the best of intentions, it was clear that Henry was on the path to one of many possible hells.

"What do you want to go there for, anyway?" Henry asked, unmoving from her position against the window. "It's no more than a backwater," she lied. "A trading post for brigands and thieves."

"Please don't lie to me, it makes this much more difficult than this needs to be."

"You didn't answer my question."

The woman sighed with exasperation. "My reasons are my own. They aren't any of your business."

"I'd say they are my business when you're holding a gun on me," Henry hissed. "I wasn't even headed there," she lied again.

"I already asked you not to lie."

"And I'm asking you to tell me the truth. Why do you want to go there?"

"I know some people there."

"Which people?" Henry pressed, convinced the woman was lying, too. "Which people do you know there?"

"Are you seriously suggesting that you know every single person in that settlement?"

"Not all of them, but plenty, so try me."

The woman sighed again, leaning closer to Henry as a guard passed their row without a second glance, slipping through the door to the staff area of the transport. "Who are you working for?" the woman asked.

Henry's breath caught in her throat. Yes, no, and maybe could all be the wrong answer that got her killed, and so none of them quite appealed. "My business is my own," she said, parroting the woman's previous answer.

"That response only works when you're the one holding the gun."

"And you're not going to shoot me on a transport and risk drawing the attention of the guards you're so painfully obviously trying to avoid, so how about we cut the horseshit?" Henry opened her eyes now, waiting for the woman to respond, and when she didn't, Henry continued. "You're wearing an oversized cloak, for one thing, and you tensed when that guard walked by, for another. And the third thing is where you're trying to go, it's not a place that Intelligence agents are allowed to go. Furthermore, if you were an Intelligence agent, I'm betting I'd have heard of you, and I haven't."

"And who must you be that you'd know of an Intelligence agent?"

"You tell me, seeing as you were ready to dictate my life's history to me about an hour and a half ago."

"You're not how I thought you'd be," the woman said, tilting her head just enough that Henry saw a flash of her dark eyes, mysterious in what they were hiding.

Henry folded her hands in her lap, careful to keep them away from her stomach. If there was anything an assassin with a gun didn't need, it was more leverage. "And what did you think I'd be like?"

"Demure."

"You've definitely got the wrong woman for that, then."

"I heard you attended finishing school."

Henry snorted. "About a million years ago, maybe."

"Fifteen is hardly a million."

"Might as well be, with how much has changed since then."

The woman shifted in her seat, keeping the gun trained on Henry. "Enlighten me. What has changed in fifteen years?"

"You're fishing for information," Henry replied, examining her cuticles. "A rookie move, and an obvious one, at that."

"I've been doing this since before you left that finishing school, don't lecture me on being a rookie. Leaving the woman who watches your six back in Chalidon, that's a rookie move. If you're as smart as you think you are, you'd know that being anywhere in the Near Systems alone right now is a hell of a risk."

"Oh, is that what the gun is for, then?" Henry whispered. "Is it because you wanted some company, and threatening someone is the only way you can get it?"

"Hardly."

"Until proven otherwise, that's what I'm going to choose to believe." Henry nestled back into the seat, closing her eyes once more. She could feel the intensity of the woman's stare, but ignored it. Whoever she was, Henry would only have one opportunity to get away from her without drawing attention. Anyone who brought a gun onto a transport looking for her was either desperate or working for the Coalition Science Academy. Her eyes flew open at the thought, and despite her prior restraint, she jolted upright, staring at the woman.

"What's the matter, did you just figure out who I am?"

"You're Coalition," Henry said.

"I am."

Henry's lungs turned to lead at the admission, and suddenly, breathing was incredibly challenging. "I see."

"Does that make you more or less likely to follow my instructions?"

"That depends on what your instructions are, if I'm honest."

"I already told you. Get me to Bradach."

"I can only imagine what you'd do once you got there, so you'll board that transport over my dead body," Henry said, leaning towards the woman. "You'll have to kill me in a transport hub filled to the brim with people. Figure out how to explain that to your superiors." She pressed her hands into the rough fabric of the seat, the worn threads biting gently into her palms as a welcome distraction. "You're losing control of this situation, whoever you are. You thought you could chase me onto a transport and threaten me?" Henry flapped the fabric of her skirts angrily. "Think again."

"Calm down."

"I'm not going to calm down, you calm down!"

The woman looked behind her, tugging the hood down over her face. "You should be quieter."

"What's the matter? Is my volume becoming a problem?" Henry shouted, standing up. It was one hell of a risky move, but she'd never been shy about making those. "Are you concerned that I might be drawing too much attention?"

"Sit. Down."

"I think I'll remain standing, actually. I'm sure when that guard comes back to make sure everyone is belted in for landing, he'd love to hear why I'm choosing to remain standing."

"He'll nab you, too. That chip in your arm isn't going to protect you if he figures out who you are."

"And who's going to tell him? You? Mysterious stranger who's clearly trying her hardest to remain unseen?"

"I told you," the woman said, advancing once again, now backing Henry against the window, "my reasons for my anonymity are my own."

"You'd better start fessing up fast, or I'm going to make sure that we both get dragged off this transport kicking and screaming." Henry cocked an eyebrow. It was a bluff, but a good one. Hyun had taught her well, and it had only taken about thirty-seven humiliating defeats to get it right.

"Alright, alright, keep your skirts on," the woman said, backing off. She sat back down, arranging her cloak to obscure not only her face, but most of her form, too. "I don't think you fully understand the position that I am in."

"Alright," Henry said. "Enlighten me."

The woman cleared her throat lightly, licking her chapped lips, scaly from dehydration or sun or both. "I need to get to Brad—I need to get to that settlement, because there is important information that I have to deliver in person."

"A likely story."

"It is the truth, whether or not you choose to listen to me," the woman said, her voice now barely above a whisper. "It is of the utmost importance. Life or death."

"For who?"

"For thousands." The woman pressed a palm to her forehead, breathing slowly as though she was stifling a sob. "Tens, maybe hundreds of thousands."

Henry watched her for any signs of subterfuge, knowing there must be more to the story. "What is the information?"

"I can't tell you."

"Why not?"

"I have to make sure it gets to the right person."

"I'll say it again. Tell me who it is you're looking for, and I might be of more assistance."

The woman shook her head. "I can't. While I know who you are, I don't know your true intentions, and I cannot risk this falling into the wrong hands. Well, any more than it already has, that is."

"Until I know who you are, I'm not telling you anything, or taking you anywhere. I'm no fool, I know there have been moles and spies all over the Near Systems. Spies for this, leaks for that, it's unending." Henry took the opportunity to glance out the window, noting that they were beginning their descent through the moon's thin atmosphere. "Three factions and counting, the Coalition, it never stops, it doesn't pause for anyone, least of all you or me."

"Please," the woman whispered. "I am begging, now." She laid the gun on the empty seat between them, leaving it covered with a section of her cloak.

Henry looked at the woman, and then down at the gun, and in that split second, missed the car door opening once more.

"You, out of your seat," the MPO shouted at the woman. "You're under arrest for suspicion of sedition and treason."

"I didn't do anything," the woman pleaded, holding her hands up. "You have me mistaken for someone else."

"We know who you are, Dr. Arteo, and we've been searching for you for weeks now. You went missing from your post. Why is that?"

Arteo. Henry stifled a gasp, not wanting to implicate herself, too.

"You thought you'd slipped the net, but I caught you." The guard smirked, proud of his find. "I'm going to get such a promotion for this." He elbowed the second guard who followed him into the passenger area. "I won't have to hang around here with losers like you anymore, right?"

"I found her, too," the second guard protested.

"Not really, though, did you? It was all me, and that's what's going into the report."

"What about that one?" the second guard asked, pointing at Henry. "She was sitting next to her, I'm betting birds of a feather, you know?"

Arteo threw back her hood, shaking out her mane of untamed curls, more a mane than a style. "She has nothing to do with this. I don't even know who she is."

"Horseshit," the first guard said. "I don't buy that for a minute."

"It's true, I was just trying to hassle her for some extra credits. It's been days since I've eaten."

"And it will be days more once you're in lockup. Come on, hold your wrists out. Don't make this more complicated than it already is. I bet if you come quietly, they won't order a public execution. Maybe if you're really well behaved, they'll assign you to a mining work camp, and you can die in peace, far from the reach of cameras and press." He pulled out a set of iron cuffs, and the second guard did the same, a steely glint in his eyes as he set his focus on Henry.

"Arteo, you'd better have that information," Henry hissed, snatching the gun from beneath the cloak. She shot one officer, and then the other, leaving them in a heap on the floor. Her stomach lurched hard at the transport's turbulence, and she turned to deposit what was left of the crackers onto the seat.

"Gods," Arteo whispered. "You shot them."

"It was them or us, come on," Henry said, pulling her through to the staff area, mercifully finding it empty. She shoved the gun down her dress, not willing to hand it back to the woman who'd held it on her, no matter what the strange circumstances were. "Follow my lead," she whispered.

Arteo nodded, matching Henry's speed and posture.

Henry burst into the conductor's booth, throwing her arms over her head. "Pirates!" she screamed, letting manufactured tears roll down her cheeks. "Or rebels, I don't know! They ran towards the front of the transport. They nearly killed us!"

The three MPOs standing scattered, two racing for the front of the transport, and the other placing a bar on the doors just as the ship landed in the bay.

"What are you doing?" Henry asked.

"Procedure when there's piracy or rebels on board," the guard answered. "No one leaves until they find who's responsible."

Henry sighed. "I really wish you weren't making me do this."

"Do what?" he asked.

Henry pulled the gun out, holding it on him. "Take off the bar."

"It was you," he breathed.

"And you're next if you don't open the door." She pulled back the hammer of the revolver. "Now," she added.

Hands shaking, he didn't even reach for the heat gun a few steps away, and for that, Henry was grateful. She didn't know how many rounds were left after taking out those two further up the transport. "Alright," the

MPO said, removing the bar. The doors hissed open, and Henry and Arteo ran through.

"We have about sixty seconds before a beacon-wide security alert," Henry said over her shoulder, walking quickly, but not running. Running would be a dead giveaway. "We don't have the luxury of sticking around for the quickest transfer." She pulled Arteo towards bay sixteen, recognizing the small symbol on the back of one of the ships, the black silhouette of an owl, with the eyes painted a bright blue. One of Captain Tansy's fleet, thank the gods. "Come on, this way."

As they approached bay sixteen, the lights flickered and went out, coming back a split second later, bathing them in red as the sirens began to sound. "Georgie is going to kill me," Henry hissed, diving behind the vessel. She stamped one foot on the ramp and shouted, "Last one there drinks from a dry barrel!" and crossed the threshold into the ship's cargo bay.

Immediately, the cargo door began to close, and the engines began to power up.

"Holy shit, Henry," Ivy said, skidding into the cargo bay. "I heard the code but I never would have thought it was you. Where's Georgie?"

"Still in Chalidon and blissfully unaware of this." She grimaced. "Don't tell her."

"Won't be long before it hits the airwaves."

"I know." Henry slumped against the wall as the ship lifted out of the bay, just seconds before a full lockdown would have prevented it. "This is Dr. Arteo. She was at Turas-Mara with the others."

"Oh, my gods," Ivy said, extending her hand. "I've heard so many amazing things about you, I'm truly honored—"

"She held a gun on me."

Ivy retracted her hand, raising an eyebrow. "You sure it's really her?"

"I'm sure. Where is this rig headed?"

"We were fueling. I was out further but hopped a few coming back this way. This ship needed some fine tuning before a big transport. Where do you need to go?"

"Home," Henry answered.

"I'll ask nav. Maybe we can get you there. It won't be fast, though. There are already six blockades between here and there."

"Remind me not to leave again any time soon, okay?" Henry smoothed stray hairs back against her head, extending her legs out in front of her. "Full disclosure, that lockdown alarm was us."

"I figured."

"I took out two MPOs."

Ivy blinked. "Captain Tansy tends to frown on that."

"If this information is as important as Arteo says it is, then it may save a lot of lives."

Arteo unclipped her cloak, hanging it over her arm. Her sapphire jumpsuit was a far cry from Coalition standard clothing, but there was something about her that still looked too much like a lackey for Henry to trust her. Maybe it was that ramrod straight posture. Arteo nodded. "I promise, this information is worth all the risks. It could change everything."

Chapter 15

Mae stood in the street, staring at that same gods-damned door. The early evening light was beginning to wane, the glow sinking further beneath the horizon with every passing moment that she waited, instead of doing what she'd gone all that way for.

The last time she'd seen them, she was being dragged away in handcuffs. They'd tried to use her, and failed.

Now, she needed to use them, and couldn't fail. Not if she wanted to get Bailey back to Bradach safe and sound. There had been no word from home. Before she left, Delia had promised to include a code word in the broadcasts if Bailey had made contact, but in twice-daily news reports, she never once said "melon."

The brick street of the historical district was even under her boots, perfectly leveled and kept up for the wealthy residents of the area. The gods forbid they should have to see something as horrifying as a weed creeping up through the cement, or the slightest hint of a pockmark blemishing the road. Mae knocked on the door, the large brass door knocker surprisingly cold in her hands, despite the day's relative warmth.

The door opened to an unfamiliar face, an older man in a suit jacket, almost balding but not quite. "May I help you?" he asked in a bored voice.

"I assume you're a new hire," Mae said, pulling off her black lace gloves as she crossed the threshold.

"Excuse me, ma'am, but this is a private residence!" he protested, reaching for her arm.

She stepped back and out of his grasp, giving him a small bow with a delicate incline of her head. "I mean no harm. My parents live here."

"The Machenets have no children," he said coldly.

"Well, that's a new development," Mae replied with a snort. "I can assure you, I grew up in this house. The sixth stair of that staircase creaks sometimes, and the windows in the upstairs bedroom get stuck. Oh, and the chair in my father's study is burgundy, trimmed with brass rivets."

"Maevestra," her mother said, flatly, from the doorway of the dining room. "How delightful."

"Telling your new staff that I don't exist, that's a new one from your book of lies, Mother," Mae said, stuffing her gloves into her pocket. "But to disown Genevieve, too? It boggles the mind to wonder what must have happened there." She folded her hands in front of her, standing unmoved. "Although I suppose the presence of this lovely man who tried to keep me from getting in is proof that you've landed on top. Again."

"Our fortunes have improved somewhat from the last time you were here, it's true."

"Where's my father?"

"He's working, Maevestra, and he's not to be disturbed."

"This is of utmost importance."

Her mother frowned. "Whatever it is, I'm sure it can wait."

"Why, is he busy scraping the bottom of the barrel for more tawdry gossip to extort people with?"

"I hardly think you're one to make smart remarks about tawdry gossip, given what you've put us through." Her mother looked to the man, still holding the brass knob. "You may close the door, Frederic. Please, leave my—leave us in peace. We have business to discuss."

Frederic did as he was told, bolting the door and heading up the stairs. He paused on the sixth step as it creaked, glancing at Mae before he disappeared to the second floor.

"You have a lot of nerve showing up here again," Mae's mother said. "Considering what we had to do to bail you out the last time."

"Please, I saved you both, and you know it. Without what I did, you wouldn't have whatever comfortable deal you have with Overseer Allemande."

"Soon to be High Councilor Allemande, if all goes to plan."

Mae raised an eyebrow. "That's quite a coup for you."

"Which is why your father is not to be disturbed." Her mother sighed angrily, pressing a stray hair back into her perfectly coiffed hair. "Do you have any idea of the lengths we had to travel to remove you from the books?"

"You didn't have to do that."

"Of course we did. You wouldn't have been able to travel back here if we hadn't."

Mae rolled her eyes and flinched, surprised at her own petulance. "You had my record expunged because it would have negatively impacted your names, not to save me." She rolled up her left sleeve, pointing at a tiny scar. "I have an alternate chip. Maevestra Machenet isn't even here in the Capital."

"You're a damned fool to be using one of those grey market chips, they're illegal." Mae's mother gave a quiet scoff, looking over her shoulder into the other room. "Not that legality has ever meant anything to you."

"The hypocrisy in here is a little thick today, don't you think?" Mae asked. "I can hardly breathe for the fumes."

Her mother sniffed airily, ignoring her. "Your sister was always the one who was going to make us proud."

"Yet you're telling your new butler that you have no children, so what happened there, I wonder? Did Gen finally get so tired of your antics that she disowned you for good this time?"

Mae's mother tensed, her shoulders rising up towards her ears. "What do you want, Maevestra? I know it must be something, because that's the only time you're here, when you can scrape something out of us before you leave us for dead again."

"Leave you for dead," Mae repeated with a snort. "How over dramatic."

"Anything could have happened to us when you were arrested, and you didn't even pause to make sure your misdeeds had been set right before fleeing the planet again." Her mother sighed, moving to the side. "You might as well sit in the dining room. Sound carries too far in this corridor."

"Afraid Frederic might hear what you do for a living? Might dig up some of those skeletons you've got hiding in the closet?" Mae laughed, crossing into the next room. "Hells, I wouldn't even be surprised if you really did have skeletons in the closet."

"Keep your voice down, Maevestra, grey market chip or no, people will know who you are."

"It's not a grey market chip."

"Then what is it?"

"For me to know, and you to never find out." Mae sat in one of the high-backed chairs, noting that the silver tea service was already sitting on the table. "Expecting someone?"

"No, I'd intended to have a quiet, calm moment to myself, but clearly that's far too much to ask for." Her mother sat opposite her, mouth set into a stern frown. "Mothers can never get even that."

"If you can't manage to get that with no children in the house and my father hiding in his study twelve hours of the day, I don't think your inability to drink tea has anything to do with motherhood." Mae reached for a teacup, pouring from the pot. The scent of ginger and lemongrass filled the air, and she resisted the urge to have even one fond memory of her childhood in that house. "What else happened with Gen? That's quite a thing to have to hide from high society."

"After your little stunt, we had to crawl back from the gutter, Maevestra. We had to make some deals that were, shall we say, slightly less than advantageous, in order to gain the social capital to do our work again. Your sister was less than thrilled about your name being all over the papers."

"Oh, so it's my fault."

"Whom else would be at fault, dear? The rest of us weren't on the front page locking lips with a general, now were we?"

"You were already in a bad position when I came back last time. I saved you, whether or not you choose to believe it."

Mae's mother raised an eyebrow, taking the teapot from her to pour her own. "We would have been just fine on our own. At least then we wouldn't have had to work so hard to expunge an arrest and subsequent imprisonment."

"Hardly an imprisonment, I was out the same night."

"You broke out, Maevestra, and we had MPOs in this house for weeks afterward with thousands of questions. It was unending until your father managed to pull some strings to get the record erased. A few MPOs were less than pleased about it, but lucky for us, their jurisdiction ends where our front door begins."

"Okay," Mae said, resenting the guilt that was settling between her shoulder blades. Even after everything they'd done, the guilt persisted, like a wildfire after a light rain. "Fine."

"That's all you have to say for yourself?"

"Yes."

Her mother scoffed, looking over Mae's head at the curtains. "What do you want, Maevestra?" she asked. "You might as well get to the point."

"I need to speak with my father."

"He's not the only one who makes things happen in this house, you know."

"I'm aware, but he's also the only one present who won't speak to me like I'm a child."

"You are a child, at least, you certainly act like one," her mother said, stirring sugar into her tea with an irritating grate of silver spoon against fine porcelain. "You always managed to get exactly what you wanted, and to the hells with the rest of us."

"No better than what Genevieve did."

"Your sister had to protect her position. I can respect that. You, however, flit all over the Near Systems, doing whatever you please, with no regard for anyone but yourself."

Mae pressed her fingertips into the bleached linen tablecloth, focusing on the feeling of fibers against skin, and not the unstoppable march of frustration that was scaling her spine. "I rarely leave my home, actually. I'm quite happy there."

"You're wasted there."

"It's better than being here," Mae shot back. She squeezed her eyes shut, aware that every word out of her mouth made her sound more like the irreverent teenager her mother saw her as. She took a deep breath and sipped at the tea, letting the gentle spice of it coat her tongue before swallowing. "I prefer being elsewhere. I think, given the circumstances, it's the best outcome for everyone involved."

"Yes, perhaps so."

"With that firmly in mind, I should make it clear that I won't be here any longer than absolutely necessary. Once I have what I came for, I will be out of your perfectly done hair, and you can return to pretending you have no children."

"Do you think it's easy for me, having both of my children pretend I don't exist?"

"I obviously know that you exist, or I wouldn't be sitting here, drinking over-steeped tea."

"It's only over-steeped because I was interrupted, Maevestra." Her mother sighed again, quieter this time, finally sipping her tea. "And it's not over-steeped, you just have a juvenile palette, probably a result of living in a place where no good tea winds up."

"I'm not a big tea drinker, anyway."

"Then far be it from you to make judgments and assertions, then."

Mae sucked her teeth, for a brief moment wondering why in any hell she ever thought this would work. "I need information," she said finally. "I need to find someone."

"You're going to need to be more specific than that, dear."

"I need you to find General Fineglass."

Her mother snorted an indelicate laugh, rare for her. "Still lovesick, are you?"

"Something like that."

"Given that General Fineglass returned to the Rim not long after your cowardly escape from prison—"

"Jail."

"The lexicon is largely inconsequential under the eyes of the law, Maevestra." Her mother lifted the lid of the tea pot, frowning. "Can I assume we're going to need more tea? Or does your delicate palette require something a bit less complex?"

"Coffee," Mae answered, ignoring the barb. She'd have to get used to it again, the constant knife-dance across eggshells, verbal sparring that never stopped. Her mother sharpened her tongue the way a master swordswoman would prepare her blade, with absolute precision and deadly intent. "Please."

"A horrid beverage, Maevestra."

"A horrid beverage for a horrible daughter. It suits, don't you think?"

"Frederic," her mother called, ringing an awful bell that sat next to the tea service, "we are in desperate need of more tea, I'm afraid."

He descended the stairs quickly but softly, and Mae noticed that he skipped the sixth step. "Of course, ma'am," he said, taking the tea set away into the kitchen. "It will only be a moment."

"And a coffee, for our visitor, if you would."

"Yes, ma'am."

Mae shifted uncomfortably in her chair, already wanting to leave. Wanting to be gone, boarding a flight back home, knowing she'd find Bailey there, but she wouldn't, not until she found out where she was. "I'm sure you're thrilled to have people to order around again," she said acerbically.

"Please, Maevestra, we wouldn't get any work done if we had to keep up with this place ourselves. Frederic is gods-sent, so polite and efficient."

"No doubt poached from another house."

"He was previously employed by the Weavers, yes, but after certain accusations about the Exchequer were made public, he was searching for somewhere else to be employed that would respect him for his work and keep the house out of the limelight."

"Funny he chose here, then," Mae replied, watching the kitchen door. "So much for your deal with the Exchequer, then?"

"He was unwilling to negotiate. He forced our hand."

"Powerful enemy to make."

"A pittance, if the reward is an ear on the High Council, Maevestra, surely you must realize that." Her mother sniffed, picking an errant piece of wax from the unburnt candles on the table. "If not, then perhaps you were never going to be the political prodigy your father dreamed you would be, after all."

"He should have realized that when I was nine years old. Is he still holding onto that, after all these years?"

"Well, you know your father. Always an idealist, a hopeless romantic. He always wanted the best for you."

"He's had a strange way of showing it."

Frederic reappeared with the tea set, steaming once again, and a cup of coffee at the edge of the tray. He slid it over to Mae with a nod. "I hope it's to your liking, ma'am."

"I'm sure it's wonderful," Mae replied.

"Mrs. Machenet, I will be taking tea to your husband in his study now."

"Tell him his daughter is here," Mae said. "Tell him I need to speak with him."

Frederic glanced at Mae's mother, who nodded almost imperceptibly. "You may tell him. I'd be surprised if he didn't already know, given the entrances that Maevestra likes to make." He disappeared again, this time taking the tray, before Mae's mother spoke again. "This thing with the general, it's not all that it seems, I fear."

"You don't need to worry about the why, I just need to get a message to her, and quietly."

"Communications are heavily monitored, Maevestra. We could be arrested for even the slightest hint of treason."

"I'm not asking you to commit treason, I'm asking you to send a wire, and I'm here asking you instead of doing it myself because I'm aware of the monitoring, and despite my brief stint of imprisonment, I'm not eager to repeat it." Mae took the cup of coffee in her hands, absorbing the warmth, inhaling the familiar, bitter scent. "That's all I am asking."

"A declaration of love? Dearest, she spent two months making the rounds with the papers, disavowing any relationship with you. Let it go. It's over."

"It is not a declaration of love, I do have some self-respect, thank you Mother, it is about another matter entirely, I just need access to your secure wire line, and then I will go as soon as I get a response. Given the delays with signals out to the Rim, I would wager a day, maybe two, if you let me use it this evening."

"You'll have to speak to your father about that. I don't know how to use that thing."

"Which is why I said that the moment you laid eyes on me, but you weren't very interested in listening to what I had to say." Mae sipped at the coffee, reveling in the familiarity. Even when nothing felt safe, at least coffee was. She hadn't had much tea since she'd been dosed by that little brat Emeline.

"Maevestra," her father declared, descending the stairs. "I thought I detected trouble."

"No trouble, not from me. I just need to use your secure wire line to send a message."

"Your little rebellious friends don't have a secure line?"

Mae flinched. "No."

"I'd heard that Obsidian Enclave has some very impressive technology. That's the word in the alleys."

"Spending much time in alleys, Father?"

He sat next to her mother, folding his hands atop the table. "We have people for that. Little birds to tell us things, passing on useful bits of information."

"Have any of those little birds said anything useful about General Fineglass?"

"Hmm." He was unmoving in his poise, and that's what made him so successful at blackmail. He never flinched, not for anything. "Perhaps."

"What is it?"

"You think you can come in here and make demands, Maevestra? After the mess you left us with last time?" He made a quiet tsk sound, pouring tea from her mother's pot. "You know that's not how things work when you're a Machenet."

"Fine," Mae relented. "What do you want?"

"That depends on what you have."

"Tell me what you're after, and I'll give you information if I am able."

Her father frowned at his tea, glancing at his wife. "Gladys, darling, I think you've over-steeped your tea."

"It's not over-steeped," her mother hissed.

He looked back to Mae, considering her for a moment. "I assume you won't give me the location of your little settlement."

"Never."

"Very well," he replied casually. "It's not as if the High Council doesn't already know where it is anyway, but it could have been a coup for us, offering that up."

"Only you could offer information someone already has, and have that work in your favor."

"Which is why you grew up in this nice house, Maevestra, why you wanted for nothing as a child."

Mae grimaced, the guilt finding more footholds in her vertebrae. "I never asked for any of it."

"And yet it was given to you, what a charmed life you've led. Anything less than charmed has been your own making. Your own choices, despite our warnings to the contrary." He sipped the tea without a wince at the overly strong flavor. "Give me information on The Splintered, and I will unlock the secure line for you."

Chapter 16

Rosie drummed her fingers against the hydroponics tray, blowing out a noisy, aggravated sigh. It had been a week of having free roam around Lucent Base, and still, she knew nothing. Zink had made sure that her chip wouldn't grant her access to any of the more interesting buildings, out of the justified fear she would immediately call for help, and so it had been seven long days of rotating between her quarters, the greenhouses, and the mess hall. The east wing of the technology building was largely empty, and functioned more like a monument to Obsidian Enclave ingenuity than a research facility. She'd memorized the layout of the base five times over, and could walk it in her sleep if she had to.

The frustration of having no contact with anyone was palpable and scraped at her consciousness like bad jam over burnt toast. The greenhouses were impressive, that much she couldn't deny. So much fresh, impeccable produce, unsullied by gnats or gastropods, crates and crates of fruits and vegetables, much more than the base could ever hope to consume itself. They'd been exporting it.

Back to their home colony, to Ceru, maybe, or to Kilper to sell it off, or a trading beacon, if there was one nearby that hadn't been obliterated in the Terringgough Gulch blast. She plucked a plum and bit into it, savoring the sweet juices that ran down her chin.

The absence of Delia was like a deep burn, the kind that hurt worse the longer that time goes on. Nerves rebuilding, restructuring, and she'd spent months trying to forget what it was like to live without her, only to have to force herself to remember if for no other reason than self-preservation.

Four more bites of the plum and it was finished, and she was left with sticky fingers and the pit, rough against her palms as she held it.

Rosie sighed angrily, wiping her hands on the thighs of her Obsidian Enclave standard-issue jumpsuit. If Zink wasn't going to give her access to what she needed, then she would take it instead. Seven days was long enough to stand around waiting, and she'd been promised she could leave, but it hadn't escaped her attention that Zink had left on a four-day mission the day before, according to the dockworker preventing her from going any further. It also hadn't escaped her that there were no gods-damned shuttles or transports in the docks.

She was stranded, just as she'd feared, and it had been Zink's plan all along.

Rosie was under no illusions as to who he was, and what he wanted, both from this war and from her, not to mention what he wanted for his people back in Ceru. He claimed he would be satisfied with peace, but establishing a fully functional research facility inside the Near Systems suggested otherwise. What were they going to do, abandon it?

She strode across the greenhouse, stopping only once to marvel at the perfect ripeness of a tomato, pushing through the glass doors into the large courtyard. The medical building was close by and seemed as good a place as any to start a thorough search of Lucent Base. Besides, they'd probably have a wire in there, maybe even one she could use to get a message out.

It didn't take long, waiting by the back door of the building, for someone to slip up. Rosie had worked in kitchens long enough to know that people took shortcuts with safety procedures, especially if they thought no one was watching. Someone, a med tech perhaps, propped the door open with a clipboard while she crept around the side of the building to eat her lunch. No doubt she didn't want to sign out and back in again at the front desk, so had done this instead.

Rosie took the opportunity, being sure to replace the clipboard once she was inside. The bigger her head start, the better. A clean stack of medical uniforms sat atop a cleaning cart in one of the corridors. She slipped a white lab coat over her jumpsuit, hoping it would give her some cover, despite knowing if anyone really saw her, they'd know who she was. Zink hadn't been shy about making that announcement at least three times since she'd arrived. Still, the illusion of authority was better than nothing, and wouldn't raise suspicion if someone only saw her from behind.

Most rooms were empty, and that was largely to be expected. Obsidian Enclave was still a backhanded player in the war, keeping plenty of distance between them and conflict with the Coalition. Further, Lucent Base had to remain under the radar if they wanted it to escape Coalition eyes, so it seemed the only patients were ones with extensive injuries. She peeked through the window, squinting past a maze of tubes and machinery to an oddly familiar face.

"What in all the gods' names?" she said aloud, pushing the door open. She reached for the chart hanging at the edge of the bed, but someone slapped it out of her hand.

"I told you, I want to see Zink."

Rosie turned. "*Hyun?*"

"Rosie, oh my gods," Hyun said, throwing her arms around Rosie. "Where is everyone else?"

"There isn't anyone else. It's just me." Rosie bent, picking up the chart. "Did you hear the announcement Zink made about me being here? I've been on the base for a week. Why didn't you come find me?"

"We don't hear the announcements in the medical building, they don't want to disturb the patients."

"Yeah, that or he didn't want us to know the other was here," Rosie grumbled. "What happened?"

"You don't know? They didn't tell you?"

"Zink scooped me up before they got back. I haven't spoken to anyone since they took me."

Hyun gave a low growl, surprisingly threatening given her usual demeanor. "He said we could leave whenever we wanted, but he won't give me wire access. He said it's too dangerous to move him right now, but Zink isn't a gods-damned doctor, he's not even a med tech."

"So what now?"

"Jasper won't survive in a shuttle, we'd need an actual ship."

"None in the docks," Rosie said.

"Of course not. That would be too easy, wouldn't it?" Hyun pressed two fingers to her temple, sitting back in the well-worn chair at Jasper's bedside. "I stayed because I didn't trust them with him. I didn't trust them to not, I don't know, use him for experiments, or..." Hyun trailed off, her dark eyes filling with tears. "Or let him die."

"How did it happen?"

"It all happened so fast. Terringgough exploded, we were racing to get out of the blast zone. Breakneck pace just about, and no other pilot could have done it, I'll tell you that much. We went through the belt. Zink chased us. We took a rock to the hull, and it smashed up the med bay. Jas took the hit, pushing me out of the way." Hyun drew in a shaky breath. "And now he's here."

"Gods." Rosie looked him over, trying to hide her horror that he was hooked up to so many machines. "But he's stable?"

"As he can be, I guess." Hyun took Jasper's hand in her own. "No signs of improvement. I just want to take him home, Rosie."

"We'll get him home. We will."

"So you haven't heard anything from anyone?"

Rosie shook her head. "No. I've barely spoken to anyone since arriving, mostly just Zink. I have a feeling he told everyone to keep away from me. He wants to convince me to go with him to Ceru, beyond the Rim. To become their mascot for the war, I guess."

"And do you want to go?"

"Of course not. I never wanted any of this, Hyun. I didn't want it the time they cornered us on Terringgough Gulch and I don't want it now. I'm no faction leader, I can barely handle puff pastry without swearing enough to make Larkin wince."

"You have the legacy, though."

"I'm not convinced anyone gives a shit about legacy except Zink," Rosie said. "I'm about as useful as a fork in broth."

Hyun tilted her head. "That's not really true, Rosie. You helped six people escape Turas-Mara."

"With help."

"You poisoned most of the station."

"As a cover!"

"And not only did you evade capture, but you wrecked their targets, for weeks, because of what you did out there." Hyun shrugged. "Believe what you want, but it's always been clear to me that you know what you're doing."

"I'm faking it."

"Aren't we all?"

Rosie snorted softly. "Yeah. I guess we are."

"I'm surprised he let you have access to this building if he's trying to keep us away from each other. To keep us from plotting, or taking over his shitty little base."

"His shitty, incredibly technologically advanced little base," Rosie corrected. "Have you seen those hydroponics bays?"

"Imagine those in Bradach," Hyun mused. "Carmen and Bailey would be like little kids in a candy store."

"Are you kidding? Imagine what I could cook with access to ingredients like that." Rosie sighed happily, almost forgetting for a moment that she was being held prisoner on a base a long way from home. "Not having to cobble a menu together from whatever wasn't rotten on the transport? Gods below, what luxury."

"More to the point, Gordon, why *did* he give you access to the medical building?"

"Oh. He didn't."

"What did you do, smash a window? Very suave. You definitely won't get caught that way."

"No, I waited for someone to prop the rear doors open. Walked right in, stole a lab coat."

Hyun sucked in a breath. "You'd better hide, then, because they're going to make rounds in five minutes." She nodded towards the clock on the wall, the gears ticking forward with an ominous, inescapable rhythm. "Lunch break is over now."

"Where can I hide?"

"You're better off leaving and coming back later."

"And just hoping someone leaves the door ajar again?"

"It worked once, right?" Hyun said. She looked at Jasper with a wan smile for a moment as her expression hardened into something else entirely. Something more dangerous. "No. I'll come to you. You're staying in the greenhouse, right?"

"Greenhouse A."

"I should have access. I'll wait until final rounds tonight and then I'll come to your door and knock three times. We can plan then."

"Okay," Rosie whispered, now all too conscious of the clock and its meaning. She grasped Hyun's hand tightly, looking into her eyes. "We're going to get out of here. All of us. I promise, if it's the last thing I do."

"Knowing Zink, it might be."

"I'd be surprised if the Cricket wasn't already on its way here for us. Captain Violet knows you're both here, right?"

Hyun nodded. "She knows, but I had to bluff. Make her think I was leaving for good, that maybe I'd join Obsidian Enclave. Hells, the food is amazing—don't tell Ned I said that—but she might just be thinking I've defected."

"She can't think that. She knows you better than that," Rosie said. "I bet they're already making a plan to get us out of here."

"If not, then we'd better come up with something fast." Hyun glanced at the clock again. "You'd better go. But we'll talk later about how we can steal a ship and get out of here."

"Later," Rosie repeated, trying to reassure her. She slipped through the door and back down the corridor, a light suspicion setting in when she didn't see a single soul there. Almost as if it had been a trap. She eased the door open, letting it latch behind her now that the clipboard was gone. She was about to breathe a sigh of relief when the vapor trail of Zink's ship appeared high in the sky, descending quickly to the docks.

Rosie half walked, half jogged back to the greenhouse, not wanting to be spotted where she wasn't supposed to be. She busied herself with pruning the berry bushes, no longer laden with fruit now that they had been harvested a few days prior. She'd hoped for some to make a pie, just something familiar to ease her mind, but they'd all been exported before she was able to steal some for herself.

"Ms. Gordon," Gregor Zink said, throwing open the door of the greenhouse. He was beaming widely, like he'd just won a game of cards or a major interstellar battle.

She glanced up at him, feigning innocence. "It's been seven days, Mr. Zink," she said evenly.

"Indeed, indeed it has!"

"Are you alright?" she asked flatly, keeping her attention on the pruning shears with each snip of a bare stem. "You seem excitable."

"Of course I'm excitable. You passed the test!"

She closed her eyes, willing her stomach to not lurch into her throat. "Test?"

"Yes, of course we had to have a test. It's data, Ms. Gordon, it's repeatable, it's case study." He closed the glass door and tilted his head, smiling. "I knew you were your grandmother's granddaughter."

"Are you going to clue me in, or do I have to guess at what you mean?"

"Perhaps the leadership gene skips a generation. Your mother never wanted anything to do with us."

"I don't want anything to do with you, either, or have you forgotten that?"

He laughed, throwing his head back with the force of it, the shallow, hollow sound echoing against the domed ceiling. "You'll soon change your mind. Come with me. I want to show you something."

"I don't enjoy these mind games, Mr. Zink."

"I don't play games, Ms. Gordon, I gather data. In this case, my hypothesis proved true!"

"What hypothesis was that?"

He sighed happily, looking at her like she was a well-trained puppy and not a grown woman. "I knew that pushed far enough, you would break the rules."

"So the medical building was bait, then."

"I don't know if I'd call it bait. I presented an opportunity for you to take matters into your own hands, and you took it!"

Rosie still refused to look up, despite the fact that now her hands were shaking. "So Hyun was in on it, then?"

"She's one of the most gifted medical minds I've ever had the pleasure of meeting," Zink explained, waving to a distant figure through the door. "She's more knowledgeable than most doctors and specialists. I think this may be due to her photographic memory."

"Explains the card games, then."

"Cards?"

"Nothing," Rosie corrected as Hyun pushed open the door. "You're with them now, is that it?" Rosie asked, resisting the urge to lose her composure.

"This is one of the most advanced bases I've ever seen," Hyun replied, taking a few steps towards her. "I couldn't just leave, not after the technology I've seen. To think I was inserting a half-baked metal rib cage a few years back, and here they have things being grown! From stem cells, Rosie! No more risk of rejection, less risk of infection, and that's not even starting on all of the treatments they've developed for illnesses."

"A few shiny pieces of equipment, and you sell the rest of us out?"

"It's about more than that, and I am hoping you will come to see that. You should join us in Ceru, Rosie," Hyun said gently. "As soon as you're settled, we can send for Delia. We'll get you a state-of-the-art kitchen, whatever you want, but we need you at the forefront of this war."

The tiny matchstick light of hope Rosie had held onto fizzled out, plunging her into depths she didn't even realize imaginable. "I don't want to go to Ceru," she said. "I want to go home."

"You have an ocean, a vast deep space of potential, Ms. Gordon," Zink said. "You cannot even begin to fathom what we could all achieve together.

"What about Jasper?" Rosie asked. "You'd just leave him here on Lucent

Base?”

Zink smiled, taking the pruning shears from her hands. “Ms. Gordon, he will live and thrive, thanks to you. Your bravery today unlocked a treatment for him that had never been available before. Now that you’ve shown your true colors, your loyalty, your bravery, now he can be treated the way he deserves.”

Rosie looked from Zink to Hyun, expecting to see a difference in expression but only finding the same encouraging smile from both of them. “So you withheld treatment until I broke into the medical building?”

“It’s not as simple as that, Ms. Gordon, please, you make me sound like a monster. I’m not a monster, I’m just a man who desires the secrets of the universe and for peace. I don’t think either of those things are impossible to attain, especially if we have you as our figurehead.”

“What’s in Ceru, then?” Rosie asked, her lips pressed firmly into a frown.

“I’m so glad you asked, Ms. Gordon. I have someone to introduce you to, he’s been so excited to make your acquaintance again.” Zink opened the door, whispering to someone just out of view, a man, obscured by the leaves of a large bush.

Rosie craned her neck, trying to see, as a dapper, well-dressed man entered the greenhouse.

“Ms. Gordon, what an absolute pleasure to meet again. I can only express my extreme dismay that our last meeting was both brief and chaotic.” He extended his hand, offering her a warm smile. “I’m Barnaby Meier. I think we can make amazing things happen together.”

Chapter 17

Alice tossed her wrench onto the cluttered workshop desk with a noisy, perturbed clatter and a heavy sigh. "This fucking ship," she grumbled under her breath.

"Are you finished yet?" Josie asked from the doorway, leaning against it casually, draped against it like she wasn't the source of so many gods-damned problems.

"No, I'm not finished yet, not unless you want this boiler to explode."

"And they said you were the best," Josie said in a bored voice. "Maybe that was a lie that Violet told you. Maybe she kidnapped you because you were the hottest mechanic, and not the best." She wrinkled her nose, tucking a lock of blond hair behind her ear. "Don't get any ideas, Green. You're not my type."

"And sycophantic pirate captains with a grudge aren't my type, either."

Josie raised an eyebrow. "Aren't they?"

"Listen, this is the third damned ship you've put me on to fix. Don't you have mechanics on your crew?"

"Good help is so hard to find these days, Alice. Wouldn't you agree?"

"Not particularly." Alice bent, examining one of the pressure gauges. "This whole boiler should be replaced. Too much sediment has built up, it's getting dangerous."

"As long as the ship can fly, we'll call that done."

"It can, for now, but it can't indefinitely." Alice tossed a screwdriver to the ground with a metallic clang, and it rolled halfway across the grate before it came to a stop under the boiler.

Josie's eyes followed the tool, nudging it with the toe of her polished black boot. "Unlike your egotist of a captain, I do try to schedule regular maintenance and repairs on our fleet. It's just been a challenge lately, given our usual mechanic connect has gone dark."

"Gone dark?"

"She was—is—Coalition, but we were old friends. Well, I was old friends with her aunt, anyway." Josie smirked. "She spoke so *highly* of you."

"I don't know what you're trying to get at, but the longer you stand there and talk at me, the longer this is going to take. I still have two patches to check and re-seal before I'm finished here."

"It was sarcasm, Green. She didn't speak highly of you at all."

"Unsurprising, given my defection."

"Still, before grey market chips became illegal, she was an excellent trade partner for new parts. Not all of us fly around in rust buckets, you know. We can't all find replacement pieces in the depths of an old beacon junkyard."

"I don't source parts from junkyards, you can never know what kind of condition they've been kept in. Rust, for one thing, corrosion, for another, and let's not even get into how often those damned gaskets will crack if they sit in a warehouse that's too cold."

Josie strolled to the workbench, picking through the bits and pieces with a frown. "I don't recall this looking quite so disorganized this morning."

"You can have tidy, or you can have done. You don't get both," Alice snapped. Her hands were aching from days of near nonstop work on Josie's ship, then a secondary, and now a tertiary. "How many ships do you have, anyway?"

"A number." Josie shrugged, giving her a petulant smirk. "Don't worry, this is probably the last one."

"Vi isn't going to let you forget this, you know."

"I'm aware that we have more rounds to go before this thing is finished." Josie picked up a gear, inspecting it as if she knew what in hells it was for, and tossed it back into the box with a quiet clank. "She should feel grateful that this is all I've done."

"Grateful?" Alice asked with a loud scoff. "Vi is right, every damned time we're down, you show up and make everything worse. You're like half-eaten candy stuck to the bottom of my boot, I just can't quite manage to scrape you off."

"That might be the nicest thing anyone has ever said to me, Green."

"You need better friends."

"My friends are fine, thank you very much, and at the end of the day, I always know that we'll come out on top. We always do."

Alice hissed out a sigh, inspecting the safety valve and frowning at a deep dent in the brass. "You need a new valve, this one is damaged."

"You can do that, right? Replace the valve?"

"Not without a valve to replace it with. I'm not a genie, Keller."

Josie advanced on her, hand on the gun in her holster. "Watch it, Green. That's Captain Keller to you."

"Regardless of your egotism, I can't magic a valve out of thin air," Alice said, ignoring the captain's menacing stance. "There are no spares in this boiler room, I've already looked. So unless you're hiding one inside that pretty purple corset you're wearing, we'll need to stop somewhere to trade for one. You can't run max speed until it's replaced, or you risk blowing the whole line out."

"Fine. We're not far from Kilper, we'll stop there."

"Fine," Alice agreed, already planning her escape. "I know a couple of parts technicians there, I'm more than happy to arrange an advantageous trade."

Josie snorted. "Do you think I'm a fool?"

"No?"

"You're not leaving the ship when we reach Kilper Station. You'd make a beeline straight for the first ship to take you back to Violet. You two are like magnets. It's extremely tiresome, and if I'm being honest, kind of gross."

"*Gross?*"

"It doesn't fill me with joy to see the person who murdered Captain Leo all married up and happy, no, Alice." Josie rolled her eyes dramatically, a hand on her hip. "She was warned to stay out of my way, and I keep finding her—you—parked right in the middle of my path to greatness."

"I didn't realize the path to greatness was paved with piracy, abduction, and extortion."

Josie laughed forcefully, bending to smack the tops of her knees. "Oh, hilarious, Alice, really, very funny. Are you really still that naïve? Everyone known for their greatness has spent a lifetime stepping on the backs of other people. It's the only way to ascend, and if Violet had any sense, she'd see that's the only way to do things."

"Leo would have left you the moment he knew you were pregnant, you know," Alice retorted, turning back to the boiler. She tightened three screws before Josie responded.

"Captain Leo pulled me up out of the mud, Green. He was rash, and quick on the trigger, and probably would have made a terrible father, you are right about that, but what am I supposed to tell my daughter, when she's old enough to ask for the real story? You expect me to look her in the eyes and tell her that I let her father's murderer go, never to be seen again?" Josie shifted her weight, the thick tread of boot sliding against the metal grate. "Violet deserves death for what she did. She should feel lucky that I've not done more than I have. My interference is a mercy, Alice, not a punishment."

"You could tell your daughter that her father was an insignificant fool who picked a fight with the wrong ship at the wrong time, that he threatened people, probably would have let us all die out there." Alice knelt, scrunching down to peer beneath the boiler. "What a legacy."

"Because your parents have such a legacy? What were they, farmers?"

"Rebels," Alice answered plainly.

"That's far more interesting than I would have expected, coming from someone as interesting as a piece of stale bread."

"I don't know much more than that, they were killed when I was young. I did grow up on a farm, thank you very much, but it wasn't with them." She strained to reach under the boiler, reaching for something lodged at the back while trying not to singe her arm. "They had a safe house in Aarq."

"I've never been."

"I don't remember it much. The door was painted a bright blue. There was wallpaper inside, peeling, but printed with birds, I think." Alice's fingers closed around something hard and metal, and she drew it out slowly. "Why was there a droid wedged beneath your boiler?"

"I don't know, did you put it there?"

Alice flipped it over, her lungs refusing to intake air as she examined it.

"Don't do that," Josie said, reaching for the droid.

Alice twisted out of her grasp, holding the droid aloft over her head, trying to pry the back off with her fingertips.

"That's not fair, you're like a damned giraffe." Josie reached for her gun, but Alice wrenched her arm back like she was about to throw the droid.

"Don't shoot me, or I throw this against the wall and we can both watch it shatter into a million different pieces."

"You break it, you fix it," Josie threatened.

"Can't fix these, they don't have typical part sizing." Alice pried the back off, examining it for a moment before replacing the panel. "Where did you get a murder droid, Josie?"

"I found it."

"Found it where? Because this looks like a much newer model than the ones we found a few years back."

"I traded for it on Kilper a few weeks ago."

Alice wiped a thick layer of dust from the droid, staring Josie right in the eye. "I doubt that."

"Why does it matter? You're hardly in any position to be calling the shots on my gods-damned ship," Josie shot back. "My business is my own, and you need to keep your enormous cyclops self out of it."

"This is a Coalition droid, is why I'm asking. Have you been doing deals with the Coalition? This mysterious mechanic, maybe?"

"I already told you, that mechanic cut us off. Which is why I had to go out of my way to poach you off the Cricket." Josie laughed. "I bet they're still sitting there where we left them, dead in the water." She climbed on top of the workbench, plucking the droid from Alice's hand. "Do you think they ran out of air yet?"

"Air filtration can run on solar for two weeks if the ship is on standby."

"Maybe." Josie shrugged. "Who knows what can happen out there?"

"If you sent a scrap team out there, I swear with all the gods as my witnesses, I will make sure that you suffer," Alice threatened. "I'll carve every last piece of tech out of every single one of your ships, and I will hunt you until you're dead."

"Relax, Cyclops, I didn't send a scrap team. Like I said, my attention is a mercy, not a punishment. I like the fiery temper though, that's new. Is that how you wound up with Violet in your bed?"

"Why are you so curious about my bed, Josie?"

"Because I can't even begin to fathom the depths of depravity one would have to plumb to sleep with a crew member."

"Your very own Captain Leo did. Isn't that how you wound up with your daughter?"

"That was before I joined his crew. Nothing happened between us once I was on board."

Alice snorted. "Sounds boring."

"And Violet is dangerous, but you're too love-struck to realize it. Do you need to lose another eye before you figure that one out?"

"That one was all me," Alice said, wiping away the dripping condensation gathering on the outside of one of the boilers. "Your condensate pipe is blocked on this one. Either that or your heat exchange is cracked."

"Let me guess, you need more parts for that?"

"No, boiling water to test for a blockage. If that's not it, I can weld the heat exchanger back together for now."

"Fine," Josie said again, climbing down off the workbench with the droid closed in her palm. "I imagine you'll need a heat gun either way."

"It would be useful, yes."

"You know, I never did understand why you left the Coalition." Josie stood in the doorway again, hesitating. "You could have had it easy."

"Hard to have it easy when you can't sleep at night."

"I sleep just fine."

"I didn't." Alice began checking the final boiler, despite it appearing fine on first inspection. "And sometimes you don't know what you're looking for until you find it." She sighed. "I know you got the damned droid from Barnaby Meier."

"And how do you know him? A mutual acquaintance, I'd wager?"

"We used to be close." Alice slid a hammer back into its slot in her tool belt, standing up. "He betrayed us more than once."

"Then Violet is as blind as she is dangerous." Josie glanced at Alice's eye patch. "No offense."

"You drag me off my ship, leave my wife and the rest of her crew in the middle of dark space, and you think a comment about lack of sight will be what upsets me?" Alice shook her head. "Just when I think I have you figured out, you do something else weird." She sorted through some spare gears and bolts, dropping them into their respective boxes. "You'd do well to be cautious around Barnaby. He'll rob you the moment he gets the chance."

"Ah," Josie said, nodding. "He sold you out to Violet. I'd heard something about that, but I never thought it was true. I thought you chased her the moment you saw her."

"It's more complicated than that."

"Worked out for you, though, didn't it?"

Alice sighed heavily. "Am I here to fix the damned ship, or to give you my life story?"

"I'm mining for useful tidbits, Green, things I can use against you later. I thought you'd have realized that by now, but maybe you're as dim as Violet is. Birds of a feather, and all that."

"Vi isn't dim, she should have kicked your ass years ago. Should have shot you, too, when she had the chance."

Josie smirked. "Ah, but she didn't, did she? Hence my comment. I wouldn't be leaving dangerous enemies out there to roam around." She opened her palm, examining the droid. "And, yes, that does mean I don't see Violet or in fact, anyone from the Cricket as a threat."

"There's going to come a time when you're going to have to eat your words," Alice said coolly. "And I'm going to relish every moment of it."

Josie's face fell, icing over into something steely, all traces of her usual mischievous bullshit gone. "It's about half a day to Kilper Station. Get settled, mechanic, it's going to be some time before you leave us."

* * *

"Gods be damned," Alice hissed, sucking on a bleeding knuckle. The exhaustion was making her sloppy. Three minor burns just that morning, and now one more graze across the top of her hand. "How many more are there?" she snapped, feeling Josie's stare boring into her back.

"Oh, I don't know. A few," Josie replied casually, flicking a speck of dust from her shoulder.

"You don't know how many ships are in your own fleet?"

Josie laughed. "These aren't *my* ships, Alice. What gave you that impression?"

"The fact that I'm sitting here in the direct path of mirrored light, probably burning to a crisp, certainly sweating like a pig, elbow-deep in another engine."

"Relax, the light out this far probably won't burn you." Josie raised an eyebrow, her stare following a bead of sweat trickling down Alice's face. "Though the rest of what you said is certainly accurate. No, these aren't my ships. I barely even know whose they are."

"Then could you kindly fucking explain why I am fixing them?"

"Trades, mostly. Labor for goods. You're more useful than I'd expected, as it turns out."

Alice wiped the sweat from her brow, feeling the grease from her hand smear across her skin. "So I'm what, an indentured servant?"

"Something like that."

"What are the terms, then? How many of these—" Alice smacked her wrench against the hull of the ship she was working on, denting the metal.

175

"—damned ships do I have to repair before you let me get back to my real job?"

Josie narrowed her eyes, leaning to the side with a hand on her hip. "The terms are whatever I damn well say they are. Get back to work." She eyed the dent with a frown. "And don't damage the merchandise, Green, or I'll add that to your tab."

"You can't just keep me here indefinitely," Alice countered.

"You'd be dead if it weren't for my magnanimous mercy, so I strongly suggest you put some effort into learning how to keep your trap shut."

"She's going to come for me, you know." Alice turned back to the engine, thrusting her hand inside again to free the blockage stopping the gears. "And when she does, I doubt she'll be as merciful as she was the first time."

"She's not the arbiter of goodness, you know," Josie said. "I know you're all love-struck, your head filled with static because she was the first woman in a decade to give you the time of day, but Violet Vear is far from benevolent."

"She wasn't the first in a decade."

"Not from what I heard."

Alice glanced up at her as she pulled a large, mangled chunk of metal from the gears. "I'm going to assume your source on that count is Barnaby, and we all know he's far from reliable."

"Oh, he's reliable for information, you just can't believe a word he says about trades and deals." Josie leaned against the ship, arms folded over her chest. "I would say I trust him as far as I could throw him, but he's small enough that I'm betting that's an inaccurate statement."

Alice snorted. "Regardless, it was seven years, not ten."

"A rounding error."

"How many more? My hands are busted up, Keller, these ships are in rough shape." Alice held up her burned, blood and grease caked hands as evidence. "Where did you find them, the bottom of a scrap heap?"

"They had the same deal that I had with that mechanic."

"The one who hated me?"

Josie nodded. "The very same. In fact, her deep resentment for you and in fact, for the Cricket as a whole, is part of the reason I decided to trust her in the first place. You really should be kinder to your apprentices, you know."

"Apprentice." Alice sat back on her haunches, holding part of the engine to the light, making sure more metal wasn't hiding in the crevices. "Trudy."

"Not your apprentice for long, then, I'm guessing."

"A few weeks, maybe, before I left to return to the Cricket." She leaned forward, placing the engine back into the depths of the ship, her torso completely inside the hull. "I am surprised to hear that she was working with the likes of you."

"More people work with me than with Violet, because at least I wear any treachery on my sleeve. She pretends to be so honorable and pristine, meanwhile she has just as much blood on her hands as any of us." Josie knocked on the hull, the sound reverberating painfully in Alice's ears. "There are at least ten more ships in the repair queue, so I suggest you get your ass moving, Cyclops."

Chapter 18

Bailey picked at a ding in the wall, flaking away chips of paint under her fingernails. She sighed heavily, draping her legs over the side of the chair.

"Stop it," Wilhemina ordered.

"I can't stay hidden in your quarters forever, you know. I thought you just wanted to sort one thing out and then we'd go? I feel like I'm bait here, just waiting for someone to figure out there are two of us."

"I hadn't expected Overseer Allemande to be watching me quite so thoroughly. I swear, every time I leave this room or leave my office, there she is with some damnable report that she wants to shove in my face." Wilhemina tugged at the lapels of her uniform, straightening the points of her crisp collared shirt. "It's like she knows."

"She doesn't know, if she knew she'd be in here already, dragging me to the brig by my hair."

"Unless what she wants is enough evidence to take me down."

"What, you think finding your supposed-to-be-dead almost twin of a sister in your office wouldn't be enough evidence? Come on, Willa, it's been days since you rolled me up here in that cart. At this rate, I should have just stayed on the shuttle. At least on the shuttle, I'd have been able to pilfer some decent food from the cargo bay."

Wilhemina sighed, picking up the purple and gold fountain pen sitting on her desk. "They do regular inspections of the transports and shuttles, Bailey, this is the only option." She signed her name, the tip scratching quietly against ominous pages. "There was a special transport here when

I was gone and Allemande hasn't told me what it was. Says it's classified, but not much is classified from me. I'm a gods-damned general."

"I'm aware."

"As soon as my information request comes back from the Capital, we will go."

"Every day we're here is a day we could be at the Archives, finding out who in hells we are and why in hells we wound up sisters."

"Half sisters," Wilhemina corrected, glancing up at her.

"Sister enough that you haven't killed me yet." Bailey pulled her legs down from the arm of the chair, leaning forward over the desk instead. "Sister enough that you helped them escape, Willa."

"Shut up," Wilhemina hissed. "My office may be largely soundproof, but it's not a guarantee. Besides, even saying that kind of thing out loud makes me uncomfortable. I didn't help anyone."

"You wrote secret notes to lead them to information."

"I wanted someone who could take the fall if they got caught, which they very nearly did, by the way."

"And why didn't they get caught?" Bailey asked, playing with the tail of her braid.

"Because I had to intervene!"

"And yet, you didn't have to."

Wilhemina let loose a small growl of frustration. "The sooner you shut up, the quicker I will get this done."

"Come on, Willa," Bailey whined. "Every day that I'm gone, Mae is going to consider dumping me a little bit more. Can't you send a secure wire or something?"

"Our esteemed Overseer Allemande has also been skulking around the wire room, like she's waiting for something."

"She can't be there *and* outside your door at all times."

"It's a small station, Bailey."

"You can't say you have private business?"

"Not on the secure line, that's not for personal affairs. I could get written up. I could get a *demerit*, Bailey."

Bailey snorted. "Breaking into the archives wouldn't get you a demerit?"

"It's not breaking in when you have access. I just need to find the right excuse to send me there."

"Then hurry the hells up. I'm getting tired of half portions of food."

Wilhemina tossed the pen back to the desk, sending a fine spray of ink to splatter across the surface. "You think I'm not getting tired of that? You're lucky I'm sharing with you at all. I could have just thrown a few protein bricks a day at you and said you could help yourself."

"This was your idea, Willa. Straighten out a few things here and we'd be gone, that's what you said. Not let's go to Turas-Mara and you can sleep on the shitty couch in my office while your stomach growls because I might be a general, but I'm scared of an overseer."

"It's not a shitty couch," Wilhemina shot back. "And I'm not *afraid* of Allemande, I'm just aware of how she operates."

"Chicken."

"Are you seriously trying to *chicken* me into being rash because you're feeling a bit bored?"

Bailey sat up. "Why, is it working?"

"No."

"The longer I'm here, the more likely someone will find me. Or, and this would really be your worst nightmare, I go rogue, slink through the ventilation system, and escape, leaving a trail of evidence a mile wide that it was you who let me onto the station in the first place."

Wilhemina stacked the papers in front of her, frowning at the delicate ink splatters. "First of all, no one is permitted in my office except me. Those orders come from above, way above, in fact. Military and civilian business is separate, and I'm the highest ranking official on this station. Second of all, you can't escape through the vents, because it's a new policy that vents be fitted with razor wire to prevent that exact thing from happening. I can only assume you and your friends had something to do with that."

"I was never in a vent."

"No, but the two I found in Allemande's office were."

"And you reported that?"

"Obviously not." Wilhemina looked at her, finally, and raised an eyebrow. "This is the only thing I know, Bailey. I've been military since I was sixteen, I can't just throw it all into the wind. There are still regulations that must be followed for the good of everyone."

"But you get to break select regulations because you're special?"

"I'm a general!"

"Yeah, so *generate* a way for us to get the hells off this station," Bailey said, leaning forward to lightly punch Wilhemina in the arm. "Let's go to the Archives, Willa. I want to know, don't you?"

"You just want to get back to your girlfriend."

"Is that such a terrible thing?" Bailey huffed softly, pulling a finger across the varnished desk with a squeak.

"Stop that."

"Wilhemina, for all the gods' sakes, you know the longer we stay here, the more likely it is that we'll be found out. Like you said, it's a small station, and I'm getting cabin fever pacing these four cramped walls every damned day."

"It won't be much longer, you need to learn some patience."

"You might be older than me, but you're not the boss."

Her sister flicked one of the metal stripes at her shoulder. "Uniform says otherwise."

"I'm starting to think this was all some kind of ruse to gently imprison me again." Bailey rolled her eyes, sitting back in the chair. "I never should have come out here, especially without telling Mae what I was doing."

"It's for the best you didn't tell her. It means she can't be dosed with truth serum."

"She's already been dosed with truth serum," Bailey grumbled. "Allemande's kid, back in the Capital."

Wilhemina set the stack of papers down on the desk, tilting her head to the side. "Is that so?"

"Unfortunately."

"I'm not surprised, Allemande has bragged to me more than once about her frankly illegal stash of several vials." She straightened the papers, picking them up again. "It's not a far leap to think her child would do the same, given access and opportunity." Wilhemina stood, adjusting her belt buckle, shining gold against the grey of her uniform. "Did your little girlfriend tell her anything?"

"Not much, she managed to get away before the full potency hit. She was arrested soon after, but seeing as the guards didn't know she'd been dosed, wasted the opportunity."

"Fools. I could spot someone dosed with truth serum from five kilometers away."

"Okay, Willa," Bailey sighed.

"I have a meeting with my head of security. Don't go anywhere."

"Where am I going to go, for a leisurely walk to the observatory?"

Wilhemina paused, her hand on the doorknob. "I mean it, Bailey."

"I'm aware, thank you."

"I'll be back soon. I'll bring some dinner. I heard it's stew."

"It's always stew," Bailey complained.

"Not all cooks are as good as the one we had here before, treason notwithstanding." Wilhemina slipped out the door, and before it closed, Bailey heard, "What do you want *this* time, Amaranth?"

Bailey paced the office ten times, corner to corner, the muscles in her limbs desperately craving something other than the few steps it took to cross the thinly carpeted floor. Luxury was foreign at Turas-Mara, even for generals. She slumped into her sister's chair, resting her head in her hands. Mae might actually kill her when she got back to Bradach. Or worse, she'd leave her.

Given what Bailey had done, she couldn't blame her, but the uncertainty hung in the surrounding air, heavy with the promise of late night arguments and Mae tossing all of her stuff out the window. The best thing she'd ever found in the Near Systems, and she'd managed to screw it up, just like she screwed everything up.

She'd let her people be taken. Many of them were still broken from their time working at the mining camp, and she'd never been able to track down the rest of them. One more failure in her impressive portfolio of embarrassments, of letting people down to such an extent that she imagined them cursing her name as they drifted off to sleep.

Whatever she'd managed to do, to fix her shortcomings, had never been enough.

Heading all the way out to Nox Beacon without a word to Mae had been one more mistake that she'd begun to regret almost instantaneously, and now as time went on, every hour brought her closer and closer to making a run for it, to steal a ship and make her way back home and never leave again, never allow herself to wonder again who she really was or where she really came from, because Hjarta was only part of the story.

A scraping sound inside the lock drew her attention, panic immediately dropping into her stomach and sending acid creeping up her throat.

"Willa?" Bailey whispered toward the door, knowing whoever was on the other side wouldn't hear it. They'd established a code, three knocks and a cough before opening, enough notice for Bailey to hide in the closet, but this was different. She stood, trying to clamber over the desk as the lock disengaged and the door hinges gave an ominous creak.

"General!" Overseer Allemande said, reeling backwards even as she pushed the door in. "But—you were just—"

Bailey froze, one leg over the desk, one foot planted on the floor. "I was just what?" she asked, trying to sound like Wilhemina. It hadn't been a problem before, not when it had been a decade since anyone had seen her in the Capital, but now it was a side-by-side comparison. Shit. She tugged at the sleeve of her jumpsuit, trying to make sure her tattoo wasn't visible.

Allemande stood in the doorway, staring. "What are you doing?"

"Calisthenics," Bailey answered coolly. It seemed that listening to her sister wax poetic about her workout routine had begun to seep in, after all. "Good for flexibility. What do you need, Overseer?"

"I, uh... you said that you had business in the wire room."

"Concluded."

"That was rather fast."

"It was efficient." Bailey took her leg off the desk, adjusting her jumpsuit. "Why are you breaking into my office?"

"I needed some... paperwork." Allemande straightened her jacket. "For the crew rotation. I had a few amendments I wanted to make."

"Unilaterally?"

"I'm allowed amendments, Wilhemina, you know that."

"You're not allowed to break into my office, though, are you? You're the civilian branch. This is military. You have no jurisdiction."

"Not yet." Allemande smiled her gleaming, sinister grin, reaching for a file on the desk marked crew assignments. "That will come to pass soon enough."

"And what is that supposed to mean?"

"It means that while you were off gallivanting at Nox Beacon, there was an important transport vessel here at Turas-Mara."

"And?" Bailey prompted, her heart in her throat because the gods-damned door was still standing open. "Come inside, Amaranth, we can talk."

"I just need the file, thank you very much."

Bailey handed her the file, nodding towards the door. "Is that all?"

"Don't you want to know *why* there was an important transport vessel here?"

"Sure. Why, then, was there a transport vessel here?"

Allemande flicked through the file, frowning at the contents. "I thought I said I didn't want night crew assignments reduced, Wilhemina."

"The crew corrections come from on high," Bailey said, repeating what her sister had said. "You and I both know there is a limit to the authority we wield here."

"This didn't come from on high, don't feed me lies, Wilhemina. I know it didn't come from on high because *I* am from on high, now. Or at least, I will be when I am confirmed as the newest member of the High Council."

To Bailey's horror, Wilhemina appeared behind the overseer, her panicked stare strong enough to bore holes through the station's hull.

"What are you looking at?" Allemande asked, whipping her head around.

Wilhemina shoved her into the office, following close behind and locking the door. "What the fuck, Bailey?" she shouted.

"She broke in, what was I supposed to do?" Bailey shot back.

Allemande reached for her concealed pistol, illegally held, but Wilhemina already had hers trained on the overseer, hammer pulled back. "Don't even try it, Amaranth."

"They'll have you for this, you know. Holding a gun on a member of the High Council?"

"You're not on the council yet, and lots of accidents can happen at a station this close to the Rim."

"You wouldn't."

Wilhemina stepped closer. "Wouldn't I? You've been watching me ever since I left the Capital, just waiting for the slightest hint of a fuck up."

"I wonder why, when you've been making dalliances with rebels," Allemande sneered. "I was right about you from the very beginning."

"And yet I still managed to escape your eagle eye," Wilhemina mocked, leaning back against the desk. "You got lucky, Amaranth. If you hadn't broken into my office, you'd be none the wiser. What were you so desperate for that you had to circumvent the digital lock, then?"

"She said it was for crew reassignments," Bailey said.

Wilhemina laughed. "That's bullshit. Come on, Amaranth, you can either tell me now, or I can send my sister to fish that vial of serum out of your quarters and we can find out what you really know. All of it, in excruciating detail. I'm sure the High Council would love to know all about your misdeeds."

"I was looking for information on your little jaunt to Nox Beacon. It wasn't hard to find out there were no missing shipments that week, Wilhemina, I'm not a fool. I thought maybe you'd engaged in a dereliction of duty to find yourself in the arms of a lover, which would have been enough for the ethics board to send you packing. But this," Allemande said, almost in awe, "this will ruin you for sure."

"Yeah, I think we've gone past the point of no return, here," Bailey said. "Not many ways to clean up this mess without bloodshed."

"If you kill me, they'll find you and tear you both apart," Allemande hissed. "Without hesitation. I am a member of the High Council. They won't overlook that."

"She's probably right," Wilhemina said coolly, gesturing casually with the gun. "However," she murmured, looking back at Allemande, "I think you're forgetting that I know plenty of your dirty little secrets, too. Enough for the council to find someone else. Hells, maybe even your daughter, how about that? Well, maybe not actually, as from what I heard, the council is less than pleased with the moves she is making in Skelm."

"Don't bring Emeline into this," Allemande snarled.

"Bailey, empty the bottom drawer of my desk. There's a box in the closet."

Allemande laughed. "You're going to run? You won't get far."

"You're not going to send anyone after us, and I'm going to tell you why." Wilhemina paused, letting Bailey pull an archival box from the cupboard and start filling it with files from the desk. "I know enough to ruin you, and we both know you don't want that. You know enough to ruin me, that much has become painfully obvious in the last five minutes, but I'm not finished with my work yet. I'm not done yet, Amaranth, so you're not going to report this for at least a week. Two, actually. You'll report my disappearance in two weeks."

"I'm supposed to be on a transport to the Capital in just a few days."

"Even better, you have cover for why you didn't notice my absence. No doubt the head of security will be the first to raise an alarm, but that gives us a few days of a head start." Wilhemina stepped closer to Allemande, using her height to her advantage. "If you report this early, I will send the entire contents of those files to the High Council. No doubt they'd be very interested in hearing all about the illegality of your methodology, not to mention the deal you made with someone you knew wasn't me, but kept your mouth shut because you wanted the investment for your sector."

"You told me that you killed her," Amaranth spat.

"I lied, obviously."

"What could she possibly have to offer you that the Coalition hasn't?"

Wilhemina glanced at Bailey, who gave her a nod as she placed the final file into the box. "I don't know the answer to that yet, Amaranth. If we both manage to live through what's coming for us, someday I'll tell you." She kicked the desk drawer shut and took the pen, placing it into her external breast pocket. "Get into the laundry bin, Bailey, we're leaving."

"What do you think is coming for us?" Allemande asked with a sharp laugh, one born more of panic than confidence.

"War, Amaranth. It's coming for us all, and you and I have been on the wrong side for too long to survive it." She gestured towards the closet. "Get in quietly, and we'll bar the door."

"It's soundproofed in here, how am I supposed to get out without alerting the entire station to your absence?"

"You figured out how to break into my office without alerting the entire station, so I'm betting you'll figure this out, too."

Bailey placed the box into the laundry bin, climbing in on top and covering herself with sheets as her sister placed an iron bar between the handles of the closet door. "I'm sorry, Willa," she whispered.

Wilhemina sighed. "I should have known this would happen. Fucking High Council, her?" She holstered the pistol, pushing the laundry cart through the office door and locking it behind her. "We're all fucking doomed."

Chapter 19

The ship landed in the Chalidon docks, right on schedule, but the dock manager took his sweet time in verifying their logs. They were all falsified, of course, and ripe for discovery, but lucky for them, he didn't seem to notice. Cass nearly flew out of the loading bay, heading straight for the Brushstroke Inn. She prayed to the old gods that someone there had heard something about the Cricket, something other than damaged relay codes and untraceable coordinates that led nowhere.

"Hold up," Tansy said, following behind. "You forget, I don't move as fast without my leg."

Cass stopped short, pressing herself against a brick building, away from the flow of passengers heading to and from the transports. "Sorry," she replied, running a hand through her hair. "Just worried. We haven't heard anything from Ivy either, not since she hopped back to the rest of the fleet."

"When she knows something, we'll know. That girl is loyal and looks out for all of us. She's on it, I guarantee."

"I hate being out of comms with so many. Feels like flying blind."

"You can fly blind, if you have the right support," Tansy suggested. "You need a good nav, and then anything is possible. I once knew a two-person team, scrappers out near the Rim. Pilot took a heat gun to the face once, he couldn't see a damned thing after. His nav was the eyes, the pilot everything else. Instinct never goes away."

"Are you volunteering to be my hypothetical nav?"

"Hells no, I have my own agenda, Calvetti, one that starts with getting my damned leg repaired."

"You don't have to wait for me, you know. You can get back on that ship and head straight for Bradach. I'll catch up when I'm able."

Tansy paused, leaning against the brick to catch her breath. "What, and leave you without a ship?"

"I've managed through worse."

"I'm not letting you talk me into missing all the fun. I'm determined I won't miss the next time you blow up an entire mining camp."

"Wasn't me."

"No, but you were there, and it's one hell of a story."

Cass continued up the street, mindful of her speed. The morning mirrored light was dim through the atmosphere that day, a bluish-grey cast to the entire city. Workers streamed to and fro, a busy network of diligent ants all doing their part to uphold the Coalition. "We could have been one of them," she said, glancing across to Tansy. "It would have been an easier life."

"Easier, maybe, but infinitely more boring," Tansy replied, laughing. "I'll take death-defying near misses over the sanitized doldrums of the Coalition. It would be a far worse death than anything else I can imagine." She swung forward on her crutches, using the momentum to crest the gentle hill. "Can you imagine the abject horror of waking up one morning and realizing that half your life had passed you by? Years and years of routine, of reaching upwards and never being able to grasp anything other than someone else's broken dreams."

"Bleak."

"A life's tragedy, distilled into neat little check boxes and time cards," Tansy added. "I'd much rather go down swinging."

"Hopefully we can avoid both going down and swinging while we are here," Cass said. "I didn't think I'd be back here so soon." A man watched her as they passed one another, and she gave an involuntary shiver. "It feels like shifting sand under my feet."

"The whole of the Near Systems is hanging on by a thread. All any of us can do is hang on and hope for the best."

"And go down swinging?"

Captain Tansy laughed, tossing a braid over her shoulder. "Yeah. And go down swinging."

The Brushstroke Inn was unassuming from the outside, cobwebs stretched across the front window, a harsh suggestion of a derelict, abandoned building. The dust looked thicker than last she'd seen it, and it had only been a few weeks. The door opened easily with a quiet creak, and Cass pulled the lever to activate the pulley elevator. It arrived, and she nodded to Tansy. "Your carriage awaits."

"See you down there."

Cass descended the stairs one at a time, still unsure of the steps despite their familiarity. But the stone was slippery with moisture, just lying in wait to give someone a concussion or a one-way trip to the incinerator. "Hey, Marv," she said when she reached the bottom. "The usual, if you don't mind."

"Didn't expect to see you here so soon," he quipped. "Not with the extra checks at the docks."

"Me neither. Complications. Payne around?"

"Here," Georgie said, turning around in a booth. "What's the matter?"

"We were out in dark space when we got a distress call from the Cricket. They're dead in the water somewhere, but the relay was bounced so many times, we have no way of knowing what in the hells is going on. Have you heard anything?"

Georgie's face paled. "No. No, I haven't heard anything, and I'm guessing no one back home has either, because Henry hasn't mentioned anything."

"Is Weaver back there now?" Tansy asked, stepping off the lift.

"She said she got back two days ago," Georgie said. "But with comms being so monitored, that's all I've heard."

"No open channels?"

Georgie shook her head. "Not that I know of. Marv?"

"Nah, too risky from here," Marv replied, filling a glass with crushed ice. "Too much being monitored. Don't want to risk any attention."

"We need to get in contact," Cass said. "We need to find out where the Cricket is, if they're not—" She stopped short, allowing the inevitable assumption to crowd into the tavern like poisoned gas.

"They aren't," Tansy reassured them. "Vi would never allow it."

Cass slid into the booth to join Georgie, her head in her hands. "I feel like I'm trying to put out a dozen different fires at once," she groaned. "No one knows where anyone is. Comms are down or limited, everything is just so…"

"Splintered?" Tansy offered with a quietly sardonic laugh. "I hate to say that's what you get for naming a faction that, but it certainly didn't do you any favors."

"Half the anti-Coalitioners think I'm dead, and the other half are happy to march behind Cole Marion, bane of my existence."

"Be easier if he went missing," Tansy said. She shrugged her shoulders. "What? It's true."

"I'm surprised to still see you here, Georgie," Cass said, catching the glass that Marv slid across the wood. "Weren't you supposed to head back with Henry?"

"My sister is scheduled to come through Chalidon in a few days." Georgie was busy tearing a napkin into shreds, piling the pieces in a neat pile on the table in front of her. "I was working on some campaign flyers and thought I might be able to help shift things here."

"She's not running for governor here, why is she coming to Chalidon?"

"Interviews, mostly," Georgie said. "Not many reporters are that interested in going to Skelm."

"Because it's a backwater," Captain Tansy offered, but cleared her throat nervously when Georgie visibly bristled at the comment. "For now, I mean. It just needs some real leadership."

Georgie turned back to her shredded napkin. "She's leading Das in the polls. She has a real shot at this."

"It's going to be an uphill battle with how much the High Council has it out for her," Cass said. "I hope she knows what she's doing."

"That's why I'm here, to keep an eye. Just in case. Then, when Emeline leaves, I'll grab the first transport to the moon bay and head home. I promised Henry I'd be home as soon as I could. She gets worried when I'm away too long, a side effect of how things were in the beginning for us, I suppose." Georgie drained her glass, wiping her mouth with the back of her hand. "My mother probably worries enough for all of us."

"The docks are going to be a damned nightmare if your sister is arriving soon," Captain Tansy said with the slightest hint of an irritated groan. "We got lucky with checks today, but I'd bet my other leg that they step it up until she's gone. They'll be worried that she'll start a riot."

"She's not going to start a riot, she's doing interviews," Georgie protested. "Although if you ask me, this place could use a little rioting. The Coalition has gotten too comfortable here. They do whatever they like, and the corruption is out on display." She waved at Marv for another ale. "And the strangest part is, no one even seems to care."

"Sounds like the Capital," Cass offered. "Sounds like everywhere nowadays." She sipped at the half-frozen drink, savoring the fiery burn of the clear liquid as it drained down the back of her throat. "If it's not the Coalition, it's Obsidian Enclave." She paused, her hand hesitating over the rim of the glass. "You don't think it's Zink who fired on the Cricket, do you? He already abducted Rosie, what's taking things one step further?"

"Could be," Captain Tansy admitted. "He seems to enjoy holding grudges."

"Understatement of an eon," Cass grumbled.

"How do we know if the Cricket is still out there?" Georgie asked.

Captain Tansy threw back her drink with a delicate grimace. "We don't."

"Marv, there has to be a secure line somewhere in this city," Cass said, turning back towards him. "We need to contact someone and find out what in hells is going on."

He laughed, deep and round like she'd told an elaborate joke. "Sure, there's a secure line. It's at the local Administration Building. Good luck getting in there to use it."

"Even if we broke in, that thing has to be surrounded by half a dozen biometric locks," Georgie said. "Besides, any hint of a disturbance and that puts my sister in danger. They're begging for an excuse to get rid of her without people rioting." She shook her head. "The one in that building is out of the question. It's not an option."

"We can't leave the Cricket in the middle of dark space, either," Captain Tansy shot back. "For all we know, they're still out there, barely fending off scrappers."

"Are we the only ones who got the transmission?" Cass asked. "Ivy said it was bounced between a bunch of relays, right?"

"That doesn't mean anything. If it was up to me, I'd be on the first ship out to their last known location."

"Given the encryption, their last formally known location was Bradach when they left. That's hardly going to be helpful," Georgie said carefully. "We should wait to hear something more, we can't just go on a wild chase across the Near Systems. We'd never find them with all the blockades and circumventions."

Cass held the glass flat against her palm, willing the almost painful cold to sink into her skin, grounding her in a reality she wished she wasn't a part of. "I'm so gods-damned tired of all of this."

"You're the one who started a new faction," Captain Tansy quipped.

"Yeah, and I've regretted that several times already," Cass replied with a sigh. "The path to success would be far easier without Cole Marion, without Gregor gods-damned Zink, and without all the monitoring that makes any kind of communication a risk for all of us." She smacked her hand against the bar and it gave a dull echo through the low rafters, nothing more than exposed brass pipes, long since oxidized, a sickly green hue to every joint and piece. "I'm tired of waiting."

"Not much else to do right now," Marv said, lingering by a small radio in the corner. It was relaying every ship landing and takeoff in an irritatingly monotone voice. Name of ship, number of passengers, time of arrival or departure, one after another. "The docks are busy, and they're only going to get busier with everything that's going on with the war."

"The war," Cass said with a slow hiss tacked onto the end of it. "I suppose it was always going to come to this, but now that it has, I want to fake my death and start over as someone who doesn't have a stake in any of it."

"I feel like you can only get away with faking your death the once," Captain Tansy said. "After that, people start to doubt the legitimacy."

"I wasn't being serious, you know."

"Shut up," Georgie said, leaning across the table. "Marv, turn that up."

He twisted the knob on the radio and the voice droned into the tavern. "The Gold Feather, bay eighteen. Four passengers. Arrival, three minutes past."

Georgie nearly knocked over her chair as she stood. "That's Emeline's ship. She's here early. Why is she here early?" She was already headed for the stairs when Cass caught her by the arm.

"Hold on, Payne, think for a minute. What are the odds it could be a trap? One set for you specifically?"

"The Coalition has no idea I'm even here."

"But it's not a leap for them to assume you might be, right?" Cass asked gently. "I've seen what kind of information they manage to get their hands on. For all we know, they're tracking all of us right now."

"No one is being tracked, don't be dramatic," Captain Tansy said, reading over a small, compact menu. "Marv, how in hells am I supposed to see what this says? The print is so small I'm going to need a magnifying glass."

"Space is at a premium down here, in case you haven't noticed," he grumbled in reply. "We can't all have huge refurbished taverns in Bradach."

"Okay, but even if we're not being tracked, which is debatable, if you ask me, that's still no guarantee that it's not a trap," Cass reiterated. "There might be fifteen agents on that dock just waiting to scoop Georgie up."

"Then find a way to go and look without getting caught. You're a rebel faction leader, but sometimes I wonder what's going on in your head," Captain Tansy mused. "I'd have taken out Cole Marion the moment he didn't offer to step down from the leader of The Scattered."

"And risk the safety of Bradach?"

"Fair point, Calvetti." Captain Tansy squinted at the menu. "Marv, I'll have a number twelve, whatever that is."

"It's whatever's in back. The Brushstroke Inn special."

"Whatever sounds great. I'm starving." Captain Tansy glanced at the rest of them. "You should both eat."

"I'm not hungry," Cass and Georgie said at the same time.

"I'm going to the docks," Georgie added, shrugging on a grey jacket lined with yellow. "You can come, or you can stay, but regardless, I am going to meet my sister at the dock. Once they've squirreled her away in one of the hotels, there's no way I'll be able to get to her, not even with a disguise. The security protocols are too much."

"I'll go, if only to make sure that you don't get yourself killed," Cass said, draining the last of the liquid out of her glass and crunching bits of ice between her teeth, trying to ignore the pain radiating in her jaw as a result. "Captain?"

"I'll stay and work on a plan to find the Cricket," Captain Tansy replied. "Vi drives me up the wall, but there's no way in any hell I can let her sit out there waiting for rescue."

Georgie was already halfway up the stairs by the time Cass started off the bottom step, rushing to keep up. "Gods, Payne, wait up, I can't fly up the damned stairs."

"No time to waste," Georgie said over her shoulder, not even pausing to hold the door open for Cass. "I can't miss this opportunity."

"Does she even want to see you?" Cass prompted, jogging down the brickwork pavement to catch up. "The last I heard, she—"

"The last you heard, she said she didn't want me dead. That's a solid improvement compared to what she said before. I just need to talk to her, and she'll see reason. I'm just trying to help."

"I get that, but we can't just fly in half-cocked when she's on a Coalition vessel, landing in a Coalition-controlled city, and there are more MPOs by the damned day. We have to be smart about this."

"There's too much going on to be smart about it all," Georgie argued.

"We'd be in stasis forever, trying to figure this all out. Sometimes you just have to make a leap of faith."

"I'd rather not leap into the jaws of death, if you don't mind."

Georgie didn't reply, she just kept walking towards the docks, mirrored light glinting aggressively from the polished metal of the ships in the bays. Georgie pulled a flat cap from her back pocket, pulling it down low over her eyes.

"I wish I knew we were playing dress-up, I'd have come prepared," Cass said, struggling to keep up. "Gods, you have a long stride, Payne. You're not even that much taller than me."

"Lifetime of timed work in the Coalition," came the reply, harsh and strangely devoid of emotion. "It does that to you."

Bays one to ten sat empty, waiting for new residents to arrive. The docks were noisy, the air cluttered with the sound of two dozen ships all at once, their engines demanding attention from passers-by. Bays eleven through fifteen were cargo ships, freight being unloaded by dock workers at a breakneck pace.

"Eighteen," Georgie muttered under her breath, marching dutifully past the workers.

Bays sixteen and seventeen housed enormous ships, hiding the one in the further bay. Cass looked to the side, spotting another man staring. The hairs on the back of her neck stood up, and she blanched, reaching out for Georgie but narrowly missing her wrist. "Payne," she hissed over the din of the docks, "just wait, something's not right."

"There she is," Georgie said, her voice thick with emotion. "Emeline!" she shouted.

Emeline turned, dressed in primly tailored charcoal skirts with lilac piping and yellow details at the cuffs, an ode to the Coalition. She blinked first, and then sighed, clasping her hands in front of her. "Georgina."

"I heard you'd be here."

"Indeed."

Cass shrank back, despite the fact that Emeline had already spotted her. Her stomach pulled, intuition resting there, uncomfortable and unpliable.

An MPO stood at the base of the ramp, casually shifting the weight of a heat gun from arm to arm as he waited for the opportunity to use it.

"I missed you," Georgie said, taking another step closer. "I hoped that I could help with your campaign. I know that you're still angry with me, but—"

"I'm not angry with you, Georgina."

"You're not?"

Emeline shook her head. "Of course I'm not." She fidgeted with her skirts, the soft rustle inaudible over the noise. "I'm not angry with you, but I can't have you around this campaign. I had hoped that my warnings would give you a clue to stay one hell away from me, but it would seem that one of us didn't get the brains in the family." Emeline nodded to the MPO at the ramp. "Arrest her."

"Wait!" Cass protested, trying to push her way back through the crowd. Emeline locked eyes with her, giving a barely perceptible shake of her head. Cass hesitated, and it was just long enough for the MPO to clap Georgie in irons.

"You can't do this, Emmy," Georgie protested, tears gathering in her eyes. "Don't do this."

"You forced my hand, Georgina." Emeline sighed before shooting a warning look at Cass. "I wish you hadn't." She turned back towards the ship, adjusting a pin in her hair. "I would advise anyone else to get lost. Get out of Chalidon, while they still can."

Cass choked on the hard knot forming in the back of her throat, dropping back into the throng of workers and passengers. She hated being right.

Chapter 20

The theater was dark, despite the lights, spaced evenly against the wall, which gave off a faintly yellow glow. Olivia shifted in her seat, tugging at the low neckline of her gown. Shimmering purple satin all the way to the floor, offset by a silvery lace corset. The boning dug into her side and she was cursing not having it altered before the event, but there just hadn't been enough time. She also hadn't expected to be invited. Despite her warm welcome back into the fold, something felt *off* with Tarand, something she couldn't quite put her finger on.

The first actor burst onto the stage, streaming with peacock feathers and gold fringe, an almost ridiculous sight, if it wasn't a performance. Olivia held the tiny glasses to the bridge of her nose, watching the stage while her mind wandered in an entirely different direction.

Work was never far from her mind, that had been true since the beginning, but the all-council meeting was looming large over her head, a storm cloud threatening on the horizon of her thoughts. Two had arrived already, and were watching from adjacent boxes. Four in the Capital, two to go, and they'd be arriving within the week. Until then, it would be a parade of public events and positive public relations for the members of the High Council who lived off-world.

Olivia had always hated the theater. It wasn't so much the garish costumes, those were more impressive than not, but the hideous nature of it, a compulsion to sit still and not move for hours while you watched a lackluster piece of Coalition propaganda. It was always the same story. A hero, down on their luck, who joins the Coalition military and becomes a savior. The details changed, but much stayed the same.

She fidgeted with her hands in her lap, rolling the edge of her matching lace gloves and unrolling it again, crushing the delicate textile between her fingers like she was the arbiter of life and death. Maybe she was, in a way, come hells or high water, no matter the cost, laws be damned, and so on and so forth.

Councilor Tarand laid her hand atop Olivia's, pressing gently. She didn't even look at Olivia, not even hesitating to reach over and silently insist that Olivia stop fidgeting.

When her hands fell still, Tarand removed her own, setting it back in her lap. Her eyes never left the stage, following every actor's movement. Meanwhile, Olivia found herself watching everywhere other than the stage. The gilded carvings laid into the walls, the gently worn tracks in the red carpet below, the jittery wobble of a man sitting three rows back from the front who clearly didn't want to be there. She related a little more than she might have liked.

The first act dragged on for what felt like hours, she wasn't sure in the dark, too difficult to read the pocket watch face. It had to be at least midnight.

"One down, one to go," Officer Abara grumbled as the lights went up for the intermission.

"Not a fan?" Olivia asked.

"I'd rather treat myself to having my eyeballs removed with a cocktail stick."

"Oddly specific, and yet relatable."

Abara granted her a sly smirk. "And here I thought you'd be a surefire theater fan, with all your well-to-do friends and your place near the High Council."

"That's just for the clothes," she replied.

"Are you not enjoying yourself, Olivia?" Tarand asked, turning in her seat. "I found it rather enthralling, personally." Her deep purple robes whispered silk against the floor. "Who doesn't love the story of an underdog?"

"Mm," Olivia agreed. "I'm just not sure about some of the narrative choices."

"What do you know about narrative choices, Ms. Guisette? You're my assistant, not a writer."

"You are correct, ma'am, as usual."

Tarand stood, smoothing the wrinkles from the fabric billowing out from around her. "How long is the intermission?"

"Fifteen minutes, ma'am," Abara answered. "Do you require assistance?"

"No, I'm fine." She turned to Olivia, laying a hand gently on her shoulder. "Could I trouble you for a drink, dear? I'm absolutely parched. I barely had time to think this afternoon, much less do anything else."

"Of course."

"Don't be too long, I would hate for you to miss the second act." She narrowed her eyes, but only slightly. "We all need to be on our best behavior right now, no?"

Olivia smiled. "Incontrovertible, ma'am." She stood, heading out into the corridor, which by contrast was bright, brash, and vaguely repulsive in its opulence. Maybe once the theater had been for the common person, but no more, not with the marble floors and gilded ceilings. She sighed, wondering again why she'd bothered to come back at all.

For information. For access.

Yet, it felt like Tarand was holding her at arm's length, even as they discussed the meeting, even as she pitched some ideas for strategy. She missed the excitement of being in space. Gamma-3 felt like a cheap consolation prize, despite the gold and the gemstones that dripped from every person sitting in the boxes.

She wasn't left out on that account, either. A sparkling sapphire choker was clasped around Olivia's neck, a gift from Tarand three years prior. Her fingers danced along the settings, feeling them poke at her skin. Once, she'd loved these events. Now, they felt like a mockery, as though the facade that had surrounded it was cracked and falling away, one shard of cheap porcelain at a time.

The lobby was bustling, busy with people all scrambling for refreshments. If she waited for the line, Tarand would give her one of those disapproving looks she was so damned good at, signaling her quiet contempt. Olivia dipped behind the bar herself, bending to reach for a glass on the bottom shelf, the rim reflecting light from the chandelier above, glittering with crystals and heavy with prisms that refracted the yellow glow from the lights into a vast spectrum of color and beauty.

She crouched lower, trying to reach the glass without the beverage tender noticing that she was there.

"Yeah, I heard," a voice said from above the bar. "I don't know anyone who hasn't heard yet."

"Gods help us if she's stationed in the Capital, I'll cut off my own gods-damned ears just so I don't have to listen to her talk," said a second voice, a woman. Olivia dare not move, but glanced up at the beaded sleeve hanging over the bar. Blush pink with gold shimmering accents, embroidery she recognized from earlier that evening. It was Florence, the right-hand assistant to High Councilor Brome.

"Any ideas what she's really up to?" the first voice asked.

"Marcus, your guess is as good as mine, but I do know that whatever it is, it's bad for us."

Olivia squinted, racking her memory. Marcus. Marcus Winters, the overseer? That was the only Marcus she knew of that had any right to be rubbing elbows with adjacent High Council staff. They were clearly talking about Allemande, but why? To what end?

"She's a gods-damned nuisance," Marcus complained.

Finally, something we agree on, Olivia thought.

Florence shifted, the beads of her dress clacking noisily as she moved, settling with an angry, disorganized rhythm against the wood. "We need to take her out before she takes us all out with her. She's gotten too big for her boots, and we all know it."

"It's more than that, she's trying to take control of sectors she has nothing to do with. My sector is my business, and she keeps trying to interfere for her own benefit." He huffed quietly, drumming his fingers against the bar. He was agitated, more so than usual. "If we don't get rid of her, who in hells can even say what kind of challenges we'll be up against this time next year."

"Agreed. None of us wanted this. It was forced on us."

Olivia nodded to herself. Interesting that Wallace Brome had voted for Allemande, but didn't want her in power. Extortion, perhaps, or bribery. She wouldn't put either of those things past the overseer, not with her track record of success at any and all costs.

Marcus cleared his throat softly, as though he were stalling for time. "Is there a plan, then?"

"Best not to talk about that here, Winters," Florence scolded. "You know better than that."

"Of course," he apologized. "My mistake, I am simply eager to see the Coalition return to its former glory. We need to balance the High Council before we will be able to truly get hold of these rebel leaders, scum, cockroaches that they are, but she's standing in the way. She is the imbalance, and everyone knows it."

"Tarand has to go," Florence whispered, her voice so soft that Olivia thought for a moment that she must have misheard. "Cecelia is impeding progress. She wants to stall new councilors being added to the roster because she fears losing her grip on the Near Systems. I say enough is enough."

Olivia shrank towards the cupboard, now terrified she'd be seen. Overhearing gossip about Allemande was one thing, but an assassination attempt on Councilor Tarand's life was another thing entirely.

"I'll have a courier send over some documents tomorrow," Marcus said, now in a louder voice. "I've prepared what I hope is a compelling portfolio, showing why my sector should be next in line for upgrades to processing and manufacturing."

He was covering now, someone must be nearby. Olivia was barely even breathing, despite the din of the busy lobby.

"Excellent, Mr. Winters. We look forward to perusing your proposal,"

Florence said. "Enjoy the rest of your evening." The gold beads were dragged back over the bar, the clatter of tiny glass fading as she walked away. Marcus Winters waited fifteen seconds and departed himself as well, leaving Olivia still crouched behind the bar, reaching for the rim of a glass.

"Can I help you?" the beverage tender asked, a worried scowl on her face. "Are you okay?"

"I'm fine. I needed a glass for Councilor Tarand." Her fingers curled around the glass now and she pulled it free from the cupboard, standing upright and trying to ignore the rush of blood pulsing in her temples. "Sparkling water, if you have it."

"Of course." The beverage tender filled the glass and stared as though she was waiting for another set of instructions.

"That's all," Olivia said, heading back to the private box entrance. Officer Abara grabbed her by the elbow, pulling her into an alcove.

"Where in hells have you been?" they demanded. "She's ready to take your head off at the shoulders."

Olivia chewed the inside of her lip. Who exactly could she trust in the Capital? "I overheard something."

"Something like what?"

"It was nothing, just Capital gossip, you know how it is."

Abara searched her face, squinting gently. "You can tell me, Guisette."

"I don't think I can, actually."

"I covered for you in that cell," Abara hissed. "I didn't tell anyone what actually happened when Calvetti escaped."

"Is that because you were covering for me, or because you wanted her to get out?"

Abara tilted their head, eyes flicking to the lights as they flashed a three minute warning. "Are you setting a trap for me, Guisette?"

"A trap?"

"Don't play games with me, we both know what you are. Intelligence. An agent. You're trained in mind games and I might be a fool, but I'm no easy mark."

"I'm not in the habit of playing mind games," Olivia finally answered.

"Aren't you?"

"I told you, it's Capital gossip, nothing more."

"Then why do you look like you want to sprint out of this building and take off in the first transport you can find?" Abara asked. "You can't fool me, Olivia."

"I look like I want to sprint out of this building because I do," she admitted. "This play is the worst thing I have ever seen."

"You can bullshit me all you want, Guisette, but when push comes to shove, you're going to have to open your mouth and talk." They leaned against the door frame, allowing Olivia room to pass. "We both know we can't do this alone."

Olivia crossed in front of them with a vague nod, still holding the glass of water. *Can't do what alone,* she wondered. Keep Tarand safe? Work together? Overthrow the gods-damned High Council? Given the recent few months she'd had, it could be any of the above. "Here you are, ma'am," Olivia said, handing over the water.

"Olivia, where have you been? I'd started to think that someone had snatched you right out from under my nose."

"I'm afraid not, ma'am. Just a long queue in the lobby."

Tarand sipped the water, stopping to give Olivia a withering glance. "You know we supersede queuing conventions, my dear," she said flatly. "Next time, do try to be more prompt? I worry when you are out of my sight. We live in such troubling times."

"Understood, ma'am."

"I had to send Officer Abara after you, leaving me defenseless in this box."

Olivia sat in her seat, arranging the fabric around her. "Don't trouble yourself in that way, Councilor. Whatever happens, I'll be fine. I'm trained for it."

"You certainly managed to come back from Terringgough Gulch un-scathed," Tarand said airily. "I suppose I shouldn't be worrying about a night at the theater."

"You shouldn't compromise your own safety," Olivia said firmly. "But I will endeavor to be more prompt in the future, as I do not wish to cause you upset."

The lights dimmed again, plunging them back into darkness. The second act passed in the same way as the first, with forgettable characters and a hero who sang a long ballad about fighting against corruption for his beloved. Olivia caught herself drowsing, her neck falling to her chest. She coughed, trying to cover her slumber, but the steely glare from Tarand suggested she hadn't covered it quite well enough.

Three more ballads and five monologues later, the cast returned to the stage for final bows. Olivia straightened her back, ready to leave the theater and get out of that dress. Something about it made her feel vulnerable in a way she hadn't before, despite all of her training.

The actors left the stage, but the lights didn't return. Olivia leaned forward in her seat, the air crackling with the electricity of something about to go wrong. It was just delayed enough, just strange enough that she knew whatever came next was going to be a problem.

A man cleared his throat loudly as he pushed through the heavy velvet purple curtains of the stage. "Good evening, everyone," he said calmly. "I am not someone whose name you need to know."

"What is this?" Tarand demanded in a hiss. "Who is that?"

"I don't know, ma'am," Olivia replied.

The man took off his top hat and bowed to the audience, showing his respect for those present. "I regret to inform you that the production you saw tonight was a farce." He fumbled with the hat, running his fingers over the black satin ribbon of the band. "The truth is, the theater has been hamstrung by the government for decades."

Tarand seized Olivia's arm, her nails digging into flesh. "Get him off that stage. Immediately. *Quietly.*"

Before Olivia could finish nodding, she was already out of her seat and pushing her way out of the box, past Abara, who tried to grab her arm. She wrenched free, running for the stairs at the end of the corridor. The heels of her polished boots skidded across shining granite floors, gleaming her reflection back at her. One flight, two flights of stairs and she was rushing through another set of heavy swinging doors, looking for the backstage entrance.

"Ma'am?" one of the actors said, chasing her down. "Ma'am, you can't go backstage!"

"The hells I can't," Olivia snapped, shrugging them off. "It's me or it's MPOs, make your choice." She wrenched open the stage door, leaving the actor standing frightened in the hallway.

"And that is why I—all of us here—urge you all to support the free election in Skelm. What can be done there can be done here in the Capital too, if only we can believe in the power of the arts."

Fool, Olivia thought. Tarand would have him shipped off to a work camp by daybreak, assuming he didn't meet an unfortunate early demise when the guards got him. She reached for the override lever and pulled it, cutting the power to the lights.

"We will not be silenced!" the man shouted as screaming erupted in the theater. It was panic, pandemonium, but Olivia could use it for her own advantage. She marched out into the darkness of the stage, groping in the near pitch black. Her hand connected with the soft wool of a suit jacket and she pulled, yanking him offstage.

"Unhand me!" he shouted.

"If you don't want to leave this building a corpse, I suggest you shut up," Olivia snapped, shoving him up against the wall. He was larger than her, but she was scarier, and that was reflected by the fear in his eyes. "Your people can't be doing this. Not here in the Capital."

"We agitate for change," he spat.

"Who are you? Scattered? Splintered? Obsidian Enclave?"

"No," the man replied, confused. "We are just people who want fair elections. The High Council doesn't speak for all of us, it never has." He squinted at her in the pin-pricked dark. "Who are the Splintered?"

"No one." Olivia released him with a rough shove. "Forget you heard that name, unless you want them to torture you before they send you to a work camp."

"What?" he gasped.

The stage door slammed open, and a team of five or six MPOs dragged him away, gone before she could say another word. She reached for the microphone, depressing the large silver button at the front.

"Good evening," she intoned with her best impression of an usher. "We apologize for the technical difficulties following tonight's performance. Please find your nearest exit using the lit bulbs recessed into the floor. Please do so in an orderly fashion, and we will have power restored as soon as possible."

Olivia released the button, breathing a sigh of relief. In the doorway, standing in sleek silhouette, was Tarand, nodding appreciatively. She approached, clasping Olivia's hands in her own.

"Dearest, I always knew I could count on you."

Chapter 21

Evie scrubbed her hands in the sink, desperately trying to rid herself of the honey clinging to her skin. Her own fault for trying something new with the tofu, but gods below it made an unholy mess. One more scrub with the soap and she rinsed, drying her hands on the legs of her trousers. She pushed through the door back end first, picking up the two plates on the counter as she went. "Order up," she said brightly.

When Larkin didn't respond, Evie turned as she maneuvered around the bar, setting the plates on a nearby table with a smile. Larkin was staring at the door.

Cole Marion gave a cocky shrug, strolling across the tavern to sit on the padded stool at the bar. He folded his hands atop the wood, his fingers steepled in the center. Evie's heart began to pound in her chest at the mere sight of him, knowing that whatever this was, it couldn't be good.

"What'll it be?" Larkin asked coolly.

"None of that silly horseshit you make here. A real drink."

Evie swung around the corner, a hand on Larkin's back. "Need any help?" she asked.

"No," Larkin answered. She grabbed a fresh glass from underneath the counter, setting it on the bar. "Whiskey?" she asked casually.

"Brandy," he replied. "Assuming you have it."

"I have it. Four kinds." Larkin set the bottles out, gesturing with an outstretched hand.

"Give me what you'd drink."

Larkin nodded, returning three bottles to their places on the shelf. One remained, a dusty brown with a faded, cracked label. She poured two shots neatly, sliding one across to Cole in a round, squat glass. "This one's older than both of us."

"Some people say you can't taste the age after ten years."

"They haven't had this."

He raised an appreciative eyebrow, swirling the glass. "I must say, that is rather nice."

"Nicer than the shit you used to get back in Skelm," Larkin said, still not even a ripple of recognition against her surface of calm.

"The shit we had in Skelm was only slightly better than watered down ethanol." He sipped again, holding the glass to the light. "I never believed what they said about you."

"And what's that?"

"That you were some assassin. Some cold-blooded killer for hire."

"Don't be ridiculous," Evie said cheerily, wiping the bar with a damp cloth. She wasn't about to leave Larkin alone to deal with him, no matter how many people were around. "Those are just rumors."

"Rumors," Cole repeated, glancing around the tavern. "Rumors can change the course of history, if the cards are played correctly."

"Yeah, well, I was never very good at cards," Larkin said, knocking back her brandy. "Drinks I can do. Cards aren't my purview."

Cole turned, his piercing gaze settling on Evie. "Bartender turned part-owner. What a coup for someone like you."

Evie grinned at him, and Larkin's hand on her thigh let her know that it was more a baring of teeth than a display of friendliness. "Someone like me, indeed."

"I just mean that most people around here don't amount to much. They're stagnant. Stalled. At least you had the gumption to get out there for a while, even if it was too much for you in the end."

"I don't know if I'd say that."

Cole laughed, sliding the glass from side to side with a resonating scrape. "I would. Bradach breeds complacency. People feel too safe here to do anything." He nodded at the nearby table. "Just look at them, for instance. Scrappers snatching up some low hanging fruit, as it were. Not one of them could be bothered to give a shit about anyone other than themselves."

"Are you confused about where we are? This is Bradach. It's a pirate settlement. Morally grey is how things get done," Larkin said acerbically. "Besides, the refugee efforts at the dock prove you wrong. Plenty of people here are busy trying to improve things, instead of holing up in a tavern, holding political shadow councils."

A smirk played at the edges of Cole's mouth, and it sank a lilting unease into Evie's gut. He sipped again, performatively, showing that he was savoring it. "Is that what you think I'm doing?"

"Isn't it?" Evie retorted. "You're not even supposed to be here anymore."

"Where would you have me go? Our bases of operation have always been mobile, movable, impermanent. And it doesn't help that Calvetti blew up Terringgough Gulch."

"The Coalition did that."

He shrugged. "So she says."

"You think she would do that herself? Risking life and limb for what, a public relations exercise?"

"Cassius Calvetti would absolutely do that, if you don't see it, then you're both fools." He drained the glass now, setting the glass back on the bar with a hollow thunk that echoed across the tavern more than it had any right to. "I guess you didn't poison that one, then," he said, running his finger around the rim of the glass.

"I wouldn't have much repeat business if I poisoned all my customers," Larkin said, calm and collected. "I don't think the reviews would be very favorable."

He leaned across the bar. "I know it was you, Flores."

"Whatever you think you know, I can guarantee you don't," Evie said, frustration creeping in at the edge of her voice. "Why don't you head back to the Bronze Bell? I can't imagine they'd be very happy to find you here."

"No one else has access to toxins like that, not without the right knowledge." He sat back on the stool, centering his weight. "Not without practice."

Evie set an empty glass down hard on the bar, the sound drawing the attention of a few nearby patrons. "You're not welcome here," she said. "Leave."

"I'm a paying customer. You wouldn't just kick me out, would you?"

"You haven't paid anything yet." Evie took his glass from him, piling it into the crate of dishes destined for the kitchen. "That was on the house. Get out."

"You don't seriously think that you can make an attempt on my life just to throw me out of your tavern, do you?" Cole asked, leaning over the bar. He was almost nose-to-nose with Larkin, but true to form, she didn't even flinch. "Get real, Flores. You're not going to know a single moment of peace until I have you thrown out of Bradach. You people want to be all high and mighty about rules and regulations just because Cassius Calvetti talked you into supporting her silly little rebel sect of ardent believers, but I think most will see things differently."

"Oh? And how is that?" Larkin asked, unmoving.

"Political activity is one thing, murder is quite another," he replied.

"One brings the might of the Coalition down on us, the other prevents it," Evie snapped. "You've been warned. Get out of our bar."

"What are you going to do, poison me again? Far too many witnesses here for that, I daresay."

Evie snatched a knife from beneath the counter and stabbed it through the hard polished wood, leaving it to stand upright. "Don't test me." Larkin gave her a surprised sideways glance, eyebrows raised almost into her hairline. Evie stepped back, letting the knife speak for itself. "I'm awfully clumsy with blades."

"Are you threatening me?" Cole asked, laughing again. "Evie Anderson throwing herself into the fray, and for what? For this poxy little bar? For a woman you know very little about?"

"Because I find you repulsive," Evie spat. "On a number of levels. And because it's my right to show you the gods-damned door when you come in here making wild, baseless accusations."

Cole tilted his head, mouth set into a frown. "Hardly baseless though, is it?"

"You don't have a shred of proof beyond silly rumors and anecdotes."

"I'm betting I'd find hemlock in your precious little garden, and that would be proof enough for most," he replied, a self-satisfied grin hanging on his face like meat on a hook. "Because what tavern needs that in their herbal stores?"

Larkin shifted now, reacting to a patron at the other end of the bar waving for another ale. She picked up a tall glass, pulled the ale, and slid it down the bar with the smile Evie had become accustomed to seeing, but it faded the moment she turned back to Cole. "You won't find anything like that in the garden. Plenty of mint, though. That stuff tends to take over."

Cole squinted at her. "Prove it."

Evie was resisting the urge to raise an eyebrow, knowing the hemlock was out there, growing in a thick patch just below the bathroom window, up against the ivy-covered brick of the exterior.

"Fine, let's go," Larkin said, tossing a rag onto the bar with a nonchalant shrug. "If it will keep you the fuck out of my tavern, I'll give you a guided gods-damned tour. Maybe then you'll keep your baseless bullshit out of my face."

"I'll go," Evie interrupted. Something within Larkin was flickering, reverting back to old habits, her voice cold and monotone. Even when they'd both been in prison, she hadn't sounded so detached as she did in that moment. "Watch the bar."

"Eves—" Larkin began to protest.

"It's not a large garden, we won't be long, and then we can get back to work once he sees himself out." Evie laid a hand on top of Larkin's, a silent gesture of reassurance. "I'll only be a minute."

"If you lay a single finger on her, I will gut you like a fish," Larkin said evenly. "I'll make sure that you're awake to feel it."

Cole twitched at the threat, stifling a wince, or the desire to run, maybe. He stood from the stool, following Evie through the tavern to the back door. Her hands were shaking as she unlocked all three deadbolts, pulling it open to reveal the waning mirrored sun of twilight. Purple streaked clouds hovered, fragile in the distance, not yet full enough with water to rain.

"We could have been allies once," Evie said, stepping out onto the grass. She turned, expecting to see the fluffy heads of white flowers, the blotchy stems, but instead saw only an established bed of mint, running rampant across the soil. She blinked at it, shaking her head.

"You always thought you were too good for me."

"We never thought that, Cole."

"Do you know what it's like to lose everything? To watch the tavern you spent your life building get ransacked, burned out, and left for the rats and the roaches?"

Evie rubbed her fingers against a mint leaf, allowing the powerful scent to ground her in the reality of the moment. "I sat in a Coalition prison, I think that's understanding enough."

"I didn't realize." His eyes fell on her tattoos, the iridescent scales trailing down one arm all the way to the wrist. "A souvenir?"

"A cover for the souvenir, maybe."

"I'm sorry," he said, and for once, it sounded like he meant it. "Truly."

"It is what it is," Evie replied, leaning against the apple tree in the corner. Thankfully, Larkin hadn't used cyanide, or its existence would have been harder to conceal. "No sense in dwelling on how terrible it was."

Cole glanced around the small garden, inspecting each of the small pots that sat on top of a shelf made of old crates. "A nice collection of aromatics."

"Larkin takes her drinks very seriously."

"Not many people growing lemongrass for cocktails." He pinched a blade of it between his thumb and forefinger, separating it from the rest of the plant. "A shame really, it lends a nice freshness that just lemon can't."

Evie waited a moment, watching him touch every plant. "As you can see, there's no hemlock out here. Just herbs and aromatics."

"Rumors always have a basis in reality," he said. "Sometimes small, but the seed of truth remains there, regardless." Cole kicked at a patch of loose soil surrounding a patch of freshly sprouted lettuce. "But maybe I had my wires crossed."

"Perhaps you did."

"My bodyguard, Amos, he was a good man."

A pang of guilt sliced its way below Evie's skin, a regrettably familiar sensation. "I am sorry for your loss."

"The funny thing is, if he hadn't died, I probably would have fired him for drinking from my private stores. Yet here I am, alive and well, and he's being incinerated."

"We live in strange times."

"I know that things have gotten a little..." he trailed off. "Dicey."

Evie picked at a piece of bark, prying it off the tree with her stubby fingernails. "That's quite the understatement."

"In another scenario, we all might have been allies. Friends, even, if Cass hadn't betrayed me." He bent, examining the shoot of a chive, reaching up for the waning sunlight. "We all want the same things, you know. Peace. Freedom. To escape the yoke the Coalition has placed upon all of us."

She let him continue, wary of where the conversation was headed. It wouldn't be long before Larkin began to worry about where she was.

Cole sifted his fingers through the soil, letting it fall back to the damp earth. "We may have different ideas of how to achieve that, but perhaps we shouldn't have wound up on opposing ends of the war." He moved to the mint patch, running his hands through the leaves. "But that doesn't excuse what she did."

"Cass?"

He turned back, reaching for something inside his breast pocket. "Your co-owner." The blade glinted in the setting light as he pulled it free, and he held it out quietly. "This is freshly transplanted, I'm not a fool. The soil has been recently turned, though I can commend her on the plant recovering so quickly. I can only wonder what was here before." He held the knife towards her, casually, but with a lingering threat.

"You'd kill me in my own establishment?" Evie asked, moving away from the tree. If she was lucky, she might be able to get over the fence, but he'd probably wind up stabbing her in the leg instead.

"In self-defense. Everyone knows she has a shadowy past, it doesn't take a genius to figure out what it was that she did." He advanced slowly, one step at a time. "I came here to clear the air, and you attacked me, Ms. Anderson. No doubt the room of patrons that just saw you ram a knife into your bar will attest to the fact that you seem unstable. Violent, even, and who could blame you when you've been broken down so far by the Coalition?" He nodded at her scars. "The story practically tells itself."

"And what do you get out of my death?" Evie asked. "One less tavern to compete with the Bronze Bell?"

"I get the adoration of Bradach, and the rallying of every rebel-adjacent pirate that hears the story of how an ex-Coalition mercenary and her little friend tried to have me wiped off the map."

"She's my fiancée, actually," Evie corrected. "And that's one hell of a stretch. You were supposed to leave Bradach, but here you sit, putting everyone in danger."

"As I said, people are complacent. They need motivation to get off their asses and fight for freedom. What better motivation is there other than defending yourself against an unprovoked attack?" He pulled up a mint plant, holding it by the tips of the leaves, knife still held out with his other hand. "See? No established roots, Ms. Anderson. Larkin isn't the only bartender who gives a shit about her ingredients. The rest of us just had to make do with whatever crumbs we could scrape from the Coalition, and deal with the ire of every one of you who judges us for it."

"I don't judge you for that," Evie said. "What I judge you for is your myopic ideas about this war, and about the people you choose to do business with."

Cole took another step towards her, dropping the plant to the ground. "Who, Gregor Zink? The man is a zealot. He has all these fanciful ideas about destiny and symbols, but gods, the tech sure is nice to have access to."

"You traded him one of the strongest weapons we've ever seen."

He shrugged. "A weapon isn't much use if you can't use it."

"He can."

"He won't. At least, he probably won't. It won't be on us, in any case."

Evie stepped backwards again, finding herself pressed against the fence. "This is your last warning to leave," she said, her voice pitched too high and wavering with fear. "Leave now, and no one has to know about this."

"We've gone too far for that, I think, don't you?"

"If I scream, they'll all come running."

"If you scream, I kill you regardless." He took the knife and slashed it against his forearms, drawing rivulets of blood to the surface. "Defensive wounds."

"No one will believe you."

"I have the might of The Scattered on my side, and the tangential support of Obsidian Enclave, and I'll also get The Splintered back under my wing once they hear that Calvetti asked you to kill me so that she could return to her position as the head of the faction."

Evie's chest thudded, heart pounding noisily in her ears. She watched him as he advanced, wondering what the odds were that she could get the knife from him. "You're a lost cause," she said. "You say we all fight for the same outcome, but you're the only one trying to commit murder."

"She tried to kill me!" Cole hissed, advancing again. "Did you think I would let that stand?" He took another step. "Did you think I would forgive and forget?"

"Larkin didn't do anything," Evie lied, and even she could hear how obvious it was. "You're mistaken."

"You see, I don't think I am." He sprinted forward, pinning her to the fence. The point of the knife was flush with her throat, a pinprick of gore that would only be a preview to what came next.

Evie gasped for air, reaching out for him but never catching. "Please," she begged. "Let me go."

"This is only the beginning of the war," he said, his voice placid water. "This never would have happened if you hadn't struck first."

She ducked down, feeling the knife scrape against the fragile skin of her neck, painful, bloody, but superficial. He tripped forward, head meeting the iron of the fence, staggering only once, but it was enough. Taking the opportunity, knowing it would be her only chance, Evie pried the knife from his hands, sinking it deep into his chest. The blade pierced through the crisp pale blue of his shirt smoothly, no different than quartering tofu for the fryer. It was strange how easy it had been.

He lay there in the garden, bleeding out as he gasped his final breaths, his blood watering the thorny brambles growing in the corner. Evie stumbled backwards against the brick, holding a hand to her neck.

"Marion, you'd better be leaving now," Larkin said, throwing open the door and stepping into the garden. She inhaled sharply, already reaching out for Evie with a desperate, grasping search. "My gods, Eves," she whispered in a hush. "What have you done?"

Chapter 22

Delia was only two steps behind Larkin, despite the fact she'd been told to watch the bar. Whatever was going on, she needed to know. "Larkin," she hissed, reaching the back door. "What in hells?"

"Shut up. Close the door," Larkin replied. "I told you to stay inside and watch the bar."

"What's going on? Maybe I can—" Delia stopped short as the door latched, looking over the garden and finding a body slumped against the fence. "Who—"

"Cole Marion," Evie whispered.

Larkin moved towards her, moving her hands out of the way. "Let me see."

"It's nothing."

"You're bleeding!"

Evie jerked away. "I said it's nothing."

"We need to get the story straight, right now," Delia said, crossing to the fence that sat parallel to the street and looking up one way and down another, grateful that there didn't seem to be any passers-by. "There's no way I can keep this from hitting reports, and if we're not the ones to break it, we lose the advantage."

"Is that all you're thinking about right now?" Larkin hissed, rounding on her. "The political spin? Evie was nearly killed!"

"And she wouldn't have been if you hadn't fucked up killing him!" Delia shot back. "What kind of assassin doesn't wait around to make sure the mark actually dies?"

"One who knows how not to get caught." Larkin's voice was heavy with regret, guilt, and rage.

Delia knew not to push her any further. She gestured to the body. "We need to get him out of here, and before anyone sees."

"No, we need to contact the authorities," Larkin replied. "Tell them that he showed up with baseless accusations and attacked Evie."

"He gave himself defensive wounds," Evie said softly, still staring at the body.

Delia pressed a palm to her forehead. "Shit." She gave the street another cursory glance, bending to inspect the corpse, still giving off warmth, much to her alarm. Not the first body by far that she'd seen, nor the most grisly, but somehow, it felt more real than those other times. She squeezed her eyes shut, trying not to think of how Rosie might end up if they didn't get to her soon enough. "We're going to need help."

"We can't involve anyone else, it's too risky," Larkin said. "The only way to keep a secret is to never tell anyone."

"Do you really think The Scattered finding their leader dead in your garden, with defensive wounds, after his bodyguard died from poisoning, is really going to pan out well for you?" Delia asked. "We need to be very careful about how we craft this. Someone needs to get a hold of Calvetti. She's going to need to step in, and do so quickly, before rumors start to circulate."

"Calvetti is bouncing from ship to ship all over the Near Systems, it's going to be almost impossible to find her," Larkin said. "Not with the frequency monitoring. Someone would hear."

"Get a secure line out to Chalidon, then, hells, send one to Lucent Base for Rosie's eyes only."

"Zink would never let her see that message."

Delia sighed heavily, still crouching down over the corpse. "I know. It's not as if we haven't tried that."

"Chalidon might be a good bet, but only if Marv can track anyone down. Georgie and Henry left ages ago, they should have been back by now."

She swore under her breath. "They should have been back by now." She stood, brushing off the knees of her trousers and adjusting the suspenders over her shoulders. "Okay, Forrest, one crisis at a time," she said aloud to herself. "Who do we know with connections to waste removal? Scrap teams, anything."

Evie grimaced, but as she wasn't holding her throat anymore, Delia had to assume it wasn't the wound causing it. "I don't think those connections are likely to help us."

"Yeah, more like fucking betray us," Larkin added, kicking a large pebble across the grass. It skidded across blood-wet blades, coming to a stop just beneath the apple tree. "What else have you got, Delia?"

"So you do know someone in disposal?" Delia prompted. "We can work around betrayal. What we can't work around is a dead body in your garden. Someone could walk down that street any moment and see him lying there."

"She's right," Evie said, trying to use her sleeve to wipe away the blood on her throat. "Who's watching the bar?"

"I told her to watch the bar," Larkin griped, jabbing a thumb at Delia. "Clearly, it didn't take."

"Someone has to watch the bar."

Delia glanced at Larkin, and then at the street. "Larkin, it should be you. I'll raise eyebrows, not to mention I can't mix a drink to save my life. Evie is already bloody, it can't be her."

"Fine," Larkin said after a long moment. "Don't let this get out of hand, Forrest."

"You have my word that I'm going to do everything in my power to keep this under wraps until we know how to play it."

Larkin disappeared back into the tavern, leaving the door unlocked. Delia pulled a handkerchief from her shirt pocket, wetting it from the outside spigot. She held it out for Evie, who shook her head twice before she took it.

"Thanks," Evie said, wiping the blood from her skin.

"Are you sure you're okay?"

"Hurts like shit, but nothing worrying." Evie rinsed the handkerchief and wet it again, scrubbing a stubborn patch where the blood had begun to dry behind her ear.

"We need to get him out of the line of sight. I'd ask for a sheet, but I'm not sure if that looks too obvious."

"There's a basement window around the side, we could probably fit him through there."

"And then what?" Delia asked. "Then we just have a suspicious corpse inside your tavern."

"Is that really so much worse than the corpse being in my garden?" Evie snapped. She shoved the handkerchief into her pocket, a tiny bloodied corner hanging out at the top. "This never would have happened if it weren't for you."

"Me?" Delia asked, already looking for the window. "How is any of this *my* fault?"

"Larkin never would have gone over there if you hadn't baited her into it."

"I didn't even know she was listening!"

Evie scoffed, pointing at the small rectangular window sitting against the foundation of the tavern. "Please, she's always listening, that's what she does!"

"And if she'd actually killed him, he'd have been dead in his office with a long enough list of leads that we could have sidestepped it until the war was over and no one cared anymore, but instead he's growing cold here, with a long line of witnesses that saw you two come out here!" Delia threw out an aggravated sigh, trying to pry the grate from the window. "Witnesses," she repeated. "Gods be damned. We can't hide him in your basement."

"Larkin already went back inside, we can't announce it to the settlement council now." Evie pressed against her temple, eyes squeezed shut. "It's been fifteen years since someone was killed in Bradach, and last time it was a drunken lout who tried to have a duel." She rubbed at her neck again, wincing. "If you don't count the spy that Cole killed in his office, but the council wasn't involved with that."

"The council wasn't involved," Delia repeated. She chewed on her lip for a moment before she resumed trying to pry the grate from the window.

"What are you doing?"

"You're not going to like this—either of you, actually—but it just might work." The grate popped free, and Delia dropped it into the grass with a dull thud. She eased the window open, eyeing the width. "I think he'll fit."

"I thought you said we shouldn't, because of the witnesses," Evie said warily.

"We have to play this very carefully. We're going to stash him for now, figure out getting him to the incinerator later. You're going to go back inside and tell everyone that Cole Marion attacked you and fled."

"That's ludicrous."

"Half the people in Bradach know that he was up to no good in the Bronze Bell. Half the people here wanted him gone anyway, and won't look too hard into why he left."

"And the other half?"

"We can only hope they don't care. He has some ardent supporters still here, but without him heading things up from his makeshift headquarters, we can only hope they will relocate." Delia crossed the garden again, picking up one of Cole's feet. "Grab the other one. We'll drag him. Be quiet."

Evie nodded, taking the other shoe in her hands. "And if someone asks me why I cleaned up first?"

"You're a tavern owner, you take hygiene seriously." Cole's body squeaked against the wet grass, coated in scarlet stickiness, thick and arterial.

"And if people start asking questions?"

"We lie, Evie." Delia dropped the corpse at the open window, nudging it through with the toe of her boot until it fell down into the basement, knocking into a shelf filled with dusty equipment. "Good thing no one is down there, that would have been a nasty surprise."

"What do you mean, lie?"

"I'm a trusted broadcaster, Evie. I can tell the entirety of the Near Systems that Cole Marion is sending me important messages about The Scattered. Then, when the moment is right, we make him a martyr."

"You think he deserves to be a martyr when he tried to kill me?"

"Obviously not, but it's the best way to be sure no one comes around here asking any questions we don't want to give the answers to." Delia closed the window, replacing the grate. She frowned at the streaky smudge of red cutting through the garden, reaching for the spigot. "We need to rinse this away."

"It will be dark soon," Evie said, looking up at the sky. "The mirrors are almost closed in."

"We can't leave him down there for long. He's going to smell."

Evie wrinkled her nose. "Gross."

"I need to know more about this connection you have with waste resources. Maybe I can dig something up on them, or maybe encourage them to deal with this problem for us."

"I don't think that's a very good idea." Evie connected a hose to the spigot, the metal creaking as she screwed it on. "She's my ex-girlfriend. Her wife is the one who works in waste resources, lots of connections with scrappers."

"That does complicate things." Delia leaned against the brick. "Bad breakup?"

"She tried to have me framed for one of her jobs that went bad. That's how I wound up in that cell where I met Larkin."

"Yeah, I'd say that's pretty bad. Well, what about blackmail?"

"We don't want to mess with Holly Ambrosia. She has too many connections, she'd tell the wrong person, we'd all get rounded up and shipped out of Bradach." Evie turned away, wiping at her face with the sleeve of her shirt. She sniffled loudly, choking on her tears. "I don't want to leave, Delia, this is my home."

"No one is going to have to leave. We'll figure this out together."

"You don't know that!"

"I'm going to do everything in my power to make sure it doesn't," Delia offered. She moved to put a hand on Evie's shoulder, but thought better of it, and let it fall to her side instead. "There's enough going on out there that there are opportunities for distraction."

"I hardly think that people are going to overlook the murder of the leader of The Scattered," Evie said with a quiet sniff. "Everyone is too spread out. It feels impossible. I haven't even cracked that damned call sign yet. I thought I was close last night, but too many of the characters weren't—" Evie stopped herself short, turning back towards Delia. "I had the cipher one character off." She handed the hose to Delia, already reaching for the door. "Of course the damned cipher was off, that's why the coordinates didn't make any sense!"

"Wait, where are you going?"

"To find out where in hells the Cricket is." Evie wrenched the door open, rolling up her sleeves. "We're going to need them, if we're all going to make it out of this war."

* * *

Delia knew, as she knocked on the door of the residence, that it was probably a bad idea. Asking old flames for favors never went well, especially when it was a friend of the old flame who'd been explicitly told not to say anything.

Still, a career in broadcasting meant that she had a few cards up her sleeves. Not as many as Mae, and not played as expertly as Hyun, but given the right opportunity, she could manage just fine on her own. Which is why, when the door opened and a very pretty brunette woman peered out, Delia granted her a winning smile.

"Holly Ambrosia?"

The woman held the doorknob firm in her hand, blocking the entrance. "Depends who's asking."

"I'm Delia Forrest."

"Right, the broadcaster." Holly leaned against the door frame, the pink silk of her dressing gown snagging on the wood. "What do you want?"

"I had a few questions for you about some scrap jobs that went wrong, oh, a couple of years ago, now."

"I don't know anything about scrap jobs, I'm not a scrapper."

"But your wife is?"

Holly's eyes narrowed. "I don't know who you think you are—"

"Delia Forrest."

"You said that already."

"I thought it wise to clarify, given your outburst." Delia smiled, leaning forward towards the large varnished door. "Perhaps I should cut to the chase. I have information that could prove useful to you. I also possess information that would be detrimental to your status here in Bradach."

"Bradach is a backwater," Holly spat. "I'd rather be anywhere but here."

"Ah, but you can't, can you? Too many people looking for you, hoping to catch you outside the safety this backwater brings. Too many people you threw to the wolves, perhaps?"

"Get off my doorstep, or I'm getting my gun."

"That won't be necessary, and besides, we both know that would only complicate matters."

Holly huffed angrily. "What do you want?" she hissed.

"We have need to access some discrete disposal."

"What is it, illegal munitions? A scrapped vessel you can't sell off?"

Delia tilted her head. "Nothing quite that large."

"Did you steal something you shouldn't have?"

"Sure, let's go with that," Delia replied. "As for size, it could potentially fit into a suitcase." While the thought of stuffing Cole Marion's corpse into a suitcase was deeply unpleasant, it was also very likely the way they'd have to get rid of him and all the evidence of what had happened, if their plan was going to work.

"And who is *we*, may I ask?"

In the distance, a ship landed in the dock with a loud thunk, the sign of an amateur pilot. It was almost dark by that time, the street lamps flickering on one at a time, offering their tepid glow to the encroaching darkness. Delia waited a long moment before she answered, knowing it could find them all thrown onto the next transport. "Evie Anderson and I."

Holly opened the door wider. "Come inside."

An unexpected request, but not an unwelcome one, assuming she wasn't being invited in to be murdered. It was probably unlikely that Holly would murder her, and besides, Delia was marginally confident she could take the woman in a fight. She followed Holly down a short corridor, opening into a beautiful living area with vaulted ceilings that stretched up high past the second floor banister. "Your home is beautiful."

"Better than most of the dumps around here, at least," Holly grumbled. She came to a stop in front of a sofa, her every movement dancelike, the silk twirling around her legs. "Sit."

Delia did as she was told, folding her hands in her lap.

"What has little Evie gotten herself into this time?"

"Oh, you know, the usual for a place like this, but everyone is so on edge lately that we don't really want to take any chances."

"Hmm." Holly sat in a tall-backed chair, crossing one leg over the other. "On edge is certainly one way to put it."

"How would you put it, then?"

"Chaotic. Declining. One step away from total destruction."

Delia raised an eyebrow. "Oh? And why is that?"

"The people in this place, Ms. Forrest. They're all missing the point, even you. Reporting on what happens thousands and thousands of kilometers away, hundreds of thousands, even millions, as if it has any effect on things here."

"Doesn't it?"

"In a sense, perhaps, but Bradach has been on the decline longer than I've even lived on this gods-forsaken rock. I was supposed to be someone, you know. I was supposed to rise through the socialite ranks in the Capital, instead I'm here, princess of nothing."

"Trust me, the Capital isn't that good. You'd have hated it there."

Holly scoffed. "That's quite a declaration to make mere moments after meeting me."

"No one likes the Capital except the ones sitting at the top, and that was never going to be people like us."

"Speak for yourself."

Delia shrugged, letting Holly hold on to whatever bitterness she was so enamored with. "Regardless, we have something that needs disposing of, quietly and quickly."

"What is it?"

"It's better if I don't tell you."

"Evie would tell me," Holly said with a smirk.

"Then she can tell you. It's not my place to do so," Delia replied. The conversation was going nowhere, and she needed to bail out of it, fast. "I'm sorry for taking up your time. I'll be on my way." She stood, pressing a palm to her forehead. Gods be damned, she'd tried to help and instead, created another loose end.

"You know, I probably owe Evie one, given what I did."

"You probably owe her more than one."

Holly stayed seated, offering up a small shrug of apology. "Perhaps, but I'm offering one. A suitcase, you said?"

"Sure."

"Leave it outside the Pig, in the alley. I'll have someone collect it before the mirrors shift back for the morning cycle."

"Just like that?" Delia asked, dumbfounded.

Holly smiled. "Just like that. But tell Evie it was me." She leaned forward, toying with the deep cut neckline of her robe. "Tell her I want to see her."

Chapter 23

Violet tossed her cards down on the table, scattering the bits of glossy card across the scratched wood. "Enough of this," she growled, standing up from her chair. "If I have to play one more round of Banríon, I swear to all the gods, I will lose it."

"We're dead in the water, Boss, I don't know what else you expect us to do." Ned swept the cards into a pile, straightening them carefully. "Though I do agree, it's less fun without the imminent threat of Hyun playing for keeps hanging over our heads."

"Yes, who'd have known that what we've spent the past seven years dreading turned out to be what we missed most."

"I hope they're alright."

"You and me both, Ned," Violet said with a sigh. "Nearly two weeks without contact."

"Nothing on the scanners, either. Well, nothing friendly, anyway." Ned stacked the cards into two neat piles, setting his back into a brushed metal case. "A day, maybe two, before we're in real trouble."

"I'm tired of waiting. What if Josie never allowed Alice to send the coded location?" Violet pinched the bridge of her nose. "What if no one is coming?"

"Then we die."

"I'm serious!"

"So am I, Boss." He stood, pocketing the case. "Rations are low. Oxygen is even lower. We're running out of options, and fast." Ned moved to the kitchen, rummaging around the pots and pans with a frustrating metallic clatter that rang in Violet's ears. "The filtration switched off this morning, not enough solar here. Unless you plan to entrap a frigate, we're out of luck."

"So let's entrap a frigate, then," Violet said casually.

Ned snorted a laugh. "Very funny, Boss."

"What other options do we have? If we do nothing, we run the risk of suffocating in a couple of days. If we do something and someone shows up, then…" she trailed off. "I don't know. We can figure that out when we get there."

"That's the most foolish thing I've ever heard come out of your mouth." He poked his head up over the counter. "Kady would never go for it."

"I'm in support of anything that gets us the hells out of here," Kady said, appearing in the doorway. "I'm so bored that I think my brain has started to leak out of my ears."

"Where did you come from?" Ned asked.

Kady waved a hand casually. "Oh, you know, I just flew in from across the Near Systems for a chat." She gave him a wry smile. "I came from my quarters, Nedrick."

"And you think we should be setting a trap for a military vessel?" Ned asked with a noisy scoff. "There are three of us, Riha. Three against a crew of at least fifty aren't odds I enjoy playing."

"Alive and in a cell is better than dead on an airless ship." Kady leaned against the door frame, her cloak dragging along the threadbare carpet. "We haven't heard a word from anyone since Josie stranded us out here. If we wait any longer, all anyone is going to find are our cold corpses."

"Thank you, Kady, I'm not sure we need the graphic imagery," Violet interrupted.

"It's visceral."

"It's going to give me a panic attack."

"Captain, all I'm trying to express is that I'm with you. If you want to set a trap, I'll happily fight at your side. Although, I do have to mention, our cannons aren't functional, and we're pretty short on ammunition."

Kady cast a sideways glance at Ned, who was still dragging things out of the cabinets. "What in all the hells are you doing over there, Beckett?"

"Just give me a minute, I'm looking for something," he shot back.

Violet sat back down at the table, drumming her fingertips against the surface. "I'm not content to be a sitting duck any longer. Clearly, something has gone wrong. Clearly, Alice's message never reached anyone back in Bradach, and as far as they know, we're all just flying around, trying to draw out Zink." She pressed her lips together, releasing them with a quiet pop sound. "I need to get our people back, and I can't do that while I'm stuck here in the middle of gods-damned nowhere."

"Where do you think Josie is keeping Alice?" Kady asked.

"I don't know, but when I find that scheming little rat, I'm going to tear her apart." Once more, the fire of rage burned under Violet's skin, searing at her nerve endings. The pain of it was making her irrational, or maybe that was the depleting oxygen. It was possible it was further gone than they realized. "I'm done playing games with Josie Keller. The next time I see her, she's getting the same as her precious Captain Leo got."

"Aha!" Ned shouted, dragging a rusted box from beneath a false board.

"You hiding contraband aboard my ship again, Nedrick?" Violet asked, only partially serious.

"You betcha, Boss," he replied proudly, prying off the lid. "Emergency supplies." Ammunition gleamed in the dim light, the sparkle of promise that would likely end in the splatter of bloodshed.

"How much?"

"Few hundred rounds for each of us." He shrugged. "Well, for you two. I'll take the heat gun."

"You've been holding out on us," Kady said with the rare and distinctive tone of surprise and appreciation tingeing the edges of her voice. "You might have mentioned that sooner."

"We were only fighting time before," he explained. "But it seems like now, I'm being outvoted by both of my superior officers on the ship."

"We'll need a plan," Violet said, nodding at the table. "Let's hammer one out. We need to be careful, strategic. Nothing bombastic, nothing risky."

Ned cleared his throat, sitting back on his haunches on the floor of the galley. "Not to split hairs here, Boss, but I'd argue that this entire idea is risky."

"How hard would it be to change our tags?"

"Change our tags?" Ned asked, laughing. "To what?"

"To a Coalition vessel," Violet explained. "After all, this rig was once part of their fleet, so it should be hypothetically possible, right?"

Kady pulled out a chair, turning it around to sit on it backwards. "It's possible. We lure them in with a standard S.O.S. We make it look derelict, then when they board us, we strike." She raised an eyebrow, leaning forward against the chair. "It's a good plan."

"And if they decide to tow us back to Gamma-3, what then?" Ned asked. "Do we just wait to be thrown into a high-security prison? We all know that there have been plenty of security improvements since we pulled that off last time."

"You're as bad as Alice," Violet growled. "What would you have us do, sit here and wait for death?"

"I don't know, Boss, I'm just trying to make sure our bases are all covered."

"Your objections are noted, Beckett."

Ned began replacing the pots and pans, stacking them quietly with a deep frown plastered across his face. "I'm not doubting you, Boss. You know I wouldn't do that."

"It certainly feels like you're not on board with this."

"No, I'm just scared." He set the final pot inside and closed the door, standing to brace himself against the counter, his brawny, tattooed arms shaking slightly. "I know we've been in worse scrapes than this, but it doesn't feel like it." Ned looked over at Violet, his face creased with worry. "I hope you know that I'd follow you into any battle, Boss."

"I'd hoped that someone would come for us, but no one has. I can't ignore the fact that we are at a crossroads. Either we begin preparations now, or we resign ourselves to destiny and put our fate in the hands of the gods."

"The gods have never done shit for me," Ned grumbled. "Let's do this."

* * *

Violet breathed deep, grateful for the finite amount of air they had left. She leaned on the back of her chair, listening to the soft, polite squeaks of the gears as she waited.

"It's done," Ned announced, finally.

"And confirmation?"

He glanced at the display, watching. "Stand by."

"Captain, I've sealed all the corridors," Kady announced, setting a heat gun down on the ground. "It's not perfect, but it should hold long enough for us to board them."

"Rations?" Violet asked, turning to face her.

"Sealed and packed. So long as we manage not to get caught as stowaways, we'll waltz off whatever ship shows up at the next port and make our way back to Bradach."

Violet ran her hands over the console, tears pricking at the corners of her eyes. "I hate to leave the Cricket here," she said softly. "Feels like abandoning one of the crew."

"She'll still be here when we make it back," Ned offered, tapping at the screen. "Confirmed S.O.S receipt. Code suggests a ship is already being sent this way."

"She might not be," Violet replied. "They might just tow her back for scrap."

"We can only hope that's not the case," Kady said, in that specifically airy tone that Violet knew meant she was lying to save her feelings. "I'm sure they'll leave her."

"Alice is going to kill me for losing the ship." The tears fell now, and she turned back to the window, brushing them from her cheeks. *If Alice isn't dead,* she wanted to say, but at the same time, allowing the words to pass her lips would give them validity and power, and the thought of that made Violet want to vomit.

"We've been in worse scrapes," Kady said.

Violet sighed, squeezing her eyes shut to stem the tide of tears. "No, we haven't. There were more of us, then. Now, it's just us."

"We'll get them all back."

"I don't even think Hyun wants to come back. She was very clear on the matter."

Kady shifted, bracing one boot against the wall behind her. "Hyun was upset, and understandably so. She may have changed her mind in the past few weeks."

"Or not."

Ned cleared his throat, tapping at the screen. "Boss, I reckon it won't be long before we have to make a move."

"Understood," Violet replied, nodding and swallowing back another beleaguered sigh. She was still the captain of the gods-damned ship, if only for a few more hours. "Kady, did you seal the galley after you took rations?"

"Yes, Captain."

"And quarters?"

"All the quarters are sealed as well."

"Excellent."

Time passed like melted sugar, burnt and sticky, holding only a thin memory of potential, now irreversible and sluggish, dragging them all to their probable doom. Ten minutes passed, and then twenty, and even that small amount of time felt like an eternity in some hellish purgatory, a waiting room for permanent torment and death. None of them said anything, each lost in their own thoughts as much as Violet was, preparing to say goodbye to her ship. Her faithful, persnickety, scrap-heap stolen ship that she never should have been flying in the first place.

Still, it was hers, or as much hers as a ship could be when it was stolen from a scrapper's junk yard on the other end of the Near Systems. It had been shiny and pearlescent in the mirrored light, the model only recently retired. Now it was a mess of patchwork metal and desperate repairs done with tape and solder.

She dragged her fingertips over a solidified bead of solder, holding part of the console together like she was running her hands over Alice. It had been her who'd made the repair, after all. Violet had never anticipated how everything would play out when she first dragged Alice onto the Cricket, and with that retrospect, it all seemed so impossibly improbable.

"One ship incoming," Ned announced, enlarging the display.

"Tags?" Violet asked, still wary about other pirates. She wouldn't put it past Josie to give away their location just to let some other crew tear them apart.

Ned grimaced, looking over at her with an apologetic haze resting heavily on his face. "Coalition tags, Boss," he said quietly. "Approaching fast, should reach line of sight in sixty seconds. Stand by for visual."

Violet paced the bridge, her boots following the familiar path in the carpet, created from years of worry. Pressure, anxiety, and fear, none of them ever far from Violet's mind. "Standing by," she responded.

The three remaining Cricket crew members stared out the window, awaiting the new hell that was set to drag them all back down into it.

"Shit," Kady shouted, just as something hit the ship, rocking them back and forth, tossing them all across the bridge like rag dolls.

"What in hells was that?" Violet demanded, picking herself up off the floor.

Kady pressed her forehead to the front window, followed by her palm, the heat from her breath fogging a neat circle around her mouth. "It's a tow line," she said gravely. "We're attached."

"Gods be damned," Violet hissed, throwing herself down into her chair as though she could fly without power. "They're going to drag us back to Gamma-3."

Chapter 24

Georgie yanked at the iron cuffs around her wrist again, knowing they would continue to refuse to budge. Anchored into the wood with a steel bolt, she'd worked at it for hours, every moment she thought the MPO standing guard outside wasn't paying attention. Trapped, and imprisoned, and Henry would be wondering why she was late in returning to Bradach. Her mother would, too, for that matter.

She sighed heavily, allowing the hint of a growl to edge in, frustration finally getting the better of her. She should have known better than to try to talk to Emeline, but she'd done it anyway, hoping things were different.

Hoping things could go back to the way they were.

They'd always been close, but what happened in Skelm had solidified their relationship, or at least, that's what Georgie had thought until Emeline had been scooped up by the military. Brainwashed, probably, re-educated, released back into the population or at least, allowed to study out on Turas-Mara before she left to begin her campaign for election.

Georgie braced as the door swung open again, expecting the same surly MPO to throw a bowl of porridge at her, slinging it across the uneven surface of the table, spraying sticky oats across the wall. She squeezed her eyes shut, preparing for the impact of the steel bowl against the wood.

"I told you not to come."

Georgie opened an eye and then another, taking in the sight of her sister. She looked so strangely grown, dressed to impress in a demure blue frock that made her look older than her twenty years. "Emmy."

"Don't call me that."

"Emeline, I—"

"Georgina, I told you not to come. Repeatedly. I all but begged for you to heed my warnings, to listen for once, instead of charging forward anyway. Your bullheaded stubbornness has now gotten both of us into trouble."

"You don't have to tell them I'm your sister."

"It's obvious that you are. There are plenty of records stating that fact, despite all the files my mother destroyed to conceal my unfortunate genetic attachment."

"It would kill Mom to hear you say that."

"It's not our mother I am worried about, Georgina, it's you." Emeline sat down across from her, a sigh escaping her as the silk of her skirts whispered against the wooden chair. "You're too impulsive, and you're going to get people killed, just like last time."

"I told you, I didn't make those decisions unilaterally."

"Regardless, you had a hand in it."

"Barely, I was just trying to get out alive!" Georgie shook her head, staring up at the half-rusted ceiling. "Trying to get you out alive, too."

"I was safe."

"How was I supposed to know that? Allemande is hardly known for her mercy, Em. For all I knew, you were locked away in some cell just like this one, having strips carved out of you. What did you expect me to do, just wait it out and hope for the best? There were already things in motion that I had no part of."

Emeline tensed, her shoulders contracting as Georgie spoke. She frowned, her mouth turned downwards into something that was almost a snarl. "Even if I'd died, it was no excuse for putting Skelm to the torch."

"There were no torches involved."

"No, just explosions, right?"

Georgie scoffed. "Using the same technology your precious Coalition used to decimate settlements!"

"I wasn't aware that the science wing took any hits from the storms that night. From what I heard, it was nothing short of arson."

"That wing was empty."

"And how many months of research do you think we lost while it was rebuilt?" Emeline asked, gripping the edge of the table. "Every action has a consequence, Georgina."

"So what are you saying, Emeline? You think I should have let them take you? I should have turned myself and all the others in? What do you think would have happened then? Do you really believe the Coalition would have let us live?"

"What makes you think that your life, the lives of the other defectors in Skelm, are worth more than the ones who died that night?"

Georgie blinked at her, leaning as far back in the chair as she could, as though it would free her from having to have this conversation. "I don't think that."

"Your actions suggest otherwise."

"I had to find you!"

"And now you have." Emeline gestured at the cuffs locked around Georgie's wrists. "Was it worth all the trouble?"

"If it means I have a chance that you will listen to me, then yes."

"I'm not interested in more lies."

"Who's lying?" Georgie asked with a shrug of her shoulders.

Emeline shot her a look across the table. "You forget, I was right there alongside you when everything started to take off in Skelm. I lived in that basement too. I worked to improve that city and you just wanted to blow it up. I guess that would be easier, wouldn't it? You don't have to take accountability when all that's left is a pile of ash and embers."

"I never lied to you, Emeline."

"Things are different now. We've found ourselves on opposite ends of the line in the sand."

Georgie huffed quietly, stifling it, swallowing back the external signal of frustration. "I came here to help you."

"By showing up on the docks, all but screaming my name? How was that supposed to help me, I wonder?"

"I wasn't screaming."

"Near enough," Emeline hissed. "Do you have any idea of the kind of pressures I am under with this campaign?"

"Of course, that's why we came here in the first place."

"We? You mean you and Calvetti?"

"No, I didn't arrive with her. I meant Henry."

Emeline rolled her eyes dramatically, and for a split second she looked familiar, much more like the petulant, stubborn teenager Georgie had left behind. "Of course, I should have known that your little girlfriend was here. Where is she now, I wonder? Planting charges beneath the dock's boards?"

"She left days ago. I stayed."

"Why?"

"Because I thought there might be a chance to see you." Georgie raised her hands from the table, the iron links clattering softly with the effort. "And it looks like I was right."

"No one likes a know-it-all, Georgina."

"Please, as if you haven't been swanning around, making declarations left and right."

"Who else is going to stick around to pick up the pieces, then?" Emeline demanded, throwing her hands up in the air. "Not you, or your little gang of pirate friends. Not Henry Weaver, who blew up the entire wing of a building to cover her own tracks before she pushed my mother down an empty elevator shaft. Not The Scattered, who I'm pretty sure only exist for the sheer purpose of getting under my skin."

"I'm surprised you haven't mentioned Obsidian Enclave yet."

Emeline gave her a sideways glance. "An oversight on my part. They're nothing more than one more faction that needs to be dealt with, paid off and bribed to stay the hells out of the Near Systems."

"Good luck with that."

"And what is that supposed to mean?"

"It means that you miss a lot when you're stuck in one place, always bowing down to whatever the Coalition wants."

"I'm hardly the picture of Coalition deference," Emeline said with a derisive snort. "Haven't you heard? The High Council wants me dead."

"That doesn't surprise me, and it's one more reason we need to get the hells out of here." Georgie blew out a puff of air, trying to get rid of the single strand of hair that continued to fall across her face. "They have more of an army than you'll ever have, even with all the rotations you've somehow managed to pull off."

"You have oats on your face."

"Tell your little MPO, she's the one who keeps throwing the bowls at me like I'm a lion and not a handcuffed janitor."

Emeline's jaw flexed. "She was instructed that you were highly dangerous. She is only acting accordingly."

"Oh yeah, incredibly dangerous, what with my total lack of any weaponry. What am I going to do, blink her to death?"

"What did you expect me to do, Georgina? Let you go?"

"I came here to help with your election."

"And I already said, I don't need or want your help! Do you have any idea of the damage you've done in showing your face here? What if a member of the press had been present? Even now I'm going to have to worry about a headline splashed across the papers about how I'm still embroiled in my traitorous past."

"Maybe that wouldn't be such a bad thing. The Coalition is losing ranks daily."

"And gaining new ones, Georgina." Emeline ran her fingers across the worn wood of the tabletop, pausing at a divot to circle it before moving on. "Most people don't care about the righteousness of freedom or of rebellion. Most people want to know that their children won't go to bed hungry. They want opportunity and stability, not upheaval. You'd know that if you ever deigned to speak to anyone outside your little rebel hive."

Georgie searched her sister's face, looking for some sign that she was still who she once was, but found nothing. "You've changed, Emeline."

"And thank the gods for that."

"The last time I saw you, you would have died before you let the Coalition win."

"I'm playing by their rules because that's how you get elected," Emeline sniped. "I'm hardly on their side."

"You might as well be, you're practically throwing yourself on the pyre of their expectations. Don't you remember who you are?"

Emeline scoffed, turning away. "Of course I remember who I am. A poor nobody with no chances who got the opportunity to make a difference. Opportunity that Ma never gave me, never gave us!"

"She wasn't able to!"

"Exactly, Georgina! What kind of opportunity will come from burning it all down? Nothing more than little piles of riches for the Haves to scoop up while the Have-Nots try to scrape together a life in the ruins. If you think it would be anything different, you're naïve."

"Naïve."

"Yes, Georgina, naïve."

Georgie snorted a laugh. "You think you know it all, don't you?"

"I know more than you." Emeline angrily brushed a hair back into her low-swept bun that sat at the nape of her neck, and turned back to Georgie, her eyes fiery with anger. "There are certain benefits that having access to the Capital can get you."

"Benefits like truth serum?

Emeline's gaze flicked away, just for a second. "I don't know what you're talking about."

"You dosed Mae Machenet."

"I suppose she's part of your little band of rebels too, then?"

Georgie shrugged. "Sure, if that's how you want to look at it." She sat back in her chair, the chains pulled taut. "Why did you dose her?"

"She was hiding something."

"And that gives you the right to drug her? You want to stand on the moral high ground, Emeline, but I'd never do something like that."

Emeline stood, almost knocking over her chair in the process. It wobbled on two legs, rocking back and forth with the force, before settling back against the table. "She's still alive, isn't she? That's a lot more than I can say for the thirty-eight who died in Skelm the night you burned it down."

"You're obviously desperate to blame someone other than yourself for that, so fine, lay it on me," Georgie spat. "It wasn't my technology, and it wasn't my idea to hold a gods-damned rally the night that the dignitaries were arriving for the gala, but sure, it's entirely and completely my fault, despite the fact that I barely escaped with my life."

"You're saying that it was my fault?" Emeline demanded. "I told you to stay away from that technology."

"They were going to kill us all, anyway! We'd all be lying in graves past the Skelmian border, getting torn apart by dust worms bit by bit. What do you think would have happened if we surrendered? Do you think your—I can't even call her your mother—that monster would have let everyone go free? Or do you think she would have pressed every one of those refugees into the factories?"

"You forced her hand!"

"You're delusional," Georgie shouted, tacking on a laugh at the end. "I've never understood why you blamed me for all of this, but it's clear now that you can't handle the weight of responsibility. How are you going to lead a settlement if you can't even accept that what happened was a culmination of dozens of factors, only a few of which either of us had control over?"

"I should have let them take you."

"What?"

"You're lucky it was me who arrested you, and not the Chalidon city guards," Emeline said, gripping the back of the chair with enough force to turn her knuckles white. "You'd be halfway to the incinerator already."

"Then take me there yourself, maybe it would help your campaign for voters to see you shove me into a pine box yourself. Emeline Allemande, famously incorruptible, unless it's by the Coalition, and then you'd better not accept any teas from her."

"The Coalition had nothing to do with me dosing Mae Machenet."

Georgie laughed. "No? I find that hard to believe."

"I was trying to find *you!*" Emeline shouted, covering her face with her hands. "I knew she was up to something with that General Fineglass, it was plain as day, so I thought she might have an idea of where you were."

"Horseshit. You've spent every moment since they loaded you on that transport denouncing my name."

"You keep saying that you came all the way here to help with my campaign, just to put it into jeopardy with your predictably brash actions. I think you came here to sabotage me, Georgina."

"I'm glad Ma can't hear this. Can't see what you've become."

Emeline flinched before rounding on Georgie once again. "Just keep her out of this. It wasn't her decisions that led to the deaths of thirty-eight innocents."

"Do you really think she'd have done anything differently?" Georgie shot back. "Do you think she'd have let those people become indentured to the Coalition, and for what? For the crime of wanting to live free? Which, by the way, they were doing just fine at before your precious Coalition unleashed those storm generators on them." Georgie pulled at the chain again, more from anger now than from hope. Still, it didn't budge, keeping her tied to the table. "Ma would have done anything to keep those people safe. To keep *us* safe."

"Lucy is the furthest thing from safe, living out there in that settlement."

Georgie's brow furrowed as she gave her sister a quiet laugh. "Lucy is doing just fine, don't you worry about her."

"She's in danger of wasting her potential if she stays there."

"Lucy is working with some of the foremost scientists in the Near Systems, and she's still a teenager. She'll do just fine out there. She's already thriving."

"Send her to me," Emeline offered. "I'll make sure she gets the best education credits can buy."

"You've got to be kidding me," Georgie said with a snort. "You really think I'd hand over Lucy so that you can shove her into some boarding school where they'll not only ignore her natural talents, but they'll brainwash her, too?"

"It's not brainwashing if it's true," Emeline argued. "Pirates and rebels both have plenty to answer for, and the thirty-eight dead in Skelm are only the tip of the iceberg. Your hands have blood on them too, as much as the Coalition."

"Hardly."

"I just want what's best for our sister. She's still young, she'd be forgiven her dalliances with rebellion. But if she gets much older, those offerings of clemency will evaporate."

Georgie narrowed her eyes, glaring at Emeline. "You'll get Lucy over my dead body."

"You're going to throw away her future, just like you almost threw away mine. What's the matter, Georgina, you can't stand to see us manage to achieve everything you couldn't?"

"Is that what this is really about? You think I'm *jealous?*"

Emeline inhaled slowly, blowing the air out through her nose, saying nothing for a long moment. "You can't be here, Georgina."

"It's not like I can leave, can I? You chained me to a table." Georgie rattled the chains again for emphasis, leaning forwards to brace herself on her forearms. "I can either help your campaign, or I can hurt it. That's up to you."

"Are you *threatening* me?"

"This isn't how I wanted things to go, Emeline."

"Then you shouldn't have come. You should have listened to me when I told you to stay away from me. You should have kept your gods-damned distance after I left Terringgough Gulch." She cast a steely glare at Georgie as she turned to face the wall, pretending to examine a knot in the wood. "I suppose that explosion wasn't your fault, either."

"I wasn't even there. It was Cass and some high councilor's pet spy."

"Olivia Guisette."

"You know her?"

Emeline nodded. "We met out on Turas-Mara when I was still there. She is a force to be reckoned with, if rumors are to be believed."

"So I've heard," Georgie replied. There was no way to know if Emeline knew that Olivia was a double agent—triple?—and so she only nodded. "She gave Cass a run for her money."

"Still is, from what people are saying." Emeline turned back to the table, her eyes fixed on the steel bolt in the center of the table. "I didn't—" she stopped short, shaking her head in dismay. "I'm going to have to report this, Georgina. If I don't, who knows who might use it to tank my campaign, and with it, any hope that Skelm will ever be a unionized settlement. And that would be on you, Georgina, completely and totally sitting on your shoulders, because you chose to come here, chose to show your face and endanger whatever future I might have left after our father left us to rot in that gods-damned apartment." Emeline sighed again, throwing open the door. "You should have listened to me."

The door slammed, and with it, the last hope that Georgie would ever manage to reach her sister, that things could ever be whole again. The moment Emeline's footsteps faded, Georgie began twisting at the chains again, willing them to shred the wood surrounding the bolt that held her in place. If she couldn't protect Emeline, she could at least try to protect the rest of her family.

Chapter 25

The Executive Building reached high into the sky, past the low-hanging clouds that proudly displayed the threat of rain. Mae exhaled softly, slowly, trying to convince herself yet again that this was the right thing to do. Her father could spin almost anything into a coup. All she had to do was deliver the information and hope it didn't get anyone killed.

"Stop fidgeting," her father said under his breath as two attendants opened the doors wide for them, revealing the polished, sparkling floors and the dimly lit grand staircase, bathed in an eerie glow that cascaded down from the stained glass windows above it. "You were raised better than that."

"Pardon me for being a little nervous to meet a member of the High Council," she hissed. "It's not every day that—"

"If you're ever going to assume my place as the head of our family business, you'll need to remember how to appropriately present yourself. No more of those red dresses, no more front page news, Maevestra."

"I already told you, I don't—"

He silenced her with a withering glare. "Not here, Maevestra."

She clamped her jaw shut as they entered the elevator, pulling at her skirts. Still no mention of melons on Delia's radio broadcast, which meant Bailey was still missing, maybe even imprisoned somewhere, and if Mae wanted to find her, she had to play her father's silly political games. She'd known it when she boarded the transport bound for the Capital, but it had never been so obvious before that moment.

"We have an appointment with High Councilor Tarand," her father announced to the attendant. "Gerard and Maevestra Machenet."

"Mr. Machenet, of course," the attendant said, pulling the shining metal grate closed and pulling several levers to the side. "It will only be a moment."

The elevator ascended through three floors, the darkness of the shaft ominous enough to pull at the ever present pit in the middle of Mae's stomach. The doors opened, revealing the opulence of High Councilor Tarand's suites, with huge oil paintings hanging on the walls, and freshly cut flowers standing proudly in crystalline vases on every table that sat flush with the wall. Something about it made Mae's skin crawl, and maybe it was the juxtaposition between the visible grandeur of the building and those who slept unhoused just three streets away, wrestling for the status to claim one of the covered doorways to rest.

Mae bit her tongue, willing the sharp pain to clear her thoughts. Bailey. She was doing this for Bailey.

"I'm proud of you, Mae," her father said, reaching out to squeeze her hand. "This is what I've always wanted for us. For you."

She only nodded and made an odd grumble of assent, not wanting to open her mouth lest a stream of angry expletives tumble out. Closing her eyes, she thought of Bailey again, letting her thoughts focus on the safe delight she'd feel when Bailey was back home, unharmed.

"Mr. Machenet, what a delight," Councilor Tarand said, ushering them into her office. "It has been a long while since we last saw each other."

"Too long," Mae's father said cordially, bowing his head to the councilor. "It's an honor to be back in your presence, my lady."

"Always the charmer," Tarand said with an airy laugh, the kind reserved for polite company and the press. "And Ms. Machenet, I don't think we've made one another's acquaintance. Your speedy exit from the Capital upon your last visit robbed me of the opportunity."

The obvious threat hung heavy in the air, even as Tarand offered up a broad smile that didn't quite reach her eyes. "Uh, thank you, ma'am," Mae mumbled. Her father shot her a look, and so she added, "It's my undeniable pleasure to finally meet you. I have to say, the rumors are true, your robes really are stunningly beautiful."

Tarand raised an eyebrow in appreciation before turning back towards her desk. "From you, that's quite the compliment. Where do you work these days?"

"I consult, mostly. A few custom pieces every now and then, mostly private auctions and the like," Mae answered. "I tend to bounce around out near Delta-4 for the most part."

"If I'd known, I would have commissioned you to make my garb for the next gala," Tarand said. "But with it happening in just a few days, I'm sure there isn't enough time to complete such an ambitious project?"

"Oh, I didn't bring my studio with me, I'm afraid."

Mae's father stepped forward, seating himself before being invited to. A quiet, polite display of power and influence, more mind games, the same ones he'd been playing since he was old enough to extort his first politician. "I'm sure you could whip up something for the councilor, Maevestra."

"Don't be ridiculous, Gerard," the councilor said. "We're just making small talk. Your daughter's formidable skills with a sewing machine aren't why you are here." Tarand sat at her desk, the length of her robes dripping over the sides of the chair, the silk almost crispy. "Your wire suggested that you have some very valuable information for me, no?"

"We do," Mae's father answered. "Or rather, my Maevestra does."

Tarand glanced from one to the other, leaning back in her chair with a quiet creak of the protesting wood. "It would seem that the apple doesn't fall far from the tree, despite my previous assumptions."

"We're very proud of her."

"Ms. Machenet, can I assume that you will not embarrass me or this office in the near or distant future?" Tarand asked.

Mae cleared her throat. "Ma'am?"

"Will my morning paper have your picture on the front page again, cavorting with one of the most highly decorated generals in the Coalition's history?"

"Oh," Mae answered. "No, ma'am. That was a... a display of momentary ill judgment."

"I should hope so. Other families wouldn't recover from a scandal like that. I'm not sure yours would survive another hit, if truth be told."

"Understood, ma'am."

Tarand folded her hands atop the desk, sitting so still she may as well be an oak tree. Unbothered, unconcerned, unmoved, the three things most needed to be a member of the High Council. "Your dalliances with General Fineglass certainly shook the Capital."

"I do apologize."

"Love makes us do ill-advised things at times."

Mae resisted the urge to pull at the hem of her cuffs, focusing on keeping her hands still in her lap. "It does," she agreed. She'd expected some level of questioning about her last trip to the Capital, but enduring it was another sensation entirely.

"I imagine that was a difficult separation."

"It... was."

"Have you heard much from the general since then?"

Mae flicked her attention from the councilor to her father, whose neutral face offered nothing in the way of advice or hints. She folded her hands in her lap, taking the opportunity to dig the short nails of her thumbs into her palms, a burst of sharp focus. "No. I don't think she enjoyed the attention that our coupling brought her."

"Wilhemina Fineglass is a complicated woman."

"She is," Mae agreed, unsure of what the councilor was actually trying to ask. "Too complex for me, I'm afraid."

"That's a shame to hear, your partnership would have been an incredible marriage of power in the capital. The daughter of the great Gerard Machenet and one of our foremost generals? You'd have been untouchable, unstoppable."

Mae opened her mouth to respond, but the councilor held up a hand. "A good thing for many of us, then, that your little romance didn't work out." Tarand shifted in her seat, pushing a handful of braids over her shoulder, and the wooden beads clacked quietly. "Even if it would have been one hell of a thing to see."

"My daughter assures me that she is through with all of that," Mae's father assured the councilor. "She is on the straight and narrow path, your eminence, here only to serve the Coalition."

"Indeed," Tarand said, deadpan, as she stared at him. "You'll forgive me a little bit of Capital gossip, Gerard, I get to indulge in it far too infrequently."

"Of course," he demurred. "My apologies."

"When did you last hear from the general?" Tarand asked, glancing at Mae.

Panic rose in Mae's throat, the telltale bile burning the fragile tissue there, urging her to expel it into the potted plant near the window. She swallowed hard, wincing at the sensation and taste. There was no right answer, because it had never been the general to begin with. She'd wrongly assumed that the matter would be closed, as her record had been sealed and expunged. "I suppose when I left Gamma-3," she answered.

"Odd that your whirlwind romance would end so abruptly."

"Sometimes the flames that burn the hottest also burn the fastest."

Tarand grimaced, a sour look settling on her face as though she'd smelled something suspiciously unpleasant. "Indeed." She tapped a pencil against the soft surface of the writing desk, the quiet rhythm somehow still echoing around the room, the sound gathering in the distant rafters. "There's no need to hide a relationship with the general, Ms. Machenet. We already know everything there is to know."

If true, then Mae was only awaiting imprisonment. A trap laid for her that she'd stepped right into, unless the councilor didn't know about Bailey. Mae breathed, trying in vain to quiet her nerves and the endless, persistent thudding of the panicked heartbeat in her chest. "I'm not hiding anything," Mae replied with what she hoped was a nonchalant tone. "I am telling you the gods' honest truths."

The councilor stared, challenging her to falter, and when she didn't, sighed heavily, setting the pen down on the desk. "Very well," Tarand said. "What did you come here to tell me?"

"Maevestra has information about The Splintered," her father said.

"She can speak for herself, thank you, Gerard," Tarand replied acerbically. "Perhaps it's time to pass the torch." She searched his face with quiet derision before adding, "Perhaps past time, in fact."

"I can offer you information on The Splintered," Mae repeated.

"They are but a fringe group, small in number. What makes you think that information about them would be in any way interesting or useful to me?"

"Because The Splintered has a leader, and her name is Cassius Calvetti."

"Ah." Tarand drummed her fingers against the wood. "Olivia, I have need of you."

The door opened, and Mae tensed. Cass had assured them all that Olivia Guisette was on their side, but Mae remained skeptical. No one renounced the Coalition that quickly, not when the Coalition had paid for their cushy life.

"Ma'am," Olivia said, standing in the doorway. "What do you need?"

Tarand smiled warmly. "These fine people are known for having extremely advantageous information."

"Of course," Olivia said, meeting Mae's panicked stare. "The Machenets are legendary, even before the front page scandal with General Fineglass."

"Yes, Dearest, I have already covered that."

"Of course you did, ma'am."

The councilor gestured for Olivia to close the door. "Ms. Machenet has information on The Splintered."

"That's impossible," Olivia said tersely, closing the door with slightly too much force. "They're such a new faction, no one has information yet."

"I know that Cassius Calvetti is leading them."

Olivia laughed dryly. "Cassius Calvetti is dead, she died at Terringgough Gulch."

"I, uh—"

"Did you need coffees, ma'am?" Olivia asked, her hand resting on the doorknob. "Teas? Refreshments of any kind? I know that informational meetings can be extremely long and *arduous*, given how long it takes us to positively verify the information given."

Tarand tilted her head. "Yes, Olivia, that would be wonderful."

"I can't carry them all myself, and Officer Abara is on break. I don't trust their replacement to not spill huge quantities all over our esteemed guests."

"Very well, I'm sure Ms. Machenet would be more than willing to assist you." The councilor offered Mae's father an oily smile. "It will be good to have a little catch up with Gerard, in any case."

"Yes, Maevestra, help the councilor's assistant."

"Ms. Guisette," Olivia corrected. "I am an Intelligence agent, sir."

He turned, giving her a patronizing smirk. "Of course you are, Ms. Guisette."

"I'd love to help," Mae chirped, standing from her seat and following Olivia to the door. As soon as they stepped into the corridor, Olivia closed the door and grabbed her arm forcefully, dragging her down a back hallway. She sequestered them in a stairwell, doors closed at either end.

"What in hells do you think you're doing?" Olivia demanded.

Mae glanced up at the corners, squinting. "Cameras," she whispered.

"Do you think I'm a fucking cabbage? There are no cameras in this stairwell. Only place in the entire building except for the toilets, and there's too much traffic there." Olivia leaned against the door. "Answer my question. What are you doing here?"

"Building collateral."

"By throwing Cass under the steambus?"

"I can't help the position I've been put in. Most of us don't have many options left at this stage in the game."

"Is that what this is to you? A game?"

"No," Mae said carefully. "That's not what I meant."

"Why are you giving Cass up?"

"I'm not telling Tarand anything she wouldn't have found out sooner or later anyway, assuming she didn't already know."

Olivia leaned forward, staring at Mae. "I'm not at liberty to discuss that."

"Of course," Mae replied with a roll of her eyes. "I'm not even sure whose side you're even on."

Olivia released a slow hiss from her lips. "What are you trying to get for this information?"

"I'm not at liberty to discuss that," Mae parroted, adding the distinct edge of sarcasm.

"I can help you, if it means you'll back off of Cass."

Mae chewed on her lip. It was impossible to know if Guisette was on her side or not, or on a side all of her own, one where the only thing that mattered was Cass, and to hells with anyone and everything else. "I'm trying to gain access to a secure line."

"Why?"

"I'm looking for someone."

"Who?" Olivia asked. "Who are you looking for?"

"Piss off," Mae retorted, making a move to push past her.

Olivia squeezed her eyes shut, leaning against the door. "Wait. Just wait." She tapped her fingers against the door frame in a quiet rhythm. "I can get you access to a secure line, but it will have to be me that sends it. Can't risk you getting found In the wire room or they'll know something is up."

"Turas-Mara, General Fineglass."

Olivia blinked at her. "Why?"

"I think that's where Bailey went."

"She's not there."

"What do you mean? How do you know that?" Mae asked, releasing the handle.

"It's being kept quiet for now, but General Fineglass is missing."

Mae shook her head. "No. Missing? Why?"

"All we know is what Overseer—High Councilor Allemande told us, and that's that Wilhemina Fineglass was exhibiting some troubling behaviors. Allemande went to check on her and was attacked as the general fled the station."

"Shit," Mae hissed. "Gods be damned to hells."

"No ideas about what happened there?"

"Only that Bailey probably had something to do with it, even though I'm not sure yet."

"Okay," Olivia replied. "Alright." She checked her pocket watch with a frown. "We'd better get those coffees, or they'll wonder where we disappeared to. Councilor Tarand has a habit of assuming the worst, so we'd better not be late." She turned towards the door, looking over her shoulder at Mae. "Don't do anything foolish, Machenet."

"I was playing the only card I had."

"Then find a new deck." Olivia opened the door, peeking out down the corridor before pushing it further ajar to let Mae out of the stairwell. "I know that you don't know me, but I'm asking you to trust me."

"If anything happens to—"

"You're not the only one trying to track someone down," Olivia shot back. "Where is she?"

"Bailey?"

"No, you turnip, Calvetti."

"She's not in—well, you know," Mae whispered, following her into a small room lined with coffee pots and tea kettles. The smell was thick and overpowering, but it was at least a welcome distraction from the bile still biting at her throat. "Last I heard, she was heading out to Obsidian Enclave."

"To get back your cook?"

"Among other things. Zink has a deal with The Scattered."

Olivia's eyebrows shot up. "Oh."

"Yeah, he's a man who tends to get what he wants." Mae poured coffee into a tall, slender mug, the kind that was almost too impractical to drink from. She added plenty of milk and sugar to both mugs, the same way she and her father both liked it, an irritating similarity born of genetics and solidified by hundreds of rainy weekends where she'd studied in her father's office as he worked. The bittersweet memory churned in her stomach, unpleasant and unbidden.

"Done?" Olivia prompted, waiting in the corridor with two mugs of black coffee. "Come on, hurry up."

Mae stumbled after her, trying not to spill from the overfilled mugs. "Right behind you," she muttered, her eyes on the coffee as she walked, willing the levels to stabilize and not escape over the lid of the mug.

"Olivia, Dearest," Tarand said, opening her arms wide. "You're back so soon!"

"No lines at the stations," Olivia explained coolly, setting Tarand's mug on the desk.

"Right now, Ms. Machenet, you have my full attention. I'm ready to receive any and all information you may have about The Splintered."

Mae sipped at the coffee, grateful for the burn it left on her lips. "Cassius Calvetti is alive and leading The Splintered."

"Yes, we've covered that," Tarand replied with irritation. "What else do you have for me?"

Mae caught Olivia's warning stare and sat up straight in her chair. "I have it on very good authority that Cassius Calvetti is heading to The Rim with an army." The lie tasted sweeter than the sugary coffee that lingered on her tongue.

Chapter 26

The ship landed effortlessly, descending through terraformed atmosphere with silent ease and coming to a rest in a wide bay without so much as a shudder. Rosie bent, adjusting the buckle on her boot that had been rubbing against her ankle.

"Are you ready to step into the place you'll want to live for the rest of your life?" Gregor Zink asked, pulling the lever to raise the loading bay door.

"We'll see about that," Rosie retorted, following him down the ramp.

"I can promise that you will be amazed."

She stifled a gasp as her vision adjusted to the searing, unrepentant light. Ceru was brighter than Bradach, so much that she was forced to shield her face from it. She hadn't felt sunlight so intense since she'd lived back on Gamma-3. Huge mirrors hung over the city, just like in Bradach, but in Ceru, there were layers of silvered surfaces, all bouncing light between one another to simulate the strength of the sun.

Huge buildings climbed high into the sky, none of them obscured by clouds, every glass panel sparkling in the light. Rosie cleared her throat in a bid to clear her thoughts. "So this is Ceru," she said. It wasn't a question, more of a proclamation.

"Welcome, Ms. Gordon."

"How long before I can leave?"

Zink visibly wilted in response to her barbed comment. "I'd hoped you would at least like to stay long enough to learn about who we are and why we are."

"I have things to attend to," Rosie said tersely. She'd long grown tired of Zink's nonsense, his game-playing and manipulations, all designed to make sure he got his own way. The journey beyond the rim had only been a few days, a tiny fraction of the time any other ship would take to cover the same distance, but the unprecedented speed had left her feeling groggy and irritable. "I already told you, I can't just abandon my life back home."

"Perhaps someday you will call Ceru home," he offered, gesturing out into the city. "All the glamor and opulence of the Capital, with none of the military police that mar the shining façade. We have a number of cutting-edge labs here, all designed to push humanity further than we've ever gone before."

"It's certainly sunny," Rosie grumbled, squinting against the light.

"We control the weather here." When Rosie raised an eyebrow, Zink chuckled, waving over a sleek boat fitted with solar panels across the top. "I know what you're thinking. That technology was stolen from us, sold to the Coalition, but not in its entirety. Still, the only thing they know how to do with technology is to weaponize it."

"Those storm generators cost hundreds, probably thousands of lives," Rosie shot back. "You couldn't keep a lid on that tech? Couldn't keep it out of the hands of the Coalition?"

Zink sighed sadly, running a hand through his greying hair. "Ceru citizens are provided for, most want for nothing. However, there isn't much I can do if one of them becomes besotted with an Internal and would do anything to be with them. Unfortunately, there have been a few cases of technology being sold in those circumstances."

"Internal?"

"Those that live within the Rim."

"And you are?"

"We are Obsidian Enclave, Ms. Gordon, I thought we'd long since established that matter." He offered her a sly smirk, but she ignored it. Zink climbed into the boat, holding his hand out to help her. "There are no steamcars or steamtrucks allowed within Ceru city limits," he explained proudly. "Ceru is accessible, sustainable, and at the forefront of exploration."

"There are no steamcars or steamtrucks in Bradach, either," Rosie replied, stepping into the boat without his help. "Hardly cutting edge."

The boat pulled away from the short dock, heading under an arched bridge through a series of interconnected canals. Rosie took in the sights of Ceru, being careful to remain stoic. Still, it was a stunningly beautiful city, rich with flora. Wisteria dripped over the sides of the bridges, and ivy climbed against red brick buildings, stretching its tendrils across in an earthen reclamation of a place that had never been meant to host human life, or in fact, any life at all.

"How long has Ceru been here?" Rosie asked.

"Over half a century," he replied proudly. "Your grandmother died to protect this place, gave her life to preserve it. I can only hope that we've done it justice, and will continue to do so as long as the human race survives."

Rosie didn't respond, choosing to ignore his desperate attempts to manipulate her emotions. It had started the moment she touched ground on Lucent Base and hadn't stopped throughout the entire journey to Ceru.

"On your left, you can see our communications tower. It has the longest range of any tower of its kind, and we are able to monitor transmissions across the whole of the Near Systems and beyond."

Delia would love that, Rosie wanted to say, but bit her tongue. Zink didn't need to know any more than he already did about her romantic entanglements. She didn't need Delia in trouble, too. "Impressive," she offered, throwing Zink a metaphorical bone. "I suppose that's how you always manage to be in the wrong place at the wrong time."

"That depends on your perspective, Ms. Gordon. From mine, I am always in the right place at the right time." Zink muttered something to the boat driver, who pulled off onto a side-canal, shaded by the edifices that towered above them. Trees lined the sidewalks, their blossoms potent and the thick scent settling heavily over the water. "This will be your home while you are here in Ceru." He disembarked, once again holding out his hand for Rosie.

"Temporarily, then," she replied, once again ignoring it. She climbed out of the boat, dusting off the knees of her jumpsuit, covered in a fine mist of water from the boat's gentle wake.

"Of course." He led the way into the building, pushing open the glittering glass doors. The high ceilings were mirrored, giving a strange infinite feel to the interior. Something about it turned Rosie's stomach, but she ignored it, having much more pressing matters to focus on.

"Do you live here, too?" she asked.

Zink laughed quietly, shaking his head. "No, Ms. Gordon. This building was designed and created for your grandmother. It is a shame it wasn't finished until after her untimely demise, but I must say, it gives me a deep joy to see you here, finally, taking your place at the helm of Ceru."

"I am merely visiting."

"Yes, for now." He stepped into a sleek elevator, pulling a wide lever on the wall. "This is the fastest lift known to humankind."

"Fascinating."

"I'd hoped you would be more enamored with our technological advancements," he said, punctuating his displeasure with a frown.

"An elevator is hardly something to swoon over."

The doors opened onto a strange floor, translucent bricks of glass instead of wood or carpet. Rosie stepped out, almost expecting them to crack beneath her feet, but of course they didn't. She followed him down a long corridor, past an empty desk that stood in the foyer. "Apologies that no one is there yet, but that desk is where you can ask for anything that you might need. Snacks, water, a haircut, fresh linens, whatever your heart desires."

"A wire room?"

"In time, Ms. Gordon. This transition will require patience."

"I think I have offered enough patience at this point, thank you." She tugged at the lapels of her jumpsuit, letting the stiff fabric fall back on itself without a sound.

"These are your living quarters," he announced proudly, ignoring her admonishment. Zink threw open a set of double doors, heavy with frosted glass that matched the walls of the corridor. "I hope you will find them suitable?" He smirked again, and Rosie's chest burned with frustration. Simple yet elegant light fixtures hung from the ceiling like planets orbiting a sun, and the far wall was floor to ceiling glass, looking out over a placid Ceru. To the right, an abbreviated corridor ending in a large room, the four poster bed just visible through the gap in the door. It was piled high with wool blankets draped over the side to drag artfully along the floor. It was larger than any quarters she'd ever lived in, significantly so.

"It's fine, I suppose," she replied, waving a hand with a particular sort of nonchalance that always irritated men like Zink. She glanced around at the stunning opulence and shrugged. "It will do."

"You're a difficult woman to impress, Ms. Gordon."

"I imagine my grandmother was more so."

She stepped through into the bedroom, running her fingers along the soft linens and poking the cushions with a curious fingertip, testing their firmness. "When will Hyun and Jasper be joining us?" Rosie asked.

"Don't worry about them. They'll be heading to their accommodations presently."

"Why aren't they staying in this tower with me?"

"Ms. Gordon, the care you have for your friends is astounding and truly admirable. Unfortunately, this structure is not set up to provide the kind of care and treatments that Jasper needs, and his companion opted to stay with him rather than somewhere else." He smiled again, but this time Rosie could see the barely concealed threat of his words. "I'm sure you understand."

"Of course," she replied. "Although I will be requesting a transport to wherever they are staying."

"It is a closed facility, I'm afraid."

"Then Hyun can come here when she's settled."

"Ms. Gordon—"

Rosie turned on him, pivoting on the heel of her boot. "This is not up for debate, Mr. Zink. If you want my cooperation in your little plot, then I, at the very least, need to see Hyun to know that she and Jasper are being cared for."

"Understood," Zink said coolly. "How silly of me to suggest otherwise. Of course you will be allowed to see and meet with your friend. That building is a closed facility, however, so I'm afraid you won't see Jasper again until he is cleared for release with a clean bill of health."

"And when will that be?"

"Healing takes time, there is no metric. For some, a few days, for others, several months."

"Months!" Rosie shouted. "I'm not staying here for months."

Zink shrugged easily. "Perhaps not, but I imagine your friend will want to stay until her partner is healed. She will be welcomed and treated with kindness until that day."

"That had better be the case." Rosie stared out the window, towering over the city below. Canals and streets stretched out into the horizon, along with other buildings that were tall, but shorter than the one she was in. Tendrils of smoke rose in the distance, and her eyes narrowed. "Rhodium mines."

"Our most valuable export. The Coalition's desperation for the ore is why we have spent decades in secrecy, and seek to maintain our invisibility. They take everything they can with brute force and leave everyone else with empty hands to starve."

"I find it hard to believe people would volunteer for the mines. What are they, convicts? Political prisoners, digging chunks of ore out of the ground?"

Zink's eyebrows raised almost into his hairline. "We are not that kind of people," he explained. "The mines in Ceru are automated. The only time people go down into the mines is to check the seams for purity, but the machines are never on when that happens. Mining this ore is a necessary hardship, I will grant you, but we aim to do so in the most ethical way possible."

"We'll see about that."

Zink pursed his lips. "I will leave you to settle in, then." He stopped, scratching at the light stubble on his chin with a quiet rasp. "What would you explore, Ms. Gordon, if you had the opportunity to? What question lingers in your mind, unanswered? Perhaps we could find a solution together, to close the loop in your mind and offer you some respite."

"I'd want to know why my grandmother abandoned her family for this place. It has a few shiny baubles, I will admit, but from what I have seen so far, it was not worth what she did."

"Abandonment?" Zink asked, playing up his disbelief. "Your grandfather lived here for a time, as did your mother."

"I think they would have told me about that."

"You can ask them yourself. They are currently living three floors down." Zink smiled, turning back for the elevator. The soles of his shoes tapped against the gleaming tiles, each step like a drumbeat in her ears. Her family, in the same building. Her family, after all that time away, running from her past and towards something that had seemed more like truth, but was turning out to be a mirage.

"Wait, hang on!" Rosie shouted, chasing after him. She caught him by the arm, jerking him backwards. "Did you abduct them, too?"

"No. They were more than willing. They didn't tell you?"

"Obviously not."

Zink shrugged again, offering his hands up. "They've had the same access you will enjoy here. If they chose not to send a wire, then perhaps they have more to say than will fit into the small box of a letter."

"I want to see Hyun."

"Not your family?"

"They've waited years to see me, they can wait a few more hours," Rosie said, trying desperately to keep her calm but aware that the flicker of unease in her voice had become apparent. "Hyun doesn't have anyone else here other than me. She needs support."

"She has the full support of the medical team, I wouldn't worry. She will get everything that she needs, at no cost to her or her crew."

"Where is the medical center?" Rosie pressed.

Zink folded and unfolded his hands, staring out at the city. "I'm not sure how to break this news to you, Ms. Gordon, but Hyun joined Obsidian Enclave. She is one of us, and will remain in Ceru even after her partner has been treated."

Rosie snorted a laugh. "Sure."

"She worked with me back on Lucent Base to encourage you to stretch your wings, Ms. Gordon. Hyun sees the infinite potential of Ceru, of expanding beyond the Rim and exploring the unknown. Who knows what medicinal treatments are out there, waiting to be discovered?"

"Yes, or surprising new weapons to threaten the Near Systems with."

"We haven't threatened anybody, unlike The Scattered." The name of the rebel faction fell out of his mouth like unchewed food. "We endeavor to progress, not fall back into the warring ways of the past."

"And that weapon?"

"Will be dealt with in due time."

Rosie rolled her eyes, pushing past him to the stairwell. "If you won't take me to Hyun, or bring her here, then I guess I'll have to go looking myself."

"Suit yourself, Ms. Gordon, I already indicated that you were allowed to go and do as you wish."

"Leave a message at the desk if you need me," Rosie said, already descending several of the hundreds of steps it would take to get to the bottom.

"You can take the elevator, Ms. Gordon. I assure you it's much faster."

"I'm fine."

"As you wish." He entered the lift, and the doors closed with a polite ding.

Rosie glanced around for cameras, finding one in almost every corner. It seemed that Ceru was no different than Lucent Base in that regard. She shielded her face, not wanting the security team watching the feeds to see the tears gathering in the corners of her eyes. Ceru was indeed a stunningly beautiful city, but in the same way that a lake glistened on a warm summer's day, all glitter and sunlight, reflecting with such cheerful aggression that it skillfully hid the horrors beneath.

One step after the next, flight after flight of perfectly uniform stairs. Rosie was grateful for her stamina from working in the busy kitchen at the Purple Pig because her calves and thighs barely even ached when she finally reached the bottom.

Zink was nowhere to be seen, thank the gods. She needed a break from his constant winnowing for information, carving pieces of her out to examine under the harsh light of day, asking too many questions about a woman who'd died before Rosie was even born.

She pushed through the frosted doors onto the sidewalk, shielding her eyes not from the sun this time, but from an immediate visual cacophony of flashbulbs.

"Ms. Gordon, how do you plan to guide Ceru into the next phase of development?" one reporter asked.

"How does it feel to be the granddaughter of Norah Gordon?" another shouted, shoving a recording device into her face.

There were at least twenty of them, all shouting for her attention, taking photos, making notes. She tried to push past them but they only surrounded her, pressing with questions, demanding answers. Rosie wound her way to the back of the tower, trying to ward them off with silence and shielding her face. If she could just get into one of the canals, maybe she'd be free to find Hyun and try to unpick this mess, try to find a secure wire to tell Delia she was alright, figure out why in hells her family was staying in Ceru as well.

It was impossible—every canal, every avenue blocked with reporters. With a swallowed growl of frustration, she pushed back into the tower, leaving them outside. It was almost as if Zink had planned the entire thing, and of course he had. Always the illusion of freedom, while keeping her chained like a disobedient dog.

Chapter 27

Alice fought with the wrench, trying in vain to loosen the rusted bolt holding down an air filtration unit so old, she was surprised it hadn't killed all the ship's inhabitants already. The wrench slipped, and the unspent force sent her knuckles slamming into the jagged tangle of wires and debris behind it. "Gods be damned," she shouted, throwing the tool to the floor with an angry, jingling clatter.

Sitting back on her haunches, Alice picked up the small wrench, turning it over in her hands. She hadn't felt so lost or adrift since the last time she was on the C.S. Stronghold, wondering where in hells Barnaby had wound up and yearning to be back on the Cricket. The scuffed metal almost glinted in the dim light of the ship's boiler room, her reflection blurry and unrecognizable, but the streaks of blood from that morning's run-in with a low-hanging doorway were still apparent.

"Josie!" she called, standing up. Alice slid the wrench into her pocket, resting a hand on her wide hips. "I'm done."

"Oh, good, I—" Josie stopped short at the top of the stairs, her arms folded over her chest. "It certainly doesn't look done."

"I am done," Alice repeated. "No more."

"I think you're forgetting who holds the cards, here."

"I don't give a shit about cards. I've been out here for ages fixing all these gods-damned ships while you profit off my labor, and I need to get back to the Cricket."

Josie's hand rested atop the revolver holstered at her waist. "Then you're forgetting who holds the gun.”

“Are you going to shoot me, Keller?” Alice spat, stepping closer. She towered over Josie, but a gun leveled the score. “Right here on the docks of Kilper Station?”

“Who would tell me no?” Josie asked, a bemused smirk playing across her lips.

“Violet would never stop hunting you.”

“Oh, I don’t know,” Josie said with a nonchalant shrug. “She obviously decided to leave you here. I heard that the Cricket isn’t parked where we left it. They left you here, Green.”

“She wouldn’t do that.”

Josie laughed, her palm still resting flat against the holster as a reminder of what she was capable of. “I’ve also heard that your beloved Captain Violet has a very colorful past.”

“You’ve spent years chasing after Captain Leo’s legacy, and for what?” Alice said with an exaggerated snort, trying to shift the conversation. “You’re stuck here in Kilper Station, same as me, trying to scrape together some credits to send back for your daughter.”

Josie whipped the gun from the holster, holding it against Alice’s chest. “Don’t ever say a word about my daughter,” she snarled.

“Just let me go, Keller,” Alice said simply. She wiped the back of her hand against her forehead, and it came away streaked with grease and dirt, a casualty from the air filter that was, annoyingly, still bolted to the floor, the broken tiles around it a strange omen about the ship. “Let me leave. This ship isn’t going to make it many more flights anyway. The air filtration system alone could cause a catastrophic failure, and half the bolts holding this vessel together are seventy percent rust. Fixing it barely delays the inevitable.”

“Yet you want to get back to the Cricket?” Josie asked, following up her rhetorical question with an ugly snort. “That thing is in even worse shape than this one is.”

“I understand that you didn’t have much of a choice before, when you were scraping together a living for the sake of your child, but you have a choice now to be the better person and let me get back to my ship. Wherever they've ended up, they'll be needing my help."

Josie threw her head back with a laugh, the sound echoing in a jarring metallic across the ship's interior hull, marked with rust spots and tarnished. "Does this overwrought do-gooder shit actually work on anyone, or just Violet?"

"You'd be surprised what decisions people will make when they are given better viable options."

"And you haven't given me shit, so keep your trap shut and get back to work."

Alice glanced around at the boiler room, shoving her hands into the pockets of her green jumpsuit. "Whose ship is this?" she asked. Cobwebs hung thick in the corners, years of little to no maintenance taking their visible toll.

"I told you to stop asking whose ship is whose."

"This thing looks like it's been sitting in a scrap heap." Alice nudged the toe of her boot into the layer of thick, greasy dust of the boiler room floor. "It doesn't even look lived in."

"It's a project vessel for an old friend."

"What old friend?" Alice asked. "Barnaby?"

"I haven't seen that fool in months," Josie replied, keeping the gun trained on Alice. "Last I heard, he was working with Obsidian Enclave as their fence."

Alice stepped backwards, almost losing her balance. "Working with them? A fence?"

"Does that really surprise you?"

"No."

Josie twirled the revolver around her index finger four times before putting it back in the holster. "You were right, though. This is his ship. He got it in a trade, it's been sitting in the docks since the last time he was here. The dock manager sent him at least a dozen wires, but he never came back for it, so I suppose it's mine now."

"It's not worth much," Alice said, kicking a screw across the floor. It bounced six times and came to rest in the space between two tiles, where the grout had long since disappeared. "You'd be better off selling it for scrap."

"You're going to fix it, and then I'll sell it to the first sucker who looks at it," Josie replied. "Honestly, Green, you don't have a mind for business, do you?"

"It's not my specialty."

"Probably why you and the rest of your crew have been all but broke since the Coalition outlawed grey market chips," Josie replied. "The rest of us are learning how to adapt."

"This ship won't fly."

"The hells it won't. You're going to be here until it does."

Alice cracked the knuckle of her thumb as it rested in her pocket. "It may well explode on ignition."

"Good thing I have a test subject, then."

"You'd take out half the dock!" Alice protested, throwing her arms into the air for emphasis. "You'd kill people!"

"Then I guess you'd better make gods-damned sure you fix it properly then, shouldn't you?" Josie glanced at the rusted air filtration system and rolled her eyes. "And hurry it up."

"Get out, I need to sleep." Alice turned away from her, stretching the thin bedroll out across the ground. She'd slept in worse places, probably, but she couldn't remember when. Her back ached with stiffness, and her knees weren't doing much better. "I've been at this for fourteen hours already, and if I don't get enough sleep, I might just mis-wire something."

"It would be your own funeral."

"At this point, I would happily choose death over having to put up with you." Alice bent, unlacing her boots. "Out."

"I'll be here first thing in the morning, and you'd better hope to every one of the gods that you've made significant progress by then." Josie picked up a gasket and threw it at the filter, where it bounced without a sound. "You'd better have at least fixed this."

"If I don't need parts, it will be fixed."

"Good." Josie glared, searching her face. "I'll be locking you in again. Can't have you running off, now can we?" She took the tool box from the rickety table with a hostile smirk. "Someone will bring these to you in the morning. I don't want to leave you with the means to escape."

"I can't fix anything without my tools, Keller." Alice flipped a long, silvery, dirt-smudged braid over her shoulder, the stray hairs poking out from the top to the tail. "Even you should be smart enough to know that."

"Use your hands, if you must. I don't care. Just do it." Josie said as she closed the boiler room hatch and locked it from the other side.

Alice waited until the reverberations of Josie's boots faded up the corridor, and the sound of the loading bay door slamming echoed through the small ship before she decided to make her move.

She was no pilot, but she'd done it once or twice. She just had to get the bucket of rusted bolts out of the docks and through the atmosphere, get to the nearest beacon, and ditch it there. No matter what was keeping Vi, she had to find her. Waiting wasn't an option anymore. She ached with fatigue, weeks of nonstop, physically demanding work, one repair after another and no Ivy to help her, no Ivy to climb into the tiny spaces between boilers, or beneath comms consoles.

Pulling the wrench from her pocket, she began working on the rusted hinges of the boiler hatch. If she could get to the bridge of the ship, she could evaluate its reliability. Really, it was Alice's ship, and she deserved to take it back.

After all, it had been Barnaby's, and he owed her big for all the times she'd forgiven him and he turned around to do it all over again. And now it was Josie's, and she could consider it payment for services rendered. The first hinge came loose, bouncing down the stairs with a noisy clatter. She waited, almost anticipating Josie would have heard it from wherever it was she was staying on the station.

No one came. Alice yanked out the second hinge, lifting the door as much as she could with the deadbolt engaged, throwing her weight behind it, feeling the metal shift under the force until the deadbolt snapped with a sickening crunch.

There was no time for waiting now. If Josie did return at the sound, and saw the door hanging like that, she would know what was going on. Alice leaped up the ladder, running to the loading bay door to disengage the pulleys. She did this by slamming the corner of an old metal crate into the gearbox, which would work well enough to keep someone out. She glanced around, looking for her toolbox, and seeing nothing more than other emptied crates and an empty loading bay.

She overturned each of the crates, willing her tools to fall out, but they didn't. She'd have to leave them behind with Josie, if she even made it out of the docks, and the loss of something so rudimentary still pulled at her. The big wrench, her favorite pliers, that nice screwdriver set Ivy had gotten her for a birthday two years back. Ivy had been so young then, barely even an adult.

Alice shook her head angrily to clear her thoughts, pushing through the airlock and leaning against the glass on the other side to get the seal to engage. One more thing wrong with the damned ship, and something that could kill her if it disengaged outside of an atmosphere.

The ship was smaller than the Cricket, with fewer quarters and shorter corridors, so it was only fifteen steps to the bridge. The console held on by one fraying wire, and Alice hissed out a sigh.

"This thing is more a death trap than a ship," she grumbled aloud.

She sat down in front of the console, rubbing her eyes, trying to ignore the exhaustion that pulled at the edges of consciousness. Kilper Station was far from dormant, even that late at night, and angry shouting drifted down the docks. It sounded like a card game, and Alice smiled for just a moment before the loss of Hyun pierced her once more. They'd all lost so much. They were all so fractured, and she hadn't heard anything in weeks. Josie hadn't even let her listen to Delia's broadcast for fear they'd find some way to pass a message to her.

She spliced two wires together, then two more. Each time moving slowly, methodically, trying to keep the fraying wires together as she worked. There was no tape or guards on the bridge, so for all she knew, the console would catch fire the moment she started the ship.

Alice gritted her teeth, splicing together two more. She stood, waiting, one eyebrow raised at the console.

It lit up, the board flashing with colors and alarms from the diagnostic system. Low on fuel, loose seals on the doors, sediment in the boilers, and, of course, the air filtration. Alice ran her hands over the buttons, assessing what was an emergency and what could wait. Once, she would have refused to leave the dock before every warning had been addressed, but the past year had broken her of that habit. They'd flown the Cricket from place to place, patching, grasping, praying to old gods that they'd survive one more firefight in dark space. The last two had nearly taken them out.

Alice's frown deepened at the thought of Gregor Zink and his ridiculous mind games, barely giving her the parts she needed to repair the ship back on Lucent Base. At least she hadn't been foolish enough to allow his Obsidian Enclave mechanics to help, they'd have wound up with two trackers and full sets of microphones wired to transmit in real time. The man had an unsettling commitment to surveillance, his very own panopticon.

The ship's systems could wait. The longer she stayed in the dock, trying to fix all the ills of the ship, the more likely it was that she'd get caught. The console had taken at least two hours to repair, and the overhead mirrors creaked with the first light shift of the day, simulating a cold, colorless dawn. Alice took a deep breath and sat in the captain's chair of the bridge, pushing the memory of the last time she'd done that from her mind. She'd find Vi. She had to. The thread binding them together was fraying but gossamer, fragile and frighteningly impermanent.

With a heavy sigh, she pressed the ignition, and to even her own surprise, the ship coughed into life, the warnings now blinking with an exaggerated menace. "Here we go," she said, pulling back on the throttle. Part of her expected that the ship would catch on fire, or explode, or fall apart. Maybe even all three.

Rising up from the dock, the radio patched in with a growled crackling. "Vessel in dock C3. What is your status?"

"Uh, leaving?" Alice replied, pressing the button to transmit her message.

"You are not cleared for takeoff, unknown vessel."

"This is the P.S Manta. Can you clear me?"

"We need your destination," the radio said.

Alice drummed her fingertips against the console, frowning at how beat up her hands were. Swollen, cracked, burnt, scratched, she looked like she'd had a fight with an entire menagerie of mechanical monsters. "Where's the nearest beacon?"

"Coalition beacon, about two hours out."

"Okay, second nearest, then."

The radio laughed, a crunching, static noise. "I figured as much. Prentiss Beacon, a bit further than that. Neutral, but the Coalition likes to suppress it, so don't expect any trade. You'll be lucky to pick up fuel. We also need your name for the logs."

"Sorry?" Alice replied, pulling back on the throttle. "I can't hear you, the radio is breaking up."

"P.S. Manta, you are not cleared for flying without this information on the books!" the radio replied, clear as a day on Gamma-3.

"I can't hear you, sorry!" She yanked back on the throttle, willing the ship to climb faster. "Come on, you fucking pineapple of a ship, *move!*"

Despite her demands, the ship remained at a constant, steady speed, rising up first through clouds, and then atmosphere, the radio shrieking at her. She leaned over and turned it off. If they were going to chase her, having twenty seconds of notice wasn't going to help.

The ship crested out of the thin, terraformed atmosphere and into dark space, and when it lurched at the shift, Alice breathed a quiet sigh of relief. The hardest part was over. She just had to find Vi.

An hour outside of Kilper Station, she turned the radio on again, bracing for the potential impact of more screeching, but she was well out of range by then. She fiddled with the knobs, trying to keep the ship on course. There was no auto-pilot and Alice was no Violet, so if anything happened, it wouldn't be pretty.

She flipped the switch to move to a secure wire, the radio silent from the lack of transmissions. "Calling out, this is Alice Green seeking assistance, over." She repeated herself three times, waiting in between for an answer that never came.

"Calling, this is Alice Green looking for the Cricket, over."

"Alice!" a scrambled voice replied, heavy with static. "You need to get back here. Something has happened."

"I can't make it there in this ship, I'm heading to Prentiss Beacon. Who is this?"

"It's—" the radio garbled. "We can't send anyone for you. No ships."

"Violet isn't back in the settlement?"

"Haven't seen her. —knows what happened."

Panic seeded in Alice's gut, sending tendrils out through every vein and pore. "I'll be there as soon as I can."

"Be careful, there are — in the — region. Oh, and—" The radio cut off, beginning to smoke from behind. Alice turned it off, staring at it. Vi was missing, and something was wrong, and she was in a ship she could barely fly, that was one bad maneuver from falling apart.

The gods be damned.

Chapter 28

Larkin cast a worried glance around the tavern for the twelfth time in as many minutes, once again anticipating that an angry mob of Cole Marion supporters would break the door down and set fire to the place, waving around heat guns and revolvers as they overturned tables and ripped down tapestries. It wouldn't be the first time something like that had happened, although so far as she knew, it hadn't in Bradach. Yet.

Evie had disappeared hours ago, waving her hand casually about some meeting she had to attend, something about suppliers and favors, Larkin had only been half listening. She was starting to regret that, given it wasn't long from closing and Evie still hadn't returned. Worry settled in her gut, churning the acid so aggressively that it splashed into her esophagus, giving her a terrible burning in her chest she couldn't ignore. It was reminiscent of when she'd taken that screamingly hot bolt to the ribs, and upsettingly so. Without realizing it, she rubbed at the raised scar that lay hidden under her loose-fitting shirt, long healed but a permanent reminder of the metal that lay beneath her skin.

"Last call," Larkin said, ringing the silver bell next to the bar. "And don't try to argue just because I'm on my own, I'll toss you out on your ear."

A few patrons laughed, but most gave her a cursory glance before returning to their conversations. Two wandered up to the bar, asking for refills on their drinks.

Larkin made them automatically, barely present in her own mind. Ale poured, cocktail mixed. She slid the glasses across the polished wood and placed the trade materials in the box below the till. More and more patrons had been showing up with rhodium, which Tansy was thrilled about, but it made Larkin uneasy. Where in hells was all the stuff coming from? The mines were all Coalition-controlled, at least, as far as anybody knew. It was a tightly restricted substance, and the market for it would begin to shift before too long. She frowned, pushing the box to the back of the shelf.

The Purple Pig began to empty out, the same way it did every night. The early birds first, giving her a nod as they exited. Then the ones that did in fact try to argue, and she threatened them with a smile, walking the tightrope between friendly barkeep and no-nonsense establishment owner with practiced perfection. They left too, grumbling. The last few to wander out apologized, leaving a tip on the table. That was nice. She pocketed something shiny, a lump of silver or platinum, she couldn't tell which. Evie always could.

The bar across the door fell with a thud, and she stood at the window, looking out at dark streets peppered with pools of yellow glow from the street lamps. Where had Evie gone? Larkin's brow furrowed, and she returned to the tables, wiping each of them down, scraping crumbs into a tray for disposal. She leaned against the shining wood for just a moment before she pushed through the swinging door to the kitchen with her hip, dumping the crumbs and setting the crate of dishes next to the sink. They wouldn't take long, but she'd hate every moment of it.

She braced her palms against the sink, waiting for it to fill. Curls of steam rose up from the basin, obscuring the polished metal tiles behind. It wasn't so much the dishes that she minded, but the lack of a distraction from her own troubled thoughts. Cole was gone, but the threat lingered.

The sink was nearly full, obscuring the dishes hiding below the surface with its glassy surface. Before she had the opportunity to plunge her hands into the water, she saw the faint shadow of something moving behind her in the reflection. Something that was far too large to be Evie.

She spun on her heel, already reaching for the throwing knives at her hip.

"I don't think so," a man said, exiting from the shadows in a deeply hooded cloak. The man who'd been at the bar every night for two weeks. Of course.

"I do," Larkin shot back, throwing three knives in quick succession. One went wide over his left shoulder, one pierced through his loose cloak and hung there, tangled, and the third grazed his shoulder.

He pressed fingers to the graze, examining the small amount of blood there. "Bitch," he said, moving for her again.

"Original," Larkin said with a laugh, dancing away from four blows he aimed at her, his meaty fists swinging through the air like cleavers. "Do you use that on all the ladies?"

It had been months since she'd trained, even longer since she'd taught. With Bradach growing, the Pig was more popular than ever, and she wasn't able to keep it all up. She had to give up training or bartending, and with Evie at her side, the choice hadn't been a hard one to make. Even so, the movements were like silk against water, autonomous and easy, like she'd never spent a day away from it.

The realization was troubling, but that was something to deal with after she got this assassin out of her kitchen. He pushed closer, his gait covering twice as much space in half as much time. "Get the fuck out!" she shouted, throwing another knife, and this time it sank deep into his bicep.

He growled out a deep scream of pain, yanking the knife from his flesh and turning back for her once more. He was tough enough to give her pause as she reached for the last throwing knife. She waited for the perfect moment to strike, leading him around the kitchen like a cat on a leash, jumpy and panicky but somehow still practiced and graceful.

"You're all out," he said with a smirk. The knife to the bicep hadn't done much, not that she'd labored under any false illusions that it would have. He moved towards her again, and she dunked a used ale glass into the hot, foamy water, thrusting it up into his face.

The man shouted, rubbing at his eyes with the crook of his elbow. "Bitch!" he yelled, his face buried as he desperately tried to clear his vision.

Disoriented by the thick, industrial-grade washing soap, he staggered back towards the door, grasping for the handle.

Larkin snatched a carving knife from the block and hurled it towards the door. It sank into the wood with a satisfying thunk, just inches from his head. He reached for the door but it wouldn't open easily, not with the knife holding the bar in place. "You're not going anywhere," she announced.

"Oh, you want to play this out?" he asked with a frustrated growl turning to face her with squinting, red-rimmed eyes. "That's strange. From what I'd heard, you were all washed up."

"Yeah, well, at least one of us washes. I could smell you from across the bar," she retorted. "Who are you?"

"I'm going to be asking the questions here," he snarled, lunging for her.

Larkin dodged his punch, ducking under it and twisting away. "We'll see about that."

The hooded man reached for a paring knife that was sitting next to a bowl of lemons, but Larkin got there first, sliding it from the sleek metal surface. He swung again, this time connecting his knuckles with her eyebrow. She staggered backwards, keeping hold of the knife with one hand and pressing the other to the fresh blood running down her face.

"You've gone soft, Flores," he growled, advancing on her.

She lashed out with the paring knife, slashing wildly in the air. The blood was running into her eyes, obscuring her vision, and panic was rising fast in her chest. She was out of practice, out of shape. The movements were there but not the speed, and only some of the precision. She'd grown complacent, comfortable in her role at the Pig.

"Soft and useless," he reiterated.

"Fuck you," she hissed, slicing a deep gash into the back of his hand.

He yelped but grabbed a heavy iron pan from the stove, swinging it at her like a bat. One hit from that and she'd be at least unconscious, but probably dead. He was taller, his reach longer, and she was at a disadvantage. "I should have poisoned you the first time I realized you were probably an assassin," she shot back, dancing around the rolling cart in the center of the kitchen. "Should have slipped it into one of your ales and let you go die in some back alley like the trash you are."

"Oh, like you did Cole Marion?" He swung the pan, crashing into a stack of glasses that all shattered, tumbling down off the counter in a cascade of sparkling shards that glittered in the amber light of the kitchen lamps.

"I barely even know who that is," she lied. This was it. Her punishment for putting the poison into his whiskey. Some lackey or a failsafe had triggered and now she was going to die. She never should have done it, but there hadn't been much of a choice. Marion was dead anyway, a kitchen knife sunk into his chest, but he never would have come to the Pig if she hadn't struck first.

"I think you know plenty." Another swing, this time rushing through the air with a threatening, empty whoosh.

"I'm giving you one more chance to surrender," she shouted, brandishing the knife. It was pathetic, really. There was no way to get close enough to him to use it, not with him using that pan like a mace. She was as threatening as a defanged cobra.

"I won't be offering the same," he said, unfortunately guessing her next move and breaking her stride.

She staggered backwards, searching for her footing. He swung again and this time only missed by a narrow margin, so close that she felt the wind from it caress her blood-stained cheek. "Piss off!"

He grinned, and his too-white smile gleamed through the shadows of the kitchen. "I'm not leaving here until my job is done."

"Or until I make a fresh corpse out of you." Larkin tucked forward, rolling behind him and slashing at his cloak with the knife, trying to find purchase against the meat of him. The hood fell, revealing a once-familiar face that stole the breath from her lungs.

"Recognize me now?" he asked, turning on her.

"Unfortunately." She darted out with the knife again, reaching flesh with the tip of the blade and pressing inward.

He roared in pain, twisting away from her but taking the knife with him, lodged in what she hoped to the gods was one of his kidneys. "I knew you wouldn't make this easy."

"You went through the same training I did, what makes you think I'd roll over and die?"

"Because you were never supposed to go domestic, Flores."

"And you were never supposed to wind up in a pirate settlement halfway across the Near Systems, were you? So I guess we both fucked up."

He pulled the knife out of himself, dripping with black blood that oozed thickly onto the floor, leaving a trail across the pristine tiles. "You think I came here to drink at this shitty tavern, and listen to turnips whine about the Coalition? Crying like little babies because they didn't get their way?" He snapped the blade from the handle, dropping it onto the floor. Holding his wound with one hand, he stalked towards her again with the pan. "You have nothing to fight me with now, Flores. You might as well give up."

"There are others. They'll come for me," she said, backing towards the door that she'd sealed shut herself. A foolish, rookie move. He was between her and the swinging door to the tavern, and she had nowhere to go. "Any minute now, they'll walk through that door."

"No one is coming for you, Flores."

Evie. Rage boiled in Larkin's gut, leaching into her veins like liquid fire. "What did you do to her, you slimy little fuck?" she gasped, wrenching the carving knife from the door. "I will carve chunks out of you, and I will enjoy every moment."

"Touched a nerve, have I?" he asked with a weak snort. "We'll see who walks out of here alive."

"I nicked your kidney, didn't I, John?" Larkin said, holding the knife out to keep him at bay. "Maybe I should give you a matching pair."

"I'll survive this little scratch, but you can't survive your head being caved in." He streaked forward, almost losing his balance. He swung the pan, and Larkin cried out at the sickening crunch it made when it connected with her side.

"That's going to leave a mark," she wheezed, still holding her position.

He blinked, hesitating for just a moment. He'd expected that to send her to the floor, but it hadn't, and it was just enough of a gap that she had the opportunity to crouch, darting around him to hold the knife to his throat. She was standing on her toes to match his height, but he didn't have to know that. "I don't have ribs there anymore, asshole," she whispered. She pressed the blade into his skin, enough to let him know that she would kill him if he so much as tried to move. "What did you do to her?" Larkin demanded.

He grunted against the knife. "I don't know what you're talking about."

"Evie, you useless sack of rotten potatoes. Where is she?"

"The brainy one who's always running circles around you?" He laughed hoarsely. "I wouldn't know."

Larkin knocked the pan from his hand and kicked it away, careening across the tiles with a metallic screech. "Don't lie to me, John."

"Not lying. I don't know where your little attachment has gone."

"She left earlier, and I haven't seen her since."

"Maybe someone else got to her. Seems to me you two have been busy making enemies all over the Near Systems. This is probably the last place you can sleep easy at night." He chuckled. "Maybe not anymore."

Larkin growled, wishing she were just a few inches taller. "Who sent you?"

"You know who sent me."

"Lionel Cabot is dead," she answered, scraping the blade against the burgeoning hair sprouting from his chin.

"That's not who sent me, Flores." He swallowed hard, the mound in his throat pushing up against the knife as she dragged it down across his skin. John flinched away from the pain, a coward to the last. "Come on, think. You know the answer."

"Cole Marion."

"Wrong again. I guess I was right that you've lost your edge."

Larkin drew the knife across his skin, just hard enough to draw a thin rivulet of blood that ran down his pale skin and disappeared into the thick black fabric of his cloak. "Don't forget who's in charge here."

"Don't you realize what you did when you took off? Not only did you leave a trail of devastation in your wake, but you put the rest of us at risk, too. Now we're all at the Coalition's mercy, and if we resist, they send another to kill us off."

"No."

"Did you really think they'd let you quit, just because you managed to put a bullet in Lionel Cabot's head? They've known you were here for some time, but the treaty kept them from sending someone to take you out. Once Marion was doing political deals on neutral ground, it changed the rules."

"Why wait to kill me? You've been hanging around here for weeks."

He coughed and cleared his throat, straining against the knife. "You were rarely alone. I'm damned good, but—"

"Not that good, clearly. I'm years out of practice and I just beat you without breaking a sweat."

"If you had ribs, you'd be dead by now."

"Lucky for me, the Coalition took care of that." Her arms ached from the angle, but she couldn't let him go, not yet. "So you were afraid to take more than one of us on at a time?"

"There weren't supposed to be any witnesses."

"I'm surprised you wouldn't have just killed them."

He wheezed, coughing again. "I would have, and I still will, given the opportunity."

"I don't think you're going to live that long, John."

"Maybe not, but they won't stop sending us. The day I stop sending updates, they're going to dispatch another. And another, and another, until the job is done. You're not safe here, Flores. You haven't been since the moment Cole Marion made the first deal with Obsidian Enclave. I don't blame you for killing him, I was tempted to do it myself just for the thrill of it. He was a nasty piece of work towards the end, a real thorn in the Coalition's side."

Larkin pulled at his neck, forcing him to contort himself backwards with a soft grunt. "The High Council can send as many assassins as they want, I'll kill each and every one. I don't care that we trained together, none of us were ever friends. We were just orphans with no one, trained to kill and be alone. It's not my fault what happened."

"The High Council will see you dead before the year is up, Flores."

"I'd love to see them try. Their first attempt wasn't very impressive."

"I almost got you, and you know it."

"Almost doesn't count." Larkin sank the large blade deep into his neck and released him, letting him fall to the floor with a thud. The gasp he tried to take gurgled in his throat, and before the moment was out, he was already dead, blood pooling beneath his huge frame.

She pulled the knife from his neck and tossed it into the sink, where it stained the crystalline water scarlet, the ripples dancing with red through the rest of the sink. Larkin sagged against the counter and sobbed, a loud, wracking cry that shook her to the core. She held herself, pressing a hand gently against her side, wondering if the hit had damaged the metal frame underneath. She would have asked Hyun, but she was across the Near Systems on Lucent Base with Jasper.

Tearing a strip from the apron hanging on the peg, she tied a tourniquet around the wound from the paring knife, grateful it hadn't been worse.

"Evie," she sobbed, burying her head in her hands. "Where are you?"

Chapter 29

Evie nodded again, pulling out her pocket watch to check the time. She frowned at the face, frozen. It must have run out hours back, because it still read seven in the evening, and it was long past that. Glancing around, she looked for a clock on the pristine walls of Holly's home, but found none.

"Anyway, so she's leaving me," Holly said with a sigh, topping up their wine glasses.

"What?" Evie asked, pulling herself back to the moment. "Your wife is leaving you?"

"Left, really. She's gone."

"But this place—"

"Is a rental I can't afford on my own anymore. That's why I was asking if you knew of any work going, something high level maybe, a scrap consultant or some such."

Evie's cheeks blew out with a huffed sigh, and she laid her hands in her lap. "Everyone is struggling lately, with the outlawing of the grey market chips. Scrappers are getting priced out of the market by Coalition teams that are faster and more efficient. We're looking for a cook to fill in while Rosie is gone, but other than that, I don't know how to help."

Holly's eyes filled with tears, and she buried her face in her hands. "Oh, Evie, this all started when I did what I did to you. The universe is punishing me, and I can't get free of it."

Evie sipped from her glass with her eyes closed, knowing the look on her face would give her thoughts away. Holly had been sneaking around for years, causing problems in every sector for the gods only knew how many people. Evie hadn't been the first, and she sure as hells hadn't been the last, either. "I'm sorry to hear that."

"No, I'm sorry. What I did was totally unacceptable, and I haven't even begun to pay you back, not even with what I arranged."

"I'd rather not discuss what you arranged, but thank you for your apology."

"You deserved better than the likes of me."

"I did, and do, which is why I'm marrying Larkin." It was the first time she'd said it aloud, and the words almost surprised her. She'd spent years waving away the idea of it, but now it was almost like a light in the distance. If they actually managed to make it there, maybe everything would be alright.

Holly jerked back in her seat. "You're getting married?"

"Is it that much of a shock that someone like me would wind up a wife?"

"No—no, that's not at all what I meant."

"Then what did you mean?"

Holly fell uncharacteristically silent, the first time in hours that she'd actually paused to reflect on something Evie had said. Somewhere, an unseen clock ticked away the seconds, and Evie wished she knew where it was. She cleared her throat. "Do you know what time it is?"

"Oh, who cares what time it is? This calls for a celebration!" Holly stood, stiffly, her hands balled at her sides. She took their wine glasses away, despite their fullness, and disappeared into the next room. "I think this calls for some bubbles, don't you think?"

"I should be getting home, it's almost closing time. I don't want to leave Larkin to do all the work. She'll have been expecting me back already."

Holly returned with a dark green bottle that was covered in a fine layer of dust. "Nonsense, don't be silly! One glass to celebrate your engagement, and that's it."

Evie chewed her lip, desperate to say no, but aware that Holly was the loose end that could get them all thrown out of Bradach if she ever decided to open her mouth. Why in hells Delia had gone to her for help, Evie would never understand. "Alright, one glass," she relented.

"You already made me wait ages to see you, Babes, don't make me drink alone, too."

The old endearment was stagnant now, ineffective, inert. Still, Evie shifted uncomfortably as Holly popped the cork with a giggly shriek, leaping away from the foam that escaped from the narrow opening. She looked up at Evie with a grin, pouring the glistening liquid into two fluted glasses. "I'm so glad you came by."

"Yeah, me too," Evie lied, taking the glass. She took a sip, the taste brighter than she expected, the bubbles tingling the end of her nose. "It's nice."

"It had better be, for what it cost. I swear Marshall is skimming extra profits off the top with this stuff."

"Considering how many blockades there are across the Near Systems now, I don't blame him."

Holly wrinkled her nose, smiling. "Gods, it's fantastic. It was supposed to be for our fifth anniversary, but this is a much happier occasion, I think." She looked down at her glass before smoothing out the crisp indigo crinoline of her skirts. "And she left it here, so now it's mine to do with as I wish. Don't you agree?"

"Uh, sure."

Holly ran a finger around the rim of her glass, drawing a quiet, high-pitched hum. "So, marriage. When's the big day?"

"We haven't really planned anything yet. It's still pretty new as a concept for us."

"You have to let me plan it," Holly said with a gasp, setting the glass down on the table in front of them, immediately leaving a ring on the polished oak wood. "Maybe that could be my new thing, event planning!"

"It's a long way off. Maybe even years," Evie deflected. "Anyway, I couldn't say no forever. Larks has been asking me for ages."

"For ages," Holly repeated.

"She wants the big dresses and the flowers and the speeches. I never did, but with how things are now, I can't deny her that. Not when it's so important to her." Evie leaned back on the settee, allowing herself to enjoy the bubbles for a moment. "She's the best thing that ever happened to me."

"I guess it's good that we didn't work out."

Evie bit back the cutting remark on the tip of her tongue, preventing a mishap with another mouthful of bubbles. It gave her just enough time to set aside the bitterness and reply, "I guess it is."

"I am sorry, you know." Holly ran a bit of the crinoline through her elegant fingers with a quiet swoosh, letting the rest fall to the ground. "Her leaving has been a wake up call, I guess," she said softly, staring at the wall opposite her plush, overstuffed chair.

"You could go home," Evie offered. "Back to Gamma-3."

"My parents bailed me out of trouble the last time I was there, but they told me it was the last time they'd be helping me. They're done with me, Babes, just like everyone else." She glanced over, her eyes glassy with tears. "Even you."

"There was a time I'd have done anything for you," Evie said, a harshness to her tone that she hadn't anticipated, but she still bore the scars as a reminder of how what Holly had done had left her marked forever. "Why did you want me to stop by?"

"I wanted to apologize."

"And then what?"

"And then ask for work, which I did." Holly sighed, draining her glass and refilling it. "I didn't expect you to come back to me, not after what I did." Holly crossed one leg over the other, laying her arm against the chair. "Don't worry, I won't say anything about Cole Marion. I can't. If I do, she'll be even angrier with me for using her position and access again."

"Thank you."

"I can't do it again, though. She's gone, Babes, and she's not coming back. She left the night before your friend showed up on my doorstep asking for my help."

"I understand."

"Cole Marion was a piece of work, anyway. Rancid little shit, and worse, the longer he stayed in Bradach. This place doesn't need people like him showing up to throw everything out of balance."

Evie lifted an eyebrow. "You once called this place a backwater."

"It is, Babes, but it's the only place I can be these days, so I'd better fight for it. I'd rather be alive in a backwater than dead in the Capital, which is what I'd be if I went back to Gamma-3."

"Mm."

Holly dragged a fingertip around the rim of her glass before she drained it a second time. "Maybe you should get going. Your betrothed is waiting for you."

"She is," Evie said simply. "It's getting late."

"Half past midnight," Holly agreed, squinting at a clock somewhere behind her.

Evie bolted up off the settee, nearly knocking over the table with the glass and the bottle in the process. "Gods, she'll be worried sick, especially with what happened to Rosie, and to Alice, and—I have to go." She rushed for the door, her boots squeaking quietly against the polished tile floor. "Thank you for the bubbles. And the apologies. All of them."

"Of course," Holly said, catching up to her. She reached around to unlock the door, pulling it open. "Thank you for coming."

"I'll let you know if I hear of anything, work-wise."

"Yeah," Holly said sadly, a pained smile stretched across her face. "Yeah, please do. And if it's alright with you, and if Larkin won't kill me, I'd like to come back to the Pig."

"Larkin won't kill you, she's retired."

"Then what happened with Cole Marion?"

"That was all me," Evie replied. "He attacked me."

"You definitely saved the juiciest part of the conversation for the moment you're walking out the door, didn't you?" Holly asked. "I'd love to hear the whole story someday."

"Maybe when this is all over, and people stop caring."

"From what I hear, not many do already."

"Holly—"

She held her hands up, stepping back. "I gave you my word I wouldn't say anything, don't worry. And my word is worth more these days. I'm trying to make a fresh start. I have to, if anything is going to change."

"It was nice to see you," Evie said, and meant it now that she was on her way out the door.

"Tell Larkin I said she's the luckiest woman in the Near Systems, maybe even beyond the Rim."

"I will."

The door closed and Evie was already halfway up the alley, almost at a run despite the darkness of the cobblestone streets. The stars past the mirrors shone brightly, but the pinpricks weren't enough to light the way, and the street lamps only pooled yellow light in circles at their bases. Evie strode from one to the next, knowing she'd have to beg forgiveness when she got home.

She hadn't even told Larkin where she was going, not really. A meeting, she'd said, and left it at that. Larkin's feelings on Holly sure as hells weren't a mystery, despite her help with the Cole Marion problem.

"Fuck, fuck," Evie hissed, jamming her key into the front door lock. Larkin had already barred the door from the inside. "Larks?" she called, assuming Larkin was still clearing tables. "Let me in, it's me."

When there was no response, Evie walked around to the back of the tavern, clumsily throwing herself over the fence. They'd have to get that damned gate fixed. She went to unlock it, but it was jammed shut. First the gate, now the door. Typical. Evie threw her weight into it and nearly fell into the kitchen, skidding in a puddle of... something.

"Larkin?" she called again, squinting into the kitchen. Evie closed the door behind her and her boot met something disturbingly fleshy. "What the—" She grappled for the light switch, flooding the room so immediately that her eyes struggled to adjust. When they did, her heart leaped into her throat.

A dead body. A man, twice Larkin's size, and covered in sticky, half-dried blood. A broken paring knife in two pieces on the floor. More blood, this time droplets in a trail that led straight to Larkin, who was sitting with her back to the bottom cabinets, hugging her knees, and rocking softly, staring straight ahead.

"Larks?" Evie said gently, despite her own terror. "What happened?"

Larkin only shook her head, squeezing her eyes shut.

"Okay." Evie sat down in front of her, laying her palms on Larkin's knees. "Are you alright?" She glanced at the tourniquet on Larkin's arm, the blood smeared across her face, and the empty eyes staring back at her. "Do we need to call a medic?"

"No medic," Larkin managed to say. "But not alright."

"Maybe, just to make sure—"

"No medic!"

Evie sat back on her haunches and nodded. "No medic," she agreed. "We need to get you cleaned up, just to make sure. Will you come upstairs with me?"

Larkin stared at the corpse in the corner. "Can't leave."

"I'll deal with that."

"No."

"Larks, I said I'd deal with it, and I will. But first, you need to let me help you clean up, because I'm not convinced you don't need a medic." Evie's heart was thudding painfully in her chest at the sight of it all, so she reached up to the light switch and turned off the kitchen lights. She suspected that it was the same reason Larkin had done it, too. "Can you walk?"

Larkin nodded, climbing to her feet unsteadily, using Evie for balance. "I'm fine."

"Yeah, we'll see about that. You said the same thing when half your torso was missing, so forgive me if I'm a little skeptical." Evie steered her to the stairs by her shoulders and led her up to their apartment, one step at a time. "Bathroom," she said, locking the door behind them, being sure to hit every deadbolt twice while Larkin was watching, and grabbed a revolver from underneath the table. "No one else is getting in here tonight. You've seen me. You know I'm a damned good shot."

Larkin smiled weakly, but it was empty. "I know."

The bathroom was the way they'd left it that morning, which was somehow surprising, given the carnage below. The faucet was still dripping tiny splashes into the sink, the bathtub still had a soap ring from the last bath Evie had taken three days prior, and the towels Larkin had used that morning to shower were still rumpled and not hung correctly.

Larkin stripped off her clothes, one layer at a time, starting with boots, socks, trousers, apron, then her vest. She hesitated, staring at the mirror. "I look terrible."

"You couldn't look terrible if you tried." Evie helped her remove the final layers, stifling a gasp at the ugly purple bruise spreading across Larkin's not-ribs and onto her back. "Larks," she whispered.

"It hurt, but I'm not dead."

"Remind me to thank Alice for making those metal ribs, and Hyun for installing them." Evie had to work to keep her tone light, when what she wanted to do was scream and cry, throw her arms around Larkin and beg to know what had happened. Instead, she turned, twisting the bathtub tap. "Shower or bath?" she asked.

Larkin shrugged, noncommittal.

"Shower then, less getting up and sitting down with that dent in your side." The bathroom began to fill with steam after just a few moments, and Evie was grateful for the reduction in visibility because it was becoming harder and harder not to cry at the sight of Larkin's beaten form. She stripped quickly, getting into the shower behind her. "Let me," she said, gently wiping away the streaks of blood. She unbraided Larkin's hair, letting the dark locks fall loose to her hips, already drenched.

"He was a patron," Larkin said.

"Here? At the Pig?"

"For weeks. I didn't recognize him. I should have, but it's been so long."

Fear twisted thorny tendrils around Evie's heart. "You knew him?"

"Training, a long time ago. He was a weird, lanky kid then, smaller than me." Larkin pressed fingertips to the bruise, wincing. "I guess he grew up."

"Why?"

"Governor. Ralph Baker, Lionel Cabot. Coalition is angry I didn't stay. I'm a loose end, Eves."

Evie nodded solemnly, taking it in and trying to not let the panic rising in her chest show on her face. "We'll take care of it."

"He said they'll keep sending people."

"The hells they will." Evie massaged suds into Larkin's hair, letting the hot stream of water rinse away the blood. "We outnumber them."

"He'd been at the bar for weeks, Eves. Waiting for the perfect opportunity to strike." Larkin let loose a tiny, strangled sob. "He waited until I was alone."

Guilt, grief, and fear flooded into Evie from the ground up, rising quickly and was almost ready to send her to her knees when Larkin continued, laying her head on Evie's chest. "I never wanted to do this again. Never, never."

"I'm so sorry, my love. You never should have had to." Evie wrapped her in a tight embrace, letting the water wash over them both. "It was self-defense. It doesn't count."

"We both know it counts, Eves."

"It doesn't."

"It counted when we were at the Armory, it counts now," Larkin said, wrapping her arms around Evie's waist as she fell to her knees in front of her. "I don't want to do this anymore, Evie, and they made me. They forced my hand, and they knew that they could. They're still reaching me, still controlling me, even now, even past so much dark space they're still making me do what they want."

"Never again," Evie soothed, dropping to her knees to match Larkin's height. "I will break down the door of the High Council myself."

"No!" Larkin sobbed, openly now, her fingertips digging into Evie's flesh. "No, you can't, you can't leave me Eves, I need you. I need you here with me. I have to know that you're safe because without you I lose everything that helped me remember how to be a real person."

"You are a real person, Larkin," Evie said, rinsing the suds from her hair gently, like you would a frightened stray. "You're real, and we're going to get to the bottom of this."

"What about him?"

"We'll figure all that out, I promise."

"You can't let them take me back, Eves."

"I won't. I promise I won't." Evie held her tight, willing herself to focus on the feeling of the water pelting against them, and not the dread that was already seeping under the door, ready to engulf them both.

Chapter 30

Delia rapped on the back door of the Purple Pig again, unconsciously tapping the toe of her boot against the cold cobblestones. "Hello in there," she called, impatience beginning to color the edges of her tone. "I have a broadcast in half an hour and Thomas isn't here for setup!"

Heaving an angry sigh, she vaulted over the broken gate and stalked around to the front of the building for the second time, even though she knew the door was still barred from the inside. "What good is having a key if you lock yourselves in anyway?" she muttered aloud, starting to worry that she would miss the morning broadcast for the first time since Rosie was taken. Still, even then Carmen had taken over, it's not as though there was no broadcast at all. "For all the gods' sakes!" she huffed, perhaps as loud as she meant to, but she'd never admit it.

"What's the matter?"

She turned, heaving a sigh of relief at the sight of Captain Tansy. "When did you get in?"

"About ten minutes ago, Weaver and Arteo were already headed to the science tent."

"Arteo?"

Captain Tansy sighed. "Long story. Ivy swapped ships a ways back, trying to get out to the Cricket before we knew it was missing." She shook her head, leaning hard on the crutch at her side. "What a mess." She eyed the door, an eyebrow raised. "Barred from the inside?"

"Seems so."

"Why?"

"No idea. No one is answering wires, either. I already tried."

"Strange." The captain peeked around the corner and nodded. "This way. There's a window in the back that's usually open. And if it's not, we can make it be open."

"What are you doing back here?"

Captain Tansy made a dramatic gesture at her leg, or rather, the lack of one. "Some bastard messed up my cybernetic pretty good. I need repairs, been hobbling around for weeks on this thing. It's fine enough, but hard to run from the Coalition on a crutch."

"Right."

"Do they usually bar the doors?"

Delia shook her head. "The front maybe, but never the back. I have a key so I can get into the basement for broadcasts."

"When did you see them last?"

"Yesterday's evening broadcast. Thomas and I didn't stick around after, he wasn't feeling well and wanted to head home, and I was—" Delia cut herself off, not wanting to elaborate further. "I just wasn't in the mood to be around people."

"You seem like the outgoing type, Forrest."

"It's hard without Rosie."

Captain Tansy nodded, pushing experimentally at a window. "Locked. Do you have a hairpin or something?"

"Don't you?" Delia asked, nodding at the artful coiling of braids atop the captain's head.

"No way am I taking this out. Give me one of yours."

Delia pulled out several pins, handing them over to the captain one at a time. In a matter of moments, she had the small window open, and grinned at Delia, gesturing for her to climb inside. "You can unbar the door for me. I'd rather not climb through that narrow window with a crutch."

"Alright," Delia said, pulling herself through the window and into the bathroom of the tavern. It looked the way it always did, but there was a strange stillness that crept its way under her skin and pushed up tiny bumps that spread across her arms in an instant. She closed the window behind her, the heels of her boots clicking quietly against the bits of parquet floor uncovered by thick rugs. Pushing up the bar, she opened the front door for the captain.

"Thank you kindly," Captain Tansy said, looking around. "Any sign?"

"No."

"Aye, Evie and Larkin, it's just us!" she called, seating herself at the bar. "You two layabouts going to get up anytime soon?"

"Maybe they slept in," Delia said, trying to convince herself of it as much as she was trying to force it to be reality. "Coffee?"

"You know me. As large as you can make it, lots of cream and sugar. A little cocoa, if they have any."

"I'll have to look." Delia pushed through to the kitchen and swallowed back a scream, stumbling back through the swinging door.

Captain Tansy was already off the stool and ready to fight her way into the next room, using her crutch like a sword, balanced on one foot. "What is it?" she barked.

"Body. Dead," Delia said.

"I guess that's why they barred the doors." She glanced up at the second floor door with a worried look, standing up again. "They'd better be alright, I can't run this place on my own. I don't even want to anymore."

"I'll go," Delia said, heading up the stairs. "Evie? Larkin?" she called out. "If you don't open your door, I'm going to let the captain break it down, because there's a dead guy in your kitchen and we need to be sure you're both alive."

The door eased open, revealing a groggy Evie, her eyes bleary and her face puffy from lack of sleep, or tears, or both. "We're alive."

"Thank the gods," Captain Tansy shouted from below. "What in hells happened?"

Evie closed the door behind her, shooing Delia back down the stairs. "Keep your voices down, Larkin is sleeping, and that's what she needs right now."

"What happened?" Delia repeated, standing back at the bar. She needed coffee, but another look at that corpse and she might need whiskey, too.

"An assassin, sent for Larkin. He was a patron, in and out of here for weeks. They trained together when they were young, and now the Coalition has somehow absorbed the rest of the assassins into their ranks. Larkin is a messy loose end that they're desperate to tie off."

"And Guisette?" Delia asked. She still wasn't sure if she trusted the spy or not, given how manipulative Intelligence could be. "Is that how they found her?"

"We don't know." Evie pressed palms to her forehead and grimaced. "I need to go and get Sandrine from the medical tent. Larkin keeps saying she doesn't need a medic, but she took a beating from that dead fuck in the kitchen. Maybe she'll listen to Sandrine."

"If not, she might listen to José," Delia suggested. "Gods, two dead bodies in two weeks."

"*Two?*" Captain Tansy said, leaning over the bar. "What do you mean, two?"

Delia and Evie exchanged a worried glance. "Cole Marion is dead," Delia whispered. "He came here and attacked Evie in the garden out back. She fought him off, but we had no friendly ships in port, so we had to call in a few favors to get him to the incinerator without any questions."

"Obviously I'd heard he was missing, but not that he was dead." Captain Tansy raised an eyebrow and sat back on her stool. "Good riddance."

"Keep that under your hat, will you? We don't need anyone poking around here, especially not now," Evie said softly. "I'm sure people will find out, eventually. We haven't heard from Cass either, so no idea how she's managing his disappearance."

"I saw her in Chalidon on Delta-4," the captain said. "With Georgie Payne."

"What in hells is Calvetti doing out there?" Delia asked. "Shouldn't she be rounding up troops, or undermining Gregor Zink, or finding that damned weapon, or something?"

"Calvetti has good instincts, I'm sure she's there with good reason."

Evie hid her face, muffling her sniffles. "This is a nightmare."

"Hopefully the stiff in the kitchen isn't anyone someone will come looking for?" Tansy asked.

Evie shook her head. "No. He's an assassin."

"Good. Go get Sandrine, José, whoever. Forrest, with me. I can't drag that behemoth out to the port myself."

Delia hesitated at the door, wondering if she'd be just as surprised the second time she saw it. "How are we going to get a body from here to your ship without being seen?"

"Carefully."

"And how do you propose we do that?"

"A crate."

"I don't know if he's going to fit into a crate," Delia said, peeking through the swinging door again. "He's taller than any of us, and his arms are like tree trunks."

Captain Tansy peered over her shoulder before pushing through the door herself. "Gods below, how in hells did Larkin fend this monster off? He's huge!"

"She took some pretty bad hits," Evie said, heading for the door. "We only have a few hours before the tavern opens for lunch."

"We'll get a move on. What's the menu?" Delia asked. "I'm not a very good cook, but I can try."

"Change it. Sandwiches, I don't care, but we have to open or it's going to look strange." She glanced at Delia. "Where's William?"

"Sick or something. I don't know, he's been avoiding me lately."

"Right." Evie slid through the front door, locking it behind her from the outside.

Captain Tansy leaned against the counter in the kitchen, and let loose a low whistle. "We've got our work cut out, Forrest."

"How in hells are we going to get this cleaned up before the place opens?"

"Sheer force of will, and a deep commitment to not getting thrown off this rock," the captain answered. "How opposed are you to taking him in chunks?"

Delia winced. "Extremely."

"Then we need something bigger than a crate." Captain Tansy looked around, her questioning stare landing on the trash bin in the corner. "That should do."

"You don't think anyone will ask why we're dragging a trash can through the streets to the dock?"

"Not if we make it look like a keg." The captain stepped over the corpse, the end of her crutch leaving bloody polka dots across the tiles. It would have been funny, if it wasn't so specifically grisly. She reached under the sink, rummaging around past containers of solvents to produce a very large canister of industrial strength glue. "Once we get him in, we glue boards and straps around the outside. It will look a little oddly proportioned, but this early in the morning, no one is going to know the difference. Help me pick him up."

Delia followed her lead, grabbing the corpse under the arms as Tansy balanced on one leg, taking his feet. Together, they managed to heave him into the can, turning it upright and sealing on the lid. Delia made quick work of breaking apart three kegs, just enough boards to cover the can. As the captain glued, Delia mopped up the blood, having to change the water six times to get it to run clear with every pass. When they were finished, it looked like a child's school project, but at a distance, it would be believable.

"Good enough," Captain Tansy announced. "I'll get a couple of my crew to come get it, and set off without me for a few days. They'll dispose of it in dark space and no one will be the wiser." She gave Delia a sideways glance. "If the broadcasting thing doesn't pan out, I think you really have a future in biomedical disposal."

"No thank you," Delia replied, her guts already in knots from what they'd done. "I don't think I have the stomach for it."

"Probably not," the captain agreed, leaving through the swinging door.

Delia followed her, finding Sandrine and José pleading with Larkin at the bar.

"Just to be sure," Sandrine said kindly, softly, taking Larkin's hand in her own. "If you don't want to do it for yourself, then do it for me, for José, for Evie. We're all worried about you, Sugarlump. It's obvious that you really took a beating."

"I told you, I'm fine," Larkin said with a laugh, but it was hollow, only a shadow of her usual gregarious self. "Honest, Sandrine, I'd tell you if something was wrong."

"Mija," José said, resting an arm around Larkin's shoulders, "we just want to make sure you're alright. It will only take a minute. Evie says you have a pretty nasty bruise."

Larkin's eyes welled up, and she pulled away. "I don't want an audience."

"No audience, Sugarlump, we'll use the back room," Sandrine said gently. "Just you and me and if you want Evie with you, then that's alright too."

"Evie," Larkin confirmed, grabbing her hand. "And then we should all eat."

"I'm on it," Delia said, well aware that Larkin shouldn't be anywhere near the kitchen that day.

"What about your broadcast?" Larkin asked. "You have to do it or someone might come knocking. If someone comes knocking—"

"We'll get you checked out and then José and I will make breakfast and help sort out lunch," Sandrine interrupted. "We'll get it taken care of." She turned in her wheeled chair, casting a questioning glance at Delia. "The kitchen is cleared?"

"Cleared," Delia confirmed. "I should prepare the broadcast. I left Carmen a note last night, but—"

"I'm here, I'm here," Carmen chirped, bursting through the front door. "Sorry Dee, I got tied up." She smirked, smoothing her skirts. "Didn't get your note until a few minutes ago. Let's go, we're already late."

Delia nodded, leading the way through the kitchen and down the back stairs into the basement. "You picked a hell of a morning to not check your messages," she muttered, pulling her notes from her pocket and unfolding them out onto the broadcast desk.

"What's going on up there?"

"Long story."

"Give me the bullet points, then."

"Huge assassin, now dead assassin."

Carmen raised an eyebrow, sitting down in her chair. "Busy morning."

"How's Roger?"

"Better than the rest of you, that's for sure. Ignorance sure as hells can be bliss. I'll let him keep it until we're done here."

Delia snorted. "How magnanimous of you."

"We're starting to get people writing in to ask about Cole Marion." Carmen dumped a satchel of papers out onto the desk. "Every one of these is someone asking for more of an update about how he's missing. No one has any information, and they're starting to concoct some pretty wild stories."

"Like what?"

"Like he was assassinated."

"Not too far from the truth, I guess, but he brought it on himself," Delia mumbled. "What else?"

"That Cassius Calvetti is the one who did it."

Delia let out a slow hiss. "Gods be damned."

"You said it."

"So what, then?"

Carmen drummed her fingertips on top of the papers, emitting a strange sort of shifting lilt of a rhythm. "We lie. Tell people he's sending us messages from a secure location. Instructions, reassurances. We could use it to our advantage, drum up votes for Emeline in Skelm, get people to move back to Cass and get enough traction to undermine Zink."

Delia blew out a frustrated sigh, fingers tangling in her messy curls. "And say what, that Cole is hiding in some secret bunker? Why would anyone believe that he was only sending information to us?"

"I'm sorry, did you know of any other competing pirate and rebel radio broadcasts around? Do we have rivals that I don't know about, and Thomas has never mentioned?"

Delia smoothed the creases from her script, reading it over in her head once more. "No, but it could cause more problems for us."

"What *doesn't* cause problems these days?" Carmen asked with a shrug. "It's an idea that could work."

"It's risky."

"All of this is risky. Being here in Bradach is risky, this broadcast is risky." Carmen pointed at the stairs behind them, jabbing with her thumb. "Folding some dead guy into a decorated trash can is risky."

Delia shuffled the papers in her hands, knowing she'd already lost the argument. "I'll think about it. How long to broadcast?"

Carmen checked the clock on the wall, and then her own pocket watch. "It's dead on. Ready when you are."

Delia nodded, putting the headphones on over her messy, sweat-frizzed curls. Carmen counted her down as she sat on the other side of the booth, pointing when the channel was live, the same way she'd always done, but now, there were expectations that Delia wasn't sure she could live up to.

"Good morning, I'm Delia Forrest," she began. "Thank you for tuning in and we apologize for any lateness you may experience in accessing our broadcast. Satellites are becoming increasingly difficult to hack." A lie, but a small one. Delia was almost worried at how easy it had been to lie.

"Emeline Allemande has fallen in Skelmian polls for the first time since she joined the governor's race in the settlement. Pundits attribute this to her absence in Skelm over the recent weeks, as she has been visiting neighboring sectors. We will keep you updated on her run in the lead up to the election coming up soon."

Delia paused to breathe, shuffling her notes. "In other news, blockades continue to cause major shipping delays across the Near Systems. If you are trying to approach any Coalition-controlled ports, we recommend exercising extreme caution, and that you remove your grey-market chips and have yourself refitted with one that will pass these checks. Burt's Bonanza in Kilper Station has plenty of these chips, available for a fee. Thank you to Burt's for sponsoring our segment today."

Carmen nodded, giving her an encouraging look.

Delia bit her lip, closing her eyes to the notes on her page. "We are pleased to announce that Cole Marion is no longer missing. His closest allies have been passing us information from a secure location to send out to his supporters across the Near Systems and beyond. He indicates his support for Ms. Allemande's candidacy and encourages any who live in Skelm or have the opportunity to rotate in for the election to give her your vote. After all, a vote for Emeline is a vote for change." Shame boiled in Delia's stomach like it hadn't since Turas-Mara, except now she was the one writing the propaganda. "He also wants The Scattered to know that he will lead you from this secure location, as there have been attempts on his life from Coalition Intelligence operatives. He will be meeting with Cassius Calvetti, leader of The Splintered, as soon as possible to discuss a treaty. Until this evening, that's all from us. I'm Delia Forrest, good day."

She set the headphones down and vomited into the bucket beneath her desk. She'd become exactly as bad as the Coalition.

Chapter 31

Cass drained her glass, setting it down hard on the bar. She glared at the radio even as Marv turned it off, the static fading with a loud click.

"Since when are you working with Cole Marion?" Marv asked, already lining up another shot of whiskey for her. "Seems strange, given the faction split."

"Your guess is as good as mine," she growled. "I don't have the slightest clue what in hells he's talking about, but it doesn't surprise me that he's off somewhere hiding while everyone else does the dirty work. It's becoming his standard mode of operations."

"Any ideas where he's headed?"

"No, although I imagine he'll be sending out feelers trying to figure out where I am. No doubt he won't use secure lines in an obvious bid to get me picked up by the Coalition, the slimy little rat." Cass swallowed down the second shot, relishing the burn as it flooded down her throat. It was one way to know that she wasn't dead. Not yet, anyway. "I'm betting he holed up on some backwater settlement or beacon somewhere, hiding in a bunker while he waits for most of this to blow over. Then he'll emerge, triumphant, convincing everyone that he was the one who orchestrated it all along." She slid the glass down the bar. "Fucking turnip."

"So what now?"

"Still trying to find out where Emeline Allemande put her sister. My contacts at the Administration Building here said they have no records of any prisoners being brought in that day, much less one that matches

Georgie's description." She sighed angrily, yanking frayed threads from the knees of her pants. "But once I find her, we need to get the hells off this rock. I need to get back to finding that gods-damned weapon that Zink got hold of, and I'd bet my left tit he's got it out at Lucent Base."

"Never been," Marv said, wiping out a glass. "Is it nice?"

"You won't have been, it's hidden by some of the most technologically advanced cloaking devices I've ever seen. If the Coalition goes down, it's going to be them that manage to do it, with all that tech and all those ships." Cass hissed out a breath. "I'm starting to wonder why I even bother."

"You can't help but bother. You're Cassius Calvetti."

"Yeah, and I never knew how much I wanted this until Cole Marion tried to take it away. Well, not tried, he did take it. Seated himself right at the helm before my body was even cold."

Marv raised an eyebrow and laughed. "You look pretty alive to me."

"Unfortunately. Being dead would be a damned sight more peaceful, and all the gods know it."

The door upstairs opened and closed with a faint jingle, and they both turned towards the stairs, waiting to see who would appear. The speakeasy had been quiet, empty over the past few days. Many had left Delta-4 with the intent to rotate into Skelm for the elections. Even more would leave now, after that damned radio broadcast.

Georgie gave a halfhearted wave, seating herself at the bar. "What did I miss?"

"Where in hells were you?" Cass demanded, resisting the urge to give her a hug. She felt oddly responsible for her, despite not knowing her all that well. "And how did you get out?"

Georgie raised her wrists, still bound by iron cuffs. A steel bolt dangled from the chain. "Emeline had me arrested. She locked me up in some block of offices, I didn't know where I was until I got out. It's on the far side of the city."

"Near the Administration Building," Marv supplied. "What can I get you?"

"Anything but oatmeal," Georgie answered. "And maybe something to get rid of these."

"I was looking for you, no one had any records. Your sister didn't report your arrest to the authorities here." He coughed lightly, clearing his throat.

"No, she didn't want it to stain her precious political reputation," Georgie spat acerbically. "That's all that matters to her now."

"Surely hiding it is worse than reporting you," Cass offered. "Getting it out in the open, and all that. Secrets fester, and they always come out in the wash."

"She didn't want people to be reminded of her affiliations with people like me."

"Pirates?"

"Rebels, I expect." Georgie held out the cuffs when Marv returned from the back with a wide-toothed saw. He cut through the chain, freeing her arms, but the cuffs remained intact. "I guess I just have a nice pair of bracelets now. Not really my thing, but I didn't get much of an option."

"I can pick that," Cass said, examining one of the cuffs. She pulled a spindly piece of metal from inside her jacket and got to work on the first one, popping it easily. "At least she didn't use digital cuff locks, those are harder to deal with." The second one released, and it fell to the floor with a loud clunk.

Georgie took a plate from Marv, setting it on the bar and loading up her fork with wilted leaves of spinach. "I guess we should be grateful that her campaign hasn't raised enough to spring for the newer models."

"We need to get out of Chalidon and off of Delta-4," Cass said. "Did you catch that radio broadcast? I think Cole is trying to smoke me out. He's wanting me to make myself known so that he can send the Coalition after me. Wherever he's hiding, it's somewhere safe and out of the way." Cass smacked herself on the forehead with her palm. "Of course," she said. "How could I have been so foolish? He made deals with Gregor Zink, sold off that weapon, he wants access to their tech. He's not in a settlement, he's on Lucent Base."

"Makes sense." Georgie cleared the plate in record time, laying her fork on top of the chipped porcelain with an ugly clatter. "Marv, any messages?"

"Nope," he said. "And I don't know if you caught it when your sister had you locked up, but you're going to have one hell of a time getting back home from here. No more trips to the transport beacon without notarized traveling papers. There was an incident and a few MPOs got smoked."

Georgie frowned. "I was expecting to come back to a flood of panic from Henry. She'd be home by now and wondering where in hells I am. But no messages? No ships headed back that way?" She tightened her ponytail, the flyaways framing her face. "She's gone and done something again, I just know it."

"Something like what?" Cass prompted when Marv didn't.

"I don't know, but it can't be good. Marv, can you get a secure line to Bradach?"

Marv shook his head. "I'm afraid not. Our line here has been compromised. Maybe that's why she hasn't sent word, there's nowhere to send it to."

"Or she didn't go home first. She got waylaid, or into trouble, or—" Georgie squeezed her eyes shut. "Or worse."

Cass ran her hands over the bar, snagging on bits of worn down wood. "Marv, are you sure you can't get a line out?"

"Not unless you want to guarantee we all get hauled in by some MPOs," he answered. "The only other ones I know of are in the Administration Building."

"We can't break in there for that, it would be wildly irresponsible. Georgie, come with me to Lucent Base, they'll have secure lines there."

Georgie's brow furrowed. "Do you really think Zink would let you use one?"

"It's not Zink I'm after, it's Cole, and I could take him in a fight if I had to. He lets everyone else do his fighting for him, he doesn't know what he's doing." Cass shrugged. "I know it's probably not the closest, but at least we can be sure we won't run into any Coalition there. And if something is going on in Bradach, we need to be careful."

"The broadcasts are still going out, that's a good sign," Marv said, leaning against the dark stained door frame. "No mention of anything in Bradach, and they always report that kind of thing."

"That still doesn't explain about Henry," Georgie said softly. "She should have been home by now."

"Maybe she is, and wasn't able to get word." Cass stood, extending her hand. "What do you say, Payne? Are you in?"

Georgie nodded, shaking her hand. "Best offer I've got right now. I can't stay here or Emeline might just change her mind on turning me in, or reporting that I was here in the first place. Can't get home the usual way, either."

"Let's get a move on." Cass nodded to Marv. "Stay safe. We might need this place in the near future, with the way things are going."

"I'll be here, same as always. Always a pleasure, Calvetti."

Cass climbed the stairs, blinking against the light when she reached the top. Daytime in Chalidon was always surprisingly bright, and it didn't help that she'd only been venturing out at night to reach her contacts across the city. Fewer eyes in the darkness, even if there were more patrols. Hoods could hide a lot about a face. "Let's get to the docks," she said over her shoulder. "Should be a transport out that way. Nothing direct to Lucent Base, obviously, but hopefully something heading for the Belt."

"And then what?" Georgie asked, matching her pace along the brick streets. "How do we get from a beacon in the Belt to Lucent Base?"

"I'll figure that out when we get there."

"Are there any beacons Obsidian Enclave are more likely to use? I mean, this side of the belt, most of those got obliterated by the blast at Terringgough Gulch."

Cass stopped, staring up at the terraformed sky like it would give her the answers, and for once, it did. "You're a gods-damned genius."

"No one's ever accused me of that before, but I guess there's a first time for everything." Georgie sidestepped a gouge in the street, the cracked bricks around it crumbling. "Henry is the smart one of the two of us."

"You've got brains too, Payne."

"You sound like my mother."

"Your mother is one of the smartest people I've met," Cass countered. "Smart enough to stay out of this gods-damned war."

"I'm not sure being a medic and refugee organizer is the definition of staying out of it."

"She's helping people heal, and that's more than I can say for me or most of the rest of us getting caught up in all of this. When it's all over, people like me will be forgotten, and rightfully so. I don't even know what I'm doing half the time, but she knows her own mind in a way I can only hope that I will."

Georgie smirked. "I'd tell her that you said that, but it might inflate her ego too much."

"I doubt that. Sandrine is a lovely woman. Raised some amazing daughters."

"Two amazing daughters, at least."

Cass shot her a look. "Stop discounting yourself. You got your family out of Skelm, you've been keeping things running back in Bradach."

"I wasn't discounting myself, I was discounting Emeline." Georgie sighed. "I really thought that if I could just talk to her on her own ground, she might hear me. I guess not."

"She has a lot to consider. The High Council wants her dead." Cass glanced around, a new and disconcerting habit she'd picked up. Always afraid she was being followed, she scanned the thin crowd for familiar faces, but thankfully, found none, memorizing these new ones in case there was another spy in the mix. Part of her hoped she'd see Olivia chasing after her with a knife. At least she knew how to deal with that. "And half the media wants to help them."

"All the more reason for her to accept my help, then!" Georgie shot back, kicking a loose chunk of brick down the street, and it bounced underneath a perfectly shining, parked steamcar. "But no, Emeline always has to do everything all by herself. Did you know that when I was getting my family out of Skelm, she sneaked off the Cricket to stay there?"

"No, but it doesn't surprise me."

"It's a damned good thing she did, because I wouldn't have survived without her there with me. We were so close, we shared everything, now she's just another stranger." Georgie growled under her breath. "And now I can't get in touch with Henry or anyone back home. It's all a mess."

"It's usually a mess, I'm learning." Cass shielded her eyes against the glare of the glass-paneled buildings that rose up out of the ground like blinding leaves. "That's why we're going to go to Lucent Base, kick Cole Marion's pathetic ass, and get you in touch with Henry. Then we can win this damned war and go home."

Georgie was quiet for a moment before she replied. "I wasn't supposed to tell anyone, but we were trying for a baby."

Cass didn't say anything, not knowing what was coming next. She didn't look elated, so maybe congratulations weren't in order. She clamped her jaw shut, scanning the docks on the horizon for a ship that would be heading to the Belt.

"It didn't take. We'll try again, of course, but I don't know, I guess I got all excited for nothing. I'd hoped so hard it would work, you know?"

Cass didn't know, having no inclination for being a mother, but she nodded anyway. "I'm sorry to hear that."

"I just want to get back to her because I know she's not taking it well. She was being so strange before she left here, like she was hiding something."

"We'll get you back there, Georgie."

"Yeah." Georgie bumped her shoulder against Cass'. "Thanks, Calvetti."

"Oh, this is purely selfish. I don't enjoy traveling alone, and it's what I do most of the time. Having some company is a nice change of pace."

"I'm not convinced you have a selfish bone in your body," Georgie said. "Not from what I've seen."

"They're there, they just manifest in strange ways. What happened with Guisette was probably selfish."

"It worked out, though."

Cass chuckled. "Yeah, maybe it's a sign that my permanent bad luck is changing. Assuming she didn't fly straight back to Tarand to sell us all out, that is."

"I feel like we would have known that by now."

"You'd think, but she's quite possibly the most manipulative woman I've ever known. Lies like she's breathing. You should have seen her with Gregor Zink, some story about being an admin data pusher named Anna Francis. Rolled right off her tongue like it was nothing, not even a flinch."

"Gods, you really do have it bad for her," Georgie said with an indelicate snort of laughter. "No wonder you almost tanked negotiations."

"I'm not the one who fired a missile at an old mining camp wired to the brim with explosive charges, now am I?" Cass retorted, laughing along with her. "Gods, I hope I see her again. I'm not sure any other woman would ever measure up."

Georgie wrinkled her nose, teasing. "And I thought Mae and Bailey were too much."

"Look there, the departure board," Cass said, pointing. "Bay seventeen, out towards the rim. Heading to the Belt."

"That's a Coalition vessel, Calvetti. Are you trying to get us killed?"

"It's a freighter, not a frigate. I'll bet it has a skeleton crew. They're stretched awfully thin these days."

Georgie shook her head. "I think we should wait for an independent ship. If we get caught stowing away on that thing, I'll be back in iron cuffs in an instant, and if you don't mind, I just got out of some."

"I'll make you a deal. We go hang out on the dock and watch that freighter. If there are more than three MPOs, we wait." Cass grinned at her expectedly, waiting to win her over.

"Fine, but if we get caught, Henry is going to kill you."

"I believe it."

"You should, she's ruthless. Once pushed Allemande down an elevator shaft."

Cass folded her arms over her chest, suppressing a laugh. "Shame it didn't kill her. That woman is a thorn in everyone's side."

"You're telling me," Georgie grumbled. "Split my family down the middle and continues to climb ladders. You heard she's High Council now, right?"

"Unfortunately." Cass leaned against a street lamp, tugging her hood over the top half of her face as she watched the freighter being loaded. Three dock hands were scuttling back and forth like crabs, ferrying crates onto the ship. There wasn't one MPO to be seen. "So far, so good," she mumbled.

"I thought they were packing these full of guards, given all the newspaper headlines about piracy."

"It's a scapegoat. These things have been struggling to keep up with shipping demands, so my contacts tell me they've suspended the regulations for staffing. But they don't want the public to know that, because it's easier to enrage people with piracy than to actually fix the rotting infrastructure of your failing government."

"You sound like Emeline."

"She has a lot of good ideas, Georgie. She's smart. I know things are fraught, but give it some time. Let her win this election and get settled, let's get on the other side of this war that's almost at an outbreak. You might be surprised."

"I doubt it."

"They're closing the loading doors," Cass said, pushing off the lamp post. "It's now or never, Payne."

"Gods be damned," Georgie hissed. "Fine, let's go."

They sauntered across the dock, casual, relaxed, and then, just before the overhead door latched, dove into the loading bay of the C.S. Stronghold's Revenge.

Chapter 32

The port in the Capital was just how Bailey remembered it: busy, crowded, and borderline incomprehensible. She was about to step off the loading bay ramp of the transport when Wilhemina yanked her backwards.

"What do you think you're doing?" she hissed.

"I thought we were going to the Archives," Bailey answered, twisting out of her grip. "In order to get there, we have to leave the ship."

"Allemande will have reported what happened as soon as we left Turas-Mara. Neither of us can be seen here, but we sure as shitting hells can't be seen together." Wilhemina pulled a ratty cloak around her shoulders, pulling up the hood. "I'm hoping they haven't pulled my authorization yet, or we're never getting in there. It's sealed up tighter than an officer's—"

"Willa," Bailey interrupted, "why wouldn't they have pulled it? You just said Allemande would have reported it."

"She won't have reported you. She'd get kicked off her precious High Council for aiding and abetting when it became obvious that it wasn't in fact me sucking the tongue out of Gerard Machenet's daughter in a broom closet. Or me making all those trade deals that were so advantageous to her sector that she was able to boost herself into one of the highest seats in the land." Wilhemina tossed a cap to Bailey. "Here, wear this. I got it at that beacon where we ditched my shuttle. Stuff your hair up in it."

"My hair?"

"Yes, Bailey, your hair. It's recognizable."

"Says the woman with the face scar."

"I can't shove my face in a hat, now can I? That's why I have the hood." Wilhemina's arms raised up, and then with a shake of her head, they fell back to her sides. "Be careful."

"What if one of us gets caught?"

"Then we're both as good as dead, so I don't recommend it. Don't talk to anyone. Don't be seen by anyone, either. There's a tavern here, the Dark Owl—"

"It's not here anymore," Bailey said quickly, trying to stem the flow of guilt and grief that flooded into her. "Marina Sykes is dead."

Wilhemina blinked. "Dead? I hadn't heard that."

"No, I suppose you were too busy out at the Rim to care that you handing her over to save our asses got her killed."

"She was just a tavern owner, it would have been a slap on the wrist, maybe a month in a work camp at a push. She can't be dead, you must have misheard."

Bailey resisted the urge to shove her backwards, or punch her, or run off the ship and find the first vessel headed towards home. "She's dead, Willa, and it's our fault. They charged her with treason to smoke out Cassius Calvetti."

"That doesn't make any sense."

"Nothing about the Coalition does." Bailey blinked back the tears rapidly gathering in the corners of her eyes and tugged on the cap, shoving her hair up to the top of her head. "Should I meet you at the Archives tonight?"

"No, I'll go alone. Too much of a risk to be seen together."

"Willa—"

"If I need your help, I'll ask for it. Here's a radio, its radius is limited, so don't go wandering off. Channel seven. Assume everything can and will be heard, so don't get wild with it."

"Why am I even here if I'm only going to be sneaking around, looking for places to hide until you do the dirty work of breaking into the Archives?"

"Because if everything goes to plan, I won't have to break in. You're here in case the plan goes to shit." Wilhemina sighed, pushing the stray hairs stuck to her forehead out of her face. "Don't get yourself killed."

"I'll try."

"I mean it, Bailey."

"Alright, Willa, I heard you the first time." Bailey stepped off the transport, squinting into the uncomfortably bright Gamma-3 sunshine. Even after just a few seconds, she could have sworn she could feel her face crisping and burning under the rays. She stepped off the docks and onto the adjoining street. This time, there was no Davey Klein around to whisk her off to a fancy hotel. She was on her own, at least until Wilhemina got what they came for.

Mae was probably going to kill her if the guards didn't do it first. Bailey grimaced at the thought, slipping into a dark, empty bookstore. The door jingled when it closed, the latch not quite catching. It smelled like Hjarta somehow, a dusty, old smell that was like being catapulted back to her home.

Her home, which didn't even exist anymore. It was taken from her, just like everything else. Her mothers. Her people. She sighed, running her fingers along the pristine leather spines. Her sister, and Mae too, most likely. Women like Mae didn't sit around waiting for their wayward lovers to wander home. She was a force of nature, and everyone knew it. Beautiful, accomplished, whip-smart, and kind, she was everything Bailey wasn't.

"Can I help you?" a bored voice asked.

"Just looking," Bailey replied, making a clumsy effort to alter her voice to sound lighter and chirpier than it usually was. "Just browsing, hoping for inspiration to strike."

"Whatever. Just don't touch anything."

Bailey wandered up one aisle and down the next, reading the titles embossed in gold or purple, every single one of them a rousing endorsement for the Coalition. It was strange. What good was a bookstore if all the books told the same story? Every tome filled with the same plot of advancement thanks to the Coalition, rescue thanks to the Coalition, everything thanks to the gods-damned Coalition.

She frowned, swallowing back the desire to set fire to the place. Coming back to the Capital had been a silly, foolish idea, and now that she was there, it was all coming into sharp focus. Selfishness. People were suffering, dying, and she was worried about wondering why she and Wilhemina were related. It was shallow and self-indulgent, and the shame of it pooled in her feet, rising up through her legs and guts like ignited fuel.

She had to get back to Mae. Back to Bradach, back to Captain Marshall, back to where she could be of use, and not skulking around one of the most dangerous places for her in the whole of the Near Systems and probably beyond. She'd taken four steps back towards the docks when the radio buzzed with static at her hip.

"Hello?" she spoke into it, slipping into a dingy alley. "Are you there?"

The radio returned nothing but static. Bailey checked the channel, frowning when she realized it was already correct. "What's going on?" Bailey asked, more urgently this time.

Once again, the only transmission was a thick, garbled static, like someone was trying to talk through a tunnel.

The tunnel. Had they already picked Wilhemina up? Bailey froze, heart thudding in her ears.

"Gods be damned into fucking hells," she hissed, heading towards the tunnel. It was going to be a long walk, one she'd made before but hadn't wanted to repeat.

If they had already nabbed her, and were taking her through the tunnel, what was over there? The hotel, to be sure, and the gardens, but everything else was centralized in the Capital. The Armory, the Administration Building, the Executive Building, those were all in the same district, not far from where the Dark Owl had been.

Even the thought of the tavern twisted in Bailey's stomach. She never should have given Marina Sykes up, and Marina was dead as a result. None of them had saved her, none had been able to, not even Cass, who was in a cell in the next hallway over. Bailey cracked her knuckles one at a time, an old habit she'd tried to cease, because it always drove Mae to shoot her dirty looks across the dinner table.

What if they hadn't taken Wilhemina through the tunnel? What if the interference was something different, like a basement of a building? What if they already had her in a cell in the Executive Building? Bailey covered her face with her hands and groaned audibly. She wasn't cut out for it. Not last time, and not standing with her hair shoved into a too-small cap, either. It was starting to give her a headache, having all that hair stuffed up there.

If Wilhemina had been arrested, then it wouldn't be long before they pulled her chip authorization. Bailey still had the chip from Officer Jones in her arm, inert, but it would work with a boost of electricity. She'd just have to convince someone to give her one, and hope that whoever worked the front desk at the Archives didn't read the newspaper, because she'd been all over the front page not too long ago.

* * *

By the time night fell, Bailey's feet were aching from being on them all day, walking up one street and down the next, wasting time, worrying, concocting wild stories in her head about how the Coalition already knew she was in the city and had sent Intelligence agents to tail her, that Wilhemina was enduring the gods only knew what in some dank cell in a basement, that Mae was already writing her off to be with someone else.

Amy and Aran were long gone, and so was their bakery. The Dark Owl was dark, but Bailey could only give it a sideways glance from three streets over, the guilt being too much to face head on. She was alone and friendless in the Capital again, except this time her face was recognizable. This time, there was no Mae to bail her out when she messed it all up.

The Archives was an odd building, domed with glass and set between all of the other Coalition edifices. The lawns leading up to the door were lush and cared for with precision, every topiary expertly sculpted, telling the story of the rise of the Coalition to come together and stamp out piracy and crime. It was a strange, threatening kind of beauty to be portrayed, and Bailey shivered as she walked past them.

Flowers lined the sidewalk, thick and lush, all of them yellow or purple, except the ones that were both. An ocean of dedication to the Coalition, presented with enough flora to overload the sinuses with its thick pollen. Bailey sneezed twice before she reached the front doors, also rounded and inlaid with metal so pristine it must have been platinum. She wouldn't expect anything less from the Coalition, not after all the displays of excess she'd seen.

With a deep breath, she laid a hand on the door, ready to push inside, when a pair of strong hands dragged her backwards into the bushes. She gasped, ready to fight but unable to see her assailant in the growing blackness.

"What in hells are you doing?" Wilhemina hissed. "I told you to steer clear of this place!"

"The radio made a sound, I thought they nabbed you!" Bailey shot back.

Wilhemina rolled her eyes, glittering in the glare of distant street lamps. "A sound. You were about to break into the Archives and almost certainly get caught, because the radio made a sound."

"It sounds ridiculous when you put it like that."

"It is ridiculous. Are you fundamentally incapable of following orders?"

Bailey tugged her arm free. "No, I was trying to get the information before they inevitably pulled your chip and locked everything down."

"What, you were just going to waltz in there and take the documents, and think that they'd all just let you?"

"No, obviously not," Bailey retorted with a noisy huff. "I still have a Coalition chip in my arm. It's been deactivated, but it might have worked if I could convince someone that it had been killed with an electromagnetic pulse."

Wilhemina raised an eyebrow. "What security classification is it?"

"I don't know, I used it for most things when I was pretending to be you."

"I'd always assumed that someone had copied my chip somehow. Where'd yours come from?"

Bailey chewed on her lip, unsure of how much to share. "Marshall. I don't know where he got it from, could be anywhere. Could be a rebel movement, could just be someone making duplicates for a few extra credits."

"And here I thought it was the result of a highly coordinated campaign. Apparently not."

"I did try to tell you that when you had me chained up in your office."

Wilhemina pinched her arm. "Don't say it like that, you make me sound as bad as Allemande. I couldn't very well let you run around, you probably would have sent your rebel pirate friends a signal flare or something and spelled out prison for both of us."

"Whatever you say, Willa."

Wilhemina sighed heavily. "It's an automated system at night, and if you have a high enough clearance—which I do, barring it being revoked—you don't have to talk to anyone."

"That's useful."

"Almost like I actually know what I'm doing." Wilhemina smirked and gave Bailey a sideways glance. "If you jump over the turnstile you should be able to follow me in, we just have to avoid triggering the motion sensors too far apart."

"Why didn't you say that before, at the docks? I could have come with you the whole time."

"Because I'm trying to keep you out of trouble, but you seem hells-bent on finding it anyway. Come on, follow me. Stay close. There's no attendant this late at night, but we don't need to be taking any unnecessary risks."

"Like breaking into the Archives to find out why we're related?"

Wilhemina grimaced, the faint scar on her face scrunched up. "Exactly like that."

The door was lighter than Bailey had expected, and she almost stumbled as a result. She stuck close behind Wilhemina, holding her breath as the chip scanned. A light flashed green and the turnstile clicked forward, much to her surprise. She hadn't realized until it worked that she'd been anticipating an alarm. Breathing a sigh of relief, Bailey jumped the turnstile behind her, following so close that it would have looked comical to any onlookers.

"Where is this file?"

"My guess is the redacted section. Top level clearance."

"And you have that?"

"Apparently still, yes." Wilhemina led them through a labyrinth of corridors and rooms, some larger than others, all of them lined with books, binders, and fat files stuffed to the gills. Everything was white inside the Archives except the spines of the books. The walls, the marble floors, the window trim, even the signs warning them to turn in any and all materials before exiting the building or face a charge of treason.

"I guess they take things seriously here," Bailey muttered after they passed the fifth sign of its kind.

"Can't have any interlopers learning state secrets, now can we?" Wilhemina asked, her tone dripping with sarcasm. "Here we go, redacted family affairs."

The room was larger than Bailey had anticipated, one of the largest in the facility that she'd seen so far. "Wow," she breathed, reaching out for a file.

Wilhemina smacked her hand lightly. "Don't touch anything. If something happens, they'll dust this whole place for prints. Despite our likeness, we don't share those. I'm also taller than you, not that it matters."

Bailey snorted a laugh, leaning against the wall. "No you aren't, I'm taller. You just wear those enormous boots all the time."

"Horseshit."

"Whatever you say, Willa."

"Shut up and let me concentrate. We don't have all night." Wilhemina pulled one box of files, and then the next, flipping through folders one at a time, her frown deepening with every unhelpful page. "I don't understand why it's not here. I've checked for my records, for yours, and there's nothing."

"Did you check our mothers' files?"

"Your mothers, not mine."

"Did you?"

"Fine." Wilhemina replaced one box and pulled another, setting it on the table. She rifled through it before replacing the lid. "General medical files, nothing from the time she would have been—you know—and nothing after, either."

"What about another room?" Bailey asked. "Another room for redacted family stuff?"

Wilhemina shook her head. "No, this is the only room for that. Whatever answers there were, they've been destroyed."

"I thought you said nothing is ever really destroyed in the Archives!"

"I thought so too, but there's nothing here, Bailey!"

Bailey growled under her breath, glancing through the small window in the white door across the corridor. "What's that room for?"

"It's for documentation on abandoned experimentation. Weapons, mostly."

"What if there's information in there about the superweapon?" Bailey asked, already pushing through the door, using the sleeve of her jumpsuit. She couldn't not look, not when she was so close.

"Bailey, no!" Wilhemina hissed, struggling to shove the box back before she followed Bailey through the door. "The motion sensors!"

"Keep up, then," Bailey said, charging across the corridor. She couldn't give Wilhemina the time to think about it or she'd never be able to see if there was anything in there that could help turn the tide of the war.

"The superweapon wasn't abandoned, that information won't even be in the Archives yet because it's an active and ongoing project!"

"There could be something though, right?" Bailey countered, pressing through the door with her hip. "Some shred of something?"

"No, it's—"

Bailey cut her off with a wave of her hand. The room was smaller than the previous one, lined with shelves. She grabbed the largest one and dropped it on the table, tearing off the lid.

"Bailey, your prints!" Wilhemina protested, scrubbing them from the box with the edge of her coat. "You have to be careful, let me do it." She wrested the box from Bailey, pulling a file from the front. "What in hells is the Alaric Protocol?" she muttered.

"How should I know, I—"

"Shh." Wilhemina scanned through one file after the next, the crease in the center of her forehead deepening. "There are hundreds of names here. More than would ever be involved in a standard lab project. It was relatively short term, studies were only done for seven years before the project was thrown out."

"So there's nothing about any active weaponry in here?" Bailey asked, tempted to pull another box from the shelves but conscious of the motion sensors lining the walls in the room. Where the previous room only had one, this room had ten.

"No, I told you that already. We'd need to get into the Armory for that, but I wouldn't make it past the front desk without being recognized." Wilhemina continued to leaf through the pages. "This study started a year before I was born. There are so many family names listed in these files."

Bailey leaned over. "For what?"

"That's what I can't figure out yet. The study was pulled so abruptly, most of the information wasn't even compiled correctly. The files are incomplete, it's hard to say."

"What could they have been doing with children?" Bailey asked. "It's not like most of them can even throw a grenade, much less pilot a ship."

Wilhemina pulled one file from the box, spreading it out on the table. Belinda Stockton and Herbert Baer was emblazoned on the front in thick black print, both beneath a red stamp that read *deceased*. "I don't know what this is," Wilhemina said.

"Who in hells was Herbert Baer?" Bailey asked, swallowing hard.

The next file to be laid on the table read Belinda Stockton and Heinrich Stewarton. Wilhemina stared at Bailey from the corner of her eye. "I guess we have to look at them."

"I mean, it's what we came for." Bailey's glance flicked around at the rest of the room. "I didn't expect to find it here."

"Me neither."

"You promise you didn't know?"

Wilhemina nodded solemnly. "I swear it." She opened the first file and recoiled gently. "It's me. Photos, birth date, medical records." She shuffled through it slowly, and Bailey's hands were burning to reach for her own. "Bailey, it was an experiment to test how to raise Coalition-compliant children."

"Why?"

"To raise them for the military." Wilhemina's breath caught in her throat and she bent, breathing heavily. "They separated me from my birth parents in order to raise me into becoming exactly what I became." She snapped the file shut, reaching for the second. "Yours is incomplete. Your—our—mother took off right after the lab informed her that she was with child again. She was part of some—some sort of family sciences division."

"She wouldn't have left you if she had the chance."

"I don't think I'll get the answer to that question in files like these. I can't know what she was thinking." A strangled sob escaped Wilhemina's throat, and she braced herself against the table. "My adopted mother always said I was born to be a soldier. I guess she was telling me the truth all along."

"I'm sorry, Willa." Bailey reached out for her, but her sister pulled away.

"You would have been too, if she hadn't run." Wilhemina gave her a strange, crooked smile. "You never would have survived basic training. No wonder this fucking experiment got dropped."

"I never did like taking orders."

"Yeah me neither, that's why I aimed to be a general. At least then it was me calling the shots." Wilhemina closed the files, placing them back into the box. "What a wasted life I've lived."

"It's not wasted, you're here now." Bailey leaned her head against Wilhemina's shoulder. "With me."

"I'm going to burn this place to the ground. Not the Archives, the Coalition," Wilhemina said after a long moment. "Every one of the people involved in this has a right to know what happened to them. Aren't you friendly with that broadcaster Delia Forrest?"

Bailey nodded. "I am."

"We're going to blow this thing wide open. This is going to shake the foundations of the government, of the High Council itself."

In an instant, the room went black, the only light coming from the emergency lamps in the corridors outside the rooms, dimly lighting the path out of the building. "Motion sensor?" Bailey whispered.

"No. Get down. Someone's here."

Bailey crawled beneath the table, shoving herself up against the solid wall of it. It was a tight, uncomfortable fit.

Boot heels clicked down the corridor, coming to a stop outside their door. It opened without a sound, the light flickering through the glass.

"General Fineglass, how good of you to return to the Capital."

"Councilor Tarand, always a pleasure."

"Your identity chip was logged the moment you entered the building, which triggered an alert. Did you know that disappearing from your station without a word is tantamount to treason?" the councilor asked. "Or did you just forget?"

"I had sensitive information about Overseer—Councilor Allemande that could only be delivered in person."

"Interesting, then, that I found you in the Archives." The councilor approached, her boots loud against the marble. "What's this?"

"Nothing," Wilhemina said, replacing the box on its shelf. "I was hoping to find more information about Councilor Allemande's daughter. I know that her parentage is rather... rebellious."

"Indeed. Olivia, dearest, finish cleaning up these misplaced files, and be sure to check for any anomalies across the hall. We wouldn't want anyone knowing we were here, would we?"

"Of course not, ma'am," Olivia answered.

"General, with me, please," the councilor said firmly. "It seems we have much to discuss."

Chapter 33

Violet threw the wrench onto the ground, and it bounced along the boiler room floor with an angry clatter. "Gods be damned into every known hell," she hissed, slumping against the boiler. "It just won't start up."

"Won't be long before we're towed into the Capital docks, Boss," Ned announced from the doorway. "I don't think we can get her up and running in time."

"Not without Alice," Violet agreed, doing her best to ignore the empty ache in her chest where her wife should have been. For all she knew, Josie could have shoved her out of an airlock at the first opportunity, and even the edges of that thought were too much for Violet to bear. She cleared her throat and looked up at her navigator. "I swear this damned ship only answers to her."

"It's a shame Josie didn't take me instead. At least then you could have gotten clear." He shifted, tracing the tattoos on his arms, his grey shirt rolled up to the elbows. "The other preparations are done, Kady and I just finished."

"That's something, at least."

"Loading bay door reinforced, the airlock secured."

Violet nodded. "I doubt it will be enough, but it's something."

"We'd follow you into the hells themselves," Ned replied quietly. "You know that, Boss, don't you?"

"That's good, because I'm fairly certain that's where I'm leading us." Violet rubbed at the bridge of her nose, constantly aware of the pulsing headache that hadn't left since Alice had. "Our only saving grace is that they must think this ship is empty. No comms, no nothing since they started dragging us through dark space."

"It let the solar generators charge the air filtration, at least."

"I'd say it was a small mercy, but I don't know what's on the other end of this for us. It's possible that it's going to be a prolonged doom." Violet stood, brushing the greasy dust from her knees, "But there's still a small chance we get out of this alive. If we do, it's getting off Gamma-3 that will be the bigger challenge."

"One I'd hoped I wouldn't be repeating quite so soon," Ned grumbled.

"But think of the stories you'll have to tell at the Pig," Violet said, playfully elbowing him in the ribs. "You'll be a folk hero."

"We both know that's the only reason I left the Coalition in the first place. It used to get me plenty of dates with dashing men."

"You could still get those dates, Nedrick."

He smirked, nudging her off. "Yeah, yeah."

"One of us has to use these stories, I'm already married and we all know Kady isn't interested."

"Kady is married too, but it's to her lab."

"And thank the gods for that," Violet said. "We'd all have been dead a long time ago without her." She closed the door to the boiler room and threaded a padlock through the latch. There was no sense in making things any easier for the Coalition rats that would board and strip the ship for parts. "I'm gonna miss this old girl. I never thought I'd be saying goodbye like this."

"None of us did, Boss."

"I thought I'd retire with Alice when this was all over, you know? Find a nice little place, get a dog, leave all this to you and Kady and the rest of them. Ivy's more than capable of being lead mechanic now." The nostalgia of a future she'd almost surely lost pulled the faint smile from her face. "But even if this hadn't happened, even if Josie hadn't turned up to make everything worse all over again, we still lost two of the best medics the Near Systems have ever seen."

"She had to stay, Boss."

"I know. But I feel we've lost them forever."

Ned rested an arm around her shoulders and squeezed lightly. "We'll see them again."

"Hopefully not inside a prison cell."

"Please, we both know Hyun could talk her way out of anything. She'd gamble with our lives and win."

Violet snorted a laugh. "You're right about that, Ned." She sighed again, leaning into his huge, solid frame. "It's been one hell of a ride," she said quietly.

"It has."

"No regrets?"

"None," Kady answered, rounding the corner of the corridor. "I set a trap in all of our quarters," she said, her arms folded across her chest. "I hope the Coalition likes flames."

"One last hurrah," Violet said. "I'm sorry the ship isn't going to you."

"If we make it out of this, you can owe me one," Kady replied. "I accept payment in the form of ships and not getting publicly executed."

"If I manage the latter for us, then I'll work on the former, how about that?" Violet countered.

"Deal."

The ship began to shudder and shake as they descended through Gamma-3's atmosphere, heralding their reluctant return to a planet they'd all hoped they'd left behind.

"Weapons at the ready," Violet said gravely, unholstering her pistol. "We don't fire unless there's no way out, in which case we make a damned spectacle. On my mark."

"Aye," Ned replied, hoisting the huge heat gun that had been propped against the wall. He held it over his shoulder, glowing orange as it fired up.

"Captain, it's been a pleasure," Kady said, pulling a short-barreled shotgun from the inside of her long-tailed coat. "No matter what happens, know that I've loved you both."

"Knock it off, Riha," Ned grumbled through a strangled sob. "You're going to make me cry again, and we all know my aim is shit through tears."

"Channel it into rage, Beckett, we all know you're a beast from the hells with that heat gun," Kady retorted, tossing him a smirk.

"They're setting us down," Violet said, glancing out the porthole window. "Let's get to the underbelly before we hit the dock." She followed Ned down one corridor, and then the next, until they all climbed down into the old secret hold beneath the bridge. She twisted the hatch closed, securing the door just as the ship touched the ground, almost throwing her from the ladder.

"Got your back, Boss," Ned said, bracing her from behind. "As always."

"Are you ready, Nedrick?" Violet asked, nodding at the heat gun. "It's time."

"I was born ready," he replied, turning to the floor. He fired the heat gun into the metal grate flooring, the red-hot bolts shooting clean through, tearing the ship apart and leaving smoldering steel in their wake.

Kady kicked the loose metal, clearing a hole just wide enough for them all to fit through. "Let's get the hells out of here before anyone figures out this ship wasn't abandoned." She jumped through, landing on the wood below. She nodded up at Ned, who followed with a louder thump.

Violet took one last look at her ship, the one thing she'd kept from the Coalition. Rescued from a scrap yard so long ago, it had saved her more times than she could count. A sob caught in her throat but she swallowed it back, because there would be time for tears later, but not for escape. She leaped through the jagged hole and staggered to her feet the moment her boots touched the docks. "Get clear of her," she hissed, motioning for the other two to follow her.

Past one ship and then another, she couldn't resist taking one last look at the Cricket over her shoulder as it was dragged up onto the docks, the workers already inspecting it for damage and scrap value. Her heart was heavy with guilt and failure, shame rising up in her like magma, hot and inescapable. She tore her eyes away, trying not to see the tears in Ned's eyes, or the fear on Kady's face.

The end of the docks came abruptly, a small wrought-iron fence marking the edge of the last bay. Violet leaped over it easily, holding out her hand for Ned to follow. He took it, lumbering over the metal with a grimace.

"Ditch the heat gun, Nedrick. Kady, stow your weapon." Violet holstered her revolver, squinting into the bright sunlight. "Gods, how I wish we knew someone in this gods-forsaken, gods-damned city."

Marina Sykes' name hung heavy in the air, unsaid, but they all tensed, and Violet immediately regretted saying anything at all. She grimaced, shaking her head. "There has to be someone here we know. Some connection we can use to get out of here as soon as possible."

"Is the Dark Owl gone? Really gone?" Ned asked quietly.

"Yeah," Violet answered. "It's gone. Calvetti said it was looted and empty. Marina's co-owner was still there, but hiding. Squatting really, and I doubt she's still there."

"Better lead than nothing," Kady said, shielding her eyes from the sun. "Gods, it's bright here. How does anyone see anything? I feel half-blind from this light."

"You don't remember it?" Ned asked, holding his face up to it. "The warmth on your skin?"

"I remember being inside of a lab most of the time," Kady replied. "Usually windowless. Couldn't let the general public see what we were working on, or the Coalition would have been done years ago." She sighed, stretching her arms over her head. "You good to walk, Ned? It's about half a mile from here."

"So long as I don't have to walk back," he grumbled, unfolding a cane from his pocket. "It's a good thing this isn't Skelm, I don't think I could handle the hills."

"None of us can handle those damned hills," Violet interjected. "Sent from the hells." She stepped up onto the sidewalk, and the others followed, blending into the morning crowd. She was grateful for the rush hour, it made them less conspicuous, less noticeable, and if it had been even a few hours later, they may not have even made it off the docks without being noticed.

It had been years since she'd been back to Gamma-3, and there was an odd feeling of familiarity swirling with a distinct presence of threat as she followed Ned up the street. She'd never lived in the Capital, but she'd been there enough as a cadet in training to know that the city had changed.

It wasn't just the shops that were different, it was the blurred landscape at the horizon, barely visible through the newer buildings that had sprung up long after she'd left for the last time in a stolen ship from the scrapyard. The city bustled with people, but there was a coldness hanging over the crowds, despite the warmth from the sun. The Coalition had pressed its populace down into a manageable conformity, almost like automatons, as they moved from one street to the next. She'd never missed the safety and vibrancy of Bradach more.

"It's on your left," Ned announced with a nod, after what felt like an eternity of walking. His gait was uneven, pained, and guilt flooded into Violet once more. "The sign has been taken down, but that's it."

Violet eased around to the back alley, knocking on the door. "Hello?" she called softly. "We're friends of—" she stopped herself, shaking her head. How dare she use Marina's name for their own gain, when none of them had moved to save her? "We're friends," she said.

"No such thing," a voice said from inside. "Piss off."

"We know Cassius Calvetti," Kady offered.

"Then you're no friends of mine. She promised she'd save Marina, and she didn't."

Violet cleared her throat. "We'd like to help you get off Gamma-3, if you'll help us find some contacts."

"No one gets out of this gods-forsaken city, not without the proper chips." The door opened a crack, and a pale, sunken-cheeked woman peered out, scraggly blond hair a halo around her face. "Who are you?"

"Captain Violet Vear. Our ship broke down in dark space. We were snagged by Coalition scrappers and towed back here."

"Then you're lucky to be alive." The woman sighed. "I'm Aven." She pushed the door open further. "You're attracting too much attention. Come inside."

"Thank you," Violet said earnestly, closing the door behind them and lowering the wooden bar over the frame. "We're sorry for your loss."

Aven stared at Ned. "It's you."

"Aye," he replied. "I never got to thank you for your hospitality last time."

"Marina always liked you. Said you were funny, you know. And you always helped out." Aven tilted her head, staring. "You made that nice soup."

"Can do again, if you've got ingredients."

"I don't have much here other than a few sprouting potatoes and onions, and whatever was left in the kitchen. I've never been much of a cook."

Ned was already pulling a dusty, stained apron from a hook, limping behind the counter. "I'll make that work."

"Marina always said you'd be back someday." Aven pulled a faded, tattered cloak around herself, grasping at the frayed edges. "Said someone like you is always in trouble. Good trouble, she said."

"I don't know about good, but I do know about trouble," Ned replied, already scrubbing potatoes in the thin stream of water from the faucet. "She was a remarkable woman."

"So you can get me out of here?" Aven asked quietly.

"We can sure as hells try," Violet interjected. "We just need a place to lay low while we figure some things out."

"You'll need Coalition-issued chips for everyone, no exceptions. You won't manage to stow away, there are too many checks at the docks here. Three inspections before the ships are allowed to take off."

Violet nodded. "Which is why I haven't been back in a very long time. What about the trains?"

"They've been doing random checks, pulling people out and sending them to work camps directly," Aven answered. "The airships are the same, and besides, no one can afford those anymore, not unless you're a high-ranking officer or something."

"What about The Scattered? Are there any underground cells here?"

"Not that I know of. There were a few, but they left with Calvetti." Aven face twisted into a deep frown, and she turned away, her eyes squeezed shut. "Not only did she fail to save Marina, she took away my last chance at escape."

"The Coalition fired on Terringgough Gulch," Kady explained. "Cass went there to try to free Marina. She made deals and held up her end in trying to get her freed. The High Council killed her, anyway."

"I suppose you're with her, then," Aven said bitterly. "The Splintered."

"In a sense," Ned replied. "We're just trying to survive the war and help as many as we can."

Aven took a deep breath, exhaling slowly. "And yet, you come to my door looking for assistance."

"There aren't many doors open to us in the Capital, so for that, we thank you." Ned diced the vegetables, allowing the silence to permeate the room before he continued as he scraped the pieces into the pot from the cutting board. "I'm surprised to find you here."

"Not many places left to go, as you said."

"If we can just stay a night or two, try to figure this out, then we'll make sure you come with us when we leave," Ned promised. "Calvetti had one hell of a tail when she broke out. As far as we're aware, no one knows we were even on our ship when it got dragged back here. As long as we move quietly and carefully, we might have a shot."

Aven sighed. "If it wasn't for him, I wouldn't have let the other two of you stay."

"I understand," Violet said carefully, a tiny glimmer of relief pricking through the darkness. "Ned is right, we promise we will find a way for all of us to get out. All of us, or none of us."

"I've heard that before, and I'm always left behind."

"On my honor as a captain, I will not."

"I'll believe it when I see it," Aven shot back. "Do you know anyone else in the Capital? Someone with money, hopefully? We'll need a lot of it to get out of here. A lot of money or a Coalition ship. Those are the only ways."

"We don't have anyone in the Capital, not anymore," Violet said. "But we may be able to find some friendly faces, if we're cautious." She glanced at Kady. "What are the odds that you can find some old lab partners who might be sympathetic?"

Kady shrugged. "Not likely, but not impossible. I'll have to put some feelers out, I haven't spoken to anyone active in the Coalition Science Academy in years. It's a shame Henry isn't here, she probably knows more than me."

"You've turned more than one against the Coalition, I have faith in you," Violet encouraged. "I'll check some rosters and see if there are any familiar names still kicking around the flight school. Ned, what about Davey? Any chance he'd be back in the city?"

Ned flinched at the name. "Last I heard, he and Amy Ballen were hanging out near Nox Beacon, trying to track down the superweapon. That was a while ago, but I can't imagine he'd be back on Gamma-3, not after what happened last time."

"You nearly got yourselves killed last time," Aven said. "Marina thought it was almost a miracle that you all made it out alive." She shuddered, burying her face in her hands. "And in the end, she was the one who paid the price for your freedom."

"We can never repay her for that," Ned uttered softly, focusing on the soup as he stirred. "Nor can we repay you."

Aven glanced up at him, tears shining in her eyes. "I haven't spoken to a soul since Calvetti left. I spent weeks praying that Marina would be freed, that she'd show up at the door smiling, cigar in her hands, but she never did." Aven drew in a shaky breath. "I listened to the execution on the radio. I shouldn't have, but I did, and now I'll never be able to forget the sound of the shot." She stood, peering into the kitchen at the pot, now starting to release tendrils of steam. "But she'd want me to help you. That's how she was, you know."

"I know," Ned replied.

"But if you leave me here," she said, turning back to Violet with a mean glint in her eye, "I'll make sure every one of you pays the same price that she did."

Chapter 34

Henry pulled open the door of the Pig, rubbing at the small of her back with her free hand. By the gods, she was exhausted, more tired than she ever thought a person could be, and increasingly concerned about Georgie's absence in Bradach. She should have been back already, and yet, her side of the bed remained empty.

The tavern was rammed full with patrons, not that it was any different than any other night. People clustered around the bar, toasting each other, laughing, while couples at small tables in the back brushed thumbs against knuckles, eyes wide to soak up each other's view. Something about it just made Henry miss Georgie even more.

"Good evenin', Sugarlump," Sandrine called over the bar. "I'm just here to check on that nasty bruise of yours."

"Can it wait? I'm slammed," Larkin said over her shoulder, shaking a cocktail with one hand and pulling an ale with the other.

"As long as you're not trying to get out of anything," Sandrine warned. "I told you, we need to keep an eye on that. Not many folks running around with dented metal ribs, Larkin Flores."

"I promise, I promise!" The bartender slid a frosty mug of ale down the slick wood and poured the shaken cocktail into a beautiful artisanal glass.

"Evening," Henry said, sliding onto a low stool next to Sandrine. "Busy day?"

"You saw the lines at the clinic, you tell me."

"And yet you're looking fresh as a daisy," Henry countered. "Here I am, looking haggard and half-dead."

"You could never look haggard, Henfeathers." Sandrine paused, sipping wine from the glass Evie had just set in front of her. "In fact, I'd almost say you were glowing."

"Hardly. I think I've slept ten hours in three days. Arteo and I have been working around the clock to try to figure out this superweapon, but it's much harder when we don't have it in front of us."

"I know, Lucy told me."

"She's been a big help in the lab. Lucy is learning so fast, she'll out-pace us all in no time at all."

Evie looped back to their table, pulling a pencil from behind her ear. "Hey, Henry. What can I get ya? No cook tonight again, so there are sandwiches and some sides. Or, this might appeal, Larkin got in some more of that nice white wine you and Mae liked last month."

"No wine, thanks. I'm exhausted and I'll wind up crumpled in your doorway. One of those fancy lemonades, if Larkin has time, and..." Henry trailed off, trying to figure out what it was she actually wanted. Food, to be sure, but nothing usual. "Do you have pickles? Oh, and mango?"

Evie raised an eyebrow. "Is this for an experiment?"

"No, just tired from the lab, you know."

"Alright, coming right up. The drink might take a few minutes."

"Thanks, Evie." Henry turned back to the table, and Sandrine was staring. She was staring like she *knew*. "So," Henry said, desperate to change the subject, "how was the honeymoon? You haven't been back that long, and we've barely had a chance to catch up."

Sandrine tilted her head, but nodded. "Oh, you know. Probably the most wonderful trip I've ever been on. We went to Zeta-6 to see the rings. Well, we didn't touch down, you know, more of a sightseeing vessel. José has an old friend with a lovely liner, I couldn't even find one complaint if I tried."

"And how is married life?"

"Don't tell Georgina, but I think I missed being married, Henrietta. He's the loveliest soul I've ever met. Kind, gracious, and one hell of a cook. He even gives me a run for my money with cornbread, which isn't something

I ever thought I'd admit out loud."

Henry nodded, glancing over Sandrine's shoulder at a particularly amorous couple in the corner, huddled around the small lamp at their table, giggling. "I'm so happy to hear that." She took the glass and plate from Evie as she passed with a distracted wave, and set them on the bar. "And don't worry, I won't tell Georgie."

"Where is Georgina? I thought you two were supposed to be traveling together."

"She wanted to stay in Chalidon a few days more to help Emeline."

Sandrine frowned and took another sip from her glass. "I keep telling that girl to steer clear of her sister for now. Em has made her intentions clear. Georgie needs to respect that."

"She's just trying to help."

"If she doesn't stop trying to help, she's gonna wind up helping herself into a Coalition cell." Sandrine put down her glass, perhaps a little more forcefully than she had intended. "When did you hear from her last?"

"When I left to come back here. There are no more secure lines into Chalidon, none that we can use, anyway." Henry sipped from her glass, savoring the lightly fizzy bubbles on her tongue while she considered her next words. "I'm sure she'll be along in a day or two."

"You do realize that whatever it is you're trying to hide is only going to make me worry more, right, Henfeathers?"

"I'm not... hiding anything," Henry protested. "Georgie said she'd be a few days behind me, that's all." Worry and guilt nestled at the back of her throat, almost gagging her. She shoved a chunk of mango into her mouth to stall the sensation. "Juicy," she affirmed aloud.

Sandrine leaned back in her wheeled chair, tapping her fingernails against the glass. "Does Georgie know?"

"Know what?" Henry daren't make eye contact. Sandrine could sniff out a lie from half across the Near Systems.

"You might be able to hide it from everyone else in here, but you can't hide it from me, Henfeathers. You passed up that wine you spent a whole week raving about last month, the pickles, the mango." Sandrine offered her a quiet, excited smile. "It worked, didn't it?"

Henry sighed, leaning across the table. "Keep your voice down. I haven't told anyone."

"Not even Georgina?"

"Especially not her." Henry took a bite of pickle, stifling a groan of happiness at the gorgeously acidic taste. "Who made these? Carmen?"

"Bailey, I think." Sandrine wheeled her chair closer to Henry. "So Georgina doesn't know?"

"She never would have stayed in Chalidon if I'd told her, you know that. And she was working with Calvetti to get word out about Emeline's election, and I couldn't take that away from her, not when she's spent years trying to fix things with her sister." Henry crunched on another pickle. "Besides, it's early. There are no guarantees."

"Have you at least seen a medic?"

Henry flinched at the borderline accusation. "No. But I only just got back a few days ago, and—"

"You'll come see me in the morning. Or one of the others, if you'd rather it wasn't me." Sandrine drained her glass. "Just to be safe and sure."

"Alright," Henry relented, knowing there was no point in arguing. "Before I head into the lab, then."

"I hope you're not working with anything dangerous."

"Not unless you consider reams of codes and data to be dangerous." Henry returned to the mango, savoring the slippery texture of the sweet fruit. "We're trying to learn how we can mitigate it, this superweapon that Zink has. None of us trust him to not use it, and if he does..." she trailed off, unwilling to follow the thought through to completion. "Arteo has some data I wasn't privy to before, not having worked in the weapons division." The plate made a small, polite clatter as Henry pushed it aside, now empty. "I don't think I ever would have eaten that before."

Sandrine's eyes welled up with tears. "I'm sorry, I just—this is such wonderful news, Henrietta, and my Georgie is going to be over the moon about it. She loves you so much, you know."

"I know. I love her, too."

"My first grandbaby, and right after my wedding, I know things out there are wild and dangerous right now, but back in Skelm, before y'all got us out, I never thought I'd know real happiness again. But here I have purpose, I met someone I love, Lucy Bee is thriving, and you and my Georgina are going to start a family of your own." Drops spilled out over Sandrine's cheeks and she laughed, brushing them away. "Look at me, being a silly old woman. Don't you mind me one bit."

Larkin appeared like she was out of thin air, already leaning down. "Sandrine? You alright? What happened?"

"Don't you worry about me, Sugarlump, I'm fine and dandy." Sandrine smiled broadly, grabbing a small medical bag she'd had hung behind her chair. "Are you ready?"

"Yeah, but let's make it quick, I don't want Eves out here on her own when the next rush shows up."

"It will only take a second. Come on, into the back room." Sandrine wheeled off towards the rear of the tavern, Larkin in tow.

Henry smiled, and allowed herself the secret joy of placing a hand against her barely visible belly, hidden beneath the table. She'd tell Georgie the moment she was back.

* * *

Henry strode into the lab, tossing her briefcase onto the desk with a soft thud, the leather sliding across recently varnished wood. "Morning," she grumbled. Not enough sleep, not to make up for the days of almost zero shut-eye.

"You're late," Arteo replied, not looking up from her notes. "What took you so long?"

"Nothing," Henry lied. The medic had confirmed she was definitely still with child, and so far, everything looked good. "Traffic."

"Here? There are no cars, how did you get caught in traffic?"

"The bakery was busy." Henry passed her a sugary pastry and un-wrapped her own. "Here. Penance, for my lateness."

"It's a good thing you never worked in my department, I'd have written you up for that." Arteo took a bite and groaned. "And then torn up the report, because as it turns out, I am easily bribed."

"Don't tell anyone else that, they'll think you're a double agent."

Arteo laughed, throwing her head back with it. "They don't have these in the Capital, so my integrity is safe for now." She slapped a file on Henry's desk. "Here, I was up late working on some of those calculations."

"Gods, woman, you're a machine."

"I can't take all the credit, Roger unpicked that equation we were both struggling with yesterday. As it turns out, that made all the difference."

Henry scanned the pages as she ate, brushing sugary crumbs from her skirts. There was no delicate way to eat a pastry, but finishing school had been a long time ago. "So what does this mean for our plan to find a counteractive device?"

"Nothing yet, unfortunately," Arteo answered. "Even if we figure out how this thing works, trying to come up with something to protect every planet and settlement is going to be a huge undertaking in and of itself."

Henry nodded, licking the sugary glaze from her fingertips. "I think the main problem is in the exponential distribution, is it not? A small hole, most places could survive that, even manage to repair the atmosphere. The way this thing supposedly tears through and continues the disintegration is what I can't figure out."

"Morning," Roger chimed, pushing through the door with a large white paper sack. His face fell, and he dropped his arms to his sides. "Oh. You've already eaten."

Henry stood, snatching the bag from him with a mischievous smirk. "I'd never say no to another, Aran's pastries are to die for."

"How'd you get on with the calculations?" he asked Arteo, leaning against his desk.

"You were right about that equation. I don't know how I missed it," she replied, accepting another pastry from Henry. "Good work."

"Rog has always been good at the puzzles," Henry said, passing the bag back to him. "He's invaluable to any team, and he knows the research inside and out."

He motioned to his head, long since healed. "I can't pull all-nighters like I used to."

"I wasn't here all night either," Henry reassured him. "Anyway, all this is well and good, but doesn't do a lot of good unless we can get our hands on the thing. No word from Calvetti on the matter?"

Roger shook his head. "No comms from her lately. What's the deal with her going to meet Cole Marion?"

"I don't know, the broadcast was the first I heard of it. Thank the gods Marion is at least out of Bradach, I don't know how much longer things would have remained calm here." Henry wrapped the second pastry up, setting it on the shelf behind her for later. She'd been getting ridiculously hungry in the mid-morning. "It would be nice if she'd let us know what was going on, though. How am I supposed to stop a superweapon I've barely even seen?"

The overhead lights buzzed faintly in the quiet for a moment, each of them considering what would come next. Henry wracked her brain, looking for solutions that refused to present themselves, willing the sugar in her bloodstream to deliver the answer straight to the forefront of her mind. Exhaustion pulled at her, and the only thing she wanted more than the answer to their questions was to ease into bed next to Georgie and sleep for half an eternity.

"Shields would be almost impossible to implement at scale," Roger muttered aloud.

"Not to mention, the Coalition already has weaponry to overcome shields, at least all the ones I'm aware of," Arteo said. "I wish this gods-damnable thing had never been created in the first place."

Henry nodded, and then frowned. "Too late for that now, I guess."

"Maybe Zink won't use it," Roger offered. "Perhaps it's better in his hands than in Cole Marion's?"

Arteo shook her head, smoothing her wrinkled white lab coat with one hand, brushing the sugar from her fingertips. "Cole is rash, but Gregor Zink is calculating. He tried to squeeze information out of me more than once about Coalition projects, but I only obliged once. It was enough of a mistake that I vowed I'd never make it again."

"What was it?" Henry asked. She could scarcely imagine a piece of technology that the Coalition had, and he did not.

"Communications monitoring. I thought it would be disseminated, used across Obsidian Enclave to monitor Coalition troop movements and analyze their patterns. Instead, it was hoarded, kept to only the ships he allowed, and weaponized not only against the Coalition, but The Scattered and neutral ships as well." Arteo's lips pressed into a thin line, and she straightened the piles of papers atop her desk. "Zink is a snake, don't let him fool you. I think he'd use that superweapon in an instant if it meant that Obsidian Enclave became the new law of the Near Systems. He's a man not only driven by progress, but obsessed with it. His sciences divisions are so overworked in their search for new discoveries, some of them burn out after half a year."

Henry ran her fingers along the desk, focusing on the uneven knots in the shining wood. "It feels like he's the only one with a shot at defeating the Coalition, and I'm not so sure it would be an improvement."

"He wouldn't," Arteo agreed. "But I don't know, maybe no one is. Maybe we're too willing to throw our fellow human under the wheels of a steamtrain in order to snatch a modicum of progress out of thin air."

"If not a shield, what about some sort of anti-matter cannon?" Roger mused, shuffling through Arteo's pile. "If the exponential activity of this superweapon means that no terraformer could possibly hope to keep up with the atmospheric degradation, what if we try something that would pull the molecules together? It wouldn't stop the tearing, but it might slow it enough to prevent a catastrophic loss of life." He laid the file on his desk and took a bite of the pastry, crumbs settling on his burgundy tie. "At the very least, it may prove better than nothing."

"Gods," Henry said, rifling through her files. She yanked open a desk drawer and began to toss study after study on top, the pages starting to slide out of their envelopes until Arteo leaped up from her chair to rescue them. "What if it wasn't anti-matter, but something more... reflective?"

"Like a mirror?" Arteo asked. "I don't think a weapon like this would be foiled by some mirrors."

"No, not like a physical reflection, not a mirror, but—" Henry held a file aloft over her head, triumphant she'd found it. "But reversing the polarity?"

"Those calculations would take years," Arteo said. "We don't have years."

"We have access to some of the most brilliant scientific minds in the Near Systems," Henry argued. "We could call Jhanvi Jhaveri, maybe others. Rog and I, we stopped those damned storm generators, we saved lives figuring that out. Hundreds, even thousands." Henry cleared her desk, laying out the correct file as though it was delicate cobwebs spun from gold. "Look here, at how those storm generators were functioning. Remember, Rog?"

He nodded. "I remember, but what does that have to do with this superweapon?"

"It's in the delivery. Anti-matter cannons would help—and we should get a team on that, actually—but if we calculated how to reverse the polarity of that thing's streams, we could neutralize it before it ever triggers."

Arteo leaned against the file cabinet, her arms piled high with old studies and papers. "It's going to take almost an unprecedented phenomenon of combined skills to pull this off."

"Get every scientist and mathematician you know," Henry said, standing from her chair. "We're going to need them if we're going to pull this off."

Chapter 35

Georgie shifted uncomfortably in her crate, regretting that she'd gone along with the plan in the first place. She should have just stayed in Chalidon until Emeline's election was over, and the patrols eased off the docks. Wood bit through her jumpsuit into her back and tangled in her hair, the unfinished knots rough against her bare skin. "How much longer?" she hissed between the cracks of two boards nailed together.

"Relax, Payne, not long. You're lucky this is a newer ship. The old ones take twice or even three times as long." Cass sneezed quietly, muted in her sleeve. "I probably shouldn't have chosen the crate with the grain, I can barely see through my eyes watering."

"It's not much better in the empty ones, trust me. I think I have at least a dozen splinters, and some in places I didn't realize you could even get a splinter," Georgie replied.

"When we get to the beacon at the Belt, we can find a shuttle hopper to Lucent Base." Cass sneezed again. "I might have to throw my weight around with that, though, so we'd better be ready for a fight if it comes to that."

"A fight?" Georgie asked, resisting the urge to jump out of her crate. "What do you propose we fight with? Are you hiding a couple of revolvers in your pockets?"

"Our fists, Payne. You can't tell me you never got into a scrap or two."

"Sure, but that was a long time ago. I was a kid."

"The instinct never leaves you." Cass snorted a laugh and then choked on it. "Just keep moving and throwing punches, you'll be alright. You've got what it takes to be a prizefighter, I'd bet."

Georgie laughed, stifling it in her collar, the blue twill fabric coated in sawdust. "I think Henry would kill me herself if I told her I was going to be a professional fighter."

"Kid like you, growing up in Skelm, I'm betting you had a few run-ins." Cass paused. "I'm betting you won, too."

"Ma couldn't defend us like that, and our father was gone, so yeah, I did now and then. Had to keep the worst of them away from the girls, you know. The bigger kids would pick on Em sometimes when she was little. She was one of the only ones at that school who didn't have parents in management at least, she got teased. Didn't take much to convince the little shits to leave her alone."

"She's grown, Georgie."

The ship's engines rumbled beneath them as they approached the beacon, preparing for landing. "She's only twenty."

"And what were you doing at twenty?"

Georgie's jaw tensed. "I don't see how that matters, Emeline isn't me."

"No, but I'm guessing she watched you a lot growing up." Cass grunted softly as the ship touched down in the bay, shifting in her crate again. "You were what, working in one of the factories? Full time, probably?"

"Janitorial, but yes."

"Sole income for your family?"

Georgie frowned, despite knowing Cass wouldn't see it. "Yes."

"She saw that. She wants to be grown. If she wants your help, she'll ask for it."

"Em doesn't know what's good for her sometimes. She does some foolish stuff, she's going to get herself killed if she's not careful, which she isn't being right now, gallivanting all over the Near Systems trying to drum up votes. I don't understand why she won't just accept my help."

The loading bay door began to open, and Cass swore under her breath, struggling with her crate.

"What's the matter?" Georgie asked, panic rising as bile in her throat.

"Cass, what's going on?"

"Too early for them to be searching the bay. Something is wrong. Get out of that crate, Payne. We might have to fight our way out."

"I told you this was a bad idea!" Georgie hissed, struggling to crack open the lid of her crate. Another sliver pierced through the calluses on her hand and she winced, pulling back. "I told you this would happen!"

"If we live, then I owe you one, alright?"

"If we live, you owe me way more than *one*, Calvetti." Georgie threw off the lid of her crate just as the loading bay door was open wide enough to let through a captain in full uniform, flanked by a small squadron of Coalition officers. "Shit," she breathed.

"Welcome aboard," the captain said evenly. "Although, you failed to notify the dock manager in Chalidon of your departure, so I feel it's safe to assume that you two are rebel spies." He took three steps forward, his hands clasped behind his back. "I am Captain Augustus Allen of the C.S. Stronghold's Revenge, and you are stowing away on my vessel."

"Our mistake," Cass replied, rising from her crate. "We thought this was the transport we'd booked tickets on."

He smirked, but the mirth did not reach his cold stare. "I'm afraid you two will be charged with treason. Come quietly, and we guarantee you will reach your destination whole."

Cass shrugged easily, casually, as though she wasn't facing down certain death. "That's very kind of you to offer us an escort to our destination, Captain Allen," she said. "I'll be sure to tell your commanding officer that your courtesy and kindness is unparalleled."

"Your destination is going to be a work camp at the very least," he replied, stepping closer again. "Although, you look awfully familiar. What is your name?"

"Anna Francis," Cass replied, shooting Georgie a sideways glance. "I work in the records department in the Capital."

"Then why would a Coalition citizen be stowing away on a freighter bound for the belt, I wonder?" He asked, clearly unconvinced.

"Long distance relationship. The records department doesn't pay enough to book a transport out here, and my heart breaks a little more every day."

Georgie shook her head, wondering why in hells Cass was playing games while they were about to die. All she could think about was Henry, and how she'd likely never know what had happened to her, would have to wonder forever why she'd never gone home to Bradach. Her mother would never know why she'd disappeared from Chalidon, Lucy would grow up without a sister, and Emeline would probably be thrilled.

"Captain, I don't think we need all these guns, do you?" Cass asked innocently, stepping out of her crate and dusting off her grain-covered knees. "We're just two Coalition employees trying to take a cheap trip to the belt. We're very sorry, and we'll never do it again."

"It's policy to arrest any and all stowaways on Coalition and privately owned vessels," Captain Allen replied, hands still clasped behind his back. "Now, I'm not a man who enjoys gore, so I'd rather not order these fine officers to fire on the two of you, but I will if you do not cooperate."

Cass grinned broadly. "Who isn't cooperating? Check our pockets if you must, we haven't stolen a single grain of wheat or handful of flour."

The captain frowned. "This isn't about theft, Ms. Francis." He turned, his greying hair a dull shine in the incandescent light of the waiting beacon outside the ship. "This is about treason. It's about treachery and espionage, and the integrity of the Coalition. If you are who you say you are, which I thoroughly doubt, then you should know all too well how much damage even a small breach can cause. I'll have to report this immediately, and you two will be detained until we can verify your identities."

"Oh, please, Captain Allen, I can't lose my job," Cass said, burying her face in her hands. "My family depends on me. I'm all they've got."

"Then you should have considered that before breaking the law and endangering the Coalition," he replied coolly. The captain nodded to the flanking squadron, who holstered their weapons. "Hold out your arms for your chips to be scanned," he said to Cass and Georgie. "For your sakes, I do hope you're not lying. There are twice as many of us as there are you, so I ask you to comply."

"I hope you remember," Cass said, turning to Georgie. "We're going to need it."

The captain's face clouded. "Remember—"

Before he could finish his question, Cass surged forward, tackling him at the knees. Georgie followed suit, the toe of her boot catching on the edge of the crate and sending her sprawling. Staggering to her feet, she swung her fist at the nearest officer, missing his jaw but connecting with his hand, sending the revolver he'd just retrieved from its holster skidding along the polished metal of the loading bay floor.

She scrambled for it, reaching, crying out when another officer cracked her on the skull with the butt of his rifle. Dizzy, the room was spinning around her, and it was all she could do to remain upright, much less throw an accurate punch. Cass was grappling with the captain and the third officer, trying to pull her away from Augustus Allen. She was losing, and so was Georgie.

It had been a foolish, ridiculous idea to try to fight their way out of it, and Georgie was paying the price for Cass' nonsense. A rifle shot rang out, the piercing metallic echo ringing in her ears. She swung wide, not even seeing who was in front of her, or which officer yelped in pain when her fist connected with something. Pulling her hand back, she blinked at the blood on her knuckles, a long-forgotten sight, but the sharp pain radiating through the bones in her hand brought a clarity that shot through the fog.

The first officer was reaching for the gun on the floor, and Georgie stomped on his hand, grinding into soft, knobbled flesh with the heel of her boot. He groaned, and it was an ugly, pained sound. The second moved back to aim his rifle, but Georgie grabbed the barrel, still hot from the last shot he'd taken, the metal burning into her flesh.

"No mercy, Payne, shoot the fuckers if you have to!" Cass shouted, landing a kick in the captain's ribs. He was reaching for a sidearm, concealed inside the jacket of his uniform.

"On your left!" Georgie warned her, wresting the rifle from the second officer and sending the butt of it squarely into his nose, blood streaming freely. He staggered backwards, careening down the ramp, covering his gory face with his hands.

"Bitch!" the first officer spat, pulling his hand to his chest, cradling it against himself. He kicked out, sweeping Georgie's legs from beneath her. She landed hard on the floor, the air knocked from her lungs. Georgie gasped for breath, her mouth opening and closing like a half-dead, landed fish. She aimed the rifle and shot, the round denting the loading bay door but missing the officer. He reached for the revolver again with his uninjured hand, and Georgie struggled to pull back the rifle's bolt for another shot.

"Get off me!" Cass shouted, but Georgie didn't have time to look or help her.

The second officer grasped at the revolver, firing with a shaking hand. The bullet zinged close enough to Georgie's head that she swore she could smell singed hair. Rolling to the side, she yanked at the bolt again, now jammed. "Gods be damned into fucked hells!" she shouted, throwing the rifle to the side. Useless Coalition garbage, and now she was without a weapon once again.

Another shot fired into the floor next to her, and she rolled again, willing her feet to line up underneath her legs. She crawled forward, yanking at the officer's left boot, stealing his balance so that another shot fired off wildly, lodging in the wall behind her. She thrust an elbow into his knee and he crumpled involuntarily, catching her in the skull with the revolver.

Vision swimming, Georgie grabbed his arm and bit just above the wrist until she tasted blood, spitting it out onto the floor in an ugly splatter of saliva and scarlet viscosity. His grip on the revolver loosened, and Georgie used his uniform to drag herself to her feet, headbutting him squarely in the forehead. They both staggered, stumbling, but she was the one left with the gun.

She fired wildly, unsure of how many rounds had been fired or how many were left in the chamber. It grazed the officer's shoulder, but he advanced on her anyway, reaching for her shoulders. He grabbed at her, his hands around her throat.

"Georgie!" Cass cried, desperation puncturing her usually calm tone.

"Help!"

Twisting to the side, the officer's hands still around her neck, Georgie fired, catching the third officer in the thigh. He fell to the ground and Cass twisted from his grasp, shoving him down the ramp with her boot. Georgie tried to fire again, finding the revolver empty.

"I've got you now, you little fuck," he growled, tightening his grip.

Georgie flailed, trying to break his hold on her and failing as static edged into her vision, unable to fill her lungs with air. She slammed the gun into the back of his skull, but it did nothing to loosen his grip.

"Get off of her, you boot-licking piece of shit," Cass screeched, running across the loading bay with the captain's polished silver revolver in her hand. The shot went through the officer's shoulder and he grunted, releasing Georgie. Cass fired again, this time at his ankles, and his boot bloomed crimson with blood. He fell to the floor, screaming.

Georgie grabbed him under the arms and hauled him off the ship, leaving only Captain Augustus Allen. She swayed on the spot, the head injury and lack of air fogging her perception of reality as it blurred around her.

"Someone will have heard that," Cass said, yanking on the lever for the loading bay door. "We have to get the hells out of here."

"We're stealing the ship?"

"Damned right."

"You're a pilot?"

Cass turned back to the captain, who was out cold. She took the iron cuffs from his pocket and imprisoned his wrists, looping the chain around a pipe against the wall. "No, but I'm sure I'll figure it out."

"A ship this size takes at least five," Georgie protested, holding a palm to her throbbing head. "We'll never make it out of the bay."

"Not with that attitude. Come on, we need to get a move on." Cass dragged Georgie through the airlock and up to the bridge just beyond it, throwing herself down into the captain's chair. "Autopilot, engage?" she asked, looking at the console. The ship refused to engage, the boilers silent as the graves they were about to find themselves in. "Manual mode."

Still, nothing happened. Georgie felt the walls closing in on them, distantly aware that the sirens in the beacon had begun to sound, alerted by one of the officers they'd dumped off the ship. "They're coming," she said, her eyes refusing to focus.

"I'm aware of that," Cass snapped. "Help me, Payne!"

"I don't know what to do, I'm just a janitor."

"You're a gods-damned rebel and a pirate, and I swear to all the gods above and below, if we don't get out of this beacon, Henry will kill me herself for getting you into this mess, and I'm not ready to die yet, so help me!" Cass began pushing every button and sliding every gauge, pulling at every lever with increasing panic.

Georgie tilted her head, staring at the side console behind the captain's chair. It looked like those nav trackers she'd had to wear back in Skelm, but what in hells would that be doing on a Coalition freighter? She pressed the central button, and the console lit up like Bradach at night, sparkling lights twinkling through open windows.

The boilers fired, and the ship's engines roared to life. She smiled at it, thinking of Henry again. Henry, so soft and beautiful, smarter than anyone Georgie had ever known, and waiting for her back home.

"Whatever you just did, keep doing it," Cass called over her shoulder. "We're getting the fuck out of here, Payne, hold on to your ass because here we go!"

Georgie was thrown back against the wall as the ship engaged, lifting up from the bay and disengaging from the lock. Dark space was ahead, and Coalition patrols behind. "How fast can this thing go?" she asked, pressing more buttons. "We've got company, Calvetti."

"Yeah, yeah, I'm working on it. Just shut up for a minute so I can think," Cass shot back, leaning into a lever directly in front of her.

The ship groaned into action, picking up speed with every passing second, the force of it pressing both of them back into their seats. Georgie gasped from the pressure of the force as they shot into dark space, leaving the beacon far behind.

"Are they still on our tail?" Cass demanded, leaning over the console.

"I don't know, I can't find the radar."

"You saved my ass back there, Payne."

"I could say the same thing," Georgie replied, searching for the navigation controls, not that she'd know what to do with them once she found them.

Cass turned, smirking over her shoulder. "I knew you were a scrapper."

"We almost died."

"Good thing *almost* doesn't count."

Georgie snorted loudly, the absurdity of it swimming in her brain. "We almost died!" she shouted, laughing. "Gods, Henry would kill us both if she knew."

"Lucent Base isn't far, maybe half a day at this speed," Cass said after a long moment. "We're going to get a secure line, and I'm going to kick Cole Marion's ass beyond the gods-damned Rim."

"Won't the Coalition be tracking this vessel?" Georgie asked, leaning back in her seat, unable to find the radar and hoping it wouldn't matter.

"I'm banking on it. Gregor Zink's secret little base isn't going to be a secret for very much longer."

Chapter 36

Olivia tucked a lock of pin-straight, platinum blond hair behind her ear, the gently flickering bulb in the lamp on the wall casting jumpy shadows over the dimly lit table. "As I said, please don't say anything to any of the other high councilors," she repeated for the third time that day. "I'm sure you understand the importance of this."

"Of course," Hanna replied, nodding sagely. "I will report this to High Councilor Jacobs at the earliest opportunity. I cannot believe that Kimura would do this."

"We are all shocked that she would try to stage such a coup," Olivia lied, shaking her head. "After all the council has done to rehabilitate her image, and she does this? It's such a disappointment."

Hanna scribbled notes in the margin of her page. "To think it would come to this is so upsetting. High Councilor Jacobs hasn't done anything to deserve such ire. I would know, I've been his assistant for over a decade. He insists that everything be done by the books. Kimura should know that, and why she would be running to the papers with such flagrantly false allegations of embezzlement is shocking."

"I just thought you should know." Olivia smoothed her palms against the papers in front of her, ignoring that the movement had smudged the ink just slightly. "If it were reversed, I know you'd come to me with any information you had."

"Of course, Olivia, I would absolutely. We all have to work together, you know. I'll admit, I was skeptical when Councilor Tarand pulled you from

Intelligence for this position, but you've only ever impressed me with your dedication and poise." Hanna reached across the table and grabbed Olivia's hand. "I won't forget this, you know."

"The times are troubled, we can't risk scandals, no matter how unfounded, especially with the council's recent expansion."

Hanna frowned. "We never thought that would go through. Councilor Jacobs only did so to trade a vote with Kimura on trade infrastructure. Now we have an imbalanced council, a new high councilor arriving today, and Kimura's trying to stab us in the back."

"It's a shame that her rebellious tendencies were never quite stamped out." Olivia patted Hanna's hand and pulled her own free, stacking the pages and tucking them neatly into a beige folder. "I know that you will show discretion, Hanna."

"Of course."

"No one can know it was me who told you. Councilor Tarand is sympathetic to your situation, but if it were to get out that she was showing favoritism..." Olivia trailed off as she stood, clutching the file to her chest. "It would only cause more upset."

"Of course," Hanna repeated. "Neither of your names will pass my lips when dealing with this little problem. And thanks to you, it will be a small problem. If this had hit the papers, the gods only know how much damage it may have done." She nodded, scooping up her own papers. "With the all-council meeting in just a few days, we're all busy enough with preparations."

"I don't think I've slept in a week," Olivia said lightly, but the truth of it was weighing heavily against her spine, her entire body feeling compressed and compact from the pressures of what she'd been doing. Orchestrating a treasonous coup did take a toll on the physical self, unfortunately for her sore, aching muscles. "I'll see you at the meeting."

"Yes, see you then," Hanna said, her focus repositioned on the notes in front of her, no doubt trying to piece together the web of lies that Olivia had so expertly spun.

Olivia eased out of the office, closing the heavy oak door behind her. At least Councilor Tarand didn't hide her away in some closet-sized room, unlike Councilor Jacobs had done to Hanna for years. Small mercies, at least, because she never had liked small spaces much.

She checked her watch with a delicate flick of her wrist and sighed, picking up the pace towards the elevator and taking it all the way down to the ground floor, exiting behind the grand staircase into the gardens behind the Executive Building. The grasses were lush, the paths paved in perfect arches with polished quartz and marble, leading out to the greenhouses at the edges, just near the fence that surrounded the building. Sleek, impressive, and topped with razor wire.

The greenhouse was warmer than the exterior, so upon entry Olivia shrugged off her jacket, laying it demurely over her arm as she walked the narrow aisles, feigning interest in rare orchids and plants from colonies that had been seeded millions of kilometers across the Near Systems. She bent to smell one as she spotted Mae from the corner of her eye.

"Maevestra Machenet, what a pleasant surprise," Olivia said loudly, straightening. "What brings you here so late in the afternoon?"

"You summoned me," Mae hissed in reply. "No note, just a location and a time. What's the deal, Guisette?"

"Isn't this orchid stunning?" Olivia asked, shooting her a look. "Absolutely radiant, wouldn't you agree?"

"Er—yes, radiant."

"So radiant that one could only hope that its twin was here in the Capital," Olivia replied breezily. "Or perhaps not a twin, but a sister orchid that looked remarkably similar."

Mae sucked her teeth, glancing back to the flower. "Two orchids in the Capital? That's impossible. Only one would have made it through customs."

"And yet, two orchids."

Mae pulled at her charcoal colored crinoline skirts, breath catching in her throat. "Where is the other one?"

"It's hard to know for sure, but I once heard of rare orchids growing in derelict speakeasies. Something about the environment that helps them thrive." Olivia crossed the aisle, feigning interest in a rose bush that had been bred to grow without thorns, but the blooms were upsettingly fragile. She glanced at the sign that read *do not touch the roses* and back at Mae. "Isn't it strange, that despite this sign and the outward show of propriety from those who frequent this greenhouse, that the blooms disintegrate regardless? Someone has ignored the instructions and done what they wanted, anyway."

"Some people don't listen," Mae replied with a heavy sigh. "Some people are more concerned with orchids than roses."

"Understandable, and yet the fragility is of utmost importance to me specifically." Olivia bent to smell the rose, its petals barely still attached to the stem. "Your father is the same, is he not?"

"My father is probably the one touching them," Mae replied.

"We're all tempted, from time to time." Olivia brushed a fingertip to a petal and watched as it fluttered, bruised and ruined, to the brick path below. "Thank you for coming. I fear things may start to move quickly. You and your—orchid—should leave the Capital as soon as possible."

Mae shook her head, hands clasped in front of her. "It would raise too many questions with my father. I've already begun wandering down some paths that I can't return to without significant blockages. I have to stay the course for a little while longer, or risk that orchids may wind up in the possession of some unsavory types." She leaned in closer, brushing against Olivia's elbow. "Some that do not have green thumbs."

"You need to be careful, Machenet. With both orchids in the city, the councilor will have more questions for you that I'm guessing you don't want to answer, and neither will they."

"But—"

"The more well-known of the orchids has already been taken into custody. A loose custody, but guarded nonetheless. I suspect she will know she is being watched." Olivia leaned away from the roses, leading Mae deeper into the greenhouse, but always walking alongside the windows. The more that saw them together, the better. "What do you think of the new high councilor?" she asked, directing her voice up to the glass, where it reverberated around the greenhouse.

"Have you lost your senses?" Mae hissed. "What in hells are you playing at?"

"I need you to cooperate," Olivia whispered, turning away from the windows. "I gave you information, so please play along or none of us will make it out of this alive."

"I think that a last-minute addition to the High Council is unprecedented, is it not?" Mae replied noisily, resting a hand on her hip for emphasis. "However, many in the Capital are concerned about the growing unrest in more remote settlements, and at the Rim. I suppose with exponential expansion, having an additional face at Turas-Mara can't hurt."

"And what about the other sectors? Have you heard anything untoward?"

Mae chewed on her lip for a moment, searching Olivia's face for clues, but Olivia didn't offer any. What they said together was largely immaterial, the rumor mill would draw their own conclusions, regardless. "I know that Marcus Winters has been vocal about Amaranth Allemande's meteoric rise," Mae replied finally. "He's also expressed significant regret that her daughter is causing problems in Skelm."

"Yes, well, it was always going to be Winters, wasn't it?" Olivia asked in an offhand tone. "That's hardly a surprise, given his previously lodged complaints."

Mae pulled her behind a large fern, its leaves broad and green in the perfectly controlled environment. "Listen, I don't know what you think you're—"

"Ms. Machenet, I hardly think that an unsanctioned radio transmission is cause for alarm," Olivia said loudly. "Cole Marion is no match for the Coalition, no matter what kind of weapon he's got his hands on."

"And *I* hardly think that the High Council is doing enough to stop the growing threat of rebels beyond the belt," Mae shot back with a questioning glance.

Olivia nodded, but barely, before guiding them both back beyond the ferns, their dotted undersides turning her stomach. She'd always hated the things. "I don't care what your father thinks is best for the Capital, my loyalties lie with Councilor Tarand, the same as they always have. Gerard Machenet may be one of the most renowned political strategists in the history of the Coalition, but he doesn't know everything, and neither do you."

"He has access to information the High Council could only dream of," Mae replied. "He is the foremost in the Capital's history, and if he says the unrest in Skelm and beyond the Belt is troubling, then I think people have a right to know."

"He's not a member of the High Council, Ms. Machenet!"

"Neither are you!"

Olivia resisted the urge to allow a wicked grin to spread across her face. As she'd suspected, Mae was playing the scene beautifully. Trust a Machenet to know just how to slide into something without asking too many questions, and leverage them for later. "That may be the case, but I am still the spokesperson for High Councilor Tarand, and it is her opinion and mine that we have more pressing issues at hand than some up-jumped bands of rebels and pirates looting freighters. If people are concerned for their safety, then they are more than welcome to hire more private security for their travels. Now, if you'll excuse me, I have business to attend to."

"You can't just walk away from this, Guisette."

"I think you'll find that I can." Olivia slipped a note into Mae's pocket, making sure that she knew she'd done it with an arched eyebrow. "This city doesn't need your father's help, and it never has. He meddles in affairs he has no business meddling in, and I for one am tired of him thinking he's the one who runs this place. As far as I'm concerned, his actions have only proved to be a detriment to the progress not just in the Capital, but across the Near Systems and the Coalition as a whole."

"That's certainly a statement."

"Indeed. Good day, Ms. Machenet." Olivia strode away, fists balled at her sides for effect. There were at least three journalists in the greenhouse, same as there always were, skulking around, waiting for a scoop. Of course, nothing would be shared without the express permission of the High Council, but it made them feel important. She stalked across the green again, slowly, making sure that the reporters saw her do it. She was betting that it wouldn't be ten minutes before Tarand got a wire about this scoop, and that was where the real challenges would begin.

She could have sworn that the elevator was moving slower that day, but perhaps it was just the impact of her shredded nerves, pulsing with every shift and sway of the pulleys as they silently pulled her back to the top floor. Pausing to steady herself, she waited at the doorway to the councilor's office. "Ma'am?" she prompted.

"Olivia, I was wondering where you'd gotten to," Councilor Tarand replied, turning in her chair.

"I was sorting out the final catering arrangements for the celebratory gala after the all-council meeting. You'd mentioned that you had some concerns about the seafood not being fresh enough, so I was making sure that the chefs were made aware."

"You always have everything in hand, Dearest, and I thank you for it." The councilor's smooth, unblemished skin shone a deep bronze in the afternoon light peeking through the gap in the heavy curtains. "You could have left that task to the event coordinator."

"I wanted to know that it had been appropriately dealt with, I know we don't want another fiasco on our hands like the last meeting."

"No, that was rather embarrassing, even if we did keep it out of the papers. If only we'd known that the previous councilor was allergic to shellfish." Tarand smiled, pushing braids over her shoulder with a rhythmic clicking of the wooden beads. "A pity he didn't survive the encounter."

"Even more a pity that Kimura was his replacement."

The councilor's smile melted into a deep frown, and she drummed her fingertips against the desk. "Any word on that?"

Olivia nodded. "The preparations are in place, ma'am. All we have to do now is wait for the opportune moment to strike."

"I could never have done this without you."

"Any Intelligence agent would have been lucky to be plucked from the masses to serve at your pleasure," Olivia said. "I know that I was."

"Still, not all are as dedicated and skilled as you, Dearest, your recent failures excepted." Tarand swiveled in her chair to face the window, squinting at the stripe of sunlight that illuminated tiny dust particles in the air like sequins. "There was a disturbing report this morning, Dearest."

"Oh?"

"A report of someone using your code name before hijacking a freighter at a beacon near the Belt."

All at once, a flood of emotions slammed into Olivia with such force that she had to brace herself against the desk to keep from toppling over. "Oh?" she asked casually. "How strange."

"How many people know that code name?"

Seven, she thought. "None," she said. "I haven't had to use it since long before I entered your service, ma'am," she lied.

"I thought so. At first, I wondered if it might be a coincidence, but then this—person—said they worked in the records department. That was your cover as well, was it not?"

"It was, ma'am." Olivia swallowed back both the relief that Cass was still alive, because no one else would have used that name, and fear that the net was beginning to close in around her. "Perhaps someone hacked into my personnel file?"

"It's possible, but there have been no breaches at the Archives of late." Tarand turned to face her again. "Not other than General Fineglass."

"You think she's connected to this hijacking?"

"I think we should resist the urge to rule it out, at least," Councilor Tarand mused. "I think there's something she isn't telling us, Olivia. Something she's hiding. Her intel on Overseer—" She gritted her teeth. "*Councilor* Allemande has certainly been illuminating, but I feel there's more to this story. You're sure nothing was out of the ordinary at the Archives that night?"

Olivia shook her head, clutching files to her chest. "No, ma'am. The sensor logs revealed that she was telling the truth, she was searching for information about Emeline Allemande's family history." She shifted the files into one arm, resting them on one hip, praying to all the dead gods that the councilor wouldn't see the lies printed plain as day on her face, that she'd erased the records of which files had been tampered with and escorted Bailey out through the back entrance, shoving a wad of rhodium into her hands and sending her off to find shelter at the Dark Owl. "Though I do agree that it's strange that the general didn't say anything to us at all about it before abandoning her post to travel back to the Capital."

"She insists we wouldn't have allowed her to come." Tarand shrugged slightly. "It's hard to know if she would have been right. I like to think myself an open-minded person, but we're all tempted by ease at times, and I find the Rim much easier to stomach knowing there is a decorated general holding things together out there." The councilor glanced at the open doorway, raising an eyebrow. "Yes, Officer Abara?"

"There was a wire for you, ma'am," they said, holding a sealed card aloft. "It's from the Coalition Courier."

"Bring it here, then," she said with a sigh, holding out her hand gracefully, as though she was a dancer in a ballet and not one of the most powerful people in the Near Systems. "Any time now, Officer Abara, I don't have all day."

"Of course," they said, handing it over. "Should I wait for a reply, or—"

"You're dismissed," Tarand said, waving the same hand. She frowned at the page as she opened it, scowling down at the printed ink. "Olivia, close the door."

"Of course." She did as she was told, returning to her seat after she'd flipped the deadbolt. "What is it, ma'am?" Olivia asked, despite already knowing what the wire would say.

"It says that they heard from an anonymous source that Cole Marion of The Scattered has a powerful weapon. It also says that other anonymous sources are concerned about the leadership in the Capital, and that the problems in Skelm are spreading." Tarand slammed the paper down on her desk, her eyes glinting like embers. "If this gets out, the Coalition will fall." She tore up the paper, letting it fall to the floor in tiny shreds of evidence. "We need to get a handle on things, and fast."

"What do you need me to do?"

"Draft an edict. The Skelmian election is off, due to risk of tampering. For the foreseeable future, Governor Das will remain in place. Get the other councilors to sign it, today. We have no time to waste. The people need to see our strength on display."

Olivia nodded, sparks of energy jolting in her veins. "Of course, ma'am," she said evenly. "I will see it done."

"And find out where in hells that weapon is, Olivia. Find it, and fast. Cole Marion certainly isn't smarter than the whole of the High Council."

"As you wish, ma'am."

Chapter 37

Mae swore under her breath, ducking into an alley mostly hidden by wisteria that dripped down off the pristine bricks, concealing a place for deals to be made in private. It was no secret, either. The proximity to the Executive Building meant that her own father had used it at least a dozen different times, with different politicians and investors, to secure his own future.

She slid her finger under the seal of the note, breaking it with a quiet snap. The wax felt strange on her fingers, unfamiliar in a way that she hadn't anticipated. Olivia Guisette was certainly up to something, but what? She certainly seemed keen to get Mae the hells out of the Capital, and that itself was cause for concern. Betrayal? Subterfuge? With Intelligence, you could never really be sure.

Still, she'd made it clear where Mae could find Bailey—at least, that's what it seemed like she was saying. Mae let out a quiet hiss. What if it was a trap? Her own father likely wouldn't mind having her out of the way, especially if it could be done in a way that didn't raise any flags against the Machenet name or legacy.

The note was smudged, like it had been written in haste, sealed before the ink was dry. Mae squinted at the barely legible letters, trying to make them out.

Get out of the city, it read. Mae pulled the page closer to her face, tugging her glasses down onto her nose. "Does that say coup?" she whispered aloud to herself. Tilting the paper didn't seem to help the legibility of the letters, but maybe that was intentional, in case of interception, or in case Mae decided to take it straight to the High Council.

She hesitated in the alley, torn in two directions. Back the way she came led home to her parents' house, more questions, more barriers to gaining access to the secure line she desperately needed to find out what in the damned hells below was going on in Bradach. If only she could get thirty seconds to ask if they'd heard from Bailey, she might have a better idea of whether or not Olivia Guisette was setting her up for a trap. The others seemed to trust her—at least mostly—but Mae had seen enough espionage that she probably wouldn't ever really trust Agent Guisette, no matter what she did to convince them.

The other end of the alley fed into one of the main streets in the Capital, and half a mile beyond that, the Dark Owl tavern, likely derelict after Marina Sykes' capture and subsequent murder. Mae folded the paper in her hand once, twice, three times, the sweat from her palms doing nothing to improve the legibility of the smeared ink. It was possible that Olivia wasn't lying, but her arrival in Bradach came with Rosie's capture and Bailey's disappearance. Intelligence was known for deeply layered operations that even her father didn't know the true depths of. More than once, they'd used him to execute a crucial part of a plan, and he hadn't even known it until after the deed was already done.

But if Bailey was in the Capital, Mae had to find her. Had to know that she was alright, had to demand why in any of the known hells she'd vanished without so much as an abbreviated wire or a note on the table, disappearing into dark space without a word, as though Mae meant nothing to her at all.

She tore the note into a flurry of tiny white pieces, dropping them into an iron trash can at the far end of the alley. Consequences be damned, she supposed. Maybe Guisette was telling the truth, beyond all reason. Maybe her dalliances with Cassius Calvetti had swayed her opinion on Coalition matters. Or, Mae was about to launch herself directly into a waiting trap.

The streets were busy that time of day, bustling with workers and merchants rushing to and fro, criss-crossing each other's paths in the golden glow of sunlight. Mae raised her face to it, savoring the warmth that settled in her cheeks as a reminder of what she'd left behind twice. Despite the natural sunlight, Gamma-3 didn't hold a candle to Bradach. For one thing, her parents wouldn't be caught dead there.

Turning down one street and doubling back on herself to confuse anyone who might be tailing her, Mae disappeared into an alley that ran behind the Dark Owl tavern, the same way she had the night they broke Ned out of a cell across town. Mae chewed on her lip, fingers resting against the boning of her corset where she'd hidden a small knife. It wasn't much, but it was better than nothing, and easily concealed in the structure of her dress.

She rested a palm against the back door, pushing gently. An unseen padlock rattled quietly, and the sound of it made her jump, every muscle already prepared to fight or to run. Mae pressed her face to the dusty glass, trying to see in through the tiny slice of visible glass, the rest hidden by newsprint glued to the inside. If it was being used for a squat, they knew exactly how to discourage prying eyes without looking too obvious.

The inside was dark, with no signs of life beyond some broken pottery laying in shards on the floor, too many to reassemble, no matter the glue. "Gods be damned," she muttered, skulking around to the front of the shop. The door was closed and locked, just like the back door, but from the street would look like any other derelict, all but burned out tavern. Was it possible that Bailey was hiding in plain sight? It seemed unlikely, but Olivia Guisette had been right before, according to the rest of them who'd been on Lucent Base.

"Hello?" she called softly, almost afraid of a reply. "It's Mae."

Long, excruciating moments passed in silence, without even a hint of a shuffling boot from the inside of the tavern. She huffed out a sigh, unconsciously stamping the heel of her boot against the brick pavement. "Open the door, gods be damned, if this is a trap I'd rather go to prison now rather than stand out here waiting for you lazy officers to get your acts together."

The padlock inside clicked, and the door eased open. "Aven," Mae said, a sigh of relief escaping from her lungs. "Thank the gods."

"We weren't sure if it was really you until that little temper tantrum," Aven replied.

"We?"

Aven stood aside, revealing most of the Cricket crew, and, by the gods, Bailey, standing in the corner looking guilty and sheepish. "Yeah," Aven said. "We." She closed and locked the door behind Mae, snapping the padlock shut. "Who told you we were here?"

"Olivia Guisette."

"The Intelligence agent?"

"The very same."

Captain Violet rushed forward to wrap Mae in a hug, but Mae was still just staring at Bailey, who was strangely unmoving in the corner. "It's so good to see a friendly face," the captain said, giving her a slight squeeze before releasing her. "Especially a face with some contacts."

"How in the hells are you all here?"

"Long story," Ned replied, nodding at Bailey. "We didn't know that Stocky was here until last night. She, uh—" He swallowed loudly and leaned against his cane. "Well, I'm sure you two can catch up on the particulars."

Bailey pushed off the wall, approaching slowly. "Mae, I—"

Without thinking, Mae reached out and swatted the sleeve of Bailey's jumpsuit. "What in the hells were you thinking, Bay Leaf?" A sob caught in her throat, strangling the breath she was desperately trying to suck into her lungs. "I thought you were dead, you absolute apricot!"

"I'm sorry, Mae, I—"

"Shut up." Mae grabbed Bailey by the lapels of her jumpsuit and dragged her in for a harsh, wanting kiss. Her eyes welled up as their lips met, and soon their kisses were moving around the salty tears that streaked down her cheeks.

Captain Violet cleared her throat. "Uh, Mae—"

Mae ignored it, refusing to release Bailey from her grip. She never wanted to let go of her again, not after all they'd been through together, not after thinking she'd lost her again. Her fingers tangled in Bailey's hair, still tied in a messy braid that hung down her back.

"Mae?" the captain tried again. "We need to discuss some particulars."

Finally, excruciatingly, Mae extricated herself from Bailey's lips, but kept a grip of her sleeve. "Alright," she replied, willing the tiny sniffles emanating from her face to cease. "Alright, yes, I'm here."

"We need a ship. We're stranded until we do."

Mae shook her head. "What do you mean, you need a ship?"

"The Cricket was towed back here by a Coalition scrap team, and it was taken directly to the scrap pile outside the Capital. We had some problems on our way out to Lucent Base, and we ran into Josie Keller." The captain's jaw ground against itself at the name, and she paused before continuing. "She took Alice."

"My gods," Mae breathed. She couldn't even imagine the worry, the utter destruction she would feel if that had happened to Bailey. "Where is she?"

"Hard to know for sure, but Josie tends to spend a fair amount of time on Kilper Station. It suits her nefarious bullshit, so I wouldn't be surprised if that's where she is."

"Has anyone had contact with Bradach?"

Kady shook her head. "No. Too hard to get a secure line unless you've got clearance access."

"I've been trying to gain access," Mae explained. "I was trying to find you." She glared up at Bailey and then kissed her again. "But I'm also out of the loop with everything else. What's this nonsense with Cole Marion?"

"Your guess is as good as ours," Captain Violet said. "We were hoping you had more information than us."

"I'm afraid not." Mae leaned against Bailey's frame, closing her eyes to savor the sweet relief that was settling into her veins for just a few moments, before the next fear moved in. "Guisette is up to something in the Executive Building. She passed me a note that said to get out of the city as soon as possible. Something about a coup."

The captain raised an eyebrow. "A coup?"

"That's all it said."

"I'm not keen to stay any longer than we have to, so she'll have no fight from me on the matter. I need to get to Kilper Station, so that I can lodge my boot right up Keller's—"

Ned coughed loudly. "If you can help us get a ship, we'd be very grateful."

"I'll do my best, but my father doesn't have access to ships or manifest logs. Not without some sort of trade, or something like that." Mae shot Bailey a look. "Guisette said your sister is here in the city, too. Is that true?"

"Yes," Bailey mumbled.

"And why is that?"

"Willa wanted to find information about why we're related."

Mae stared. "Willa. You gave her a *nickname?*"

"We're getting off-track," Kady interrupted. "Can you get us a ship or not?"

"Not immediately," Mae admitted. "If I'm able to do this, and at the moment that is a very big *if*, it will take at least a few days to organize. I wouldn't hang all of your hopes and dreams on me managing it, my father is watching me like a hawk. He seems to think I'm up to something."

"No one ever accused Gerard Machenet of being unobservant," Aven grumbled. "I think he was in this tavern more often than most, securing deals."

Mae tilted her head. "He was?"

"At least twice a week. Never had any alcohol, only tea."

"Interesting." Mae snaked an arm around Bailey's waist, relieved that she was alive but still burning with quiet rage that she'd left in the first place. "Do any of you think Guisette might be up to something?"

"It's not out of the realm of possibility," Captain Violet admitted. "She hasn't turned us in yet, at least so far as we know, but that doesn't mean she won't."

"I think she's trying to get rid of us, get us out of the city."

"Why not just have us arrested?" Ned asked. "That would be the easiest way."

Mae shrugged. "Maybe we're bait. Maybe she's trying to get us all rounded up and implicated before she springs the trap. What kind of coup could she be talking about? There's no way anyone can take down the High Council as a whole, not even individual members. They're all much too connected, too protected for that." She chewed on her lip, considering. "Not even my father could do it, and trust me, he tried. He's had a vendetta against High Councilor Jacobs for years."

"It's best to get out of the Capital as soon as possible," Captain Violet asserted. "Whatever Guisette is planning, it's not good for us. Whether it's a warning or a threat, I don't want to be around to find out. We need a ship, any ship, Mae. Big enough to get us all out of here and out to Kilper Station for Alice."

Mae nodded. "I'll do my best." She frowned, aware that her brow was creasing. She didn't want to leave until she knew what Olivia Guisette was up to. Call it curiosity, or a genetic predisposition to self-preservation, but something about the agent's demeanor had gotten under her skin.

"How angry are you?" Bailey asked, after the others filed back into the basement. "On a scale of one to breaking up?"

"Do you really think I'd be back here, sucking up to my parents, if I was going to split up with you?"

Bailey shrugged. "I'd hope not."

"I can't believe you didn't tell me you were going. Do you have any idea how worried I've been?" Mae demanded, finally releasing her. "And for what, so you can go gallivanting across the Near Systems with General Fineglass?"

"Wilhemina," Bailey corrected softly. "And I'm sorry. I had to know where we came from, I—I had to use that comms link Guisette gave me, had to see if it worked."

"It could have been a trap, Bay Leaf."

"It wasn't."

"That you know of. For all you know, General Fineglass is set up in some cushy accommodations, collecting a fat bonus for getting all of you in the same place at once. One fell swoop, and we're all done for."

Bailey shook her head. "Willa wouldn't do that."

"You don't know her!"

"I know her more than anyone else, and she wouldn't. She broke into the Archives, she deserted her post on Turas-Mara. Allemande saw both of us, she knows that I'm alive and Willa's been protecting me."

Mae blew out a slow sigh, resisting the urge to grab Bailey by the shoulders and shake her. "If Allemande knows about you, then we're all in more danger than I thought."

"Willa will set it right."

"Or set you into a cell and throw away the key."

Bailey stepped back, shaking her head again. "No, Mae. I know that you're much smarter than me, you grew up amid all—this—but I need you to trust me, just this once."

"You want me to trust you?" Mae demanded with a scoff. "After you take off without a word?"

"Yes, I want you to trust me. Make me pay for it the rest of our lives if you want, pull that card out any time you want me to take out the trash, or pass on a job, or pick up crates from the port for you so that you don't have to listen to Abigail complain, but right now, in this moment, I need you to trust me." Bailey took Mae's hands in her own, staring her down with those huge gods-damned eyes that always melted every inch of Mae's resolve. "I need to find Willa. Councilor Tarand took her from the Archives."

"How do you know that?"

"I was there."

"Gods, Bailey."

"Olivia Guisette smuggled me out the back entrance." Bailey tilted her head. "I don't know what she's up to, either, but I do know that she saved me and covered my tracks. Willa found some evidence that we were part of an experiment to breed children for the military."

Mae jerked back. "What?"

"It's why we're sisters. Except my mother took me out to Hjarta, and Willa... Willa was left here on Gamma-3."

"Gods below," Mae breathed. "How awful."

"We have to find her, Mae. I can't leave her here."

Mae sighed. "Guisette seemed to imply she was being held somewhere, but it doesn't sound like she's in a cell. A monitored apartment, maybe. My father has landed more than one dignitary there after some scandals broke that shouldn't have."

"So you know where they are?" Bailey asked, pulling her closer with excitement. "You know where Willa is?"

"The apartments are all across the Capital, it's nothing centralized. It has to look like they're being given the choice to stay there, when in reality they're being watched at all times." Mae turned her head, resting her face against Bailey's chest. "Your—sister—will know what it is. She won't make any missteps if she knows what's good for her."

"Can we rescue her?"

"She seems more than capable of rescuing herself, Bay Leaf."

Bailey hugged Mae tight, her chin resting on top of Mae's head. "She needs us, Mae. She can't get out of this one without help. Not when she abandoned her post, no matter what she told the High Council. Not when Allemande saw the both of us in the same room, proving Willa lied to her about killing me."

Mae breathed in Bailey's scent, a spicy sweet smell somewhere between cedar and cinnamon, knowing the respite was only temporary. "Allemande won't want that information getting out, it would jeopardize her new role as a member of the High Council."

"Exactly," Bailey agreed.

"She's going to try to kill Wilhemina, then, if she hasn't already." Mae retreated, her hands clasped around Bailey's neck. "Leave it with me. We'll break your sister out."

Chapter 38

Rosie drummed her fingers against the windowsill, staring out, strangely, at the rainiest day she'd seen since she lived on Gamma-3. Terraforming usually disrupted weather cycles, manipulated by bioecological humidifiers. The Coalition may have taken that technology and squandered it with the storm generators, but Ceru used it to turn a lifeless, rocky planet into a haven of lush greenery and steady, beating rain.

Through the droplet-covered glass, she could still see the outlines of umbrellas down on the street, the journalists out there waiting, always waiting, never discouraged by her disinterest or outright swearing. Hyun was somewhere across the city, hopefully with Jasper as he received the treatment Zink had promised.

She still hadn't been to see her family.

Zink hadn't returned, either, which made her think this was another one of his tests to be sure she was worthy of the honor she'd never wanted in the first place. She stood, pressing her palm against the cold glass, and then her forehead, watching as three raindrops raced down the window before they converged into one long stream. Her family would be wondering why she was still hiding on her private floor. It was time to face them and try not to buckle under the weight of their shattered expectations.

She was in the elevator before she had enough time to talk herself out of it, and when the doors opened onto a beautiful floor, with marble columns and crystalline sconces on the walls, Rosie had to steady herself. It wouldn't kill her to face her mother, but still, anxiety burned in the pit of her stomach, reminding her that she'd only finished her breakfast an hour ago. No one needed to see those eggs revisited. Hells, she'd barely gotten them down in the first place. For all of Ceru's beauty and impressive technologies, their chefs needed some work.

Rosie laid a hand on the doorknob to the apartment before she retracted it. This wasn't home, and maybe they weren't either, anymore. Sometimes, a family ceased to feel like home, through too much distance, or desiccated dreams, or a forgetfulness of who they were in the first place. She knocked instead, clearing her throat and tugging at the collar of her jumpsuit to straighten it.

Her grandfather opened the door first, jerking backwards away from her. "Rose," he breathed. "What are you doing here? Didn't you get our letters?"

"What letters?"

"We sent them to that beacon you told us you were working at." He drew in a shaky breath, his bottom lip wobbling. "We hoped you'd come for us."

"I haven't been on Nox Beacon in a long time," Rosie replied carefully. "I was transferred to Turas-Mara, and then—" she shook her head, unable to admit her failures to him. "It doesn't matter. I wound up in Bradach, and then Gregor Zink dragged me out here." She chewed the inside of her cheek. "I only just found out you were here," she lied.

He nodded, ushering her inside, double locking the door behind them. "Intelligence agents found us back on Gamma-3. We fended off the first few, but they kept coming, always with more questions, always threats, Rose." He eased himself into a plush, high-backed chair, the grey velvet almost shining, even in the overcast light from outside. "We knew that we couldn't stay."

"Where's Mom?" Rosie asked, casting a cautious glance around the room.

"I'm here," her mother said, standing at the end of a corridor that separated the bedrooms. She was wearing the same jacket she always had, green waxed canvas and frayed at the cuffs, but now it hung around her shoulders, making her look even smaller than she was. Clearly, she'd lost too much weight, and too fast. Her mother raised a thin eyebrow, arched over gaunt cheeks. "Unfortunately."

"Mom, it's good to see you."

"I told you, Rosie, didn't I?" her mother asked, arms folded over her chest. "I told you that digging any of this up would lead to trouble. I tried for years to get you to hear me, and you never did."

"I'm—I'm sorry," Rosie stammered. "I didn't mean to, I—"

"Did you tell them where we were? Who we are?"

"No, of course not. I didn't say anything about either of you." Rosie squeezed her eyes shut, knowing her actions back on Turas-Mara would have triggered an investigation into her family. You couldn't give an entire station moderate, intentional food poisoning and disappear without anyone following that up. "I'm sorry, I did what I felt needed to be done."

"At our detriment."

"Mom—"

"And now we're out here at the ass-end of nowhere, in a city I'd hoped I'd never see again."

Rosie took a deep breath, willing her shoulders to release their tension. "Things are changing in the Near Systems, Mom. We can't hide forever."

"Rose is right. It was always a matter of time before they uncovered our past, or at the very least, started to ask uncomfortable questions. I only took us to Gamma-3, to Dubhmoor, because at the time, that was the safest place for us." He shrugged, the shoulders of his knitted sweater rising and falling as he did, warping the robin designs stitched into the yoke. "Times change."

Rosie's mother rolled her eyes again, shoving her hands into her pockets. "You were always more sympathetic to this nonsense."

"It was never nonsense, Nadia." He folded his hands in his lap, staring at her with wide hazel eyes. "You must know, after all this time, that it was more than that."

"I don't want to discuss it." Rosie's mother stood straight, squaring her shoulders. "I want to go home now. Rosie, can you arrange that?"

Rosie's grandfather stood, pushing himself out of the chair by the armrests. "We can't go back to Dubhmoor. Can't even go back to Gamma-3, and you know that, but you're angry, and while I understand why, it doesn't seem fair to put that on Rose. We haven't even heard her side of the story yet." He nodded at the chair he'd just vacated. "Sit, Nadia."

"I'm fine."

"Sit down, Nadia."

Rosie's mother threw herself into the chair like a petulant, sleep-deprived toddler, her stare fiery with rage and disappointment. "Fine, then. Talk."

"They were torturing prisoners out at Turas-Mara. Holding people longer than the laws allow, researching weaponry so terrible you wouldn't even believe something like it even exists." Rosie tilted her head before she continued, shocked that her mother hadn't interrupted her yet. "I couldn't sit by and let them do it. I... I temporarily disabled most of the station's personnel, and escaped with the prisoners on a High Council ship."

Her mother was very quiet for an unsettlingly long moment. "Well, you're certainly your grandmother's granddaughter." She sighed, pressing fingertips to her temples. "Maybe all this nonsense skips a generation."

"I know you won't understand it."

"I understand, Rosie, but sometimes it's not our responsibility to be the ones to throw ourselves onto the pyre. Sometimes we have responsibilities that extend beyond ourselves. Your actions on that station are what opened this investigation into us, we were having to deal with it only a couple of months after you left."

Rosie stood straight, her brow furrowed. "That can't be. What happened on Turas-Mara wasn't until I'd been gone almost a year. I worked on that station for months without incident, and before that, I was on Nox Beacon, minding my own business."

Her grandfather grinned. "See, Nadia? I told you Rose wasn't the reason."

"Tell me about the Intelligence agents who showed up to question you," Rosie said, standing by the window and squinting out into the foggy rain.

"I don't know, Rosie, they were agents. I didn't exactly take their badge numbers, I was too busy panicking that we were about to be arrested."

A terrible, sickening realization dawned over the horizon in Rosie's mind, and anger washed up through the marble floors and rushed into her feet first, rising inside her so fast, she didn't know what would happen when it reached her head. "Zink," she hissed. "Gregor Zink. If they had been real Intelligence agents, my guess is that you would have been picked up immediately, not gently harassed over a period of months until you agreed to leave."

"No, Gregor Zink was very understanding, more than willing to help when we finally reached out," her grandfather protested. "I had worried that all those avenues would be closed to us."

"He wanted you to ask him for help." Rosie squeezed her eyes shut, her jaw clamped firm enough to make her back teeth ache from the pressure. "He's been behind all of this, even from the start." A growl escaped from between her lips, unbidden. "Regardless," she continued, "we need to find a secure line. If I can just get in contact with Bradach, find out what's really going on, then maybe we can try to sort out this mess." She moved to the window, glancing down at the reporters below. "Have they been harassing you, too?"

"We don't have key cards to the ground floor," her mother said. "We've been in here since we arrived. I suppose I can't complain too much, not with someone else doing all the cleaning and the cooking—although that leaves something to be desired, if I'm being honest."

Rosie laughed. "You're telling me. I don't understand how they manage to make sandwiches so bad."

"Bread like sawdust. You're telling me they have automated rhodium mines, and not one good bakery?"

"Maybe it's another one of Zink's tests," Rosie said, almost resigned to it. "I'll tell you more about that later. I need to get to my friend across the city." She glared down at the black umbrellas crowding the pavement, wriggling like damp ants. "We're going to give those reporters what they want, an exciting scoop."

"You're using us as a decoy," her mother accused.

"Yes," Rosie admitted. "Hurry up, I'm sick of looking at the walls in this place. Grandma had strange taste."

"This isn't what she wanted, Rose," her grandfather said softly. "She was never like that. I know there are plenty of legends, that many remember her differently—even you, Nadia—but we were together every day from the moment we met. She wanted a place for people to grow and thrive, and she paid for it with her life. Protected every person who lived here by refusing to give up the intel." He swallowed hard. "She was flawed, but so are all of us, in our own ways. I ran and hid when Obsidian Enclave needed someone to step into leadership."

"I'll go, but only if I can be honest," her mother interrupted, tilting her chin. "I'm not sugarcoating her legacy for some reporters."

Rosie almost smirked. "I don't care about that. Let's go." She strode back into the main hallway, calling for the elevator. Her mother and grandfather joined her, and it began its descent to the ground floor, where the reporters were waiting, calling through the glass the moment they appeared.

"Ms. Gordon, who are these people?"

"What are your plans for Ceru?"

"Who will be appointed as the new chief on Lucent Base?"

"Where will Obsidian Enclave go next?"

"How do you plan to follow in Norah Gordon's footsteps? How will you uphold her legacy?"

Rosie pushed the door open, immediately flanked by reporters, all thrusting cameras into her face. She held up her hands, asking for silence. "I would like to introduce you to two people who know more about Norah Gordon than anyone," she called out over the din. The reporters quieted, backing off, piranhas waiting for the red meat. "Her husband, Anton Gordon, and her daughter, Nadia Gordon. My mother and grandfather have been in Ceru for nearly a month, and Gregor Zink hid it from you."

The journalists erupted, flashbulbs nearly blinding her, all shouting out questions over one another as they demanded answers for all the questions she'd just planted.

"My mother would be rolling in her grave," Rosie's mother shouted, drawing their attention. "She wasn't a good mother, but she wanted the best for Ceru. You're all being lied to."

Rosie sidled away, blinking against the fat raindrops that fell into her eyes and collected on her eyelashes. She didn't have the first clue where the medical center was, nor where she would find a secure line to get word to Bradach, if there even was one that was unlocked. Zink apparently hadn't left anything to chance.

The sound of wet footsteps drew up behind her, and she spun on her heel, ready to redirect another reporter, even if she had to do so with more force than she'd like.

Barnaby held a hand up in surrender, opening an umbrella with the other. "Ms. Gordon," he said, offering it to her. "I am at your service."

"I don't want Zink's lapdog following me around," she retorted. "No doubt you've already told him that I escaped, anyway."

He offered the umbrella again, rain gathering on the epaulets of his pristine trench coat, darkening the taupe fabric there. "Much to the contrary, I assure you. Gregor Zink is but a stepping stone to you."

"I've heard about you from Captain Violet," Rosie shot back, but this time took the umbrella. "Theft. Scams. You sold Alice off to a pirate vessel. You're a con artist."

"Former," he corrected. "The winds have shifted of late. It's no longer easy or advisable to sit on fence posts or remain neutral." Barnaby bowed his head, and a tiny waterfall fell from where the precipitation had collected on his flat cap. "I can tell you where the medical center is, Ms. Gordon." He raised his face to meet hers again, large eyes almost pleading. "I can tell you what Gregor Zink is planning."

"You mean other than imprisoning me in a concrete tower?" she asked acerbically. "What's next? Is he going to turn me into a puppet to appease the masses?"

Barnaby nodded towards a nearby bridge, shining even under the cover of clouds and dripping with lush plants, the greenery vibrant and inviting. "The medical center is a ten-minute walk into the next district. Let me prove that I am telling you the truth before our conversations evolve any further." He leaned in close, water ricocheting from the umbrella down onto his coat. "A reminder, Ms. Gordon, that Gregor Zink is rather fond of surveillance." His gaze flicked towards a series of small black boxes affixed to the underside of the bridge's railing.

"Understood," Rosie replied, following him, now holding the umbrella so that they would both benefit from its protection. He didn't seem like the sort of man who was frequently uncomfortable, and it was clear from his shifting, squelching gait that he was unaccustomed to walking in the rain.

They plodded along in relative silence, the noise of the rain dampening the quiet shuffle of pedestrians and the smooth hiss of the tram that cut across two large intersections, one that sliced through a small parade of retail shops with immaculate window displays, and another surrounded by tall, nearly identical buildings with matching silvery metal supports and gently tinted glass windows from the street all the way to the top floor. She'd never have found her way without a guide, not when every building looked the same.

"Here we are," Barnaby announced, directing her through the front doors. "The medical center of Ceru."

It was bustling with personnel, everyone busy and no one even looking twice in Rosie's direction. Doctors and medical techs in near-matching uniforms, the only differentiation a colored band around their forearms, embroidered into the coats. "Excuse me," Rosie said to a man working behind a desk. "I'm looking for Hyun Park. She would have arrived with a man by the name of Jasper. He was brought here for some extensive medical techniques. I know that you probably won't tell me where he is, but—"

"He was slated for extensive testing," the man interrupted. "But they never made it to the medical center. They left on the same transport they arrived on." He shuffled through a stack of index cards, straightening them against the desk. "Was there anything else?"

"Tests," Rosie repeated, taking a step back. "No, that can't be right. He was transferred from Lucent Base for extended care and surgeries. It was ordered by Gregor Zink himself."

The man sighed, flipping through the cards once again. "I'm sorry, ma'am, we don't have a record of anything else." He glanced at her over a pair of round, silver spectacles. "I can't offer any more information without a security clearance."

Barnaby leaned over the desk, dripping water across the polished wood. "My good man, you are speaking to Rosie Gordon, the only granddaughter of Norah Gordon. I would expect that she would command the highest security clearance."

The man behind the desk stared, oblivious to the growing stream of water streaking across the surface. "My apologies, Ms. Gordon," he said. "I was not informed that we would have the pleasure of hosting you today."

"I'm just trying to find my friends," Rosie explained. "But you're telling me they were never here?"

"No, ma'am. They were never here." The man stood, leaning in close. "You didn't hear this from me, but the paperwork suggests that Zink was the one who requested they be re-routed back to Lucent Base." He sat back down, shuffling the cards and brushing the water away as though nothing had happened.

"Thank you," Rosie said, pulling away from the desk. She pushed back out onto the street, holding the umbrella aloft even as the rain began to die off. Not even Zink's cameras could see through the black fabric that kept her dry.

"I'm sorry," Barnaby said as he caught up to her, and for once, he sounded genuine. "I don't know why Zink sent them away."

"Tell me what Zink is planning," Rosie demanded, feeling the icy steel settle in her voice.

Barnaby reached around the back side of a pillar, wrenching a small black box away with a quiet grunt. "We have about five minutes before that microphone loss is logged and they start pulling the camera footage," he whispered gruffly. "What you said isn't far off the truth, Ms. Gordon. He does want to use you as a kind of political puppet. If you go along with his ideas, he has the entirety of Ceru and Obsidian Enclave eating out of the palm of his hand."

He fell silent as several school-aged children trundled past, stomping in the puddles with squeals of glee, sending a spray of water cascading back to the concrete. Barnaby cleared his throat. "These games he plays are to keep you occupied, trying to find the truth even as he is three steps ahead of you, covering his tracks. He wants Ceru for himself, and he'll use you and your family to convince everyone it's what your grandmother would have wanted."

"Why tell me this?" Rosie asked, watching the street for more interlopers. "Why risk your cushy position as a merchant adviser?"

Barnaby exhaled a breath through his nose, wringing rainwater from his drenched handkerchief. "Ms. Gordon, aside from finding Gregor Zink a truly irritating sort of man, I would say that one can make a fair pile of credits in a coup."

"A coup," Rosie repeated. "I'd need an army for that, and ships."

"Done and done, Ms. Gordon," Barnaby replied. "All you have to do is ask, and they will give you the stars on a silver platter." He glanced down a side street and frowned. "We'd better be leaving now, Ms. Gordon. A coup waits for no woman."

Chapter 39

Alice coasted the ship into the beacon on fumes, the boilers cold from lack of fuel and the engines spluttering angrily, the horrible wet hacking sound a sign of the vessel's ill health. She parked in a bay, leaning her head back in the chair. Never again. She never wanted to pilot a ship ever again. How in hells did Vi keep track of everything all at once? It was more than Alice could handle, and the steady, pulsing throb in her temples was proof of it.

She powered down the ship, not that it mattered much. That hunk of junk wouldn't be going anywhere, not without plenty of coercion. Still, she wasn't done with it, not unless she could hop aboard a transport, which seemed unlikely without an active Coalition chip and a fat pile of credits to pay for the journey. Alice groaned aloud, wishing against everything that she could just be done with this journey. Being the one to make all the plans and do everything was a raw gods-damned deal.

The beacon was mercifully quiet, with no MPOs in sight. A rare blessing from the old gods, perhaps, a reward for not losing her cool. Or it was merely a coincidence, and she was four seconds away from being clapped into some iron cuffs and carted off to a work camp on some derelict asteroid. She tensed at the thought, the muscles in her shoulders already aching from the constant effort. Alice bent at the base of the loading bay ramp, rubbing her knee. It was an old injury, but one that loved to flare up at the worst possible moment.

Dim light was glowing from incandescent bulbs on the walls, bare and without shades, but functional, nonetheless. The place didn't have a single iota of style or comfort, but it at least seemed like a place where people wouldn't ask too many invasive questions. Alice sighed, sitting down on a rusty bench, sliding her boots back and forth against the dirty tile floor, stains long since embedded into the untended ceramic.

"Fancy meeting you here," a familiar voice said.

Alice turned and gasped, throwing her arms around Ivy's shoulders. "Ivy, what in hells are you doing here?"

"Evie triangulated where the Cricket was and where Josie took you. It wasn't hard from there to figure out which beacon you'd head for." Ivy shrugged, green curls bouncing at her shoulders. "And here I am."

"What are you, some kind of navigator now?"

"I picked up a few things flying around with Captain Tansy's fleet."

Alice raised an eyebrow in admiration. "Obviously." She hugged Ivy again, keeping her hands resting on Ivy's shoulders. "I missed having you around. No one else anticipates what I need next, I have to actually tell them."

"I learned from the best."

"You grew your hair out." Alice rested her hands flat on her thighs, rubbing against the green twill. "It suits you."

Ivy tossed a curl over a shoulder with a giggle. "It was time for a change. You know how it is."

"I don't think I've changed my hair in twenty years," Alice admitted. "Biggest change for me was this." She snapped the eye patch against her face with a short laugh. "Vi says it makes me look tough."

"So, where are we going?" Ivy asked, casting a dubious glance at the ship across the beacon. "I sincerely hope that's not yours."

"It is."

"It actually flies?"

Alice laughed. "Barely. I need to find out where Vi and the others ended up. Can your new skills figure that one out?"

"No, but I have it on good authority that there was no one to be found."

"What? Why? I sent coordinates!" Alice protested, standing up off the bench. "Someone should have gone out there!"

"They didn't get them decoded until the Cricket had already been towed. Captain Tansy sent a ship out there, I was on it. There was nothing and no one there. Flight logs suggest the only ships that far out were Coalition scrappers."

"Shit," Alice hissed. "Fuck. Gods be damned into hells, lemon-ass wire codes and Josie gods-forsaken Keller making everything worse, as usual."

"No mention of captures in the Coalition press," Ivy offered. "They might have made it off, or at least managed to hide out somewhere in the Capital."

"Gods." Alice paced behind the bench, three steps in each direction before changing, the soles of her boots quiet against the tiles but still squeaking softly. "That doesn't mean they weren't taken. Is anyone trying to do anything?"

"We only just figured it out yesterday," Ivy apologized. "Secure lines are hard to get in and out of the Capital, nearly everything is monitored and we can't risk giving away their position if they are hiding out in the city."

"No, of course, that makes sense."

Ivy turned around to face Alice, grabbing for her elbow to stop her in her tracks. "This one might be up to just us. We can't find any of the others."

"Rosie?"

"No word."

"Bailey?" Alice asked. "Maybe Captain Marshall—"

"He's volunteered his ship for refugee transports, he's working with Captain Tansy now. Besides, he's all the way on the other end of the Near Systems, they'd never get here before someone starts asking questions about that piece of junk you have dry-rotting in the bay over there." Ivy snorted a laugh. "At least no one will try to steal it."

"It was hardly my first choice, Ivy," Alice shot back. "So what, then? We... try to hop a transport to the Capital?"

Ivy shook her head. "I have a better idea. We've been working on trying to figure out some exit paths for people stuck on Gamma-3. Captain Tansy's had a few people working on it for months, actually."

"And?"

"And there's a small area, a few hundred miles from the Capital, where there's a gap in the radar signals."

Alice began to pace again, shaking free of Ivy. "That's impossible. Gamma-3 and the Capital are the most heavily monitored places in the whole of the Near Systems. I'd say in the galaxy, but given all the cameras on Lucent Base, I think Gregor Zink has that on lock."

"It's a small area, it used to be a small settlement a long time ago."

"Where?" Alice asked, stopping to wait for Ivy's answer. There was something hidden there, something like a word on the tip of her tongue, something she almost remembered but didn't. "Where is this place?"

"It's called Aarq."

Alice let out a breath, puffing out her cheeks with the effort. "That's where I'm from."

"Where you grew up?"

"Yeah." Alice shot her a look. "So don't say it was *a long time ago*, Ivy, I'm not that old. Yet."

"Captain Tansy said there used to be a safe house there for rebels during the last uprising. She talked to some people who were there, back then. A refugee woman we grabbed out of Red Top. She was trying to get her great-grandchildren to—well, you know where."

"Yeah." Alice was frozen on the spot, her legs refusing to move. "And she's sure of this?"

"As much as you can be with that kind of intel," Ivy replied with a shrug. "Either way, Aarq could be the key to getting people on and off of Gamma-3, at least until the Coalition figures it out."

"They did last time, they will again," Alice said vacantly. Her family. Her parents. Everyone all but wiped out during the uprising, leaving her to grow up on a farm up north, cut off from everything she'd known. "If they haven't already. Could be a trap."

"Captain Tansy already made a trip down—well, one of her ships did, she's back in—you know." Ivy stood, thrusting her hands into her pockets. "Might be our best bet."

"What if we get down there and can't leave?" Alice asked, staring at the rusting ship across the beacon. "That thing might make it there, if we can get fuel, but getting back is another question."

"I don't know, I'm not the one who stole it," Ivy replied. "Pity you couldn't steal something that looked less like a death trap."

"Might keep us out of trouble. Or might draw enough attention to get us scrapped, it could go either way." Alice draped an arm around Ivy's shoulders. "I'm glad you're here."

"Wouldn't be anywhere else. I learned a long time ago that you all need me to show up and bail you out." Ivy laughed, resting a hand casually on her hip. "But without you and the captain, I'd still be hustling card tables and getting into trouble."

"Hear anything from your parents?"

"A little. Mom's pleased I gave up the cards, but I can't say she's thrilled that I'm a mechanic. She says it's not befitting of a lady."

Alice snorted a laugh. "You want me to talk to her?"

"What, and remove all doubt that I'm cavorting around with criminals? No thanks, I'll pass." Ivy grinned up at her and adjusted the tool belt at her hips, pulling the strap tighter and notching it. "As much as she hated the card table hustling, she would probably hate rebellion more, and my dad basically does whatever she says."

"I understand."

"It's better like this. They like me better when they don't know what I'm doing, and I like them better when I don't have to hear their opinions." Ivy shrugged. "There are more important things in life than keeping people who want to put you into a box happy."

"Agreed." Alice sighed, looking at the P.S. Manta. "We'd better get to work."

"Yup. I guess we'd better."

$$* * *$$

Aarq was different than she remembered, and while that shouldn't have come as a surprise after decades away, something about the crumbling structures and cracked brick roads turned Alice's stomach. They'd paved over everything she'd known as a little girl, and replaced it all with Coalition-issued, standard buildings and signs, everything yellow and purple and above all, grey. They'd left it to rot.

Alice stepped off the ship, trying not to vomit her meager breakfast onto the concrete of the dock. She swallowed back the bile, and it burned in her throat. "It looks different now," she said.

"Captain Tansy said the Coalition basically steamrolled this place after the last uprising." Ivy gave her a sideways glance and a raised eyebrow. "You okay?"

"Yeah," Alice replied, shaking her head. "I'm fine. Different is fine. At least we're here and unscathed. I didn't think that was going to work."

"You thought I'd lead us into a trap?"

"No, of course not, I just—" Alice cut herself off with a quiet grunt. "We need some supplies, and we need to get to the Capital."

"Gaskets?" Ivy asked, pulling a pencil from behind her ear and making notes on a small pad of paper. "Bolts?"

Alice nodded, ticking things off on her fingers, giving the grey sky a wary glance. It looked like rain. "Add calipers, socket wrench, vise..." her brow furrowed as she struggled to remember the other items on the list.

"Heat gun?" Ivy offered.

"We'll need one for soldering." Alice frowned at the growing bullet points in Ivy's notebook. "It's going to be a challenge to pay for all of this. I don't suppose you've come across a Coalition-issued chip laden with credits, have you?"

"Unfortunately not." Ivy slid a pack of cards from the back pocket of her jumpsuit and raised an eyebrow in question. "I could hustle for it."

"Ivy, no."

"Do you have any better ideas?"

"You're out of practice!" Alice challenged.

"Not exactly, I've been playing in locales here and there." She shuffled the cards deftly between her fingers, the soft rustle of the cardboard inaudible against the whistle of wind through trees on the horizon and a rumble of distant thunder that only reminded Alice of Skelm. Ivy began the shuffle again, not even looking at the cards. "It's a hard habit to drop."

"And here I thought you'd gone on the straight and narrow."

"Unless a better idea presents itself, I think this is the only idea we've got." Ivy paused her shuffle and straightened the cards, fitting them back into their sleeve. "Yes or no, Al."

Alice growled under her breath. "Fine. But don't get caught. I already have plenty I need to explain to Vi when we find her, I don't need to add losing you to a work camp to the list." She hugged Ivy tight, squeezing her around the shoulders. "Be careful."

"I'll be fine." Ivy craned her neck, looking up at the clouds. "I'll be back by sundown. If I'm not, then you can worry, but not until then."

"Deal."

Ivy grabbed Alice's hand and stared, unblinking. "I'll be fine, Alice."

"You'd better be. I'm going to need you to get the hells off this rock."

"Sundown," Ivy repeated, releasing Alice and disappearing down an alley.

Aarq swallowed her whole, just like it had so many others. Alice shook her head, trying to rid herself of the thought. There was no use in dwelling on it, or in worrying about Ivy, but some thoughts couldn't be restrained. Some thoughts creep under the doors in the mind, leaching into the walls, poisoning the water just enough that it isn't noticed until it's too late, and things are too far gone.

Alice turned, pacing the streets of the abandoned settlement, wondering if things with Violet were too far gone, too. They'd been growing apart over recent months, never able to get a moment's peace, and so they spent all their time arguing, sniping at one another until the lights went out at night. Violet always fell straight to sleep, no matter what. Alice would lay there for hours, picking apart every argument in her mind until she was awake too early, angrily banging on the boilers and flinging tools across the workbench.

She'd spent so much time resenting how things were without realizing how much worse they'd become. A common affliction, but a deadly one. Alice kicked at a loose pebble with the scuffed toe of her boot, sending it skittering along the uneven pavement. Aarq had been mostly grass and farms when she'd left, or rather, when she'd been sent away. She understood now why her parents had done it, but the injustice of it never stopped burning in her belly.

A few people wandered the streets, cautious and quiet. Most of the buildings had padlocks and chains over the door handles, but it wasn't a surprise. The Coalition had a nasty habit of rushing in to fix a place, patting themselves on the back when the gleaming new office buildings were constructed, and then abandoning a place as quickly as they'd taken it over, leaving nothing more than the charred skeletal remains of a settlement.

She stopped in a small cafe, spotting the grey circle next to the register and sighing with relief. Most places didn't accept grey market chips anymore, not after the law changed. In truth, she was surprised to find somewhere on Gamma-3 that still did. She chose four sandwiches, two for her and two for Ivy, as well as several bottles of juice, making sure to choose Ivy's favorite. It wouldn't be as good as the freshly squeezed stuff at the Pig, but it would do nonetheless.

The chairs inside the cafe were old and creaky, the unfinished, untended wood groaning as she sat at a table in a dark corner, ready to spend the day waiting for Ivy and trying to distract herself from the worry. She'd never had children, never wanted to, but her fear for Ivy never left her chest, always pulling a ring of anxiety tight around her lungs. Ivy was a smart girl and capable, she'd be fine. She'd gotten out of worse scrapes before.

Alice exhaled a long breath and unwrapped the first sandwich, savoring the sweet jam that spilled out over the sides. It had been weeks with Josie, weeks with nothing more than bread, water, and a pile of over-boiled greens that were so vile, she could barely stomach eating them. She'd become so spoiled with Ned's cooking on the Cricket, and Rosie's in the Pig, that she'd forgotten how awful most of the food in the Near Systems really was.

Long, excruciating moments passed. She'd meant to save her second sandwich for when they were back on the ship, but she ate it anyway in a desperate attempt to press the time forward.

Time crept. After the sandwiches she'd bought for herself were long gone, the two for Ivy wrapped delicately in waxed paper, Alice walked back to the dock and glared at the derelict ship sitting rusted in its bay, the oxidized metal gleaming orange in the glow of the sunset.

Light dipped down below the horizon, and Ivy didn't show.

The street lamps flickered lazily, and still, Alice stood alone on the dock, the panic steadily mounting in her mind, clouding rational and reasoned thoughts with wild suppositions. Ivy could be in trouble. She could be hurt, or imprisoned, or dead.

Carefully, Alice unfolded an old scrap of a map from her breast pocket. She'd carried it with her for years, ever since Vi had given it to her. A key to her past long since rusted, but if it held clues of where a resistance might be hiding, it could help in finding Ivy. Buildings that no longer stood were circled in red or green on the map, the ink faded and vague. One building marked with green and gold painted stars sat in the top left corner of the map. A mill. Alice squinted into the growing darkness, up the hill to where an old grain silo still stood.

Having no other leads, Alice marched back across town to the mill and pounded on the door, the splintered wood rattling at the latch. "Open up!" she shouted, her voice echoing across an empty courtyard.

A woman yanked open the door with a hand on her hip and a steely glare that almost made Alice lose her balance. "Who in hells are you?" the woman demanded, half Alice's height but twice as intimidating.

"I'm looking for someone. A friend."

"Get lost, lady. This is a closed game." The woman moved to slam the door, but Alice shoved her boot in the gap, wincing at the pain as the door ricocheted against her ankle.

"Wait," Alice pleaded. "A game? Like cards?"

"What are you, some kind of addict? We don't serve people like you here. Like I said, it's a closed game."

"My friend went looking for a game. I'm hoping it was this one."

"Come in."

Alice stepped over the threshold, and no sooner she did than the door was barred shut behind her, and two men were at her sides, grabbing at her arms. "Hey, piss off!" she shouted, pulling away from them.

"Alice!" Ivy shrieked from the far side of the room, cuffed around a chair. "Alice, I'm sorry, I—"

"So this is *your* little thief, then," the woman said, leaning against a sturdy wooden card table that sat in the middle of the old mill, a bare light bulb hanging from a beam above. "We were just about to teach her a lesson."

"What lesson would that be?" Alice managed to eke out, despite the dryness of her mouth.

"That you can't hustle a table of hustlers." The woman tossed her head, flinging around a tangle of brunette curls that framed her face. "I assume this is a joint effort? What was it? Alice?"

"That's Ms. Green to you," Alice spat. She regretted it immediately, because it sounded ridiculous coming out of her mouth. That kind of thing only worked for Vi.

The woman leaped down from the table, approaching with her mouth set into a frown. "Your name isn't Alice Green. Who are you, really?"

"I'm not lying, that's my name. I'd have you scan my Coalition chip, but it was deactivated years ago."

"Let her go," the woman said to the men. She got closer, eyeing Alice from her short height. "Where are you from?"

"Here, originally. Haven't been back in a very long time."

"Who owned this mill?"

Alice blinked. "The Gonzales family, I think. I don't know, it was a long time ago."

"What were your parents' names?"

"Ira and Bethany." Alice stepped forward and away from the men who had restrained her. "Why?"

"Why is exactly what I should be asking you," the woman said. "Why would you come back here after all this time? What are you after?"

"I don't know what you're talking about."

"Your parents. They—you do know, right?"

"You couldn't have known them, you look like you're half my age," Alice said. "They died a long time ago."

"My parents did." The woman held out her hand. "Gloria González. Pleased to meet you."

"Can you also release my friend?" Alice asked, shaking her hand. "Whatever happened, I'm sure it was a big misunderstanding."

"Oh, she's good," Gloria said with a laugh. "She'd have gotten away with it, too, if Pyotr over there hadn't gotten scammed by her a few years back out on Delta-4." She nodded towards a hulking man in the corner, who was cracking his knuckles one at a time. "Why is your friend here trying to hustle us, Alice Green?"

"We need credits. Our ship is on its last legs, and we have others from our crew who are missing. The captain, her second, and the navigator. Their ship got towed back to the Capital from dark space." Alice took a deep breath. "It's a very long story."

"Release the girl," Gloria said without turning around. "Pyotr, get these two a couple of chips."

"Thank you," Alice said. "Thank you, honestly, I—"

"If you weren't who you are, this would have ended differently, but then I suspect that's why you chose Aarq for this little mission."

"We chose this place because there's a radar gap," Ivy said, rubbing at her wrists as she approached. "Only place on Gamma-3 you can land without lots of extra scans and questions."

"A convenient story," Gloria said. "Alice, is this true?" She crossed her arms over her chest, tattoos covering every inch of exposed skin there. "You can tell us."

"Yes," Alice admitted. "I didn't want to come back here. It's... different."

Gloria waved a hand in the air. "Yeah, you know the story. Coalition wants to squash rebel activity, so they all but burn the place out. You can't grow anything here anymore, they built on all the fertile land. Your parents are probably rolling in their graves."

"Their graves," Alice repeated. She'd never stopped to wonder where they'd been interred.

"Out past the trees, about ten miles out. People wanted to be sure their graves wouldn't be disturbed. I don't think any of us really remember where they are anymore." Gloria's face fell. "I'm sorry for that."

"It's alright."

"They saved my family, you know. Saved so many that passed through here, hiding them, setting them up with falsified documents, with chips, papers, you name it." Gloria took the chips from Pyotr, handing them over. "These are for you. It's not a fortune, but should be enough for fuel and repairs."

"Thank you," Alice said again. "I don't know how we can ever repay you."

"This is our repayment to you," Gloria replied. "This is atonement. We're even, now. No more guilt." She brushed her hands together three times and held them up before reaching to shake Alice's hand again. "Don't stay here in Aarq. Leave as soon as you can. If you brought a ship, it will attract attention sooner or later."

"We will."

Gloria stepped back, appraising Alice and Ivy both. "Who do you fight for?" she asked.

"I don't even know anymore." Alice pocketed the chips, making sure they were safe. "Whatever side we're on, it's not the Coalition's."

"Good." Gloria nodded towards the door. "Get out of here. And kid, if you're going to hustle, you need to get better at recognizing people you've screwed over."

"Don't worry," Alice said, steering Ivy towards the door by her shoulders, "she will not be hustling ever again."

Chapter 40

"Calling Lucent Base, asking clearance for landing," Cass said, leaning against the console, the blinking lights casting an odd glow against the glass of the front viewing window. There was no response, but she'd expected that, arriving in a Coalition rig. "Lucent Base, come in. Requesting clearance for landing."

She smirked, glancing over at the navigation panel. "We might have to wing it," she called over her shoulder to Georgie. "I knew they'd do something like this."

"Wing it?" Georgie asked, standing stiffly at the navigation panel. "We barely made it here in one piece."

"Don't be so dramatic, Payne, we haven't even gotten started yet." Cass leaned over the transmitter once again. "Lucent Base, if you don't grant me clearance, I'm coming in anyway."

The radio crackled quietly for a moment, and Cass couldn't help but envision the absolute panic and disarray that would be in their comms tower, increasing exponentially with every message she sent. As far as they knew, a Coalition ship not only knew where they were, despite the cloaking shields, but knew the name of the base. They'd be scrambling, probably dragging Gregor Zink from his quarters at that very moment.

"Last chance, Lucent Base," she boomed into the microphone, her lips almost touching the metal. Her voice was probably blowing out their speakers. Good.

Three seconds more of static before the hesitant reply came. "Identify yourself."

"I don't think I will, actually."

"We have missiles locked and loaded, Unidentified Vessel. Exit our airspace immediately or be obliterated."

Cass snorted a laugh. "That's hardly a way to treat an esteemed guest, now is it?" She rested a hand on her hip, laying against the holster she'd stolen from Captain Augustus Allen. It was nice to have a reliable sidearm for once. It had been too long. "Grant me clearance."

"You have fifteen seconds to exit our airspace," the radio crunched.

"Okay, here I come!" Cass replied with a cackle, pressing the ship down through the shields. It was so strange, watching a whole base appear out of nothing, where only dark space had been mere moments before. No missiles came, which she appreciated, despite having known that it was a bluff. No way was Obsidian Enclave prepared to start randomly firing on Coalition vessels.

The ship descended into the docking bay, the clamps clicking into place as the loading bay door unsealed with a loud hiss. "You ready, Georgie?" Cass asked.

"I don't know about ready," Georgie replied with a grumble. "I'm just hoping this doesn't get us killed."

"Don't worry, it won't."

"That's what you said last time."

Cass shrugged. "And look! We're not dead!"

"Tempting fate, Calvetti." Georgie shook her head with a tiny, almost imperceptible smirk. "But I'm learning that's kind of your whole thing."

"If you want to be part of The Splintered, you'll have to get used to it."

"I don't know if want even comes into it. I'm only here because you dragged me along."

Cass led her through the doorway to the bridge, the revolver at her hip half out of the holster. She had to be ready for anything. Henry would kill her if anything happened to Georgie. "Dragged you along to get you what you wanted, which is a secure line, no?"

"Fine," Georgie said with a dramatic sigh. "But no funny business."

"But that's what I'm best at!" Cass gave her a playful nudge to the shoulder, knocking her off balance. "Get ready, just in case these fools are trigger-happy."

"But you said—"

Cass descended the ramp onto Lucent Base, waiting for Gregor Zink or Cole Marion to appear. Instead, she got a half circle of Obsidian Enclave soldiers in armor surrounding the dock. "Good afternoon, friends," she chirped in an obnoxious tone. "I was summoned here by Cole Marion."

"No one summoned you here, Calvetti," one of the soldiers replied. "And you just brought a tracked ship to our shielded base. Get back on it and leave, immediately."

"I don't think I will, actually."

The soldier lifted a heat gun onto her shoulder, aiming it directly at them. "Do it now, or face the consequences."

"You're not going to kill me, it would be a whole thing." Cass approached, knocking the heat gun from her shoulder. "Take me to Cole Marion."

"He isn't here. Now leave, before this gets ugly."

"Of course he's here. He made a point of publicly summoning me, no doubt to shore up support in his faction." Cass shrugged, nonchalant, still resting her hand against the holster. "Bring him out, and that weapon he's hiding."

"We don't know why Mr. Marion made such an announcement on the broadcast, we have never hosted him nor that weapon on this base, regardless of ownership. Truth be told, Gregor didn't trust him."

"That's the smartest thing I've ever heard from Zink." Cass wandered around the half circle, looking each soldier in the eyes. "Cole Marion is certainly not to be trusted. That's why I know that he's here, hiding somewhere. No doubt he thought he could drag me past the Belt to have me dealt with by Obsidian Enclave, making him the innocent party." She wheeled around, pointing back at the first soldier. "Who has that weapon now?"

"That's classified."

"Georgie!" Hyun pushed through the semi-circle, throwing her arms around Georgie. "Thank the gods you're here."

"We've been so worried," Georgie replied. "How is Jasper?"

Hyun shook her head sadly. "No improvement as of yet, but Gregor said the treatment takes a while to take effect." She tilted her head. "Where is Rosie?"

"She's not here?" Cass interjected. "She's supposed to be here. The others were on their way back."

"We all went out to Ceru—their city beyond the Rim, you know—but Zink sent Jas and I back as soon as we arrived, he said the treatment would fare better here on Lucent Base." Hyun's hair was tangled, falling down past her shoulders in a nest of knots. "The others never arrived. I thought you'd be bringing Rosie back. She's still out there?"

"The Cricket went missing," Georgie replied, hugging her again. "We think it was towed back to Gamma-3, they ran into problems with Josie Keller. Don't worry about Rosie, we'll find her."

Hyun stepped back, covering her mouth with her hands. "The Cricket is missing?"

"Unfortunately."

"I never should have left," Hyun said, shaking her head. "I should have—they could have—" she inhaled slowly, letting her hands fall to her sides, balled into fists. "I'm going to make Captain Josie Keller pay for what she's done if I ever see her again. What about the crew? You got them in time, right?"

Georgie bit her lip. "The ship was towed with the crew. We don't know where they are."

Tears filled Hyun's eyes, and her hands clenched and released in a strange, unpredictable rhythm. "No. No, that can't be. Captain Violet would never let that happen."

"They were dead in the water, no mechanic. Josie took Alice."

"Josie Keller deserves whatever is coming to her," Hyun said in a low voice. "We'll never forgive her for this."

"They might yet get out of it. We haven't heard of any arrest reports, and you know High Councilor Allemande would be crowing about it," Georgie soothed. "It's possible they got off the ship before it landed on Gamma-3."

"Did you really endanger an entire base just for a family reunion?" the soldier interrupted. "We have more important things to be dealing with than your petty missing person's reports."

Cass pointed at the soldier, staring her down. "Where's Cole Marion?" she asked. "The little scamp dragged me out here, no doubt to cause more problems."

Hyun shook her head slowly. "Cole Marion isn't on Lucent Base."

"Then why—"

"I don't know why he told Delia that, but he's not here." Hyun sighed, shoving her hands into the pockets of her embroidered trousers, the threads frayed. "I'd know if he was here. He isn't."

"Gods be damned," Cass spat. "It's a trap."

"You're bringing the Coalition to our doorstep!" the soldier shouted. "How is this a trap for you? Where do you think we can hide from them, now that they have these coordinates?"

"We have a hostage too, a Captain." Cass nodded towards the ship. "You can have him, if you want him."

The soldier pointed the heat gun at her again. "What in hells are we supposed to do with a hostage?" she demanded. "All you've brought is liability."

"I've brought you leverage," Cass replied coolly. "You should be more grateful."

"Leverage is useful, this is a ticking time bomb."

"I don't have time to argue. We need access to your secure line." Cass started to cross the line of soldiers, but one pushed her back. "If you want me off your base, the fastest way is to give me what I want."

"Or we could just kill you," the soldier said, adjusting her position. "Kill you, and obliterate the ship, and shove the hostage out an airlock. How's that for a deal?"

"I don't really think that's a very good deal," Georgie said, clearing her throat. "We're only here because—"

"I don't give one good gods-damned fuck why you're here," the soldier said, advancing on them with the heat gun, the end of the wide barrel glowing orange from the bolt inside. "Leave now, or face the consequences."

"You don't scare me," Cass replied, stepping close to her. "Bluffing doesn't work on a bullshitter. The Coalition learned that the hard way. Twice. Do you want to add Obsidian Enclave to the list?"

The soldier hesitated, the gun wavering. "Turn off your nav comms."

Cass waved her hand in the air. "Already done," she lied. "I'm not fresh out of training."

"We'll need to see to the hostage."

"He's in the brig, the second door on the left once you're through the airlock. Anything else?"

"Someone will need to be in the wire room with you to monitor communications."

Cass tilted her head from side to side, considering the terms. "They can sit outside the room."

"Fine." The soldier lowered the heat gun, motioning for several to board the ship. "Make it quick, and you'd better be blowing up that ship as soon as you leave."

"I'd like to disembark first, if that's alright with you." Cass strode towards the comms tower, letting go of a deep breath slowly, quietly, so that no one would know how scared she'd really been. "Thank you for your cooperation."

"I didn't think that was going to work," Georgie whispered, catching up to her. "That was incredible."

"Oh, you know, all in a day's work," Cass replied. "Let's get you in touch with Bradach. I don't want your woman tearing me to shreds the next time I make it out there." Something inside of her deflated, leaving a hole where the promise of Bradach had been. "*If* I ever make it out there again. I doubt they'll be lifting their political ban any time soon."

"Cole certainly didn't care about that."

"I do."

"Where do you think he is?" Hyun asked, following on the other side. "I haven't heard anything since the broadcast."

Cass gritted her teeth. She'd been so sure that the little rat was hiding out on Lucent Base, she'd come prepared to take him down, and he was in the wind, once again, and so was Gregor Zink. "I don't know. A rebel settlement, if I had to guess, but there are dozens of those. I can't just make wild guesses, we'll lose too much time."

The soldier accompanying them unlocked the comms door with the chip in his hand, showing them inside. "Secure channel on the left," he said.

"The deal was for you to wait outside," Cass said, waiting for him to leave.

"I'm going," he said, rolling his eyes. The door latched closed, and Cass took stock of the room. It was efficient and clean, just like the rest of Lucent Base. No sign of clutter anywhere, and everything was so pristine that she could only imagine the maintenance rotations. Back on Terringgough Gulch, her wire room had always been covered in a fine layer of mining dust. The stuff was everywhere, in gears, on clothes, hanging in the air.

"Secure line to Bradach, come in Bradach," Georgie said, already grasping the microphone like it was a lifeline. "Georgina Payne from Lucent Base, come in, Bradach."

"Carmen here. What in the gods-damned hells are you doing out there?"

"Long story. I'm with Cass, she came looking for Cole Marion. Is he still hiding out in Bradach?" There was a long silence over the line, crackling gently with static. "Hello? Did I lose you?"

"I'm here," Carmen replied. "Don't worry about Cole Marion."

"What's that supposed to mean?" Cass interrupted, taking the microphone from Georgie. "He's gallivanting all over the Near Systems, trying to goad me into making a mistake, and you're telling me to not worry about him?"

"He won't be a problem anymore."

Cass rocked back on her heels, understanding seeping into her. "He's dead?"

"Are you sure this is a secure line?"

"Positive. This place is locked down tighter than High Councilor Allemande's undergarments." Cass braced herself against the desk. "What in hells was that broadcast, then?"

"Insurance."

"It would have been nice to have a heads up. I left Delta-4, we nearly got our asses kicked, and it was for nothing?"

"We had no way of contacting you with how much is monitored these days. So Georgie is with you?"

"Yes, I'm here," Georgie reiterated. "Where is Henry?"

"Probably on her way up from the sciences tent, I already sent someone for her." Carmen waited a moment before continuing. "Rosie isn't there?"

"They took her to Ceru," Hyun chimed in. "Beyond the Rim."

"Shit," Carmen hissed. "It will be months before we can reach her. Delia is going to lose it."

"Less in an Obsidian Enclave ship," Hyun offered. "I saw her before she left, she was doing alright. Healthy, not hurt. For all we know, she's joined them by now."

Georgie pushed her way to the microphone again, leaning over Cass' shoulder. "What about everyone else? Is everyone else alright? My Ma?"

"Everyone is fine, more or less," Carmen replied. "A Coalition assassin showed up for Larkin. She's alright, but we're all on edge. Rumor has it they'll send another."

"For Larkin? Why?" Georgie asked.

The radio prickled with static. "Because she knows too much."

"Hello? Georgie?" the radio chimed.

"Henry! Are you alright?"

"Yes, darling, I'm quite alright. I met Dr. Arteo and Jhanvi Jhaveri. They're both here now, working with the rest of us. We've discovered an ingenious way to counteract the superweapon, so long as we can determine every possible algorithmic outcome—" Henry laughed lightly. "You don't need to hear all that. Georgie, I have something to tell you, I'm—"

"Shit!" Carmen shouted, and in the background of the radio transmission, the unmistakable sound of Bradach's intrusion sirens wailed.

"What's going on there?" Cass demanded, grabbing the microphone. "Carmen? Henry?" she called, but the line was dead. Horror pulsated through the air, weaseling its way into her veins, pumping through her every cell with every terrible beat of her worthless heart, locked in the silence with the others.

Georgie was the first to break the quiet with a strangled sob, throwing herself towards the door. "We have to go, have to get there."

Cass didn't argue. They would never get there in time to save them from whatever was happening that very moment, but they'd be drawn to the smoldering remains, regardless. She drifted behind Georgie, following her through the door.

The soldier with the heat gun stood there, a terrible smirk on her face.

"What did you do?" Cass roared. "Tell me what you did, you worthless, half-chewed pomegranate!"

"You fuck me, I fuck you," the soldier retorted.

"I think I would have remembered asking for that," Cass said, revolver already out of the holster. "I'm already involved with someone, and she's much more intimidating than you."

"That wasn't a secure line," the soldier said simply, smiling, almost grinning with the sick pleasure of it. "You just broadcasted not only whatever you said, but Bradach's location. Don't worry, I made sure that the Coalition heard every word of it from the moment you connected. Lucky for us, there was a ship nearby with direct comms installed."

Cass pulled back the hammer, nearly blinded with rage. "You fucking snake. You horrible, disgusting, nasty piece of work, you'd be better off as bio-fuel."

"Your bluffing didn't work this time, Calvetti," the soldier said, tossing fiery hair over her shoulder. "Zink always said you'd come back some day, trying to call all of the shots. He was right."

"I'm only here because I was summoned here!"

"By your own people, by the sounds of it."

Georgie rushed forward, grabbing for the revolver, but Cass didn't relinquish it. The trigger pulled, and a shot went wide, the bullet lodging into the wall of the comms tower. "No, Georgie," Cass shouted, wresting the gun from her. "I'm not letting you do that."

"She—they—" Georgie tried to say, but the sobs strangled in her throat. She swayed on the spot, but Hyun braced under her, making sure she didn't crash down to the white concrete. "Gone. All gone," she moaned, burying her face in Hyun's shoulder.

The soldier's face fell, watching Georgie. "I hope you're happy," Cass said, shoving her. "Doing Zink's bidding, making sure that innocent people get hurt. You assholes are no better than the Coalition, and I will see each and every one of you suffer, if it's the last gods-damned thing that I do."

Chapter 41

Bailey sighed for the fifth time in three minutes, leaning up against the doorframe of the Dark Owl. "What's taking her so long?" she wondered aloud, turning to bang her head against the wood. "This is taking too long."

"Relax, Stocky," Ned soothed, sitting on the floor with his leg propped up on a crate. "She'll be here."

"She's mad that I left without saying anything, and that it was for Willa."

"I mean, she is a Coalition general, Stocky. What's your plan for when you get her out?"

Bailey chewed on the side of her finger. "I don't know. I hadn't thought that far ahead yet." She groaned, banging her head again. "It's my fault she got caught in the first place. If I hadn't sent that letter, she'd still be out on Turas-Mara."

"Maybe." Ned shrugged, flipping open the top of an old, dusty bottle of whiskey. "I say you saved her from the terrible fate of having to deal with High Councilor Allemande."

"I still can't believe that pumpkin wound up as a member of the High Council," Captain Violet said, holding her empty glass out for Ned to refill it. "Of all the people."

Kady shifted, taking a bite out of a loaf of stale bread. "It could be worse."

"How could things possibly be worse?" Bailey asked. "We're all stuck here, hiding, waiting for some way off this gods-damned rock. Willa is under close monitoring who knows where, we haven't had word from anyone else and can't find them, and there's about to be enough security on the docks to ferret out even a mouse as a stowaway with the all-council meeting."

"It could be worse, because we could be dead or imprisoned already." Kady shrugged, taking another bite. "Anyway, at least we're not on our own. We have shelter."

"Yeah, for now maybe," Bailey grumbled. "How long before the Coalition figures out that we're here and sends in a squad to flush us out?"

Ned dragged himself to his feet with a pained groan, holding his leg with one hand and the bottle with the other. "It's not like you to be this negative." He poured whiskey into the empty glass Bailey had left on the windowsill, water-stained with the dregs of the previous night's drink at the bottom. "If you don't relax, you're going to wind up doing something foolish, and we can't afford that right now."

"My sister is probably going to wind up getting the shit kicked out of her," Bailey said, picking up the drink.

"Maybe she deserves it," Kady mumbled under her breath.

Anger flashed in Bailey's vision, rage boiling up to the surface. "Deserves it?" she demanded. "She put her life on the line for Rosie and Delia, helping them escape. Leaving all those notes. She left Turas-Mara with me when Allemande discovered us!"

"What else was she going to do?" Kady asked. "Try to convince her that you were nothing more than a hologram?" She gave a derisive snort, returning to her bread. "Fat chance of that."

"She could have thrown me to the Coalition right then and there, actually," Bailey shot back. "Could have told Allemande I'd managed to smuggle myself aboard, that I'd faked my death, or that I was another interloper who'd had surgery to look like her."

Kady glanced up at her, cheeks full of bread before she swallowed. "Sure."

"I've failed so many times in my life," Bailey said quietly, taking a sip. The taste was familiar, warm with a gentle smoky burn as it slid down her throat, but it wasn't what she wanted. She set the glass down, leaning gently against the rim with the flat of her palm. "I lost so many on Hjarta."

"You got most of them back," Captain Violet offered, shooting Kady a look. "That's more than many would have done."

"And there are still some out there that I didn't!" Bailey countered, tears springing unbidden to her eyes for the second time that day. "I left them to rot."

Ned shook his head. "You didn't leave them to rot."

"It doesn't matter, because wherever they are, they're probably cursing my name, and rightfully so. I abandoned them." Bailey swallowed back the lump in her throat, pulling at the split ends of her braid. "I can't fail Willa, too."

A knock at the door spurred her to wrench it open, dragging Mae inside. "What happened?" Bailey demanded. "What's the plan? Where is she?"

"One thing at a time, Bay Leaf," Mae said, reaching up to cup Bailey's face in the palm of her hand. The gentle, affectionate touch calmed her, and she bent to kiss Mae lightly.

"Alright," Bailey said. "One thing at a time."

"Things are going to start moving fast, if Olivia is doing what I think she's doing."

"And what is she doing?" Aven asked, standing at the top of the stairs. "Because whatever it is, she's not doing it fast enough."

"She's manipulating the press." Mae waved a hand in the air, breezing past Bailey. She took the glass of unfinished whiskey, brought it to her face, frowned, and set it back down. "Shame you don't have any nice red wine in this place."

"Fresh out," Aven deadpanned.

"Guisette is trying to start a coup, and I'm hoping we can use that to our advantage. Tarand and Kimura will be distracted, trying to suppress the news articles and broadcasts as well as prepare for the all-council meeting. My hopes are that General Fineglass—"

"Willa," Bailey insisted.

"That Wilhemina Fineglass is loosely guarded as we approach the all-council meeting in two days," Mae finished. "She's being held in a lodging block on the other side of the city, out past the tunnel."

"Near the hotel?" Bailey asked.

Mae nodded. "Yes. From what I can tell, she's had several meetings with High Councilor Tarand, but that's all. There is usually a full MPO squad stationed in that building."

"There's no way we can take out a squad on our own," Captain Violet said. "Not without weapons."

"We don't want to take anyone out. That draws attention, and attention will get us killed." Mae shook her head, linking her arm with Baileys. "A small strike team to get in and out, lead General—Wilhemina back here." She glanced at Kady. "Do you have your chip disabler?"

Kady whipped the small, snub nosed silver gun from a side holster, giving off a slight glare in the dim, incandescent light that coasted over the surfaces of the mostly abandoned tavern. "Never leave home without it."

"Good." Mae fished something out of her skirt pocket, holding it out. "This is the contact for someone who might be able to get you off-world. He owes my father a steamtruck load of favors from being bailed out over the years. My father has never cashed in on that debt, saving it for a rainy day, I imagine, but I'm going to go ahead and do it for him."

Ned took the slip of paper, holding it close to his face. "I can't read this. Here, Kady," he said, handing it to her.

Kady took it with a smirk. "I keep telling you, Nedrick, you need spectacles."

"Yeah, yeah," he grumbled, draining his glass of whiskey. "I'll get around to it, eventually. It's not like I've had many opportunities, Riha, or have you forgotten?"

"Wait," Bailey said, untwisting her arm from Mae's. "How do we know for sure that this guy won't turn us in, won't alert a bunch of MPOs the moment we show up?"

"Because I will make his life like living through multiple hells if he does," Mae answered casually. "Mention my father's name, that should put the fear of the gods into him.”

“I’ll go,” Captain Violet said, taking the paper from Kady. “My mugshot is the one most out of date.”

“You look the same as the day you first showed up in Bradach, Boss.” Ned poured himself another glass of whiskey and held it up in the captain’s direction. “Still as fresh-faced as ever.”

“Cut the shit, Nedrick,” Captain Violet replied, laughing. “I’ve got the scar now,” she said, gesturing to the shining slash across her face.

Kady stood as easily and gracefully as a swan gliding through a placid lake. “Are you sure, Captain? I’m more than happy to go. I might even be more intimidating.”

“My father’s name will be intimidation enough,” Mae interrupted. “Captain Violet, Ned, you two can head to the docks as soon as Bailey and I leave to liberate Wilhemina Fineglass. It may take some time to locate him, he does his best to remain under the radar. Kady, if you would, you can meet us in the woods to disable her chip and then meet the others at the contact’s bay. If the timing all works out, you can all be on a ship headed for home first thing in the morning.”

“Hold on,” Bailey said. “You all?” she repeated, a sick realization twisting in her stomach. “You’re not coming with us?”

“I think it’s best for me to stay in the Capital until after the all-council meeting. It would raise too many red flags to disappear before then.”

“Mae, no!” Bailey almost shouted, stepping backwards from her. “No, you have to come with us. It’s far too dangerous here for you to stay here alone.”

“I’m not alone, Olivia Guisette is still working in the Executive Building. I think she has proved herself to be trustworthy, and she’s going to need my help if she’s really trying to instigate a coup. The gods know my father certainly won’t help her.” Mae tugged at the taffeta of her crisp cerulean jacket, straightening the hem. “I promise I will be alright, Bay Leaf.”

“No, I won’t let you!”

Mae reached out and grabbed the cuff of Bailey’s jumpsuit, dragging her into the back room. “We’re not going to have this argument right now, especially not in front of the others," she hissed.

"I don't care if they hear me tell you that I don't want you staying here, when it could very likely get you killed!"

"Oh, so you're the only one who gets to make life or death decisions without consulting the other?" Mae waited for a response, staring Bailey down with a perfectly shaped, arched eyebrow and one hand on her hip. "No?" she prompted.

"You're still mad," Bailey said with a sigh.

"Of course I'm still mad, you pineapple. You left without even telling me where you were going or why!"

"I knew you'd say no."

Mae snorted a sarcastic laugh. "Damned right I'd have said no to you offering yourself up to a Coalition general on a silver platter."

"She's my sister, Mae."

"Bay Leaf..." Mae trailed off, letting her hand fall to her side. "I need to stay. I need to do this, just like you needed to do that."

"But I don't want you to," Bailey protested.

"Then we're even." Mae wrapped her arms around Bailey's waist, burying her face in Bailey's chest. "It will be fine. I'm a Machenet. We're basically unkillable, as my father has deftly demonstrated."

"I still don't like it."

"That's fine." Mae checked the dainty watch on her wrist, white gold with a hand-painted face, the numbers shining past the shadows of the back room. "Shift change is in fifteen minutes. We need to go now, if we're going to get your sister out."

"Alright." Bailey wriggled from her grasp, bending to tighten the laces of her boots. "We're not done talking about this yet."

"We are one hundred percent done discussing this," Mae said, kissing her full on the mouth. "It's done. A done deal, Bay Leaf. If you don't want me running around the Capital trying to get myself killed, then you should think about that before you run off without telling me again."

"Fine," Bailey grumbled. "Let's go."

* * *

The street lamps surrounding the lodging building flicked off, letting the night's darkness swoop in around them like a velvet cape. It was a new moon, and there was only the faint, distant glow of the city from the other side of the tunnel.

"Why did the lights go off?" Bailey asked.

"Because I blackmailed someone in the Administration Building," Mae answered simply. "It was a fair trade, given that she's apparently been siphoning funds from the discretionary budget for years."

"How did you find that out?"

Mae shrugged. "My father keeps tabs on many people."

"I hope this works," Bailey said. "I don't think I can have another failure on my conscience."

"You're not a failure, Bay Leaf. I keep telling you this, it's like you don't hear me."

Bailey turned, searching for Mae's silhouette in the darkness. "Of course I hear you, but I let a lot of people down."

"You saved more than you didn't."

"Wouldn't have had to at all if I hadn't been a coward back on Hjarta."

"We don't have time for this, Bay Leaf." Mae eased open a chain-link fence, the hinge groaning quietly in the quiet night. The nearby hotel gardens were awash with insects, their summery hum puncturing the silence with a strange, cyclical rhythm. "Contemplate this later, we need to have our heads clear right now."

"Alright, fine," Bailey relented, following her around the back side of the building. "Where's the circuit box?"

"Up there, to your left. It's pretty high up, you might have to—"

Bailey easily reached up, flipping open the box. "You were saying?"

"Sometimes I forget just how tall you are."

"Shorter than Alice."

"Not by much. I know your inseams." Mae pressed a palm against the exterior brick, leaning in close. "Flip the first three, and the last five," she whispered.

"Why not all of them?"

"Because we want this to look like an electrical fault, not a breakout."

Bailey nodded, despite knowing that Mae probably wouldn't see it. Dutifully, she pulled each of the switches down with an uncomfortably loud click, and waited. "Did it work?"

"Oh, it worked." Mae pulled her by the hand. "Come on, we have to get inside. This is the first thing they'll check once they realize that the power is out." She stopped underneath a window. "Boost me through this."

"I'm not boosting you through a window, Mae."

"Now or never, Bay Leaf. I don't really care if we leave here with or without this sister of yours, but I'm getting the feeling that you do."

"You're bossier in the Capital."

Mae snorted a laugh. "Just do it."

"Step on," Bailey said, interlacing her fingers and crouching, knees bent. Mae was slight enough that it was easy to raise her up off the ground, high enough that she was able to slither through the open window. Bailey followed, jumping and grabbing the frame. It responded with a loud, echoing crack, and she froze, still hanging there.

"Bailey, come on! Inside!" Mae whispered.

"They'll have heard that," Bailey protested.

"All the more reason to hurry the hells up!"

Bailey pulled herself up and through the window, landing softly on the other side, and extending her arms to catch Mae. "I'll never get tired of that."

"Of what?"

"You, in my arms."

"Okay, lover girl, stay focused." Mae kissed her briefly, pulling her down the empty, darkened corridor. "Time enough for that later, assuming this works."

"Assuming?"

"Yes. I'm assuming this will work."

Three corridors in, the lights were still out, and the distant sounds of voices echoed through the building, drifting through the halls with muffled, unintelligible syllables. "They're going to look at the circuit box soon, hurry," Mae prompted. "It's not far now."

"How did you find out which room she's in?" Bailey asked, voice barely above a whisper.

"You don't want to know. Look, here it is." Mae knocked lightly on the door. "General Fineglass, this is housekeeping," she said.

Bailey scrunched up her face, staring at her. "What are you doing?"

"Trying to get her to answer the door, obviously."

"Willa!" Bailey called through the door. "Willa, it's me! Come on, let's go!"

The door flew open, and there was her sister, a dark, hulking silhouette, her eyes glinting with unadulterated rage in the scraps of light glancing off the tiled floors. "What in hells are you doing here, Bailey?"

"Uh, saving you?" Bailey responded.

"You absolute fucking grapefruit, you foolish little—"

"Hey!" Mae interrupted. "She's risking everything to—"

Willa scooped Bailey up, hugging her tight, almost too tight, but that was probably a foregone conclusion given her workout regime. "You came for me."

"Of course I came for you," Bailey said, muffled against her sister's coat. "But we have to go. They'll be turning the lights back on soon."

"My chip—"

"We have a solution," Mae said. "But you have to come with us right now."

Willa nodded, releasing Bailey. "I don't think we've met, despite what the papers think."

"It was a pleasure not kissing you," Mae retorted. "Follow me, the back stairs are around the corner."

"There are cameras on the outside," Willa said, following them. "They'll see me leaving."

"We cut the street lights, they won't see anything," Mae replied, ushering them both through a heavy steel door. "Blackmailed someone for it, cashing in an old family debt."

"Gerard Machenet really is a bastard, isn't he?" Willa asked. "Er, no offense."

"None taken. My father is the worst of humanity." Mae nodded towards the stairs, her face bathed in the red glow of the emergency lights. "Down to the bottom and take the second door on the right."

Willa nodded, leading the way. She wasn't in her uniform now, only a set of soft, Coalition-issued athletic clothes, grey cotton with yellow piping on one side, and purple on the other, all of it strangely hued in the glow.

"Quiet," Bailey prompted. "You have heavy footsteps."

"If you'd served twenty years in the military, you'd have heavy footsteps, too."

"Shh!" Mae hissed. "Stop moving. Someone is outside that door."

All three froze, backing against the railing of the stairs, barely even breathing for the noise. Mae interlaced her fingers with Bailey's and squeezed, and Bailey wasn't sure if it was reassurance or a warning. She squeezed back anyway.

"Who the fuck forgot to cycle the power station?" a voice from outside yelled. "Honestly, you're all a bunch of fucking lemons. I'm applying for a transfer the first chance I have. Look at this, half the gods-damned circuits blew."

"If you had to babysit a general, you'd forget to cycle the power station too," a second voice shot back.

Bailey laid a hand on Willa's shoulder in reassurance, and her sister covered Bailey's hand with her own.

"Fuck you, man," the first voice said. "I'm sick of your excuses."

"Whatever," the second yelled.

Switches flicked noisily, and at the last one, light flooded the stairwell. Mae's grip on Bailey tightened, almost enough to cause pain. She was surprisingly strong, but that came from all the work she did with her hands.

"Get back to work, asshole," the first one called.

Bailey willed the door to stay closed. She wished it and prayed to the dead gods for it, but it opened anyway, revealing an MPO who jerked backwards in surprise.

Quick as a flash, Wilhemina leaped down the final five stairs and was on him in half a breath. She snapped his neck like a twig and he fell lifeless to the ground.

"What the fuck!" Mae hissed.

"He would have told," Wilhemina countered. "What did you want me to do, let all of us get caught?"

"I told you she was a monster," Mae said, pulling at Bailey. "I told you, I told you."

Wilhemina bent over the corpse, pulling at his arm. A gun fell from his hand, already cocked and ready to fire. "He was going to shoot Bailey, and me, and you."

"How did you see that gun?" Bailey asked.

"I'm the one who didn't escape the bullshit experiment." Wilhemina pushed open the door, peering out. "Come on, let's get out of here before someone comes looking for him."

"Yeah," Mae said, shaking her head. "Yeah, Kady is waiting just past the tree line with the chip disruptor."

"Good." Wilhemina looked back over her shoulder at the dead soldier. "I'm sorry. You deserved better." She sighed, squeezing her eyes shut. "Could have been either of us, Bailey. That's the worst part of all."

Chapter 42

Violet pressed a hand against her hip, ready to fight her way onto the ship if she had to. "What do you mean, you won't take us there? Didn't you hear what I said?"

Norman Thibo fidgeted with his hands, pulling at his sweaty fingers, shoulders hunched as he stood on the ramp of the vessel. "I did, ma'am, and please give Gerard Machenet my deepest apologies, but I can't take you there."

"Listen, pal," Kady said, stepping forward to jab a finger into his chest. "Mr. Machenet isn't going to take kindly to being ignored. You owe him, and you know it."

"Anything else. I will do anything else for him," Norman pleaded, mopping his brow with a stained handkerchief from his pocket before running it across the remaining beads of sweat lingering on his bald head. "That place isn't safe."

"It's plenty safe!" Violet countered, for once allowing Kady to continue her physical intimidation. "Safer than you're going to be here if you don't cooperate."

"No, no, you don't understand!" Norman said. He sighed, jamming the yellowed cotton square back into the pocket of his pin-striped trousers. "Please, we can't talk about this out in the open."

"I think we can," Kady said loudly. "Perhaps we should let every occupant of this dock hear about what it is you asked Mr. Machenet to cover up for you."

"No!" Norman stepped backwards onto the ship, gesturing for them to follow. "Come inside, please, I can explain. Please don't tell Mr. Machenet. Please." He twitched his fingers again, brow deeply wrinkled with worry. "Please," he echoed for the third time.

Violet nodded, and her two crew members followed the man aboard. The dock was quiet that time of night, and the street lamp closest to the bay flickered for a few quick moments before returning to its usual amber glow. She rested her hand against the revolver at her hip, ready for Norman to ambush them, even if he didn't seem the type. He looked more likely to bolt like a frightened animal, but then, frightened animals sometimes lashed out.

"Alright, talk," she said after the loading bay door closed. "Out with it."

"First of all, thank you for agreeing to hear me out." He stepped backwards and away from them again, brushing the edge of a Coalition-issued metal crate, with the yellow and purple insignia stamped on the side, the paint still fresh.

"Don't thank us yet," Kady warned. "You're not out of the woods, Mr. Thibo."

"Please don't tell Mr. Machenet that I refused his favor."

Violet stepped forward, a slow-motion chase across the ship's loading bay, lit only with the emergency lights. The darkness unnerved her, and so she was determined to keep eyes on him. "We will tell Mr. Machenet whatever we please," she said evenly. "Now, explain to me why you can't take us to Bradach."

"I don't know where it is."

"Horseshit." Violet pulled the page Mae had given her from her pocket, brandishing it at Norman. "From what I hear, you've been working as a fence for over a decade."

"That's true, that's true," he relented. "Okay, you have me there."

Ned cracked his knuckles, towering over the man menacingly. Violet was suddenly glad for the dim lighting, so Norman wouldn't see the smirk that crossed her face, knowing that Ned didn't have it in him to be the muscle for a deal. Lucky for her, his hulking frame looked the part. "Listen, buddy," Ned boomed. "We aren't in the mood for games, and the boss here has a reputation for a reason. We aren't interested in your excuses or in your lies. Just tell us the truth, and no one will get hurt."

"Please," Norman said, stumbling backwards over another metal crate. He hissed in pain, grabbing at his ankle. "Please, I can explain."

"Explain, then," Violet said. "Otherwise, we'll have no other choice but to tell Mr. Machenet that you spat on his generous deal." She advanced on him, hand still on her gun. "Did you think that Mr. Machenet would give out free services to a pathetic little low-life like you?"

"Of course not." Norman hopped on one foot, cradling his ankle as he leaned against the crate that had done the damage. "Of course not," he repeated, rubbing at it. "Listen, if you don't already know, then I can't tell you. It contravenes the code."

"Code," Violet said, her hand falling to her side. "Norman, that's for people who have never been there before, and it's where our ship makes berth."

He shook his head. "No. No, if you had a ship, you wouldn't need me."

"My ship is—" Violet stopped short, a sharp stab of regret and grief bursting like a dam in her chest, letting loose a flood of wishes and dead dreams that would drown them all, if she wasn't careful. She cleared her throat, pausing to let him test putting weight on his ankle. He was fine, of course, but a dash of grace tended to help negotiations. "My ship is indisposed at the moment." Violet pressed her thumb and forefinger against the bridge of her nose. *The Cricket is gone forever,* she thought. *Gone, and scrapped, and the rest incinerated, and it's all my fault.*

"If I take you, and you're not supposed to be there, then I lose my livelihood. I can't—" Norman mopped at his brow again, hands shaking. "Please, you can't possibly understand the kind of predicament this puts me in."

"We aren't interested in your excuses," Kady said. "Take us to Bradach."

"I can't."

"Gods be damned, man, that's our home!" Ned boomed. "Boss, tell him!"

Violet sucked her teeth before advancing on Norman again. "Ask us anything about Bradach, we can tell you the answers."

"That doesn't account for much of anything anymore, I'm afraid," Norman replied, holding his hands up in defense, as though she was already pointing a gun at him, and not standing with her hands on her hips. "There have been spies. They could have told you anything. Oh, hells, I just know this is some kind of trap. I just don't know why Mr. Machenet is playing these games with me."

"We know all about the spies," Violet interrupted. "I saw one of them wind up with a bullet in his head in the upstairs room of the Bronze Bell." She raised an eyebrow. "Satisfied?"

"If you truly knew Bradach, then you'd…" Norman trailed off. "Then you'd *know.*"

"Know what?" Kady demanded, joining Violet at her side. "What would we know?"

"You see?" Norman said, backing up to the airlock door. "You don't already know, so you can't possibly be from there. I'm sorry, I can't help you." He pressed a button, and the airlock hissed. Before he could disappear to the other side, Ned strode forward, yanking him back into the loading bay.

"What do you know?" Violet asked, her tone steely even as her spine began to compress with worry, one vertebra after another crunching with the pain of unknowing.

"I can't tell you," Norman said again, trying fruitlessly to wriggle from Ned's grasp. "You'd know if you knew!" He was starting to panic now, sweat beading on his scalp and dripping down to splash against the collar of his grey shirt.

"Tell Mr. Machenet that Norman here wasn't interested in paying his debt," Violet said coolly, glancing sideways at Kady. One look told her that her second in command was just as worried as she was, and it wasn't because Mae's father clearly had an even more terrifying reputation than they'd already assumed. "Tell him the debt was refused."

"No!" Norman shouted, wrestling with Ned's grip. "No, no! I couldn't take you even if you knew the reason!"

"This vessel looks perfectly space-worthy to me," Violet said. "Your refusal has been noted." Her insides were crumbling one moment at a time, her stomach clenched in an unwinnable battle of being desperate to know, and never wanting to find out.

Norman yanked himself away from Ned's clutches, dusting off the blazer that matched his trousers. "It's not about my ship. She's safe and space-worthy, that much is true, and I can't have you spreading lies about it. I have enough problems on my plate." He sighed. "Listen, if I could help you, I would, but I can't, and that's all I can say on the matter."

"Tell us right now," Kady said. "Right now, or I swear on every single dead god rotting in their unkempt graves that I will make sure that Gerard Machenet knows exactly what kind of slimy weasel you are."

"Alright!" Normal yelled, backing away from her, winding up in the corner of the loading bay like a cornered animal. "Alright. But you didn't hear this from me."

"I haven't heard a gods-damned thing yet, Mr. Thibo, so start talking," Violet said.

"Broadcast," he said, still holding his hands up, still standing on one leg. "Broadcast, transmission, wire link."

It was Violet's turn to advance on him, and so she did. "What is this, some kind of game to you? I asked for answers, not riddles."

Norman squeezed his eyes shut. "You could be Coalition!"

"Do I look like Coalition?"

"That doesn't mean much anymore, they've got spies all over the gods-damned place. I heard there are spies in every faction."

"Not all of them," Violet replied. "The Splintered are a small, dedicated group. We are not spies."

"Broadcast," Norman said again. He locked eyes with Violet, taking out his pocket watch and flipping it open, the gold chain sparkling in the red light of the loading bay. He shook his head slowly. "Transmission." He shook his head again. "Wire link."

"For all the gods' sakes," Kady muttered, rolling her eyes. "Stop playing games with us. What about Delia's broadcast are you trying to make a point about?"

Ned checked his own pocket watch, staring at it. "We missed it this evening. We missed it because Mae was giving us instructions." He rounded on Norman. "What happened in tonight's broadcast?"

"Gerard Machenet didn't send you?" Norman asked with a barked laugh of relief. "It was his *daughter?*"

"If you think his daughter isn't at least twice as terrifying as he is, then you have another thing coming," Kady snapped. "She controls everything that goes on in this gods-forsaken city, her father is just the face of it."

"She was on the front cover of the papers not so long ago, caught in a broom closet with a general," Norman said, snorting.

"You have no idea what you're talking about," Kady said. "You're so clueless that it's actually embarrassing."

"Says the crew who's so deeply involved with Bradach that you didn't even know that they got raided." Norman clapped a hand over his mouth, scrambling for the airlock again.

It was a good thing that Ned was ready to catch him, because Violet was having to struggle with the idea of remaining upright. Bradach, raided. *Raided.* Raided and gone. Or worse. "The superweapon," she breathed.

"If comms are down, how did you know?" Kady demanded. "Tell us!"

"There were a few ships getting ready to dock when the Coalition vessels showed up. They hightailed it out of there, obviously. Word gets around when you're actually pirates."

"We *are* pirates, you rancid pile of rotten fruit," Violet whispered, alarmed at the menace in her own voice. "We're some of the best gods-damned pirates in the Near Systems." She nodded at Ned. "Let him go. He can't help us. He can't help anyone, by the looks of him."

"That's not true," Norman protested, "I—"

"Zip it," Violet barked, cutting him off. "Open the loading door."

"But Mr. Machenet—"

"Listen, we don't give a rat's gods-forsaken ass about your debt. You can take that up with him." Violet gestured towards the front of the loading bay. "The door. Now."

Norman nodded, ducking under Ned's arm to pull the lever. The pulleys squealed with the effort, and Violet had a flash of Alice oiling the Cricket's door the month before, hanging from a fly system, grinning down at her as grease dripped from her brush to the floor. Gods, she hoped Alice wouldn't head back to Bradach. Let her have heard the same news and let her stay the hells away from whatever was happening.

They disembarked, standing once again on the darkened dock, listless and without direction.

"What now, Boss?" Ned whispered.

"We need to find someone who knows what happened," Violet answered. "We need to—I don't know. Get back there. Do something." She nodded at Kady. "What's the status on Bailey's sister?" She still found it strange that they were helping a Coalition general break out of a monitored apartment, but regardless, she couldn't be talking about that openly, or using her name where someone might overhear.

"Affirmative," Kady replied with a nod. "Probably headed here, if I had to guess."

"Then we need to catch them before they wind up in view of any cameras, because we won't have the quick escape we'd hoped for." Violet finally moved her hand away from the revolver, but the same aura of danger lingered, laid heavy on her shoulders just like a burden. "They'll be close by, I'd imagine."

The wooden boards of the dock creaked under their feet, the usual nighttime bustle absent in light of the upcoming all-council meeting. Norman Thibo would have been the only merchant with enough Coalition-approved credentials to get them off-world, but even he couldn't help them. No one could.

Off the docks and back onto the pavement, Violet watched the horizon for Bailey and her sister, who should have been approaching with Mae. "Something is wrong," Violet murmured.

"Aye," Ned agreed. "It's too quiet, Boss."

"Kady, what happened when they left the lodging?" Violet asked.

"I'm not sure, Captain. They seemed a little shaken up, but that would be standard, given the plan and what they'd done. Gen—Wilhemina seemed upset."

"Doesn't she usually?"

"Different," Kady replied. "We didn't have time to discuss it. I zapped her chip, and all but ran down to the docks to meet you."

"Hmm." Violet's hand drifted towards the holster again, a comfort, something familiar, a failsafe, but she stopped herself. Two revolvers and a heat gun were hardly a challenge for the might of the Coalition, especially in the Capital. "Let's walk up a few streets. Maybe they were waiting for a signal, or watching to see if the ship powered up."

She led them up three roads without a word, crossing junctions where steamcars were curiously absent. The city was locking down for the all-council meeting, giving it an odd, ghostly aura that set Violet's teeth on edge. She paused, just outside the yellow circle of a street lamp, watching for movement and finding none other than a couple of fugitive rats rummaging through trash in an alley. Even the might of the Coalition couldn't rid the city of its vermin.

Finally, after what seemed like an eternity, the trio emerged from an alley at the top of a gentle hill, Mae's skirts almost luminescent in the glow of the street lamps, flanked by the two strangely similar women. Ned was about to call out to them when Violet clapped a hand over his mouth, having to reach up above her head to do so.

"Shh," she hissed. "Something is wrong."

Behind the trio, a small squadron of MPOs, guns pointed at each of them.

"Shit," Kady muttered.

"We need a distraction," Violet announced in a whisper. "Or this is it for them and for us."

"But Boss—"

Violet scanned the darkened windows, squinting past the glare of the glass. "How much juice does your heat gun have, Nedrick?"

"Four, maybe five shots, but—"

"Is that what I think it is?" Violet asked Kady, nodding at a building across the road. That close to the docks, the buildings were mostly industrial, whether printing presses or warehouses.

Kady followed her stare, nodding. "Looks like it. Solvent."

"Will it ignite with a bolt?"

"Captain, you want to blow up a building?" Kady asked, incredulous.

"Why not? You blew up a lab. Ned, power your gun. Hurry up, they're already making their way up the street."

Ned folded up his cane and slung the gun over his shoulder, the bolts inside already growing warm. "At maximum heat, one shot," he confirmed.

"Then we'd better hope you don't miss."

"Captain, this is hardly keeping a low profile, wouldn't you say?" Kady whispered, her eyes watching the group progress further away from them. "We'll have to loop back around, because this will draw attention."

"That's the idea, Commander Riha." Violet so rarely used Kady's command designation, but as they were probably about to die or be thrown into a cell, it seemed appropriate. She sighed, flattening a palm against the exterior brick of a building. "I'm so tired of running."

"Four seconds to max temperature," Ned announced in a whisper, and already the heat was rising from the gun's wide maw of a barrel in silent wavy tendrils, like an oasis in the desert. "Three, two, one—" He fired, the force of the gun jerking his arms skyward. The bolt screamed through the air, crashing through the glass.

It was too dark to see where it had landed, and Violet waved the other two off as she stood, regrettably rooted as she waited the eternity to see if her foolish plan had worked. The building remained unlit, the only damage the sparkling shards of glass littered on the ground.

One guard peeled away to investigate, but that wasn't enough to save them.

"Please," Violet hissed, backing into the shadows. "Come on!"

All at once, the world lit up. She shielded her eyes, covering her face from the blast. Strong arms dragged her from behind, pulling her into an alley, and she knew that Ned had waited for her, the foolish, wonderful man that he was. The only sound was the ringing in her ears, her vision blinded by the brightness of the explosion.

The second building exploded, starting a chain reaction throughout the industrial district that sent bricks and flaming bits of debris flying through the air.

They were running. Not so much running as stumbling, grasping along brick to escape the growing blaze. Ned dropped the empty heat gun and snapped open his cane, the same one Marina Sykes had given him. He pushed himself along, half-dragging Violet because she was fixated on looking backwards, marveling at what they'd done, wondering if the flames would engulf them all before the night was through.

They struggled, and tripped, and clambered along empty city streets, their faces hidden from cameras by the growing cloud of thick, black smoke. One more street to the Dark Owl and the sirens began to sound, a screaming, wailing sound that pulled at Violet's ears.

When they collapsed through the door of the tavern, half-blind and half-deaf from smoke and sirens, she was only half-aware that of the six of them who had ventured out, only five had returned.

Chapter 43

Henry had been hiding in the basement for hours, wedged beneath the wire desk with Carmen. No one had opened the door, or called for them, or whispered beneath the crack what was happening. Larkin's voice was barely audible above the din, directing someone to remove the bar over the back door.

"Why would she be letting someone in, when they haven't even—"

"Did she just say siege?" Carmen hissed, already dragging her yellow skirts up over her thigh to reveal a garter strap holding a large knife against her bronzed skin.

"We can't just rush up there, we don't know what we're dealing with!" Henry countered. "Could be Scattered, looking for Cole, or could be Obsidian Enclave looking for an easy annex, or hells, it could be Coalition!"

Carmen shook her head. "It couldn't be Coalition. William has been feeding them incorrect coordinates for months, intercepting every coded message, altering it, and sending it on." She leaned forward, peeking out from under the desk. "My bet is on Scattered. We knew that ruse wouldn't hold forever."

"I can't believe you didn't tell us about that."

"Easier to keep secrets if fewer people know about it." Carmen squinted at the stairs, shushing Henry when she tried to respond. "We should get up there, we have the advantage on our side. We can flank from outside, we just have to fit through that window."

"I'm not doing that," Henry said firmly. "Whoever is here, trying to manipulate us with force, needs to be given a stern talking to."

Carmen snorted. "I don't think that's going to do much, Weaver. Don't you remember what happened the last time you took matters into your own hands? I had to help carry you, half-dead, back to the hideout in Skelm."

"It's different this time. I'm not hiding in a cargo bay stuffed full with chemical solvents." Henry tugged at her cropped jacket, straightening it over her waistband, which was already uncomfortably tight. "If it is Scattered, we just call Cass back on the wire and she'll tell them he's there with her."

"They're going to want more proof than that."

"Ma'am!" a voice shouted from the other side of the basement door. "There's a cellar or something here."

"Search it," came a muffled, disaffected voice. "Kill anyone who resists."

Henry scrambled out from under the table, holding her hands over her head by the time the MPO shot the lock off the knob. "Don't shoot!" she pleaded, sinking down to her knees. "My friend is under the table. Don't kill her, either."

The MPO smirked. "Not yet, anyway." He descended the steps, followed by three more soldiers. Nodding at the table, he tilted his chin. "You under there, come out. No sudden movements."

"Fucked gods," Carmen grumbled, shimmying out, holding her palms up. "The Coalition?" she whispered as one of the soldiers placed her next to Henry, steering her by the shoulders.

"By order of the newest member of the High Council," the squad leader announced. "Her Honor, High Councilor Amaranth Allemande."

Henry's stomach twisted into a knot, and her hands flexed in and out of fists at her sides. "What does she want?"

"To clear out this colony of pirates and leeches," the leader said easily. "Same thing though, really."

"Are we under arrest?" Carmen asked.

"You might as well be," he replied. "Don't try anything, or we'll shoot.

Pile of bodies in the street outside already accounts for that." He shrugged. "Feels the same as clearing an abandoned building of roaches, if you ask me."

"You never should have come here," Carmen said. "This isn't going to end the way she thinks it will."

The leader stepped forward, pressing the tip of the barrel of his rifle to Carmen's throat. "And why is that? You have secret traps down here, or something? Rigged explosives?"

"No."

He pointed the rifle at Henry, keeping his eyes on Carmen. "I'll ask again, but this time, I shoot your friend if you don't give me an appropriate answer."

Henry had the flash of a thought that she could easily pull the rifle from him, given his slack grip on the stock, but a glance around at the other MPOs in the basement kept her hands at her sides. "There's nothing down here," she said with a light shrug. "There is a wire desk beneath that sheet, but you won't find anything else down here."

"Blood smear by this window," one of the other guards said.

"I cut myself doing garden work," Carmen offered, showing off a long scratch that ran across her forearm, jagged and lightly swollen. "Thorns."

"I doubt that." The leader nodded again, this time to an MPO standing near the wire desk, who unearthed it with a dramatic flourish, yanking off the dusty white sheet that covered it. "Looks like you two have been running quite the little operation down here." He smiled, and it was cold, not even a hint of warmth or sincerity. "Which one of you is Delia Dodson?"

"Forrest," Henry corrected, stepping forward. "I am."

"Wait—" Carmen started, but a guard silenced her with a firm crack of rifle butt against jaw, and she staggered backwards, holding her face with a quiet whimper.

"You run the pirate broadcasts?" the leader asked, an eyebrow raised. "You don't sound like her."

"It's a stage voice," Henry lied. She hoped Delia was hiding somewhere else, because they'd kill her if they found her. The reality that she'd just offered herself up to the Coalition hadn't really crossed her mind. "If you're going to arrest me, then arrest me." Henry folded her arms across her chest, a gentle, non-threatening display of defiance. "Might as well get this over with."

"All in due time." He turned, stepping back to the stairs. "Ma'am! Two down here, radio operators."

"Good. Bring them to me," said a voice that Henry was desperately wishing she didn't recognize.

The leader jerked the barrel of his rifle to the side. "You heard her. Up. Both of you. Don't do anything foolish, or we'll be forced to take action, and I really don't feel like cleaning up a mess today." He flicked a piece of lint from the grey wool epaulet on his shoulder before placing both hands back on the rifle. "Move it."

Carmen went first, following one of the guards. She tossed her head easily, dark curls bouncing. "Don't worry. We've been through worse, right?"

"Yeah," Henry replied, willing her to stay calm and not reach for that guard's sidearm. They didn't yet know what was waiting for them upstairs in the tavern, and one wrong move would find them all dead and sent off to the incinerator, just like Cole Marion had been. Henry shook her head, still absorbing that piece of information. Once, they'd all shared secrets, but everything had become so fractured, so secretive as the war intensified.

"Through to the tavern," the leader said, following up from the back. "Take them straight to the high councilor."

"Aye," the guard in front said, pushing through the swinging door. "You two, get in there." She shoved Carmen through, and then Henry, making sure that both felt the rifle in their backs as they went. The Pig was all but destroyed, every bottle smashed against the carpet, ugly stains spreading like malignancy from the bar out towards the overturned tables. Evie and Larkin, both handcuffed, kneeling in puddles of good wine and whiskey. Larkin's eyes burned with quiet, dangerous rage, despite her restraints.

The squad leader leaned against the bar once they were all through. "Delia Dodson and her operating technician," he announced. "Found them in the basement."

The newest high councilor turned, top hat in hand, thumb and forefinger running along the brim. "That isn't Delia Dodson."

"Forrest," Henry corrected again, standing firm.

"Ms. Weaver, how nice to see you again," Allemande said, her voice saccharine sweet. "The last time we saw each other, you were on the wrong side of the line. Again." She glanced at the other soldiers. "Where are the others?"

"We cleared the building, ma'am. There's no one else."

"Impossible. This one is never seen far from her rebel paramour. She must be here somewhere, I already found the mother down at the medical tents."

"Georgina isn't here," Henry said, for once so grateful to the dead gods that they'd kept her away, safe from the invasion. "She is meeting with Obsidian Enclave."

"Obsidian Enclave is hardly even fit to lick the mud from my boots. They have a few pieces of interesting technology, but it's nothing we can't replicate or steal. We've done it before."

"Poorly," Henry shot back. "You forget, Inspector, I've seen the inside of Coalition labs."

Allemande took a revolver from the guard standing next to her and pointed it at Henry, who instinctively flinched, laying her hand flat over her stomach for a split second before she realized, but it was long enough. "Ah," Allemande said coolly, not lowering the gun. "A whelp. You and Georgina Payne have chosen to procreate, then. An interesting choice, given the environment you'd be raising a child in. This backwater is hardly suited to child rearing."

Carmen leaned over, nudging Henry with her shoulder. "You never said! Congratulations!" she whispered.

"Thanks," Henry replied, still staring straight ahead. She didn't want to give the guards any more reason to fire on them.

"Bradach is a far sight better than the hole of hells you call Gamma-3," Evie snapped, glaring.

"That is enough," Allemande said, not even turning to look at her. "I have plenty of plans for you, Ms. Anderson, don't you worry."

"Maybe next time you can slice up something else, because these tattoos were a lot of work, and I'd hate to besmirch the artist's talent." Evie raised her arms slightly, the iron chains jingling as she did, the scale tattoos barely concealing the scars beneath.

Allemande glanced at her, and then at Henry, and then turned slowly to Carmen. "Another betrayal."

"I was never on your side," Carmen hissed. "You murdered my people at Fort Gelad and took the rest of them into servitude—"

"I offered them opportunity," Allemande inserted. "A pity that you chose to shun my hand up out of the mud of that settlement." She sighed quietly, lowering the revolver to her side. "No matter. The gods have seen it fit to allow me to correct the mistake I made the first time." She flicked her wrist towards Carmen, and the squad leader aimed. Carmen reached for the knife beneath her skirts, but the muzzle of the rifle sparked with the explosion, and she fell to the floor with an empty, dull thud. Already, blood pooled from her forehead, soaking into the wood below.

"No!" Henry tried to scream, but the only thing that emitted from her lips was a guttural, wheezing gasp as her lungs betrayed her ability to speak.

Allemande made a soft tutting noise and turned back to Evie. "A waste. She had the potential to be so efficient, but she chose to use her skills for treason."

Evie choked back a sob, a small moan emitting from her lips in the shape of a quiet *no*. Larkin faced forward, unmoving, her stare fixed on the empty shelves behind the bar. There was no expression on her face of recognition or realization. She was blank, like a new canvas ready for paint, or a cloudless sky waiting for rain.

One of the guards stepped over Carmen's body, his boots crunching against broken glass. "What do you want us to do with her?"

"Send her to the incinerator with the rest," Allemande said, waving a hand in a deeply unconcerned manner.

"No, wait," Henry said, holding her hands up. "Wait, let us bury her."

"Oh, I think she deserves the same end that she gave Cole Marion, don't you?" Allemande asked easily. "You people act like the Coalition is nothing more than a long list of regulations, unworthy of protection, but you kill your own just as simply as you make yourselves lavish breakfasts." She handed the revolver back to the guard next to her and wiped her hands with a bleached handkerchief from her breast pocket, embroidered with the yellow and purple crest of the Coalition. "So much for The Scattered being the saviors of the Near Systems. You killed their last leader."

"Cassius Calvetti is still alive," Evie said between sobs. "She's out there, and she's coming for us. She's coming for *you*," she spat.

"She is more than welcome to try," Allemande retorted. "I think I have proved today that I have the upper hand, in weapons, in personnel, in technology, and more importantly, in strategy." She cast a disappointed glance at Carmen's corpse, limp, half of her against the wood, and half against the blood and alcohol soaked rug, her eyes still wide with surprise. "Sometimes, it is prudent to play the long game instead of jumping into the fray unprepared. A lesson I learned the hard way, I'm afraid."

Henry squeezed her eyes shut, willing herself to stay in the moment, and not wonder who was lying dead on the cobblestones outside the tavern, if one of them was Sandrine, if another was Lucy. They were her family, through and through, as though they'd been a part of her life since the very beginning. She struggled to swallow back the lump in her throat in order to ask the question she was afraid to let past her lips. "Lucy?"

"Ms. Payne will be relocated to Gamma-3 and put into reeducation until she is ready for accelerated learning programs. From what we found her doing in the sciences lab near the docks, I'd say that won't take long." Allemande laid a hand on Henry's shoulder. "I trust that you trained her?"

"We all did."

"Mm. Well, I can assure you, Ms. Weaver, reeducation is best for her. Luckily for your child," she said, nodding at Henry's stomach, "they will grow up in the Coalition, and will have no need for reeducation."

"What is your fascination with us?" Henry demanded, wrenching away from Allemande's grasp. "Is it because you worry that someday Emeline will change her mind, come back to us, shun you forever?"

"Emeline has nothing to do with this," Allemande snapped.

"I bet it eats at you that we got her off Turas-Mara," Henry said. "That she got away from you the first opportunity she could, and went back to the one place you begged her not to go."

"Emeline was never my prisoner. She is doing work putting Skelm back together after my successor ran it into the ground." Allemande stepped back, nudging Carmen's body with the toe of her boot. "Get this out of here, it's making me feel sick."

"Aye," one of the guards said, picking Carmen up by the ankles and dragging her across the carpet to the front door. Inexplicably, Henry's first thought was that he was going to give Carmen friction burns pulling her across the floor like that, and when the realization hit that it wouldn't matter, her knees collapsed from under her, sending her to the floor.

"Cuff her," Allemande said. "And prepare her for transport. She'll be headed to the work camp on Gamma-3 until she gives birth." She gave Henry a strange, hungry look. "No sense in wasting potential talent. Ms. Weaver is a brilliant mind, no doubt her child will prove just as gifted."

Henry held out her wrists for the cuffs, the weight of them dragging at her limbs as the soldier clapped them around her. "I hope my child grows up to destroy you," she said evenly. "I hope they dismantle your precious Coalition brick by fucking brick."

"Language, Ms. Weaver. What would your parents think?"

"My parents are nothing more than cowards. Weasels, lying in wait, unwilling and unable to hold even one conviction that isn't to stay quiet and stay out of the way while the Near Systems burn around them," Henry spat, her chest heaving with the effort of trying to remain in control, even as Carmen's body was pulled through the front door and tossed carelessly into the bed of a Coalition steamtruck along with others. Through the small opening in the door, Henry searched what she could see from the bodies in the truck, praying to treasonous gods that she wouldn't find Sandrine's face. The only face she did recognize was the tailor from across the square, his white apron crimson with blood.

"Your parents served the Coalition for decades with faith. It's a shame their daughter was so easily corrupted by the first rebel that came along."

"She wasn't the first," Henry replied. "There were others."

"No, Ms. Weaver, there weren't. You need to learn that lying to me is ineffectual. I always figure it out in the end." She turned towards Evie, smiling at her. "After all, captured rebels told me for years that they didn't know Ms. Anderson here, that she wasn't the leader of a rebel cell, that she had nothing to do with The Scattered or the rest of it, but I found differently, didn't I?"

Allemande frowned at the empty shelves, rustling the grey skirts of her purposefully tailored dress. "Contraband. Miscreants. A wire desk in the basement. Maps upstairs to every rebel settlement, codes. Ms. Anderson, you are behind every move that unseated me since you broke my jaw back in Skelm." She held Evie's jaw in her hand, a glint in her eyes. "I've dreamed of the day I'd get my hands on you again, and here I stand, and there you kneel, in your proper place at last."

"If you touch her again, I'll kill you," Larkin said calmly, her stare still fixed at the wall. "I will take you apart, High Councilor Allemande, limb by limb."

"Ah, Ms. Flores, you're in cuffs if you hadn't noticed. You may have bested Ralph Baker, fool that he was, but you cannot best me."

"I killed the assassin you sent."

"I didn't send him dear, that isn't my department." Allemande pulled Larkin's hood down, exposing her exhausted, gaunt face. "You hardly look ready for a fight, in any case."

"Don't touch her," Larkin repeated.

"You're not the one giving orders here," Allemande replied, stepping around Larkin to face her. "You'll be dealt with soon enough, and quietly. Heavens forbid that word about you and your ilk get out. You made a useful weapon, Ms. Flores, but the time has come for you to be decommissioned." She turned to the guards with a delicate sigh. "Get them loaded onto the transports with the rest. Put the torch to this place when you leave."

The door slammed open, an MPO holding her side as she crumpled to the ground. "Councilor," she rasped, "A contingent of rebels." Blood oozed from her lips, her face losing color by the moment. "One of them—crutches—crack shot, she—"

"Find her," Allemande ordered to the guards. "Root her out and kill her, whoever she is."

Chapter 44

Delia handed Captain Tansy another box of ammunition, using her spyglass to look out over the burning settlement. Smoke rose thick in the air, and scuffles were still breaking out at the edges of town, where the terraformers' boundary lay. The docks had been locked down by the Coalition for hours.

"Thanks." The captain flipped open the box and loaded more rounds into her steamrifle, snapping the cartridge shut when it was full. "How's the Pig?"

Delia swallowed back the lump in her throat. "Burning."

"Bastards. I'll put holes into every single one of them for what they did to that place." Tansy braced against the window frame, taking aim at an MPO on the street below who was dragging someone back to a transport. "I built it with my own two hands. Mostly, anyway."

"It was a beautiful place."

"I bet you're glad your girl isn't here to see this."

"I hope Rosie is somewhere safe." Delia looked through the spyglass again, searching for their friends. "No sign of them."

"We'll find them before that transport takes off. There's no way you would have missed them being marched down to the docks."

"I hope not." The MPO Tansy had been aiming at crumpled to the ground, cradling her arm and dragging herself into the shadows of a nearby alley. Delia's stomach twisted again, and something underneath her skin burned, for justice maybe, or for freedom. Sometimes, she'd seen that the two were the same, really, in the end. "Do you think we'll make it out of this?"

Captain Tansy gave her a sideways glance before taking aim once more. "No." She took aim, letting out a long, slow breath, and fired, the weapon recoiling into her shoulder. "No one gets out of something like this. All we can do is take out as many as we can before someone figures out we're up here on the roof."

"Who would have thought that in the end, it was the Bronze Bell that offered us safety?" Delia asked, nodding down towards the street. "Twelve-o'clock, with the heat gun."

"Got him." Tansy fired again, and she sighed, following it up with a bitter, empty laugh. "We all thought this place was untouchable. We were fools."

"It was Cole's fault."

"That monster Allemande would have found a reason to come here, regardless." Tansy snapped another round into the chamber, setting the muzzle of the steamrifle against the window frame. "We should have seen the end before it came for us."

"No one could have known."

"Mm." The captain shifted the crutch under her arm, trying to hide the pained expression that crossed her face. "I'm almost glad I didn't get my leg back before I go out. It would be a gods-damned shame for a piece of tech so beautiful to wind up in the incinerator." She scowled, taking aim again. "Although the fuckheads probably would have ripped it off my corpse." Captain Tansy fired, staring down at the street. "Good riddance."

"I can take over," Delia offered, holding her hands out for the gun. "I'm a half-decent shot."

"I'm better."

"You look like you're in pain."

"Good thing it won't last much longer."

Delia glanced up at the sky, cloudless. She preferred the chaos of the storm generators back in Skelm to the encroaching, organized order of MPOs stalking up and down streets, dragging out anyone they could find.

"That transport must be full by now," she said, closing her eyes and imagining Rosie waiting for her at the end of a broadcast back on Turas-Mara. Rosie, the only woman she'd ever really loved, and she wasn't even going to have the opportunity to say goodbye. "What will they do with the rest of us?"

"Bring in another transport. Or let some burn, and the rest starve." The captain nodded towards the comms tower, which was already being dismantled. "No news in or out. I doubt anyone is even coming for us." She squinted out the window, starting to aim, and then stepping out of view of the window, her back against the wall. "If the gods are kind, no one is coming for us. They'd set down right into a trap."

"A shame we don't have more weapons."

"If I could get to my ship, we would, but no doubt these slimy shits have already looted it for all its worth."

The horizon beyond the docks was pale with the light of early evening, the mirrors above Bradach doing their work despite what was going on below, neutral and unimposing. "It looks like some of the ships are being stripped for parts, but it's hard to see which from all the way over here, even with the spyglass."

"They'll have started with mine," Captain Tansy replied bitterly. "I've been flying under their noses for years, and they've hated me for it. How could anyone want to leave the great Coalition?" She gave a dry, humorless laugh, so different from her usual tone. "How could any one of those refugees think that they deserve something better than a short life in a mining camp, when the Coalition is so gods-damned benevolent?"

"This won't be the end, you know. Cass is still out there, and Rosie, and—"

"It's the end for us, Forrest." Captain Tansy peeked out the window and flinched. "They're narrowing down where we are now. It won't be long."

"We could move to another rooftop," Delia offered, unsure what else to say when the cobblestones were running with blood, dripping down from the backs of steamtrucks loudly bouncing across the settlement.

"Nah. Can't move fast enough without my leg." The captain leaned out the window, taking aim at a window across the city. The gun fired, and the glass shattered, raining down over a small squadron of MPOs below. "Maybe that will put them off the scent for a few more minutes."

"I'm sorry I never had the opportunity to fly with you, Captain," Delia said as a lieutenant pointed up at the roof, gesturing to his underlings. "It would have been the trip of a lifetime."

"I don't have much need for journalists on my ships," Captain Tansy replied with a wry smile. "But I would have welcomed you with open arms and some fresh coffee." She growled quietly under her breath. "Fucked gods, what I wouldn't do for a cup of coffee right now." She snorted back a derisive laugh, leaning the gun against the brick interior with the quiet scrape of metal, barely audible above the noise of the steamtrucks struggling to cross the cobblestones, and the shouts of others making fruitless attempts to resist. "Larkin is going to be pissed. She just bought that coffee machine a few months ago."

"I don't think we have long, Captain."

Captain Tansy rubbed at her armpit where the crutch had been resting. "I know." She inhaled slowly, quietly, holding the breath for a moment or two before exhaling between her teeth as a whistled hiss. "Let me load up before our last stand, eh?"

Delia nodded, tossing a box of ammunition and finding the bag empty. "Last one."

"I doubt we'd have time for more, anyway." Wordlessly, the captain loaded the steamrifle once more, dust particles dancing in a sunbeam invading through the open window. "The lieutenant first."

"Three-o'clock," Delia answered. "Near the entrance to the park."

Snap. Lock. Fire.

"Down," the captain answered in a dangerously neutral tone. "They can see us now."

"Incoming!" Delia shouted, ducking down behind the brick. A barrage of shots embedded themselves into the crumbling brick exterior, left untended for years by the owners of the Bronze Bell, long since loaded onto the prison transport. A flurry of bullets zinged through the window, blasting the far wall to shreds with chunks of it crashing down onto the unfinished wood floor. "What now?"

"We're cooked," Captain Tansy answered, clutching the steamrifle to her chest for a split second before firing wildly through the window once more. "We're outgunned."

"Shit," Delia whispered, peeking through the spyglass. "They're taking Henry somewhere."

"What about the others?"

"I can't see Evie, Larkin, or Carmen. As far as I know, they were the only ones left in the Pig after the sirens started. Everyone else ran for the docks."

"Fools," the captain said sadly, racking in another round. "Are they taking Weaver to the prison transport?"

"No, they're aiming for another ship, as far as I can tell."

"Why would they do that?"

Delia eased out a breath, despite the heavy thudding in her chest. "I'm going down there."

"You'll die, Forrest."

"I'm going to die either way. I'm not going to sit here and just—just wait for death!" Delia threw down the spyglass, the lens cracking when it met with the floor. "I'm going."

"And what are you going to do when you get down there? Run?" Captain Tansy shook her head, but there was a hint of a smile playing at the corners of her mouth. "Punch someone?"

"Never been very good at right hooks," Delia answered. "But I will be gods-damned if Rosie finds out I went down a coward."

The captain pulled a revolver from her hip, spinning the chamber and snapping it back into the gun. "I'll lay down as much covering fire as I can, but you'd better be fast, Delia." She nodded towards the back stairs, a steely glint in her brown eyes. "Once I'm out of ammunition, the game is over. Make her proud." Captain Tansy squared her shoulders, throwing down the crutch to lean against the window instead, even as a round whipped past her head. "You're a damned good broadcaster."

"And you're a damned good captain."

"Damned right I am."

Delia nodded, crouching, her spine already protesting the position with the grinding crunch of vertebrae against vertebrae but it was only background noise for her mission as she slipped through the doorway and down the back stairwell, coated in thick, greasy cobwebs and a delicate sheen of slippery sawdust, collected there from years of unfinished renovations. The wooden stairs creaked under her weight with every step, protesting her presence, begging her to stay with Captain Tansy on the top floor.

Each stair brought her closer to her own inevitable demise, and with it, the screams and shouts of others trying to run, to survive the betrayal their sanctuary had wrought. Bradach was no longer safe, and maybe it never had been in the first place. Nowhere was safe from the malignancy of human violence, of that deep and inexorable quest for power, for pain, for subjugation, for loathing and fear of the other, and by the gods, maybe she was tired enough of it all. That was what led her to the back door of the Bronze Bell, two moments away from throwing away her own life in the desperate, selfish need to have meant something.

In the first moment, she laid her hand on the tarnished doorknob, closing her eyes to remember her Rosie one last time, regretting every moment they'd ever spent apart. In the second, she shouted to the captain that she was ready, and she pushed herself out into the sunset light, still an assault on her retinas. The captain was already laying down fire, shooting down across the cobblestones with a terrible racket as shots ricocheted against buildings, shop signs, steamtrucks, and corpses. No matter how the day ended, Bradach would never be the same. The streets would always remember when they ran red with the blood of its residents.

Ducking behind one building and then another, Delia sprinted from shadow to shadow, already winded, her lungs already protesting, but she ran anyway, chancing a look over her shoulder and regretting it when she saw that the Bronze Bell was surrounded, and the firing was beginning to slow. The captain was down to her revolver, and conserving what she could. The pit in Delia's stomach widened, threatening to pull her down into the bile to dissolve her one pound of flesh at a time. One more sacrifice. One more failure.

She was wheezing, doubled over with the aftermath of running, when she caught sight of Henry, cuffed at her wrists and being shoved down to the docks by the muzzle of a rifle at her back. Three military police officers flanked her, pushing her until she stumbled and fell to the ground. When she stood, her palms were bloodied, but she still looked back at the Purple Pig, still streaming clouds of acrid smoke into the mirrored sky.

Delia bounced against the balls of her feet, searching for the others and not finding them. One of the MPOs gestured towards Henry with a shrug, tapping the stock of his heat gun. They were going to kill her. The other two nodded, one casting a nervous glance down an empty side street.

A steamtruck drove by, laden with bodies dressed in the grey military uniforms. The Coalition had suffered losses that day, too. They'd won, but it came at a cost, and the remaining winners were skittish. Delia chewed her lip, darting behind one of the science sheds and nearly sprawling out across the street when an overturned cobblestone caught the toe of her boot. She swore under her breath, hoping no one had seen her.

"What now?" one of the MPOs said.

The second looked up the hill towards the Pig. "Dunno. She said this one isn't for the prison transport."

"What the fuck are we supposed to do with her, then?"

Henry lifted her wrists, the orange mirrored sun catching the metal and shining a glare onto the street. "You could free me."

"Shut up," the first said, shoving her down to her knees. "I say we zap her, say she tried to overpower us. We've got enough shit to do without having to send two to watch her."

"Could throw her in the brig."

"And then what, genius? You heard the high councilor, this one is crafty."

The third one rested his hands against the holsters at his waist, giving the prison transport a worried look. "If we don't get the hells out of here soon, there's going to be trouble, I just know it."

"Pipe down, Wilson, we're all going to be fucking heroes when we leave. The platoon who liberated the great secret settlement, who tore a great big gods-damned hole right in the center of their plan." The first guard stared as a steamtruck rumbled past, struggling against the loose road. "Heroes, Wilson, heroes with something to go back to when it's all over. Promotions." He kicked at a rock. "Women."

"The only women who'd have you are in your dreams," Henry chided easily, her voice clear and calm despite her cuffs. "You three are a sight to bring on sore eyes."

"I said, *shut up*," the guard said, shoving her down again. "Gods-damned pirates and rebels, thinking laws don't apply." He nodded at the one with the heat gun. "Do it. I'm tired of listening to her."

Henry moved to stand, bracing her palm against the knee of her skirts, and thrust herself forward, slamming her head into the seconds's stomach, sending him reeling. The heat gun went skidding along the pavement, but before Delia could scramble for it, the third guard whirled around, aiming at Henry with his pair of revolvers, freed from their holsters. "Don't you even fucking move," he hissed, stepping closer.

None of them had noticed Delia yet, creeping closer with every half-second that passed. Henry was almost within her grasp, not that she knew what she was going to do when she reached her.

The guard cocked the revolvers one at a time and aimed.

Delia threw herself between Henry and the guard, almost surprised when the pain hit at the same time as the sound of the gun's explosion reached her ears. Pain, tearing through her gut, hot and destructive. She landed next to the heat gun, pulling it closer to her.

"Delia!" Henry shouted, but her voice was muted, like she was under-water. The whole world sounded like that in the moment, muffled and hidden despite the bright intensity of the day. She was standing, knocking the revolvers from the guard and kicking the guns away with the toe of her perfectly polished boot. Henry was pretty in that prim and proper way, even as she used the iron of her cuffs to slam her fists into a guard's face.

The heat gun was already warm in her hands, primed, ready to inflict the end of the universe. Delia's vision swam in front of her, and she was only passingly aware that the uncomfortable dampness seeping through her once-crisp white linen shirt was, in fact, blood. "Tell Rosie I tried," she mumbled to no one, because the other four were still scrabbling for the revolvers.

"Forrest!" Henry shouted, tripping backwards. "The heat gun!"

Delia pulled the trigger, sending a red-hot bolt into a nearby steamtruck, zinging through the metal and exiting the other side a molten, tangled mess of aluminum and steel. She pulled again, this time taking out two of the guards at once, the huge bolt scraping between them, sending them both to the ground screaming, but not before one fired back, a red-hot twist of metal slamming into Delia's arm, filling the air with the scent of scorched flesh.

"Get off of me!" Henry shouted, wriggling from the grasp of the final guard. "Don't you know how to treat a lady?" She ducked under his arm, snatching at one of the revolvers, half-hidden beneath a bush. She shot him in the chest, letting him fall to the ground in a disorganized heap of flesh and twisted uniform, the fabric hanging oddly off his unconscious frame.

"I'm sorry," Delia murmured, quietly wondering why things seemed so dark all of a sudden, but resisting the obvious answer. "I'm sorry I didn't do enough."

"You did plenty," Henry reassured her, already pressing against the gunshot wound, tearing a tourniquet from her skirts with her teeth. "We have to get you stitched up. Come on, there has to be somewhere—"

"No," Delia interrupted. "Tansy. Bronze Bell."

"That's halfway across town!"

"She's going to die, Henry," Delia whispered, tears gathering in the corners of her eyes. "We can't all die. Some of us have to live."

"You saved my life, Delia, I'm not leaving you here." Henry picked Delia up by her ankles, and with considerable effort, dragged her behind a park bush. "The others are still up at the Pig, behind, in the garden. I'm going to get you help."

"No!" Delia shouted. "Captain Tansy. Her ship. Pilot. You can get out." She shook her head, letting the tears stream freely down her cheeks, even as the warm light dried them where they lay. "Tell Rosie. Tell her, Henry."

"I'll tell her," Henry replied, holding Delia's hand. "I'll tell her."

Chapter 45

Evie shifted her weight, the hours of kneeling and standing taking their toll on her back. She'd massage the sorest muscles if she could, but her hands were still chained in front of her, the heavy iron rubbing her wrists raw. She'd hoped that she wouldn't be back in cuffs so soon, especially not at the hands of Allemande.

The Purple Pig was all but burned-out, the smoldering remains of her life quietly crackling with each new crumb of fuel it found. Every code, destroyed. The plume from the lab down by the docks suggested the same fate for the backup files stored behind Henry's desk. Years of work, gone in a matter of moments. Up in smoke, the moment they were discovered. Her life's work, reduced to ashes.

Larkin hadn't said anything for hours, not to Allemande nor anyone else. She stared straight ahead, unmoving from where they'd put her on the opposite side of the garden, just outside the Pig's back door. Cinders were smeared across her face in a messy swipe, and Evie could only watch her from beneath the apple tree, now empty of fruit for another season.

High Councilor Allemande latched the wrought-iron gate behind her, clasping a padlock around a new chain to seal it shut. "Ms. Anderson," she said, tugging a pair of crisp white gloves on over her long, bony fingers. "I must say, it is a relief to finally catch up with you again. I'm just sorry our last meeting was so abbreviated."

"Oh, you know, I had somewhere to be," Evie replied, aiming for a breezy tone, but the words tumbled from her lips, clumsy and stilted, each syllable rushing into the next. She'd never been as collected as the others. She hated that about herself. "Next time, I'll send a note."

"An Asset Protection team is already on their way for you." The high councilor cast a passing, roving glance over the remains of the Purple Pig. "For you, and your rebel assassin, and Dodson, wherever she is." She tugged at a branch on the tree, frowning at it. "I must say, I am surprised you managed fruiting trees here. Most terraformed settlements haven't managed such feats."

"You just killed the woman responsible for the fruit trees," Evie replied, taking a breath to swallow back the lump lodged painfully at the back of her throat, mingling with bile.

"Trees or no trees, she was a traitor, Ms. Anderson. Though I do suspect you will soon yearn for the same end as Ms. Rojas, once Asset Protection gets their hands on you. I daresay you will find me rather merciful in comparison."

Evie blinked into the mirrored light from above, the day just barely beginning to fade into what would be twilight on Gamma-3. "I'll die before I'll breathe a word about any of it."

"We'll see about that." Allemande sighed, tugging at the cuffs of her gloves. "I did so want to break you myself, but I have a higher calling now, or perhaps you hadn't heard."

"We heard."

"Excellent, I am most grateful to know that news of my appointment to the High Council has reached even the most rebellious of ears." She sat on the bench near the fence, watching Evie carefully. "Your code breaking files were most interesting, Ms. Anderson."

"I bet."

"You could have been such an addition to the Coalition. You could have soared, Ms. Anderson, but instead you chose to roll around in the muck with pirates and rebels, murderers and thieves all."

"Rich words, coming from you." Evie twisted her wrists in the cuffs, wincing at the pain but relieved at the redistribution of the weight from the iron chain that held her. "Given everything you've done."

"All I've done has been for the Coalition. My actions are unimpeach-able."

"You violated Coalition decency codes on Turas-Mara."

Allemande raised an eyebrow, but the rest of her expression remained neutral and unreadable. "I can only guess how you came by that bit of inaccurate information, and my guess would be Delia Dodson, traitor that she's become." The high councilor showed off a performative yawn, stretching her arms out in front of her delicately, more like a dancer than a politician. "Where might she be, I wonder?"

"I don't know."

"Come now, Ms. Anderson, Asset Protection will go much easier on you if I'm willing and able to vouch for just how cooperative you were. Now, Ms. Dodson. Where is she?"

"Forrest. And I don't know. She wasn't here when the sirens went off."

"And William Dodson?" Allemande asked, a strange sneer settling on her face. "Where does he sleep?"

"Why?"

"I like to reward my informants." She waited for a reaction, but Evie didn't give her one, and neither did Larkin, if she was even listening. Allemande frowned. "You had a traitor in your midst all along, Ms. Anderson."

Wherever Delia was, Evie silently prayed that she was tearing William's throat out with her bare hands. Evie shrugged easily, the chains rattling softly. "I don't remember. I've never been there, but he's in one of the buildings across town, as far as I'm aware."

"He didn't spend much time in this establishment?"

"Only when helping research for broadcasts, but lately that has been—" Evie tried, and failed, to stifle the sob that erupted in her throat, quiet but patently noticeable. "Lately, that had been Carmen's job," she finished.

"General Fineglass said I was a fool to broker a deal with him before he left Turas-Mara, that he was a liar and a con-artist, but I was proved right in the end." She smoothed her grey skirts, the wool stagnant in the terraformed air. "Then again, I was right about the general, too."

Evie only nodded. If the general had escaped, then that's where Bailey was. At least some of them had managed to make it out, even if she wasn't going to. No one was coming for them, and Bradach would be left a smoldering, burned-out ruin, just like the legion of abandoned mining camps and settlements strewn across the Near Systems, left to rust and rot once every resource had been scraped from it.

"You seem disaffected by the news of treason in your ranks, Ms. Anderson."

"I don't have ranks."

"I suppose you fancy this an egalitarian society then, do you? Every person for themselves, is it? The biggest brutes win and take all?" Allemande made a noisy tutting noise, grating, like birdsong before dawn when sleep wouldn't come. "That's hardly the right model to build a new federation upon."

"No one is building a new federation here," Evie answered. "People were just making lives for themselves the only way they could."

"Through thievery? Ransacking trade vessels, pillaging anything you could get your filthy hands on?" The new high councilor shook her head, letting loose a stray hair that fell into her face. It was nothing more than a wisp, but she tucked it away immediately, an irritated expression settling on her face. "The Coalition offers the only real safety and security one could find in the Near Systems or beyond."

"Obsidian Enclave has three times the technology, maybe more."

"And they, too, will be dealt with in due course. They thought they could hide in their little settlements beyond the Rim, scraping by an existence, developing technology they can't even use properly. Once we take back the realm beyond the Rim, return it to Coalition hands, we will soar, Ms. Anderson. The entirety of dark space will be at our command, and you're going to miss it all." She gave Evie a thin-lipped smile, tugging at the hem of her jacket. "What a terrible shame."

"They're going to kill Emeline, you know." Evie said it loudly, her voice echoing against the sooty brick. Larkin locked eyes with her for just a second before looking away again, offering nothing in the way of communication. "They won't let her live."

"Keep my daughter's name out of your filthy, rebel mouth," Allemande spat. "You know nothing of which you speak. I am privy to everything that the High Council orders, and—"

"No, you aren't. They told her to stand down, she refused. Do you really think the other council members will let that lie? The first truly free election in Skelm, maybe in that entire sector?" It was Evie's turn to shake her head, and she laughed for good measure, watching for every sign that she was getting under Allemande's skin. "You're a fool if you think your status will protect her."

"Everything I do is to protect Emeline."

"Horseshit."

"Language, Ms. Anderson, I will not be spoken to in such a manner." The councilor stood, brushing imaginary dust from her skirts as she rose and crossed to Larkin. "I do not doubt that you would resist a great many methods to protect your treasonous friends. After all, I left evidence to that the first time we met, Ms. Anderson, and you left me with a broken jaw the second, but I would imagine, quite rightly, I think, that you would be far more motivated if I made you watch as I carved chunks out of your beloved assassin here."

"I wouldn't do that if I were you." Evie could hear her own voice shaking with terror, but she spoke anyway. "She easily put down the one you sent for her."

"Yes, the High Council signed off on that." Allemande clasped her hands behind her back as she circled Larkin like a vulture that didn't know its prey wasn't quite dead yet. "Though it seems he left a mark or two."

"He was amateur," Larkin said, deadpan. "Training has gone down the drain."

"Yet he gave you a run for your money."

Larkin laughed, empty and hollow. "I'm out of practice and dispatched him in less than three minutes. He was a useless addition to the guild." She stared straight ahead, still unmoving. "You needed an army to come here and take what was ours, and you did so under false pretenses. You have violated the doctrine."

"The saddest part is that you think the doctrine matters," Allemande replied, stopping to appraise Evie, her cold stare raking over her like she was meat. "We could have come in here any time that we wanted, and no one would be the wiser, no one would care, because piracy sickens anyone with a shred of moral dignity." She tutted softly, patronizing and oddly paternalistic. "We allowed this as a courtesy until you took too many liberties."

Evie shrugged again, broader this time. "Your victory here won't save her, you know." Smoke curled into the sky above, quickly darkening with the smog of dozens of different fires burning across the settlement. "The rest of the High Council already decided."

"And how would you have come by that information?" Allemande demanded.

"You're not the only ones intercepting transmissions," Evie lied. Olivia had to survive the cull if the Coalition was to fall. She was the only one with access to the High Council who could dismantle it from the inside out. "Obsidian Enclave offered us technology in exchange for information."

"Obsidian Enclave are hermits who rarely leave their home beyond the Rim," Allemande said with a righteous scoff. "They're hardly a credible threat, even if they did interfere at Terringgough Gulch."

"They have a settlement within the Near Systems with enough artillery to destroy all of Gamma-3." Evie offered her a broad grin. "They have the weapon the High Council has been so desperate for, and they're ready and willing to use it directly over the Capital."

Allemande's lips curled upwards like tendrils of steam, a contorted, twisted grin that fractured Evie's memory of the last time she'd seen it, when blood ran thick over her arms. The overseer rubbed at the brim of her top hat, waiting for a long pause. "The Obsidian Enclave doesn't have that weapon, Ms. Anderson. The Coalition does."

The blood in Evie's veins slowed to a crawl. "No. It's impossible, Gregor Zink had it."

"Gregor Zink was a little light on credits and very helpfully offered it up for a tidy sum, no doubt needed to continue importing resources that their pathetic city has no access to."

"You're lying," Evie shouted. "And even if you weren't, what makes you so sure that you're safe now? How long before this escalates into a galaxy-wide war?" Evie rattled the iron chain, the metallic clang oddly dull. "Until your daughter is caught in the crossfire?"

"Your smug, cocky attitude will vanish the moment Asset Protection arrives, I can promise you that."

An unexpected breeze disturbed the smoke rising from what was left of the Purple Pig and rustled through the leaves of the apple tree above Evie's head, a sound that once brought her great comfort but was now a sad reminder of everything they'd lost that day. "I'm surprised you didn't go into Asset Protection, given your enthusiasm for torture."

"I am not a sadist, Ms. Anderson. I do not enjoy the work." Allemande tugged off her gloves, pressing them into a deep pocket of her skirts before laying a palm against the soot-stained brick. "My ambitions have carried me to the highest office in the Near Systems and beyond, something that Asset Protection never could have done. They are no more than effective executioners." She pulled her fingers away from the edifice, frowning at the black smears against her porcelain skin as she rubbed her fingertips together to dislodge the dirt. "Ah, see here, Asset Protection has finally arrived." She removed the padlock, replacing it once the Asset Protection team had entered the garden, both in head-to-toe black, with wide hoods like Larkin's, and a sash of throwing knives belted across their chests.

"Ma'am," one of them said, a long brunette braid exiting the hood and laying limp across the black wool of her jacket. It was all Evie could see, the woman's face shrouded by fabric.

"You're late."

"There were three checkpoints between base and here, we arrived as soon as possible." The Asset Protection officer cracked her knuckles, one at a time, the fingerless gloves she was wearing showcasing bitten-down fingernails. "I think you'll find that no one could have gotten here any faster."

"You will address me as High Councilor Allemande, thank you."

"Of course, ma'am, my apologies. Your appointment is recent, is it not?"

"No less valid," Allemande snapped. "These two need reconditioning and information extraction before we leave the settlement at first light."

"Ma'am, our policy is to—"

Allemande pulled one of the throwing knives from the officer's sash, holding it up to the fading sun, where the polished silver glinted, throwing a glare across the ash-laden window above their heads. "I don't recall inquiring about your policy," she said. "What I do remember, however, is telling you what needed to be done. The prison transport leaves as soon as the settlement is cleared, and the rest of the ships leave at first light. Are we clear?"

"Of course, ma'am—er, High Councilor Allemande." The officer nodded to the other, a broad woman with her hands shoved into her pockets, lurking near Evie. "We work them against each other. Shouldn't take long, if your intel was correct."

"It was, you can be sure of that," Allemande assured her. She checked a pocket watch with a quick flick of her wrist, letting the chain rattle against itself in her haste. "I have somewhere to be, a meeting I need to call. I trust you can handle this?"

The officer nodded. "Where should we bring them when we're finished?"

"Hmm," Allemande murmured. "Leave them here. Chain them to the fence. I'll have someone pick them up later, to deliver them to the Asset Protection team back on Gamma-3."

"Aye," the broad officer grunted, already advancing on Evie. It hadn't been long since Cole Marion had done the same thing, but Evie was cuffed now, with no chance of escape. The iron had already rubbed her wrists raw, the skin inflamed and swollen with several large blisters forming at the sides.

The other officer approached Larkin as Allemande padlocked the gate behind her, the sound of her boots against the pavement fading as she walked back towards the docks.

"What's it going to be?" the officer asked Larkin, circling around her. "Are you going to make this easy on me, or difficult?" She gestured towards Evie with one of the knives, slid silently from its sheath. "Or are you going to make me carve up your girlfriend there?"

"Wait," Evie said. "Don't. I'll tell you everything."

The broad officer snorted a laugh. "That didn't take long. You're telling me that fancy-pants new High Councilor Allemande couldn't handle this herself?" She shook her head, pressing Evie against the tree by her shoulders, the bark digging into her skin. "Start talking then."

"Eves," Larkin said in a warning tone, "don't."

"I'm tired," Evie said, swaying on her feet. Her exhaustion wasn't a lie, and it sold the story. "Bradach has been a pirate settlement for decades. I grew up here."

"Family?" the officer asked, staring her down.

"Long gone. Years ago now, haven't heard from them." Evie stared up at the mirrored light, filtered down through dozens of branches and countless waxy green leaves. "They could be dead, for all I know."

"You'd better hope they're dead, because we'll find them either way."

"The Bronze Bell was a base for The Scattered, for a time. Cole Marion is dead, incinerated. I killed him myself, right where you're standing." Evie tilted her head. "If you look closely, I bet you can still see the bloodstains."

"And what of the crew of the Cricket?"

"I don't know where they are. We got an encoded distress signal, but there was nothing and no one there when we looked." Evie shrugged. "Maybe they're dead, too."

"Maybe you're the last plague rats to flee the ship," the officer said. "Maybe we have a little fun with you before we go, just to be sure you're telling the truth."

Evie twisted her forearms, showing off the tattoos and the scars beneath. "It won't be my first time."

"Good, I hate breaking in a virgin."

Across the grass, the other officer had Larkin pinned against the brick, sneering in her face. Evie couldn't hear what she was saying, but Larkin was staring directly at her with a strange, detached look in her eyes, nodding along to whatever the officer was saying.

"Wrong move," Larkin announced, as she pulled two throwing knives from the sash, and, still cuffed, thrust them upwards into the officer's neck, sending her to the ground grasping at her throat.

Evie's officer bellowed out a shout, flinging knives across the patch of muddied grass. Larkin dodged each one, advancing until she was close enough to grant the broad officer the same fate as the other. She fell to the ground, her hood falling back over her shoulders to reveal a pair of crystalline green eyes, wide with fear as she exhaled her last gasp.

"Unlock me," Evie said, holding her cuffs out.

Larkin took the cuffs in her hand, but instead of releasing the padlock, she attached it to the fence. "I have to keep you safe," she said, her voice husky and hollow.

"No!" Evie shouted, wrenching at the cuffs. "Don't you dare leave me here!"

"Stay in the garden," Larkin said, vaulting over the broken gate. "I'll come back when it's clear!"

"Larkin!" Evie protested, but it was too late. Larkin had already disappeared down a dark alley, knives clutched in her hands.

Chapter 46

Georgie slumped against the doorframe of the bridge, trying and failing to remember how to breathe, her sweaty palms braced against the worn knees of her jumpsuit, the sound of terrible sirens still echoing in her ears. Henry, in trouble. Her mother and Lucy, in danger. Or worse—they could all be dead already. Georgie groaned, the repressed audible representation of her insides crumbling into dust. At least so far, she hadn't vomited.

"No time for that Payne," Cass said, throwing herself into the pilot's chair. "We need to get the hells out of here." She swiveled to face Georgie and nodded at the navigation console. "Come on, I need you. Hyun has her hands full with transporting Jasper, she's probably in the med bay now taking care of him."

"I'm no good at navigating," Georgie mumbled, pressing her head back against the smooth, unblemished metal of the Coalition ship. "No good to anyone." She stifled the cry that was begging for release at the back of her throat. Henry, Henry. Gone. All of them, gone. Her mother. Lucy. Everyone at the Pig. Gone. Gone, and because she had to stay for Emeline, had to try one more time, and once again it had wrought ruin on everyone around her.

"Georgina Payne," Cass said, staring her down. "Put your ass in that nav seat. I need you."

"They're all gone, Cass," Georgie said, hot, angry tears welling in her eyes. "There's not going to be anything left when we get there."

"We don't know that."

"We'll never get there in time."

Cass yanked at the controls, sending them deeper into dark space, the window in front of her crystal clear, with far distant stars that twinkled dangerously at the periphery of the ship. "This is a fast vessel, and we're closer than you think."

"If you know where we are, then you don't need me as a navigator." Georgie slid down to the floor, her head in her hands. "Gone," she said again, unable to process everything she'd lost all at once. Her future, burned to the ground in an instant. She'd spent far too much time daydreaming about having children and babies and family that it was like losing all of that, too. She'd never hold a child in her arms, never learn how to be a mother, never hold Henry in her arms as their babies slept, finally, after weeks of restless nights. Little by little, whatever was left of her filtered into the floor, leaving her nothing more than a desiccated husk.

"Payne!" Cass shouted, pulling hard on the steering. "We're too near the Belt for this shit, Payne, I need you on nav!"

"What's even the point?"

"Because if I know everyone back there in Bradach, they're giving the Coalition a hell of a time. They aren't going to roll over, they're going to fight back, and I will be gods-damned if I'm not there to help. Now get your ass off the floor and help me, damn it!" Cass glanced over her shoulder at Georgie and scowled. "Payne, there's no way your mother isn't holding off at least three of them by herself. Come on, we're in a Coalition tagged vessel. There's enough chaos that we might just make it through the blockade."

Georgie stood, easing herself into the navigation chair. "The Coalition knows we have a hostage, we're going to have every gods-damned ship in the sector after us."

"Not if every gods-damned ship in the sector is parked in Bradach."

"This isn't a gun ship, how in hells are we supposed to get anything done?" Georgie squinted at the nav maps, trying to make sense of it. It was a mystery how Ned managed to decode some of the maps just by looking, and knowing coordinates by rote, knowing exactly where everything and anything was. She puffed out her cheeks, staring at the radar. "Asteroid, port."

"Thank you." Cass easily maneuvered the ship away from the threat, her shoulders still tight up around her ears. "It's not a gun ship, but we have a hostage to trade, and we might just be able to get out of there unscathed with some of our people. It's worth a shot, and it's better than nothing."

"But—"

"Calling all frequencies, I repeat, calling all frequencies," Cass announced into the radio. "This is Cassius Calvetti, scourge of the Coalition. I am piloting a stolen vessel, and I have valuable hostages aboard." She breathed, a long inhale and an equally long exhale. "Now is the time to take up arms. Cole Marion is dead, killed by Coalition forces. Long may his memory be a comfort to us."

Georgie signaled that another asteroid was ahead on the starboard side, and Cass nodded silently, piloting the ship around it. So many obstacles, and they weren't even going through the Belt, just around it.

"Rumors of my death were planted in order to keep me quiet, but I can assure you, the time for silence is over. The Coalition has instigated an illegal attack on Bradach, the place so many of us call home, where so many make berth, and we are under siege. Join us in fighting back against the tyranny of this government." Cass laid down the radio just as an asteroid swiped the side of the ship, sending her sprawling against the rich purple carpet. "What in hells was that, Payne?"

"Sorry, that one wasn't on radar." The nav desk blinked up at Georgie, too many sensors in too many places. "It doesn't look like anything other than cosmetic damage."

"I guess I should be grateful for that." Cass dusted herself off, sitting back in the pilot's chair. "I don't know if that will have done any good. I'm sure some will think it is a trap. Most, even."

"A bold claim to say that the Coalition killed Cole Marion."

"He'd be alive if he hadn't been warped by what happened after Skelm," Cass answered. "He used to laugh, once. He'd joke around with others and help with loading up supplies, he had a passion for making things right." She sighed softly, rubbing at her temples. "He was corrupted by the same rot that ruined the Coalition. Power, greed, hunger, it's all you start to feel after a while."

"How did you manage to survive it?" Georgie asked, tightening her ponytail. "Why didn't the rot get you?"

"Spent too much time alone in a Coalition cell, I'd imagine. And I know that Olivia wouldn't have one single iota of interest in someone like Gregor fucking Zink."

Georgie jerked back from the display as a large red circle appeared. "Er—incoming transmission, Captain," she said cautiously. "Do we... accept?"

"No. It's probably a Coalition vessel trying to harangue us."

"No ship tags."

Cass turned around in her chair. "No tags? Nothing at all?"

Georgie shook her head. "No. Looks like a land transmission would."

"That's impossible. We're way too far out for a land transmission to reach us in dark space, there aren't even any beacons left in this area to boost a signal, not after Terringgough Gulch."

"So... accept?" Georgie asked, her hand hovering over the button.

"Alright."

Georgie searched for the button, pressing four of the wrong ones before finding the correct lever. "Patching through," she said finally, almost grateful for the job and the distraction from what would soon almost certainly be searing, unsustainable agony that she'd never recover from. "Patched."

"This is Cassius Calvetti. Which underpaid Coalition peon do I have the honor of speaking to?"

"Cass?" came a garbled, static-ridden reply. "The connection is terrible, where are you?"

"Rather not say. Who's this?"

"Rosie Gordon."

"Fucked gods," Cass replied. "It's damned good to hear your voice,

Rosie Gordon. Are you alright?"

"I'm fine." The speaker buzzed angrily, only letting every third or fourth word through. "Did you get that?"

"No, Gordon. Go again."

"Zink lied about almost everything. Hyun isn't here."

"I'm here," Hyun said, stepping onto the bridge slowly, bracing her hands against her knees with every step up the short set of stairs. "Good to hear your voice, Rosie."

"How's Jasper doing?" Rosie asked.

Hyun flinched, sucking in an uneven breath that caught in her throat. "He didn't make it."

"What?" Georgie demanded, almost flying out of her chair. "But back on Lucent Base, you said—"

"Zink lied about that, too. They'd kept me from monitoring his vitals, locking away anything that might have helped me understand. There was no treatment, there never was. He just wanted to separate me from the rest of the crew, make them easier to pick off." Hyun swayed on the spot, brushing messy hair out of her face. Georgie was there to catch her right as Hyun's knees collapsed from beneath her, huge, wracking sobs choking her. "He lied, Rosie, he lied, he lied."

Cass stared for a moment before she returned her attention to the window. "Bastard," she whispered.

"He didn't improve because he was never going to," Hyun continued between muffled cries, her face buried in Georgie's jumpsuit. "Zink chased us through the Belt. He caused that crash. He killed Jasper." Hyun threw her arms around Georgie, barely able to string words together through her grief. "He killed Jas, he killed him, he killed him," she moaned, over and over.

All Georgie could do was hold Hyun and rock her gently, trying to hold back her own tears. It wasn't her time to grieve, but she feared it wouldn't be long before it was her turn, staring at the smoldering ruin she'd once called home. She wouldn't shush Hyun, or tell her that it was alright, because it wasn't. Sometimes, death was just death, unfair and sharp as it sliced parts of a person away, along with people they'd loved so much that they'd become part of one another. In death, separation, it was learning how to be reborn, painful, disorienting, and without consent.

Georgie squeezed her eyes closed, willing herself not to cry, to stay strong for Hyun, who lay crying in her arms, bereft, lost, and broken.

"I took him off the machines myself," Hyun said, clutching at the twill fabric of Georgie's jumpsuit. "I thought if it had to be anyone, then it had to be me."

"Why didn't you tell us?" Cass asked gently.

"I knew you'd never let me. You're many things, Calvetti, but what you aren't is someone who gives up. It has made you a good leader, but would make you a poor med tech." Hyun sobbed anew, pressing her face into Georgie's shoulder. "Sometimes, you can't heal what's broken."

The ship hummed with its efficiency, a quiet thrum, a stable rhythm that pulsed beneath the floor of the bridge, running all the way down to the boilers. No proximity alarms, no invasion sirens, no gunshots, no one to plead with to earn back Jasper's life. No boat to send back to the other side with promises of return when business had been finished. Tears seeped through the fabric and lay against Georgie's skin, a physical, unpalatable reminder of just how much they'd all lost.

They'd lost freedom, justice, and they didn't even yet know the toll that they'd have to tally when they reached Bradach. A dark, terrible day, worse than the storms in Skelm, worse than being left behind, worse even still than when Emeline was taken. Hope died in Georgie, withering, the leaves curled and limp, replaced with the stark nothingness of bitterness and revenge, a fallow field ripe for the spilling of blood.

"I'm coming to meet you," Rosie said finally, her voice thick with emotion and static. "I'm coming back to Bradach."

"But Zink!" Cass protested. "He'll never let you leave Ceru."

"Zink can kiss my big ass," Rosie retorted. "What's he going to do, shoot me in front of all these gods-damned reporters? Where's Delia?"

"We don't know. Probably in Bradach," Georgie answered softly. "When we got through on a wire, it was Carmen and Henry. Then—" Georgie inhaled, steadying herself. "Then the sirens went off, and the line was cut."

"It's enough," Rosie said. "Enough already. We've already lost so much, we don't even know—I don't want to lose anything else."

Cass cleared her throat quietly, flicking her stare from the window, to the nav panel behind her, to the radio in quick succession. "We're going to—"

"I'm not losing anyone else, Calvetti," Rosie said, an unfamiliar harshness to her tone. "Not one more person."

"We're going to need more people, Gordon. There are only three of us on this ship, plus a hostage."

"You're taking hostages now?"

Cass shrugged, despite the fact that Rosie couldn't see her. "It wasn't really part of the plan. I improvised."

Static hissed through the speakers. "They'll kill you for that, Calvetti."

"They can add it to my tab. The way I see it, theirs has been due for a long time." Cass squinted out the window at some asteroids in the distance, looping together too far from the Belt. "I need you back on navigation, Georgie."

"Aye," Georgie replied, squeezing Hyun around the shoulders. "I'm gonna be right here, okay?" she asked, surprising herself with how much like her own mother she sounded, the quiet drawl dragging out the final syllable. "Just right here, I promise." Disentangling herself, she eased back into the chair at the nav console, doing her best to monitor what she saw there. "Port, and then starboard."

Cass nodded, punching coordinates into the main console. "Gordon, we'll see you when we get there. Punch Zink in the face for us."

"He's going to have worse than that when I'm done with him." Rosie exhaled a frustrated breath. "I'll see you when I see you. Don't get yourselves killed."

"I'll do my best."

"If you—if you find Delia, tell her I'm coming. Tell her to wait for me. Tell her I'm sorry I didn't leave sooner, that I didn't figure it out earlier."

"Tell her yourself, Gordon," Cass said lightly, but light like an eggshell, and not light like a cloud. Fragile, and they all knew it. Dangerous, and they all saw it for what it was—a reckless attempt at hope when the light had all but gone out. "Over and out."

Chapter 47

Larkin moved through the city in the midst of a strange, foggy haze that had settled within her. She'd left Evie in the garden, refusing to remove the padlock. At least there, she would be safe. There, she wouldn't have to see what Larkin was already doing.

There'd be no going back, not after that. Evie had only seen a tiny sliver, a fragment of what Larkin was. After all, she'd spent most of her life trying to forget. Trained from a young age by someone who promised he would help them, but no doubt he'd been in on it too. It all came from the top. The sick, diseased, rotten-at-the-core High gods-damned Council that had spent years maneuvering her with puppet strings, letting her think she was her own woman, but she never was.

She'd hardly killed anyone they hadn't directed her to.

The fools at the Armory, maybe. She couldn't even be sure about her attempt on Cole Marion's life—maybe that had all been orchestrated, too. They must have known she'd kill the assassin they'd sent for her.

"Hey!" an MPO shouted, pointing his steamrifle at her. "Stop right there!"

Larkin jerked the gun's barrel, only passingly aware of the burn of the metal against her skin. The dish water at the Pig was sometimes hotter. The Pig. The only thing she'd ever let herself build, hoping for a bloodless future, and they'd taken it away. They'd ripped it out from underneath her, the same way they always did.

The officer's neck was fragile in her hands as she twisted, the crunching stealing the life from his eyes as he fell to the cobblestones. It was strange how soon the muscle memory returned. One fight with a half-trained assassin in the kitchen was all it had taken to unleash the monster that always lay within her, dormant, waiting for the opportunity to strike.

Evie was how she'd spent years tamping it down, resisting the urge to disappear into the night again, untractable, unfound, unloved. Larkin hadn't left because how could she, when what she'd spent so long searching for was staring her in the face? Love. Family. The opportunity to build something out of bricks and not blood.

She watched as the lights in another guard's eyes faded, her hands clasped hard around his neck. "You never should have come here," Larkin whispered as he sank down, slumped against the ashy brick of an empty, burned-out shop. Mae's shop. For some reason, Larkin pushed inside, running her fingers along singed fabrics, the smell of smoke heavy, impenetrable, and choking.

"Larkin!" someone hissed, emerging from beneath one of the large cutting tables in the back. "Thank the gods, I thought I'd die in here. That guard has been posted outside the door for hours, I couldn't get out, I— "

"Abigail."

"Thomas is here too, he's in the back. Are you alright?" Abigail asked, reaching out for her.

Larkin dodged it, stepping backwards. "Evie is in the garden," she said simply. "Don't know about anyone else." She left the way she'd entered, the bells on the door oblivious to the surrounding horror. Abigail was trying to follow, calling after her, but no, Larkin couldn't let her see what she really was—a weapon. One more tool of destruction.

There was good reason for people to hate those who stole life from others. Even better reason to fear those who did it without guilt. Larkin was a programmed monster, built for destruction, and she let it carry her through Bradach. Five, maybe six MPOs already, she'd lost count—plus the two Asset Protection officers who were still laying dead on the crisp, dried-up grass. Tears pricked at her eyes but she blinked them back, attributing them to the smoke.

After all, she was an assassin. She was merciless. She was death made flesh, a trained killer who thought nothing of shoving her thumbs into a man's eye socket just before she gutted him like a poor-quality fish, not that anyone in Bradach had seen fresh fish for years.

Passingly, she wondered if they could build a lake in Bradach, extend the terraformers. Would Rosie teach them all how to cook fresh fish, fat from farming?

Then, she remembered that the city was already burning around her, irredeemable. Rosie was gone, and that had been Larkin's fault, too. She'd let herself grow complacent, and they'd snatched Rosie in the early morning hours, right from under Larkin's nose.

Never again.

They wouldn't take something from her ever again, even if that was only because she'd die that day. Everyone would be better for it, if she made a mistake. If she let some up-jumped MPO skewer her at the end of a knife, or pump the rest of her full of lead and iron, or take out the other side of her rib cage that was still just flesh and bone. She wouldn't survive it a second time.

If she was gone, the others could feel safe. No more assassins. Evie would thrive, and find someone better, who wasn't as damaged, or as much of a failure, or as quietly dangerous as an assassin hiding in plain sight.

It was no wonder that it had been easy for him to find her. She hadn't exactly gone out of her way, and regrettably, she'd done it on purpose. She'd known they'd send someone for her, and Larkin had figured it would be better to see them coming than to be surprised by it, so she never bothered changing her name when she went into business at the Pig. If they wanted her, she was easy enough to find, and they had, and she was.

The mirrored light was fading now, turning to night. Floodlights from a steamtruck cast an eerie pallor over the stained brick of the buildings, smoke still hanging thick in the air. It would take the terraformers weeks to filter out all the particulates. Maybe they'd all be dead by the time the Coalition came back for them, scooping their lifeless bodies into mass graves, bulldozing what was left of the settlement just to begin again as some sort of military outpost that they'd abandon five years later.

Hope had always been a lost cause.

It had laid dormant, just beneath her skin, for years. She ignored it, because for someone like her, hope was nothing more than a strong poison. Fatal, if she wasn't careful.

And she'd been right. Her complacency led to the destruction of everything. She hadn't been watching, too focused on trying to forget the horrors she'd wrought. She'd spent too many nights sneaking back down to the bar for a nightcap, and then another, the only way she could get to sleep without remembering wide-open dead eyes staring back at her.

There had always been a reason that she preferred poison. At least then, she didn't have to witness the aftermath. She ran a thumb over the ring Evie had given her. Safe for now. For now. For now. Words echoed in her mind like a threat, and dragged at her with a constant, aching worry.

Larkin didn't know what she was looking for, as she moved through the city, one alley at a time, striking out in the growing darkness, darting between stray flecks of light, keeping to the darkness the way she always had. After all, it was the darkness that had truly given birth to her, and it was the darkness that would soon come to reclaim what it had lost.

The docks were swarming with military, like roaches in a trash heap. All of them with their heat guns and their steamrifles, cocky, arrogant, overconfident because they'd yet to learn how many they'd lost, and how many they had yet to lose. The sirens began again, and Larkin wished she could hide from it, but she couldn't. There was no noise loud enough in the entirety of the Near Systems and beyond that could drown out the inevitable.

She lurked, waiting for one to stray from their pack and into her waiting arms. A wolf, waiting patiently for prey. "There's nothing wrong with being a wolf," Evie had once said. "They have to eat, just like the rest of us."

Maybe that's what Larkin was doing, as she snatched an MPO from her route and snapped her neck like it was porcelain. Fragile. Too fragile, as if her spine was begging to be broken. She looked up at Larkin with dull eyes, and Larkin turned and vomited into the alley, not that there was much in her stomach other than bile. It foamed against the cobblestones for a few moments, the coarse bubbles glistening in the lamplight, before dissolving back into nothingness, indistinguishable from the dampness brought from blood, and water to quench the fires, and the terrified piss of too many who'd mistakenly thought Bradach was a safe haven.

She found herself in front of the Bronze Bell, standing hidden across the street. The building was surrounded, if only by a few. Others had peeled off when the sirens began anew, shrieking across the city with their warning song. Maybe there was another invasion. Maybe it was nothing at all.

Larkin traced the form of the building upward, looking in every dark window from her vantage point atop the dumpster. What were they waiting for? Who was inside the tavern? She tilted her head when her gaze fell on the top floor, some sort of glint sparkling from a broken window, but from beyond the shattered glass. She crept closer, dangerously close to an MPO in front of her until the building next door exploded, raining glass down on everyone who stood in the street.

More of the squadron scrambled, some rushing into the blaze anticipating warfare when it was likely just a result of too much booze meeting too much heat. The explosion had been largely superficial, not structural, but the soldiers hadn't been trained to see that.

Larkin had.

She'd spent most of her childhood throwing herself at anything dangerous, just to learn how to survive. She wasn't sure she wanted to survive the siege of Bradach. Maybe it was best if she died along with the rest of them. The road back from the horrors she'd wrought would be too hard to travel, too fraught, with too many apologies and pleas for forgiveness and sleepless nights, and—Larkin stopped to drag a lone sergeant into the alley and put a knife into his temple. One more casualty. Collateral damage. He was in the wrong place at the wrong time, but that had been her own life's story. One long string of terrible coincidences leading her to that moment, as his last words were too garbled with gargled blood to even decipher.

No matter. His words didn't matter. Nothing mattered, not anymore. Nothing except making sure Evie made it out alive.

So much of it was automatic. She didn't even have to think before taking the knife from an MPO's belt and using it on him. She didn't have to consider the consequences when she threw a stolen, perfectly balanced knife into the throat of the squadron's commander. It was a good thing that Asset Protection valued quality weapons. The crowd in front of the Bronze Bell was beginning to thin, as half of them split off to look for her.

They'd never find her. She was a shadow herself. She was the reason to fear the dark.

Three more silenced by the knives, and she was irritated when she reached for more and found none in the sash. Perfectly balanced was all well and good, but more would have been preferable. Instinctively, she rounded on the heel of her boot, ready to return to the Pig for the knives that waited there, before remembering that the inside of the tavern had been reduced to ash.

Nothing left there except shame and regret.

They'd taken everything from her. Everything, because Evie wouldn't want anything to do with her after that night, even if they both made it out alive. No one loved a killer. No one loved a monster.

The sirens continued to scream, and it was disorienting to all except Larkin. The sound was an irritation, but it was background noise, a drone, something to internalize and harmonize with, always quietly satisfied when the bone crunch lined up with the rhythm of the repeating squeal. Before long, and before she realized, the Bronze Bell was left undefended. She stepped over four corpses on her way to the door, and pushed inside, silently floating up stairs that creaked under anyone else. She knew where the weak steps were, dancing around every ill-fitting nail and screw that pushed up out of the old, worn wood.

She almost expected Cole Marion to be sitting at his desk on the second floor, but he wasn't. The room was empty, the same as it had been since

Evie killed him. That had been Larkin's fault, too. She never should have let that happen. She should have stayed and made sure it was him who had died, but she'd been weak.

The third floor was empty, too, housing nothing more than peeling wallpaper and the thick scent of burnt casks. She wondered how much the MPOs had stolen of the booze before spilling the rest. A waste. A shame, even for the low-quality swill they served there. Fools. Everyone knew that quality surpassed quantity any day of the week.

She pushed the door open to the attic, staring into the muzzle of a steamrifle. "It's empty," she said, pushing it away.

"Oh, the gods are good," Tansy said, reaching out for Larkin. "They've had me pinned in here for half an hour, at least."

Larkin sidestepped the embrace, picking up an empty ammunition box from the floor. "Someone was in here with you."

"Delia."

Larkin raised an eyebrow. "And now?"

"She went off to find Henry, they were taking her down to the docks."

"Allemande wanted her for something special." Larkin shrugged. "Henry is pregnant."

"Gods," Tansy breathed, leaning against her crutch. "What's it like on the ground?"

"Messy."

Tansy stepped closer, reaching a hand out once more, her brow furrowed. "Are you alright? You look—"

"You should leave. This place can't be defended by one person." Larkin's breath almost caught in her throat, snagging on something too close to an emotion, and she shook her head to rattle it loose. "The Pig is gone."

"I know. Saw the smoke from here."

"Avoid the docks."

"Where's Evie?" Tansy asked quietly, as though she was afraid of the answer.

"The garden behind the Pig. They sent Asset Protection." Larkin used the edge of her black cloak to wipe blood from one of the knives she'd retrieved from the neck of an MPO. "She's still there."

"Alright."

"I sent Abigail and Thomas there, too. Haven't seen the others, not yet."

Tansy nodded slowly, slinging the steamrifle over her shoulder and tucking the revolver back into the holster. "I'll head there. See if there's... anything I can do."

Larkin picked at the drying blood beneath her fingernails, unable to say aloud that Carmen was already gone. "I don't think we can do anything."

"Looks like you've already done plenty," Tansy said, eyeing the splatters of blood across Larkin's black vest, almost invisible but not quite. "I've always wondered what you could do. I guess now we know."

"Yeah. Now we know." Larkin all but leaped back down the stairs, desperate to get away, to ignore that Tansy knew now what she was. A demon, if those were real. A nightmare, if they weren't.

The siren was silenced once again, and the streets of Bradach replied in kind, growing quiet despite the echoes of screams that still lingered in the small spaces, like the droplets of blood dripped down from a windowsill, or the trail of oil and fluids that led down to the docks, or a satchel left against a building, uncollected, its owner probably already half-incinerated.

The city would never be the same.

People would never forget the horrors that had been visited upon them, even if they survived the night. Larkin breathed deep the smog of combat and almost relished how it seared her lungs, the burning there not so unfamiliar. She ran a hand along her dented rib cage, leaving a strange crater in her side. The bruise still hadn't faded and gods, if only things had turned out different.

If only she'd never killed Lionel Cabot in the first place.

If only she hadn't joined that school, if she'd stayed on the streets where she belonged, trying to scrape a living out of dirt and promises.

If only she hadn't dragged Evie down into the mess and the muck of it.

She'd make the decision easy for the rest of them. She'd throw herself at the docks, onto a sacrificial pyre of blood and greed, taking out as many as she could in the desperate, wrenching hope that some would live on.

The docks were well lit, even at that time of night, the lamps flooding each bay with warm yellow light that radiated from every post, pooling at the bottom. Lights didn't care who was using them or why, and so they lovingly lit the path for the Coalition to stampede through Bradach with guns and misery, scraping away everything in one fell swoop.

Larkin killed one guard messily, letting the slice in his throat spray out over the wet wood. She wanted them to find her. She shouted as she snapped the neck of another, throwing the body down to the ground, contorted and unnatural. Still, in the chaos, no one noticed. She blinked, unsure how someone could be so unaware that they would be oblivious to death knocking at their door.

Strong, weathered hands pulled her down off a crate, and for a moment she was relieved that it was the end. She was ready to give herself over to death, to allow her life's blood to seep out onto the dock, to wish Evie a better life with her dying breath, until she realized that she was looking up into José's kind eyes, heavy with concern. "Mija," he whispered. "You can't take them all out by yourself."

Larkin didn't reply, she only stared.

He pulled her through a thick hedge into a small clearing, the same place he would still sometimes pitch up a stand of paella. Sandrine was there, and her arms were already open to receive Larkin.

"Larkin, Larkin," Sandrine said, already embracing her, tears flooding down her cheeks. "I don't know where my other daughters are and you're the only one I've got left. You can't leave me, too."

Chapter 48

Alice punched the fake ship tags into the main console, fingers already trembling, but beyond her own fear, beyond her terror that everything was falling apart around her, she had to find Violet. Her wife, her captain, her confidante—needed her, and that was that. "You ready?" she asked.

Ivy nodded, pushing her long green hair over her shoulder. "As I'll ever be," she answered, eyes glued to the navigation panel.

"Here we go, then. Let's hope I did it right, this is usually Kady's area of expertise." Alice checked the logs for the twelfth time and pressed the radio transmission. "Gamma-3, this is C.S. Kite, requesting permission for landing."

The radio crunched and crackled for the longest moment of Alice's life. "Denied, Kite. The Capital docks are closed for High Council business."

"Requesting permission to land at the nearest airfield, then."

"What is your purpose for landing?" the dispatcher asked.

To rescue my wife and friends and use my advantage to destabilize the Coalition, Alice thought, and if her hands weren't all but tied to the controls, she would have been pulling at the ends of her braids. She cleared her throat quietly and pressed her lips together to suppress a nervous intake of breath. "Our ship needs repairs."

"You'd best land at the scrapyard, then. Only problem is, no transport between there and the city. Airspace is restricted for the next fortnight, no trains in or out, no docking privileges for anyone who isn't with the High Council."

"No problem."

"You'll be stuck at the airfield until the limits are lifted."

"Understood."

"You'll have to sleep on your ship, there are no accommodations at the scrapyard."

Alice chewed her lip. "Understood," she repeated.

"Use the northeastern slipstream, set down at the scrapyard, and get off the landing pad. Welcome to Gamma-3, Kite."

"Thank you kindly, dispatch." Alice flipped off the radio and with the motion, disturbed the meager breakfast she'd had hours earlier, and it settled in the back of her throat until she swallowed it back down. "Well, we're in," she said.

"Hard part is over," Ivy agreed.

"I don't know about that, we still have to get the hells off Gamma-3 after we find the others. They'll figure out our tags are fake pretty soon after we land. This ship isn't going to pass as anything other than a security breach." Alice leaned into the controls, steering the rickety, half-dead ship through the atmosphere, cringing when the angry rumbling tore a strip from the exterior. Leave it to Barnaby to wind up with something in such disrepair that it was more of a liability than an asset. "We might have to steal some transport to get to the Capital. That must be where they are."

"How do we find out if they've been imprisoned?" Ivy asked, leaning against the console on her forearm. "And if they have been, how do we get them out?"

Alice shook her head. "Gods below, I don't even have the first idea. We can only hope that we find Mae or Olivia." She swallowed hard again, trying to clear the burning bile. "And hope again that they haven't been picked up, too."

The scrapyard came into view as soon as they descended through the clouds, a strangely organized mess for what it was. The landing pad was smack in the middle, a circular pad of pavement amidst the towers of scrap metal, left to rust until someone showed up to rescue them.

The landing was rough, skidding across the pavement without the landing gear, because she'd forgotten to lay it down. Ivy grimaced, clutching the edges of the navigation console with white knuckles, not even daring to look out the window until they came to a complete stop. "We're here," Alice tried to chirp, but the churning in her gut made it come out more like a threat than a celebration. "Let's get the hells out of here."

"You don't have to tell me twice," Ivy replied, finally releasing her clutching grip of the console.

"Losing an eye makes depth perception a little challenging," Alice said, more defensively than she had intended. She snapped the eye patch against her face for emphasis, ignoring the sharp sting of pain as she did it. "Next time, you land the ship."

"There are a couple of steambikes over there. A little rusted, but I'm betting between the two of us we can get them working in short order." Ivy nodded at a scrap pile through the window, already making her way to the loading bay door. "Should only be, what, a couple of days' ride from here?"

"Not much between here and the Capital," Alice said, following her through the ship. "Might be a hungry trip. Not much of anything worth eating left on board to take with us."

"It's better than walking."

Alice stepped out of the ship into the warm Gamma-3 sunshine and shielded her face, jerking away from it. The cloudless sky beat down on them both. "Okay," she said. "Doesn't look like there are any attendants, which is good news for us. I'm betting all non-essential guards have been relocated to the city for this all-council meeting." As Alice's vision adjusted, she found herself staring in disbelief. "Ivy," she said, tilting her head. "What in every known hell is our ship doing in this scrap yard?"

"What?"

"Over there, under a fresh shipment of rusted sheet metal." Alice strode across the huge scrap yard, her mind racing with enough thoughts to take out even the most advanced ship's console. If the Cricket was there, where in hells was everyone else? She climbed up the side of the ship, finding footholds on an adjacent pile of abandoned parts, most of them long outdated. "Ivy, it's our ship." She pushed off the sheet metal with a loud grunt, sending it down to the ground with a noisy clatter that echoed across the yard. "Ivy!"

"I heard you!"

"It's the Cricket!"

Ivy stood near the landing pad, resting a hand on her hip. "I can see that."

"We can fix it!"

"And then what? You heard dispatch, flight space is restricted for a fortnight."

"Yeah, I mean, only if they catch us, though, right?" Alice flashed what she hoped was a winning grin, but Ivy was unmoved. "Come on, I can't do this by myself."

"We will absolutely get caught."

"There's no one around!"

"Not right now, but every minute we stand here debating is another opportunity for someone to show up and throw us into cuffs. I don't know about you, but I'm not interested in experiencing that today." She pointed at the steambikes again. "Those won't take as long to fix."

"They won't get us off Gamma-3, either."

"We don't even know if we'll be able to find the parts we need."

Alice scanned the scrap yard, swiveling from her position atop the ship. "I've been here before for parts. Not for years, a decade, maybe? Look, over there, I can see the tail end of a boiler that might fit. And look!" She kicked at a pile of scrap, dredging several rubbery seals from beneath a pile of leaves. "Gaskets!"

"If this gets us killed, I'll never forgive you."

"If this gets us killed, you won't have the opportunity to hold that grudge." Alice slipped down from the ship's exterior, already trying to pry open the loading bay door. There was a trick to it, if she could just find the latch.

"It's lower," Ivy said, watching.

"Are you trying to tell me about my own ship?"

Ivy shrugged. "It's your wife's ship, and the latch is lower."

"How do you know that?"

"I might have skipped curfew a time or three."

"Ivy Hill, you are a pirate. We do not have curfews."

"That's not what Kady said."

Alice snorted a laugh, catching the latch and pushing up the door. "She's just trying to keep you out of trouble." The door creaked with resentment, the pulleys seized. "Strange. How did these get all messed up?"

"Could be the result of sitting in a scrap yard, is my guess," Ivy retorted with a smirk. She climbed onto the ship behind Alice, surveying the cargo bay. "Gods below, it's a mess in here."

"Smells awful," Alice agreed. "This place needs to be aired out. I'll start with the quarters." She stopped at the charging deck on the wall, laying her hand against it. "BEEP!" she called, pressing the large green button on the front. "BEEP, wake up."

The tiny droid chirped quietly, the power lights weak but present. It disengaged from the lock, floating just over Alice's shoulder.

"Don't worry, we'll get you some more power soon," Alice soothed. "Just hold out a little longer. We need you for some light." She pushed through the airlock, concerned at the lack of security protocols, despite the ship's location and condition. "The sooner we get circulation moving, the better we'll be able to test filtration before we test her out," she said to Ivy, keeping an eye on the yellow beam of light emitting from the front of the tiny droid. "That should only take a few hours, assuming we don't run into more problems."

"We're going to get caught."

"Not if you stop pouting and help. Go drag that boiler over here, we can check the connections. Make sure you don't damage the components, they can be—"

"You do realize I've been hopping ships for almost a year with Captain Tansy, right?"

Alice stopped fussing with the lock on Kady's quarters, her fingertips already raw from rubbing against the textured metal. "Of course I realize that."

Ivy gestured across the scrapyard with the delicate flick of a wrist. "That boiler will work, it has the old connection ports, which we can swap out for the bronze ones. I left some in the boiler room."

"Where?"

"You know," Ivy said with a shrug. "With the rest of it."

"My only regret in life is that I didn't make sure you had a better organizational system than me." Alice yanked on the lock, but before she had the opportunity to be smug, fire spat out from above the door. She shrieked, an embarrassing sound emitting from her throat, and leaped out of the way, patting out the small flame on her shoulder. She squinted into the relative darkness until BEEP swiveled the beam of light, illuminating an elaborate rig across the door. "Who the fuck put traps on my ship?" she demanded, tearing off the blowtorch with one angry motion.

"Your wife's ship," Ivy corrected again. "And my guess is that it was her."

"She has no appreciation for this vessel," Alice grumbled, pulling at the wires that had connected the lock to the torch. "Never wants to stop for repairs, never lets me do work the right way. I swear this thing is probably held together by glue and hope at this point."

"I'll be sure to tell her you said that."

"Don't you even dare."

"Trouble in paradise?" Ivy asked, quietly, as though she wasn't sure if she was crossing a boundary or not. She took the dismantled trap from Alice's hands, winding the wire around her hand into a neat ball.

Alice didn't respond at first, biting her tongue as she checked the other doors in the corridor for traps, removing the ones she found. "It's been hard lately," she said finally. "And now I don't even know where she is, or if—" she stopped herself short, unable to even say her biggest fear aloud. "Yeah," she finished. "Trouble, I guess."

"We'd better get this rust bucket fixed up, then, so you can tell her that you're sorry."

"Ivy, if we get the Cricket moving, and we find Vi, I swear on my life I'll never complain about her again."

"Your wife or the ship?"

"Both."

"Circulation is starting to move," Ivy said, wedging open the final door with a wad of the wire. "Bodes well for filtration."

"Yeah, we'll need new filters, but I doubt we'll find those here in the scrapyard. If we do find any, they're probably disgusting."

Ivy nodded. "Moldy."

"At the very least." Alice kicked a chunk of loose metal on the floor, and it skidded down the hall, coming to a stop just short of the stairs to the bridge. "I worry that they're locked up, Ivy. I can't do this stuff without Vi. I can keep the ship flying, but I can't do the rest of this. It's impossible."

"Wherever they are, we'll figure it out." Ivy picked up the metal, pocketing it and heading down the fork that led down to the boiler room. "And as far as the filters go, I'm sure these can hang on until we hit a beacon." Ivy twisted her cap around the wrong way and laughed lightly. "So long as we don't actually *hit* the beacon. I don't know if I trust you to pilot any more ships, Alice."

"I have *one* eye!"

"Then it's a good thing we're going to find the captain." Ivy threw her hands up in frustration, the gesture only just visible without the ship's running lights. "The boiler door is padlocked."

"For all the gods' sakes, Vi," Alice hissed under her breath. "Didn't Ned have a hatchet in the galley?"

"No, I think that was a revolver."

"There must be something on this damned ship." Guilty, Alice rubbed a seam on the wall, running her fingers over the rivets. "Sorry. I didn't mean that."

"Yeah, it's not the ship's fault that there's a padlock." Ivy bent, pulling a pin from her hair, letting down a loose, wavy curl.

"What are you doing?"

"Larkin taught me." Ivy's tongue stuck out just slightly as she worked, mumbling curses under her breath until the padlock popped free, clattering down to the ground. "Huh. I didn't think that was actually going to work."

"That might have been useful information *before* I almost set my face on fire."

Ivy released the boiler room door, coiling the heavy chain around her arm. "You're the one who taught me to observe before taking action."

"Not quite what I meant, though, is it?" Alice grumbled. She pushed into the boiler room, coughing at the cloud of dust that rose up from the floor. "Gods, it's a damned mess in here."

"It always looks like this."

"I have a system!" Alice protested.

Ivy dropped the chain on the workbench, already sitting on the floor with a wrench, loosening the nuts keeping the old, broken boiler in place. "Should be a quick replacement if we work around each other."

"I thought that was already the plan."

"You're irritating when you're right, do you know that?" Ivy asked, pulling herself to her feet. "I'll get the boiler. But if I get busted in the time it takes to drag that hunk of shit over here, I'm going to hold a grudge against you to the grave."

Alice rolled her eye dramatically, throwing her hands up in defeat. "Fine, I'll go with you. But if your complaining is what gets us caught, then the grudge is mine."

"Deal."

Chapter 49

Bailey's legs ached from running. The Capital was a dense, sprawling city, some parts hilly, the roads paved with wide, smooth bricks that were beautiful for driving, but a frustration to climb with wet boots, soggy from the dew that rested on blades of grass before she tore through them in their desperate escape.

Smoke had already begun to seep beneath the doors of the Dark Owl, leeching through the gaps in the old, frustrated windows, the scent heavy with the arid, chemical stench of solvent. The Capital was in chaos, not that you'd know it from the lack of sirens. They'd stopped almost as soon as they'd started, silenced by some poor grunt.

"Bailey?" Wilhemina called, staggering back to her feet. "Bailey!"

"I'm here," Bailey replied, pulling her sister by the arm, the fabric of the informal uniform soft under her hands. "Gods, we almost didn't make it out of that."

"There are only five. Who's missing?"

Ned massaged his leg as he leaned against the wall, half of his face covered in soot. "Kady," he replied, bleak, his voice hollow and scared. "Kady is missing."

"I'm going after her," Captain Violet announced, pulling herself to her feet. "If we move now, we might be able to get her back before they've booked her."

"Don't be ridiculous," Wilhemina chastised. "We barely made it out of that mess, and you want to go back?" She shook her head. "It's foolish.

Ridiculous."

The captain laid her hands on her hips, looking as imposing as she could for someone nearly a foot shorter than both Bailey and Wilhemina. "I don't know who you think you are, but you don't call the shots around here."

"And you do?" Willa asked, and it was more earnest than Bailey had anticipated.

"Er—yeah, I do, actually," Captain Violet answered. "We don't leave people behind."

"Who said anything about leaving anyone behind? I'm only saying that heading straight back out onto the streets after blowing up most of the industrial district might raise a few too many red flags. Hells, I'm surprised you've all managed to hide out here this long without getting dragged back in." Wilhemina leaned against the door frame, and it squealed with a creak under her muscular weight. She folded her arms, waiting for a response, and when the captain only stared, she continued. "And so I would recommend we wait until she's booked in, because the holding cell is only one set of bars to breach, and not three." She shrugged. "Although I would imagine my access has been revoked by now, given I murdered an MPO in our escape."

"What?" Captain Violet demanded. "I thought we agreed to keep things quiet! Now we're dodging murder charges, too?" She pinched the bridge of her nose, pacing the worn wood of the floor, caked with mud, soot, and the old, forgotten remnants of spilled ale. "For all the gods' sakes, I'm starting to think we're never going to make it off this gods-damned planet."

"She saved us," Bailey interjected, finding herself standing between the captain and her sister. "Willa saved us. That MPO would have killed all of us, and no doubt gone looking for the rest."

"He was just doing his job," Wilhemina said softly. "The same thing I did for twenty years."

"Need I remind the rest of you that Alice is somewhere out there, probably being—" Captain Violet stopped short, visibly flinching from her own words. "And Bradach, and Rosie, and, and, and. We don't have time for any of this, we need to get off of Gamma-3 and the hells back home to pick up whatever pieces are left after all of this."

"The docks are closed, Captain," Mae said, looping her arms around Bailey's waist. "We won't get a single ship out until after the all-council meeting."

For everything that had gone wrong, for all the terror laying thick in the air, for each uncertainty that tainted the future, Bailey couldn't help but lean back into Mae's embrace, silently thanking the dead gods, laying unreachable in their graves, that she had her woman back, and that she was safe, digging her fingers into Bailey's hips as though she was trying to keep her from floating away. She pulled Mae's arms closer around her, grateful for the distraction and the reminder, pressed tight against her, the soft crunch of crinoline like a whispered, thankful litany.

"No trains, either," Wilhemina said. "Roads closed, too. They won't be taking any chances."

"We can't stay here and just wait," the captain protested. "We need to get back to our people."

Mae pushed her chin into Bailey's back, her voice muffled by the ash-dusted twill jumpsuit. "High Councilor Kimura has jurisdiction over security in the Capital."

"I thought that was Tarand."

Wilhemina shook her head, still standing with her arms folded over her chest. "Tarand just thinks she should have jurisdiction over everything. It's Kimura."

"And Allemande?"

"The Rim. Turas-Mara and beyond it, probably including whatever in hells is out there with Obsidian Enclave." Wilhemina shrugged lightly, letting her shoulders fall back down. "Some kind of huge settlement, the scouting missions said. I don't think I've ever seen her so excited as when those reports started to come in."

Captain Violet stopped her pacing, pausing to jab a finger at Wilhemina. "This is your fault, you know. If they hadn't been trying to spring you from that block, Kady wouldn't be in custody right now."

"With respect, you don't know that she's in custody." Wilhemina shrugged again, earning her a sharp glare from the captain. "From what I hear, your crew is pretty crafty."

Outside the darkened window, the warehouses still burned across the city, lighting the horizon with a strange hue that crept into the midnight clouds, green, ominous, and spreading. Bailey pressed against the glass, the cool sensation almost surprising, given the heat of the blast they'd felt not so long before. "Kady may be in the Administration Building. When they arrested me for my crimes, they took me before a judge—well, it was Overseer Allemande then, as Kimura was apparently trying to escape."

"So she says," Wilhemina commented. "So that she could dismantle the rebellion from the inside out."

Captain Violet raised an eyebrow. "You think she's lying?"

"She's almost certainly lying, and I'm betting Tarand knows it." Wilhemina nodded towards the window that faced the Executive Building, its facade dark and unlit, except for one lone window on the top floor. "I'm betting she's in there right now, trying to figure out who started those blasts, and how to spin it to the press, because if this lands on her head, she's finished."

Aven was pressed against another window, staring out into the street. "Someone is coming," she said carefully, picking up a large crowbar next to the door. "Someone hooded."

"Kady?" Ned asked hopefully, limping to join her at the window. "Maybe it's Kady?" He opened the door, ignoring the protests of the others. After all, agents and MPOs could wear whatever they liked, and travel wherever they pleased, even in the midst of a city on fire.

"Do you have *any* idea what you've done?" Olivia asked as she entered, yanking down her hood as she slammed the door.

"Speak of devils, and they appear," Wilhemina said acerbically.

"Of course," Olivia said, throwing her cloak to the floor. "Of course you're here, and not where you are supposed to be."

"You can't be here," Mae protested, picking up the cloak and dusting it off, folding it delicately over her arm. "You could have been tailed."

"I wasn't. Every on-duty MPO in the city is currently combing the industrial district." Olivia flung herself into a worn, overstuffed chair, sending a flurry of feathers into the air. "Do you mind explaining what in hells happened?"

"An explosion," Captain Violet explained, now mirroring Wilhemina's crossed arms. "Because otherwise, three of us were going to wind up imprisoned. One of us already did!"

"You've certainly removed any doubt that the general is working with rebels and pirates, haven't you? I might have been able to fix that, but no, you had to throw yourselves into the ring and set half the gods-damned city on fire." Olivia growled with frustration, burying her head in her hands. "The all-council meeting is tomorrow, and now everything I've put into motion has been put into jeopardy by this. How am I supposed to do what I promised when you keep interfering?"

"I'll go," Wilhemina said, squaring her shoulders.

"What?" Olivia asked, stifling a laugh. "Don't be ridiculous. You're going to be public enemy number one in the morning."

"It's at least four hours until daybreak. Let me go and bring Kady back."

Captain Violet shook her head, already pulling her revolver out of the holster and checking the chamber. "No. Absolutely not, I am not entrusting the safety of one of my senior officers to someone so *recently* reformed."

Bailey kissed Mae's hands and unraveled herself from her grasp, moving to stand next to her sister. "I'll go too."

"No!" Mae protested, pulling at the frayed cuffs of Bailey's sleeves, frowning at them for half a second. "No. I just got you back, I'm not letting you throw yourself back into that mess."

"You all have to admit that this is the best shot. Confusion is easier in the chaos." Bailey shrugged under the weight of Willa's hand clapped on her shoulder. "I'll go too," she said again. "For Kady."

Olivia rolled her eyes, drumming her fingers against the worn arm of the chair. "I swear to the gods, if you make this any worse, then I'll—"

"Listen, Blondie, I know you run these streets, but I've been around longer than you," Wilhemina challenged. "You keep the High Council and its councilors busy, and I'll deal with this."

"I don't think you quite understand the gravity—"

"I was out on Turas-Mara for years, I know all about gravity. And Allemande, and if I know her, she's the one terrorizing that settlement." Wilhemina folded her sleeves down, buttoning them at the cuffs. "Am I correct in assuming she hasn't arrived for the meeting yet?"

"Yes," Olivia replied carefully, now digging her fingers into the chair. "But some of the others are angry that she disobeyed orders."

"Do members of the High Council even receive orders?" Mae asked, running a strip of fabric from her skirts through her fingers. Bailey had seen her do it a thousand times before, and always when she was nervous. "I thought they did as they pleased."

"High Councilor Allemande is new to the inner circle. Some are less than pleased with her work thus far." Olivia tugged a pocket watch from her pocket and sucked her teeth, standing again and taking her cloak from Mae. "I need to get back to the Executive Building, Tarand will wonder where I've gone." She pointed at Wilhemina, and then at Bailey. "You two had better not screw this up."

* * *

Bailey tugged her undershirt up over her mouth and nose, her eyes already watering from the dense smoke that wafted through the Capital's streets, creeping down every alley as inevitable as a twilight shadow. "So what now?" she asked, nudging her sister. "What's the plan?"

"No plan," Wilhemina answered, not even turning to look at her. "We just go and get the job done."

"But Olivia said—"

"And like I told her, I've been around longer."

"But that doesn't mean—"

Willa stopped abruptly, grabbing Bailey by the shoulders and shaking her gently. "Don't you get it, Bailey? Once this is over, no matter how things shake out, I'm finished." She let her hands drop back to her sides with the quiet hush of fabric, the smudges on her face still visible in the darkness. Someone had turned off all the street lamps, but that was only a boon for them, despite its purpose being to keep Capital residents calm and ignorant. Ash floated through the air, and it twisted like a knife in Bailey's chest because all she saw was one more home burning, even if it wasn't her own.

"You'll go home with us," Bailey assured her.

"And then what? You think a bunch of rebels and pirates will welcome a Coalition general with open arms?" Willa shook her head. "No. No, there's nothing left for me, not here or anywhere else." She shoved Bailey lightly. "You shouldn't have come."

"I'm not letting you do this alone."

"You should have. I'm just the shit on the bottom of your boot, Bailey." Willa offered up a sad smile, heartbreaking because she hadn't even chosen any of it for herself. "Thank you for coming for me. Going down in flames is at least more palatable than quietly rotting away in a cell."

Bailey wanted to argue, but swallowed back the urge as another explosion rocked the city, the rumbling beneath her feet an ominous reminder of what was at stake. "If they nabbed Kady, we need to grab her before processing."

"Why?"

"She's ex-Coalition. Blew up a lab once, so I've heard."

Willa smirked and kept walking, her boots quietly slicking along the surface of the sooty bricks. "I remember that. Weapons lab?"

"Yeah."

"Higher-ups were so angry, they locked everything down for a month. They wouldn't even release her name, for fear some of her coworkers would join the cause."

"Is that what they'll do to you?" Bailey asked, immediately wishing she could take back the question. "Sorry, I just meant—"

"Probably." Willa squinted into the growing darkness, the thick cloud of smoke starting to blot out the delicate, fragile light of the moon. "Administration Building is just ahead."

"It looks empty."

"Trust me, we're not about to be that lucky. Chances are that this is a trap, Bailey." Willa approached the side of the building, crouching through the long shadows that melted into the night, as seamless as they were dangerous. "There's no other reason for it." She turned, grabbing Bailey by the shoulders once again. "You have to let me go in alone, Bailey."

"Absolutely not. You expect me to let you do that alone?" Bailey pulled away from her, trying to ignore the wounded pull in her chest. "You're my sister."

"I'm no better than a machine, programmed to do what I'm told."

"Is this what you were told?" Bailey demanded in a hiss, gesturing at the metal grate Willa was already pulling on. "Breaking Kady out of a holding cell, that's what the Coalition wanted from you?"

"No."

"I don't blame you for what you were before," Bailey said, tears springing to her eyes but it wasn't the smoke that brought them forth, it was quiet desperation for something that felt like family again. "We've all made mistakes. I lost so many people, Willa. I hid, and I watched as they were loaded onto transports. Not like you, charging into battle without so much as a second thought. I could never be as brave as you are."

Willa tugged at the grate again, freeing it from the brick facade with a noisy clatter that made both of them flinch. "It's not bravery, it's foolishness."

"Then that's one more thing that shows you're my sister." Bailey reached up to pull herself into the duct, but Willa pulled her back down, dragging at her tightly laced boots.

"This one is on me, Bailey."

"Let me come with you."

"None of you will make it out unless there's more chaos and distraction than they can deal with. The industrial district was a good start." Willa straightened her braid, tucking away the strays that had formed the hint of a reddish glow around her head, in silhouette from the dampened moonlight. "They can't catch us both, Bailey, do you understand? Everything falls apart if they catch us both."

"I don't want them to catch either of us," Bailey hissed, still reaching up for the duct. "Willa, come on."

Wilhemina shook her head, almost imperceptibly, and dusted the ash from her shoulders with swift, sharp flicks. "I'm going in alone. I'm going to get Kady and get her to the docks, and you need to leave the moment you can." She drew in a deep breath. "When you've already lost everything, there's nothing left to lose."

"Willa, no!" Bailey protested, but her sister had already disappeared into the grate, leaving only a faint imprint of her boot in the grass that would be gone with the first strong breeze.

Chapter 50

Olivia drained what remained of her coffee, the fifth that day. There wasn't much else to keep her awake when she'd spent sleepless night after sleepless night trying to keep the Coalition together while also quietly ripping apart the seams under the cloak of destruction and chaos.

"It would appear we are running late," High Councilor Tarand said, sliding easily into her chair. "Let's begin." She smiled easily, her eyes shining with false promise as she looked out over the all-council meeting.

"We aren't all present yet," High Councilor Kimura objected, sliding the folder in front of her across the impeccably polished wood table, the sheen of it more of a glare beneath the harsh incandescent lighting from overhead. "I motion we wait until all councilors are present and accounted for."

"Seconded," said High Councilor Jacobs, running his finger around the rim of his empty glass. He took a silver flask from beneath his robes, taking a generous swig. "Surely with everything at hand, we should delay until we can form directives about the Rim and what lies beyond it."

Tarand pursed her lips, drumming her manicured fingertips against the table. "Our newest addition was given ample time to travel to the Capital, but has apparently chosen to ignore our invitation. We don't have the time nor the luxury to continue delaying the inevitable, not when the city remains on fire."

Jacobs chortled, screwing the lid back onto the flask. "Cecelia, you act as if a small, accidental explosion in the industrial district is somehow cause for alarm. You forget, I manage hazardous materials every day in my role. Solvent is particularly hazardous, it isn't the first time it has caused damage." He tucked the flask back into his robes, nary a care that not so long ago, he'd signed Marina Sykes' execution warrant for selling the same thing he couldn't go more than a few hours without. "Rebel activity in the Capital is negligible, and they are without resources. It's not as if the weapon is still unaccounted for."

Tarand flinched, and Olivia mirrored her before clearing her throat. "Of course it isn't, sir," she agreed. "It is well within custody."

"Then we should wait for High Councilor Allemande." Jacobs leaned back in his chair, folding his hands over his robes, the stiff fabric folded over itself to the floor, where it dragged against the immaculate carpet.

"Thirded," said High Councilor Brome in a bored, disinterested tone. "There's no sense in starting without her, especially given what's going on in Skelm. When will she arrive?" He cast a spurious glance at Tarand, no doubt due to the lies Olivia had fed his assistant. "Cecelia?"

"High Councilor Allemande is currently dismantling a pirate settlement," Olivia offered brightly. "I'm sure everyone at this table would agree that is of top priority."

"I don't agree," Brome said. "There will always be settlements that need clearing. We put one down, and halfway across the Near Systems, another grows in its place. This one is no different."

Olivia smoothed out the unwrinkled paper in front of her, palms against the smooth texture. "High Councilor Allemande feels differently."

"This settlement is nowhere near the Rim. Why does she feel she has jurisdiction? From how we've always done things before, Councilor Kimura has control over issues regarding crime and the subsequent meting out of punishments." Brome shrugged, tapping the end of a pencil against the stuffed file in front of him. "Why should things change now?"

High Councilor Fredericks gave a derisive snort, tossing her mane of fiery curls, a contrast to the drab, grey robes that she wore. "Perhaps some of us think that High Councilor Kimura shouldn't have been in charge of that at all, given the conditions in which she joined us."

The light overhead flickered gently, drawing Olivia's attention, and she couldn't help but wonder if the fire in the industrial district had reached the power plant. If it had, then the long-dead gods were still listening to her desperate prayers, muttered in dark stairwells as she nearly tore her dress in half with sweaty, nervous fingers.

"I beg your pardon?" Kimura asked, standing up from the table now. "I recommend you take that back, ma'am, before we have issues of slander on our hands. I was cleared of any and all wrongdoing, and thoroughly explained my position." Kimura shifted uncomfortably in her robes, tugging at the fabric that never hung quite right on her frame. "In fact, it was my advancements during that time period that helped to uncover this settlement that Amaranth Allemande is currently dismantling."

"So you support her bid, then?" Tarand asked innocently.

"I didn't say that."

"It was implied, Flora."

Kimura leaned against the table, hands flat against the wood, pressing down into it as though it would give her the answers that Olivia was hoarding inside her own mind. "I didn't imply anything, I am simply explaining the conditions of my release and promotion." She curled her fingers, nails scratching harmlessly against the lacquered surface. "Again."

"You can't blame certain members of this council for being suspicious, Flora," Tarand continued in a breezy tone. "The conditions of your ascension were unusual, to say the least."

"And yet, I never missed an all-council meeting, nor did I ever directly ignore an invitation to pursue my own specific goals." Kimura's jaw was clamped, flexing beneath flawless skin. "My feelings on our newest member's actions are, apparently, irrelevant."

Jacobs stood too, jabbing a finger at her from across the table. "Horseshit, Flora. You had the power to go after this settlement at any time, but you left it to a new recruit to clean up your gods-damned mess."

"Bruce, please," Tarand said, speaking over him. "This is not the time for petty interpersonal conflict."

"I'd hardly say that any of this is petty. You're losing control over the Capital, Cecelia, and everyone can see it. You're so concerned with how the rest of us are doing our jobs that you seem to think that you're now beyond reproach." Jacobs shook his head, laughing. "Just because you spend most of your time up to your neck in horseshit from the media here in the Capital doesn't mean you have the right to think you're above the rest of us. Maybe if you concentrated on your own duties, we wouldn't be looking at half the problems that we are."

Tarand exhaled softly, letting the tension thicken over the table. "Thank you for your thoughts, Bruce." She gestured around to each of the other high councilors, one at a time. "Anyone else agree? Flora? Meredith?" She paused. "Wallace?" When no one spoke, she smiled demurely, clasping her hands in her lap once again. "It would seem that you are on your own, Bruce."

"I'm just the only one who's frustrated enough to say something. No doubt Flora at least agrees, considering what I've been told."

Kimura jerked her head back, incredulous. "What you've been told? Are you listening to rumors again, Councilor Jacobs? I haven't said a gods-damned thing about High Councilor Tarand, not at this table nor anywhere else. I strongly advise that you take back the comment before I am forced to file an official motion to strike that from the record."

"So you deny that you find Cecelia to be one of the most pompous, frustrating infants born of privilege you've ever met?"

Olivia chewed the inside of her cheek until she tasted iron, spending every crumb of focus on maintaining the hopefully neutral expression plastered against her face. It was working. Somehow, it was working, against all the odds. They'd tear themselves apart, and she'd be on her way back to Cass before she knew it.

"Of course I didn't say that!" Kimura shouted. "Where are you hearing this?"

"One can access nearly any bit of information, if you just know where to look," Jacobs said. "Which is one more reason why this immediate invasion of a pirate colony that's been trafficking goods for us for decades seems all the more suspicious. Bradach is hardly a secret, and yet by morning, it's going to be plastered across every newspaper."

"Force them to pull the stories, then," Tarand offered. "I have contacts there that I can lean on."

Jacobs snorted. "I'm not surprised that's your solution."

"And how would you have us contain this, then?" Tarand demanded. "Perhaps, if we ask very nicely, they won't print that the all-council meeting is on indefinite hold because one of us decided to take a fucking detour." She flung a fountain pen at the table, sending a fine spray of ink to rest in tiny droplets on the surface. "You have no idea what it takes to keep a firm rein on the press."

"What difference does a few days make, Cecelia?" He picked up the pen, turning it over in his hands. "Explain it to me."

"It makes us a target, you persimmon, and you know it."

"The docks are locked down, as are the rails and the roads. All airspace from today onwards will be tightly and aggressively controlled in Capital jurisdiction. Tell me, what are you so concerned about?" He pressed a fingertip to the edge of the pen, drawing ink from inside that bled into his light skin, staining it. "If the weapon has been contained, which it has, then we have no real concerns. Every threat called in has turned out to be a hoax."

Olivia resisted the urge to smirk, because she was the one who had made dozens of calls, flooding the tip line from wire desks all over the city. Every late-night wire, every false tip to push them off-guard and closer to collapse.

"Fine," Tarand said evenly, pushing herself up and out of her chair. "I can't force you to see reason, unfortunately. If you want to laze around and wait for Amaranth to stroll in whenever she sees fit, then be my guest. However, if any of you get tired of waiting for that woman, you know where to find me." Without even turning her head, she summoned Olivia with a sharp flick of her wrist. "Ms. Guisette, with me. We have plenty of work to keep us busy, even if the rest of our colleagues are choosing to shirk their duties."

"How about you adjust your tone, Cecelia," High Councilor Fredericks uttered quietly, dangerously, and Olivia knew it wouldn't be long before the High Council began to crumble beneath the weight of itself. "You are not a regent, you are a member of this council, and you will behave as such."

"Just because you're the oldest surviving member doesn't make you a god," Tarand retorted. "You may have been here longer than the rest, but don't think we can't see the blood on your hands."

"I had nothing to do with Lionel Cabot."

"You keep saying that, and yet it's no secret that you were the one so concerned about his instability. He might still be sitting here, instead of Kimura, had you not arranged for him to be dispatched."

Fredericks smiled easily, pausing to take a long sip of her tea while keeping her eyes locked on Tarand. "I don't recall you offering up any objections, Cecelia. He was just as much a danger to you as he was to the rest of us."

Tarand tossed a handful of braids over her shoulder with a series of noisy clacks emanating from the wooden beads at the end of each one. "At least when he was in Skelm, we didn't have upstarts two heartbeats away from starting a revolution. We didn't have press following her around like desperate puppy dogs looking for a story."

"No, we had a member of the High Council who was failing at his job to hide in plain sight, to keep his mouth shut and his hands to himself until we came up with a new rotational plan, rather than working with the gods-damned Scattered to invent new things up at the armory." Fredericks pushed away her teacup and saucer, the porcelain scraping unpleasantly against the table. "We voted, and we agreed. You agreed as well."

"Perhaps I shouldn't have," Tarand shot back.

"Perhaps. But what's done is done, and now, we all must live with the consequences, and that includes remaining civil. We will reconvene when our newest member arrives."

"You don't have the authority—"

"Thirded," High Councilor Osei said. "There. That's a quorum, Cecelia."

He stood, his robes dragging elegantly along the ground. "It's done. When Amaranth Allemande arrives, we will continue this meeting, and we will recognize her efforts in regaining the weapon from rebel hands."

High Councilor Tarand floated through the door and down the corridor, with Olivia trailing after her, not nearly as unimpeachably graceful in her movements.

"Ma'am," Olivia said, closing the office door behind her, "I'll get to work finding High Councilor Allemande."

"Send her an ultimatum, Olivia." Tarand hovered by her office window, holding back the heavy velvet drapes, staring out at the greenhouses and gardens beyond. "Bradach or her daughter."

"Ma'am?" Olivia asked, doing her best to ignore the searing panic that had already begun to flood into the empty space in her chest, between where her lungs ached for different air, and where her heart thudded reluctantly, having been unceremoniously torn away from the one thing that had ever made her feel truly alive. "You want me to call in the hit on Emeline Allemande?"

"It's far past time, I think you'd agree. We've given her warning after warning, and yet, she continues."

"But the rest of the council—"

Tarand flung the curtains shut, rounding on Olivia. "The rest of the council is only as good as its weakest member, and let me be clear, Ms. Guisette, neither Flora Kimura nor Amaranth Allemande can handle the pressures that this position entails. When Bradach is silent, and Skelm is back under the control of Governor Das, and the Capital is more prosperous than it's been in fifty years, they will all thank me for my work and then spend the rest of their days with their mouths shut."

"Of course, ma'am," Olivia replied, scribbling notes into the margins of her notebook, her handwriting messy and uneven, a pox on the crisp whiteness the page had once been. "Who shall we call in?"

"I don't care, just get it done."

"John would have been closest, but he hasn't checked in."

"No, he was sent for that assassin in Bradach, no doubt to clear her out before Amaranth landed." Tarand brushed against Olivia's arm, gentle and pleading. "What was the last report?"

Olivia swallowed hard, staring down at the floor, studying her boots, unsettled that the previous night's mud was still caked onto one side. "Heavy casualties."

"On their side?"

"On both, ma'am."

Tarand swore under her breath, raking everything atop her desk to the floor with loud, obvious clatters. The inkwell smashed against the wall, sending a dark, ugly blotch to drip down the pristine paint, rolling across the carpet with splodges that the wool eagerly soaked up, changing it forever, irreparable and stained. Three fountain pens rolled beneath the desk and out of sight, and the overturned folders sent papers exploding over their heads, floating down like an early snow.

"Allemande called for reinforcements about eight hours ago."

"Gods be damned. How far out are they?"

Olivia bit her lip. "They probably landed recently, if not, then they will be soon."

"How many?"

"Seven squadrons."

Tarand sat down in her chair, burying her head in her hands. "How has it come to this, Olivia? Undermined by one of the most irritating women I've ever had the displeasure of meeting. A woman who, despite all of our valiant efforts, managed to secure that weapon before we did."

"I don't know, ma'am."

"I suppose I should be grateful that our troops were able to bring it back to the Armory, but still there are questions that I cannot seem to find the answers to."

There was a strange sense of time in that moment, as black ink slid down the wall, as the carpet absorbed the excess, as the last of the pages landed noiselessly on the office floor, as Tarand lifted her head and stared, and Olivia had never seen her look like that before.

Vulnerable, twisted and tied up with a quiet, violent rage.

"I know it was *you*, Olivia."

She was already backing up, reaching for the door knob, instinct overtaking intellect. "I'm sorry?" she asked innocently, hearing the crack in her own voice, a telltale beacon of her own indiscretions. "What was me?"

"Who has been telling lies about the members of the High Council?"

"I don't know, ma'am. I only know that it's my solemn and sworn duty to protect your reputation."

"My reputation."

Olivia swallowed hard, her fingers curled around the files and the papers in her hands, three paper cuts at once slicing into the creases of her hands. "Yes, Councilor. I don't know who is lying to the other members, but it's best we keep this under wraps, no? After all, we have the weapon back in the Armory, and—"

"It's been you all along." Tarand stood, backing Olivia into a corner. "You've been undermining me for years, Ms. Guisette."

"No!" Olivia's heart pounded blood to her ears, and all at once the room was starting to close in around her. "No, I would never, I—"

"I prayed to the gods that I was wrong," Tarand said. "When you came back from Terringgough Gulch with nothing more than scrapes and bruises, I wondered then how you'd done it, but I told myself it was because you were the best of the best." She toyed with a lock of Olivia's hair, letting it cascade through her elegant fingers, beset by stacks of rings that lined each digit. "Personally picked from the Intelligence agency, my perfect right hand who would help me ascend."

The councilor's eyes filled with tears, the huge droplets spilling out over her cheeks, leaving wet tracks before they fell onto her robes, darkening the fabric there. "Kimura insisted I have you tailed, even as your work remained as high a standard as always."

Olivia shook her head, a desperate refusal of the truth being told to her. "No," she whispered.

"I wondered what you were doing in that greenhouse with Mae Machenet. I thought perhaps you were shoring up a victory for me, using her father's connections to bury the other councilors under enough allegations of fraud to silence them. But then, no headlines surfaced to that effect, so I wondered if you were playing house with her. The entire Capital knows now that she prefers a high-profile paramour." Tarand tilted her head, causing more tears to splash down across her collar. "I thought, maybe, you were looking at her the way you used to look at me."

The councilor sighed sadly, brushing a thumb over Olivia's cheek, taking a tear with her. "I still don't know what that was. You've always been careful, Olivia, but this time, not careful enough."

Olivia swallowed hard. "Ma'am, I never—"

"Save your precious breath, my dearest." Tarand kissed her gently, caressing her shoulders with an unfamiliar tenderness. "You must know I cannot let this betrayal stand, and so you've left me no choice but to dispatch you myself."

Chapter 51

Mae straightened her skirts, brushing the soot from the crisp taffeta. The Capital's sky was almost orange that morning, the sunlight filtering down through thick clouds of solvent-inspired smoke to lay limp against the brick in the streets, and wash itself lazily across the face of the Executive Building. Bailey had returned in the wee hours, but without her—whatever she was. Watching Fineglass so easily snap the neck of that soldier was more than enough to give Mae pause, even if it had saved her own skin.

She approached the door to High Councilor Tarand's office, nodding at the guard posted there. "I'm here to see her," she said simply, knowing Olivia must be inside. If she could just get her into that stairwell again, they could figure out how to spring Kady and Fineglass from wherever they were being held. Gods below, problems on top of problems, a never-ending skyscraper of horseshit to unpick and deal with.

The officer nodded, the glare from the overhead lamps shining across their head. "Of course, Ms. Machenet."

"I'm surprised you remember me."

"Your face is hard to forget." The officer shifted, lowering the butt of the steamrifle to the floor. "Be careful," they whispered, their lips barely moving as they spoke.

"What? Why?" Mae hissed in reply, bustling closer.

"Ma'am," the officer called through the closed door, "Ms. Machenet is here to see you."

The muffled muttering from inside came to an abrupt stop, and silence wavered, circling the paths of irrevocable destiny, before Tarand replied, "Thank you, Officer Abara. You may send her in."

Mae stepped over the threshold into the office, expecting to see Olivia glaring back at her, but finding her own father's smug smirk instead. "Father," she said evenly, not letting on that explosions of panic were in that moment reducing every single internal structure within her to rubble. "It's good to see you out of bed so early. I know how you like your rest." She smiled, tilting her head innocently at him. It was a lie, of course, but it was one that would scrape its way beneath his skin and irritate him for years.

She bowed her head gently towards the high councilor, hands clasped in front of her. "Madame High Councilor, thank you for seeing me."

"I've been expecting you."

"Oh?" Mae asked, still hiding behind her plastered-on smile, wan and empty. "I must say, my journey was rather an impulsive one."

"Please, sit."

Despite every instinct within her telling her not to, she sat, arranging her skirts around her and hoping that neither her father nor the high councilor would notice the burned flecks of fabric that hid in the folds, singed by embers after the blast. "It's surprising to find your office devoid of your assistant, High Councilor."

Tarand narrowed her eyes, pushing back from the desk and standing, looking out the window at the gardens beyond. "Ms. Guisette has been given a special mission, which regrettably takes her away from my office."

More panic bloomed in Mae's chest, and she wondered just how much she could withstand before the horror of it all swept her out to sea like a targeted tidal wave. "Oh?" she asked again, simply, and continued to ignore her father. Whatever the reason he'd beaten her there, it wasn't good.

"Yes, she's a very busy woman. Too busy, if you ask me."

"For your sake, I hope she returns to you soon."

Tarand toyed with the velvet of the curtains, crushing it between her thumb and forefinger, the excess cascading from her hands to the floor, where it lay in an artful heap. Mae's hands itched for it, for the security of something real that hadn't and wouldn't change. A seam was a seam. Fabric was fabric. Applications of techniques for specific outcomes that she could do half-asleep while Abigail rambled about some new man she was dating. *Abigail.*

The high councilor sighed demurely, letting the curtains pull away from her hands. "Ms. Machenet, while I am unsurprised to find you at my door, I must say I had hoped that I was wrong."

"I'm sorry?"

"You've created yet another mess for us, Maevestra," her father said, one leg crossed over the other, the horrible grey of his suit not at all the right choice for his complexion. It washed him out, and she'd told him that for years. It was one more quiet insult, no doubt intentionally planned. "I'd hoped that after the nonsense with General Fineglass, you would calm down and settle into your new role for the family business." He shrugged, opening his hands to show empty palms. "Perhaps not."

"I'm afraid I don't know what you're talking about," Mae said carefully, aware that the status quo was rapidly disintegrating beneath her boots. She'd only gone there because Bailey had begged her to, and it may yet prove her own demise, or at least imprisonment. "I came here to tell the high councilor that I have information about who was behind the explosions in the industrial district last night."

Tarand raised an eyebrow. "It never ceases to amaze me, Ms. Machenet, that you somehow always seem to be in the wrong place at the wrong time for a girl of your family's stature." She nodded before turning back to them, throwing open the curtains to allow the tainted sunlight to trickle in through the window, hazy and duplicitous. "But go on."

"It was a squadron of rogue MPOs," Mae lied, her face set in stone. Her father was watching her every move, and she couldn't give him a single bargaining chip to hold her with. "I saw them myself. The explosion originated at a warehouse along an intersection. You can check there, if you want to verify my story."

"The explosions in the industrial district were caused by an unfortunate, anomalous accident," the high councilor replied, running her fingers over the spines of books on their shelves, perfectly aligned, no doubt by Olivia. "They were not caused by a squadron of rogue MPOs."

Mae swallowed hard, aware that a net was quickly closing in around her, and resisted the urge to thrash or run like a cornered animal. "Ma'am, one of them fired a Coalition-issues heat gun bolt into a drum of solvent."

"Do you think I cannot run my city, Ms. Machenet?" Tarand asked.

"Of course not, ma'am."

Tarand arched an eyebrow as she circled the office, stopping behind Mae's chair and resting her hands on Mae's shoulders, pressing down on her so much that it almost hurt. "Why would you come into my office and lie to me, Ms. Machenet?"

"I would not lie to you, ma'am. You can check everything I have said. I thought you should know, given the importance of the all-council meeting."

The high councilor waved her hand casually in the air, disturbing the flecks of dust suspended, the ignorable gesture wreaking chaos on what had already been. "I've ordered the meeting to be delayed for the time being."

"Because of the explosions?"

"No, Ms. Machenet, because we are awaiting the arrival of our newest esteemed colleague. From my understanding, your family is already well-acquainted with High Councilor Allemande, are you not?"

"We are," Mae's father interjected. "We assisted her with some challenging situations the last time my daughter was visiting the Capital."

"Then I should say that I am surprised that Ms. Machenet did not try to seduce her, too." Tarand's eyes glinted like molten gold as she spoke, her glare made even more threatening by the orange glow outside. "Though given what I have heard about Amaranth Allemande, I doubt she would have made much headway."

Mae stood, the compulsion too much to deny. "I'm afraid I don't know what you're talking about," she said, her jaw set firm because if she allowed herself to feel anything other than the sting of outrage, she would crumble faster than the destroyed warehouses on the other side of the city. "I have no interest in High Councilor Allemande, nor anyone else."

"No?" Tarand asked, pushing her back down into the chair. "I thought your love for General Fineglass was unparalleled. Has the fire of love cooled so soon?"

"It is difficult to remain in love when someone traipses through a press tour denouncing their association with you and reassuring the Near Systems that she is happily married, in fact."

"Ah, but everyone with an ear to the ground knows that he filed for divorce quite a long time ago." Tarand finally released her, continuing to circle around the office like a half-starved shark, desperate for a fresh catch. "Where is General Fineglass, Ms. Machenet?"

"I'm sorry?"

The high councilor turned, staring, but her face was surprisingly neutral, much to Mae's frustration. "I am growing tired of these games, Ms. Machenet. I am not a fool, no matter how much you may think I am one. You are here to throw me off the scent."

"Ma'am, I cannot answer your questions if I don't understand them." Mae lifted her chin, aware that her father was watching, too—but if neither of them knew where the general was, that was only positive, assuming they weren't lying to her face, which they probably were. "I have not seen General Fineglass since the last time I was in the Capital. Is she even here?"

"Maevestra, as your father, I am duty-bound to clean up the messes you continue to leave in your wake, trails of destruction and havoc that leave your poor mother in floods of tears." He sighed sadly, a performance, and not a very convincing one. "If you just tell High Councilor Tarand where the general is hiding, we can all begin to rebuild the relationships of trust that you have insisted on destroying."

Her father's pitiable expression did not match that of Tarand's hunger, and so Mae sat back in her chair, convinced that only one of them knew why they were all there, and she was standing dressed in yesterday's High Council robes. Mae folded her hands in her lap and gave a wistful glance at the window. "I'm not sure where she is, ma'am. I wish I knew, if only to tell her how much of my heart she broke. Alas, my heart belongs to another, these days."

"So it would seem," Tarand said airily. "You know, Gerard, I'd always assumed that someone like you would have a firmer grip on your children. It would seem that even the most ruthless have an undeniable soft spot for their daughters." She sat again, the chair creaking quietly from the movement. "When I first saw Ms. Machenet cavorting with my Olivia, I assumed that it was your doing, Gerard."

For once, Mae's father looked surprised, and she relished it. Good. Let him be on the back foot for once, always trying to play catch-up, forever behind the evolving news of the situation. He cleared his throat in a demure, polite fashion. "It was," he lied.

"It was?" Tarand asked, a hint of brevity to her voice, as though she knew that he was inventing new narratives for the press to devour.

"Of course, Madam High Councilor," he said. "There were concerns among several investors about the future, not just of Turas-Mara, but all enrichment beyond the Rim." He shrugged lightly, his hands still firmly clasped. Olivia wondered if Tarand could see that he was digging his short fingernails into his palms, or if it was only her conditioning as the daughter of one of the most feared men in politics that had trained her to do so. Her father laughed, matching Tarand's pretended tone. "We both know that investment drives progress, ma'am."

"Indeed it does, and if I wasn't sitting here looking at you, I'd think those words just leaped from the mouth of Amaranth Allemande." Tarand plucked a pen from the desk drawer, hovering poised over a blank sheet of paper. "No doubt you are beyond thrilled at her promotion, Gerard."

"I am only happy when the Coalition is served well," he replied. "The safety and continuation of the Coalition is my only goal."

"Yes, I'm sure that lovely house you live in has nothing to do with it," Tarand replied with half a chortle tacked onto the end of the sentence, but it was the kind of laugh you'd hear from a hyena right before she finished you off. "Ms. Machenet, I need for you to tell me where you are hiding

General Fineglass."

Mae waited a beat before she replied, the only sound in the office that of her own rustling skirts as she shifted her legs beneath her. "I can say, High Councilor, with complete and total unimpeachable honesty, that I have no idea where General Fineglass is. Until this conversation, I wasn't even aware that she had returned to Gamma-3." She demurred, clamping her mouth shut because the meeting had already been off the rails since before she'd even arrived, and she clearly wasn't going to glean any sort of information about Kady or Fineglass, other than that the latter probably wasn't in custody—although, with Tarand, anything was possible.

"I had hoped you would cooperate, Ms. Machenet. Your father always did speak so highly of you."

"I doubt that," Mae replied without thinking.

Tarand flicked her wrist towards the door. "You may leave, you're boring me."

"When will Ms. Guisette return from her new assignment?" Mae asked, trying to keep her tone breezy but feeling the crack in her own voice as she spoke. "I have some... personal business with her."

The high councilor's eyes narrowed, hardening over. She tossed the pen at the desk, sending a spray of ink across the previously blank page, its ivory delicacy shattered by uneven globs of viscous black. "Ms. Guisette will return when she has completed her assignment, Ms. Machenet, and even when that happens, I can promise you will have no business with her at all." Tarand continued to stare Mae down, completely ignoring her father, just as she had for most of their meeting. "A girl of your breeding should be more careful about who you're letting up your skirts."

Mae stole a glance to the side at her father, who probably should have said something at that, but instead, he was examining his cuticles, pretending he hadn't heard what Tarand had just said. Typical Machenet behavior, shoring up your own status just to throw anyone else to the wolves. She stood and braced her hands against the back of the wooden chair, the lacquer smooth under her fingers. "I will keep that in mind, ma'am."

"Your poor father can only bail you out of your personal messes so many times before this city will tire of your headline-stealing antics, Ms. Machenet."

"Last I checked, my face had been nowhere near a headline since last I was here."

"Only because my office—Ms. Guisette specifically, I might add—quashed the reports of you two cavorting down in the greenhouses, as though every political operative and journalist couldn't see you whispering behind ferns about only the gods know what." Tarand huffed out a terse, angry sigh, returning her focus to the marred page in front of her. "Both of you, get out of my sight."

Mae opened the door, aware that her father had yet to move from his seat. In the corridor, Officer Abara grabbed her hand to shake it with more enthusiasm than she had anticipated, and she nearly recoiled from them until she saw the opportunistic strength in their eyes, staring.

"Ms. Machenet, always a pleasure," they said, nodding. "I've always been a fan of your work." They released her hand and tugged at an epaulet on their shoulder. "Very sharp."

"Er—yes, of course. Thank you," she said, shoving the slip of paper they'd deposited in her palm down deep into her pockets.

"Maevestra," her father growled behind her, "it's time to leave."

"It looks like your deal with Allemande didn't benefit you as much as you hoped it had. What were you doing here, anyway?"

Her father grabbed her by the elbow, pulling her towards the elevator, the scuff of their boots against plush rugs quiet but audible on the hushed top floor. "Cleaning up your mess, as usual."

"And what is it I've supposedly done now, I wonder?"

He huffed angrily, a growl dying in his throat. "A squadron of MPOs, you say? Looks like you would have gotten a pretty close look at them."

"Nothing was booked, relax."

"You cannot keep putting this family into jeopardy," he hissed as they approached the lift.

"Funny you should say that, when you were broke the last time I showed up to bail you out," Mae replied, loud enough to make him visibly uncomfortable. "When I showed up last time, you were all but destitute, with Mother having to consider selling the house to keep you from it."

"Keep your voice down, Maevestra, haven't I taught you anything at all?"

"Oh, you've taught me plenty. Why is it that you think I'm able to outsmart you, time and time again?"

He steered her onto the elevator, frantically pulling on the lever to close the doors. "If you will recall, Maevestra, it was me who expunged your record after you disappeared last time."

"To save your own ass!" she shouted now, barking out an incredulous laugh as the elevator descended floor to floor, the glass behind him looking out over the polished marble at the entrance of the building, five stories below. "You've never lifted a finger unless it was of some benefit to you."

"I don't appreciate the tone you are taking with me."

The elevator doors opened, and Mae stepped out into the foyer. "Stay away from me, Gerard. And that goes for Gladys, too."

"Genevieve never would have embarrassed us like this," he said quietly, a warning, hostile tone. "Never once did she wind up on the front page of the papers, or have us called into a high councilor's office like an obedient lapdog."

"That's because Gen wrote you off," Mae answered simply, fumbling with the paper in her pocket, already desperate to know what it said. "She knew you were poison, and now, so do I."

Her boots clicked against the marble, a messy echo lingering just above the floor as she unfolded the paper that Officer Abara had given her. There was only one word.

Reeducation.

Chapter 52

Henry peeked out the window at the settlement beyond the Bronze Bell, hazy and broken and painfully, wrenchingly silent. The fighting had continued for two days already, and with the Coalition gunships still in the dock, there was no sign of a ceasefire. Near the docks, the ashen remains of the sciences tent, with smoldering pages still blowing in the breezes from the Coalition ships' engines. All their work, lost to fire and damage, stolen out from beneath them right as they were on the cusp of a breakthrough.

It was hard to know who was alive and who wasn't. Movements were a challenge when there were MPOs everywhere, lingering in every corner, beneath every eave, thick as bacteria on a culture plate down at the docks. She had moved to other buildings three times already with Captain Tansy before they returned to the Bronze Bell. How strange, that a place they'd once reviled was now their unwanted salvation.

"How are you holding up?" Captain Tansy asked, loading in another cartridge they'd stolen from a Coalition restocking wagon.

"Fine, I guess," Henry replied, stretching her legs out in front of her, the heels of her boots scraping against the unfinished wood of the attic. "At least the ships stopped coming."

"Prison transport left last night. I guess it was finally full."

Pushing the dirty, torn bed sheet that acted as a curtain aside, Henry once again stared into a maw of nothingness, Bradach broken and smoldering. Half the buildings were burned out or collapsed, and the other half were being used by rebel squatters or Coalition soldiers as makeshift base camps.

"Allemande's ship is still here."

"Strange, I'd have thought she'd leave for the all-council meeting," the captain said, taking aim at a window on the other side of the city and pulling the trigger. Distant glass shattered with the quiet rustle of the pieces landing against the cobblestones, so many torn up and overturned now due to the steamtrucks. "Maybe she was uninvited."

"If only we were that lucky," Henry said. She found herself looking to the sky again, squinting into the heavy, ash-ridden clouds that sank lower and lower with every passing hour, willing Georgie to appear out of the mist and simultaneously wishing that she never would. As much as Henry required rescue, the idea of Georgie being in peril made something in her stomach twist. Instinctively, she held a hand over her belly, pressing gently against the swelling there.

"Any word on Delia?" the captain asked.

The question scraped razor blades of anxiety across Henry's skin, and for a split second, she tried to jerk away from it, before realizing that no, she would have to weather the storm. There was no going back about what she'd done, leaving Delia lying under a bush with a messy, ineffective tourniquet above a missing limb. "No," she said, and the odd finality of it bubbled up under them both like rancid, over-boiled milk. "I haven't heard anything."

"If she hadn't—"

"I know," Henry said, her chest growing tighter with every passing moment. "I shouldn't have left her there."

"Not much more you could have done."

"I still shouldn't have." Henry ran the tattered fabric of her skirts through her fingers, the once crisp blue muddied in her hands. "They took Lucy, Jhaveri, and Arteo, too. I should have fought harder."

Captain Tansy took the muzzle of the steam rifle out of the window and leaned it against the wall, bending to massage where her leg ended. "Then you'd probably be dead, too," she said quietly, slumping down against the wall. "Not that I'm convinced any of us will get out of here alive."

"I wish we could go back to before any of this happened."

"A few days aren't enough to make a difference. They were going to come here, regardless."

Henry peered through the broken spyglass, splintering the orange sky into uneven, jagged pieces. "I mean, before any of it. Before the storm generators, even. I should have taken Georgie and her family somewhere else, somewhere quiet, the moment I had the opportunity to."

"You didn't know, Weaver. None of us did."

"Still," Henry pressed. She pushed herself up onto her knees, watching as a small ship, a shuttle perhaps, descended through the atmosphere. "A shuttle," she said, her breath uneven and ragged.

"Whose?"

"Hard to tell. Not the Cricket's."

"No, that ship can't hold on to a shuttle longer than a few weeks. The gods know I've heard Alice complain about it enough back in the Pig." Tansy leaned out the window, staring at the smoldering ruin down the street. "That's gone now, too."

"It's all gone," Henry agreed. "We lost weeks of work at the lab. I would swear by the gods we almost had that algorithm beat." The shuttle touched down in the docks, nestled between two huge gunships. Even with the broken spyglass, she couldn't quite make out the words emblazoned along the side, but when the doors opened and a slim, petite figure emerged, she couldn't help but swallow back a strangled sob at the sight of her. "It's Emeline."

"Georgie's sister?"

"Yeah."

"Allemande's kid?"

"Something like that."

The captain stole a glance before ducking down beneath the windowsill once more. "What in the hells is she doing here? Every reason I can conjure up has nothing but bad news for us. Didn't that kid drug Mae?"

"She did," Henry said with a nod, already moving for the hatch.

"Where do you think you're going?"

"Georgie stayed behind in Chalidon to talk to her sister. Emeline might know where she is, might know if she's—" Henry stopped herself short, tugging at the dirty fabric of her skirts. "I need to know."

"I'm coming with you."

"No! I can't have anyone else on my conscience," Henry protested, pushing the captain's hands from her arm. "I'll be careful. If anything goes wrong, I'll just activate the sirens again."

"If they haven't blocked access yet."

"Then I'll run."

Captain Tansy snorted a laugh. "Yeah? You do much running recently, mama hen?"

"I'm perfectly capable."

"Nope." The captain slung the rifle over her shoulder and snatched the crutches that were propped against the brick. "If there's one thing I know, it's that Georgie is a real pain in the ass when she's upset, and I just don't think I can be dealing with that. I'm coming. I'll cover you. End of discussion."

"Then I'll stay," Henry lied, already plotting how she'd sneak out the moment the captain was asleep.

"You're a bad liar, Weaver. A brilliant, kind of intimidatingly intelligent scientist, but an absolutely, unequivocally bad liar." The captain waved a hand at the hatch. "Come on then, let's go. We don't have all day. Well, we do, but I'd rather not be out in the open any longer than necessary."

"Maybe it would be better to move at night?" Henry asked, still thinking about her lie and how, if she kept her cool, it just might work.

"That kid could be anywhere by then. Right now, we know she's on the docks, and no doubt Allemande is going to appear any moment to yank her aboard that Coalition vessel, so come on." The captain nodded at the hatch again. "I said, come on."

Henry huffed out an aggrieved sigh and pulled back the wooden floorboards, climbing down from the attic back into the Bronze Bell. "You're a difficult woman to argue with."

"Let's just say I'm adept at knowing my opponents." The captain checked out three windows before waving them forward. "We're clear for now, assuming those roving bands of MPOs moved back uptown after last night. Larkin tore through that squadron, the bodies filled two trucks."

"Any sign of her since?" Henry asked, despite already knowing the answer.

"No, but I'm less worried about her than the rest of them. If you'd have seen her, you'd agree."

"I don't know, Evie said she was pretty shaken up after that assassin got into the Pig after hours." Henry eased down the steps one at a time, overly conscious about the quiet staccato echoes emanating from her boots with every stair. "Gods, I wish this wasn't happening."

"No one wishes for this, Weaver."

Henry ran her fingers over the peeling wallpaper, resisting the urge to tear at it, to take out her fears and frustrations on the old, worn out glue that barely held it in place. "Some do. The ones who made the storm generators do. The ones who made that superweapon do." She paused at a soot-stained window, pressing a palm against the cool glass and hoping against all hope that Georgie was okay, wherever she was, and that wherever she was headed, it was far from Bradach. "For some, bloodshed is the only thing that drags them out of bed each morning, the possibility to rip life from someone else."

"As much as I wish I could disagree with you, I can't."

"Yeah." Henry continued down the steps, and when she reached the first floor, jiggled the knob before opening it, half-expecting a mob of MPOs to leap from the mid-afternoon shadows and throw cuffs on them before they knew what was happening. Yet, the streets were strangely quiet, with nothing more than whispers on the stilled breeze, thick air hanging over all of it, suffocating enough to remind her why the superweapon was a danger in the first place, wherever in hells it was. "Coast is clear."

"When we get near the docks, we should cut through the park. There are some good trees there to hide in."

"Trees?"

"You have a better idea?"

"No," Henry admitted, slinking out into the street. Cobblestones cracked under her boots, chunks of rock coming loose and littering the streets with a fine powder that coated the road. Mirrored sun was magnified through the dusky haze, and she squinted into it, willing herself to see clearly, but willpower was rarely enough to tackle something as tangible as a city reduced to rubble. "Let's just keep our cool."

"I'm cool as a candied cherry," the captain retorted.

"Oddly specific."

"You never know what small things you'll miss until they are gone." Captain Tansy motioned for her to move across the street, aiming for the shade of one more burned-out building, the top windows still leaking smoke into the sky, with curling tendrils like the melon vines that once grew in the community garden. By the looks of it, the garden had been razed, cut down to the ground and mulched to make room for more Coalition transport across the settlement. The captain followed, using her crutches to swing across the street in one fluid motion. "If I make it out of this, I'm getting upgrades for the next leg. One with attachments."

"Attachments?"

"At least three knife compartments and a gun," Captain Tansy answered. "And a flask."

"Anything else?"

"Two flasks."

Henry pointed up at the trees just beyond the short fence that shot high into the sky, above the worsening smog that continued to sink down across Bradach, suffocating it with ash and soot and the burned up, desiccated dreams of everyone who had once lived there. "Think you can climb that one?"

"Not a problem. I'll try to cover you the best I can if anything goes sideways." Captain Tansy eased open the gate, the shrill shriek of the hinge freezing them both in their tracks until they were satisfied that no one else had heard it. "But I won't do anything unless there's no other option."

"Keep an eye out for the others."

"I'll keep two eyes out, how about that?" The captain grabbed a low-hanging branch, hoisting herself into the tree until she was barely visible amidst the foliage. "Don't get caught, Weaver."

"I'll do my best."

"I don't want to deal with Payne if she finds out I was the one who let you do this."

Henry rolled up the dirty, ashy cuffs of her sleeves, frowning at the frayed threads peeking from the button holes. Mae would be aghast if she saw it, but then, no one knew where in hells she was, other than somewhere on Gamma-3 trying to track Bailey and her sister down. A mess, all of it. All of them cast to the edges of the Near Systems, cut off and spread thin. The Coalition never would have been able to take the settlement if they'd all been in one place, but that was explicitly the point. Divide and conquer. "Georgie won't find out," Henry said, waiting at the trunk of the tree.

"She's still there on the docks, talking to someone. The dock manager, maybe?" Captain Tansy called down from her perch in a hushed whisper. "There's a squadron about to rotate back into the city, probably to collect wounded. They have a stretcher and two steamtrucks. If you go now, you might be able to—"

Henry didn't wait for more instructions. She strode through the ruined park, stepping over branches and singed tomato leaves, her heart squeezing in her chest because it was only three days ago that Carmen was out there pruning, laughing away her complaint that Bailey had left her with the brunt of the work. Her body had probably already been incinerated, if the thick plumes of smoke belching out into the atmosphere were anything to go by. Henry choked back the sob whispering in the back of her throat and pushed through the opposite gate, waiting behind a hedge until she saw the glint of Captain Tansy's scope sparkle from the leaves.

"Emeline," she said from the hedge, quiet but firm. "What are you doing here?"

"You shouldn't be here," Emeline replied, unmoving, still looking over forms on a clipboard. "You should have left."

"We didn't know."

"You should have known, then." Emeline flicked a glance in Henry's direction, but returned to the papers in front of her. "It's no surprise to anyone that this has been in the works since Cole Marion opened a base of operations here."

"Cole Marion is dead."

"Yes, I'm aware. Calvetti's announcement across every frequency made sure of that."

Henry stepped out from behind the bushes, hesitant, afraid someone would snatch her up before she had the chance to fight back. "Where's Georgie, Emeline?"

"She's not here?"

"No."

"Last I saw of her, she had ripped an iron bolt out of a table and escaped."

"Escaped?" Henry hissed, still too afraid to set foot on the dock itself, staying rooted in the gritty mud of battle instead. "You imprisoned her?"

Emeline narrowed her eyes and tossed down the clipboard, where it landed atop an empty crate with a noisy clatter. She dragged Henry onto the waiting ship, up the loading bay ramp. "Better it was me than an official booking, don't you think? I told her not to come, and she did anyway. What was I supposed to do, welcome her rebel self with open arms?"

"She was trying to help you!"

"I don't want or need help from rebels, Henry." Emeline sighed, squeezing her eyes shut. "I shouldn't even be here. I should be back in Skelm. The election is so close, yet I was dragged out here because the high councilor is concerned that there will be an attempt on my life." She toyed with a splintered piece of wood, wobbling it back and forth until it snapped off the crate and fell to the ground. "I cannot ignore the orders of the High Council."

"Is that all you care about?"

"Yes."

Henry couldn't help but notice that Emeline looked far older than her twenty years, the weight of her decisions pulling at the corners of her eyes.

She looked weary in a way a girl that age never should. "You can ask how they are, you know."

"Lucy is on the prison transport." Emeline's voice was tired, frustrated—ultimately unhelpful.

"We tried to save her, we—"

"She never should have been here in the first place. I told Georgina to let me take Lucy, to enroll her in a good school, and she refused."

Henry pushed her hair, dirty and matted, over her shoulder in an unkempt clump. "Lucy was doing just fine here, and your mother—"

"They never should have been here!"

"But they were."

"What do you want from me?" Emeline demanded. "I can't single-handedly reverse a High Council decision to invade an enemy settlement."

"Talk to Allemande. Get her to leave."

"She's been after this place for years. There's no chance, and that's why I tried to tell Georgie, but she wouldn't listen." Emeline kicked at a crate. "She never gods-damned listens!"

Henry waited, resting a hand on her stomach, an automatic, unconscious gesture. "You have more in common than you don't," she said finally, leaning back against one of the crates. "Stubbornness runs in your family."

"Not with Ma." Emeline's glance flicked to Henry, and something like pain flashed across her face. "Are you...?"

"Yes."

"Georgie didn't say."

"She doesn't know. I haven't seen her." Henry shrugged lightly, as though it was a shopping list or something else equally as dull, and not the singular driving force in making sure she found Georgie and got them all safe. "You're going to be an aunt."

Emeline only stared, and stared long enough that when footsteps sounded up the loading bay ramp, she almost hesitated a moment too long to shove Henry out of the way.

"Emeline," High Councilor Allemande said, wrapping her in a tight embrace. "I'm so glad that you're here."

"Now that I've proved I'm not dead, I need to get back to Skelm."

"I forbid it."

"I have an election to manage."

"The election is off, Emeline."

"What?" Emeline stepped backwards, almost stumbling over where Henry was poorly hidden. "You can't do that."

"It wasn't a unilateral decision. Governor Das will remain in charge in Skelm until things can be sorted out. Clearly, now is not the right time for this. The Coalition has more pressing matters to attend to than a silly election." Allemande stepped back, casting a critical eye over the loading bay. "You pushed too hard, Emeline, just as I said you were in danger of doing. I cannot hold the rest of the council at bay."

"Did you even try?"

"They were going to kill you, Emeline."

Emeline made an odd sound in her throat, somewhere between a laugh and a sob. "Tell me something I don't know. They've had eyes on me since I left Turas-Mara."

"I wish you hadn't. The Rim is so lonely without you." Allemande tightened her necktie, straightening it in the dull reflection of a porthole. "Come back with me when this is all over. We can start again, and I will be able to convince the High Council that you aren't a danger to what we are trying to achieve."

"I'm not coming back with you." Emeline pursed her lips, her hands balled into fists at her sides. "I'm going home to Skelm, where I will still be standing for election."

"You can't!"

"Who's going to stop me?" Emeline demanded, shouting now. "Are you going to stop me?"

Allemande mirrored her expression, lips pressed into a thin line. She clasped her hands in front of her, fingers tightly laced in front of her perfectly tailored dress, not yet wearing the robes of the High Council. "I would rather that you didn't force my hand."

The crates were all emblazoned with the Coalition logo, and through the slats in the wood boxes of ammunition sparkled like a forbidden oasis in the desert, a dangerous mirage. Henry dipped her hand into a crate, stealing two boxes at a time and carefully, silently shoving them into her bra. If she was going to get caught, she may as well make the inevitable imprisonment worth it.

Emeline rocked from her heels to her toes, back and forth, stiff and unyielding. "I don't need your protection."

"I'm not trying to protect you, I'm trying to make sure you don't throw your career away on frivolous nonsense. Drop this election, Emeline. Join me in the Capital for my ascension, and then we can go home to Turas-Mara. In a few years, no one will remember your temporary foolishness, and we can get to work priming you for a career we'll both be proud of."

"Over my dead body."

"You never used to speak to me this way. What is it, then? Your rebellious nature come to the surface? Latent anger that you were separated from Skelm? Boredom?" Allemande looked strangely desperate as she stood there, clawing for reason in a sea of chaos. "Your traitor sister has already been relocated, Emeline. She isn't here."

"I'm well aware of where Lucy is."

"I suppose you know everything now, do you? No need for your mother anymore?"

Emeline drew in a ragged breath. "I never needed you. I never needed anyone."

"I pulled you from the—"

"Mud of the warehouses," Emeline finished. "Yes, you've said as such before." She wrung her hands, her shoulders tense and raised up high. "I'm going back to Skelm."

"You can't."

"I don't care, Mother," Emeline said quietly. "I didn't fight this hard just to be forced to stand down on the eve of victory."

"Then you've forced my hand."

Emeline stood her ground, arms folded tight over her chest. "Good."

Chapter 53

Evie buried her head in her hands because she couldn't let the others see just how much she wasn't keeping it together. Delia was still out cold, her head lolling from side to side on the chaise as the bloody stump at her shoulder leaked scarlet fluid into a horrible puddle on the marred marble. Roger hadn't spoken to anyone since Evie had told him about Carmen. There he sat in the middle of the floor, staring at a blank wall, his face plastered with tear tracks that skidded down across his five-o'clock shadow, disappearing where his dirty collar met his neck.

"Hey," Holly said, handing her a steaming mug. "You look like you need this."

"Is it really that obvious?"

"Maybe not as obvious as some, but I was around you long enough to recognize that look." Holly sat down, smoothing her skirts over her knees.

"Oh, yeah? Was it the same look I had as when you set me up?" Evie breathed in the steam, blossoming with some sort of herbal tincture that Larkin would have been able to guess immediately. Still, she was grateful for it, and for the shelter. She sighed, wrapping her hands around the cup. "It doesn't matter now anyway, I guess."

"There was some movement out at the docks, but I couldn't see what exactly."

"More ships landing?"

"Just one, a shuttle, I think."

Evie took a sip, savoring the floral taste before swallowing it down.

"Whoever was on that shuttle probably isn't any friend of ours."

"We seem to be in short supply of those, these days."

"Gods, how I wish you weren't right."

Holly tugged at the hem of her peach-colored dress, stained with soot at the knees, elbows, and across the left side of the middle torso. "I haven't seen any of the others yet. I thought maybe someone was in the attic of the Bronze Bell, but no shots for hours."

"Maybe they ran out of ammunition."

"Maybe," Holly agreed. "We can only hope this place doesn't get raided again."

"The damage looks pretty bad," Evie said, trying not to notice the remains of the blown glass vase, now nothing more than shards on the ground, or the bloody handprint on the wall from when Roger had dragged Delia in from the park, saying he'd found her beneath a tree, unconscious.

"It's alright. I never much liked this place anyhow." Holly cracked a sad smile and ran her fingers over the crystal coffee table, one of the few things in her home that had yet to be demolished or destroyed. "I always said Bradach is a backwater."

"Not enough of a backwater to keep us from getting raided, obviously."

"Maybe we should have just told everyone Cole Marion was dead."

Evie shook her head, disturbing the steam rising from the teacup. "That's not a productive path to travel. We could never know what may or may not have happened." In the distance, the sound of more explosions, mines being detonated perhaps, or they were shattering the mirrors and dooming them all for good. Or it was the terraformers, breaking down from the strain of trying to filter an entire city of smoke from the polluted air. "Thank you for letting us stay here, in any case."

"I'll be spending the rest of my life trying to atone for what I've done," Holly said quietly, and the end of her thought was punctuated by the sound of a far-off blast. "Although, given the status quo, I don't anticipate that will be for much longer."

"Lucky you," Evie said. "An abbreviated sentence."

"Where's your—where's Larkin?" Holly asked, now leaning against the bay window as she looked out over Bradach streets.

Evie joined her, instantly regretting it. The city was burned, in ruins, the smoldering, flooded remains of the only place she'd ever really called home. The mirrored light burned orange through the smoke, and somewhere out near the docks, the unmistakable flash of steam cannons. "Wait," she said. "Who's out there?"

"Hard to tell."

"Are there reinforcements? Did someone come for us?" She heard the dangerously unrepentant hope in her own voice, willing herself to tamp it down. Disintegrated hope was a more lethal poison to survival than any blade, no matter how sharp. "We should get down there."

Holly grabbed her by the elbow, pulling her back beside the door. "For what? To give those MPOs something to shoot at?"

Wrenching away, Evie was already halfway out the door before she had the staggering realization that the firefight above the atmosphere could very well be the Coalition obliterating more rebel ships. Her arms fell to her sides, and she slipped back into the house, bolting the lock once again. "You're right. We should wait. It's too hard to see through all this gods-damned smoke."

Roger stood, his blood-streaked boots squeaking against the dirty marble tiles. "I'll go."

"What? No!" Evie protested, already blocking the door. "We can't lose anyone else."

"It's what Carmen would have done," he replied softly, running his hands through his mop of dirty brown hair. "She'd have been the first one shooting back."

Evie swallowed back the lump in her throat, willing herself to ignore the nagging memory of Carmen's body hitting the floor with that empty, dull thud. "You're right, she would have been."

"Don't try to stop me, Anderson."

"I wouldn't dare. In fact, I'll join you. Larkin is out there somewhere, so are many of the others, and I'm not leaving them to rot. Whoever is trying to take potshots at the Coalition, we should help them." Evie slung a steam rifle over her back, shoving boxes of ammunition into the pockets of her trousers. "Here," she said to Roger, tossing him a heat gun. "Can you handle that?"

"I'll manage." He hefted it over his shoulder, adjusting his stance until he was rock-solid and unmovable. "I've got about ten shots, looks like."

"It's enough to rake a hole in a few ships."

Holly shook her head, standing in front of the door. "Have you two lost your senses? You can't go out there! Just look at what they've done to the city! To our friends!"

"That's exactly why we have to go." Evie grabbed Holly's hands, squeezing them almost too hard. "Stay here with Delia. If I find others, I'll send them here, alright?"

"And if you don't come back?"

"Consider our score settled." Evie nudged past her, wrenching open the door once more. "If I don't come back, tell Larkin not to look for me if she ever shows up here. Although, Larkin has never been your biggest fan." She almost smiled before the weight of the situation saddled itself upon her shoulders once more, draining away any more thoughts of levity. "Thank you, Holly."

Holly searched her face, but nodded. "Of course. I'll make sure Delia stays out of harm's way."

"You'd better." Evie released her, blinking in the strange sunset glow of noon, the mirrors above powerless to clear the smog from the city's streets. They'd all be lucky if the terraformers didn't explode under the strain of it. "What's the plan, Roger?" she asked.

"How good are you with that steam rifle?"

"I'm alright. Not as good as Captain Tansy, but I make do." The silver bolt was strangely cold under her fingers as she tugged at it, loading in a round and snapping it into the chamber. "This one isn't a quick reload, so don't do anything that's going to pull a crowd, alright?"

Roger flicked at the heat gun's gauge, setting it to maximum with a soft click, the inevitable death march towards the docks lying ahead of them, one broken cobblestone at a time. "Not until the moment is right."

"This isn't a death mission, Rog. We just need to find out whose ships are out there past the atmosphere." Though Evie said it, she didn't quite believe it herself. Lies were so easily told when uttered to grant comfort to others. There were several squadrons between them and the docks, and more MPOs patrolling there, despite the chaos in the sky. Even at a distance, their scopes glinted like forbidden treasure, begging them to slip into range, darting from shadow to shadow as they moved through the settlement.

The Pig had finally stopped burning, though the ruins continued to smolder, soft crackling as the heat consumed whatever was left. The rugs that had laid over the wood floor, perhaps, or a chair that hadn't been taken in the initial blaze. Watching MPOs toss lit bottles of accelerant to smash across the bar had been almost too much to hold within herself, until Larkin leaving her chained to the fence had surpassed it.

She wasn't angry.

Larkin had slipped away from her, and it hadn't been the first time. Back in Skelm, with Ralph Baker. Not so long ago, with the assassin in the kitchen. Just like both of those times, Evie would clean up the mess, because there was nothing so dangerous as a woman whose intended had been threatened. She held the steam rifle close to her chest, waiting for the opportunity to use it, and dreading that she would have to.

"Four, up ahead," Roger muttered under his breath, gesturing with the wide maw of the heat gun. "If we skirt around these buildings, we might be able to miss them."

The street lamps above them flicked on, dimming the sparks of explosion barely visible beyond the haze and the atmosphere. Golden pools of amber light settled into the cracks of the cobblestones, illuminating the trails of dried blood, spatters that dragged along the streets to the incinerator at the far end of the settlement. The four soldiers hadn't seen them yet, huddled around each other despite the relative warmth of the evening, even as the shadows grew longer with the settling of the mirrors back into their outward-facing positions. They were sharing a light, the dancing curls of smoke dissipating into the smog.

"Imagine smoking at a time like this," Evie replied, ignoring his suggestion. "The whole gods-damned city is burning, more smog than air at this point, and they're hells-bent on inhaling more." She shook her head, settling the butt of the steam rifle against her shoulder. "I'd give anything just to go back to before any of this happened, and they're all sharing a cigarette like none of this means anything."

"It doesn't, to them."

Evie slipped behind a building, the windows blown out. Even the shattered glass on the stones had lost their sparkle, covered in soot and ash, and they crunched angrily underfoot. "I wish I knew where the others were, I wish—"

"What?"

An overly familiar cloak hung caught on the broken spike of a wrought-iron fence post, the wide hood dragging down to the ground, the tip of the fabric sapping muddy, blood-tainted water from a puddle below. Her stomach twisted, and for a moment she couldn't quite remember how to breathe. Her lungs refused to inflate, and she just stared, approaching the abandoned garment with the same apprehension as a wild animal or an explosive with a lit fuse, the spark growing ever closer to detonation. "No," she whispered, the sound of it strangled in her throat. "No, no."

"What is it?"

"Larkin's cloak," Evie replied, finally close enough to brush her fingertips against the damp black wool beset by lint and flecks of ash. "Someone must have gotten her."

"Maybe she decided to stay on her own?" Roger offered, but even his extension of sympathy was tinged with his own grief, with a longing that would never find fruition, with a deep sadness that spoke to the future they'd all find themselves within soon enough.

Evie shook her head. "No," she said again, "Larkin wouldn't leave me."

"Left you handcuffed to the fence, Evie."

"She wouldn't do what she does without this, don't you get that?" she snapped, yanking the cloak from the fence with an angry tearing sound. "She wouldn't!"

"Maybe—"

She didn't wait to hear him, despite her awareness of his own horrible story, that he'd never see Carmen again, but neither would she, and Larkin was gone too, and probably Delia, too, if they didn't find her a medic soon. The bolt slid back easily with a smooth motion and a soft click, and before she was even aware of her own motions, one of the four soldiers fell to the ground, dead.

Another round. Another slide of the bolt. Another guard was motionless as he bled out onto the street.

Someone was screaming. Maybe it was Roger, she didn't know. Maybe it was another squadron, moving into position to sink lead into her skin until her body surrendered. It didn't matter anymore, not when she'd lost everything. The Pig. Her friends. The love of her ridiculous, implausible life. She never should have had any of it, but she had, and the loss was worse than anything Allemande or Asset Protection ever did or could have done to her.

The two MPOs left rushed her, one reaching for the barrel of the steam rifle, the other aiming a revolver. She rammed the muzzle into the first, knocking him to the ground, and smacked the gun from the other, snatching it out of the air with more poise than she'd ever exhibited before. Maybe it was Larkin's influence. Maybe it was the adrenaline scorching through her veins and turning her vision red.

She spun the chamber and shot both before reloading her steam rifle. Evie didn't even wait for Roger, she jumped over the fence into what was once the community garden and shot two more. Beyond the crushing din of the blood pounding in her ears, she couldn't hear the shots being fired.

An officer, a segregant perhaps, she couldn't tell by the dirtied chevrons on his shoulder, leaped from a half-burnt bush and wrapped his skinny arms around her legs, sending her down to the ground hard. Something in her ankle snapped, and fluid rushed in, but the pain was distant, like a ship rising through the clouds, or a boat drifting out to sea, and none of it mattered, not if there wasn't anywhere or anyone to go home to. She had nothing, and was nobody, and she would be gods-damned if she had to watch the rest of her city burn to the ground.

Evie pressed the revolver to his temple and fired, barely noticing the thick spray of blood and skull coating her trousers, but oddly and painfully noticing the charred apple that fell to the ground with what she could only assume was a dull thud, if she'd been able to hear it over the ringing in her ears. Larkin would have told her to wear ear protection, but Larkin was gone.

The revolver was empty, and she rifled through the sergeant's pockets for ammunition, finding none. His sidearm was missing, which explained why she'd been tackled. She dropped the smaller gun on the ground, staring for a moment at her ankle, which had already begun to swell and bloom with vibrant purple and midnight blue, the bruises spreading up and disappearing beneath the twill fabric.

A Coalition sniper fired a shot, and it lodged into the ground next to her. She rolled from it, aiming with the steam rifle and watching as a body fell from the fourth-story window. She'd never have made that shot without Larkin's training all that time ago. All that time, and still not enough. No amount of minutes or precious seconds ever would have been enough.

Evie reloaded the steam rifle, aware that it was her last shot before she was out. The end was coming, and the sky lit up with a series of explosions that flickered across the ground, the street lamps paling in comparison. A soldier fired a shot, but it went wide, grazing her left arm. She didn't even flinch as she fired off her final shot, catching him in the shoulder. He advanced, aiming, pulling the trigger one time after another, but none of them sent her to the ground.

When she reached him, she slammed the butt of the rifle into his face, once, twice, three times, until someone was pulling her off of him, someone was yelling, someone was pulling at her clothes and shaking her.

"Evie!" Larkin screamed, pulling her from the park.

It must have been a dream, a passing fantasy before she died. Maybe the shot that grazed her arm had been worse than she thought. Maybe it was all a hallucination. Evie stopped fighting her and followed, waiting to die, waiting for her consciousness to fade away like so many autumn leaves.

"Evie, are you trying to get yourself killed?" Larkin demanded. "What were you thinking?"

"You're dead," Evie replied simply. "I found your cloak."

"I left it there, so they'd stop looking for me. I—after I took out so many last night, word was spreading that there was an assassin in a cloak. José thought that if they believed I was dead, it would give more cover." Larkin's hands were pressed against the sides of Evie's face, and she was staring into her eyes, and gods, it was almost as though she were real.

"I'm sorry I couldn't save you," Evie sobbed. "I never wanted this."

"Gods be damned, Eves, I'm not dead!" Larkin wrapped her arms around Evie's shoulders and squeezed hard, the graze in her arm splintering with pain, and the shock of it sent her crumpling to the ground, at least, she would have, if Larkin hadn't been holding her up. "I'm not dead. Almost, maybe, but José and Sandrine found me down at the docks."

"Why didn't you come back for me?"

"I did. You were gone when I got back to the garden."

"You left me chained to the fence!"

"For your own safety."

"Horseshit, Larkin." Evie pulled away, reality settling back in, her ankle exploding with pain. "I told you never again with that."

"I'm sorry."

"I said never again!"

Larkin pulled her tighter, leaning them both against the brick. "And now I see why." Her breath lingered in Evie's ear, warm and familiar. "I always said you were a natural shot."

"Roger, he—"

"He's with Sandrine. He's taking her to Delia."

Evie sighed. "Oh." Another explosion far overhead brightened the dark sky, the reflection oddly visible in the mirrors overhead, facing outwards. "What is that?"

"Can't you see the emblems? Those are Obsidian Enclave ships." Larkin kissed her once, twice, three times, hungry and desperate and grateful and terrified. "Rosie came back for us."

Chapter 54

Bradach had been put to the torch. Buildings burned out, their lonely shells visible even from the docks. Smoke still hung overhead, the terraformers unable to keep up with the uptick in particulates. Rosie's stomach churned at the sight of it, already too aware of what it might mean.

"Commander Gordon, what is our next move?" one of her cadets asked, his cap slightly askew as it sat on his head. He was young, too young for whatever he was asking her to send him into. "Should we disable the Coalition ships?"

Rosie sucked her teeth and shook her head, still surveying the ruins of her home—or at least, what had once been her home. So much had changed in such a short period of time. "No," she answered. "If they want to leave, let them leave. This place has seen enough corpses."

Even then, the defeated vessels above the atmosphere floated, inert, waiting for a scrap team to pick apart the leftovers of so many lives. Guilt burned in her chest even as she knew that she hadn't really had a choice. None of them had. It was one pressed-against faction against another, some directed by Capital generals, cozy in their high-rise offices. The pirates in Bradach were just trying to survive. Her own cadets had followed her into battle based solely on her name.

"What of the remaining squadrons?"

She squeezed her eyes shut, willing it all to be a horrible dream, a nightmare born of quiet anxieties about the end of herself. When her eyelids raised once more, gaze fixed on the half-burned apple trees in the park, something pulled at her. Carmen would be so upset when she saw the damage.

"Round them up. Ship them out."

"And if they fight back?"

"Do what you must."

"Aye," the cadet replied, too eager for bloodshed. He'd spent some months waiting for the opportunity to prove his dedication to Obsidian Enclave, and if he wasn't careful, he wouldn't even last the day. They may have managed to land at the docks, but the fight was far from over.

"Cadet, don't take any unnecessary risks," Rosie cautioned. "No one clears buildings alone. Packs of five or more."

He nodded, jogging off towards the end of the dock where another one of her transports was landing to pass on her instructions. Strange that so many listened to her, as if she knew what she was doing, as if she hadn't stolen a bunch of ships from under Gregor Zink's nose the moment she knew what had happened. Too little, too late. It was almost a family legacy.

"Rosie!" Larkin shouted, sprinting onto the dock. "By the gods, you came back! How?"

"Where is Delia?" Rosie asked, returning Larkin's embrace. "Where is she?" The damage the city had seen was enough to strike fear into the core of her, knowing that it wasn't a guarantee that they'd all make it out alive. "Larkin!" she prompted, wriggling from her grasp.

"I can take you to her, but you should be prepared."

"Prepared for what?" Rosie demanded, tears already springing to her eyes, unbidden, usurping her authority even as cadets poured from the transport with their weapons, siphoning off down back alleys and kicking in the ash-covered doors of abandoned businesses and homes. "Prepared for what, Larkin?"

"She took a hit for Henry. She's... she's not doing well, Rosie."

"What does that mean?"

"She has yet to wake up." Larkin wrung her hands, a gesture Rosie had never seen from her before, and that realization sank deep into the core of her, an inescapable reality that wouldn't fade as a dream come morning, but solidify into a terrible existence. "She lost a lot of blood. Sandrine has seen to her, but there are so many wounded."

"How many?"

"We stopped counting."

"Gods," Rosie whispered. "I'm sorry I wasn't here sooner."

"I'm surprised you're here at all. Zink let you leave?"

"He's back on Ceru. I didn't exactly take these ships with his blessing." Rosie nodded towards another transport as it set down in the dock with a dull rattle, the wood creaking from the shifting pressures. "I don't know if he chased after us or not."

"He sold that weapon back, you know. To the Coalition."

"I was worried that would be the case," Rosie said with a sigh, a headache already settling at her temples. "There was no sign of it in Ceru or on Lucent Base, and it's too volatile to be kept outside an armory for long. We can only hope the Coalition won't use it on their own people."

Larkin pushed a few hairs from her forehead, smearing ash across her skin. "We lost Carmen, Rosie."

"Fucked gods," Rosie eked out, choked by the sob that rose thick in her throat. "What happened?"

"Our newest high councilor led the raid here. Had Carmen killed for her treason aboard Turas-Mara." Shots fired in the distance, and Larkin flinched. "She was protecting us until the end." She squinted up the street, past the overturned cobblestones to a set of houses off the main road. "We have a kind of makeshift med bay. We don't have many medics, and it's starting to become obvious that's what we're doing there. We've been relocating people as we find them. Easier to allocate resources. Come on, I'll take you."

"Delia—"

"Is waiting for us," Larkin finished, answering her question without knowing it. "The past few days have been rough. I don't even know how many casualties, and some we haven't even seen yet. Evie has a broken ankle, Roger is devastated, and I don't know how to tell you this, but William is a traitor."

Rosie stepped over a bent steamtruck wheel, the edges pockmarked from the gravel. "No doubt he got mixed up in nonsense again, the fool. Surprise, surprise." She inhaled deeply, the smog searing her lungs, and part of her already longed for the seclusion and safety of Ceru. "Does Delia know?"

"Not yet. I don't think she heard before—well, before."

"She said he frequently got mixed up in trouble. Gambling, debts, fooling around with Barnaby Meier. I suppose it shouldn't be a surprise that when offered a juicy commission on selling us out, he jumped at the chance." Anger burbled up inside her, clawing at her throat like bile. "He always said he loved Delia. I wonder how he'd feel knowing he's the reason she's—she's—" Another sob dragged at her, but she swallowed it back despite the desperate tears stinging her eyes. "Is she going to make it?"

Larkin didn't even look at her, she only kept walking, twirling the small throwing knives in her hands with every step. "I don't know."

"Where is he now?"

"We haven't seen him. Our guess is that he left Bradach with High Councilor Allemande. She was looking for him, to reward him, she said. That was before they burned down the Pig." Larkin nodded towards the blackened brick, the sign missing, the building all but unrecognizable. "None of this feels real."

"I keep hoping I'll wake up and all of this, every moment since they took me, will have been a dream." The smoky haze sank lower, and it only made the strange, sleepy quality of the city more prescient. The apartment blocks across the park, where she'd once lived with Delia, had singe marks around every window, and one of the buildings had already begun to collapse under the weight of itself. Bradach had burned, and Bradach was dead. Strangely, she found herself gripped with the urge to sift through the ashes of her home for something tangible, for something to take to Delia to bring her back, but that wasn't how any of it worked.

"On your left," Larkin said after a long moment and several dozen paces, nodding up at a large, ornate door.

"Whose is this?"

"Evie's ex." Larkin rolled her eyes as she pushed open the door. "Don't ask."

Despite the warnings, Rosie hadn't been prepared for what waited inside the large house. So many wounded, lined up against the wall, waiting for treatment. The ones worse off, laid across the floor with nothing more than thin sheets under their bodies to insulate them from the chill of the marble tile. Children crying for their missing mothers, people groaning quietly with pain, one father feverishly showing a wrinkled photograph, singed at the edges, desperate to find his son.

Carnage, and plenty of it. Death. Destruction. Despair.

Rosie couldn't help but wonder what it was all *for*.

Was there ever really a justification for warfare? For burning a city to the ground over a few stolen crates of vegetables and tech? For separating families under the guise of liberty, of something that might look like justice, but only if you closed your eyes?

"She's in the back room with the others that needed more care. We moved her a few hours ago." Larkin edged past three teenage boys huddled in the corner, each one of them hugging their knees and staring straight ahead at a blank wall. "In here."

Rosie sucked in a breath, but it didn't refresh her lungs. It was an empty but necessary action, automatic, yet she was strangely aware of it. "Delia?" she whispered, approaching a narrow chaise longue. "Dee?"

She pulled back the blanket, praying to the gods that Delia would make it. Obsidian Enclave had a lot of technology, but there was only so much to be done once someone went septic. Fabric slipped through her fingers like time. "Larkin!" Rosie cried, stumbling backwards. "Her arm!"

"I tried to tell you, she—"

"You didn't say she lost a limb!"

"Shh," Sandrine chastised kindly, bustling from one patient to the next in her wheeled chair. "The others are resting." She paused in front of Rosie, taking her hands. "Delia is in rough shape, Rosie, but she's been hanging on. I don't think she's going anywhere, even if we have to wait a little longer for her to find her way back."

"How long has she been like this?"

"Roger found her yesterday afternoon, under a bush in the park. Henry said that it wasn't long before that." Sandrine released her, turning to adjust a pillow under Delia's head. "She saved Henry's life."

"Delia, my Delia," Rosie said, emotion crumbling in her like bricks without mortar. She shook her head, trying and failing to understand how she'd left Bradach bustling, healthy, composed, and returned to find it sacked, a crumbling ruin of its once-impressive glory. "You know, the night before I was taken, Delia said that she saw so much potential for this place—for Bradach. She thought it could be for pirates what Lucent Base is for Obsidian Enclave, a place for progress and research." She sat at the edge of the makeshift cot, delicately, barely even resting her weight there. "I told her that of course it would be with her broadcasts at the helm."

"It was that, for a time," Sandrine replied. "We all worked so hard for this place, and now we have lost so much." Her delicate drawl hesitated over the word *lost*, trepidation reflected in her eyes. "I shouldn't even ask, not considering—but did you hear from my Georgina?"

Rosie nodded. "She's with Cass Calvetti, headed here, last I heard. They can't be too far behind my troops." The words still felt unfamiliar in her mouth, her tongue incapable of finding its way around the development that after a lifetime of simultaneously fearing and revering her grandmother's legacy, it was, in that moment, her own.

"Oh, thank the gods," Sandrine whispered, brushing tears from her cheeks. "They took my Lucy. I don't know where she is. It's only by luck that Henry managed to find Emeline down at the docks."

"Emeline is *here*?" Rosie asked, aware that her bewilderment was palpable. "Why?"

"I was summoned." Emeline hesitated in the doorway, holding several trays of instruments. "I brought the things you asked for, Ma."

Sandrine nodded, taking the stacked, white ceramic trays from her. "Thank you."

"Ms. Gordon," Emeline said, folding her hands in front of her skirts. "Interesting to find you here as well."

"I brought Obsidian Enclave."

"I imagine that's the ruckus I heard?"

"Yes." Rosie laced her fingers with Delia's, squeezing gently. "I instructed them to dispatch the rest of the Coalition troops."

"To kill them, you mean."

"No, dispatch. They've been asked to leave Bradach."

Emeline raised an eyebrow, her face marked with soot and someone else's blood. "Too bad the others didn't get that instruction. Do you have any idea how many bodies—"

"Your pissant mother killed Carmen, did you know that?" Larkin spat. "You stand there all high and mighty like your hands don't have blood on them, too."

"Not in my ward," Sandrine said sternly. "These people have been through enough without having to listen to another spat."

Larkin growled, pushing past Emeline out of the room. "I'm going to go check on Evie."

"I didn't have to stay here, you know," Emeline said after she'd left. "High Councilor Allemande was called away on important business before you arrived with your ships, Ms. Gordon. I was free to return to Skelm and await the election results."

Rosie brushed a hair from Delia's face, caressing her pale, gaunt cheek. "Then why didn't you?"

"There aren't enough medics in this place."

"I imagine most were taken on the prison transports," Rosie replied, and her acerbic tone earned her a warning glance from Sandrine. "I brought several of my own, I will direct them here, along with the small amount of supplies we brought."

"You should have brought more. I thought Obsidian Enclave was supposed to be the paragon of technological advancements? So advanced that you built a superweapon to—"

"The technology to build that weapon was stolen from us and manipulated into weaponry. I can't help what Gregor Zink has done in my absence, but—"

Emeline hissed out a quiet breath. "*Us.*"

"Yes, us. Sometimes you can't escape your fate, no matter how far you try to run from it. My grandmother set mine into motion years ago, and it finally caught up to me." Rosie rubbed her thumb against the back of Delia's hand, willing her to wake up and throw her arm around Rosie like almost nothing had ever changed. "I can't leave Ceru to Zink. He is too easily tempted by an easier life, by power. We've lost so much, and I can't stand to lose anything or anyone else."

"The first sensible thing I've heard since landing here," Emeline said after a long moment. "It would seem that everyone else is driven by bloodlust."

"You can't blame people for wanting to strike back against those that hurt them. That hurt their loved ones." Rosie was still looking down at Delia, monitoring the rise and fall of her chest with each and every shallow breath. "I can't say what I would do if I found the person that did this to her, even if they were just following orders."

Emeline knelt next to a patient on the floor, mopping their brow with a damp cloth, and it came away muddied with ash and blood combined. "Orders are a weak excuse when the orders are to do this."

"And yet, you are the only one of us here on good terms with the Coalition."

"They want to kill me," Emeline said.

Sandrine flinched at the words but chewed her lip, keeping silent as she tended to another patient whose quiet moans of pain echoed loud in Rosie's ears.

"I suppose that shouldn't surprise me, given the situation." Rosie considered her words carefully, aware that Sandrine would hear her, and aware that Emeline never wanted to discuss it. "And so why is it that you hate your sister so much for what she did, yet the burning of Bradach is morally unquestionable? Have more not died here than—"

"I never said any of this was unquestionable. You think I enjoy this? Watching as more people suffer and die for the whims of people who don't care a fig for them?" Emeline shook her head, rinsing out the rag in fresh water. "And yet, my—High Councilor Allemande—was given the ultimatum to take me back to the Capital by force, and she did not."

"Why?"

"Because she hates piracy and rebellion, not democracy."

"Some would say that rebellion leads to democracy," Rosie challenged softly. "It's not as though the Coalition makes it easy for change to take place."

"There are some at the top who have become blinded by their greed, their avarice," Emeline answered. "The High Council is not fit for purpose. It is run by people whose own self-interest has poisoned them. Tarand. Kimura. Jacobs. All of them." She sighed again, taking a clean cloth from the stack and moving to the next patient. "They would have us all suffer and die if it meant their lives were left unchallenged."

"I can't say that I disagree with that assessment."

"Commander?" the same cadet called from the doorway, wringing his cap in his hands.

Rosie stood, keeping Delia's hand in her own. "What is it?"

"There's been some unfortunate news." His eyes traveled to Emeline, and then to her mother. "Perhaps we should speak in private."

"Casualties?" Rosie prompted. "Gregor Zink?"

"There was a broadcast sent out across all frequencies, ma'am."

"Cassius Calvetti?"

He shook his head again. "No, ma'am, from Governor Das, she was the leader for a place called... Skelm?"

"What of Skelm?" Emeline demanded, climbing to her feet. "What happened in Skelm? Did they cancel the election?"

"Skelm is no more," he said quietly. "The governor said that we—that Obsidian Enclave fired some sort of weapon that disintegrated the atmo-sphere."

"We didn't do this," Rosie declared, finally releasing Delia's hand. "Emeline, listen to me. We did not. We didn't even have hold of that weapon, we've spent months trying to track it down after Cole Marion played us for fools."

Emeline stood motionless, tears streaming down her cheeks. "It couldn't have been you. It was the Coalition." She brushed away an angry tear. "High Councilor Allemande is the one who bought it back from Zink."

Chapter 55

Violet was sitting on the floor, her head leaned back against the unfinished brick interior, fretting still about all the things she could not fix when General Fineglass kicked in the front door of the Dark Owl, Kady slung over her shoulder.

"I got her," the general explained, stepping over the threshold to reveal someone behind her, someone in an MPO's uniform. "This is Officer Remy Abara. They worked aboard Turas-Mara with me for a time, and they helped Rosie and Delia escape with the others."

"Okay," Violet said, gesturing for Ned to close the door behind them. "What is Officer Abara doing here, in our hideout? Wearing a tracker, I would imagine?"

Officer Abara held out their arm, showing off a barely healed, gnarled scab. "No tracker."

"How were you getting into the buildings, then?"

"I implanted it into a wristwatch. That wrist watch is back at my apartment." They helped the general lay Kady down on a haphazard pile of blankets, propping up her head with some makeshift cushions. She had a dark bruise over her left eye and cheekbone, the ugly, mottled skin crawling out from her eye socket like mycelium. Abara straightened, tugging their sleeve back down. "I'm here because I know where Olivia Guisette is being held."

"Where?" Mae demanded, disentangling herself from Bailey's embrace. "Where is she? You gave me that paper that said she's in reeducation, but none of our contacts have any record of her."

Abara shook their head. "No, they wouldn't. She's being held in the basement of the Executive Building."

"Why? The reeducation camp is outside city limits, the travel ban expired last night with the all-council meeting delayed, and—"

"High Councilor Tarand insisted that Ms. Guisette not find her way into the general population reeducation camps. Said she preferred to keep Ms. Guisette close." Abara rubbed a hand over their bald head, shining dully in the muted light from the lamps atop the dusty, unused bar. "I can't get her out alone."

"Why help her?" Violet asked. "For all we know, this is a setup."

"It isn't a setup," General Fineglass said firmly, and her authoritative tone rankled just under Violet's skin, despite the fact she'd just rescued her second in command. The general—Wilhemina—stretched her arms over her head, her shoulders popping audibly. "Officer Abara and I kept each other's secrets on Turas-Mara. If they wanted clout for a big bust, they would have done it the moment I let Rosie and Delia escape."

"Willa, what in any known hell?" Bailey asked, hands on her hips. By the gods, it was still so strange to see them side by side, looking so alike. It was hard to believe they were only half sisters. "You left me outside that building. I thought you'd been captured!"

"I told you, I didn't want you to get caught." Wilhemina shrugged easily, leaning back against the bricks with her bulky arms folded over her chest. "I am not going to lose you again, Bailey."

"You can't just make these decisions by yourself, Willa."

"Fine. The next time we try to break someone out of lockup, I'll keep you fully apprised."

Violet sighed, rubbing at the bridge of her nose, desperate to massage away the headache there. "We're going to have that opportunity soon enough, I would reckon. We can't leave Olivia Guisette here, not after what she did for us. Officer Abara—"

"Remy," they corrected.

"Remy, how many do you need to get her out of there?"

They picked at the badges and stripes along their chest, as if they could erase the service they'd paid to the Coalition by removing the embroidery. "Three, plus me. The general—er—Wilhemina, her sister, and one more."

"I'll go," Ned announced, already scrambling to his feet.

"Sit down, Nedrick, I'm going," Violet said. "Captain's orders. You need to stay here with the others in case anything else happens, and in case Kady wakes up."

"She will," Remy said. "They sedated her, but she's alright."

"Good."

Wilhemina took two large revolvers from the holsters at her hips and reloaded them with two quick snaps, examining the barrel. "We'll need to keep a sharp eye. The riots are spreading across the city."

"What riots?" Violet asked, and it was somewhere between hope and dread that the possibility lodged itself. "We haven't heard anything."

"Not up this way, no. Seems like despite the reports that it was some sort of industrial accident, your explosion down at the warehouses has inspired some quiet rebellion supporters to take to the streets." The former general pushed off from the wall with her boot, the sole scraping softly against the brick. "We should use the chaos to our advantage. With any luck, forces will be scattered, and they won't be paying as much attention."

Remy nodded. "We can use my chip, I'll pick it up from my apartment and loop back around to meet you at the back entrance. Cut through the fence, don't scale it. There are proximity sensors. I'll leave now, and see you there." They slipped out the door, leaving it unlatched.

"You ready, Stockton?" Violet asked, checking her own revolver. The size of the former general's weapons made her own feel insignificant, somehow, but there wasn't any time or opportunity to rectify such a vain concern. "General?"

"You can just call me Willa. I should probably start getting used to that." She swiped a sweaty, fiery lock from her face, tucking it behind her ear. "As it turns out, I don't really know who I am."

"You're one of us," Ned replied gruffly, already bent over Kady and attending to her, pulling a blanket over her unconscious frame. "You risked your hide for us. You're one of us."

Violet said nothing, because although she knew that he was right, he usually was about these things, Barnaby excepted, she wasn't yet convinced of the former general's true allegiances. Lifelong military types were rarely so easily swayed. "Alright, you two, we'd better get a move on if we're going to meet Remy in time." She stowed her weapon, folding her arms over her chest tight, almost a hug, but never quite good enough. Another painful reminding flash of Alice's absence. Alice, wherever in hells she was.

"I don't like this," Mae asserted, taking hold of Bailey's lapels. "Wilhemina, you'd better bring her back to me."

"On my honor as a rebel," Wilhemina replied. "I won't let anything happen to her."

"You'd better not."

"You are far more terrifying than any enemy combatant, Ms. Machenet. I have no intention of breaking my word." Wilhemina nudged the door open with the toe of her boot. "We'll be back, and with Ms. Guisette in tow."

"Don't do anything foolish, Bay Leaf," Mae said, kissing Bailey softly. "If you die, I will resurrect you myself just to scold you. Are we clear?"

"Yes, Mae," Bailey replied, stepping away from her. "Keep the doors locked. If there are riots, there's a chance they'll try to loot this place in the hopes there is some alcohol left."

"They're months late on that count," Aven said bitterly, stepping up from the basement, her arms bulging with more threadbare blankets. "Good luck, Captain."

Violet nodded. "We'll get us all out of here, one way or another."

* * *

Gamma-3 had no terraformers, and so the toxic clouds of solvent-laden smoke drifted through the streets, unbidden and heavy. Violet tugged her shirt up over her mouth and nose again, pressing her chin down to her chest to hide from the fumes already burning in her lungs. Distant, but audible, people were chanting, screaming, but it was unintelligible beyond the din of a burning city. Shadows formed at the edges of buildings, chasing away any hint of light from the street lamps that had been extinguished, though it was hard to know who'd done it. Creeping, unsettling darkness chased them through the streets all the way to the fence surrounding the Executive Building, all of them silent the entire journey, with no sound other than the far-off, delicate crunching of buildings folding in on themselves, and the quiet shuffle of boots against the pristine pavement.

Though, judging by the sound of the approaching crowd, the streets wouldn't remain that way for much longer.

The general pulled a small tool from her pocket, snipping through the chain links one at a time with shallow snaps that echoed eerily over the empty courtyard. The greenhouses beyond were dark that time of night, and empty, the midnight foliage pressed greedily against the glass, desperate for drops of sunlight that wouldn't arrive until morning. That was if the greenhouses were still standing in the glow of day, and the nearing sounds of glass shattering did not bode well for their future.

"Through here," Wilhemina said, holding the flap of fence open. Bailey went first, and then Violet followed, hand already resting atop her holster. Whatever they'd find inside the Executive Building wouldn't be good, and the angry roiling inside her stomach would only be a precursor to what awaited them.

The security cameras on the walls hung inert, no sign of their telltale red blinking lights. At least this Remy had managed that, but it was unlikely to be enough to get them out unseen and unharmed. Violet had seen too much for too long, and had watched the last rebellion fail, leaving nothing more than blood and broken dreams in its wake.

With a noisy creak, the back door eased open. "Good, you're here," Remy said, ushering them inside. "I can't go with you, but you'll take these stairs all the way to the bottom. Guisette is in the furthest cell in the rightmost corridor."

"How is she?" Violet asked. Transporting an unconscious body would make their mission far more difficult.

"I don't know, I haven't been down there. High Councilor Tarand has had full control over who has access."

"Guards?" Wilhemina asked.

"One or two, no more. Guisette isn't even supposed to be down there, Tarand is contravening protocol for reeducation. She doesn't want to draw too much attention, because the other members of the High Council would use it against her, especially now." Remy tugged at the hem of their jacket. "The council is disintegrating. Allemande arrived at the docks about an hour ago, so they'll be caught up with all of that. If you're quick and quiet, you might manage to make it out unseen."

"What about you?" Violet asked, already staring down the stairs into the thick blackness of the building's basement. "What happens after this?"

Remy gave a strange, strangled laugh. "I don't think any of us know what comes after this." They ran a hand over their head, resting there for just a moment. "I'll get out when I can, but leaving now would compromise your mission."

Overhead, a light flickered and went out, only deepening the darkness. Wilhemina rested a hand on Remy's shoulder. "Thank you."

"I was always proud to serve under you, ma'am."

"We won't leave you behind, soldier."

"Get out of here as soon as you can," Remy chided with a sad smile. "Don't risk many lives for one, General." They leaned into the adjoining corridor with a concerned frown, hands flexing into fists at their sides. "You should go. Don't linger, don't wait. In and out, quick as you can. The longer you're in here, the more likely this all falls apart."

Wilhemina hesitated for just a moment before she retracted her hand from Remy's shoulder and nodding. "Understood, Abara," she said, squaring her frame with a curt nod. "Go. We'll take things from here."

Remy gave them one final nod. "Don't get dead."

"Don't get dead," Wilhemina echoed. She sighed heavily, waiting until

Remy's footsteps had faded up the corridor. "Captain Violet, you stay here and watch our six. Bai and I will head down and collect our agent for transport."

Violet wanted to argue, but didn't. "Alright," she agreed. "I suppose you two are much stronger than me."

"We're going to pry the bars apart," Bailey offered proudly, cracking her knuckles. "Steel has nothing on us."

"One successful mission, and my kid sister thinks she's untouchable," Wilhemina grumbled, already heading down the back stairs, the damp concrete sounding slick under her boots.

Bailey snorted a quiet laugh. "Please, as if you aren't constantly full of yourself."

The silence that lingered after their footsteps laid heavy against the stairs, the reinforced rear door of the building, the corridor lined with perfectly polished marble floors, the gods-damned lush green grounds outside. Something about it was ominous, pressing, but there was nothing for Violet to do but watch and wait and pray to dead gods a broken litany of broken promises. Even if they made it out, they had no idea what had happened in Bradach. Who they might have lost. Who they hadn't.

There was no telling how long the pair were gone. It might have been ninety seconds, it might have been half a year before their frenzied steps shuffled up the stairs.

"We got her, let's go," Wilhemina said.

Violet squinted at the woman in front of her: bald, with uneven, mousy brown stubble across her scalp, a broken eye socket, and plenty of bruises that crawled up and over her forearms. "Are you sure this is her?"

"It's me," Olivia answered. "Thank you, Captain."

"Let's get the hells out of here, back to the safe house."

Olivia pulled away from Wilhemina's grasp, shaking her head. "No. We need Abara."

"They told us not to wait, Ms. Guisette."

"I'm not leaving without them." Olivia's jaw set firm, and she crossed her arms over her chest. "Not after all this. I'd have slowly rotted away in that cell if they hadn't intervened." She shook her head emphatically, the rags she was dressed in damp and dirty. "If you don't go, I go myself."

"You'll get yourself killed," Wilhemina protested.

"Then you'd better come with me." Olivia ducked under the former general's arm and stalked off up the stairs, leading the way to their doom, probably.

Violet followed, a sick feeling growing in the pit of her stomach that continued to pull her gaze backwards, always looking behind them, expecting to find a soldier and the muzzle of a gun. "Where is Abara stationed?"

"Tarand's security detail," Olivia explained, pushing through the door at the top of the stairs, edging out onto the top floor. "They'll be near her office."

"We're all going to get dead," Wilhemina muttered under her breath, and Violet couldn't help but nod in silent agreement.

"Shut up," Olivia hissed, looking both ways down the corridor before crossing it.

Remy Abara wasn't waiting outside Tarand's office, and the heavy oak door was slightly ajar, and their voice emanated from within. "Of course. I will call to convene the other high councilors at once."

"We could have done this sooner if you hadn't disobeyed a direct order, Amaranth." The quiet swish of a cloak, and the creak of a chair. "Now, we are days behind schedule, made worse by the accidental explosions in the industrial district."

"You don't give me orders, Cecelia. We're equals now, or didn't you get that memo?"

Wilhemina shifted her weight. "We need to leave," she whispered.

"Not yet," Olivia countered. "Not until we have Abara."

"Equals, that's rich, Amaranth. You're an addendum, a note in the margins of history to keep the investors at the Rim happy. The gods know we couldn't let Fineglass be the face of expansion. She's about as personable as an ill-tempered, rabid dog." Wilhemina scowled at this, her face scrunched into an angry frown.

The door creaked, and fear shot through Violet like an immediate poison. Tarand cleared her throat noisily, the sound of it echoing out into the empty hall. "And as for Skelm, we both know that was an inevitability."

"I didn't secure that weapon just for you to use it on our own settlements. You destroyed the strongest producing district in that sector, you pathetic excuse for a councilor," Allemande shot back. "This is going to set us back years, I hope you know that."

"Needs must, Amaranth. Perhaps you will learn that one day, if you manage to hold on to your title. I doubt that, though. The destruction of Skelm is unfortunate collateral damage, but an easy way to quell any signs of rebellion. No one likes a faction who kills innocents."

"And if they find out that you staged it? That after we bought it back from rebel hands, you turned it on our own people? What then, Cecelia?"

"They won't." The chair creaked quietly, and Violet was trying to will Remy to exit the room, allowing them to escape before the rest of the gods-damned council showed up. "They won't, because no one found out that I sent that missile to Terringgough Gulch. They won't, because once we use it against Bradach, there won't be anyone left to prove that."

Violet's breath caught in her throat and for a moment, she wondered if all the air had been sucked out of the room, if someone had used that superweapon against them in that split second between knowing and realization. Her hand flew to her mouth, and if she had been able to breathe, she would have gasped.

"Cecelia, you can't," Allemande pleaded, her voice for the first time small and desperate. "My daughter is in Bradach."

"If you had followed orders to bring her here to me, she would be safe, wouldn't she, Amaranth? Instead, you disobeyed my instructions and left her there to keep causing problems, to continue destabilizing the Coalition. Unfortunately, sometimes, consequences cannot be avoided." Tarand sighed loudly, long and drawn out, a theatrical performance. "I myself had to put my own right hand to the sword when I discovered her treachery. If only you had—"

The sound of a small blade being pulled from its sheath. The gurgle of aspirated blood. The high councilor slumped in her chair, barely visible through the open door.

"Now. We need to leave *now*," Wilhemina said, pulling at Bailey's sleeve, tugging at Olivia. "We need to get off this rock right gods-damned now."

Remy burst through the door, leaving it open in their wake. Allemande, standing over Tarand with a small pen in her hands, blood splattered across her new high council robes. She stared at them in wonderment, her mouth opening and closing wordlessly. Abara locked eyes with Olivia and there was anger there, and something else, and they started to shout, screaming for more guards. "Breach!" they yelled. "Amaranth Allemande murdered Cecelia Tarand!"

"Abara!" Olivia screamed. "Come on! Now!"

Remy hesitated for a split second before Wilhemina shot across the corridor and hefted them over her shoulder, growling, "I said *now!* This place is going to be crawling in about ninety seconds!"

* * *

The door to the Dark Owl was ajar as they approached, and panic rose in Violet's throat until she realized why. At the sight of her wife, she was unable to stifle the sob that burst forth from her lips. "Alice," she whispered.

"You left my ship in a scrapyard, Vi," Alice said, the small droid hovering at her shoulder. "You're lucky I had no other plans."

Violet was rooted to the spot, unable to believe that her wife was standing there, smirking, smug as all hells, and the gods be damned, she had every right to be. "Alice," Violet said again. "You're here."

"Please tell me you have that ship," Wilhemina said, revolvers resting in her hands. "We need off Gamma-3 yesterday."

"What happened?" Alice asked. "You look like you saw a ghost."

"Might have done. Allemande killed Tarand. Guards swarming the place as we made it out. I'll be shocked if she winds up alive. The other council members don't take kindly to murder."

Alice jerked backwards in surprise. "Gods," she whispered.

"The Capital is going to be a damned war zone by the morning. Load up and let's move out, or we're going to get caught in one unholy hell of a clusterfuck." Wilhemina nodded at Kady, still groggy, hunched over on her makeshift bed. "And I don't think any of us are particularly in the position to be fighting for our lives."

"We're fueled and ready," Ivy said, already hefting Kady's pack onto her own back. "They might refuse clearance, but at this point, I don't think it matters."

"Move out," Violet said, still staring at Alice and wondering if it was a dream, or a hallucination, or a nightmare-in-waiting. There was time yet for that glimmer of hope to disappear in a puff of smoke. "I said move!"

* * *

"Hey," Alice said, resting her hands on Violet's shoulders. "Come to bed. Kady's come around, she can pilot while you sleep. You look like you need a bath and some soft sheets."

Violet had barely even looked at her since they boarded, not that it had been difficult with Alice down in the boiler room with Ivy. She nodded, swallowing back the lump in her throat. "Yeah."

The ship felt dangerously familiar, as if everything terrible that had happened had only been a dream, and they'd go home to Bradach and find everything right where they'd left it—the water ring she'd left on Larkin's bar, the quiet whispers of fabric in Mae's shop, the giggles and laughter from the refugee camps. Even their bedroom was the same as she'd left it back on the docks in the Capital.

"I thought I'd lost you," Violet finally whispered when Alice closed the door softly. "It had been weeks, and I—"

"It's alright, Vi, I'm here."

"It doesn't feel true."

Alice approached slowly, opening her arms to wrap Violet in an envelope of comfort. "I feel real, don't I?"

"Yes," Violet admitted, her face buried in Alice's jumpsuit.

"I never want to pilot this damned ship again, Vi. I don't know how in hells you do it, I almost crashed it at least three times. Too much to keep track of, I—I'm sorry, you know. About before."

"It doesn't matter, Alice."

"Of course it does."

Violet looked up at her, all silver hair and soot-smudged nose, and brushed a thumb over her cheek. "I can't fix this ship for the life of me, Al."

"Is that why you rigged it up with traps?"

"Kady's idea."

"Mm. Remind me to thank her for that. Almost singed my face off."

Violet pulled her closer again and laughed into her chest, squeezing her arms tight around Alice's waist. "You saved us again, Mechanic."

"Oh, you know. It was part of the job description." Alice pulled away, cupping Violet's face in her callused, warm hands. "And you've saved *me* enough times to know that."

"Are you talking about the ship or our marriage?"

"Yes," Alice answered, leaning in for a deep, painfully tempting kiss.

Violet parted her lips for her, groaning softly when their tongues met. It had been so long. So much time wasted over petty nonsense, when it could have been love in every moment, the way it had been before the war had begun. She reached up with wanting fingers, toying with the toggles on Alice's jumpsuit but not undoing them, just waiting there.

"Touch me, Violet, or I might die before we even reach the battle in Bradach," Alice whispered in a husky, greedy tone.

The toggles came loose easily, dropping the jumpsuit to the floor in a heap of fabric and promises. "I love you," Violet said between kisses, pushing Alice to their bed, climbing on top of her when they reached it and silencing her with another all-consuming kiss, and for a moment she almost forgot what was waiting for them on the other side of the journey. She stripped off her shirt first, and then her trousers, and then everything else.

Alice was staring with that hungry look, that starving desperation that Violet had never been able to get over, even when she'd tried. Resisting Alice Green was an exercise in futility, and it always had been. Violet bent, sucking a nipple into her mouth, pulling a quiet hiss from Alice's lips. She ran her hands over Alice's body, every scar, every stretch mark right where she'd left it, her hips like a heaven's cloud under Violet's fingertips.

"Please," Alice said, looking down at her from the head of the bed. "Don't make me wait, Vi."

Despite hating being told what to do, Violet relented, trailing lower over Alice's stomach, hovering where her ample thighs met for just a second, just long enough for Alice to quietly whine, before she traced up one side and down the other, inching closer until her tongue found its goal and lingered there, languished, even, teasing when she knew it could be over in seconds if she maintained the same rhythm. She pushed in only to pull back, smiling against Alice as she groaned her delighted frustration, pressing down against Violet's face in a desperate search for friction.

Before long, thighs were shaking on either side of Violet's head, but before she could even revel in her victory, she found herself flipped over, resting underneath Alice, who leaned over her, panting, her hair mussed, a mischievous glitter in her grey eye. "I think it's your turn, Captain."

Violet settled back into the bed, the gloriously soft bed that hugged every curve of her as Alice's hands roved across bare skin, delicate in her touch, despite the greedy fervor.

"I love you, I love you, I love you," Alice chanted in a voice lower than a whisper, more a litany than a prayer, three words spoken after every kiss pressed against Violet's skin. The unspoken hung heavy in the air outside their door, the knowledge they may never get the chance to love again once they reached Bradach.

Violet's gasp when Alice settled her lips to Violet's core reminded her how to breathe after so many weeks of suffocating, of being so desperate for air but so unable to quench the need. She breathed now, steady at first, and then ragged as she was pushed to the precipice and over it, muffling her loud moans with the pillow as she pulled Alice back up to her. "Alice, Alice," she sobbed, clutching at her. "This can't be the end. It can't be."

"I know," Alice soothed, curling around her. "I know."

Chapter 56

Georgie drummed her fingers against the loading bay door controls, impatient, dread coursing through her veins at what they might find. Hyun hadn't said much since they'd left, her face drawn and hollow, devoid of her usual charm and glitter, but she stood there next to three crates of medical supplies, waiting alongside her. Georgie resisted the urge to punch the door, despite knowing that wouldn't help. "Come on, come on," she hissed under her breath, willing the latches to disengage.

"You ready for this, Payne?" Cass asked, leaning against the airlock door frame.

"No. Are you?"

Cass sighed, ruffling the mop of disheveled hair atop her head. "No." She rested her hands on the holster at her waist, still carrying the stolen gun, their hostage still detained in the brig. "Getting down here was hairy enough, I don't want to see what the streets look like."

"We're lucky we weren't shot out of the sky."

"My guess is that if the Coalition vessels above the atmosphere weren't distracted by those Obsidian Enclave ships, we would have been."

Georgie sucked her teeth, still waiting for the latches. "Small mercies."

"It might get bad out there, Payne."

"I was in Skelm the night of the storms, you don't have to tell me." One pang for the guilt of the thirty-eight that had died that night, followed by a tidal wave of horror at what they'd only just learned. Skelm—her home—was no more. It had been stripped of every living thing, down to the rats that used to scurry along the warehouse floors. Jess. Bale. Erin. So many more, all gone in barely an instant.

"I would say that I can't believe they fired on their own people, but given what happened on Terringgough Gulch, I was rudely disabused of that naïve notion." Cass approached the door, pulling the revolver from her hip. "Latches detached."

Georgie nodded, pulling on the lever, listening to the pulleys creak and groan with the effort of dragging the huge door up and out of the way. She wasn't sure what she was expecting, but it wasn't the thick, barely breathable haze that greeted them at the docks. It stung her eyes and throat, the same way that Skelm once had. Skelm, which was nothing more than a ruined settlement, pockmarked with abandoned warehouses and factories, the Administration Building devoid of bodies because they, of course, had made it out unscathed. The rage was so overwhelming, it was about to drag her under its venomous undertow when Henry emerged from the smoke, holding a lantern to light their way, the glow strange in the twilight smog.

"I was hoping it would be you," Henry said, handing the lantern to Sandrine, rushing forward, and all at once the universe seemed to tilt on its axis, righting itself, if only in a small and unforgettable way. "I've been so worried."

Georgie scooped her up, squeezing her because she was real, and alive, and not hurt beyond some scrapes and bruises, and she was standing there, and not halfway across the Near Systems. "Henry, gods above, I almost died of worry. There are no comms at all, we couldn't—"

"They disabled the tower," Henry said, pointing to the broken spire, rising up into the dark smoke like a grasping, desperate, disembodied hand. "Seems like they took some lessons from Gregor Zink."

"Or the other way around," Cass said, stepping off the ramp. "Hard to tell, these days." She tipped an imaginary cap to Sandrine, sweeping into a bow. "Ma'am. Thank you for keeping everything in line."

Sandrine almost smiled, but a ghost of something flickered across her face. "I try, Ms. Calvetti."

"Ma, what's the matter?" Georgie demanded. "Where is everyone else? Did we take back the streets? Is it dangerous? Should we leave? Where's Lucy?"

"Georgina, a lot has happened," Henry said gently. She ran her hands along Georgie's arms, lingering, and pulled them to her stomach. She didn't say anything else, but she was searching Georgie's face for a response.

"No," Georgie said, laying her fingers flat against Henry's barely bowed belly, a curve so soft and gentle she wouldn't even have noticed it. "It can't be. You said it didn't work."

"I didn't want to get your hopes up, and I didn't want to keep you from Chalidon."

Georgie fell to her knees, pressing her face against where Henry's shirt met her skirts, tears already leaking down her face. "I can't believe you're pregnant," she sobbed, unable to stem the flood waters of emotion surging at the base of her. "I thought—I was terrified I'd never see you again, when we heard the sirens over that final transmission at Lucent Base, and now you're here, and you're telling me that we're going to be mothers."

"There's more, I'm afraid," Henry said, stroking Georgie's hair gently. Somewhere, on the other side of the city, there was a series of pops, tiny explosions that could only mean gunfire. Henry drew in a deep breath, letting it go as a quiet, sad sigh. "We lost Carmen."

"No," Georgie moaned, clutching at Henry's skirts. "No, Hen, tell me it's not true, tell me that you're lying!" The heavy wool fabric pulled through her fingers as she dragged her hands over it, grasping for shore when she was drowning. "Please, Henry, tell me it's not."

"She was trying to protect us." Henry tilted Georgie's chin upwards. "Delia took a hit for me, George. She's not well."

"I'll head to the medical station," Hyun announced, stacking the crates onto a wagon. "At least I can be of some use there."

"I'll go with you," Sandrine said, but Hyun shook her head. "Stay with your family, Sandrine. I'll go." She dragged the wagon up the hill, towards the ruined remains of The Purple Pig, and Georgie could barely say what all they'd lost.

"Jasper died," Cass explained. "Zink lied. There was no treatment."

"Gods," Henry breathed, her fingers still twisted in Georgie's hair.

"Hyun detached him from the machines herself."

"No," Georgie's mother said, her hands flying to her mouth. "That poor thing. I can't even imagine."

Henry ran a thumb over Georgie's cheekbone, her face still so pained. "Lucy was put on a transport for the Capital, to attend a school there."

"I'll kill them all," Georgie said, hauling herself to her feet, ready to board the stolen ship and go after Lucy herself. The Coalition had already stolen one sister from her, she wasn't about to let them do it again. "I will, if I have to do it with my bare hands."

"The ship has been diverted." Emeline stood to the side, her hands clasped in front of her. "I stole a Coalition radio last night and made the order, posing as my—as High Councilor Allemande."

"Em." Georgie released Henry finally, feeling her jaw clamp defensively. "I thought you wanted Lucy to go to that school. Isn't that what you demanded of me when we saw each other last?" She shook her head, her thoughts swimming from too much, all at once, and it was about to pull her under. "You know, there was a time I would have kissed the ground, thanking the gods for bringing you back to me, Emeline. But now, I'm just tired."

"Are you still angry about what happened in Chalidon?" Emeline asked, a hand braced against her hip. There was an exhausted quality to her stance that matched Georgie's own. "I told you not to come. That place was swarming with MPOs."

"You chained me to a table."

Emeline snorted a derisive laugh. "I let you go! You think I didn't know you were yanking on that bolt every time you thought my guards weren't listening? I told them to let you escape."

"Why even lock me up, then?"

"Better for me to do it for optics than to hand you over to the Coalition, or would you rather that I'd thrown you into a maximum security detention facility? Thanks to you and your friends, those are basically impenetrable now."

"I wasn't there for that."

"It doesn't matter, George." Emeline leaned against a wooden dock post, almost slumping against it. "None of it matters because we're all knee-deep in blood. Forget worrying about blood on just our hands, we've spilled enough to weigh on the conscience for a lifetime."

"We?"

Emeline squeezed her eyes shut, pressing her palms to her face in a desperate attempt to stem the tide of tears waiting there. "Skelm was my fault, George," she whispered.

"It wasn't your fault, Em," their mother interrupted, wheeling herself closer.

"She warned me, Ma!" Emeline shot back. "She told me that if I didn't go with her, I would regret it. She told me that my choices were reaching the point of no return and still I stayed." She pulled at her skirts, her knuckles white with the grip, as though she was trying to tear the fabric apart with her bare hands. "I stayed! I stayed, and now every living thing in Skelm is dead. All those people, Ma." She crumpled to the ground, her head in her hands. "All those people."

"Allemande did this?" Henry asked.

Emeline nodded. "She must have. All those promises about building it back to its former glory, about pushing forward into the future of the Coalition, and she lied to my face."

Georgie just stood there, waiting to know what to do. Life was busy crumbling around her as she shuffled her boots against the dock, casting a silly, childish wish into the universe that none of it had ever happened. But it had, and people were gone, and lives destroyed, and that was that. The horrors compounded as they rolled along, pulling anything and anyone into its strange gravitational pull. The inescapable, awful drag of death, rippling out like a quake, leveling everything in its wake.

There was Henry, standing in the suffocating night air, and glowing nonetheless. A lantern in one hand, the other resting against her stomach, and how in any hell was Georgie supposed to be able to protect her? She couldn't do a damned thing against war, or famine, or whatever would happen to Bradach now that it had been all but burnt out, the city's corpse still being fought over in the far district. Another quiet, far-off explosion finally pulled her back into the reality of the moment.

"We should get inside somewhere," Georgie said. "It sounds like there are still skirmishes in the city."

"Localized to a couple of neighborhoods," Sandrine replied, laying a hand on Georgie's arm. "Obsidian Enclave had the docks under control from the second transport they pulled in."

"There is still a fair amount of fighting up beyond the atmosphere," Cass replied. "We managed to sneak through because Rosie's forces knew we were coming, and this is a Coalition ship." She eyed it, standing back to observe the scratches and scrapes in the paint. "Might be mine now, though."

"Calvetti," Emeline said from the ground. "You honored our deal."

"Yeah. As did you, if memory serves."

"I didn't think The Scattered could be honorable."

Cass turned, and a small smirk played at her lips. "I'm Splintered now, not Scattered, or had you missed that memorandum?"

"I heard something about that, but from what I've heard on the ground, most were just waiting for you to come back. Whispers traveled fast that you weren't as dead as everyone feared. Or hoped." Emeline stood again, dusting off her skirts. "Does our deal still stand?"

"Seems a bit redundant now, Em."

"I want you to help me punish the ones responsible for Skelm." Emeline's eyes glinted with a fiery horror that Georgie hadn't seen there before, not even before she was taken during those demonstrations. "I need your forces to round up everyone who did this, starting with the High Council."

"Forces?" Cass said with a forced laugh. "You're looking at them. Your sister, a med tech, and a stolen ship."

"You could command the whole of The Scattered."

"The Scattered are barely hanging on, Emeline. They're spread out over the Near Systems, half of them are starving, despite my best efforts to keep trade routes open. Most don't have a ship. The ones that did are probably dead already. I am the leader of a dying faction. I'm betting plenty of them don't even know I'm not as dead as Cole said that I was." Cass glanced at Henry and sucked her teeth. "Were you involved with the Cole thing?"

Henry shook her head. "No."

"Shame. I'd like to shake the hand of the person that did it. Cole Marion was responsible for a lot of the deaths that have happened since I got locked up. Sending ships in unprepared, ignoring intel. He was a selfish fool, and from what I understand, he died doing selfish, foolish things." Cass shrugged lightly. "Sometimes, you have to take out the head of a problem, like dealing with a snake."

"Then help me," Emeline pleaded, pulling at Cass' arm. "Help me get justice for Skelm, Calvetti. Gordon already said she wouldn't press Obsidian Enclave into more conflict. She's betraying the memory of Skelm because she's too scared to act."

Georgie chewed on her lip, her hands on Henry's shoulders. "It wasn't so long ago that you hated me for taking action in Skelm."

"Your actions killed thirty-eight people," Emeline said. "Thirty-eight people whose families didn't deserve to mourn."

"Those storms would have killed everyone, Em," Georgie said. "And I couldn't leave those refugees there. Whole ships full of desperate people from small settlements that had been targeted by the storm generators. I did not mean for people to get hurt, but I carry that on my conscience, anyway. How many lives can you carry on yours, Em? Because once you start down this path, it's not an easy road back."

Georgie offered up a desperate shrug as tears pricked at the corners of her eyes once again. "I can't make things back into the way they were, with you and Lucy at home safe with me in a struggling city, crushed under Coalition control. I can't keep you little forever." She nodded towards their mother, laying a hand on her shoulder, too. "But leaving meant Ma and Luce had a fresh start. Ma got married, Em! She got her chair, she could do what she loved again, and you have no idea the work she's put in here. People know her. They respect her. She wouldn't have had any of that if we'd all have stayed in Skelm."

"Don't *lecture* me, Georgina," Emeline spat. "I know full well what's happened since I—well, since I—" she stopped short, her balled fists falling to her sides. "How did we get here, George?" she whispered.

"You won't like my answer."

"No, probably not," Emeline agreed. "I am tired of being knee-deep in blood, George. Tired of always looking over my shoulder, sick and tired of people so desperate to undermine workers for half a percentage more in profit." She shook her head again, hands pressed to her temples. "That's what it always comes back to, isn't it? Credits. How many credits can you stuff into your bank vault, impervious to the knowledge that it's all dripping with guilt and blood?"

Henry patted Georgie's arm, wriggling from her light grasp. "Georgie, I need to get back to the medical staging area, Hyun will need help."

"Are there many injured?" Georgie asked.

"We ran out of blankets two days ago."

Cass jogged back up the ramp, disappearing for only a moment, before returning with a large stack of linens. "We have these from the emergency pods. I'll join you." She nodded at Georgie. "I've got her, Payne."

"José will be wondering where I've got to, and that man does worry," Sandrine said, wheeling after them. "Come up to the big place on the corner, near the square, when you're ready. You can't miss it. Big gate in front."

Georgie sat at the edge of the ship's loading bay, her legs dangling off the side as smoke drifted, ever so slowly, dragging itself across Bradach's ruined skyline. "Maybe I should go, too."

"Wait." Emeline sat down next to her, rearranging her skirts so that they cascaded off the ship, a grey and yellow waterfall of fabric. "I hear congratulations are in order."

"Yeah, I guess they are."

"You don't sound excited."

"I'm terrified, Em." Georgie sighed quietly, trying to forget when they'd watch the mirrors turn in the evenings back in Skelm. They were younger, then. Younger but still, always, forever in trouble of some sort. Sometimes, that's just how things were. "Terrified because how can I come back to this and think my child will have a fair shot in life?"

"We didn't."

"No, we didn't."

Emeline nodded silently in agreement. "You know, it's strange. You always felt like Dad shouldn't have gone to that meeting if he wanted to keep us safe. I always thought he went in order to fight for a better future for all of us. Now, it's just... I don't know. The truth lies somewhere in the middle, I suppose." A tinge of what was once a twang had returned to her voice, a ghost in the way she shaped her vowels risen to the surface after years of being buried beneath Capital propriety.

"I can't keep fighting. They need me. I've had some lucky escapes, but sooner or later that luck is going to run out, and the idea of leaving Henry alone with a baby—I can't do it, Em. I can't."

"Lucky escapes? I told you, I let you leave," Emeline replied, poking her playfully, something she hadn't done since Skelm.

"Not that one, birdbrain," Georgie said, poking her back. "When we stowed away on this ship, we didn't realize we'd end up stealing it. We still have a Coalition captain in the brig."

"You'd better not let the remaining forces in the city find that out. They're scrambling because they don't have leadership. That radio I stole was one of the only ones left, and they're the ones who stripped out comms." Emeline shifted abruptly. "A captain. Georgie, I have an idea, but I'm going to need your help."

"Is it going to be dangerous?"

"Probably."

Georgie sighed. "Fine. But if I die, Henry might kill you."

"Deal."

Chapter 57

Delia had never been a soldier. She'd never been particularly brave, making quiet, explainable moves throughout most of her career. Thomas had nearly died because of what she *had* done, and she'd have to face that the rest of her life. William—well, if she ever caught him in Bradach again, she may very well kill him herself. Despite having an extensive vocabulary, there were no words known to her to appropriately explain the amount of betrayal he'd foisted upon all of them, and for what? More gambling debts, perhaps? Desperation? Extortion?

Light danced across her closed eyelids, and she groaned quietly. Sleep was such a welcome respite from all of it, and for that, she was a coward, too. Resting when she should have been fighting, pretending to be asleep while Sandrine bustled around the other patients, putting those who could to work caring for others. José's deep baritone rumbled from the doorway, something mumbled, but Sandrine replied "Yes, Dear, if you don't mind," and his heavy footsteps faded back into the main room.

Delia knew there was something wrong with her. The others wouldn't have let her sleep for so long if there wasn't, but she hadn't been able to bring herself to open her eyes and assess the damage. There was pain, but it was everywhere, and it was muted. Sandrine had been shuffling around her bed once every couple of hours, attaching something to the tube that disappeared into Delia's right arm, and every time it sent her back to a blissfully empty sleep.

She knew, really, but the longer she kept her eyes squeezed shut, the longer she could pretend it hadn't happened. She should be grateful it hadn't been worse, but she'd always been too concerned with her own nonsense. Too long, and too much, and despite all that rest, she was still so tired.

"Hello, Ms. Forrest," Sandrine murmured at her side, taking Delia's hand in her own. "Welcome back."

"How did you know I was awake?"

Sandrine chuckled lightly, softly under her breath. "I am a mother to four who always manage to find themselves in trouble. I can always sense it."

"Four?"

"Larkin is mine, too. She is José's, so she is mine." Sandrine examined the tube in Delia's arm, frowning slightly. "I think we should keep you on this drip a while longer."

"Does that mean I can go back to sleep?"

"I think, perhaps, we should tell Rosie that you are awake, at least. We were awfully worried about you, Ms. Forrest."

"Rosie?" Delia asked, trying and failing to push herself into a sitting position. Something was *wrong*, but she knew that if she didn't look to her left side, it couldn't possibly be real. It was a strange dream, or a nightmare, or a hallucination. "Rosie is here?"

"She's been at your side almost exclusively since she arrived." Sandrine smiled, taping over the tube once again. "I'll give you two a moment."

"Dee? Oh, my gods, Dee!" Rosie said, practically skidding into the room, the soles of her boots screeching noisily against the marble.

Delia reached out to hug her, without thinking, and nearly vomited when the sight finally sank in. Her left arm ended just past the shoulder, the bandage ratty and blood-soaked, crispy at the edges where it covered cauterized skin. "My arm," she whispered.

"You saved Henry's life, Dee. Henry and her baby."

"Baby?"

"She's pregnant, Dee." Rosie stroked her face so tenderly, so gently, that Delia almost didn't feel it. "It was all I could do to keep Georgie from barging in here to cry all over you. Sandrine had to put her to work clearing buildings. Most of the Coalition is gone. Their ships certainly are by now, at least from the docks. They've retreated to the skies, now."

"You're with Obsidian Enclave now?"

Rosie nodded, a stray curl escaping from beneath the cap she was wearing. It was frizzy, with a dull gleam under the yellow incandescent bulbs overhead. "I guess so." Her touch was so light, tracing the contours of Delia's face over and over, as if she was trying to memorize it. "Gregor Zink did his best to waylay me, but as it turns out, when you spend years promising the second coming of Norah Gordon, and she eventually shows up, people won't ask too many questions when she wants to take a third of the fleet and fly out to battle."

"What happened at Lucent Base?"

"I wasn't at Lucent Base, Dee. They took me beyond the Rim, to their city. It's beautiful, more than I'd ever imagined. Ceru has so many technologies that could help the Near Systems."

"It sounds like you want to go back there." Delia struggled to push herself up on her elbow, fumbling for a moment until Rosie helped lift her into a sitting position. Delia grunted softly from the effort, holding the bandage on her gut with her one remaining arm. "Do you want to go back there?"

"We don't have to make any decisions yet. I want you to visit with me, see if you feel the same way." Rosie pushed a matted lock of hair from Delia's face, tucking it behind her ear. "But not until things are settled here, which will take some time, and not until you are feeling better."

"I don't know if I'll ever feel better," Delia whispered, tears already surging to the corners of her eyes, and she was unable to stem the tide of them as they dumped out all over her soot-stained face. "I can never hug you again, Posy."

"Sure you can, Dee." Rosie chewed on her lip for a moment, concern rippling across her beautifully rounded features. "Captain Tansy said she might know someone who can make you one hell of a prosthetic."

"If they aren't dead after this."

"Not here, across the Near Systems. This engineer knows his stuff. I think you should go with her when things are settled."

Delia wiped the tears from her cheeks with the back of her hand, sniffling noisily. "Settled. I don't even know what that means anymore." She closed her eyes again, willing the tears to stop. "We've all lost so much."

"Ceru could be a fresh start."

"What about cooking? You always wanted to be a chef, Posy. I don't want you to give up on that."

"I am a chef. Working at The Purple Pig was some of the best months of my life, but I—I feel a different pull now. It's new, and I don't have any idea what Gregor Zink is going to do when I get back, but there are some parts about this that just... fit." Rosie shrugged lightly and brushed some ashes from her shoulder. They floated down to the marble, disintegrating as they landed.

"Commander?" a cadet asked from the doorway, holding her cap in her hands.

"Shaw," Rosie replied, turning to face her. "What's the matter?"

"We found a small squadron in an old warehouse down near the docks. They might have been trying to retake them." Shaw pulled at her ponytail, a nervous gesture as she picked at the ends.

"Did we lose anyone?"

Shaw shook her head. "No, ma'am. They lost a few, it looks like. They were uninterested in surrender."

"Very well."

"The rest of the Coalition ships have departed. What should we do with them?"

Rosie sucked her teeth. "How many?"

"Seven. The three who attempted to fight back have already been sent to the incinerator."

"Divide them into our fleet's brigs. No more than three to a brig, I'd prefer two to a cell. Send a few other cadets to post up outside, we don't need any mishaps."

"Aye, Commander." Shaw backed out of the room, still twisting her cap in her hands.

Delia raised an eyebrow. "Commander, now?"

"A lot changed while you were napping." Rosie traced a finger across Delia's face before pulling her closer for a delicate, fragile kiss. "I seem to remember you like that side of me, too."

"I like every side of you."

"Dee, something happened while you were out."

The abrupt shift in tone sank a stone into Delia's gut, and it wasn't just whatever painkillers Sandrine had put into her drip. "What happened?" She squeezed her eyes shut again, not wanting to know. "Who else did we lose?" She'd heard from others in her drifting in and out of sleep that they'd lost Carmen, but it was a loss too painful to speak aloud. "Who else?" she repeated.

"Skelm."

"Who was in Skelm?"

Rosie inhaled, ragged, torn, exhausted. "We lost all of Skelm. The Coalition used the superweapon against it. Emeline was—is—beside herself, it's all we could do to keep her from boarding one of our ships and flying off on her own. There's nothing left, Dee. Nothing but rusted factories and empty warehouses."

"Why?"

"The election, maybe, or there was rebel activity there that we didn't know about. The governor got out in time, she recorded a statement from the safety of Delta-4. She had warning, but we don't know who warned her."

Delia shifted on the sheets, sweaty from days of cycling fevers, the yellow patches sending out tendrils across the linen weave of the fabric. "What has the response been?"

"Hard to know without comms. I have some working on the spire, but they aren't engineers. I didn't bring any with me, there wasn't time. Emeline stole a Coalition radio off one of their ships, but it's mostly combat transmissions, nothing about Skelm." Rosie poked the bag that hung over the bed and it crinkled quietly. "I imagine they will be blaming the attack on us—on Obsidian Enclave, that is—or The Scattered, just as they did with Terringgough Gulch."

"What are you going to do?"

"Are you asking me as a reporter, or as the woman who shares my bed?"

"Both." Delia laced her fingers with Rosie's, trying not to think about the odd, ghostly feel of the limb she'd lost. "Not that I can do much reporting with a broken comms spire."

"On the record, Obsidian Enclave will assert we had nothing to do with the blast. That the technology to alter atmospheric conditions was stolen from us and perverted into a weapon of death. That we have the comms logs to prove it, and that we claim no responsibility. Obsidian Enclave vows to continue our tradition of research and exploration beyond the Rim." Rosie blew out a lungful of air, rustling the papers on the nearby table. "Off the record, I have no gods-damned idea, given what Zink did."

"I don't know that your comms logs will convince Coalition supporters."

"And that's why I have no idea. I don't want to get any more mixed up in a pointless war than we already have. Look at Bradach, look what's happened here, I—I can barely stand to look out at it, at the carnage, the blood-drenched streets. If the same happened to Ceru, there would be no recovering from it." Rosie kissed her again, this time a little more fervent, and less like she was handling a fragile egg. "My family is there now. In Ceru."

"No doubt your mother still hates me."

"She hates everyone, Dee, it's nothing personal." Rosie leaned forward, resting her chin on Delia's shoulder. The weight of her, the realness, almost drew tears to Delia's eyes once again. "My grandfather asked about you. He was surprised to hear that we reconnected on Turas-Mara."

"Fate," Delia said.

Rosie huffed a quiet laugh, and the breath hugged Delia's ear for just a moment before it dissipated into the air. "Fate, maybe. I can't say it was a thrill for me." Her brow furrowed, painting deep lines into her perfectly round face. "Are you in pain?"

"Yes, but it's manageable. I'm not looking forward to when Sandrine takes whatever is in that drip away from me, I'll tell you that much." Delia moved to reach for the cup of water on the table next to her and flinched away from it when her arm did not reappear at her side. "We should give this bed—cot—whatever—to someone in worse shape than me."

"You lost an arm and got shot, Dee. Just give yourself a second to breathe before you start throwing yourself back into action."

"I'm aware, Posy, it's been on my mind since I dragged myself to consciousness."

"Er, Commander?" Shaw asked, standing again in the doorway.

"If there isn't room in the brig, we can figure something out," Rosie replied, standing up from the makeshift bed. "We just need to get them out of the city, we can't have them milling around, calling their ships back down. Bradach won't stand another wave, we're barely hanging on as it is."

Shaw shook her head hard, trying to interrupt. "No, ma'am, there are more Obsidian Enclave ships out past the atmosphere."

"More ships?"

"Yes, Commander. They are calling for us to leave the city or risk expulsion from Ceru."

Rosie sighed heavily, pressing the tips of her fingers to her forehead. "Is Zink with them?"

"Commander Zink is leading the rest of the fleet, yes."

"Tell him to meet me on the docks. Tell the others to wait, don't let them leave without talking to me first. If we leave Bradach now, leave it undefended, then the Coalition will only swoop back in." Rosie growled under her breath, fists balled at her sides. "It will all have been for nothing."

Delia swung her legs over the side of the bed, steadying herself with her remaining arm, off-balance and unsure without it. She kept reaching out with a limb that was no longer there. "I'm coming with you," she said, tugging on her boots.

"You're staying right here, Dee, because you're still unwell," Rosie ordered. "I won't have you making yourself worse, and Sandrine will have my head on a platter if I'm not careful with you."

"You might be able to order me around in some scenarios, Rosie Gordon, but this isn't one of them." Delia pushed herself off the bed with a soft grunt and slid the needle out of her arm, grateful she wasn't squeamish. "The last time Gregor gods-damned Zink was in this city, he bundled you off somewhere beyond the Rim and I didn't see you or hear from you for weeks. No, thank you, I don't want to relive that. At this point, I'm not sure I could."

"Dee—"

"Just give me a minute." Delia straightened, tilting her head side to side for a moment until things came into a clearer focus. She regretted it once she saw the smear of blood streaked across the tiles in the corner, not knowing if it was hers or someone else's. "I'm going to give that man a piece of my mind. Gods-damned bastard took you away from me, and he's lucky I'm missing an arm, or I'd strangle him myself."

Shaw cleared her throat. "Are you Commander Gordon's paramour?"

Delia snorted a laugh. "Uh, sure. I guess, yeah."

"You'll love Ceru, ma'am. We have ten different comms desks and a fully formed press corps. Some of us have been avid listeners for years, you know." She clasped her hands behind her back, giving Rosie a curt nod. "I'll send your message to the rest of the fleet, and we will be waiting for you on the docks."

Chapter 58

Larkin's fingers brushed against the small throwing knives tucked into their belt, slung from shoulder to hip. The Obsidian Enclave ship was landing at the docks, and after so much had gone wrong, over and over again, she couldn't imagine that it wouldn't be the same. "They'll have better weapons than the Coalition," she grumbled under her breath.

"Rosie will handle it," Evie said, pulling Larkin's hands away from the knives. "You don't have to kill everyone who crosses us."

"That's hilarious, coming from you, Eves. It was only a couple of days ago that I had to pull you off an MPO."

"I thought you were dead. You went on a rampage and left me cuffed to the fence."

"I'm allowed a rampage every now and then," Larkin explained, leaning against her. "It's an unfortunate side effect of being raised to become a ruthless assassin."

"You don't look so ruthless to me."

Larkin smirked. "Nah. I think it's mostly out of my system." The ship descended lower and lower, through the thick, smoky clouds, before settling noisily in the bay, the bright silver of the exterior gleaming even in the haze-dimmed, mirrored light. "Unless Zink tries to pull something, and then I might just find the motivation for one more."

"Don't jump to any conclusions."

"I'm not jumping, I'm waiting."

Evie exhaled a laugh through her nose and wrapped an arm around

Larkin's waist. Her grip was firm and strong, steady, dependable. She was the rock Larkin had always needed, and never known until they were thrown together in that prison. Evie was chastising her, but she had her own hands braced against the holster at her hip. "I wonder if things will ever feel normal again."

"What's normal?" Larkin asked, melting into the casual embrace. "I don't think any of us have had normal for a long time."

"I want our normal back, Larks. I want the Pig and rushing to open for lunch and arguing about the price of bread. I want waking up late with you and looking out the window at Carmen's garden. I want your overly fancy cocktails."

"They aren't overly fancy!"

"Ten ingredients is a bit much."

Larkin scoffed, the loss of Carmen still too sharp to parse. She shoved it away, locking it in a box at the back of her mind, a tragedy for another day. "I want that too, you know. Someday. I fear it's a long way off."

"Maybe."

"Always the optimist, Evie."

"Someone has to be."

The ship's loading bay released, the air hissing around the ramp as the pressure equalized, kicking up a cloud of soot and dust as the ramp extended and the door began to lift. Gregor Zink looked different than she'd imagined. He was wiry and short, greying hair tidy and freshly cut, his white suit just as unblemished as the rest of him. Larkin had expected someone who was large and imposing, towering over everyone else, but he was just another man, mostly unremarkable.

"Where's Ms. Gordon?" he asked, his voice unsettlingly pleasant, given the circumstances.

"She's on her way," Larkin answered, shifting her torso to be sure he saw the knives draped across her chest. "We're the welcoming party."

"Things look rather different than when I was last here," he said, hands clasped in front of him. "A shame, really. I always liked Bradach."

"No thanks to you," Larkin hissed. "You gave away our coordinates."

He tilted his head to the side. "I think you'll find that you had a mole, at least, that's what I heard." He shrugged easily, blinking at the charred trees in the park. "And if you are referring to the incident on Lucent Base, your friends will be able to confirm that I wasn't even present. I was in Ceru with Ms. Gordon."

"A pity you didn't stay there," Rosie retorted, striding up the path with a confidence Larkin hadn't seen in her before. Self-assured, calm, and by the looks of her furrowed brow, ready to give Zink several hells' worth of a right hook.

"Ms. Gordon," he said, smiling. "It would seem we have some snags to iron out with regards to the use of Obsidian Enclave vessels. There are appropriate clearances that must be submitted, in writing, and in the event of war, we have a referendum." He squared his shoulders, nodding to himself. "It's unsurprising that these customs are foreign to you, given your upbringing."

"What would you have me do, leave Bradach to burn under Coalition control?" Rosie demanded. "Let it be put to the torch, so that you can remain gloriously uninvolved beyond the Rim?"

"These are not our conflicts."

"Horseshit, you've involved yourself in enough inter-system nonsense, you're just careful to never be seen causing problems, all the while you're creating chaos in the undercurrent."

"Ms. Gordon, I—"

"Now is the time to act, Mr. Zink. We cannot remain in Ceru with bloodless hands while the Coalition uses horrifying weaponry against its own citizens. What kind of progress can we even claim, if we allow the Near Systems to collapse?"

Gregor Zink listened attentively, nodding as Rosie spoke. "Ms. Gordon, you've seen what life can be in Ceru. You've seen our advancements, our commitment to research and exploration. If we spend all of our energy chasing across the galaxy to right wrongs, we'd never get anything done. Why should we muddy ourselves with conflicts that do not involve us?" He asked. "I did what was best for our people, nothing more and nothing less."

"You involved yourself when you killed Jasper." Hyun stepped forward, out of a deep shadow into the pool of amber light from a street lamp that grew up out of the dock. "Your hands are far from clean, and they certainly aren't bloodless."

He inhaled slowly, exhaling before he continued. "I did everything I could for him."

"You chased us through the Belt. You're the reason the ship even took that hit in the first place."

"Your ire is better left directed at the pilot of your ship." He extended a hand to her, an offer of peace, but a transparent and self-serving one. "There is no conflict between us. You are a gifted medic, and you would be more than welcome to join us in Ceru."

Hyun spat on the ground, leaving his offer hanging in the night. "I'd rather drag myself across crushed glass than serve you."

"Who said anything about serving?" he asked in an irritatingly bemused voice. "You would be an esteemed colleague of Obsidian Enclave, of course."

Rosie stepped between them, shielding Hyun. "I suggest you stop trying to poach people, Mr. Zink. Just because you got your way once doesn't mean you should make it a habit."

He made a strange sound in the back of his throat, half a laugh and half a cough. "I wouldn't say that I got my way, Ms. Gordon. I just had to fly halfway across the Near Systems to retrieve a third of my fleet."

"*Your* fleet?" Rosie asked. Calm, relaxed, one eyebrow raised like she'd been born into leadership. Maybe she had. "I seem to recall you begging me to take up the mantle for Obsidian Enclave. My birthright, remember? Who are *you*, exactly, other than someone who sold everyone else out to the Coalition?"

Zink's demeanor cracked, just for a second, anger flashing across his face. "I'm the person who stepped up when your family abandoned us in Ceru. I'm the one who kept the gods-damned engines running when your grandfather left us to rot after Norah died. Ms. Gordon, you can't really think that you'd show up and be handed the position of commander on a silver platter, now did you?"

He offered up a sad sigh, lacing his fingers together. "I'll tell you what we're going to do. Because of your lineage, I won't have you court-martialed when we return. You and I will work side-by-side to grow Obsidian Enclave, and continue our research beyond the Rim." He paced a circle around Rosie, but she didn't flinch, and Larkin was internally proud. Zink was a slimy rat, and she could smell the sleaze from across the dock. "This was too bold, Ms. Gordon. I'll be informing the rest of my cadets that they are to return to their ships immediately, and we will have to convince the paradigm not to punish the cadets for following you into an ill-fated, unsanctioned battle."

Rosie laughed. "You kidnapped me, Mr. Zink. Begged me to lead. You set traps for me to step into, you played games with my life and the lives of my family and friends. How well do you think the reporters would respond to that? As I recall, there were already some uncomfortable questions being asked, no?"

"Are you threatening me, Ms. Gordon?"

"Why don't we ask the fleet who they'd rather follow?" Rosie replied, stepping forward to stop him in his tracks. "If they choose you, I'll stand down."

"And if they choose you?"

"I guess we'll find out, won't we?" Rosie reached forward, taking the radio from his belt. "Enclave fleet," she said into the speaker. "This is Rosie Gordon, a commander of the fleet. Gregor Zink has been found to be selling off technology and weapons to the Coalition to line his own pockets. If you agree with his decisions, land in the docks and arrest me for unlawful seizure of Obsidian Enclave ships. If you'd rather fight for justice in the Near Systems and beyond, I invite you to continue with your previous orders to escort Coalition ships out of our airspace."

They waited, and the ships stayed just out of view, more of a shadow above the clouds than anything tangible, and the seconds dripped into long minutes.

"Well," Zink said, his voice now cold. "I suppose we will have much to discuss in Ceru."

"You have caused so much pain, Mr. Zink. Pain, and heartache, and damage, and for what?" She nodded at Hyun, encouraging her. "I think that someone else should get to pass judgment on you, sir."

"Judgment!" he shouted, incredulous. "Everything I have done, I have done for Obsidian Enclave. Every life lost is one saved in Ceru."

Rosie shook her head calmly. "No. That's not the truth, Mr. Zink. You antagonized us into destruction. You almost ruined Obsidian Enclave for your own greed and hubris. You stole me away and forced me into service."

"You seem more than comfortable in your new role, Ms. Gordon, I hardly think this should be cause for my punishment." He glared past her, staring out at the ruined city. "You should be thanking me."

"Gods below, you really are a piece of work, aren't you?" Delia asked, leaning against a charred tree. She wavered, unsteady on her feet, but Larkin was there before she fell, catching her around the waist and guiding her to an overturned crate to sit down. Delia sucked her teeth, staring at Zink. "There's something deeply wrong with you, and I'm not sure it can be repaired."

"What do you love most, Zink?" Hyun demanded, circling him. "Maybe we should take that from you, just as you took Jasper from me, and so many from these streets. Maybe you should suffer as we all have."

"He loves nothing more than power," Rosie answered, not even giving him the opportunity to open his mouth. "He has ruled Ceru and Lucent Base for so long, he thinks that he is some sort of king. A monarch, and one none of us asked for."

Zink tried to wriggle from Rosie's grasp, stepping backwards, ducking away from her. "That's rather rich coming from you, Ms. Gordon, given how you have anointed yourself as a new leader of Obsidian Enclave. It seems that you crave power, too."

"I never asked for this," Rosie said, letting him edge his way towards an abandoned Coalition shuttle. "You foisted it upon me, you never gave me a choice, and now you have to reap what you have sown." She took a deep breath, reaching out for Hyun, linking their arms. "You are hereby banished from Ceru and from Lucent Base."

"You don't have the authority!" he protested. "The paradigm will never accept this."

"I'm sure they will, once they receive my full and uncensored account of what has happened here, and at Terringgough Gulch when you foiled that deal, and across the Near Systems with every back-room deal you made that sold us out." She advanced on him casually, as though her hand wasn't resting on the holster at her hip. "That tech wasn't stolen, Gregor."

"Of course it was."

"Your story didn't check out. You sold it off to the Coalition, and for what? Why? What could be worth all of this death and destruction?"

He didn't answer. Zink took three more steps backwards, edging towards the shuttle. A coward, turning tail and running. All that bluster, all the manipulation, the secrecy, and it had ended right where it started—with running.

"You won't get far in a shuttle, Gregor." Rosie had an arm around Hyun's shoulders, steadying her. "I doubt you'll even make it to the nearest beacon."

"What do you care? You're the one sending me to my death, Ms. Gordon. Your grandmother—"

"Was flawed," Rosie finished. "As are we all, I'm sure you'd agree." She nodded towards the shuttle, the cap wobbling slightly on her head, ill-fitting, yet it stayed in place, regardless. "Norah Gordon did plenty for Obsidian Enclave, but left her family to scramble, to struggle to scrape together the pieces of our shattered life. She sought power, too, and that quest led her to her grave. Those fit to lead are the ones who never wanted to in the first place. I did not choose this, Gregor, but I'm here now, and you made me your problem."

"I never should have gone looking for you," he spat, fumbling behind him for the door's exterior lever. "I should have left you rotting in Dubhmoor. I was the one who arranged the cook position at Nox Beacon, you know."

"I figured that out a long time ago."

"You have me to thank for this new life you've fallen into," he snarled. "You don't deserve any of it." The lever released, and the shuttle's door raised, the metal sparkling in the amber glow of the lamps. "It won't be long before you're begging me to come back to Ceru."

Hyun barked out a derisive laugh, cold and shallow. "You're a fraud," she said. "You cloak everything in games, so that we won't see you're an empty vessel." She unlinked from Rosie and pursued him as he scrambled into the shuttle, afraid that Hyun would kill him after all. "I am not a violent person, Zink. I dedicated myself to healing, and I've seen far too many broken bodies to inflict that kind of pain." She pressed against the glass, her palms flat on the window. "But if I ever see you again, my morality might just crumble because you took him away from me. And I'm never going to stop looking for you, so you'd better hope that our paths don't cross again."

She released the shuttle, and it rose up out of the docks, disappearing into the hazy smog above them, the flickering lights of the battle still sparking across a darkened sky.

Chapter 59

Cass was never meant to be the leader of a rebellion, but by chance, a strange genetic anomaly mixed with being a halfway decent shot and an expert with explosives, she was catapulted into it by force. Before everything had changed—before the Coalition began firing on its own people, before she wound up at a Scattered hideaway busted up and broken, she'd wanted something so much different for herself. Once, she spent her time staring up at the sculptures in the Capital, her fingers brushing reverently along the marble. She soothed the itch in her hands with rock, with quartz, clumsy implements but chipping away at the rough surface to reveal something hidden inside used to reveal her soul, too.

War stole everything like beauty and replaced sculptures with guns. Hands once desperate for creation had developed a trigger finger, and it dragged at her. It was so much more than exhaustion; it was bone-deep and inexorable.

She was never meant to be a leader of the rebellion, but there she was, sitting at a table with the shiny, brand new leader of Obsidian Enclave, and a girl who probably would have won that election, if the High Council hadn't stolen it, paying their own price with thousands of others' lives.

Her hands rested on the makeshift table, a splintered door balanced on two stacks of cinderblocks, harvested from the wreckage that was suffocating the city. The rough wood bit into her palms, but it was a reminder to allow herself honesty.

"Our fleet has seen off the remaining Coalition forces," Rosie said, setting a small radio on the table. "A few set themselves in pursuit to chase the majority back to Gamma-3, although I don't know what they'll find when they get there."

Emeline nodded carefully, her hands folded in her lap. "Some transmissions from the Coalition radio suggest that several of their fleet have already gone rogue. There's considerable chaos, and vague reports of rioting in the Capital." She scribbled something onto the page in front of her before continuing. "I've offered up Captain Augustus Allen as a show of goodwill, and it sounds like the Judge in the Capital is willing to let this proceed without further attack or interruption. He's taken charge now that the members of the High Council have been killed, imprisoned, or chased off Gamma-3."

"It will be good to get the spire repaired here," Cass said. "We need to find out what's happening out there, and people need to know what happened here, too." She sighed, blinking up at the single bulb flickering yellow over their heads. "Things are starting to change fast."

"That's why I called this meeting." Emeline stood, drawing in a quiet breath. "I want to propose a new alliance, between what remains of the Coalition, and Obsidian Enclave, and the rebellion."

Cass chewed on the inside of her cheek, trying and failing to envision what that would look like. "I'm not sure that's even possible. How would we get rebels to accept the Coalition?"

"The High Council will be razed to the ground for what they've done," Emeline replied. "In its place, we will need something new, elected leaders, and—"

"Are you hoping to be one of those leaders?" Rosie interrupted.

"I only ever wanted to help Skelm." Emeline's face fell, and tears gathered in her eyes. "But Skelm is gone. There is no one there anymore, no one that needs my advocacy. I'm not yet sure where I belong, but I do know that it's on Gamma-3, in the Capital, in some regard. Someone has to rally people, to put an end to chaos, to organize." She shrugged, swallowing back the sob that almost escaped her throat. "I'm not good at many things, but I feel called to do that, at least."

"An alliance, then," Cass said after an uncomfortable silence, one where everything they'd lost threatened to bubble to the surface. "The Scattered, and Splintered, whoever is left of us, will want the Coalition to pull back their military. The smaller settlements will want to be left alone to thrive as they see fit." She shifted her weight on the stool beneath her, the wood creaking gently from the force. "No more work camps. No more mining colonies."

"We need rhodium," Emeline protested. "How can we progress? How can we maintain what we already have without it?"

"There is technology, automated mining equipment," Rosie offered. "I'm sure Obsidian Enclave can offer to share the blueprints in exchange for autonomy. Ceru is a beautiful city, advanced, ready to explore the stars, and we'd like to continue that without being impeded." She tugged at the button on the cuff of her jumpsuit, hanging on by one single thread, and she snapped it. "Turas-Mara can be a place where this alliance is shown to the rest of the galaxy, where our scientists can work together towards common goals."

Emeline nodded, sitting back down on her stool. "What about piracy?"

"Piracy is piracy," Cass replied with a laugh. "You can't stop it, you can only try to provide reasons why it's unnecessary. Loosening the grip on trade routes will help. Captain Tansy said that over the past six months, the majority of smuggled crates are medical supplies." She shrugged loosely. "And booze."

"That will be a harder sell, unfortunately. Despite most of the higher-ups in the Capital indulging themselves, most prefer it to be swept under the rug." Emeline straightened her jacket, and smoothed her unwrinkled skirts. "However, after this much upheaval, we won't have the resources to police the sales and trade of alcohol." Emeline let a tiny smirk slip, the first since she'd heard about Skelm days prior. "Who doesn't enjoy a sip now and then, anyway?"

"I'm telling your mother," Cass said, snorting back a laugh.

"Who do you think gave it to me, Calvetti?"

"My credits were on Larkin for that, honestly. I'm surprised she hasn't scraped together the ruins to craft you something exquisite."

Rosie cleared her throat quietly, bringing them back to the topic at hand. She was a much better leader than Cass had ever been, and she was brand new at it. She'd be a gods-damned powerhouse in time, a force to be reckoned with, the leader that Ceru deserved, especially after years of Zink's lies. Rosie slid a stack of blank pages and several fountain pens across the table. "We should write all of this down and sign it. If all three of us agree, and sign, and announce this on the radio when the spire is repaired—we can get Dee to announce, of course—then it will be easier to pull everything into line."

"I'll sign whatever you want, just don't make me write it." Cass leaned back on the stool, balancing on the back two legs, one foot braced against the table. "I've never been good with words."

"Good enough to rally the rebellion behind you, Calvetti," Emeline challenged. "Factions ready to follow you into battle. That *have* followed you into battle."

"A fluke."

"And you dragged yourself across the Near Systems, half-dead and on the run from the agent you wound up... well—anyway, you went all that way just to make a deal with me."

"How did you know about that?" Cass asked, setting the stool back level on the tiles with a loud whine from the joints.

"She talked about you."

"What did she say?"

Emeline raised an eyebrow, and in that moment she looked so much like her sisters that Cass had to suppress a laugh. "It was more what she didn't say. Regardless, that isn't my point. This document, however fragile and cobbled together, needs to equally represent everyone at this table. Rosie is right, it's the best way to get ahead of whatever is coming next."

"For the sake of my sleep deprivation, I sincerely hope that what's coming is a vacation." Cass sighed, and took a blank page and a pen from the center of the table, and began to scratch out her terms in cramped, almost illegible writing.

They worked for hours like that, mostly in silence, except for the few lively debates that broke out about trade routes and fuel beacons, and the future of all current strip mining operations on asteroids within the Near Systems. Cass' head was pounding from it all when one of Rosie's cadets appeared in the doorway with an odd, left-handed salute, almost punching herself in the shoulder.

"Commander, there are some new ships landing in the docks. A few pirates, here to help with the wreckage. A few are asking about you specifically. It's a ship called the Cricket."

"Who do they have?" Cass asked, and when Shaw began to shrug, she didn't wait for the answer. She pushed past the cadet, running through the makeshift medical area, out the door and through the ruined streets, nearly falling flat when the toe of her boot caught on a broken cobblestone.

She knew what she was hoping for, but didn't dare speak it aloud, or even allow herself to quietly hope, because it was so soon, and she was probably still in the Capital with Tarand, and maybe she'd betrayed her, and maybe she'd been arrested and was toiling away on some toxic waste colony out in the stars.

But there she was anyway, despite all the odds against them.

"Olivia," Cass choked out, already having to swallow the lump in her throat. She took Olivia into her arms, gently, because she was covered in bruises that disappeared down past the collar of her white jumpsuit. "You came back."

"I told you I would," Olivia replied in a shaky voice.

Cass rubbed a hand over Olivia's head, the short, cropped hair uneven and brunette under her fingers. "You're not a natural blond?"

"Why, is that a deal-breaker?"

"Obviously," Cass said with a smirk that faded the moment her eyes fell on another bruise, deep purple and indigo, traveling from wrist to elbow along the bone. "What did they do to you?"

Olivia shrugged, but tears pooled at the rim of her eyelid. "Nothing much worse than we did to you, I would guess." She buried her face in Cass' jacket, her tears darkening the taupe twill. "Tarand is dead."

"What in hells went on down there?"

"She knew that I was sabotaging her at the end. Spreading lies to the other members of the High Council, undermining the meeting, passing as much information as I could to Mae Machenet." Olivia gripped Cass' waist tight, almost a crush, but Cass didn't protest. "She threw me into reeducation, just a few cells down from yours. Wanted to keep a close eye on me, I suppose."

"Did you kill her?"

"No." Olivia let out a shaky breath, pulling closer. "Amaranth Allemande did. They arrested her before we even got to the docks. Last we heard before comms went dark, the riots had spread out from the Capital, hitting all the bordering regions. It's probably planet-wide by now."

"I'm sorry that Bradach isn't a more welcoming sight."

"It will be," Alice added as she passed, tucking a wrench into her tool belt, a small droid hovering above her shoulder. "First, we need comms. Sounds like everyone here is out of the loop." She stood back, something between rage and despair settling into the fine lines on her face before she spoke again. "We've certainly got our work cut out for us."

Captain Violet sidled up behind her, one hand on her holster, always on guard, and the other resting at the small of her wife's back. "It's never going to be the same, is it?"

Cass shook her head, still holding Olivia tight against her chest. "No, it won't. Change always comes, and there is always a cost. Sometimes, there is a terrible price to pay. We can only hope that we learn from our mistakes."

The nightly news

Good evening, I'm Delia Forrest with your nightly news report. Wherever you are listening from, know that terrible things have happened here in Bradach, and across the Near Systems on Gamma-3, and in the Capital.

One week ago today, the Coalition violated the peace accord with the help of William Dodson, invading this settlement with violent aims. Both sides suffered terrible losses, casualties that have torn a gaping wound that will take years to scab over. Many will not trust my words, and I can't say that I blame them. One week ago, events were set into motion that cannot be taken back, and the Near Systems are in chaos. Riots, looting, false news reports have abounded in the following days. I can promise you that everything I say is true, corroborated by multiple witnesses, and provable, should any other journalist wish to take up the mantle.

As it stands, here is what we know.

First, that the High Council ordered a weapon to be fired on Skelm to quash the first free election in decades. Everyone in Skelm died shortly thereafter. Governor Das was given prior warning and evacuated in time. She made her last report from somewhere on Delta-4, and has since disappeared.

Second, the High Council itself is in chaos. Their newest member, Amaranth Allemande, formerly an overseer, killed High Councilor Tarand in her office over a dispute about the use of the weapon deployed against Skelm. It is understood that as such, she may have saved Bradach from Skelm's fate. She is currently under arrest, facing interrogation from the Judge in the Capital. Councilors Brome, Jacobs, Fredericks, and Osei were found boarding a transport off Gamma-3, and are currently detained in their homes until an investigation can be concluded about the weapon. High Councilor Kimura maintains her innocence in that she was a part of the rebellion all along; her story has been corroborated by several members of both factions and she will be released pending certification.

Third, there is a signed and ratified document, a peace accord between Rosie Gordon, leader of Obsidian Enclave, Cassius Calvetti, de facto leader of what remains of the rebellion, and Emeline Payne, who was projected to win the election in Skelm and organized the diplomatic and safe return of Coalition Captain Augustus Allen from rebel imprisonment. This agreement lays out new policies on trade routes, imports, resources, and exploration.

William Dodson handed over proprietary information to the Coalition, including coordinates. He also brokered the sale of the superweapon from former Obsidian Enclave member Gregor Zink and former high councilor Cecelia Tarand. William Dodson escaped Bradach during the fighting, and has not been seen since. If you have seen this man, please contact our station with any information regarding his whereabouts.

We cannot and will not forcibly demand those still fighting to lay down their weapons. We have all suffered incalculable losses. Too much blood has been spilled to serve the financial interests of others, and these three leaders are asking for peace. We can rebuild cities. We cannot heal the heartbreak of so many dead who were taken from us. Join us in peace. Set down your guns and pick up tools instead.

We will all need patience as we push into this new era together, as old regimes are toppled and new, democratic ones installed. Cassius Calvetti is standing down as leader of the rebellion, and asks for others to join her in pivoting her efforts towards reconstruction.

For all of us that have felt the sharp sting of loss, being asked to set aside old grievances will be the hardest thing we ever achieve—but if we dedicate ourselves to progress and fellowship, we can achieve it together.

Thank you for listening, and good night.

Epilogue

Time passed, as it always had. Old wounds slowly turned to scar tissue, and before any of them realized it, things had changed. The Near Systems had stabilized, and the rebellion faded like a candle burning through the last droplets of wax. Bradach was rebuilt, brick by brick, though the cobblestone streets were lost forever. Progress marched through the city, bringing steamcars along with it, and an influx of curious tourists desperate to visit the pirate settlement. They would never know how different it had been before the war.

A new tavern stood tall in the center of what used to be the old park, surrounded by apple trees that shouldn't have survived the fires, but had nonetheless. A sign hung above the freshly painted pink door, emblazoned with glittering text: The Fuchsia Phoenix, because some things really were lost forever.

Cassius Calvetti rubbed the sculpture of a laughing pig as she passed, proud of her work because learning to create when so much had been destroyed was one of the hardest things a person could do. It shone in the bright mirrored light of early afternoon, gleaming prettily with its white marble. It had all but melted under her hands, begging to be made real, and so there it sat outside the tavern, known to locals, but the tourists would never understand why it was there. No one spoke of The Purple Pig, not anymore.

A little girl sprinted by with peals of laughter, pushing past Cass into the tavern. Her brand new dress was already muddy at the knees, and Georgie sprinted after her, harried. "Carmina!" she shouted, but her daughter was already inside.

"That's what you get for naming her after two revolutionaries," Olivia said, slipping her arm around Cass' waist, her pink hair shiny and pin-straight, falling down past her shoulders.

"Carmen and Marina both had more regard for fabric," Mae replied, stepping out from inside. "Don't worry, I'll get the mud out before the ceremony. I came prepared." She pulled two washcloths and a solvent from her bag with a wry smile. "If it wasn't Carmina, it would have been Bailey or Willa."

"Aren't they back from work yet?" Henry asked, leaning against one of the wooden fence posts that lined the path to the tavern door, protecting the flourishing garden from careless feet. The silver plaque at the gate was emblazoned with Carmen's name and an etching of fruit trees. "It starts in less than an hour."

Mae shrugged. "You know them, always losing track of time. The family reunification clinic had a new intake of soldiers today, fresh from Gamma-3." She squinted up at the sky, the color beyond the mirrors a fantastical display of stars. "I hope that ship is from Ceru, or this wedding is going to be late."

"When has Delia Forrest ever been late?" Olivia asked, flipping her hair over her shoulder. "Gods below, that last art show was a nightmare. I had to pressure that last buyer into not devaluing Cass' work. I'm going inside where the wine is. Mae, do you want to split a bottle?"

"You don't have to ask me twice," Mae replied, following her through the doors.

The tavern inside was modern, with stained glass that cast a spectrum of colors over the polished bar and delighted the tourists. The floors were new, the wood waxed to perfection for the occasion. Captain Tansy was sliding drinks across the bar, cracking jokes with the patrons and telling tall tales that only had a tiny kernel of truth to them, but it was all part of the charm of The Fuchsia Phoenix. Aven rolled her eyes, pulling glasses of ale without a second thought.

Alice leaned against a stool, tugging at her waistcoat and trying not to laugh at Captain Tansy's nonsense. Violet did nothing but egg her on more, a show for the tavern's patrons that always earned them good reviews and repeat visitors. "How many of them did you take on at once?" Violet asked between sips of the finest whiskey, flown in from Delta-4. "Twenty?"

"At least thirty," Tansy answered casually. "And I only had one leg that day." She tapped an empty glass against her prosthetic with a delicate clink, waggling her eyebrows.

"Thirty?" Captain Josie Keller asked with a scoff. "I hit at least fourteen ships the day we took Bradach back."

"Did you?" Holly Ambrosia asked, trailing a finger around the rim of her empty wine glass. "I'm not sure I've ever heard that story."

Josie leaned in close, dragging the wine glass away. "You should let me buy you a drink and tell you, then."

Tansy coughed out a noisy laugh, standing back from the bar and ringing a large, bronze bell that hung over her head. "Alright, everyone out. Private function. If you don't have an invitation, come back tomorrow. I hear we have a guest chef arriving at the docks. You won't be disappointed."

Tourists and locals filed out, some of them grumbling, leaving every table empty except for one, where Hyun sat with Roger, sharing a bottle of good white wine, the condensation dripping down and pooling against the mosaic tile of the tabletop. When he took her hand, she didn't pull away, despite the sadness that still lingered over both of them like a heavy velvet blanket.

Georgie pried her daughter from the staircase as she squealed and giggled, Henry holding the fabric taut as Mae blotted the mud from the dress.

"I didn't think it would take three pirates to handle a five-year-old," Bailey said, pushing through the back door, her suit impeccably tailored.

"You haven't met enough five-year-olds," Willa muttered, tugging at her burgundy dress. Remy Abara chuckled loudly, already lining up at the bar for a lemonade.

"Stop that," Mae chided over her shoulder. "I already told you, you're going to pop a seam if you don't cut it out."

Willa's hands dropped to her sides, and she sighed. "A lifetime in military uniform doesn't adequately prepare you for social events."

"Are we late?" Rosie asked, bursting through the front door. "Gods, I hope we're not late."

"We're not late," Delia said, following her in, shrugging dramatically with her cybernetic arm, the faint blue glow visible through the sheer emerald green sleeves of her shirt. "But for the record, I did tell you we shouldn't have stopped to look at that anomaly on the way from Ceru."

"We have a duty for research, Dee. I couldn't just ignore it." Rosie embraced them all in turn, ending with Carmina. "You are at least twice as big as the last time I saw you."

The little girl replied with a devious cackle, wriggling from her mothers' grasps and disappearing up the stairs once more.

"If nothing else, she's going to make sure those two are ready on time," Alice shouted across the tavern.

Larkin appeared on the landing at the top of the stairs, dressed in white, the glittering fabric draped artfully over her to the floor. For the first time since she was small, her long dark hair fell loose past her waist, adorned with twinkling gems and sprigs of tightly-knit blossoms that matched her dress. "We are on time, thank you very much," she said. Evie appeared behind her, crisply dressed in an aubergine suit.

"Where is everyone else?" Evie asked, lacing her fingers together with Larkin's.

"Outside," Violet answered. "In the back. Dr. Arteo and Jhanvi just finished with the lights, and Davey Klein just showed up with some of the other Scattered from back in the day. Hawkins and his husband just pulled into port, they have Abigail and Thomas with them. They're back from that trip they took to Zeta-6."

Sandrine wheeled out of the kitchen with Lucy, wooden spoon in hand. "I think José is just about finished with the food, he'll be right out. I think he wanted to clean up before the ceremony." Carmina threw herself onto Sandrine's lap, laughing and trying to lick the spoon in Lucy's hand. "There's my little jackrabbit," Sandrine cooed, pulling the little girl in for a tight squeeze. "Are you excited for the wedding?"

"Are you kidding?" Georgie grumbled, leaning against the bar. "She's barely slept for days. She must get this from Henry's side, the gods know I was never like this."

"Oh, Georgina, you were just the same at that age." Sandrine released the wriggling Carmina, who shot off out into the garden beyond the doors. "I'm just so sorry you had to grow up so fast. It wasn't fair on you." She patted her daughters' arms. "Either of you. Or Emeline." Sandrine leaned to the side, watching Carmina run laps around the wooden chairs on the lawn. "She's going to crash early tonight, I hope you know that."

José pushed through the swinging door of the kitchen, looking dapper as always. "Mija," he said, looking up at Larkin with tears welling in his eyes, collecting in the gentle creases. "Are you ready?"

"I was born ready," Larkin replied, taking Evie's arm and descending the steps one at a time.

"Might as well get this show on the road," Tansy said, throwing the deadbolt on the front door. "Come on, everyone outside. We have a wedding to attend."

The back garden had been transformed into a magical landscape, with perfectly painted white wooden chairs lined in four rows on either side. The aisle was created from scattered piles of apple blossoms that Carmina had already strewn over the clover.

"Hey," Georgie whispered as Emeline took the seat next to her.

"Hey yourself," Emeline replied.

"Wasn't sure you'd make it with everything back on Gamma-3." Georgie nudged her sister playfully. "How's everything going?"

"Oh, you know. Always some new crisis. There are still plenty of people angry that Allemande wound up on house arrest and not in the incinerator."

"Shh," Violet chided. "No talk of uprisings at the wedding." She laughed quietly, muffling the sound with Alice's sleeve.

Georgie exhaled a quiet chuckle. "You'll never convince some of them that she didn't save Bradach. I guess in some twisted way, she did." She gave her sister a sideways glance. "Do you still visit her?"

"Sometimes," Emeline answered. "She doesn't have anyone else, Georgie. She has nothing and no one."

Catching her daughter as she ran past, Georgie directed her back towards Henry at the start of the aisle, holding Carmina's basket of extra apple blossoms. "Yeah," she said simply.

"Alright, you two, enough," Alice muttered. "Look, they're about to start the ceremony."

The ceremony was beautiful, just as Larkin wanted. She'd planned the entire thing, from commissioning Mae for their outfits, to the six-tier cake made by Amy and Aran at their new bakery up the road, to Captain Tansy as the officiant, to the glittering lights that swung gently in the breeze, dripping from every branch as the mirrors shifted away, turning day to twilight. For better or for worse, they both repeated, and both cried in each other's arms, and there wasn't one dry eye present, not even Carmina's, even though she was far too young to understand everything that had to happen, every horror and tragedy that led to these fleeting moments of joy.

After, when everyone had congratulated the newlyweds, Ned was busy dancing with Barnaby under the trees, pressed together despite everything that had happened. Ivy and her girlfriend swayed beneath the glimmering lights, giggling softly to one another as their skirts twirled lazily in the moonlight, and Violet couldn't help but flinch from the pang of her own forgotten youth, even as she'd spent recent years rediscovering it. She sidled up to Kady, pressing a small key into her hands. "It's time," she whispered, and tears slid down her face once again. "It's past time, in fact."

"But Captain— " Kady protested, standing from her chair, wobbling slightly because she'd already had several glasses of strong ale.

"It's just Violet now, I think," she corrected. "Captain Riha, the Cricket is yours."

"Where will you go?"

"We'll travel for a time, and then settle here when we've seen what there is to see. Rosie invited us to spend some time in Ceru, so a few months there first. We're traveling back with them in a few days' time." Violet sighed, brushing the tears from her cheeks. "I'm tired, Kady. Alice is tired. We stayed with the ship until things felt stable, but I'm not sure there's much more work for us to do. I promised her a retirement back when she first joined us, and I think it's time I honored my word."

"The ship won't be the same without either of you," Kady said, her voice thick with emotion.

"It will grow into something else, just as it did before. You have Ivy, and you're a better pilot than I ever was, you've proved that in the past few years. Alice and I are rattling around on that ship like spare parts." Violet patted Kady's arm, watching as Larkin and Evie spun themselves into another frenzied twirl, egged on by Bailey's stomp and holler fiddle playing, and her sister accompanying her on the bass, plucking furiously with a face of such intense concentration that she almost laughed. Kady wandered off to tell Ned, and Violet took the opportunity to slip away into the shadows where her wife was waiting.

"It's done," Violet said, leaning her head against Alice's chest.

"Are you alright?"

"I will be." She looked up at Alice. "*We* will be."

"Do you ever wonder what would have happened if we'd never met?" Alice asked, draping an arm around Violet's shoulders. "Where would we be?"

"I don't know," Violet answered. "But despite all of it, I'm glad this is where we ended up."

Stars blinked above them in the vast, unexplored expanses of dark space, twinkling with their forbidden secrets. Nothing was ever really over, even when the dusty books were unearthed and returned to the Capital, nor when keys were passed on. Despite everything that had been, and everything that would be in the distant and mysterious future, Violet was sure of one thing. It was never too late to start over.

End of The Cricket Chronicles

Keep reading for a sneak peek into another series by Ryann Fletcher, The Vane Dossier.

Craving more Cricket Chronicles? Join the Patreon for additional scenes, vignettes, and deleted chapters:

Patreon.com/RyannFletcherWrites

Preview for Rhapsody in Flames (The Vane Dossier: Exhibit A)

Verdance was a strange name for a city that spent half its year barren, with nothing more than icy wind to keep its residents company. The dense cloud cover pressed the frigid temperatures down, resting deep in the bones of anyone who was foolish enough to be outside at dusk.

Still, she found her fingers reaching for her cigarette case and a match book, the tiny flame insufficient to heat her frozen hands as she walked, the dying spark withering in the biting wind. The end of the cigarette blazed into life, the bright, saturated orange ember a stark juxtaposition to the dark, grey evening as it drew in around her, the cold as inescapable as the shame that she'd never managed to quit. She'd gotten close, once, before everything caved in on itself, before she was left on her own to survive the Verdance winters, before she was forty-eight years old and surviving on a diet of smoke and booze, heading home too late in the evening after another disappointing day.

She stopped outside her building, wanting to go inside, weary from the cold and hungry for the relative warmth of her apartment, for the feeling of her fingers defrosting, but she wasn't about to cut a smoke short. Breath curled from her mouth as she leaned against the brick, the roughness chewing through her thick winter coat as if it was delicate silk. In Verdance, nothing was gentle. Not anymore. Not since the Rupture tore everything apart.

Another inhale and she closed her eyes, savoring the taste of ash and tobacco as it gathered at the back of her throat, whispering for more. She was almost out of cigarettes. The paper burned slowly at first, struggling to catch in the biting gusts that swept past her shoes, old and creased, yet polished to an almost mirror shine. She struck another match, but the flame was extinguished before it met the end of her cigarette. She grumbled under her breath, hunting in her pockets for another book of matches, and finding none. Of course. What else could she expect from Verdance other than disappointment and irritation, laced with a side of contempt and a heaping portion of begrudging duty to the city that had taken her in all those years ago?

Going to bed without a smoke was like going to bed hungry: unfulfilled, agitated, and filled with a general sense of injustice. A quiet, gnawing need chewed through her thoughts, interrupting anything that wasn't a meditation on just how much of a disappointment she was to herself.

Virginia pulled her coat close, her breath rising from her lips in frustrated tendrils as she fumbled for the key to her building. Shadows, it was cold. She regretted that she'd waited so long to return home, but there was an unwelcome emptiness that sometimes crept under her door, seeping into her like half frozen molasses.

The key slid easily into the lock, and she shoved the heavy metal door open with her shoulder. The corridor was almost as cold as the outside. Her landlord was cheap as the grave, and it showed in the frosted hand railing that led up the stairs. Her worn brogues slid against the wood, the panels creaking with every weary step.

Fourth floor. Apartment J-22. Virginia froze at the sight of the dark silhouette standing outside her door, already slipping her fingers into the silver knuckles she held in her pocket. "Who are you?" she demanded.

"I live across the hall. I'm your neighbor," the figure responded, the hood of their cloak obscuring their face. Virginia never spoke to any of her neighbors, and as such, didn't know their faces. She didn't know their names, either, and that's how she preferred things to remain.

"What do you want?"

The overhead light in the corridor flickered, the crass yellow glow painting them both in a jaundiced tone, the amber shadows a strange contrast to the deepening darkness outside the window at the end of the hall, the side table beset with dead flowers someone had left there months before. The figure twisted their hands, wringing them anxiously. "Someone on the second floor told me that you're a private investigator."

"If you're looking for your long lost family or whatever, you can come to my office on Phoenix Avenue. Number eleven."

The figure shifted uncomfortably. "It's kind of an emergency."

"Call the cops, then."

"I can't."

Virginia pressed her fingers through the knuckles, balling into a fist, hidden inside the deep pocket of her overcoat. "If it's illegal, I can't help you." Her shoulders tensed, waiting for a fight. It wasn't impossible that one of the runaways she'd returned home had grown up and come looking for revenge, or whatever passed for justice in Verdance those days.

"No, it's not illegal, it's..."

"Spit it out."

"My brother is missing, has been for two weeks. He's..." the figure tugged at their hood. "Different."

"Right." Virginia stepped closer, releasing the grip of her fist, but keeping the knuckles in place over her still-frozen fingers. "What is he, then?"

"Do you promise you won't turn him in?" The figure asked, a tinge of desperation coloring the tone at the edges, betraying their aims more than their nervous fidgeting had.

"Can't promise that until I know what he is. You know the law."

"I know, I know, but they said you could help, you know, in situations like this." The figure chewed their lip and pressed their palms together in a gesture that looked a lot like praying, the way people had every Sunday before the residents of Verdance had largely abandoned the churches after the Rupture.

Virginia sighed, rubbing at her temple. "You aren't going to give up, are you?"

"No, ma'am," the figure replied, shaking their head. "My brother is all I've got left in this world, and I won't abandon him. Please, I'm desperate."

"Come on, inside." Virginia kept the silver knuckles around her fingers, even as the frigid metal bit into her skin. "No sense in talking about this in the hall." She pressed to the door, looking over her shoulder at the figure. "Step back. I've been around the block enough to know that you look like someone with plenty to hide, and I have no desire to bleed out on the floor today."

"I'm sorry." The figure stepped back, leaning against their own door on the other side. "I'm Ursa."

"You already know my name, so I'll refrain from sharing it." Virginia opened the door, flipping the switch on the wall. "Come on."

Ursa entered the dimly-lit apartment, her pale hands almost translucent even under the incandescent bulb. "Your apartment is nicer than mine," they said.

"So what's the problem with this brother of yours?" Virginia asked, flipping the deadbolt. She had little interest in small talk, and even less in the matters of interior design. Besides, if her apartment was that much nicer, she could only imagine the state of Ursa's. The entire building was old, drafty, and poorly maintained, but it was better than the streets, if only by a narrow margin.

Ursa clasped their hands in front of them, pulling back their hood. "He went missing."

"Yes, I gathered that much, but I'm going to need more than that to go on."

"He has the ability to shape shift."

Virginia tossed her keys on the table with a loud clatter, already bored of a case she could already predict the outcome of. Missing people were a dime a dozen in Verdance since the Rupture. "He shift in front of the wrong person, maybe? Plenty of crews always looking for someone who can easily slip the net."

"He's a good kid, he—"

"Kid? How old is he?"

"He's twenty."

"Hardly a kid, he's an adult," Virginia replied, bracing a hand against her kitchen counter. "Cops probably wouldn't help you anyway, not for a grown shifter. They might file a report, but that's all you'd get out of them these days." Virginia sighed again, the weight of another hopeless case already settling into her chest. "You know as well as I do that—"

"I do know, and that's why I came to you. Some say... some say that you're the best."

Virginia let loose a derisive scoff. "Depends who you ask."

"The last time I saw him, he was heading off to work that morning." Ursa tugged down their hood, revealing a delicate frame and a fine dusting of scales, barely visible along their collarbone.

"You too, huh?" Virginia said, gesturing.

"It runs in the family."

"What day was that, when you last saw him?"

"Thursday, two weeks back."

Virginia pulled a small notepad from her pocket, leaning against the wall as she scribbled barely legible notes on the unlined pages. "Anything unusual?"

"No."

"No new friends he's been hanging around, no new crews hanging around his neighborhood?"

Ursa closed their eyes. "No. Benjamin is a quiet boy, he lives here with me. So unless you know of any crews—"

"There aren't. I make it my business to know who's hanging around this neighborhood." Virginia took a small notepad from the inside breast pocket of her coat, worn and bent at the edges, the accompanying pencil worn down to an almost useless nub. "Alright, how about work? He have any problems there?"

"He's always been shy. He used to have bullies in school, but he graduated a few years back."

"Names?"

"I don't know," Ursa replied, shaking their head. "I'm sorry, I... it's hard, you know, trying to work, to keep a roof over our heads, to stay hidden, and—"

Virginia held up a hand. "Yeah. I get it." She scribbled a few notes in the margins, sucking her teeth as she wrote. "Where does he work?"

"He works as a janitor in the school on Ninth Avenue."

"The preparatory school?"

"He's worked there for about six months. It was hard for him to find a job. You know how it's been."

Virginia nodded. "He's not the only one, that's for sure." She was already calculating how she'd get to the school without hitting rush hour traffic. "Parents?"

Ursa straightened their posture, worried eyes now steely. "As far as Benjamin and I are concerned, we have no parents."

"I know the feeling," Virginia mumbled.

"What?"

She glanced up, blinking away the comment. "Nothing. Okay, no ransom notes, no other clues? He vanished?"

"I know that he didn't turn up for work that day. He walks, I was still on shift." Ursa pulled at the edge of their coat, pulling threads from the fraying cuffs. "The school said there was nothing out of the ordinary."

"Hmm. I think I'll be the judge of that." Virginia pursed her lips. It would be an early start, then. She hated schools. Little dens of chaos and trauma, ripe for abuse. "I'm going to need a description."

"Here's a photo." Ursa handed over a wallet-sized picture, almost overexposed. "I know it's not very good, but it's the only one I have of him."

"It's enough. Eye color?"

"Same as mine. Grey."

"Does he..." Virginia gestured to her own collarbone, an eyebrow raised. "Visible?"

"No."

"Well that's something, at least. Not as easy to spot."

"There was a time we were proud of our differences, Ms. Vane."

"That was before all these crews made it their business to snatch up anyone who can be useful to them. Before the government made it their business to do the same. It's all part of the same cycle." Virginia snapped the notepad shut. "Without sounding indelicate, I am not a charity." She slid a card across the table. "These are my rates."

Ursa nodded. "I'd pay anything to have Benjamin back, even if it means mortgaging my own kidneys."

"Is there any chance at all that your brother took off?"

"No."

"Are you completely sure? Young shifters have a knack for disappearing into the wind, only to reemerge a year later a few states away."

"I am completely sure that my brother wouldn't do that. He knows that we're all each other has. We have to stick together. He's been doing well at work, and he was about to start some night classes for architecture in the spring."

"You wouldn't believe the number of kids I've pulled out of backstreet drug dens, completely messed up on Nether."

Ursa shook their head again. "No. It won't be Benjamin. He wouldn't touch that stuff."

"You'd be surprised. Not every mythic can cope with how things are these days."

"He wouldn't."

"Alright," Virginia said, holding her hands up. "If you say so."

"You have to find him, Ms. Vane. He's all I have left in this world. Without him, I—I don't have much reason to keep on trying to get us out of this place."

"This apartment, or this city?"

"Both."

Virginia nodded, the deep, inexorable need to escape not an unfamiliar one. "Verdance is not the same place it was twenty years ago."

"Is anywhere?"

"No. Not since the Rupture." Virginia studied Ursa's face for a reaction, finding none. "I'll head to the school first thing in the morning, see if I can't track down a lead. Chances are he's just hiding out somewhere. It's rarely anything else."

"Thank you, Ms. Vane."

"I'll keep you updated." Virginia unlocked the door, opening it. "As soon as I know anything, you'll know, so don't be creeping around my door at night. You're lucky I didn't make the assumption that you were trying to jump me."

"Do many people—"

"More than you want to know."

Ursa pulled their hood back up before stepping into the corridor. "I apologize for surprising you at home. With my schedule, I'd never get to your office during opening hours."

"Good night," Virginia said, closing the door. Shadows, the adrenaline was just sitting in her veins now, itching for some kind of release. She locked the door, checking it three times to be sure, still on edge. It wouldn't have been the first time that some grave slug had tried to wait for her at home, though historically, it had never ended well for the other party.

She hung her coat on the hook, unholstering her pistol and laying it on the counter. The silver knuckles rattled against the stained wood, dappled with water rings from years of sticky summers and condensation that dripped down the side of a glass as she pored over another fruitless case.

The radio crackled with static as she honed in on the police frequency, bent over the counter as she adjusted the knobs, the fuzz over the airwaves a constant frustration. Police scanner radios were technically illegal, but always useful. She had a few open cases that had hit a dead end, and any news could jog a new lead. She examined the photo Ursa had left, black and white, one of the edges folded and yellowed from being carried around in an empty wallet. Benjamin was a good-looking kid, with a sharp jaw and wide, soulful eyes. Photos rarely told the full story, but he didn't seem like a troublemaker. More like a sad boy with a broken family and no friends to speak of other than his sibling.

Virginia poured gin into a glass, swirling it around. She'd forgotten to get food on the way back, and there was nothing more than stale crackers in her apartment. The taste was off, as though they'd absorbed the flavor of failure right through the cabinet doors. She pushed them away with a betrayed scowl, sipping at the gin instead. The taste was acrid in a welcoming way, like a half-burned pine forest after a lightning storm, or the smell of rain against ash as it washed down the city's storm drain. Both familiar. Both drawing memories to the surface she'd prefer stayed buried.

Odd, then, that it was her choice of drink, given its effect on her, and there was no explanation for why she continued to indulge in things that only reminded her of pain.

She sank down into the overstuffed chair in the corner, patched with mismatched thread and fabric from years of use. The radio droned on with reports of alley fights, crew sightings, and some slimy fungus of a man being arrested for fraud. The last one would probably be front-page news in the morning. It's not as though Virginia Vane was the only one with an illegal police scanner. The damned journalists all had them, too. So did the attorneys.

Gin skidded down her throat, nestling warm in her stomach. It was a comfort on cold nights like those, when the chill crept beneath the windowsills like fingers from the grave, waiting to welcome her into their frigid embrace. The landlord was uninterested in turning the heat on unless the pipes were in danger of freezing, so she'd gotten used to the glacial winters. They beat the humid, cloying summers, at least.

A gentle scratching at the window pulled her attention, even though she already knew it would be that damned cat again. "Alright, alright," she relented, pushing herself out of the chair with a heaving effort to open the window just wide enough to let in the little beast, and an icy draft followed after. "You're late for dinner," she scolded, turning to the kitchen to open a can of tuna. She hated the smell, all metallic and fishy, but it was the only thing the cat would eat, and from its fragile, underweight frame, she knew that wherever it belonged, it wasn't finding enough there.

She dumped the tuna into the cat's bowl and watched it eat, each bite dainty and polite despite the ribs visible through the solid black fur. The cat sat after it finished, licking its chops and showing off an impressive set of fangs.

"You can stay the night," Virginia offered. "It's damned cold out there."

The cat responded by leaping up onto the side table again, staring wistfully out into the frozen night.

"As you wish." Another frigid gust sparked through the window as the cat slunk back into the night, disappearing down the fire escape and into a back alley.

Virginia plunged back into the chair with a quiet exhalation of breath, not so much a sigh as an admission of guilt. She pressed reading glasses onto her face, skimming a book on demonic entities she'd gotten from the library. It was a rare copy, out of print now—the researcher who wrote it had spent the rest of his days as an academic outcast. A pity he had been proved right with the Rupture, but only after he'd spent ten years cold in the grave. She'd spent years trying to track down a copy. The local librarian found one in three hours.

She was so immersed in the chapter about symbiotic possession that she nearly missed the police dispatcher calling for a unit to attend the scene of an unidentified body. Young male, between seventeen and twenty-three, found half-buried in the quarry at the outskirts of the city. Virginia's stomach clenched, knowing what it probably meant.

Tugging her coat around her shoulders, she was halfway down the stairs of her building before the dispatch call even ended.

About the Author

Ryann Fletcher is a writer who lives with her wife and too many craft supplies. She writes sapphic science fiction and fantasy, and likes to cook.

You can connect with me on:

- https://ryannfletcher.com
- https://twitter.com/IMRyannFletcher
- https://facebook.com/RyannFletcherWrites
- https://instagram.com/RyannFletcherWrites
- https://www.tiktok.com/@ryannfletcherwrites
- https://patreon.com/RyannFletcherWrites

Subscribe to my newsletter:

- https://ryannfletcher.com

Also by Ryann Fletcher

Rhapsody in Flames – The Vane Dossier, Exhibit A
After the Rupture happened, everything changed.

Virginia Vane is a disgraced former cop who couldn't leave the casework behind. A jaded private investigator in Verdance, she spends all of her free time working on cold cases involving mythics. When her ex shows up as the new sheriff of police, she's thrown into one of the most frustrating murder investigations of her life – and the bodies keep piling up all over the city.

She knows the local crews are behind it, but she can't prove it – not yet. First, she has to find what they've all been looking for – an inferno witch.

www.ingramcontent.com/pod-product-compliance
Lightning Source LLC
Chambersburg PA
CBHW051305190726
48290CB00001B/14